TO ESSAY

RUSANA BARDARSKA

Translated from the Bulgarian by

Christopher Buxton, Zornitsa Hristova & Rusana Bardarska

Originally published in Bulgarian as *Опитът* by Janet 45, 2020

First edition, 2025

Library of Congress Catalog-in-Publication data:
Names: Bæurdarska, Rusana author | Buxton, Christopher translator | Hristova, Zornitsa translator
Title: To essay / Rusana Bardarska ; translated from the Bulgarian by
Christopher Buxton, Zornitsa Hristova & Rusana Bardarska.
Other titles: Opitæut. English
http://id.loc.gov/resources/hubs/e28247b8-8055-d8fb-abe7-b910a223c01a
Description: First edition. | Rochester, NY : Open Letter Books, 2025.
Identifiers: LCCN 2025026963 (print) | LCCN 2025026964 (ebook) | ISBN
9781960385468 ebook | ISBN 9781960385451 paperback
Subjects: | LCGFT: Fiction | Essays
Classification: LCC PG1039.12.U735 (ebook) | LCC PG1039.12.U735 O6513 2025
(print) | DDC 891.8/134 23/eng/20250--dc26
LC record available at https://lccn.loc.gov/2025026963

Cover design by Matt Avery
Dorothea Tanning, Self-Portrait, 1944, oil on canvas; 24 in. x 30 in. (60.96 cm x 76.2 cm)
San Francisco Museum of Modern Art, Purchase, by exchange, through a fractional gift of Shirley
Ross Davis © Artists Rights Society (ARS), New York / VG Bild-Kunst, Bonn
photograph: Katherine Du Tiel
Cover Image, “Self-portrait, 1944” by Dorothea Tanning © 2025 Artists Rights Society (ARS), New York / ADAGP, Paris.

Open Letter Books
Rochester, NY | Dallas, TX
www.openletterbooks.org

CONTENTS

This is a book.

THE SEVENTH DAY

(Prologue)

When I was a child, I thought people only died on Sundays.

My first encounter with the so-called "fundamental question" took place early on in a rather non-traumatic, even comical manner. In Lom, where I was born and spent the first seven (so-called formative) years of my life, there were funeral processions going down the main street every Sunday. We used to live smack in the middle of that street in a municipal building we shared with three other families, where my grandmother bred hens in the backyard.

It was only later that I learned what dying really meant, and that it didn't only happen on Sundays, the only day off people had at the time, and that funerals could, in urgent cases, be held on a working day, too. In my childhood, those lucky enough to be buried on Sundays were paraded in open caskets up and down the main street. A brass orchestra in front, mostly gypsies, then the casket with four or six pallbearers, once again, gypsies (whose number seemed to depend on how heavy the casket was), with mourners at the back and onlookers at the sides, lining the sidewalks. Trumpets, trombones, clarinets, drums, and other highly inappropriate instruments would unsurprisingly play funeral marches in impossible arrangements. The repertory comprised a total of three "numbers": Chopin, Beethoven, and Shostakovich. Each time, my father would routinely announce the name of the composer then scrunch his face, as if pained by the band's interpretation. Because this was not merely a procession but a relay that juddered between the two ends of the street, where caskets were replaced and a new round of marches would start—Chopin-Beethoven-Shostakovich(x2), then again, Chopin-Beethoven-Shostakovich(x2).

You fe-e-ll-ll victi-im in an une-equa-al fi-ight . . .[1]

They seemed to be doing the Shostakovich bit best because they always played it twice—and Dad didn't grumble and mock, but hummed along. I hadn't heard Shostakovich's "Funeral March" yet so I didn't know how rich and elaborate the music actually was. At any rate, even in this simplified version, this was the only piece adequately performed by the Lom Orchestra. Years later, when I was a Pioneer and then a YCL Komsomol member,[2] I would stay stock-still at the never-ending Last Post ceremonies for the "fallen heroes" and I would listen to the same funeral march (until I fainted due to low blood pressure), and think how, in fact, all humans were victims in the unequal fight with death. Later yet, when I made the Shostakovich waltzes the soundtrack to my euphoric moods, I finally grasped why that "piece" sounded somewhat decent when interpreted by the Lom City Brass orchestra—it turns out Shostakovich really liked brass orchestras.

The same orchestra did weddings as well, which led me to think that Goran Bregović, who was born in the Balkans at approximately the same time as me, must have listened to similar stuff as a child, which helped form his "Orchestra for Weddings and Funerals." I also found out that, like funerals, weddings could be staged at the drop of a hat, albeit for other pressing reasons.

My parents were not too concerned about the impact funerals would have on me, but they did worry about all the rumpus the brass orchestra produced at twenty-minute intervals right under our windows (we lived on the first floor). My brother—a chubby, curly-headed, wide-eyed baby I loved pinching with doubtful benevolence—would wake up and start bawling with fear and exhaustion; I'd laugh into my cupped hands, watching Mom take him away to the bathroom (the only room not facing the main street), Dad would fuss around, harping on about the million times he had said the baby should sleep in its stroller in the riverside park, and Mom would snap back from the bathroom that my brother refused to fall asleep there. When I got bored with this sequence, I would retreat to the balcony—my presidium—and wallow in the death parade. Another round, another old lady, her face and her frame were so

1 A funeral march originating in Russia around 1878, later sung for the fallen of various uprisings, culminating in the communist October Revolution of 1917. It continued to be sung in the Soviet Union thereafter. Subsequently, it was incorporated into Shostakovich's *Symphony No. 11, Op. 103*, "Mov. III." The translation here renders the opening stanza as it was sung in Bulgarian with traumatic elongation of vowels.

2 Child and youth organizations in the Communist period. Membership was compulsory and expulsion (e.g., for church attendance) would seriously impact future education and career opportunities.

tiny that one of my first conclusions about death was that it made people shrink. Four light-footed gypsy men carried the coffin down the street. The next round, however, featured a hefty fellow with ample moustache and a necktie, disproving my theory. He was carried by six men, all crouching under his weight.

I was certain that only the adults could die. One Sunday, though, the oblong box was smaller and it contained . . . a little girl, like me! A man and a woman of my parents' age walked in tow with some elderly folk, wailing so loudly you could hear them over the banging and clanging of the orchestra. Why were they crying? Immediately I snuck out and started walking down the street, alongside the procession. I had to know exactly what had happened to that little girl. I asked some lady who stroked my hair and blubbered, "Oh, dear, dear, my child, an awful tragedy . . . Where are your parents? Are you lost?" I wrenched myself free of this old bore and slipped back home unnoticed.

My parents had already told me—out of goodness knows where—that when people grow old (growing old was defined as the final stage of being an adult), they get tired and *fall asleep forever* and we lay them to rest ("yes, in wooden boxes, in . . . the ground"). The word *forever* was problematic, but my parents promised to explain it when I was old enough (which, of course, didn't happen and the explanations I could find elsewhere introduced another problematic word, *never*). Neither could I fathom why the living, i.e., the robust rosy-cheeked ones, were crying. Dad had told me that they were very sad because they could no longer talk to the person who had "fallen asleep forever." The box in the ground with the sleeping person inside provoked a deep disturbance in my imagination, even though that person would *never again* wake up.

When I got back from the little girl's procession, Mom and Dad were discussing something in the living-room while Grandma had taken my baby brother to the bathroom. I asked my parents why there were children who "fall asleep forever" when they were visibly not "old" or "tired." Mom told me off for having gone to the balcony and ordered me to sit down and start drawing. They were hiding something. So, in revenge, I snapped back, "One Sunday you'll fall asleep forever, too."

My intentions were totally innocent—after that "one Sunday" I'd be able to go out and do what I wanted while Mom and Dad were *asleep*. But my words had an unexpected effect on my parents—they went quiet and pondered.

Then summer came, and on Sunday nights the funeral processions were followed by a tractor driving down the main street spraying the air profusely with a white mist (DDT or something of the sort) that was supposed to keep mosquitoes away. My parents were worried how poisonous it was. Dad closed all the doors and windows so the little provincial town went peacefully quiet.

I guess it was this problem-free perception of death as a feature of the week and part of the cycle of sleep and wakefulness that led to the encounter with my grandfather, the one I was named after. The thing was, he'd died seven years before I was born. When I told my parents and Nana that I'd met Grandpa on the upper street, the one that led to school, that he'd been riding a bicycle, and that he'd stopped, smiled at me, waved, then jumped back on the bicycle and disappeared around the corner, complete silence fell over the room. Then Nana decreed that I should be escorted to school. In practical terms, that meant that she would have to do it because my parents worked from dawn to dusk.

"But she walks the streets all day, not just on the way to school," Mom said.

The impending peril of being kept under lock and key and having my half-paralyzed, limping Nana accompany me to school just because my Grandpa had interrupted his nap and gone for a bike ride prompted one of my first observations about life, namely that truth and freedom are hard to reconcile. Years later, when I came to know that in general (with the exception of *singular events* . . .) dead grandfathers don't take bike rides around the neighborhood, I reconsidered the concept of truth, too. What is true and what isn't? What about the stuff other people refuse to acknowledge as truth? As a student in philosophy courses (in which we learned about the idealists and their father Plato, only in the broadest strokes, so we could denounce them) and Western Literature (especially lectures on German Romanticism) I often thought of my grandfather on that bike, and later the ghost in the ossuary monument.

Learning my lesson from Grandpa's Sunday jaunts, I decided to spare my family the truth about the monument to the heroes of the September Uprising[3] and its inhabitants. The sculpture atop the monument (two men and a woman with submachine guns and raised fists) stood at the center of my childhood jungle—the town park. We were playing hide-and-seek and I huddled in the portico at the base—thick glass shielded by a tangle of wrought iron. I squeezed my face through the metal features and pressed my nose against the glass. There was something in there, shrouded in white veils, it was moving or dancing—trying to brush away the veils. A real ghost! And it was lurking under the materialistic grandeur of the communist heroes stuck up above. I didn't know what a ghost was because at that time there were no horror sto-

3 An unsuccessful armed insurgency in 1923, initiated by the Bulgarian Communist Party, on command from the Communist International in Moscow, in an attempt to overthrow the government that had come to power by a coup d'état. It led to a meaningless civil war, in which terrorist tactics were used by both the communist party and the government.

ries for kids in Bulgaria, no equivalent of the *Goosebumps* series or horror movies. The word "ossuary" didn't ring a bell, either, though there were quite real ghosts and dead grandfathers idling around. I got a bit scared standing there, benumbed, watching the thing move. I told myself that I would only run away if it started coming toward the door. I was so engrossed, I completely forgot I was hiding and got spotted by the other kids. All was well, except that my head got caught in the ironwork and the kids had to ask a lady for help. While everyone was fussing around me, that thing stopped moving, the white veils turned into long white curtains covering something that looked like a big cabinet. Later on, I realized this was the ossuary itself—a place for storing bones, human bones, of course, those of the heroes aesthetically sculpted atop the pedestal. I scraped my ears but my head was finally pulled out. I decided not to tell the kids and the lady, or my parents and Nana. Only I would know the *truth*. Otherwise Nana might suddenly decide I needed to be escorted to the park, which was just across the street. All Mom had to do to summon me home was to step out on the balcony and call my name.

I was quick to forgive Nana's role as my chaperone, though with walking at the speed of a tortoise, I had to drag her all the way to school. Most days she made me disgusting toast for breakfast, which I threw from the balcony or shoved under the bed that we shared. (When an oil-and-paprika slice landed on the beehive head of a lady comrade and the hiding place turned into an ant-hill, I changed tactics but never told anyone about my ingenious disposal methods.) But on other days Nana made crepes with white-cherry jam. Oh, the sweetness! And yet, what I most appreciated about her were the books that she read to me and the interesting things she told me. She would say, for example, that words came from other very old languages which people had spoken a long time ago, and the words we use today might have meant something else back then. That piece of information piqued my interest immensely and bred lots of unrelated thoughts in my tousled head. For instance, I wondered how people had decided to call an apple an *æpəl*, what was the connection between the apple itself—this red apple that I had to eat—and the word *æpəl*. What had *æpəl* meant in the fairytale past, and would the people in the fairytale future think of an apple when they saw this assemblage of signs? That took me further ahead—I separated the world from the words for it and even started coining words of my own. I liked *apple*, but *ballpoint pen*, for example, wasn't much to my taste. Once I put my new words into use, I instantly figured out what the existing ones were for—no one understood what I said. Mom nervously insisted that I cut out the nonsense and eat my apple. So, the true purpose of words was for people to understand each other when they talked and to grasp the meaning of what they read. If I wanted the new words I'd invented to be understood, everyone had to know what they meant and agree to call them by those names. But everyone had conspired that *æpəl* would mean this fruit here and all other red, green, and yellow ones, too, while *ballpoint pen* would be the other thing that we write with that isn't a pencil.

Primed by this weekend existentialism and the semiotic distrust of words, I started school. In second grade, we began studying a second language, Russian. Nana said it wasn't a "real foreign language" because it would be of no help to me in a "truly foreign country." That sounded pretty vague at the time. Yet Nana, a former teacher who read Pushkin and Lermontov in the original Russian, revealed to me something truly amazing through that language, which was not so foreign after all.

One of the first things we covered in class were the days of the week. How easy it was! The words were almost the same as in Bulgarian. Except for Sunday—*vo-skre-se-nya. Voskresenya.* A far cry from the Bulgarian word for Sunday—*nedelya.* I asked the teacher what *voskresenya* meant. She blinked and said, "Sunday, I already told you." I recited Nana's lesson and patiently explained about the history of words, about Russian not being an altogether foreign language because it shared so many words with Bulgarian, and that many, many years ago Bulgarian and Russian had been the same thing—Slavonic. Nana had, for instance, explained to me that *ne-delya* (Sunday in Bulgarian) means *not to work, not to deal with anything, to rest, to unwind.* She had pointed out other words in Bulgarian with the same etymological root and had linked them with similar words in Russian. In my mind, her explanation was totally in line with the fact that old and tired people would fall into eternal sleep on the day for *not working,* but I kept that to myself.

After that etymological detour, I returned to my question: "What does *voskresenya* mean?"

The teacher was, to put it mildly, impressed, and, yes, she confirmed that Bulgarian and Russian were once the same language, hence the days of the week sounded almost the same. "But the word for Sunday is . . . different . . . No, *voskresenya* doesn't mean 'doing nothing,' it . . ." Hemming and hawing, the poor woman didn't know what *voskresenya* meant and quickly moved on to numbers and counting in Russian.

But I had my Nana, and that night she told me what that weird word stood for.

"Yeah right, she didn't know what *voskresenya* means, did she! Darn communist!" Nana growled.[4]

4 The literal meaning of the word *voskresenya* is *resurrection,* meaning Christ's resurrection. Communists are not supposed to believe in religion.

I had no idea what the Russian word for Sunday had to do with the communists. All I knew was that communists were yucky and that we were not like them. I'd had the blue chavdarche[5] scarf officially tied around my neck a year before, which mostly meant (to me at least) that I'd grown up and was already a schoolgirl. And yet I had been deeply impressed by the ceremony promoting me to the rank of a chavdarche—loudspeakers and strange ponderous words, a litany of heroes . . . and once again that mournful "*You fell victim in an unequal fight . . .*" that somewhat puzzled me at the time. I quickly put the blue scarf to use as a dancing veil. I got so carried away that I hit my chin on the edge of the bed, split it open, and had to have three stitches, all without anesthesia (that part of the jaw could not be desensitized). That was how I came to associate the blue scarf, one of the first symbols of the communist regime I was growing up in, with a jar of rounded needles, with my screams, with my father and two nurses pinning me to the examination table while the bald doctor threaded the needle in and out. Meanwhile, the monumental heroics of the ossuary—another first symbol—were completely overshadowed by a very *real* (and, should I say, rather "appropriate") ghost.

As for that odd word *voskresenya*, Nana told me a suitably eerie story. Once upon a time, there lived a lad named Khristo (she'd called him Christ, but I'd never heard that name, so I tweaked it a little bit). This young man was also paraded up and down the main street of some far-away town. He hadn't fallen asleep yet, though he got a good beating because he was a very good person. I couldn't get my head around why on Earth you'd go beating someone for being a good person, but I didn't want to interrupt Nana.

"In the end, they put him up on a big wooden cross and he *died.*"

Nana spared me the details of how exactly you attach a person to a big wooden cross and how beating, as she called it, was related to *dying*. There was no internet at the time, and no books in the library told this story, so I couldn't have all the gaps filled in. I had never gone to church because Nana, Mom, and Dad were atheists.

"So, he fell asleep forever?" I clarified.

"No, not forever, that's the thing," Nana raised a finger. "He *was* re-sur-rec-ted, *vos-kras-nal* on Sunday; that means he came back to life. V*os-kras-vam* comes from the word "cross" and means to come back to life after *death*. And here we get to the word *voskresenya*—the Russians name Sunday this way because Christ rose from the dead the night leading into Sunday."

My little brain was going at full speed. That was the first time I heard the words *die*, *dead*, and *death*. They didn't sound like *falling asleep*, be it *forever*, nor like *sleep*, be it *eternal*. So . . . wow, fancy that—there is another scenario for the Sundays, not only

5 Communist equivalent of being a Brownie.

falling asleep forever! You could actually wake up or *be re-sur-rected.* It turns out that my Grandpa, the one on the bike, hadn't just woken up, he had been . . . *re-sur-rec-ted.*

Nana observed me carefully and stroked my hair as though she was consoling me about something. We were both silent.

"Nana," I swallowed," is this . . . a true story or it is a fairytale?"

Nana looked down and stopped stroking me. Then she sighed.

"Please, tell me!"

"I . . ." she took up hesitantly, "I don't believe that story is . . . true. Neither do your mom and dad. But millions of people around the world do. They're called Christians—after the name of Christ. We don't believe Christ really rose from the dead. But we follow his commandments to be good people," Nana continued, more animated, "not to hate, envy, beat, or kill each other. To help other people. To love each other, to treat everyone like a brother or a sister . . . Now it's time for you to go to bed." Nana rose up and limped away to the sink. "Come brush your teeth."

Whenever adults don't want to tell you something, they always tell you to brush your teeth or wash your hands, eat your toast, do your homework, or go to bed. But the question, the only and most important one, was already ripe on my young lips.

"Nana, was it only Khri . . . Christ who was re . . . sur-rec-ted? Do people rise . . . from . . . the *dead*? You . . . because you're already old and tired, will you also . . . *die*?" swiftly rolled out of my mouth the new word, replacing the old *fall asleep*. "Will you come back to life afterward . . . will you be *re-sur-rected*?"

Nana was fussing around at the sink. She was rubbing a soap cloth against the muddy stain on my red coat. She didn't speak.

"*Смертью смерть поправ*,"[6] she said with her back turned to me. I didn't understand a thing. Nana explained, "That's in Russian. And in church-Slavonic."

"What does it mean? That you'll rise from the dead?"

"No, pumpkin," Nana turned around and gazed out the window. "No one does. Christians believe that they will, but that's a dream, a fabrication . . . something to console themselves with."

Well, I did see Grandpa riding a bike down the street, I thought, but I kept my mouth shut. Nana turned her back to me and continued cleaning my coat.

"Nana . . ." I said hesitantly, "if you have to be Christian . . . to rise from the dead . . . then do it Nana, please! Please, believe in that Christ!" I begged her and started

6 *Trampling down death by death.* Canonical Orthodox expression, usually proclaimed at the midnight Easter service, meaning the death of death, i.e., the elimination of human death, obtained through Jesus' sacrifice and resurrection.

weeping, not knowing why. Nana dropped the rag, sat beside me on the bed, and hugged me with her non-paralyzed arm.

I was weeping under Nana's arm; I had no apparent reason to do so but she kept stroking me, anyway. I already knew it wasn't Grandpa I had seen. Somewhere deep inside I already knew that the answer to my question applied not only to Nana, but to Mom and Dad, to my baby brother, to my aunts, my cousins, to all of my girlfriends, my teachers, to everyone, absolutely everyone, to every human being on Earth . . . Myself included.

Years later, when I was a philology student, I thought about the Sunday funeral processions of my childhood and the story of the word *voskresenya.* Language hadn't simply named the new thing; *through* language I had learned the most important thing in the world. All Slavs had focused on the fact that their God, the grandfatherly figure Bulgarians believed in, twiddled his thumbs on the seventh day. Russians, however, were more mystically inclined, so their language remembered this as the day of Christ's resurrection. The conservative memory of language had prevailed against the thoroughly non-transcendental materialism of communism as the people awoke from "the opium trance of religion"[7] (although Russians were not exactly jolted into sobriety). Language thumbed its nose at ideology. It was hard to believe that Stalin and Lenin hadn't imposed a new name on Sundays. Neo-Latin and Germanic languages call the seventh day of the week "God's Day" or simply a sunny day (most probably because there isn't much sun in the North). That sunny day of God, even in its cloudiest, rainiest, and iciest North-European versions, had become inextricably linked with "Frère Jacques" and the procession of peaceful, neatly dressed people, a community, taking off time from work and going to church.

Eleven years after this unusual lesson, when my Nana died on a cold April Sunday, I was nineteen and I wrote in my diary:

On Sunday, God took a rest, while his son Christ rose from the dead. We, humans of all languages and religions—some wasting our time on a Sunday, others going to church—we all die, irretrievably, on the seventh day of our lives.

They say life truly begins the first time a loved one dies. I still wonder if I should be counting from Nana's death or from the first time death peeked behind the curtains of my Sunday children's theatre. In any case, I find death a riveting and meaningful beginning to every story about life.

7 As per Lenin.

TIME IS IN US

Time is in us and we are in time.
Vassil Levski

The setting: 1976, the Military Club in Plovdiv for a school celebration of the Centenary of the 1876 April Uprising.[8] Kids in their Communist Youth uniforms dart around the hall and the stage; behind the curtains their leader hands out final instructions; the music teacher prepares his charges for the deafening fanfare (that was sure to drown out the recital as our bugles had no pianissimo mode). The hall, full of children, is buzzing. I gaze at the familiar face of Vassil Levski, the Apostle of Freedom,[9] blown up above the stage. I read over and over, syllable by syllable, his familiar words as if I were seeing them for the first time, to make sure they really say what I think they do: "*Time is . . . in . . . us . . . and . . . we . . . are . . . in . . . time.*" I'm trying to visualize what time is and how it sits huddled inside me and how all of us are binned in some other time. These words of the Apostle spark my deepest interest.

That night I asked Nana to show me the specific location of time in her body; I also asked if she knew where it was inside me. She stroked my "clever head" and said nothing.

8 An armed uprising of the Bulgarians against the Ottoman Yoke in 1876. It is considered the peak of the Bulgarian liberation movement despite its cruel suppression and the atrocities committed by the Turkish army.

9 Vassil Levski (1837–1873)—a Bulgarian revolutionary, a national hero. He set up the underground revolutionary organization, was caught by the Turkish police, tried, and hanged.

I learned no more a few years later when my history and literature teachers would cast historic time into noteworthy events and personalities, or into literary plots and characters; whereas my physics and math teachers seemed to use some other, absolute kind of time that they called *t*. The two kinds of time had nothing in common; our humanities and science teachers didn't seem to be on talking terms. I asked Mom where historic time or the physico-mathematical *t* was located inside me—I hoped, she would know the latter at least since she was an engineer like Dad and had studied physics and calculus.

"Pff, I have no *time* for that, I have to make dinner. Go ask your father."

Dad never cooked or did the laundry; he didn't do any cleaning, either, so he had more time to talk to me. Dad's engineering expertise lay in power stations. Shortly after we left Lom, he had to go back to his home area for several months, to launch the first unit of a nuclear power plant. Dad didn't say what kind of time I had inside me, nor did he point out its specific location, but he did tell me some other rather astounding things. Especially about the *t*-time and electricity.

"What does electricity look like?" I asked.

"Ahh, you don't need to know that—if you get an electric shock, you're dead on the spot. Don't you dare touch light bulbs, exposed wires, or wall sockets!" he said sternly, wagging a finger at me.

"What if *you* get an electric shock?" I gasped.

"I won't, because I know how to work with the current."

"Well then, since you call it a current, does it look like water? What color is it?"

"No . . ." He paused, wondering how to continue. "Look, electricity is not matter, it's not a material thing with mass and so on, it doesn't weigh anything, it has no shape, and you cannot see or touch it."

"How do you know it exists?"

"It makes things react to its energy."

"What is energy?"

"Ugh . . . that's one of the most difficult questions to answer. Just like the ones about mass. Or gravity."

"But you're an energy expert, aren't you?" I insisted.

"I can explain to you what electricity is," Dad said as he drew lines with a few plus signs at one end and a few minuses at the other—these were the wires down which the invisible, shapeless, and weightless electricity ran. It looked very simple.

"But there are different types of energy," he continued. "And, in general, energy is not the same as electricity. How can I explain this to you?! Let's take our star, the

Sun . . ." Then Dad got caught up in a jumble of explanations, only to conclude, out of nowhere, "If God exists, if we have a soul, a consciousness, or whatever you choose to call it, then, to me, this is energy. Or a field. The thought that makes our legs move, the food that is transformed into the strength to move our legs—everything is energy. Everything contains accumulated energy, everything can be charged."

God knows what I had gathered from these messy explanations, but one of my school essays in the socialist-heroic genre, dedicated to the first atomic power plant, with my Dad in the main role, of course, ended in the solemnly poignant phrase, "And down the wires the electricity slowly ran." My literature teacher was visibly moved by that finale—and the entire essay—and regaled me with an exalted A+. Dad laughed so much reading that sentence that he had to wipe tears from his eyes. After this he told me about *speed* and *distance*.

I was startled to find out that time doesn't flow the same way on Earth and in the skies, especially if you travel at the speed of light, or if you're on a planet much larger than the Earth and therefore caught in a stronger gravitational pull. I closed my eyes and tried to figure out how *fast* 186,000 miles per *second* is and how *far* one light-*year* is, but even that disheartening *attempt* gave me a good idea how vast the heavens were. Stunned by that boundlessness, I concluded that in the *speed* of light there was no *unit of time*—what use is a tiny little second as a measurement?!—but only a *unit of distance*, and not just any distance but the unreachable far-flung distances of outer space. Likewise the light-*year* is not a unit of time, either, but only of distance and space. Dad complimented me and noted that, at the speed of light, time actually stops, it disappears.

"But," he went on, "a second is not such a small unit of time; there are much smaller units, in which many things could happen."

I couldn't think of anything that could happen in a quarter or a tenth of a second, and Dad didn't elaborate. I thought I'd figured out why time would flow differently on a larger planet—well, that bigger planet would take much longer to turn on its axis so that the day could change into night!

"Okay," I asked. "But what kind of time is this? How do *we* measure it? With the same seconds, minutes, hours, days, and years we use here on Earth?"

"Well, yes . . . We have no other units of time," Dad admitted.

He didn't know how to explain why we measure the speed and distances of outer space with our incommensurate earthly ideas of speed and distance, in our earthly units of the second and the year, and the laughable earthly distance of one kilometer or mile, from our home to the local park or to the town library.

"Oh, so the speed of light can be different if we don't measure it with our earthly seconds and kilometers?" I persisted.

"No, it's a *constant*, it doesn't matter how you measure it," Dad remarked.

"Yeah, yeah, but doesn't it matter *who's* measuring it and how long our earthly second, day, night, and year are to *them*, how long our earthly kilometer is to *them*?"

My Dad lit a cigarette and opened his mouth to say something, then closed it.

"If someone from the Earth, a *human*, goes to that large planet," I kept pondering, "how would time flow *for them*—the way it does on Earth? One day means one rotation of the Earth around its axis, one year, the rotation of the Earth around the Sun, three more spins of the Earth around the Sun and I'm legally a grown-up and I can do whatever I want?"

"And my hair turns white," Dad said before returning to the question. "In general, yes, but if that person comes back to Earth, especially if he comes back fast, after one *Earth* year spent on that gigantic planet, he may return only to find his daughter is an old lady now."

The last part didn't impress me in the least because it seemed even more surreal than the speed of light and the light-year. But it suddenly dawned on me what Levski, the Apostle, was saying! Of course, that was it! Time—our human, earthbound time, the one we spend on the Earth—is really inside us! We *em-body* it! We grow up and grow old and we measure these processes with our Earth time, which is determined by the size of our planet and which we have decided to measure by the Earth's rotation around its own axis and around its star.

"Why is the day twenty-four hours long?" I asked.

"Because that's how long it takes the Earth to spin around its own axis. Come on, you've studied that in elementary school!"

"No, I meant who decided that the time the Earth takes to rotate around its axis is twenty-four hours? Why isn't a day twenty or twenty-eight hours? Who decided how long a second or an hour should last? Who decided that an hour must have sixty minutes in it? And why does everything go in tens, but the seconds are sixty and the hours twenty-four? Who decided how long a meter should be and how heavy a kilogram should be?"

Dad didn't know everything, and he didn't have the time to dig up the information in the library, either. I had to rack my brain on my own and I finally declared that *t* must be some kind of a constant correlation between velocity, distance, mass, volume, and gravity, whereas our human time was used to tally other things, like human life and history or natural phenomena, with our own human measurements. I said nothing about the Apostle. Dad agreed that, yeah, that had to be the case, and oddly enough concluded that I would take up philosophy or writing, and not physics and math. That's why he was surprised that I—his daughter, the poetess—got an astounding A+ on the math exam I took, almost unconscious with fever, to get into the English high school. But that's another story.

And yet, in high school it became clear that words, and not numbers, would be my forte. Numbers were so imprecise and obscure. With lots of effort and practice, I managed to solve the algebraic equations, but I was dumbfounded whenever something started leaning toward infinity. Mom would patiently explain the rules and algorithms, but I kept going back to the question of infinity.

"What does 'tending to infinity' mean? There should be an end point to this diminishing. There can't be infinity in the infinitesimally small!"

I don't think Mom had given infinity much thought outside the realm of mathematics—not in the boundless Universe, measured in light-years and numbers raised to great powers, and not in the infinitesimal recurring number of some negative exponent. Bothered by my weird questions and nervous that I was wasting her time when there was laundry and cleaning to be done, Mom snapped at me.

"You don't have to imagine it, it's a law, an axiom, the whole of nature proves it, you take it for granted and you learn it."

The number π and other infinity-approaching mysteries in algebra turned my gaze in the opposite direction—to the infinitesimal, and during my next conversations with Dad, I naturally broached the subject of quantum physics.

"Okay, but what about the very small planets, or all those atoms, quarks and so on. Shouldn't time flow faster there?" I asked.

"Sounds logical." Dad took a puff of his cigarette, fell silent, and then after a little while continued. "Actually in the opposite universe, in the world of the infinitely small, some particles travel so fast that they can be simultaneously in different locations and states, that is they don't need time, t, to get from one state or place into another. Practically, that eliminates time."

I couldn't imagine how one thing could be simultaneously here and there, like this and like that. Translated into my human world, that meant that I could be simultaneously fifteen and fifty (a senior citizen, as I thought at the time). Or that my late Grandpa could, actually, ride his bike around the neighborhood. But Dad interrupted these disconcerting thoughts with yet another astonishing idea.

"Imagine for a while that the Earth is . . . an elementary particle in an unfathomably huge . . . pea. Our pea, i.e., the visible and conceivable Universe, is just one in a bushel of peas or in another world we know nothing of. Or vice versa—imagine a terribly miniscule civilization living on an electron inside a pea. There, time will flow at full tilt; the whole evolutionary process will take place within . . . one human day. Although, who knows, the atom's density is huge. And should humanity ever establish contact with another civilization, the first thing they'll discuss, in my opinion, will be the matter of *time*."

I was dumbstruck.

Pondering the relativity of our human measures, of our units of time, size, mass, and velocity, as well as the possibility that intellect could live on a millionth of a pea, had a profound effect on me and completely changed my *perspective*. I felt gigantic and omnipotent at once, I peered at not just every pea, but into every absolutely innocuous item from the material world. Everything, myself included, contained some part of Mendeleev's table, and—ultimately—quantum particles. At the same time, I felt like a miniscule fly that would live for just a moment in another's chronological system, like the hundredth or the thousandth digit after the decimal dot of π, a millionth or a billionth part of a pea in a can.

In my history class we were bashing through *historical time*: revolutionary committees, hideouts with co-conspirators, persecution, dining on a handful of olives, no love, a notepad for keeping a pedantic account of the revolutionary committee's expenses, betrayal, shoelaces caught in the wooden fence, execution by hanging, nightfall, Sofia's outskirts, ravens, a gallows, oh, Mother Bulgaria . . .[10] And suddenly—time! Time is in us and we are in time. It was as if Garibaldi had made a statement, a highly relevant one at that, on the black holes in the Universe.

Naturally, our history teacher had a historical explanation of these words. The Apostle had wanted to say that the imperatives of time, i.e., history, the historical circumstance, in this case the Turkish yoke, construct us as historically conscious personalities and determine our ideals and the meaning of our lives, in this case freedom and self-sacrifice. The idea that my life goals and deepest desires depended on where and when I was born stuck in my head for further investigation. But that explained only the second, far clearer part of the Apostle's mysterious aphorism.

10 References, like in a stream of consciousness, to iconic moments of the heroic guerrilla life of the Apostle, Vasil Levski, including his organization of committees, his execution, and to the poem of the national poet Hristo Botev who lamented the tragic loss.

My teacher talked a lot about years and dates but not about *time*, its human measures and meaning, its relativism or the personal knowledge we have of it. In her historic timeline, the Apostle and Paisius, Saint Euthymius, Boris I,[11] Lenin, Marx, Darwin, Gutenberg, Charlemagne . . . all stood equally removed and mummified, no matter whether we were separated by seventy, one hundred, two hundred, five hundred or over one thousand rotations of the Earth around the Sun.

Comrade Petrov, my literature teacher, was far more interesting, managing to breathe new life into the herbarium of long-gone heroes and authors. It was as if he carefully took their pictures off the walls, examined them, and blew the dust off their faces, causing them to brighten and yawn, wake up from the long sleep and begin to . . . talk! The dead history from our history classes came alive in his classroom. Comrade Petrov would focus our attention on some details in the books—what the people were eating or wearing, how the author had gone about recounting or describing one thing or another, how he'd structured his story and chosen his words. So, we slowed down our mechanical reading that only focused on the dialogue and the next plot twist. And, oh, how his eyes would light up, how dramatically our teacher would shake back his hair when we were analyzing Yavorov, Smirnenski, Dimov,[12] Cervantes, Tolstoy! The miracle and the power of great literature . . .

Literature classes left me with a lasting, less-than-canonical approach to the classic writers and their works—not as godlike mythological creatures who "had fashioned works mere mortal hands could not,"[13] but as companions I could talk with, people who had created or seen something and wanted to tell me about it—masterfully, manipulatively, with an excess of drama or with epic detachment. This conversation across dozens or hundreds of years brought the authors and their worlds back to life. To me, these writers were alive, more so than many of the living people around me. Because they were talking to me, I could read their thoughts, I could feel their feelings. Many of the living ones didn't look like they had any.

Comrade Koleva, my physics teacher, didn't speak about *time* at all, it was the constant *t* in all formulas and that was it. I, however, suspected that her occasionally hysterical buoyancy camouflaged a profound depression. Maybe she had secretly thought

11 Paisius of Hilendar (1722–1773), a Bulgarian monk, a key figure in the Bulgarian National Revival, author of the first written history of the Bulgarian people. Saint Euthymius of Tarnovo (1325–1402), the last Patriarch of the Bulgarian Church (1375–1393) before the dismantling of the Bulgarian state and church by the Ottoman Empire. Boris I, Bulgarian tsar (852–889) who converted Bulgaria, a mighty but pagan state, to Christianity, adopted from the Orthodox Byzantium.

12 Peyo Yavorov (1878–1914), one of the greatest Bulgarian poets, founder of modern symbolic and existentialist trends in Bulgarian poetry. Committed a suicide. Khristo Smirnenki (1898–1923), a Bulgarian poet, great master of socially engaged poetry. Dimitar Dimov (1909–1966), a Bulgarian playwright and novelist.

13 Citation of a poem by Ivan Vazov (1850–1921), the so called patriarch of Bulgarian literature.

about *t* in another, non-scientific, human perspective and had pondered the *experience* of life as a pea in a can? It was only natural that I was my literature teacher's favorite, but I had no other explanation for the special affection my physics teacher had for me, since physics definitely wasn't my strong suit.

After I found out that time is inside us, in our flesh, that humans *em-body* earthly time, I took to caressing my Nana and secretly inspecting her wrinkled skin and wilting flesh, I would peer into the fading green of her eyes and think about touching seventy years of time. Time could be felt, heard, and seen! History was being de-mummified and was rising from the sarcophagus! My maternal Grandfather was born four days before Tsar Ferdinand declared the Second Balkan War[14] and Nana fifty one days after that. I stroked her and she, having already made the decision to die, hastened to tell me stories about the boarding school for war orphans, where she was trained as a teacher. She showed me the pictures, she told me about the September Uprising. Altering her voice, Nana reenacted the conversation between her mother and a wounded rioter who scurried across their backyard in Brusartsi, on the night of September 24th, 1923. My great grandma, the war widow, was shucking corn with my ten-year-old Nana. "Come here, boy, wait, let's dress your wound." "Eh, missus, missu-us, we're dying and you're shucking corn," said the boy as he zipped past the gate. Bullets flying around, the Lom barracks were being stormed, screaming, shooting, smoke, and the widow was shucking corn to feed her three children. Her brother, Nana's uncle, took part in the storming and ended up in the hold of a barge. Nana and the widow brought him mugs of corn porridge, but the watchmen kept pouring them into the Danube, cursing, right in front of their eyes.

Later on, in the night, the barges were sunk. "The boys drowned like rats," Nana sighed. I shut my eyes in horror as I pictured the metal guts of the barges and the miry waters of the river engulfing the screams, the bubbles, and the thousand globules of terminal breath. I stroked Nana's thin hair, I held her wrinkled, paralyzed arm, and gently pinched the flesh of time.

Mom's father, i.e., my other grandpa, was still alive, but quite sick. His failing kidneys and his ice-cold feet weren't just a memory from the dank trenches of the 1944–1945 winter, but the sick flesh of time itself.

The discovery that my Dad was born forty-three days before Germany invaded Poland left me aghast. This was not simply a historical date in some abstract distant past, I had a living link with the past right next to me. Pretending I was checking if

14 In June 1913.

Dad was clean-shaven, I touched his cheeks as if they were a relic from the past, and his birthday seemed magical to me.

Once, in a fellow pupil's home, I saw a photo. My classmate had a much older brother; they were born some ten or twelve years apart. The young man was already married and had a child, so my classmate was a young aunt. The black-and-white photo in the glass cabinet featured a five- or six-year-old boy in white shirt and shorts alongside a typical old Bulgarian man—wiry, shrewd, with a sheepskin cap on his head. The old man was holding the boy by the hand; his squinting eyes looking up at the camera. I asked my friend about the photo. "Oh, these are my brother and my grandfather. Grandpa died before I was born." My friend knew nothing more and couldn't understand my interest in that photo. Her mother was ironing nearby and must've been listening to us because she left the iron and told me . . . the story: ". . . all those wars, crises, riots, misery, drought, rainstorms, and hail, they were 'crushing and memorable years, Lord,'"[15] so the men in the family got married at a later age. The old man in the photo was born in Koprivshtitsa, in the besieged Koprivshtitsa, in the midst of the April Uprising! Once again, some boys had risen up, shot their guns, and died. The wise old men of Koprivshtitsa were negotiating the number and weight of gold coins it would take to buy out the besieged village from the Turks. Not wanting to provoke the Turks with smoke coming out of the chimney, the women did not light a fire and bathed the newborn with cold water. If he could endure that . . . And he did. He lived for eighty-eight years. When the baby grew up to be forty-nine, my friend's father was born; and in that photo the April Uprising survivor was eighty-six years old and holding the hand of his grandson—a . . . *con-temporary* of mine (if we don't count the large age gap between my friend and her brother). I listened, hypnotized and unblinking, looking at the brother in the photo . . . the young father who had just entered the room. The April Uprising wasn't a mummified history, it was time *em-bodied* in that grandpa, time touchable and enclosing, in its wiry wrinkled grasp, the hand of this young man here. It had stepped into the time of his grandson, i.e., into my time.

I'd been touching the flesh of time, but I knew little about it, I didn't yet *em-body* it myself, I didn't know what it felt like, I didn't know how much ten, twenty, or thirty years were, or whether they would go fast or slow. When I was sixteen or seventeen, my temporal horizon consisted of a few more or less conscious years of *experience*

15 References, again like in a stream of consciousness, to iconic literary originals, in verse and prose, which describe the hard life of Bulgarian peasantry at the end of nineteenth and the beginning of twentieth century.

and an infinite luminous future where I was forever young and immortal, and my parents remained the way they were. My childhood was a despised prelude, a form of timelessness that I wanted to distance myself from as quickly as possible. Eh, if only the Earth could circle the sun two or three times faster. Purely theoretically, I knew that my parents would grow old, that I myself would grow old and that everyone would ultimately die, but at seventeen, this was merely abstract and extremely fictitious information that hadn't become knowledge, let alone consciousness and experience.

Later, as time went on, as time *con-solidated* and *em-bodied* itself in me, my children, my men, my parents, and everything that happened to me, I began to understand how much five, seven, ten, fifteen, twetny, twenty-five, thirty, and even forty years were. Today, when I'm writing these lines, I know how much forty-seven years are—from the first meaningful memories down to this *word*. Earth years, human years, my years. Personal knowledge of time is inversely related to the decrease of personal time.

In 1976 we marked the 100th anniversary of the April Uprising, in other words, a little more than twice the time I already know. Only twice as much! So, the April Uprising isn't some mummified piece of history after all—it is someone's "yesterday," a generational "yesterday," which held the small hand of my personal "today."

I was looking at my late grandmother, shrunk and disfigured by prolonged agony and ugly death. The dichotomy between body and spirit in its most extreme. In front of me lay about forty-five kilograms of ugly, and soon to be malodorous flesh. Nana was now gone. In fact, my grandmother had been gone for months. My innocent swashbuckler youth came to an abrupt end—the cautionary sight would often swim into my head when I dolled myself up and preened in front of the mirror. *La belle Roussane* . . .[16]

With her death, Nana finished our dialogue about Christ who came to life on the seventh day unlike everyone else. Nana wasn't going to rise from the dead, and that not because she didn't believe the story.

With Nana gone, I lost my direct connection with the First World War, the September Uprising, and the repressions of Communism—they returned to the official,

16 Reference to the painting *La belle Rosine—Deux jeunes filles* by Antoine Wiertz, displayed in the eponymous Brussels museum. The painting shows two women standing against each other—one is alive, beautiful, and naked, and the other one is a skeleton. Remnants of a sculpture are depicted under the skeleton—an allusion to the function of art. There is an inscription on the painting, saying that good appearance is only a matter of *time*.

mummified, textbook version of history and to that imaginary, meaningless historic time, where one hundred and one thousand years were basically the same thing.

In a personal story about time, even a relatively short one, you can't avoid clocks and watches. The tick-tock of clocks—those mechanisms invented to count our human seconds whereby light, let's say the light of our own star, travels 186,000 miles during that second—always bothered me. The sound of personal time running out staves off sleep. Tick-tock, tick-tock, tick-tock. Chinese water torture has something to do with the ticking of the mechanical clock. If, instead of plopping water drops on a person's head, you leave that person alone, completely focused on the sound of the ticking clock, very soon they'll go insane, too. At least I think so. I'd be off my rocker. Electrical clocks don't tick, mobile phones have replaced mechanical watches and kept the passage of time out of sight; we don't hear it, we don't think about it. Our personal time is overwritten by some circular everyday time, in which we have lots of everyday things to do.

I have an acquaintance who collects wristwatches—old and new, broken and functioning. It's an expensive passion to have. I fundamentally don't understand hobbies—I can't fathom how a person can take pleasure in acquiring, possessing, contemplating, and displaying stamps, butterflies, coins, and beer coasters. Collecting wristwatches, though, piqued my interest. My acquaintance really did have an idea, vague as it might have been, that every old and usually malfunctioning wristwatch had tick-tocked away someone's time.

As a student in Vienna in the early 1920s, my grandpa (the one on the bicycle) bought himself a pocket watch—a thin, elegant Longines. The hydro-engineer kept his Longines on a silver chain in his waistcoat pocket. He would wind it up each morning after breakfast, after shaving, to mark the beginning of the new day. When Grandpa got sick and bedridden, the Longines sat on the night table and he kept winding it up every morning to mark another day he had lived. Then he motioned for Nana to wind up the watch for him, first with his hand and later with his eyes only.

Grandpa died on a chilly February morning in 1960. Nana wailed and glanced at the watch—it read 5:28. Tenderly, Nana closed his eyelids, washed him with the help of a neighbor, then ran around arranging the funeral; Dad and my aunt arrived in the afternoon. In the evening Dad sat by his late father for a while. He took his watch in his hand. He found out the watch had stopped at 5:28. My dad marveled at the coincidence but thought that the watch just hadn't been wound up. He wound it up, but the hands didn't move. He took it to the clockmaker who, after admiring the Swiss beauty of time's delicate insides, told him that either the mainspring or the main wheel were irreparably broken. The watch had been working flawlessly for thirty-nine years and had stopped the minute Grandpa died. Was this a coincidence or a shockingly literal metaphor for the end of Grandpa's personal time?

Nana kept that permanently *deadlocked* watch in the little drawer of her night table. She had told my parents that she wanted to take it to her grave. She was an atheist, I had never seen her make the sign of the cross or go to church. She had told me the story about Christ rising from the dead only to explain the meaning of the word *voskresenya* (*resurrection*). Why did she want to be buried with Grandpa's watch since she didn't believe in the afterlife? And why that particular watch? I never asked. Probably since once, when I was still a child, she terrified the hell out of me because of it.

As a playful and rather inquisitive kid, I used to rummage in everything, and Nana's drawer was no exception. I inspected that watch a few times, and one time I tried turning its hands. I found out it didn't work and, disappointed that it wouldn't make much of a treasure, I discreetly placed it back in the drawer the way I had found it—under Nana's passport and some other documents. That evening Nana came into the living-room, limping briskly toward me, and . . . slapped my face! Startled, I held my burning cheek and couldn't believe what had just happened—my Nana, who made crepes and knit cardigans for me with her single, unparalyzed hand, she who read books to me and told me wondrous tales, my Nana was looking at me with livid green eyes. Never before had I seen such expression on her face. She held the forefinger of her better arm in front of my face:

"Don't you dare touch the watch in my drawer again!" she intoned, turning around and limping out of the room.

Mom had tried to defend me, but my father stopped her. They were both silent. I felt deceived by Nana, who didn't seem to be the person I knew. I felt abandoned by Mom and Dad, who said nothing and didn't bother to console me. Heavy tears rolled down from my eyes. Only then did Mom come over to give me a hug.

"Let me tell you the story of that watch," Dad said. "You'll see why it's so important to Nana and why she got so upset."

"But I didn't break it or anything! It wasn't working when I touched it," I sobbed.

"Did you move the hands?" Dad asked.

I didn't lie. Later, when I heard the story, I found out I had thoughtlessly dipped a child's hands into the magic of time. Having met Grandpa on a bike in the street didn't make up for that. A few days later, I had a discreet peek in the drawer—Nana had turned the hands back to 5:28. Her green eyes were again full of vitality and affection and her better hand touched me as tenderly as before.

Years afterward, as I was studying for my Ancient Greek Literature exam, I suddenly remembered that episode. It felt like as if I had unwittingly desecrated Grandpa's grave, and that had provoked Nana's *wrath*.

When Dad made some money, he got himself a Longines, too—a thin, plain, leather-strapped thing. I've often caught him gazing wistfully at the watch, obviously not really checking the time, making sure he wasn't late to something, or admiring its beauty.

Tick-tock, tick-tock,
how much time I have in stock?
Tell me, watch, and do not lie,
how much time before I die?

In an outburst of black humor, I got the idea of writing a letter to the Longines company to offer them my family story and metaphor for commercial purposes: "Longines—for as long as you're here. It will tick with your ticker, it will stop with your flicker."

A few years ago, I saw another watch—a massive, heavy, technoesque thing. The engraving on its back said, "The first watch worn on the Moon. Flight-qualified by NASA for all space missions." The guy wearing it was also part of an engineering clan, a German guy full of childlike admiration for gadgets and the human technological genius. He had visited Cape Canaveral a few times to watch spaceship launches. A lawyer by education and a banker by profession, he solved integral equations for fun (equations that often lean toward infinity), exhibited enviable knowledge in music, and a surprisingly cultivated taste in the visual arts. All in all, an exemplary product of the German mania for harmony and precision (hence the talent for composing trains, cars, rockets, and music), holistic development, and self-improvement (hence the penchant for philosophy, art, and sports). His father was a German engineer who had built railroads and developed mines in Africa, his grandfather—an engineer as well, and a friend of Niels Bohr—and his great grandfather built railroads in Siberia, as engineer-in-chief to the Russian Emperor.

The engraved assurance that the watch will work in *all* space missions impressed me immensely. I found it funny how *in space* that human watch and its round face would continue to measure, in human seconds and hours, the *earthbound* time. Furthermore, it would tick-tock the circular earth time, while time in the Universe, and our personal time as well, are linear.

I inquired if that technological marvel around his wrist would still work at a speed of 186,000 miles per second, and, if so, what kind of time it would measure, whether it would keep on ticking and how it would go about it inside a black hole containing, they say, antimatter and thus anti-time, whatever that is, and, if we went to the big planet of my teenage reflections, which rotation would the watch take into account—that of the big planet or that of the Earth. The German guy admitted he didn't know and no one knew. Yet.

All boys, even grown-up ones, and especially German ones, dislike questions to which they do not know the answers, and situations where they feel helpless. I gave him back the watch and changed the subject to something more down-to-earth. But I kept thinking about his watch. If our clocks only measure terrestrial time, which exists only insofar as we think of it, embody it, and measure it, our earthly time would have no meaning outside our lives, the life of humankind, and the life of all living things on Earth. If the *t*-time is more of a constant relation between certain quantities in the Universe, a function of distance and velocity, then that thick ugly watch with the overweening declaration was an instrument for the *temporal colonization* of space or at least for the definition of a cocky macho baloney of humans to that effect. Weird things cross a person's mind while making love.

Apart from the universal *t*-constant, relative time, historic time, aesthetic time, and the earthy time we embody, which is eating up our flesh in a linear and irreversible fashion, while misleadingly rotating, there is one more sort of time—individual time. (Plus economic time, to which the next chapter is devoted.)

It's such a pity Hawking did not seriously consider psychological time—he only jokingly classified it as either fast or slow, depending on whether one is having a good time or getting utterly bored. Pity indeed. Because time in our consciousness is a singularity. Unique for every individual, and may have nothing in common with the remaining kinds of time. This time opens up fascinating pathways to things that Hawking and other physicists found otherwise utterly engrossing, like time travel, the multiverse, and quantum teleportation. Simply put, the likelihood of late grandfathers riding bicycles.

Let's take dreams for example. What kind of time are we in when we're dreaming? What kind of time do we embody while we're sleeping (inasmuch as our consciousness is something material or at least a function of matter)? I have always been puzzled by dreams. Not just the stories my own (sub)conscious mind tells me, not just the images it projects and the morals it draws, but most of all by the *chronotopos,* or *the space-time* of dreams—where and when is it happening? Why do we assume this is unreal and only accept the reality of here and now when awake? All in all, that same mind has invented "real," wakeful time, as well, which, as it turns out, is only as real as far as my consciousness allows and is applied to complete some task. Why do we discard the reality of other times and spaces which that same consciousness has conceived? Just because they serve no practical purpose? Or they can't be shared and relived with others? There is no memory in sleeping, Bulgarians say. I strongly disagree. Some of my most fundamental memories and ideas are from dreamland, from a dozen of prescient dreams, which reality and real life cannot possibly configure or explain. Besides, even if we slept all life long, we would still age. Imagine, a continually dormant mind, which remains in childhood, while the flesh is being tick-tocked away by the biological clock. Definitely, different times are at work.

In fact, I suspect that time doesn't exist in dreams. Dreams are not just a processing of the present or the past, and they are not crystal balls of the future, either. I think that in our dreams we are what we are, what we were, and what we will be—a total self, dwelling in a total chronotopos. Could it be that dreams are the chronotopos, or the time-space, of consciousness and being?

A Bulgarian writer once said that sometimes he'd wake up and not know where he was—the cityscapes of good old Europe looked too much alike. I have had (and written about) the same feeling. But I've experienced something else, too. In the same drowsy state, I don't know *when* I wake up, in which moment of my life; who is sleeping beside me, whose warmth and whose leg I feel; have my children already been born, which body, face, and haircut will I be "wearing"; will I head to school or to my workplace, and, yes, where am I—in which one of my homes? After one such awakening, eyes still closed, I touched the person lying next to me—no, that was not Nana, I identified the man and that gave me a clue where I was in time and space. I stood naked in front of the large mirror and took a long look at myself, trying to figure out the meaning of *now.*

Looking at the latest loved one whom I lost, I thought that death is not only the end of personal time; it's also an end for the mind that configures and makes sense of all kinds of time. Time—in all of its varieties—exists inasmuch as there is a mind to make sense of it, measure it or embody it. Outside our minds, out there in the Universe, there is just one kind of time—*t,* which is nothing but a ratio between other variables, an objective ratio between objective quantities, which can be expressed differently, depending on the size and movement of the celestial body, inhabited by the mind contemplating it, as well as on the em-*bodiment* and the overall shape of existence of that mind. As a matter of fact, this consciousness may not be stationed on any celestial body; it may measure time in countless other ways regardless of its location, its speed of movement through the Universe, and its form of existence.

Knowing *t* does not automatically imply knowing time. The ability to operate with *t* is no proof of a mind contemplating its own existence *in time*. "I think, therefore I am" is only true if the thinking goes beyond mere rational knowledge and the manipulation of objective variables, physical and mathematical laws, implying *t.* Robots and computers use *t* and think unimaginably faster than humans, and yet they don't *exist,* they don't have a self, being, and consciousness, they do not have an idea of time and they are not scared of it. For me the quarrels between Bergson and Einstein were about precisely that—the former was thinking of human time, and the latter about *t.* It follows that the nothingness, or the non-being (as Heidegger would call it) is fundamentally an absence of consciousness and time, while *t* would be always there.

As I was getting ready to write about time, I googled the answers that my Dad couldn't give me and that he had no time to research in the library.

Our earth time units are the product of practical necessity and are literally created "in our own image," i.e., the human measure. The early measurement units were based on the length of a foot, the width of a finger, the distance between the nose and the outstretched arm of a *king,* three barleycorns arranged lengthwise, a Roman soldier's stride. Napoleon is credited with regulating not only the administration of the state, the legal system, the army, and urban planning, but also the way of measuring things, which used to be quite frivolous, as we see. From 1801 on, distance would be measured in fixed (yet still human, terrestrial) units—one meter would equal one ten-millionth of the distance between the Equator and the North Pole along the meridian running through . . . Paris, where else?! The French would cast a visual representation of one meter as the distance between two marks on an iron bar which would remain a *material* standard kept under a lid for more than two hundred years. And how convenient—1,000 meters, i.e., 1 kilometer, would prove to be practical for drafting the boulevards in the renovated French capital or for planning French army campaigns.

Time was trickier to measure. The only reference points humans had was the alternation between day and night, the regular change of seasons, and for the particularly inquisitive, the movement of stars across the nocturnal sky. All of those were recurrent, predictable, cyclical, circular.[17] Circular—in the most literal and geometrical sense of the word—because human units of time are derived from natural reference points and the . . . circle. Ancient Babylon introduced the base sixty arithmetical system for measuring time that we use to this day. The Babylonians calculated that the year has 360 days (although the Chinese beat them to it, noting that it was more like 366 days), which in turn is related not only to the real duration of our planet's rotation around its star but also with their observations that the Sun moves across the sky and vis-à-vis certain stars with approximately one degree per day, i.e., by the end of the year it has made a full circle. Today the circle still has 360 degrees. The Chinese were the first to divide the year into twelve months corresponding to the twelve most obvious constellations, while the Babylonians divided each month into thirty days.

The story of hours is "human, all too human." No one knows for certain who, when, and how had the day divided into twenty-four hours, instead of twenty or twenty-eight as my adolescent self had suggested, nor how people decided that one hour was to have exactly sixty minutes. Even Google doesn't know the answer. Different theories justify the division with arithmetic convenience—allotting equal time (twelve hours), to both day and night; others point out that sixty is a multiple of twelve, the twelve constellations, the twelve months, or our human measure of ten fingers plus two palms, the easiest means to count with. Even before they had any idea about the elliptical orbit of the Earth around the Sun, or about the axial tilt, people noticed that days and nights were fairly different in length in summer and winter, depending on how warm or cold the climate was, whether you lived in the North or the South. So, they counted the hours differently—a winter hour was different than an hour of summer, a Northern one differing from an hour in the South. There wasn't much need for precision—no working shifts, no ship or chariot schedules, no danger of vessels colliding, no TV programs to follow, no precisely fixed breaks at school, in the field or in the workshop, and not much international traffic. The Greeks "fixed"

17 Well, the full orbit around some cycles and circles is rather slow—the Earth's axis (which determined the starry scenography in the distant past in the absence of machinery and scientific collaboration between different geographical points) makes a full circle of its "wobble" every 26,000 years.

that in the sense that they set the twenty-four hours to equal length, season and location notwithstanding. And yet, people kept using those seasonally and geographically fluctuating hours well into the Renaissance, when the first mechanical clocks were invented.

Time goes full circle, they said. That's the way it has been since time immemorial, and it will be like that till *the end of time.*[18] But the things that have to be timed—pregnancies, lives, deaths, loves, wars, kingships, histories, i.e., the all too human stuff—are unpredictable, linear, irreversible, and unique. (Some are even too singular to have a real plural form, they are so individual and unique.) They occur in linear one-directional time.

Time has that wondrous ability of switching gears—depending on whether you're young or soaring on the wings of love, triumph, or fame, enjoying "la dolce vita," if you're dreaming or waiting for something, if you're stuck with a boring job, or hungry, rotting away in a prison cell, or languishing with an incurable disease. The cosmic *mise-en-scène* notwithstanding, maybe this is the actual reason why time units aren't based on the human body, not even on regal "gold standards" like the heartbeat of some sanguine, lewd, and belligerent king—or a mushy, melancholic, and sickly one.

What we measure and how we measure it are two separate things. In regard to time, the former question is both fundamental and overwhelming to humans. It took ages to break time into minutes and seconds (milli-, nano-, pico- and the like) it took ages for the *t* of economy, physics, and math to replace the mellow, inaccurate, quaint, and ruthlessly irreversible human time. These were later phenomena, which accompanied the development of human knowledge. The Babylonians, the Chinese, the Greek, and the Arabs had no use for that *t*. They would rather reflect upon *things* (things like atoms or water displacement, triangles, remedies, and so on) than mull over *time*. Day-to-day intervals had to be measured, one way or another, while cosmic time took care of itself; you could keep track if you were that inquisitive. Ancient scientists did not include *t* in their exploration of physics, astronomy, or math. Newton was the first to consider time itself, not its measurement. Yet, because he remained so strikingly pious, he left time to be tackled by divine reason, setting it apart from physics and the Universe and, eventually limiting his inquiries to good old measurement. Broadly speaking, the "discovery" of *t* was almost concurrent with its relativization. Einstein explains that there is no such thing as an absolute time, that time flows in different

18 Interesting that in Bulgarian, we have don't have a suitable translation for *the end of time*, as used for example in pop songs—"I will love you till the end of time." But Bulgarian does have *the end of the world*, which, if we apply Einstein's space-time, is actually more encompassing.

ways, depending on the relative speed of movement, that it is the fourth dimension, that the only absolute thing is the time-space, and that it's where we live—not just in time and not just in space.

Why don't we have other units of measurement for the unthinkably vast time-space of the Universe or the unthinkably small time-space of the quantum world? Our terrestrial year and kilometer produced the innocent and melodious yet monstrously conceived hybrid term, the "light-year"—a good fit, perhaps, for the four-dimensional time-space but a very bad fit for our human consciousness. The same goes for the infinitesimal, with negative degrees for size and positive ones for number.

But things aren't that relative, and they're not all that human. While I was writing and editing my story of time, human weights and measures were fixed anew, on the basis of absolute benchmarks. So, it was no accident that I'd pondered and wondered about such things even in my childhood. They were rather odd, indeed. From the 1960s to this year (i.e., 2019, when this book was originally completed) the seven principal units of measurement, including the second (for time), the kilogram (mass), and the meter (distance) have been redefined not as human-based *things* and fixed *material* standards, but as the expression of physical *constants* and *correlations*. Each of the chosen constants is determined vis-à-vis another one and, hark, represents *a fundamental characteristic of the Universe* that is *invariable* (at least within the temporal horizon of humankind). This way, the meter is determined with respect to the speed of light in a vacuum.[19] In 2019, the kilogram was abandoned to the same fate—*Le Grand K*, the prototype they keep in Paris, will be relocated to a museum. From now on, mass, measured in kilograms and their derivatives in the decimal system, will be defined by chunks of energy and the Planck constant. This constant comes from the infinitely uncertain world of quantum physics, but at least it's a constant. And time . . . Oh, time and its princess, the second, capable of discerning a *pea* through a mountain of mattresses, is defined by the period of atomic decay to Cesium 133 and is gauged by a cesium atomic clock whose ticking is not managed by Swiss springs and cog wheels, but rather by microwaves with a specific frequency, i.e., it, too, is of quantum order.

I won't bore you with more technical details about the other units of measurement (Ampere, Kelvin, mole) that will be defined again by universal constants. On May 20, 2019, these constants will be *eternally* fixed at the values they are currently attributed. The fundamental constants are identical across the Universe and do not change with time. [20]

19 299,792,458 meters per second.

20 At least that is how humans think. For the time being.

This attempt of humankind to transcend its anthropocentrism and the consequent idiosyncrasy of human measurement units paradoxically confirms how impossible it is to actually do so. What we get from deriving the main units of measurement from universal constants are weird decimals that look (to us) so random when set against Universal absolutes, that their human origin becomes hard to ignore. They were made "in our image." A second is not sacred; nor divinely related to some key microwave frequency or the journey of light. The fast-paced ticking of the clock reminds me rather of the beating of the human heart. The only answer to the question I had in my adolescence—who has decided that the second must last as long as it does—is us, humans. Because time is in us.

A (RELATIVELY) SHORT ECONOMIC (HI)STORY, OR, A CRITIQUE OF PURE MARX

*What good will it be for someone to gain the whole world,
yet forfeit their soul?*
Matthew 16:26

I was born into a poor engineers' family. That was the opening sentence of the autobiography I had to write for a homework assignment. I must have been thirteen at the time; at school, we were practicing this "genre"—utterly pointless and meaningless under communism. The autobiographies of all communist heroes started out like that. Well, it was true that their families were described as "peasant" or "working-class," whereas both of my parents were engineers, just like my grandfathers, my two aunts, and my uncle, and yet, all things considered, we *were* commendably poor, indeed, so I decided that the heavy engineering "element" wouldn't compromise the poverty part. The sentence sounded like a proper opening line for my life story and for the autobiography as one of the genre forms for relating it.

But my literature teacher, and more importantly the Pioneer/YCL/Party Secretary who had also read my homework, thought otherwise. The representative of the Communist Party to students and teachers, she had an impressive *university* degree in Pedagogy of Pioneer and YCL Activities. The Secretary started with the statement that engineers in "our socialist homeland" were not poor and that the "techno-scientific intelligentsia" was the pride and joy of our country.

"The other source of pride," she added, "is the artistic-creative intelligentsia, but it is like a spoiled, difficult child."

I had no idea what that convoluted 'artistic-creative intelligentsia' was, and it didn't sound all that good anyway, but I held fast to the poverty bit and insisted that my family wasn't rich.

"Fine," the lady comrade said, "but no one is rich. The purpose of communism is to eliminate the rich and you shouldn't malign the communist ideal by saying that engineers are poor."

"So, the goal of communism is to make everyone poor," I concluded, but the comrade pretended she hadn't heard me.

Having been taught that the communist order was the ultimate goal, the ideal, the final destination of history, and socialism simply an intermediate stage, I had concluded that communism would cancel out not only the grand narrative, but all human biographies as well. I had written that as a footnote to the word *Autobiography*, i.e., the title of my homework. That also got me lambasted; the comrade said it "tarnished the sacred *humanism* of the communist ideal." Not that I knew what humanism was. But we had to recite Georgi Dimitrov[21] by heart, and he'd said that the wheel of history was turning and would continue to turn until the ultimate victory of communism. I had always pictured the wheel of history very vividly—huge, mountainous, apocalyptic, majestic, grandiose, booming and clanging and trampling over all the little people and their biographies until it flattened them into a thin, homogeneous strip. That wheel would finally reach communism and stop, and then all the people would be identical, they would live identical lives and would have no distinctive biographies, so the CV would logically disappear as a genre.

In this particular case, however, we were discussing the proper way to start one's life story, my life story in particular. And the proper way to write about it. It was crystal clear that poverty was considered a virtue and I wanted to know why a peasant or working-class family could be poor enough to spawn heroes, and an engineering family couldn't. Besides, my family was indeed poor. The communist Secretary and I got into an awkward discussion of what it meant to be poor or rich. When I gave some unwelcome examples of kids from visibly well-to-do families, the lady comrade gave

21 Georgi Dimitrov (1882–1949) top ranking Bulgarian communist and ideologist, close ally to Stalin and member of the Politbureau of the Russian Communist party (1943–1945), General Secretary of the Communist International (1935–1943), Prime minister of Bulgaria after the end of WWII (1946–1949), who established the communist dictatorship.

up and sent me and my teacher back to class. The rich kids were part of the sacrosanct party elite, but at that age I hadn't yet understood this.

My parents were summoned to a meeting with Pioneer/YCL/Party Secretary. Coming home, Mom and Dad were visibly amused, but they nevertheless warned that I should stop writing that kind of stuff.

"But . . . how come? It's the truth! I want to be a hero, too!" I asked in confusion. I already knew that sooner or later I would 'fall victim in an unequal fight,' but I didn't want my death to be pointless and trivial, I didn't want to "not mean anything,"[22] I wanted to be a hero and die in the name of some ideal, something beautiful that would benefit all humankind. Of course, I hadn't informed my parents about this plan; I didn't want to upset them.

"Sometimes you can't say the truth. Period." Dad thought for a second and then added, "Besides, we aren't poor. You don't know . . . you don't remember what poverty actually is."

My Dad fell silent. I had really good memories, but kept them to myself. Not because he didn't look like he wanted to talk about it, but because my memories of that "real poverty" were magical. Like all first childhood memories. My parents had sent me to a weekly crèche and after that a kindergarten, not only because they were working and my paralyzed Nana was unable to look after me, but because the crèche facilities were better than our hearth and home. Even so, my first childhood memories were precisely of those Saturday evenings and Sundays, in the tiny house with a single all-purpose room, the cellar with Nana's bed in it, the outside toilet in the little garden, a visit to which constituted a whole adventure for me. The violet irises in our little garden were taller than me, glistening with the sun. At night, Mom's wooden-clogged footsteps were the sweetest lullaby to my ears—click-clack, click-clack. Falling asleep, curled up by Nana's side, I sometimes wondered why Mom walked around the garden at night. Years later, when we no longer had a garden and Mom no longer wore wooden clogs, I realized it had been my own heartbeat booming in my ears. Or the memory of my mom's heartbeat that I had listened to before I was born.

"As for becoming a hero," Dad said after a while, "your autobiography won't make you one. At least its beginning won't. We are neither peasants nor workers. We aren't party members, either."

---

22 Reference to a poem by the Bulgarian poet Nikola Vaptsarov (1909–1942), which he wrote in prison, the night before he was executed. Vaptsarov was a communist and member of a guerrilla sabotage and terrorism group, sponsored by the USSR and the Communist International. He wrote socially engaged poetry describing the hardships of proletarian life and his faith in the communist moral and future. The poem referred to claims that the life and personality, and death indeed, of the individual did not mean anything in the fight for the bright communist future.

"Yes, I know, you are the techno-scientific intelligentsia," I chirped, not knowing what the last part was about.

"And so," Dad smiled and narrowed his eyes, "if you want to be a heroine, you'll have to be an *intelligent* heroine. Or a *literary* one."

A couple of years later Dad told me that he and Mom didn't have "proper" lineage, either. My grandpa, the engineer, had studied in Western Europe, and then he had become a prominent member of the Social-Democratic Party, so the communist regime considered him "a hostile element of the bourgeois intelligentsia." To make matters worse, he came from a big and wealthy "kulak" family. My genealogical curse seemed to go back to the Adam and Eve of our clan. On Mom's lateral branch, it was no better—my chances of getting a proper heroic origin were stunted by her deeply religious Protestant family. Which didn't stop the Party Secretary of the technical school where Mom was a teacher, from making her patrol churches on Christmas and Easter eves—to make sure that neither she nor her students would indulge in the "opiate" of religious holidays. All the while, her own father was attending Nativity or Easter services.

That memorable opening of my biography was preceded by my pre-biographical, pre-historic, pre-economic, and pre-geographic childhood.

At night, in Nana's cellar and (later, when my brother was born) in the state-subsidized apartment on the main street of Lom, in one of the rooms which served as a kitchen, dining-room, and bedroom for Nana and me, the two of us would climb into our spacious bed and set off on a journey around the wide world, across the boundaries of time and space. We read together about the Eiffel Tower, the Louvre and Versailles, the bridges of London, the Coliseum of Rome, the skyscrapers of New York, about Tokyo, which, Nana said, was the size of Bulgaria. That made Tokyo a difficult destination to picture because I had no idea how big Bulgaria was. We studied the photos and the drawings, reread some of the lines, and she explained the things I didn't understand. It appears that later on, in kindergarten, I had told such convincing and elaborate stories of what I had "seen," swearing that I had been there (it wasn't really a lie if you think about it), that they called in my parents for something of an interrogation. It was obvious that none of us had visited all those places, and yet the amount of vivid detail bespoke a person who had really been there. My mom was questioned about being secretly in contact with her cousin and her family—doctors who had absconded to the USA.

Children are unaware of the material world and its economical workings. To them, the worth of an object isn't determined by its quality or its price, (mis)calculated in money or other material objects with a price tag on them. To them, things have a value which has nothing to do with their practicality or aesthetic appeal. A gorgeous lucky marble, a bicycle (the greatest luxury), a doll, a glitzy little ring on a nail-bitten finger, a strip of lace, a bright, strong elastic band—these things have a competitive value only in a child's world, in whose pre-historic and pre-economic world they cost exactly one other lucky marble, one bicycle, one doll, one ring, one scrap of cloth, or something just as cherished. Childhood is the era of natural exchange, of inordinately precious and utterly useless treasures.

When we were kids, our only direct encounter with money was our breakfast allowance, i.e., the pocket money for syrup, boza[23] or lemonade, and a greasy piece of banitsa,[24] a rigid wafer bar, kadayif, or, as a last resort, marzipan. Ten or fifteen stotinki[25] weren't what you would call money; they were more like tokens because they could get us very specific things—and nothing more, and nothing different.

Against that socio-economic background, in that pre-economic time of mine, I was dumbfounded when Dad brought home four big cardboard boxes of . . . Kinder Surprise chocolate eggs! Determined to lift his family out of poverty for good and to finally get us a car, a Russian Lada to be precise, Dad went to work in Libya for a few years. The Party kept 80% of the dollars that the brotherly *jamahiriya* paid to the socialist *gastarbeiter* engineer. With the remaining dollars Dad managed to buy a Lada without having to wait for ten years, and had enough left for a new fridge, a cooker, a piano for me, a ring for Mom, jeans, and chocolate for everyone. There were exactly 160 eggs in the boxes on the dining-room table. Laid in comfortable plastic egg cartons, individually wrapped in foil. Even the foil wrappers were already a treasure for us kids. Once I recovered from my sheer amazement with the heavenly combo of actual chocolate and diminutive toys—those astonishingly delicate little dolls, Indians, animals, cars—I got sick to my stomach and threw up, having eaten (secretly, of course) ten of those eggs in a row. My parents checked the content of the open box and, deducing the cause of my sudden "affliction," limited my access to the treasure and established an instructional rationing policy. Their plans were impossibly long-term for my time horizon. My brother and I would receive one chocolate egg per day after having eaten our mandatory healthy breakfasts, lunches, and dinners, and after having written

23 A traditional drink made of slightly fermented wheat or millet gruel mixed with water and sugar, very popular throughout the Ottoman empire.

24 A type pf Bulgarian pastry made with Filo dough. Usually served for breakfast with yogurt.

25 The Bulgarian equivalent of a eurocent.

our homework (I was in second grade, i.e., eight or nine). And not only that, but right after the "consumption," we had to brush our teeth because my parents thought chocolate caused tooth decay. I was horrified by the idea of washing away the taste in my mouth with the terrible Pomorin-brand toothpaste. You might as well disinfect happiness itself! My brother had it easy—he didn't go to school and he didn't have any homework to do; if anything, he had to cut back his food intake (Mom was in a silent fight with Nana about his weight while I was busy hiding away the unwanted pieces of toast) and he was still dangerously tempted to eat the toy along with the chocolate.

This was the first objectively valuable piece of material treasure I owned (well, yes, in theory I *shared* it with my brother). I was quick to find the stash as I had dealt with such obstacles before when I tried cherry liqueur and coffee. (I found liqueur delightful and coffee distasteful, but then again, I was too young to have tasted the pairing of coffee-and-cigarettes or concoctions like cappuccino and frappé that were still not to be found in Bulgaria. Now that I think of it, coffee was hard to find, too.) But after that I had to face a truly insoluble dilemma. It was definitely no fun to pig out on chocolate till I puked, nor to endure all those breakfasts, lunches, dinners, and snacks just to get the damn egg—and then kill the taste with the acrid toothpaste. My biggest concern was that I couldn't show my treasure to the other kids. Mom and Dad had told me that it would be quite vulgar to parade something that other children didn't and couldn't have. Yes, I could treat a couple of my closest friends to an egg, but only in secret. It would be better if my friends didn't tell the other children, either, so they wouldn't start craving the thing. If and when I wanted to do that, I was supposed to tell Mom so she would give me a couple of eggs for the treat.

That didn't suit me. I wanted to show the miracle to the entire population of kids on my street. I wasn't concerned that they didn't have chocolate eggs of their own—and never would. I was only worried that they wouldn't have equally valuable treasures to give me in exchange. The Kinder Surprise egg came from another world and was so perfect that, deep down, I hated it a little. Besides, the little delicate toys were so beautiful that they didn't stir my imagination at all—they couldn't be anything different, or more wonderful than they already were. They stood out, awkwardly, in their complete perfection, among the colorful rags, the sticks, the paper napkins, the tattered dolls, and the hairbands of our lives. I also noticed that the same tiny toys cropped up time and again, while our personal treasures were always unique. And yet, the thin two-layer brown-and-white chocolate could not be bought with a ton of wafers, kadayifs, or fake marzipans in exchange.

Using the conceptual system of economics, I would say that I had capital or family assets at my disposal. I could use those assets, which I had no share in compiling, to buy anything from the poor laborers of the children's world. I could have bought out all their treasures, I could have taken all their pocket money and enriched myself further, and I could have become a total monopolist among the children in my neighborhood. This perspective, however, was not only unappealing but utterly abhorrent. How could I play with the kids if I had everything and they hated me? How could we keep playing together if they were mourning their most sacred treasures, now irreversibly lost? How could our small kingdom continue to exist if our entire system of values was shaken and transmogrified? Of course, I was still too young for such convoluted thinking, but today I know that this was at the core of my dilemma.

I solved it by transferring ownership—I simply gave the eggs away to the kids in the neighborhood, methodically emptying the two "sealed" cardboard boxes and "sealing" them again every single time. So the first cardboard box, the legitimately open one, was meaningfully emptied by my parents at a rate of two chocolate eggs per day, while the other two were violently emptied, so to speak, with revolutionary pizzazz, within less than two weeks. In the course of these two weeks our small world was strewn with red-and-white pieces of foil and shiny little balls. It wasn't just the magic of the chocolate egg but the wonder of getting it freely, just like that, without having to covet and crave, without hating someone who had it, the magic of making your own collection of tiny delicate toys "for free," without sacrificing your most prized possessions or crying because the whole of your "treasure trove" was worth less than a single chocolate egg, without resorting to bribery, subterfuge, or taking sides. If that was what Communism was about, it was awesome! But you had to have kids and enough "natural resources" like chocolate and toys, for example.

I remember that my euphoria was darkened by the envy of some children. Even though I handed out everything I possessed, even though these children got their Kinder eggs, they envied me. Now, not for the eggs, but because I was . . . what I was, that I had done what clearly neither they nor their parents would ever have done. They envied me and sneered at me all at once, because I was so "stupid" to hand out the treasure. This particular kind of spite would accompany me all my life, including in the workplace.

When Mom and Dad were reassured that I hadn't tried to eat everything by myself, they didn't fret over the two empty boxes (they did mind the empty cherry liquor bottle, though, which I had definitely consumed alone). There would have been a peaceful conclusion, if the era of "communism" had not overlapped with the time when I was constantly losing stuff. The combination of losing things and giving them away really soured Mom's mood. Around that time, I used to "misplace," i.e., forget somewhere and lose, my winter jacket,[26] my woolen cardigans and sweaters (knit by Nana with her one good hand), beanies, gloves, scarves, schoolbags, and sports clothes. My mind was always too preoccupied to think about such paraphernalia. All these things were elements of a mandatory material world that had no value for me. I didn't perceive them as real gifts or keepsakes, either, because I couldn't play with them. My parents, however, paid a high price for these "mandatory" objects—not only in money that had to be calculated anew in the family budget, but also in nerves, "connections" and compromises and the time needed to hunt them down in the empty stores. Mom was really mad with me (and brought up the Kinder egg "case" in a rather unpleasant way) when I got home without a jacket and without acknowledging the falling snow. I mean, the snow was "acknowledged" with two hours of play in the schoolyard but not with the idea of having to put my jacket on. I developed a phobia of losing. Of losing stuff. Every night, at bedtime, I performed my "Last Post" ceremony, with a check-list, for my personal inventory of belongings—a jacket, some sweaters, a pair of gloves, a scarf, a pair of sweatpants, some woolen socks, a beanie . . . Occasionally, some items would heroically disappear, though.

The era of losing things left, deep in my heart, a spontaneous sympathy for all kinds of *losers* and abandoned souls. I am inclined to think—with no justification, as it has turned out many times—that these kinds of people are as innocent as children, unfit for the adult economic world, that their deep nature cannot find peace within itself and cannot reside in the shallow settlements of materialism.

I was growing up; my recorded biography had (unheroically) begun; I had started turning into a woman; I was accepted at the elite English High School; I entered the adult world of material things: the world of vanity, economy, money, history.

We were poor, but then again, everyone was poor, so that was no reason to worry, to compete, to feel ashamed, inferior, and insecure. There was nothing wearable in the shops anyhow. But my mother, despite being a representative of the "engineering in-

---

26 I remembered my winter jacket many years later when in the affluent Western Europe, I was editing the Bulgarian translation of mathematical and logical tests (PISA). In one of the problems John had four jackets—all in different colors, with and without lining. Peter had . . . I can't recall what and in what number. As I was adapting the problem for Bulgarian students, I not only changed the names to Ivan and Petar, but also replaced the jackets with books.

telligentsia," was also an exceptional seamstress who made me quite a few pretty outfits from *Burda*[27] magazine patterns.

Money had only relative value, something like our childhood coupon rations. Even if you somehow managed to earn more than you needed for essentials, there wasn't where or on what to spend it. We weren't allowed to travel, much less to the West. You couldn't eat gourmet food, or buy real estate; jewelry, yachts, clothes, bags, shoes . . . were all nowhere to be found—and there would have been no way to buy them. Since people couldn't *have* the things they wanted and couldn't get to know the world "firsthand," they plunged into a sort of "correspondence course" to explore not just the capitalist world but the world as a whole. We read a lot, and traveled virtually, and studied the languages of countries we were never going to visit. We read about the belle époque, royal palaces, seaside resorts, castles, natural phenomena, oceans, sharks, deserts, stars, and the Universe. They watched TV series with aristocratic characters set against a background of posh interiors, lawns, stables, and swimming pools. We listened to classical music, most of the children learned an instrument or joined a choir. People decided to *be* and not to *have* because they couldn't have, anyway. Insatiable and cognitively omnivorous, we acquired a provincially elaborate hyper-erudition about everything. It started from school. Our pretentious tedious erudition gave us self-confidence, but it rarely led to originality of thought.

We read a lot of poetry, too. It seems that people during the communist regime were not only better educated, but more sensitive as well. In fact, intimate emotions were politically safe and a good way to vent, so love poetry and the banal soundbites of popular "universal" psychology and philosophy were encouraged. Besides, this mushiness was deeply rooted in the bottomless sentimentality of the Slavic soul. Yevtushenko[28] used to boast that only in Russia could you fill a stadium with people who flocked there not to watch a football match, but to hear some poetry.

Books and films ridiculed the desire to *have* as a lowbrow thing. Ah, how pitiful and laughable, how "spiritually inferior" those little people were—the ones who spent years scrambling to acquire a Russian car, some kitschy furniture, a pointless villa, the rare masterstrokes of the local garment industry, to find their own people in important places, or dollars which could get you a few rags and trinkets from the Corecom,[29] the little people who took odd half-legal private jobs mending Russian cars, TV sets, or

27 German housewives magazine, very popular in the '70s and '80s.

28 Famous poet in the USSR.

29 From French "Comptoir de représentation et de commerce"—a chain of duty-free stores that operated with foreign currency in Bulgaria between the 1960s and the 1990s.

fridges, the ones who churned out cheap crowd-pleasing art. We used to laugh a lot . . . We ate a lot. And drank till we could forget it all.

I grew up against this socio-economic background and then "had to find my way in life." It was crystal clear that I wasn't going to become the next engineer in the family—and that I wasn't going into the exact sciences at all. After learning to read at the age of five and indiscriminately gobbling up everything the librarians of Lom and Plovdiv allowed me to borrow; after accompanying Dad to the rehearsals of the Lom Amateur Orchestra where he played the cello; after my high-school Bulgarian teacher started taping my analyses on a voice recorder and playing them to the other classes; after joining a student literary club, majestically named "Academy of Poetry," after getting a poem published in a magazine . . . after all of that, I knew there was nothing I would rather do but read (well, *essay*, to write, if I dared) and analyze (perchance translate) some texts, and enjoy (play, if I could) some music.

There was nothing unknown, extraordinary, or magical about the adult life looming on the horizon. In a few years, I would have to face one of the few life scenarios that would stem from my choice of education and of a spouse and, if the first two didn't imply it, decide on my ethical position about becoming a Party member or adopting more or less reprehensible strategies or compromises for avoiding feudal bondage to the designated town or village where I had to live and work.[30] I was clearly going into the humanities, so that outlined the rest of the future: study philology (or philosophy, or psychology for that matter; all were equally useless economically), then head straight to being a teacher, give birth to two children and raise them, dividing my time on Earth between the classroom, the kitchen, the kids, between sitting in front of the TV or at the table, eating, and drinking.

All prudent grown-ups told me to go into law as a solid, traditional course of study and a good route to a secure and well paid job. But what kind of law could be practiced in a state where the supreme rule of law was the ideology of the Communist Party?! There were no such things as human rights, civil rights or private enterprises, hence the branches of law that would govern them were missing. Private property was reduced to one flat and one car per family (to buy either of them, you had to be on a waiting list for about ten years). People got formally divorced so they could buy a second apartment, but they would continue to make love in secret, or to keep their affairs just as secret. Although there were no prenuptial agreements, family law and criminal

30 In communist times, upon graduation, university students were allocated to compulsory jobs, usually in remote small towns or villages. Residence was fixed at a specific place and one could not move freely. Marriage (to a resident of the aspired bigger city or the capital) or an academic career were the only escapes, apart from a career in the Communist party nomenclature.

law were the only areas of justice, which had some legal substance to them. And since during the communist regime there was little crime (communist citizens were a new breed of humans, you see) at the end of the day, the only flourishing niche of the legal business was divorce, genuine or pretended. Bourgeois society brought forth the marriage of convenience, Communism gave birth to the divorce of convenience.

There was yet another, peculiar kind of law, let's call it political although this might sound like a contradiction in terms. Its "legal" basis was rooted straight in article 1 of the Constitution.[31] Nobody commented upon it, nobody specialized in it and nobody practiced it officially. All the malcontents, dissidents, illegal émigrés and their families, adversarial culture smugglers, the secret audience of *Radio Free Europe*, the *Voice of America* and *Deutsche Welle,* the long-haired boys and the short-skirted girls . . . all of them were guilty by default, according to the regulations of this political law, and no lawyer could plead anything but excuses, mitigating circumstances, immaturity, bad influence, confusion, and so on.

I, however, didn't care about people's "dirty laundry," nor about their money; I was interested in their souls and, above all, in the cosmic imprints in their human minds. Besides, I saw lawyers as morally suspicious: too ready to scoff at truth and defend anything for money.

Dad was the only one who encouraged me to match my area of study with my eventual career ambitions and to choose a job where I wouldn't "keep my eyes on the clock, counting the minutes until the end of the working day."

Censorship and ideological dictates were everywhere (just like the Secret Service informers), but the humanities still had a liberal halo. I thought if I stuck to analyzing classic Western and Russian authors and writing about the human soul, love, and the stars, I could avoid ideological conflict by digging into purely human feelings and purely literary problems. On top of it all, my favorite savant-litterateur had straightforwardly declared that if the most intelligent representatives of a nation do not occupy themselves with literature, then that's one boring nation. Come on! Me—boring?! Bulgarians—boring?! Going hungry was way better than being boring.[32]

I wanted to *be* and I didn't care about money. It hadn't crossed my mind that I would have to take care of someone, a child, for example, and that I would need money for that, too. Yes, I thought every now and then, theoretically, it would be nice to have a cute, pink, sweet, and cheerful baby—someday. Flaubert said somewhere that when

31 Stipulating the leadership role of the Communist party and the working class in the "socialist state" governance and in the society at large.

32 My self-affiliation among the most intelligent representatives of the Bulgarian nation was so blunt and unconscious that it's embarrassing to think about today.

young women reflect upon their future families, they don't go beyond the romantic glow of their wedding ceremony. That's to a certain extent how I felt about children—my thoughts stopped at the banal pink or blue imagery and didn't go any further, even when Rada was already kicking at my insides, energetically reminding me that she was on her way and that she would need food and a warm bedroom, that she would need clothing and schooling, that she would constantly lose things, as I had, and many other details.

In short, after oscillating between majoring in philosophy, psychology, or literature, I chose the last, with a side helping of linguistics. My goal was to teach at university, in other words to read and interpret, and write to my heart's content without looking at my watch, maybe even get a salary for doing what I loved, and to use that salary to pay for necessary material stuff like food, clothes and footwear, electricity, and cigarettes. I'd started working right after high school (teaching English to the kids at the local community center), I kept working my way through college (same job, but with adult students) and that, together with the scholarship I was awarded for academic excellence, allowed me to make ends meet. Maybe Dad was so full of idealistic advice not just because of my limited life choices and the lack of financially remunerative careers under communism, but also because my studies did not cost him a dime. There again, like most Balkan, men he invested all his ambitions in his son; the daughter would be a mother at most.

When it came to my choice of man, there were no surprises here either—I married an artist, a man of spirit who seemed to inhabit the same non-materialistic abode as I did. However, it quickly transpired that someone had to work, and work hard, to earn a decent salary that would cover at least the minimal family budget. Our simple economic needs left little opportunity to have two spiritual persons—or, shall I say, three children—in our family of three. I gave up on all academic and writing daydreams, I threw away tons of summary notes (whole handwritten books with records of what I'd read during my literary studies, having no money for photocopying), I wept and got stuck into work. In one of the dozens of newly sprouting publishing houses. I edited other people's texts and some authors undermined my creative streams. But most of the time I was engaged with textbooks.

By all accounts, especially simple economic ones, my personal biography was stuck in the rut of the mundane world. In the meantime, the wheel of history had continued to turn, but instead of rolling forward toward communism it seemed to have rolled backward to capitalism.[33] The planned economy did not survive the arms race with

33 In this sense, the words with which we strained our throats at meetings were not precise. "Lift up your

Reagan's Star Wars, totalitarian regimes collapsed, the Iron Curtain and the Berlin Wall tumbled down, and suddenly the time was proclaimed for democracy and the transition to a market economy.

I was swept along by the crowds in anti-communist marches and demonstrations, although once again, as before, I felt ridiculous standing among thousands of people and chanting crude political slogans. In the past, my uneasiness was balanced by the obvious nonsense of the slogans, which I found quite amusing. Now the rallying cries sounded out good things, but I felt just as uneasy.

After the ecstasy of democracy and the hopes for normal life it raised, we went through hyperinflation and winters of cold and hunger when everything I earned as an editor was only good enough for bread and yogurt. Sitting on the shoulders of her father, a.k.a. the Artist, three-year-old Rada banged an empty frying pan in hunger demonstrations, which should have been ancient history. In a few years, things seemed to go back to some form of normality; in other words, I could feed my little family again and pay its modest bills. But a modest income wasn't enough for half of the educated, working twenty- or thirty-something-year-old Bulgarians, who decided to leave the country. Besides, Bulgaria began to resemble a Latin American nation dominated by gang bosses, with fingers in the pies of racketeering, prostitution, and narcotics, along with the armament and gasoline businesses. Highly lucrative assets were allocated and reallocated by shoot-outs that took place in broad daylight on the city streets.

Behind those "dramatic historical upheavals," however, my personal story had ground to a standstill. In theory, history had opened new possibilities for travel, work, and education, but in my own life, it was too late to fight for a scholarship at a third-rate American university. I was completely incapable of setting up my own startup company or working in the gray "economy." It was no longer an advantage to have poor-peasant or working-class roots, or come from a family of anti-fascist guerrilla fighters. Now you had to be the offspring of a Communist Party elite or a descendant of a formerly wealthy family, now due restitution of its properties expropriated by the communists in 1947. These victims of the communist regime and their families could finally speak out, they could decry the wrongdoers and tell everyone about the atrocities, they could even go into politics, but they had no access to the economic resources. Capital was red, it remained in the hands of the communist nomenclature and its secret services, as well as their Russian comrades. The emerging "transitional" or

eyes, see this world, life today is moving forward, and not backward." There was no way human life could go backward, but society and the economy definitely could.

black market economy had even less need for writers and literary scholars. There was freedom of speech and convictions so the literati could write whatever they wanted, as much as they wanted. And starve to death.

In short, once again I was not at a good (re)start-position—I had neither the right pedigree nor the requisite qualities to be among the winners. And so, free of any materialistic and career-related temptations, I kept on working for the publishing house. The Artist, unbothered by any concerns about the family budget, created brilliant etchings which were no less extraordinary in their technical precision and aesthetic value than those of Albrecht Dürer. They will certainly receive recognition in a couple of centuries, when people will revise their opinion of the empty canvases of the twentieth century, and will pay a king's ransom for the Artist's elaborately engraved copper and zinc plates. That, however, will happen in the eternity of art, in that *ars longa* which is *post-mortem* to our *vita brevis.* In *vita brevis,* the economic return from the etchings yielded a twenty-year-old, third-hand German car.

To me that was the era of the lottery, the can and the moon. I would buy a lottery ticket every week and I spent all of my scarce personal time alone in the loo—a personal space indeed. No, I wasn't reading on the can. I was thinking about things, but most of all I was daydreaming. I was thinking how, at the end of the day, I was the protagonist in the whimsical, artistic version of—finally—a rather trivial scenario. I was cast in the role of the Artist's wife and muse, that devoted woman who has the noble duty to provide for the family while inspiring the Artist so that the Artist can do his creative work—the one who has the honor to share her humble fare with the crème of the local bohemia and be sung to by them.

The Artist's wife had also started taking part in the drinking sprees, to forget and not to weep. In my can-meditations, I felt like I'd been sentenced, as though my life was over. Looking ahead, I saw decades of exhausting work: good, peaceful work, to be sure, but not what I had been dreaming about. I was going to waste half of those decades on the nice job, which would provide the financial means for my family and me to . . . survive, nothing more. I had married for love, I had not been corrupted, I had not been tempted away from the straight and narrow (as I rather vainly told myself), and I had preserved my "soul and values." And yet, I didn't know what to do with them. I had no time to actually enjoy them. In the confines of the bathroom, I would often tell myself to shove those soul and values up the . . . you-know-what.

Most of my bathroom time, however, was spent dreaming—dreaming of hitting the jackpot. I came up with a simple use for that jackpot. It was easy, as it had been with the Kinder eggs. I didn't dream of yachts, diamonds, sports cars, designer clothes and bags, or vacations at fancy resorts. If I had wanted these things, I would have had a hard time indeed deciding how to spend my imaginary jackpot. Instead, I dreamt of having just enough money to allow me not to think about money. Then, I wouldn't have to squander all of my precious time on working hard. Then, I wouldn't have to repress the intriguing thoughts buzzing around in my fragile skull, setting them aside for prosaic calculations about how to pay the electricity and heating bills at the end of the month, about whether I would be able to buy Rada a winter jacket, about how to give my brother pocket money, how to help my parents until the next salary or pension. One night, after I had spent more than an hour in the loo, I formulated my first law of money: The greatest freedom money can bestow is not the freedom to do whatever we want, contrary to what most people think. We do what we really want anyway and our desires consciously or more often unconsciously follow a moral imperative formed by family, religion, culture, education, society, and the time in which we were born and brought up. But under all circumstances this has little to do with money. Consequently this is my first law about money: the greatest freedom that money gives us is the freedom to not think of money itself, but allow one's spirit to live beyond the mere survival of the body.

In the bathroom I was dreaming about money and formulating laws, and during my nights I was listening to the alcoholic snores of the Artist on my left and Rada's burbling on my right, contemplating the stars and the moon through the skylight, thinking about time, the Universe, and the meaning of life.

An artist's wife, however, is not supposed to think about these kind of things, which are the Artist's territory. Somewhere around the house there was even a book entitled *The Artist's Wife*, in which I cannot now remember what genius imparted advice to young artists about what woman to marry.

I ran away from the family bathroom and moved into another one, a really private one, so to speak. I left the Artist and my noble role at his side, taking seven-year-old Rada with me. I rented a tiny, run-down apartment where I didn't have to go the bathroom to think and daydream—the whole apartment looked and smelled like a repurposed lavatory. Well, I couldn't afford another home. I was just as rash with the divorce as I had been with my marriage—I had no idea how I'd get by, where I'd live with my child, and, all in all, what my life would be as a thirty-four-year-old divorced woman, with a useless degree in philology, in the post-communist society in a period of a prolonged transition to a market economy and EU membership.

I started writing in the evenings, after Rada had gone to bed. I got up at 4 A.M. after three or four hours of sleep. I worked my ass off at the publishing house so I could pay the rent and make sure Rada was not deprived of anything. I was determined that my so-called creative pursuits would not affect our budget in any way. I tried to ignore the uncomfortable question that kept popping up: what the hell was I doing, at midnight, at 4 A.M.? The Artist knew he was an artist, his talent had been certified with a diploma and demonstrated through numerous aesthetic productions. I was writing weird stories without a clear goal, and without any confidence in their aesthetic value. The only thing I was sure of was that I was doing something totally different from the "daily drudge," from merely earning a livelihood and achieving a humdrum "survival." And that "something" was turning me into another person, into a woman completely different from the one everyone knew. After a few good moments composing a few good paragraphs, I realized that the other world I lived in, the one of writing, gave me sensations that no other human joy or pleasure could give me. To my own surprise, my stories weren't critical or realistic. They didn't describe my bathroom visions, garnished with psychological and sociological introspections. I might have described the dramatic historical events I was witnessing, restructuring the narrative and embellishing them with timeless, universally human love stories, with acts of kindness, compassion, the heroic exploits of everyday characters, the crushing of the little man, and so on. But I didn't. Instead, I wrote about writing, I wrote about the writer *herself*, I wrote about the footprints left not by our actual biography but by the biography of our spirit, I wrote about the reflection of the stars in our eyes and the materialization of time in our flesh.

And then, the publishing house I was working for sent me to the Frankfurt Book Fair. For the first time in my life I traveled on a plane, for the first time in my life I set foot in Western Europe—once a bourgeois-capitalist rival, now a democratic role model whose European community post-communist Bulgaria wanted to join. The cultural shock was inevitable and started while I was in transit; not only was I flying for the first time in my life, but I also landed in the largest airport in Europe. Afterward, at the Book Fair, I was lost for words, for it wasn't just an important book fair, it was the biggest in the world.

And yet, the most derailing moment of my cultural shock was quite intimate. I put aside, for a rainy day, three quarters of the whopping amount of German marks that the Book Fair had paid me as daily allowances for a one-week stay (under a program for young publishing professionals from East-European countries). The sum was enough for me to live comfortably for a couple of months with Rada back in Bulgaria. With the remaining quarter I ate a sandwich a day at the Fair, I bought a doll and a toy pram for Rada, a second-hand coat for my mother and small presents for the rest of my family. For myself, I decided to indulge in a Campari, to be savored at leisure in a busy place. I could spend hours over a drink or a cup of coffee, watching the people passing by. Or looking at nothing in particular, allowing myself to be transported into another place. I like busy, noisy places in big cities (which I had hitherto taken to mean Sofia and Plovdiv), I like how anonymous and detached they make me feel. Later I realized that the Parisian cafés were invented for people like me, who, apparently, aren't that few and far between.

All the trainees had received tickets for a concert at the Old Opera House. The concert program wasn't really much to my taste but I had nothing else to do, and besides, the very idea of attending a concert in Frankfurt's Old Opera House sounded thrilling. About an hour and a half before the concert was due to begin, I seated myself in a posh bistro at the central shopping street near the Opera. Just Campari, on the rocks. It was a warm October day, late afternoon, I was sitting by the Old Opera House, smoking, drinking Campari, looking at passersby, at the buildings, the sky, thinking about Plovdiv, my life so far and to come, about the manuscript I had finished writing and wasn't sure deserved to be a book.

And then, two women walked past me, one right after the other. The first one was closer to being a girl, about twenty, maybe a student, tall, with a blonde ponytail, jeans and moccasins, white shirt, soft jacket, and a dark-blue, soft leather backpack—a beautiful, slender, agile thing. She stopped nearby, slung off the backpack, reached inside and pulled out a phone, a mobile phone like the ones I had first seen in the hands of the colleagues from the foreign publishing houses, and started talking—in English. I eavesdropped shamelessly. She was a student, the academic year had just started and she had rented a very good flat in the center of Frankfurt, yes, just for a year, because she was on an Erasmus scholarship, she wanted to improve her spoken German and most of all learn the German terminology in . . . (I couldn't get what she was studying), yes, in a month she was going back to Edinburgh for a weekend.

I was trying to listen like a mature woman who wasn't a student anymore, who was already a mother, a working woman who had come to Frankfurt on a business trip. But I couldn't stop the stupid, unexpected moisture in my eyes. The girl put the phone back in her backpack and hurried away. Then another woman passed by. I recognized her from the Fair, she was a deputy copyright manager in a large American publishing house, a bit older than me, perhaps thirty-eight or forty years old, and not exactly a beauty, but . . . pretty, sexy, well-groomed, a well-to-do woman of taste and culture, educated, well-paid and well-employed, a woman who bought the rights to books that would receive gigantic print runs. She was strolling around, having finished her shopping, two designer-brand paper bags hanging from her arm. What small purchases were in there? A scarf? Some lingerie? A piece of jewelry? I burst into tears, barely managing to put on my sunglasses and fish the tissues out of my bag so I could pretend I was blowing my nose. No, it wasn't envy or social hostility I was feeling, nor my own insecurities. I was crying because I had no access to Erasmus scholarships when I was a student, because I couldn't travel around the world or read the authors I wanted; I was crying because the low horizon of the high street in Plovdiv was making me claustrophobic, and because I was living in a lavatory. I saw how ugly my life was, hopeless and boring, how ugly and unkempt I was, myself. I thought about how I had to break my back so that, ten years from now, Rada could study in a third-rate European university—if, of course, she could get a scholarship or a job. The confidence in the intellectual superiority of my vast erudition, my exotic and authentic spirit and culture, was melting away in tears. The typed manuscript in my Plovdiv drawer seemed to me ridiculous and pitiful in comparison with the large posters of stellar authors, with the book business as a whole. The elaborate Dürer-style etchings of the Artist appeared to me provincial and old-fashioned compared to the huge blocks of color on the all-but-untouched canvases in the local galleries.

I sniffed discreetly, pretending I was blowing my nose, and repeated to myself like a mantra that this was vanity, vanity of vanities, and all is vanity, that what I envied was material, consumerist affluence, that these women *had* a lot, but *were not* a lot, in that superior, spiritual sense; that shallow geographic curiosity, and accessibility, was not enough to fathom the world, and the human being. I reminded myself that I had written my manuscript and the Artist had made his etchings under the same low provincial skies; I tried to convince myself that our artworks were worthy, as they reflected universally human fears, hopes, and dramas, including the torments hidden within these two women. At worst, I thought, we belonged to a lost generation. Despite its despair, this formula contained some pathos and decadence charm, which gave me comfort.

I went up to the bathroom of the bistro to fix what little make-up I had on and to apply some foundation to my flushed nose. Red-eyed and still in the middle of my "crisis of values," I headed for the empty second balcony of the concert hall. Where a blue-eyed stranger, as visibly bored as I was, struck up a conversation in French, inexplicably convinced that it was my native tongue—it seems I looked like a weedy French intellectual. As to the stranger, he was a divorced German jurist from Frankfurt, working for a European institution in Brussels, who had made a donation for the restoration of the opera in his hometown and had come to enjoy the result.

One July morning, blind chance—which we, mystically inclined Slavs, call fate—had sent my first husband, the Artist, to the Plovdiv covered market, where I was on duty that particular day at the fish stand as part of an obligatory course in "industry practice." The odds of a handsome, talented, single artist meeting a local, poetry-writing "beauty," albeit in a cloud of unthinkable stench, were low, but somewhat logical in the provincial scale. The odds of me arriving from provincial Plovdiv and my lavatory-style flat at that particular boring concert, on that particular evening, on that particular balcony in the Frankfurt Old Opera house, just to meet my second husband, were more or less fifty million to one.[34] The analysis of chance is a legitimate branch of science, extending from calculations of probability to chaos theory.

It seems that my two spouses came with two different socio-economic systems. The Artist belonged to the "ripe socialism," as we were taught, or the end of communism, as it became to be universally known; the Jurist belonged to capitalism—should I add "ripe" or "European"? European capitalism still possessed enough dynamism and social mobility that, with a large helping of chance, I could move from one political order to another, and from one class to another. Together with the eight-year-old Rada, I left the sunshine of my post-communist, long-transitioning homeland and moved to the old, beautiful, multicultural, colonial, capitalist, art deco, surrealistic, delicious, snug, gray and rainy, dirty and traffic-jammed Brussels, the capital of the European Union.

Unlike the credo of the Bulgarian literary guru and his classification of boredom along literary lines, the Jurist divided the thinking part of humanity into two major groups—those who had studied law and those who hadn't. As a typical German, my husband had a deep admiration for the spiritual and for art, but he preferred works of time-tested quality, i.e., the classics, which he knew by heart and reread every now and then. He distrusted contemporary art, created by bohemians and intellectuals, who hadn't studied law and didn't have serious jobs. Since my husband was definitely one of

34 My calculations are based on the male population over a certain age and on the territory of the EU, which was just starting to open its fortress gates to some East-Europeans.

the most intelligent and well-read men I had ever met, and since the most profound philosophers, composers, and psychologists were all German (or at least German-speaking), Germans definitely weren't a boring nationality. I accepted that "first, my intellect and potential needed to be invested in a good and secure job" and that writing would be "for later, in your spare time." As I had absolutely no competitive edge in the democratic, Euro-capitalist world, I had to learn French, European law, and a vast body of information about the history and machinery of the European project, which I found otherwise, laically and lyrically speaking, inspiring and historically great.

While I was in training, acquiring the needed qualifications to become a European official, the most significant Bulgarian publishing house had decided to publish my manuscript, and a Bulgarian literary guru gave my book an ecstatic review. Good, he did not know how I was drifting away from literature to bureaucracy at that time . . . The Jurist was proud with me and sincerely rejoiced my literary success, which nevertheless did not amend his "general plan" for my development and integration into the western world.

My husband descended from an eminent German-Swiss clan of lawyers, medical scientists, and hereditary social democrats; he himself was a loyal member of the German Social Democratic Party and had adopted a staunch leftist stance regarding the equitable allocation of resources and values in society. This didn't prevent him from liking sophistication and luxury. The humanist bourgeoisie breeds social democrats. On the other hand, like most Germans, he was especially sensitive to things like hunger and distress, responsibility, guilt, politically correct tolerance and humanism, etc. I benefited from, or rather endured, the historically constituted guilt of a Western European for having abandoned Eastern Europe in the paws of the Russian bear, of a German for the atrocities, committed by his forefathers, and of a bourgeois for the injustice of capitalist society. Besides, all this was packed in the Protestant moral that life resumes to duty to family and society, duty served by hard work and sacrifice. Obviously, art did not qualify as hard (and remunerated) work in my husband's mind. That's why, without wanting it, I became the soother of all his guilt, whereas the only thing I really wanted was refused me. Galatea Doolittle first had to be educated and work.

I unsuccessfully tried to persuade my husband that Germans are built on a larger frame and that my size did not mean I had been starving. To him, the German size 34 indicated a teenager or someone who was unhealthy. I had to eat more. One of the first Bulgarian words my husband learned was the imperative "eat," both directed at the willowy Rada, who kept her dreaminess at mealtimes, and indirectly at me.

Talking about food, its abundance and, most of all, quality was one of the first things that struck me in Brussels, along with the all-around splendor of the houses. We ate with heavy silverware; the food was accompanied with vintage French wines that my connoisseur husband stocked and sorted by year in a wine cellar in our basement. My cheap jeans (too cheap, but also too tight for "a woman of my taste, status, and age") were replaced by silk and cashmere. My neck, fingers, ears, and wrists were decorated with jewelry. I went to horse races (with a spectacular hat), opera (in an evening gown), casinos (in plunging necklines), top restaurants, parliamentary sessions and political meetings (in elegant business suits). For the first time in my life I had a study (the attic in our large house), but I was only supposed to use it to learn French, European law and the economic geography of Europe—and most definitely not to write (and smoke).

I'm begging the reader to forgive those lines; it was not vanity and self-conceit that made me write them. These details are pertinent to the messages of this story, and of the book as a whole.

I told my husband about my tendency to lose things and recited to him my poem about the lost items, thus I obtained the "right" to wear jeans every other day when I did not have to be in a "presentable" outfit. The jewelry was peacefully resting in a jewelry box, so there was no need to operate last-post check-ups every evening. The only two pieces I was wearing at all times, but tight enough not to get lost, were the diamond ring, which my husband gave me when he asked me to marry him, and the wedding ring. While diamonds have a "purely" earthly origin,[35] the chemical elements of gold and platinum can only be formed in the merging of neutron stars. They have come a long way to Earth to *settle* in mineral deposits here. Today over 90% of existing diamonds are synthetic, yet despite the efforts of generations of alchemists, we still don't have any synthetic gold or platinum. Since there have been no *recent* (in the cosmic sense) mergers of neutron stars in the local cosmos, gold and platinum are available in limited quantities. That's why they are so expensive and have such "solid" value that it is worth making a capital investment,[36] in a wedding ring and other adornments, symbols of *eternal* love for the women we share our lives with, or as gifts for other women (or why not men) who we care about. Such things occupied my mind as I was looking at my embellishments. I was trying to picture when, where, and how the material they were made of had come into existence. No, not in the sense of ore deposits in Siberia or children slaving away in African diamond mines. Of course

35 Yes, diamonds are made from carbon, which may come from outer space, but the polymorph allotrope of carbon, i.e., diamonds, are made on Earth.

36 And for paying off debts as Putin has recently reminded us.

jewelry was, above all, an expression of love. And deepest friendship. Diamonds are not a girl's best friend, intelligent and loving men are.

Let me go back to the perishable alimentary substances. So, that was how things were going to be, I thought. Before getting the magic Kinder egg, I was once again obliged to eat the compulsory healthy stuff; before I could be allowed to be a child again, I had to become a real adult—to have some practical, useful knowledge, and a real job with a real salary. And all that in Belgium—the country of chocolate wonder. I couldn't just be a disengaged outsider who observes capitalism and writes honestly about it, with a free conscience. I had to become a participant in it, a professionally competitive one at that: to engage and integrate—in other words, to corrupt and betray my spirit in exchange for the material rewards Euro-capitalism had prepared for me. Besides, material comfort and the bureaucratic job I was aspiring to, fully stood to dry up my zest to write.

Ironically enough, my class-consciousness catharsis, so to say, was happening in the country featuring the only—to my knowledge—still existent and thriving Marxist party. Yes, that is the same Belgium, which Karl Marx described as "the snug, well-hedged, little paradise of landlords, the capitalists, and the priest." It seems Herr Marx left a strong legacy here.

One evening my husband and I devoured a stellar Michelin menu for two that cost a few months' worth of my parents' pensions, combined. We were sitting at the famous Swan restaurant on Brussels's Grand Place where, legend had it, Karl Marx had written *The Communist Manifesto*. I had the feeling that there, at that table, in that gourmand-spiritualist session with the ghost of Marx, my consciousness would finally change as if touched by a magic wand. I had grown nervous with waiting for the inevitable change of my *Bewußtsein* (consciousness) as a result of the total change in my *gesellschaftliche Sein* (social conditions). The enduring disharmony in that fundamental balance tormented me (even though I knew that the life of Marx himself was a perplexing refutation of his own ideas). Up until that moment, the only thing that had changed with my improved social status was my weight. I had to complement my new West European physical and behavioral profile with jogging in the nearby park and sweating in the gym around the corner.

While we were having dessert, I made a decision. Since I had to—temporarily (as I hoped)—renounce being a writer (right after I had actually become one) and since my consciousness was about to be transformed, I decided to take notes. To look around with a critical eye while I could still do so, before I would be completely immersed in the grandeur of bourgeois life and get used to it. To keep track of who I had been, what

I had thought, and what my former consciousness had been. I felt like a child who was growing up while wandering in a thick forest, leaving a trail of white pebbles and colorful marbles so she wouldn't forget where she'd come from and where she'd been, marking her trajectory so she could find her way back amid this labyrinth of tempting alleys.

And so, I was living in an unstable dialectical situation, swinging back and forth between the spiritual and the material, between the desire to *have* and the desire to *be*, between reality and consciousness, whose change I anticipated, enthralled. I recorded my "growth spasms" and my old consciousness in little notes on white paper slips, which often turned into white balls, accidentally crumpled, by me or our cleaner. Paths of these tiny paper pebbles, would most often lead to the bin.

In the first few years of my new life I often became confused in by the consumerist monotony. I drove a nice, brand new German car but I would occasionally plop down on the passenger seat beside total strangers; I would try to unlock other people's cars or clean the snow off them because I always forgot where I had parked mine, and because I did not perceive my car as a unique entity which could be identified and which identified me. At the supermarket, I would sometimes drop the next round of purchases into someone else's cart—the carts all looked the same to me, there were no dinosaur eggs in mine to set it apart after a foray to the shelves. We were buying the same things; the store with its consumerist abundance engaged neither my mind nor my eyes, so they could not distinguish the personal assortment of things I had chosen.

I traveled—freely and with enough money. Landmarks and destinations I had seen in my mind in the magical nocturnal flights with Nana, now appeared to me in broad daylight. In spite of my grateful enthusiasm, I was actually disappointed with their touristic banality. After long weekends in splendid European cities, I would emerge from sleep and find it hard to recall, in my semi-wakeful state, where I was. The interior of the hotel room and the view outside the window didn't help much—a square, a cathedral, a shopping street, always clean, colorful, neat, beautiful, rich, and expensive. Poverty and ruin, and creativity and spirit fighting against them, and sometimes winning that fight, laughing at them, make some things, places and people unique. But just a few of them, though. As a matter of fact, my disorientation can also be explained by the shared culture and heritage of Europe. Motorways follow old Roman roads, the urban planning of the city centers is so similar—a castle perched on a hill (a fortress whose defense function has become obsolete), an open-air market, and a cathedral; these things used to bring together the secular and the spiritual but are currently transformed into a pedestrian zone, fanning out into a web of small streets leading toward the city walls, now replaced by a ring road.

My catch-up education and adaptation were rewarded with success in three job competitions,[37] in between which my son Mikhael was born. There I was—a happy mother of two, an employee of the European Commission, the beloved wife of an intelligent, caring, and wealthy man, a happy deviation from the emigrant model outlined by Bulgarian novelist Georgi Gospodinov. He wrote somewhere that men of science, computer specialists, and businessmen had left Bulgaria while men of letters had stayed, and those literati who did emigrate had to give up their professional vocation for working as shop assistants, secretaries, or nursing home attendants. I didn't just work for the European Commission, in full harmony with my faith in the European project, but I worked with language, the Bulgarian language, in fact! Somewhat surprisingly, in the end it was precisely my philology background and linguistic knowledge that were most useful not just for me, but for my country's interest—for colleagues and the transformation of Eurolect into Bulgarian. A dream job! I worked with excitement and I didn't look at the clock—the hours rolled by imperceptibly and, as a matter of fact, often weren't enough for me, so I stayed at the office long after the working day was over to perfect everything and share all of my ideas.

A friend of Rada's, one of her classmates from the European school, once told me that he respected me a lot because I was "self-made" like his father—a refugee from the Lebanon war who had arrived in France without a penny in his pocket but progressed to become a highly qualified dentist and the owner of a large dental clinic in Brussels (where, as a matter of fact, he had hired a Bulgarian dentist). I kindly thanked the boy for his "appreciation of my achievements" but I couldn't stop thinking about his "compliment." There hadn't been any civil war in Bulgaria and I was not a refugee! My "self-made" credentials were unquestionable, but . . . was the result what I wanted? I didn't want to become a prosperous dentist! I wanted to be a writer! Eh, if the dentists had been writers.[38]

These perfidious questions made me notice that perhaps my consciousness had not "evolved" as expected, it felt pretty much the same. I looked over the sixty something pages of notes on my computer and they only confirmed that my old consciousness was intact and working at full speed. Where the hell was my long-awaited new conscious-

---

37 One can become an EU official only through notoriously difficult open competitions, comprising several eliminatory rounds, attracting usually thousands of candidates for 100 or so posts.

38 A paraphrase of Woody Allen's classic "If the Impressionists had been Dentists."

ness hiding? I was fed up with that schizophrenic dichotomy. From the deathbed of my supposedly old personality I had already given Rada my words of wisdom, preaching spiritual wealth and passing along my historical accounts about communism. But judging by my own words and thoughts (in the salvaged paper slips that I had copied into my computer), my old personality was showing through, remaining a dispassionate witness to everything that was happening, and tormenting me with its neurotic anxiety over the passage of time and the meaninglessness of almost everything, vexing me with its inexhaustible desire to write about time and other meaningless stuff. I had everything that was supposed to make me happy, yet I wasn't.

A theory (also employed by economists, of course, they never miss a beat!) suggests that every person has a certain capacity for happiness, something inborn like a genetic predisposition, a limit. Material acquisitions can only temporarily increase the level of satisfaction or happiness, but humans soon roll back to their natural state—more happy or less happy. Was I of a naturally unhappy disposition, or was there something specific that regulated my happiness levels?

Ani Ilkov[39] once wrote that in the early 1990s Bulgarians were learning to travel abroad, but later they became somewhat snobbish about world travel; that when a poet is not a tourist any longer but lives his daily life abroad, he may stop writing; that the world has become shockingly accessible, big and interesting enough to induce an inner balance that could make you stop writing. Hmmm, where was that bloody balance?!, I was murmuring to myself . . .

A female friend of mine, a Hungarian, with whom I shared my concerns, pointed out that it was much better to weep in a Porsche.[40] I'd say that it is definitely more comfortable, but also more hopeless because the Porsche usually comes late in life. In line with the automobile imagery, I can say that I was stepping, with some malicious joy, on the accelerator of my consumerist power, so I could get to maximum speed and declare: "This car cannot fly."

I suppose that at this point the kind reader may finally express his or her indignation at my poorly disguised egotism, at what may seem like bragging, at my overweening vanity, and the crocodile tears. The reader may note that nothing prevented me from writing; on the contrary, I had all the comfort in the world to facilitate the magniloquence

39 A contemporary Bulgarian poet.

40 My friend, who was indeed driving a Porsche, actually paraphrased a famous remark rewritten from François Sagan or Ogden Nash.

of my creative ambitions . . . in my free time, as the Jurist had suggested. The point is that I did not have free time, I had neither freedom, nor time.

My and my husband's earned income, i.e., our salaries, generated an excess, which turned into capital through investment—in our case, in real estate and some stocks. However, when you have family, when you achieve success in professional life, when you have a high social status and earn more than you need, you find yourself on a merry-go-round. A nice home is a must—in the form of a big house, but you need to invest your financial excess as all your fellow riders do, in more real estate. You buy a second house or an apartment, but then you take another loan, which spurs you to work non-stop so you can pay the installments (although the rent you get out of the real estate helps). You can't afford to take unpaid leave because you need to repay your loans. Any lady's handbag (well, possibly a bigger one) would do, just as any car. But once you get on the merry-go-round, and in your particular social wagon, you can't appear in public with just any handbag or vehicle. Every new handbag or car is more expensive—what you buy is prescribed by your growing income, your social status, and your increasingly refined caste taste. Your children would learn more or less everything they need to know at any decent school, but one day they, too, will need a good starting position on the merry-go-round, so only the best and most expensive schools and colleges will suffice to prepare them and give them a competitive edge. Besides, your children have grown up on that same merry-go-round and are used to the best and the most expensive stuff. And there's no break—you work all the time to pay the ever-multiplying loans, the increasingly pricey handbags, cars, vacations, food, wines, cosmetics, hobbies, schools, and colleges. The paid leave is spent on family vacations or dedicated to the kids whom you otherwise see for no more than an hour a day. You can't afford to think about unpaid leave. You become a *slave* of the merry-go-round, of its money-needs-money prime perpetuum mobile. You spiral upward, each round faster and higher, in self-sustaining chains of cause-and-effect. Constantly comparing yourself with your peers.

Spiraling on the merry-go-round you leave no traces of yourself.

The image of the merry-go-round led me to discovering the second law of money. Once you've acquired enough money and you're free not to think about it (in other words after the first law has come into effect), before you know it, you've already been sucked into the whirlpool of greed for *more*, a fundamentally human desire. *Human greed* dictates the second law of money, which states: "The more (money) you have, the more (goods) you desire, so the more (money) you need." With this paraphrase of Marx's fundamental economic rule for *Mehrwert* (surplus value, money prime), it turns out that the rule isn't based on any characteristics specific to capital or heartless capitalists but on characteristics found in all humans—in the universal, Biblical human, crucified between the insatiable greed for more and the consciousness that life can't be satisfied by a cornucopia of possessions.[41]

Hence, logically, the last economic crisis and the ubiquitous concept of constant economic growth (which survived the crisis even though it came out a bit scruffy) not only brought Marx back into fashion but provoked moral judgment on the greed of financial sharks and the global script for human progress in general.

In this context it is fascinating to read the first few stanzas of the Internationale, and particularly their translations into different languages. It is a good example of the transition between the first and the second law of money:

Debout! les *forçats* de la *faim*, the French original says.

Die *stets man* noch zum *Hungern* zwingt,[42] the German version goes, and Google Translate confirms that the translation is correct.

Arise! ye *prisoners* of *want,* the English text elaborates further, as though with some distant premonition about the financial crises.

The Bulgarian version speaks directly of "*slaves* of *labor*" which is a paradoxically true mistranslation. We really become slaves of the material world, of *having* and, eventually, of our human greed, and hence of labor, effort, education, and all other means for satisfying that greed.[43]

Bulgarian translators have committed one more (purely linguistic?) error. By his key concept of *gesellschaftliches Sein*, Marx wanted to say that changes in our *social conditions* or *well-being* lead to changes in our *class*, or in other words, *social* and *political* consciousness. However, the canonized Bulgarian translation states that "The *human condition* (or the *being)* determines *human* consciousness." The *human condition,* or the *being,* and *human* consciousness have a much broader, universal, philosophical meaning than Marx's *social conditions* and *class consciousness.* However, this double mistranslation is paradoxically correct. It is our biblical, Shakespearean, Kantian, or Heideggerian Being, our existentialist *human condition* as doomed mortals that shapes our *human consciousness.* And in my personal *experience*, consciousness and human condition are rather resistant to the fluctuations of social conditions. As for *class*

41 An inaccurate quotation from the Bible (Luke 12:15).

42 Literal translations: Arise, convicts of hunger (French); persecuted/forced/spurred by hunger (German).

43 The monstrous cynicism of another historical slogan proves the same thing in reverse: "Arbeit macht frei . . ." As a matter of fact, this slogan has been first used by the Weimar Republic in a campaign for reducing unemployment.

consciousness, history shows that it is indeed quite flexible, depending on quite practical and quenchable needs and their satisfaction.

The Bulgarian mistranslation is strange, particularly since Slavic languages make a very clear distinction between social, living conditions (*bit*) and the human condition or state of Being (*bitié*). Are these accidental mistranslations? Didn't communist ideology attempt to usurp Being, the human condition and human consciousness as a whole, not just social conditions and class consciousness?

Marx denies the existence of non-material values and the transcendental. According to him, art is not the fruit of some immanent human essence or need, with some unique and unmeasurable *value*, but an ordinary type of production that creates its own consumers. In Marx's logic, art is just a form of merchandise *evaluated* according to his formulas about the labor time invested in this merchandise. The cricket's chirping does not count as work. And the ant doesn't think about songs or dances until it has stocked its little pantry.

Marx considers religion as the opium of the people. For him, the transcendental, be it art or religion, has no value because it's pragmatically useless: "Nothing can have *value* without being an object of *utility*," he said curtly.

The third and fourth laws of money are related to time.

I wanted to stop working, or at least stop being a "slave of labor," I didn't want to spend all my more or less wakeful and conscious time at work. I was done with my homework, I had eaten all the healthy compulsory stuff and I wanted my chocolate eggs, even if it was just to give them away. I wanted to have time for non-utilitarian thoughts, for useless notes, for doing nothing, time for gallery-going and grasshopper recitals,[44] time to listen to music, time to read books (and not just Commission papers), to take a rest from family vacations and, Lord have mercy, just maybe to write. But all those things required *time*, the kind of personal spare time that I didn't have. The only chance I had was to *buy* it, i.e., take an unpaid leave. But that would mean taking a couple (or more) of my monthly salaries out of the family budget and possibly inducing a financial crisis (or even insolvency of some branch of our family enterprise and public sale of the mortgaged real estate). Money can't be invested in something as impalpable as time.[45] I felt deeply insecure and wary of depriving my family of so

44 A grasshopper recital was all that my attempts to play the piano or guitar amounted to, so I wanted to take lessons in both instruments.

45 Ironically or not, we do make such investments . . . but they are all turned toward the future, the time when we won't be able to work, i.e., retirement. That investment is looking more imaginary than ever, albeit for

much money for the sake of something so uncertain as the outcome of my *essays* at writing. Did I have the right to do it? Did I have the talent? Did I still have something to say? Creative work, spiritual legacies, and so on and so forth are very beautiful but highly risky undertakings with zero guarantee of material or immaterial return on the investment in time and effort.

And there was the paradox—although my family was now wealthy, I was once again playing the lottery and dreaming of winning "enough money." This time "enough" meant my annual income, which I would use to redeem a year of freedom from the family budget so I wouldn't have to work.

So, here is the third law of money: the most *valuable* thing you can buy on the merry-go-round, with the currency used thereon, i.e., with money, is time. Free time, the right to jump off the merry-go-round, land on the ground and spend some time without going in circles. Strangely enough, that "law" of mine goes directly against the ubiquitous business mantra that time is money. I have just proved, very easily at that, that actually money is time, because the most expensive thing you can buy with money is time—human, existential, individual time. Apparently, the whole confusion stems from our starting point, namely what we perceive as a value, which has a certain price. Behind that business axiom we find once again Herr Marx.[46] After drafting a few formulas for the human working hour and the surplus value produced thereof, Marx concludes that "Time is everything, man is nothing: he is, at the most, time's carcass." Of course, Marx has always referred to nothing more than *labor time*—to him, the human being does not live in any other time. And the capitalists of the twentieth and early twenty-first centuries who repeat that time is money only mean *economics* time, and stock markets, investments, interest rates, exchange rates, price margins, efficiency, competitiveness, and other cogwheels of the merry-go-round where time is priced in money, indeed, the money you can gain, or the economic value you can produce, for a unit of that time.

While I was working, earning, investing, paying, and happily riding on the merry-go-round, longing to write and playing the lottery, hoping to buy time and freedom for my spirit and thought, death intruded. In a comparatively humorous economic story like this one, I won't write about death, the shock and sorrow in the wake of its imperial visit

different reasons. Besides, we might not even live up to the "bright future."

46 Even though he himself had never worked, at least not in the sense in which he conceptualized labor and working time, while killing time over a beer at The Swan.

and the end of someone's biography—these are topics for another story. I'll stay on the economic wavelength.

It had never occurred to me that in addition to origin, education, and hard work, money may come from inheritance. Up until then, my social and material progress had been the result of my work, efforts, and qualities, not a birthright or some kind of family capital invested in my education, my property, or my future estate. To the excess of our salaries, which had generated family capital, inherited capital was added. Paradoxically, I was becoming a genuine *capitalist* (of course, on a rather humble scale).

The money I needed so badly to buy myself freedom and time had materialized after all. But it cost death. And it brought me a new, monstrous kind of freedom called loneliness . . . After I "won" that ghastly lottery, I developed a superstitious fear of money and never again played a game of chance. I understood why I had always found the concept of life insurance disturbing.

Money has no smell, the Roman emperor Vespasian said. Yet nobody had warned that extra money might imply even more work and time to "deal" with it. Gentle reader, I hope it never crossed your mind that I would rush off to spend my acquired and inherited capital on material and non-material whims. I was responsible. I ran a marathon through the infernal world of heirs, legal proceedings, notaries, and tax inspectors, where everyone who could chisel something away, did so. Then I had to invest the remainder with forethought and responsibility, so I could guarantee good financial returns for my children. I couldn't squander the money, with selfish recklessness, on *time*, which might, in turn, have been wasted on uncertain, non-material *values*.

The encounter with death, revealed to me the fourth (and the last, so far) law of the economic material world. Time on the merry-go-round is fast, circular, and cyclical. It flows from one work week and month to the next, from one weekend's grocery shopping to another, from one monthly salary to the next, from one credit payment to the next, from one round of maintenance and repair to the next, from Christmas breaks to summer holidays and over again, from a school or an academic year to the next. From one financial crisis to the next real estate or stock market crash. You ride on the merry-go-round, you buckle down to work because of everything you have to pay for, spurred by deadlines at work and at home. You keep running in a mechanical spiral, in that self-explanatory, self-sufficient, precipitous cycle of reciprocal dependences.

That circular and cyclical economic time of the merry-go-round, a close relative of Marx's labor time, flows deceptively fast, or slow, and seemingly monotonous, so that it slyly obscures both the circular time of nature's calendar and the linear times—the *t* of physics, the historical time and, above all, human personal time. I have always found physics both fascinating and absolutely incomprehensible, and yet I didn't need to be a physicist to fathom the obvious proof of Einstein's theory about the relativity of time.

If you jump off the merry-go-round and feel the solid unmoving ground under your feet, once the dizziness has gone away and you see yourself in the mirror, you touch your aging body, then you look closely, beyond any mundane banality, at the faces of those you love, or at your neighbors, you find out that beyond the frenetically rotating platforms of the merry-go-round, beyond the shiny and enticing trinkets, beyond the "sound and fury," your personal time on Earth, measured in other kinds of rotations, orbits and deadlines, has proceeded at a totally different pace, one-way, non-circular, and irreversible, with no chance of return and catching-up. In the routine, mechanical orbits of the merry-go-round, while you were gyrating in the gaudiness of the amusement park and playing the Monopoly game, your spirit or your consciousness, your forgotten human non-economic *self* has walked the greater part of the short promenade under the stars. Like a sleepwalker. You have not left shiny white pebbles to track your path through the black nocturnal woods. You cannot find the way back to yourself, while the end of the forest is already looming ahead, the light shining white at the end of the tunnel and the daffodil meadow right after it. This nightmare startles you in your sleep and you finally open your eyes for real.

That personal time under the stars is something you cannot buy. My father had forgotten to clarify that it was the wall clock at the office I shouldn't be checking, or, later, the clock in my smartphone—but I should have kept my eyes (and ears) on the personal clock tick-tocking inside my body and my mind.

But can you spend all your time on the solid ground, in the fairy woods? How do artists, writers, composers, philosophers, or genuine fundamental physicists, in short—those who occupy themselves exclusively with the human spirit and the transcendental, make both ends meet? What do they receive, here and now, for the value they produce, or rather create? I'm not sure, but I guess that is the purpose of wacky crowd-pleasing art, applied arts and utilitarian crafts, gallerists, publishers, grants, trusts and foundations, patrons, enlightened monarchs, ateliers, creative writing schools and courses, scholarships and awards. There is an audience to buy what you have produced, even though it is only time (not the Marxist working time) that will tell its real value, and not the market demands of your own lifetime where art *is* a commodity, indeed.

I am uncertain about something else, too. Is it possible to combine aesthetic creation with a nine-to-five job? Most certainly not all artists were poor; some of the immortal ones were quite well-off, too. There are hundreds of examples that financial security is not a proof for lack of genuine creativity. On the other hand, it's true that money tempts the spirit, or lulls it to sleep.

I remember the funny pyramid of needs and necessities, according to which we first have to satisfy our basic needs of food, water, shelter, security. Then come our social needs—to work and to become socialized in a community. At the very top, humans may only possibly have some aesthetic needs or existential concerns. A magazine aptly stated that, once people have enough to eat, they start to wonder about the meaning of their lives. As for me, I've always thought about the "fundamental questions," whether hungry or well-fed.

Economists and financiers pare down human psychology and behavior to a few rules (invariably rather primitive ones), so they can frame and profile the individual in the world of money. To them, a person is just a human resource, a workforce unit, a hired hand; to them you are only alive during working hours, or you are a jobless bum "living off handouts" from the welfare state, or a retiree who goes on living too long. Or, outside of the job market or the welfare state, you are a client, a buyer, a representative of a target group, the known or unknown quantity in a dynamic equation of demand and supply. Or you are a loan-taker, a tax-payer, an heir, an entrepreneur, an investor . . . Only in one or more of these roles, and in compliance with rules and models, the human being can enter into the field of economy and money. Financiers and economists forge nice simple pyramids, functions, and equations to explain and predict human behavior, psychology, motives, goals, and even levels of happiness.

A Nobel prize winner in economy (Gary Becker, 1992) claims that "the economic approach is a comprehensive one that is applicable to all human behavior." The same author asserts that the ultimate overarching goal of all humans is to get maximum utility from the resources they have acquired or invested in, or, simply put, to *have* more. The same author considers children as *marital-specific capital*; they are not ordinary *goods* only because the demand for them is not concomitant with the family income growth. Other authors explain the declining number of children in increasingly affluent families in terms of . . . the growing price of parental time. You get the picture: if parents are more educated, they earn more, so a unit of their time is obviously worth more, so they want to spend more time working, instead of raising children. In short, we come back to the dictum that time is money. According to that line of thought, a dowry is defined as a collective investment (by the bride's family) in progress (that is, the growth of a new enterprise, which is the marital couple). Prenuptial negotiations in arranged marriages bring to mind the merger of two enterprises. And marriage, when you look at it, is nothing but a merger. According to that frame of reference, my first marriage should be defined as the merger of two bankrupt enterprises during a deep depression. But, in another frame of reference, it was the attempt of two children to fly, or *a portrait of the artist as a young man*. According to these same theories, my second marriage would be defined as my husband's decision to make a capital investment in a promising *start-up* from a former communist country with all the risks thereof. While in reality, it was the *taming of the shrew, sense and sensibility, pride and prejudice*.

A genuine writer[47] has dispensed with all that nonsense and pointed out that utility is a highly immoral concept and that culture, the individual, and ethics cannot be reduced to simple functions and equations. They belong to the realm of the humanities, of literature, religion, art, and philosophy. I would add astronomy and fundamental physics, insofar as they are or should be intellectual disciplines and not merely exact sciences. Economics deals with the material world, not even the world of matter, but of *subsistence* and *well-being*, so it should give up its sneaky attempts at *existence* and *being*, where the human being experiences some different kind of "hardships," which are definitely not of a daily, material and financial nature. Economics is only interested in death with regard to trusts and estates, the transfer and management of capital, the availability of personnel, retirement funds and so on, and not as an existential category.

What do philosophers think about the material world of money? Kierkegaard writes about the *aesthetic existence* of humans which, despite its misleading name, is not necessarily related to art because by "aesthetic" the philosopher means superficial, visible, material, real. This is life, here and now, with all of its natural beauty immortalized (i.e., preserved for a few hundred years) by painters and poets; this is life with all of its material trimmings and all the pleasant experiences they entail, and all other pleasant experiences caused by engaging with other people; this is life with its inevitable misfortunes, difficulties and woes; this is life with its devils and saints, with its social conditions and struggles. This is the life that is beautiful or wonderful, after all, or

47 John Lanchester, *The New Yorker,* July 23, 2018. I have loved this writer all the way back to his book *The Debt to Pleasure*, which at the time I bought for a dozen friends. A beautiful translation into Bulgarian by Andrei Andreev and Zornitsa Hristova

so we tell ourselves sometimes, while making lists of the things that make it worth living. And yet, this "wonderful, wonderful" life is inferior, as it does not bring meaning and purpose, so human consciousness operates in constant anxiety, pain, and despair, somewhat numbed or exacerbated by beauty and pleasure or misfortune and misery.

Then comes Heidegger. He writes about the *short-lived being* or the *brief existence*, i.e., about our everyday, our daily life here and now, amid objects, in the pursuit of objects, in a family and society and dedicated to family and society. Being and consciousness are swallowed and smothered by objects, by possession, by the dictates of society. In your brief existence on earth, you are not a personality and you don't have human consciousness. No revolutions in your social environment can repair this degrading existence.[48] The human condition or Being, not the social conditions, is where our consciousness resides. For Heidegger, the human conception of time, of one's own existence in time,[49] and of death constitute the fundamentals of Being and consciousness, all this housed in language.

Usually after some wake-up calls,[50] where fate rouses you from your somnambulant life, there comes a moment when you want to jump off the merry-go-round. Back to solid ground and dark woods, back to linear times and back to yourself. People call this a midlife crisis and try to cure you, instead of encouraging and assisting you. You are consumed with fear. How can I leave all of that? Am I not spinning around for the ones I love, for the ones who are truly important? Will they understand me? Or are you just terrified by freedom and the opportunity to *essay*? Because . . . is there anything left of me myself, or do I have a personality that is worth jumping off for? Do I still possess that human consciousness, that spirit, those thoughts and ideas I'm pining to express? Do I still have any human content to fill and animate that imaginary self? Is there anything left for me to *be* in what's left of my personal time? Will I find the white pebbles that I dropped in the forest? Do my words, in those tiny paper balls, have any value? Look! . . . My pockets, crammed full of banknotes, have torn at the bottom and all of the pebbles and paper balls have scattered unnoticed. So, I end up being the poorest person on Earth, an empty shell, indeed only a *carcass* of bygone time. Questions, doubts and fears . . . even more difficult for a woman. In the zenith of material, professional, maternal success, I was going to fail as a human being!

48 Did you hear that, Marx?

49 Not on the merry-go-round of one's *working hours*, dedicated to the production of surplus value. Did you hear that, Marx?

50 Most often related to health, love, or death.

The next Christmas season I made a decision. I listened for almost an hour to the wall clock, mercilessly tick-tocking my personal time. I realized that my uncommodifiable, and most probably uncompetitive, yet unique human content was weathering away, that the frenetic rotation of the merry-go-round was blowing away the microscopic layer of stardust from my retina.

I finished my latest annual agenda planner, moving the few uncompleted tasks ("due to circumstances beyond my control") to the first page of the new one, for the next year. Then I considered the most important and arduous tasks in my personal and professional life for the New Year, the ones that I usually wrote on the first page of the new agenda. Lawsuits, children, property management, repairs, the office . . . everything was all right, stable, on track. I made a few calculations and they showed that I could buy a few months of unpaid leave, i.e., I could afford to buy time. And then, at the bottom of the first page of my new agenda, I wrote something so microscopic that I could one day, if necessary, deny the existence of those barely readable words:

trying to write.

Sorry, Marx! "*Karl* Marx," one of the James Bonds in my head snarled but I couldn't identify which one. "Yes, thanks, that's right—not one of the Marx brothers whose ideas of human nature and of natural and other exchanges seem to be way fairer." Once again: "Sorry, Karl!" It didn't work for me. I can't keep waiting for that redemptive-murderous change of my consciousness. My social conditions have changed dramatically but my human condition hasn't; my thoughts and aspirations survived money. You lost the game to Heidegger. In the end of the day, my human consciousness, my idiosyncrasy, my pebbles, my paper balls, and my personal time are my greatest "competitive advantages," but in a larger *historical* context, so to speak, not in the context of the advanced capitalist society but in the context of the starry sky above us. Besides, to tell you, the wheel of history has not reached communism, but just rolled back to capitalism.

It was Christmas. Time of miracles, and of fairy tales about these miracles. Love reigns supreme, in both of its "distillates"—as an opium for the pious who love God and the whole world, and as an existential anesthesia for the depressed atheists and studious agnostics who love, sometimes rather carnally, the Other, their neighbor in the chronotopos. Compassion and charity are the greatest virtues at that time of the year, the rich become good and the poor get rewarded for their goodness. I prayed for the miracle to work for me, too. In my own way. I silently cast one Christmas spell after another—how I'd change my life on January 1st, how I'd write, how my human

Being would give shelter to my human consciousness, which was still alive but already drifting away into the white death of mundane life. To encourage the miracle to happen, I decided to try to exercise my own magical powers, long since grown rusty. As a preparation for my new life and a warm-up for my writing *essays*, I wrote this economic (hi)story to offer it as a symbolic gift and message to my children. Just like Christmas stories are meant to be.

That Christmas season, a close friend gave me a lottery ticket as a good luck wish. Superstitiously I wanted to bin it, but you are not supposed to throw away a gift (at least not immediately). So, I pretended I had completely forgotten about it, though it lurked quietly in my wallet. On the day before Christmas, at noon, I ran out to stock up on cigarettes in the nearby kiosk. I stood in the queue and waited my turn. I paid for the cigarettes and, upon leaving, handed the lottery ticket to be checked automatically at the cash register. That wicked thing was on its way to the garbage. The radio was on: you could barely make out the lyrics of the song but I knew they were about "a lady who's sure all that glitters is gold and she's buying a stairway to Heaven." That sounded like a befitting message from destiny. But why was that guy behind the register taking so long? And why were his eyes getting wider than pancakes? Why was he screaming like crazy? I couldn't hear my favorite song. What was going on here?! I looked around—the people in the queue had turned to stone. I seemed to be temporarily unable to understand French. Or maybe I had gone deaf—I could only hear the part of the song where the lady finds out that all shops in Heaven are closed. Oh, no . . . not that!!! Just my bloody luck . . . Hell, my very personalized Hell, was crashing down on me, with the shrill falsetto of a bald-headed Belgian guy, in that nondescript shop for cigarettes and a few other bare necessities. The shop assistant was neighing.

But Providence took mercy on me. Baldy stopped making animal sounds and started muttering something under his nose; then he swiped the ticket through the cash register again, and again, getting so nervous that he reached over to turn off the radio. Then he opened a notebook to compare the ticket number with the ones written down there. Then he started to apologize—it was a technical error, he was terribly sorry. He asked me whether I was fine. The woman behind me, concerned about the look on my face, suggested they call an ambulance. "With a therapist," the man behind her added. Or maybe they should call my husband, the bald guy suggested. I smiled, relieved, and then burst out laughing. It's a mistake!! I'm not winning anything!! No one is going to die!! I won't spend another two or three years of my precious personal time in investing and I won't dedicate the rest of my personal time to property management. The only downside to the fortunate cancellation of my lottery win was that it deprived me of the opportunity to schedule a séance with the ghost of Dostoevsky, which would have been dedicated to gambling, human *spirit,* moral punishment, and, possibly, the next law of money. Yet, given the alcohol spirit implied in the encounter, I felt more of a relief.

To everyone's amazement, I gave Baldy's cheek a kiss and rushed back home to finish this story.

BRUSSELS, BELGIUM

Who hasn't been to this city—Marx and Engels, Moses Hess, Victor Hugo, Verlaine and Rimbaud, Baudelaire, Byron, Charlotte and Emily Brontë, Joseph Conrad, Julio Cortázar, Hergé, Audrey Hepburn . . . Some were even born here, by coincidence, not for some intrinsic connections with Brussels and Belgium. Exiled from Germany, Marx had been a regular in the *House of the Swan* on the *Grande Place*. He lived on the same street as Engels. Victor Hugo spent years here in political exile. In fact, he had two addresses—one for his family and another one that he shared with his lifelong mistress. He finished *Les Misérables* in Waterloo. After leaving his wife and son, Verlaine also came to live here, sharing a hotel room with his same-sex lover, Rimbaud. Then, he fired a shot at him in an episode that went down in history as *le drame de Bruxelles*. It is here that Baudelaire fled from his creditors and it is here where he suffered a massive stroke, one that would put an end to his life a year later. The lifelong exile Byron stopped here on his way to warmer, more picturesque and heroic destinations. The Brontë sisters lived here in a girls-only boarding house and studied French; one of them even fell in love (under the influence of the language perhaps). Cortázar was born here at the Argentinian embassy where his father worked, but Brussels remained no more than an accidental birthplace to him because immediately afterward his family had to flee from German-occupied Belgium to Switzerland. Audrey Hepburn was also born here by chance, in a British-Austrian-Flemish family of noble descent. Her multilingual childhood in Brussels and the multiple relocations of her family around the world, following the professional commitments of her parents, bring to mind a lot of the present-day European youth that is being raised in Brussels. Even in the TV series *The Crown*, Brussels is a destination of expulsion and exile, where Princess Margaret's unwanted favorite was dispatched.

Brussels is a city of exile, emigration, hard work, *gastarbeiters*, a city of holes and corners to hide, of privacy, of escape, a short stop on an emigrant's route, a city to let loose, to have scandalous love affairs, a city to drink and eat, the incidental birthplace of non-incidental people. A liberal and discreet, unobtrusively comfortable and luxurious, pragmatic and mercantile, populous, anonymous, international and, today—global, *nowhere*. A city with no cultural nest of its own, with no history, time, claims, and norms; with no questions, conditions and judgment. A transit zone.

To me, Brussels isn't exactly the capital of a geographically and culturally concrete foreign state. In my head Brussels isn't part of Belgium, a country which has remained unfamiliar and unloved. To me, Brussels is a global non-national *abroad*, a whole world outside the borders of my homeland. Brussels is the name of an otherwise comfortable cultural vacuum. Something like a miniature non-virtual version of the global village. The Mini Europe Park with its kitsch exhibits is emblematic in this sense, even beyond the vapid EU symbolism.

Besides business, administrative and shopping centers, European institutions, Parisian boulevards, splendid Art Nouveau, Art Deco, and neoclassicist buildings and sculptures on virtually every corner of the city, Brussels has entire neighborhoods where you wouldn't know you were in Europe if somebody just dropped you there without any background information. As a matter of fact, one third of the population of Brussels (which is approximately 1.2 million people) is Muslim, more than 10% are of African origin (mostly, but not exclusively, descendants from the former Belgian colonies Congo and Rwanda) and about 230,000 are expats like me. It turns out that native Belgians count for less than half of the city's inhabitants. They, in turn, are divided into Walloons and Flemish. So that Brussels is bilingual. Officially. Actually it is francophone.

I got some idea of Belgian geography, I read through a humorous history of the country, which is constituted in itself by paradoxes so it needs almost no added humor to make you laugh. For these twenty years, I have met about a dozen Belgians, some of whom are my neighbors, if you could call that getting to know someone. I feel zero interest in this country, and zero emotion (I even feel offended by it and judgmental in recent years). Yes, I do recognize the native Belgian accent, I say *septante* and *nonante*,[51]

51 Instead of *soixante-dix* and *quatre-vingt-dix*, as they say it in French French, literally "sixty and ten" for 70 and "four times twenty and ten" for 90. In French you calculate when counting—for example, if you want to

I live next to the Godiva factory, the Belgian beer is really worth it, and the restaurants are the best.

Sometimes I repeat to myself "I live in Belgium," still trying to attribute some personal sense to this objective fact. When all the people you know are foreigners, expats like you, and the host country itself is a federation with three different separate administrative and linguistic communities (and myriad other oddities) and without a clear national identity, you can't really feel like a foreigner and you don't have to integrate; besides, there is no need to. There is no specific national culture, language, mentality, cuisine, tradition, history, and literature to get to know and interiorize, to adopt, to get to love or not, to integrate yourself in or segregate yourself from. I can't find new spiritual foundations in chocolate, beer, mussels, comic books, or Georges Simenon. There is nothing specifically Belgian in the works of Maeterlinck, Verhaeren, and Nothomb.[52] Rubens, Bruegel, and Bosch are Flemish, not Belgian. What cultural wealth there is is pre-Belgian. The same counts for Bruges, Ghent, Antwerp, Leuven. Magritte is probably the only artist who can be defined as uniquely Belgian, in my opinion, and only because of the hyper realistic twilight in his paintings and the middle-aged *petit monsieur* with the bowler hat.

I miss any authentic Belgian content.

I am simply located somewhere on the map, and that somewhere is two and a half hours from Sofia,[53] one hour and fifteen minutes from Paris,[54] where my daughter went to college, two hours and twenty minutes from London where some of my in-laws live (the train goes under the Channel, can you believe that!), two hours and twenty minutes from Frankfurt, a crossroad in my private life, less than two hours from Amsterdam, and equally removed, by plane, from most of the European capitals. I'm practically making use of one of the advantages of the city, for which it was chosen to be the EU capital sixty years ago. But Belgium has other advantages, too: it is not a Great Power, it doesn't tip the scales of European politics, and it epitomizes pragmatism and compromise.

To me Belgium is a welfare state and mostly economic topos. Brussels is the place where my home is, where I work, earn, and spend my money, socialize, receive medical care, send my children to school. Only the birth of my second child here had a chance

say 97, you say "four times twenty and seventeen."

52 Funny enough, but the artistic identity of this most famous contemporary Belgian writer is based on her non-belonging to Belgium and everything Belgian. Child of diplomats, she grew up around the world.

53 When I was a student, I lived at the same 2 1/2-hour distance from my "city of return," Plovdiv. Back then, however, I spent these two hours on a train rather than airborne.

54 On a high-speed train, the same goes for all further destinations.

to create an intimate connection between me and that city. But it didn't work. Brussels remains the accidental birthplace of my son.

The cosmopolitan nature of Brussels is superimposed on a multinational, multilingual, politically engineered young country where national identity is a very problematic concept, hinging loosely on common king and football team and, to an ever lesser extent—a common religion. Not even common taxes! Taxes are different in the different administrative counties. "We are Belgians" echoes heavily against the murky background in one of the most popular local commercials, in which Belgian football players advertise Belgian beer. It sounds like a spell, like a mantra, beyond any rational argumentation. But comes out in . . . English. A typical compromise *á la belge*.

My intimately familial, linguistic, and cultural hodgepodge, or, to be politically correct, diversity, continues, or rather comes as a result, of the social Babylon around. Babylon is an evergreen metaphor for the multilingualism and the cultural diversity of Brussels. The political evergreen follows—like the tautological and illustrative literary project "Babylon" I took part in years ago. A Flemish literary society had invited a German poet for a week in Brussels on a creative trip, a.k.a. symposium, to write something about the city in a genre of his choice. The work was then to be translated in all official EU languages, the translators would successively read their translations, the reading would be recorded, and a CD would immortalize the project. The poet had obviously taken the trouble to delve into the geography, history, and symbolism of the city. The resulting poem was a bit unclear with cryptic and somewhat frightening imagery, but otherwise expressive—the German words clattered like hooves on cobblestone, and the abundance of internal rhymes enhanced the natural sonority of the language. Since I didn't speak German, I used the two verbatim versions, in English and French, made for me by my husband and daughter. These were two literal translations with a spattering of synonym suggestions here and there. I interpreted the vague bits according to my own understanding, I fixed the rhymes, including the internal ones, too, I adapted whatever I could, even emailed a few fellow translators (institutional translators like me who spent the rest of the time translating EU legislation and Commission reports) detailed explanations of my translation choices and the degree of freedom I had allowed myself. It turned out well—both my translation and the project. It was skillful, but it didn't inspire me. Some time ago, I searched the internet to check if something had happened with the online publication (as it had indeed happened once with my endless book . . .). Everything is all right—it is still my voice reading my translation, although I do not understand the monkey as a visual background. But who knows, maybe it fits well. The monkey plays a more humane role than many of the humans in the film *Le Tout Nouveau Testament.*[55] A few years ago, in the center of Paris, I froze in front of a film poster that announced that "*Dieu existe. Il habite à Bruxelles.*"[56] And *à Molenbeek, plus précisément,*[57] as I learned a week later when I watched the film *Le Tout Nouveau Testament.* Oh, they laugh, these Belgians, and approach even the most fundamental questions in such a humane way!

There is something of our Bulgarian Bai Ganyo or his creator Aleko Konstantinov[58] about the Belgians. Or there's something Belgian about the Bulgarians beyond our first constitution and the architectural design of our National Assembly.[59] Only this "something" has made me feel a sense of kinship toward the Belgians. "*Petit pays, petits gens, petits esprits,*"[60] one of their kings condescendingly sighed. The fool in French anecdotes is a Belgian. The Dutch and mostly the French mock the Belgians for their stupidity, absurdity, pettiness, pragmatism, for their lack of grandeur and spirituality. After it turned out that Brussels is the actual terrorist center of Europe, Trump compared the city, and more specifically the Molenbeek neighborhood, to a "hellhole." But despite everything, the Belgians manage to laugh at themselves, to accept themselves as they are—even with a sense of pride.

And they try to split the country every five or six years with a sporty, rather than political or nationalistic, zeal. Yet, ultimately it always boils down to Brussels, which is impossible to divide. Years ago, when Belgium was setting a world record for the longest period of time a country could go without a government, while functioning smoothly and almost imperceptibly, I was still reading the Bulgarian daily press, and not watching the local news, so I had absolutely no idea about the political crisis in Belgium. One morning, on my way to the office, I noticed the Belgian flags hanging down from balconies and windows all around. I thought that, perhaps the Belgian football team had won an important match. I learned from the *Bulgarian* press that the Belgians were protesting against the inability of their political class to form a government . . . That goes to show to what extent I live here.

I have two more flag stories, both quite telling. Years ago, when Germany won the world football championship, everyone at home was happy. The little German citizen, my son, and his German au pair hung the German flag from our balcony,

55 *The Brand New Testament.* A co-production with Belgian participation, filmed in Brussels.

56 God exists. He lives in Brussels. (French)

57 In Molenbeek, to be precise. (French)

58 Bai (uncle) Ganyo is a Bulgarian national anti-hero, a Falstaffian character who personifies backwardness, opportunism, bad manners, etc. The author of the eponymous book, Aleko Konstantinov (1863–1897), was one of the most refined, educated and open-minded writers of his time.

59 Both being modeled after their Belgian counterparts.

60 A little country, little men, little souls. (French)

overlooking a busy boulevard. There was nothing unusual about that—when there is a football championship, many different national flags are displayed out of cars, windows and balconies. The Belgian national flag is very similar to the German one. Still, it's not the same . . . And there are two days in the year—the Belgian national holiday (July 21st) and *L'armistice* on November 11th—when only the Belgian flag may be displayed, and not to celebrate football. The Belgian national holiday, July 21st, is a public holiday and a non-working day for EU employees in Brussels, just as June 23rd is a public holiday for our colleagues over in Luxemburg. A sign of respect to the host country. On November 11th, the Belgians celebrate not just peace but their victory over the Germans in the World War I. In 2018 there were grandiose parades for the centenary. November 11th, on the other hand, is a normal working day for European institutions, while the rest of Belgium has the day off. It is an onerous task to create a union or a federation out of victors and vanquished. May 9th follows the same logic: it is a holiday and a non-working day for EU employees—not because it's V-Day but because it is the Schumann Declaration day, on which in 1950 the French Minister of Foreign Affairs released a declaration that marked the beginning of the European Union.

To go back to the story about the German flag. At the end of the football championship, we hung it from our balcony and . . . forgot about it. Then, on November 11th, the slightly different German flag was looking highly provocative. My neighbor hissed at me from the balcony to immediately get rid of that German flag. I obeyed in an instant.

The other story is about the Bulgarian flag and the cheerful, pragmatic amnesia of Belgian administration. Once upon a time, the Belgian state didn't like me and didn't want me. Even after I married my second husband, who lived and worked here, the local administration didn't want to give me Belgian ID and right of residence. It would not accept official Bulgarian ID papers, translated by sworn translators, with apostilles and all. I had to lay out my family tree all the way back to Adam and Eve. One day, at the Brussels airport, a couple of policemen took me away from passport control. It turned out that in the meandering of the bilingual and highly unwelcoming Belgian administration, I "featured" as a bigamist—simultaneously married to both of my husbands. After my initial astonishment, I had a good hearty laugh, which embarrassed the police officers, before they, too, started laughing at my comment that male polygamy wasn't actually such a bad idea if it didn't come with two mothers-in-law . . . I went on to become an employee of the European

Commission, I got a diplomatic ID card, Bulgaria became a member of the EU and I didn't have much to do with the local authorities any longer. Years later, however, I had to declare my income at the municipality. Shortly after, I received a rather unusual letter from the same authorities who had refused to accept me as one of their citizens years ago. I read the letter a few times to make sure I got everything right. The Belgian administration was bidding me an exuberant welcome on the territory of the municipality, although I had already lived there for over eight years, and was writing to inform me that on March 3rd, the national holiday of my country, the Bulgarian flag would be raised in the Town Hall in my honor. On that date I went to there to check discreetly—an impressive-sized Bulgarian flag was indeed gracing the lobby . . .

This belated hospitality was immediately cashed in. Soon after the Bulgarian flag was thus honored, the Belgians treated me to a monstrous inheritance tax, well exceeding the already sky-high rates stipulated by law (actually the highest in the world). The rich former colonial state needs deep tax rivers for various purposes. One of the things that unites Belgium is its "comprehensive" federal luminosity which makes the country something like an entertainment park that can even be seen from space. You know you're in Belgium when all the roads and motorways are festively illuminated and you can drive with your headlights off. The welfare system here is one of the most generous in Europe, especially toward unemployed and mostly non-Belgian mothers of many. All those things cost money, which comes from taxpayers, including foreigners, and excluding some Belgian citizens with bank accounts in Panama and Switzerland, for whom the state reserved the *laissez-faire* approach . . . In this way this step-mother state emptied not only the pockets, but the heart of her continuous resident and potential citizen, too.

For the rest, everyone is welcome in Brussels. There's something for everyone here. There are shops and housing for both the rich and the poor. There are countless food shops and spice shops, wig shops and extension shops, specialized clothes shops, and only male hairdressers, you name it, so that everyone can be transported to his or her homeland. Apart from the numerous cathedrals, the center of the city features a monumental mosque and a synagogue. Temples of a humbler scale are provided for all religions. There are prestigious Catholic schools and universities. And liberal ones. Brussels is also fully tolerant toward sexual orientation—there are powerful LGBT communities and numerous bars and clubs for them. Belgium was the second country in the world (after the Netherlands, as one would expect) to legalize same-sex marriages.

Civilized tolerance and pragmatism regulate prostitution as profession, which naturally attracts taxation.

Belgium can be more surreal than its own Magritte. Only in Belgium can you see a defunct Boeing 707 on the roof of a warehouse in the middle of a field. Only in Brussels can you see streets which have four (4!) names—one official, in French and Dutch, and one "artistic," from the comic books, also written in French and Dutch . . . Only in Brussels can you see three hundred stark-naked cyclists, mostly male, crossing one of the busiest places in rush hour.

After a year or two, you get used to the way things "work" here. It looks like "the infamous Polish plumber"[61] failed to overcome Belgian administration since you cannot find him anywhere. The fact that you have booked an appointment with a handyman to fix your washing machine or something, or with a technician from the phone company to have a look at your internet connection, does not mean, in the first place, that anyone would ever come. Usually, no one would even bother to call—to warn, apologize, or reschedule the appointment. In case they happen to come, it would be two or three hours after the fixed time, when you have already given up waiting at home and have just arrived at the office. In this very moment, you will get a phone call to hear the exciting news that you will be "honored" "right now, in about twenty minutes." You have to dump whatever you're doing, on the spot, and fly back home, trying to keep your nerves intact. Because Brussels is the slowest city in Europe—a fact that has been ascertained and measured by a satellite. The traffic is horrendous. The old Brussels was not planned for so many cars. But it has been subsequently devised and "arranged" in such a way that if a car breaks down or runs out of gas, the entire internal ring is blocked. And when there are summits or strikes, it's better just to stay at home.

And the police car sirens have clearly attained world fame now that they even feature in the repertoire of Sheldon Cooper in faraway California. Completely deserved. The police don't just fail to manage traffic jams, it's more like they provoke them. And especially around sleeping Brussels between two and four in the morning, when there's no car driving on the streets, police sirens blow up a storm, effectively showing off their power and waking all the citizens, so they know who's watching over them.

61 A stereotypical image used by the conservative political parties in Western Europe during the enlargements of the EU in 2004 and 2007, to scare the voters with the influx of cheap workforce from Eastern Europe.

One of my first "creative" ideas inspired by Brussels was a proposition to a tourist agency to sell a long weekend pack with the slogan "Come to Brussels to get a good sleep!" The guaranteed gray sky, clouds, rain, and wind would drag you back to your bed or to the massage table in the steamy SPA. Garnished with good food and alcohol, that makes a perfect combination. A long relaxing weekend for neurotic people . . .

. . . "*I didn't even know where Bruges fucking was.* [pause] *It's in Belgium.*"[62]

62 The opening line in the iconic film *In Bruges.*

MOM'S MEN

Mom died a year and three months ago. Absurdly, abruptly, and on the spot. She got hit by a car while riding her bicycle down one of Brussels's most beautiful boulevards. She was forty-five and had quit smoking about a year earlier.

We were in a lot of pain. But it didn't come straight away, and is still to come for my little (half)brother Michael who's six and has just begun to comprehend that he will never have a Mom—that there is no Mom anymore.

I think that, in a way, Christian[63] immediately knew what had happened. Maybe because he's old and has seen death before, he's already been through this. I didn't get it, though, not in the beginning, not in those first moments when the police called but did not say Mom was dead, they just said that . . . Actually, I don't know what they said. Christian picked up the phone, he said "yes" three times, tried to say or ask something but stopped, wrote something down on a piece of paper and hung up. He stared at the piano, then shifted his gaze to my nose and opened his mouth but could not say a thing, and then he cleared his mind and finally managed to utter, in French:

"Your Mom was involved in a car accident. Please, go pick up Michael from the birthday party and stay home with him. I have to go now."

"Is she alive?" I asked mechanically, without fully realizing what I was saying or what the possible answers could mean.

63 Christian is my stepfather, my Mom's second husband. From now on I will call him simply Christian, and my real father, in other words my biological father and my Mom's first husband, I will call "Dad."

Rushing to get his shoes, as Christian said "yes" over his shoulder, I was already putting my shoes on, too—Michael could be picked up by the mother of his friend, Martina, I could call her on the go and he could stay at their place. It was *my* mom we were talking about, that I was old enough and I was going with him. Christian didn't say a thing, I wasn't sure he was even listening as he was already flying out of the door, brisk as usual.

Now that I think of it, he was also in shock and either needed me or was simply too overwhelmed to worry about me at the moment. We drove silently. Some ten, fifteen minutes. It seemed odd that Christian, normally a nervous and often arrogant driver, was not driving like a madman this time, while I wanted to get out of the car and yell at everyone to make way because Mom . . .

The second we turned onto the beautiful boulevard, we saw that the traffic was slow because of the accident. I immediately spotted the white sheet with the weird red stains—in the distance it looked like a giant white and red flower. It was Saturday, at noon, the sun atypically blazing, and there was the giant white and red flower in the low-cut daisy-studded grass, cars inching forward, trams clattering, police officers and onlookers standing on the pavement, a police car with a silently rotating blue emergency light. As we were approaching, some white tent was being spread over the white and red flower. It looked somewhat innocent and hippie, as if there would be an open-air concert or something. An ambulance had been parked nearby, at an angle; it seemed the driver had been in quite a hurry. A policeman was holding a weeping woman in his arms, a young woman with long chestnut hair, and talking to her. Later on, I learned that she was the woman who'd hit Mom and that she was not to blame for the accident. Three men and a woman in white coats were putting some medical gear back in the ambulance and pulling a stretcher out. Then there was me and Christian stepping closer, a second policeman asking him something in Dutch, Christian showing his ID card, the officer's eyes on me. A stranger popped up by my side, a young woman with short hair and glasses. The officer was telling her something in Dutch, *it must be the daughter*, I guess. Christian headed toward the tent, then came back to me, hugged me, and just said: "*Ne regarde pas.*"[64] The woman with the short hair turned me toward her, talking to me in Dutch, then in French, but I wasn't listening, I was looking around, in the opposite direction to the white sheet, at the beautiful sunlit houses across the street and the cars flying past in the opposite lane, everything seemed unreal, as if I was watching a movie or having a dream I would soon wake up from. Now and then a few words would register, so I learned that the woman by my side was

64 Don't look. (French)

a psychologist and that she was going do her best to help me. Help me with what? I was trying to look straight into the sun, I squinted and for some reason remembered how, after Michael was born, Mom used to joke that she had given birth in French but was hoping to die in Bulgarian. Well, she died in Dutch because death had reached her in a *commune flamande*.[65]

Then I eavesdropped on the doctor, a nice young man with film star looks, explaining to Christian that Mom had no helmet on (she didn't even own one to begin with), that she had flown off the bike and hit her head on the curb, most probably breaking her cranium or the cranial base, that the ambulance had arrived three minutes after the call, from the hospital just around the corner, that they had tried to revive her for forty-five minutes on site, without moving her, including twenty-five minutes after losing her pulse, but she had never regained consciousness and they couldn't get her heart working. The doctor spoke in French, but his accent was terrible and he kept replacing the French words he didn't know with Dutch or even English ones. Christian didn't like Dutch, but had learned to speak it out of respect for the country he'd lived and worked in for more than twenty years. Besides, it was similar to German. The doctor went silent, looking at Christian and expecting his questions, then turning to the psychologist who kept her eyes on Christian while holding me by the hand, as if I was a kid. Christian just stood there, head bowed, like someone who was carefully searching for words. The doctor looked at the psychologist, signaling her to go home with me. Then he added that my mother had lost consciousness immediately, that she hadn't suffered, had not felt a thing. I was surprised at my own voice as I asked caustically in French, "What makes you so sure?"

No one had told *me* yet, in any language, that Mom was dead. Or maybe I hadn't heard. I had not understood. I hugged Christian and he started stroking my hair mechanically, his whole body trembling, I stroked his bald spot and squeezed his shoulders so he would stop shaking. The Prussian inside him winced, the helpless, grief-stricken human creature recoiled inside its hole, and Christian switched—in a physically perceptible way—to "emergency protocol." He asked the psychologist to go home with me and wait for him to return. He gave me another hug, told me to go home, promised he'd be with me in "two hours" and whispered, "*Courage. Je serai toujours avec toi.*"[66] Then he called Martina and asked her to have Michael stay over "because . . . I'll explain tomorrow. In any case, please, don't get Michael worried; tell him that we . . . we have a lot of work to do." The psychologist was still holding my

65 Dutch-speaking municipality. (French)

66 Be brave. I'll always be with you. (French) Much later while I was making the final editing to this text, I found out that the second sentence was in fact a phrase from the Bible.

hand and pulling me toward the police car. Christian resolutely refused an autopsy and asked that they take "her" (yes, that's what he said, and not "the body") straight to a funeral agency. The last thing I heard was, "Please take *her* into the ambulance, and make these people go. Let's put an end to this circus."

The bespectacled woman proved to be stubborn and strong and she managed to shove me into the police car. We drove away; the last thing I saw was how they carried a stretcher covered in a clean white sheet out of the tent. Christian strode alongside it toward the ambulance.

People, streets, cars, the sun . . . I stared at the succession of scenes behind the car window, thinking that the children's party would be over any minute; Christian had taken Michael there three hours ago. Three hours . . . Three hours ago, Mom had kissed Michael "bye-bye," asking him not to stuff himself with birthday cake, then she'd called from the door that she was going to the office by bike because she had forgotten some report and she was going to pick Michael up on the way back. I could pinpoint the moment that turned out to be my last memory of Mom—in the kitchen, spreading cream cheese on a small piece of toast, with me telling her I was going out to a disco that night, after studying all day for the "maturas,"[67] of course. Mom was wearing jeans, dark blue moccasins, and a gray cashmere sweater, and her hair was wet. One of the dark blue moccasins had been peeking out of the sheet bundle when the paramedics were moving her to the stretcher. I was thinking that I was the one who should make the call to Bulgaria—to my dad, to my grandparents, I was the one who had to make it, if only because they didn't speak any foreign languages and Christian didn't speak Bulgarian. I was wondering if Dad would grieve. If his second wife would be even more jealous of my late mom and me. The bespectacled woman was watching me, visibly concerned, and awkwardly trying to give me a hug.

There we were, at home. Mom's morning coffee was still sitting on the table, unfinished. Only then did I collapse on the floor and finally break into tears. No—I was screaming, shrieking, I was bawling, grotesquely, my own voice unrecognizable to me, and writhing with pain on the floor. The psychologist lay down by my side and tried to hug me again. Then she had me sit up and drink a glass of water with some sort of powder in it, a tranquilizer probably.

Then I called Dad. Him first. I shouted at him, I couldn't control myself, telling him that Mom was dead, that she'd been gone for two hours. He was silent, for a long

67 A type of matriculation examination taken by students at the end of their secondary education, which they must pass so they can apply to a university.

time, as I was crying and howling, and in the end he just said quietly, "May God forgive her soul."

"What is there to forgive?! There's no God," I started shouting again. My dad was silent.

"Do you want to come back to Bulgaria . . . and stay with me . . . just for a little?"

"It will really be just a little, don't you worry, just the tiniest amount, I won't bother you," I was yelling and choking on my tears. "Don't worry. Christian will take care of me. He's a good person, a German," I shouted, I barely had any voice left from all the anger and pain. Even my tears had dried up.

The bespectacled woman didn't understand a word of Bulgarian, but the tone of my voice made her think that another sachet in my water wouldn't hurt.

Later on, I felt sorry for Dad and regretted everything I'd said. The psychologist explained that I had been in shock.

It was very painful announcing the news to my grandparents, we stood in front of the computer screens for hours, sobbing, Grandma especially.

I cried for a month, silently and inconsolably, like the endless rainy days and nights, which followed that blindingly sunny April day. I didn't know how to continue studying for the maturas, how to take those damned exams, how to go to the prom, how I'd move out of the country and study in a foreign university, how I'd come . . . home, to Christian and Michael, and whether that would still be my home without Mom in it. But Misho would need me. How would I live without Mom? How were Christian and Misho going to live without Mom? Christian was already planning on hiring a nanny for Misho. The psychologist came once a week but conversation with her wasn't going well—Christian told her that he was doing fine, so did I, and Misho kept playing around us.

For a long time I couldn't come to terms with the fact that Mom was gone. Gone not for a week or a month, and not for the duration of a business trip. Forever. That was the first time I had to face "forever." And "never." Christian kept giving me awkward hugs, stroking my hair and gently asking me not to cry in front of Michael whose face swelled with tears whenever he saw me weep. Christian didn't cry in front of us, but I could hear him at night, across the three floors of our spacious house, I heard him wailing and howling in the cellar. His heavy steps echoed up and down the house all night. During the day he spent a long time rinsing his eyes—in the master bathroom, the kitchen, the guest bathroom—but they would only turn out redder, even bloodshot, and Michael would begin to fear him and come snuggle into me. Christian took Misho to sleep with him in the big master bed. Did he not want to be alone there, or could not sleep at all?

Or did Misho have nightmares and scream in his sleep? I could sense something else about Christian—some sort of bitterness that Mom never bought a helmet although he had reminded her every time, had even bought her one but she forgot it somewhere and lost it, that she left us so absurdly and so early, and most of all—irresponsibly, without thinking that she needed to be healthy and live long, that she needed to take care of us so we had a mom and he had a wife. To Protestants life is above all obligation and stoicism.

I served as an interpreter between Christian and Mom's relatives in Bulgaria—as they were trying to decide how, when, and where they ought to bury Mom. Should her body be transported to Bulgaria by air? My uncle, Mom's brother, had learned that the European Commission would cover the expenses. That way we could bury her next to my great-grandmother and great-aunt, bury her in the grave where Grandma said she would be buried, too, when "her time came." I didn't get why only the women in the family were buried together in that grave, separate from their husbands. It wasn't the right time to ask. Christian tried, in the most courteous and delicate French, to tell my grandparents that Mom had been his wife and that he wanted her to be cremated. (I searched that word in Google Translate, which was on throughout the "negotiations," but I still wasn't sure about the translation—what did burning [kremiran] have to do with cream?!) This wasn't just his personal protestant tradition, Christian explained patiently. He wanted the urn to be laid to rest in his family tomb in Frankfurt where one day his own ashes would be laid beside hers. Where "our children," those were the words that he used, could come visit both of us. My grandparents, my uncle, and his wife, lined up on our Skype screen like some sort of committee, said nothing about the cremation—as far as I could gather, the idea was totally incomprehensible in the Orthodox tradition. My grandma kept weeping and saying that she wouldn't have a grave to "shed a tear and plant a flower on." Grandpa suddenly insisted that Mom's name should be engraved on her gravestone in Bulgarian. Christian immediately agreed that her name would be written "in Bulgarian, *too.*" Then he tried to talk them into accepting, he said he'd pay for their tickets and stay in Frankfurt so that they could come to Mom's grave at least twice a year. In the end, this normally stately and composed man addressed Grandma and said, his voice faltering, that he loved her daughter immensely and believed their relationship to be written in the stars, even though it was a second marriage for both of them. He used the present tense, *I love her*, but I switched to the past as all of us had been speaking about Mom in the past tense already, *loved*, and then I corrected myself. There was silence at the other side of the computer screen, Grandma sobbing, head down, my aunt wiping her eyes and blowing her nose, my uncle and grandpa all bristling and hostile, as if it was a matter of military negotiations and national interest. I had heard Mom hint humorously that she was a firm atheist (no, wait, was it agnostic?) and that language was her only homeland so I thought that all those discussions only mattered to the living, not to Mom.

All in all, two weeks after that sunny April day a funeral service was held for Mom in the Russian church in Brussels (Christian had declared the Bulgarian church too small and ugly, "that's no church," he'd said). The priest spoke in Old Slavonic, which was equally incomprehensible to everyone. There was no translation. The coffin was closed—in typical Protestant fashion, and not because the body had been disfigured in any way. Christian explained this to Grandma. She had not insisted on seeing her child, but only because she had always been shy and timid. I could feel that she wanted to, though. At the same time, however, she was too scared to look. I myself didn't know if I wanted to see my late mom.

There were too many people, I didn't know most of them. Christian, my grandparents, my uncle's family, and I were sitting at the front. Dad had not come to the funeral, although Christian had extended an invitation and offered to pay for his ticket and accommodation. Michael was sitting in Christian's lap. They were the only ones who weren't crying—Christian wanted to spare my little brother. He kept explaining to him how Mom had fallen asleep because she had many little wounds and she couldn't wake up and that she would go up in the sky in that box. I wondered how Misho would picture that. And then, all those strangers lined up to give us their condolences, to kiss and embrace us. My cheeks went ruddy, then raw, so Christian gave me an antiseptic cream.

Only the immediate family was allowed into the crematorium—Mom was cremated after all—and everyone could say something before the coffin was taken out. All of us spoke, through sobs and tears, mostly saying how much we loved Mom, what a wonderful wife, mother, daughter, and sister she had been and how much we were going to miss her. Grandpa said what a "radiant child" she had been. His words sounded out of place, for some reason, but I translated them nevertheless. Then Grandpa recited a stanza from a poem Mom had written at seventeen:

I'll ramble round the non-being and return
In blossoms white as snow, in someone's memories,
Or in my daughters' very secret reveries
Or in the electronic dawn of this world.

I translated it word for word, and I totally lost the rhyme. After everything was over, I thought about that poem. Why Mom wrote she would have daughters and how she knew that the virtual world would eventually replace the real one? She had written "electronic," and not "virtual" because in . . . let me do the math . . . 1984 . . . computers and such were unheard of in communist Bulgaria.

I translated from German into Bulgarian when Christian was speaking and from Bulgarian into French (my active German was still not that good) when my relatives were. As for me, I spoke French out of respect for Christian, translating every sentence into Bulgarian. I wanted to speak about Mom, what a terrific Mom she had been, but what I actually blurted out was a quote from an obituary I had seen in Plovdiv. Actually, it was the first sentence outside my primer that I'd stopped to read out to Mom, "You'll live forever in our hearts," I had read flawlessly twelve years ago. Mom had not smiled, or paused, she had just said absent-mindedly, "Well done. Now you can read."

Twelve years ago I hadn't understood what I'd read at all, nor what this paper on the wall was. Now I knew. Granny brought the necrologue that they'd pinned to their block entrance door in Plovdiv. The necrologue comprised several sentences, including the one I'd read to mom as a child.

I had to speak last, but after that sentence I burst into tears and could not continue, I couldn't even translate into French. The celebrant expressed her condolences and finished off the ceremony in French.

I'm not sure about the legal side of the affair but I think that, probably with my consent, Christian could have made the decisions regarding the funeral himself. In any case, the urn—a dark brown, shiny, tall metallic object, hermetically sealed and marked by a miniature label with Mom's name and dates of birth and death on it—is still in his study. I try not to look at it whenever I go there. I wonder how heavy it is, though, and as much as I'm ashamed of my curiosity I know that one day I will secretly take the urn and hold it for a while.

What do I myself think? I don't know. I'm confused. Mom was Bulgarian. She had spoken to me only in Bulgarian, she had nudged me to read, in Bulgarian, Bulgarian authors she had hand-picked for me. She had explained certain things to me. I remember how I had been reading some Bulgarian novel, I can't recall which one, it was historical, though, and Mom had said that "we should view the individual person against the background of his or her family, country, people, culture, language, and history." Looking at things this way, perhaps we should have laid her in Bulgaria, beside my great-grandma, my great-aunt, and the place where her own mother, my Granny, would eventually be buried. I know that Dad wants to be buried on a hill in the Rhodope Mountains, he's shown me the exact place. Will his second wife be buried there, too? On the other hand, however, it's been eleven years since Mom left Bulgaria, most probably never to return. She was Christian's wife, they had Michael together, Christian loved her and had the right to have the urn with her ashes placed alongside his own family, where he would eventually lie. Even if the "background" was German and Protestant, even if the inscriptions were in German. All this would be simpler for Misho. As for me, I'm confused—I was eight years old when I left Bulgaria, I grew up in Brussels, in the so called reconstructed family, I'm Christian's daughter for all administrative purposes, and he does treat me like his own child—a little stricter, perhaps, and a little bit colder, but I think that's his Prussian streak speaking, and not the lack of biological ties. Besides, he acts like a real father to me when it comes to health, boys, school, or college. French is my . . . how should I put it, not my native tongue but what they call a first or primary language. My mother tongue is Bulgarian—but in a very narrow sense of the word. Yes, I have read a short history of Bulgaria, I know the basic facts, but what is Bulgaria to me? I'm studying in Paris now, perhaps I'll finish my studies in the United States, coming "home" here, Brussels, and then who knows where I'll go to live and work, and build my own "homestead," who knows whom I'll be building it with and where that person will come from. Now that I think of it, Bulgaria is beginning to look small and distant like a postcard of my smiling uncle and grandparents standing in front of the Amphitheatre in Plovdiv, squinting at the blazing sun. And it doesn't matter if I'll visit Mom's grave in Frankfurt or in Plovdiv, and Dad's grave on some mountain hill once every couple of years. What will I explain to my children about their grandparents? Will they even want to know? I'm thinking about all of that when I'm standing before my mother's urn. What would she have wanted? She had never mentioned where and how she wanted to be buried. I don't know if it was because she had never given it a thought or because it was of no importance to her.

Christian and I decided to give Mom's clothes and shoes away to a charity that sent them to second-hand shops in Bulgaria. I didn't tell Christian that when I was six Mom had bought me a winter jacket from a shop like that. I've remembered the shop because the jacket was really nice, it was red, and I tried to imagine the girl who had worn it. I kept Mom's beige cashmere sweater which she put on in the winter nights she spent behind the computer screen; it would always bear the smell of her perfume (and cigarettes? Did Mom smoke a few secretly after officially quitting?). And I kept a scarf. I couldn't find Mom's most elegant business suit, which she only wore when she had important occasions at work. Faltering, Christian explained to me that he had given that suit with a white blouse and "whatever else they needed" to the funeral agency. So Mom was . . . cremated in those clothes. She was dressed for work when she left this world.

I also decided to keep a silk dress, a dark blue polka-dot number that made Mom look like a movie star from the 1960s; she had worn it, though rarely, for as long as I could remember. And indeed, one of my first memories of Mom is her wearing it on the High Street in Plovdiv, and me longing to grow up as beautiful as she seemed to me, in that particular outfit. I had asked her to leave the dress to me when she died (I don't remember that part, Mom had told me about it, chuckling, when I was fourteen and had just bought a dreadfully short and tight dress). The silk dress looked classy and expensive but it hadn't been bought from any designer store; my grandmother had made it, adapting a magazine pattern to follow Mom's simple design. I told Christian there would be no need for him to buy me a prom dress because I had already decided to wear that one. It fitted me perfectly. That way Mom would be there with me—at the prom and the party for my nineteenth birthday. Christian looked uneasy at first; he was ready to buy me a gown, he said, and yet on the day of the prom it was not merely grief glimmering in his tearful eyes but a measure of marvel and pride.

I found two hats in the closet. I had never seen Mom wear them. She didn't like wearing hats, even in the coldest of days. I tried one of them, bearing inside a label *Second Coming*,[68] without giving it much thought, but as I was posing in front of the mirror, Christian asked me, a bit curtly, to take it off. Shortly after, he apologized and told me that it was just a dear, and very painful now, memory—he'd given it to Mom as a special present when they attended a horse race just outside of Köln. I left it with him, although I didn't know what he would do with a woman's hat.

Mom rarely wore her jewelry, which mostly comprised gifts from Christian, but she never took off her wedding band and her diamond engagement ring. And yet, here they were in the jewelry box. That meant Christian or the funeral agent had slipped them off the fingers of my late mother. She wore her watch, every now and then, as a piece of work-appropriate jewelry. Christian suggested that I could take all of Mom's bijoux, including the watch, as long as I took good care of them and only wore them after I graduated, got married, and started working. In fact, he suggested they remain

68 A name of a shop.

in the box for the time being. He wanted to keep the diamond ring for Michael's future wife and asked me to make sure that his wish would be fulfilled if he wasn't around anymore. He said nothing about the wedding band but gently put it back into the box where he had already left his own—he had taken it off after the funeral.

Mom's personal belongings turned out to be very few—a basket of cosmetics, six shelves of Bulgarian books, a few medium-sized IKEA boxes stuffed with many surprisingly silly (to me) letters and postcards from her friends, a relatively big box of work-related archives from the time she'd worked as an editor more than twenty years earlier (old books and above all English textbooks and grammar books which looked quite outdated), a hairdryer, an epilator, two photo albums (it felt strange to see Mom as a radiant child indeed, my uncle as a chubby naked baby, a young version of my grandparents, and a photo of Grandma when she was just a couple of years older than me). As the chances for Michael to read in Bulgarian were close to zero, we donated the Bulgarian books to a local library, which had opened a section in Bulgarian, given the growing population of Bulgarians in Brussels.

Mom had also decided to keep, in a passe-partout, a very poetic color drawing by my father (did I mention that he is an artist?). Despite the surrealistic (I'm not a specialist, I'm shooting in the dark here) deformation, I think that's Mom in it. And I think I understand why she hadn't put it in a frame and hung it, here, with Christian. I asked Dad on the telephone whether he wanted it back as a souvenir, but no, with thanks, he didn't want it, or any souvenir at all from Mom, he had "enough memories."

There was also a watercolor, which looked like an illustration to some poetry or a children's book—a paper swallow floating above the rooftops, rain falling down, and in the groove a boy and a girl hugging each other under an umbrella. Mom had showed me that watercolor and told me it was made by one of Dad's friends, a very talented Bulgarian artist who had emigrated to Canada and, after ten years of toiling away as assistant animator at a virtual-game studio, was one night found dead in the gutter. The man had gone mad. What was the moral she wanted to pass on to me? Were the boy and the girl Dad and Mom? Or another unhappy emigrant story? I could not ask Mom anymore.

I guess that was all. Plus the mobile phone, obviously, and also her glasses and the computer. And Mom's planners, of course! But I'll talk about the planners later. Mom's glasses were quite delicate, rimless, with thin gilded wires for the ears and a nose rest. She wore them when driving, watching TV, or riding her bike . . . Inexplicably, this fine little thing had survived the encounter with the pavement. I tried them on—they looked good on me, but I still didn't need the diopters. Christian gently wiped the lenses and the tiny rim, placed the glasses in the little box she kept them in and put them away. The mobile phone had crashed on the pavement with Mom, it was cracked all over and had died forever, at the same moment when she'd lost her consciousness for good, as her doctor supposed. Christian emailed the mobile company to shut down the number and they suggested he listen through the voice messages that had remained unopened. I thought that wasn't a bad idea and that we could even send a text message to all of her contacts to tell them about her death from her number. Christian wouldn't hear of that—those were Mom's contacts, not his, we had announced her death through the official channels in Brussels and Plovdiv, and besides, bad news travels fast, all those calls and messages were for Mom, not for him, it wasn't right to pry in the personal correspondence of another person, even if it was his own wife. He turned down all the offers, returned the SIM card to the company, and even gave them the broken phone to use for spare parts. That was Christian for you—decent and frugal to the core.

It was the same decency and respect that made him unwilling to snoop in her computer. I wondered if he was scared—by what he might see in the phone, the computer, the planners. Afraid he might find some secrets of hers, which he'd rather she took to the grave? Or maybe he realized that in her intimate world Mom had been speaking and writing in Bulgarian and it would be inaccessible to him, anyway?

Mom's computer had no password, but her email password wasn't saved and none of us knew it. I was thinking about Mom's email—nope, not what was in it and who she had been writing to. Like Christian, I preferred not to know. And, frankly, I was sure, there was nothing and nobody to know about. I was wondering rather how an electronic address "dies," how electronic death happens. Perhaps the personal messages would have stopped arriving by the end of the first month after the news had reached everyone. As for spam and unsolicited ads, however, it was very unlikely. Perhaps, in a year or so, some distant acquaintance or a former co-worker from Bulgaria would email Mom, not knowing that she wasn't alive anymore. And her email wouldn't send an automatic reply . . . But what would happen to the existing inbox and outbox, the files and the photos—will they be locked in a virtual safe after one, five or ten years? Or does the box get automatically "incinerated" if no one opens it in two, five or ten years? Is its content really destroyed without a trace? Or it will stay forever?

It was easy with Facebook. Four or five years ago, when I was a teenager (which I no longer was since my twentieth year had begun), I mocked Mom for being old-fashioned and backward. So she set up a Facebook profile to prove, as a joke, that she wasn't that much of a "boomer." I was Mom's friend on Facebook so I posted a message about her death on her wall. I received condolences, kind words, and grief-stricken postcards from almost all of her three hundred contacts. Now I am looking for ways to shut down her page.

Mom and I communicated by text messages mostly. I still have hers on my phone, they are so dear to me. But perhaps one day I will delete them. Or maybe I won't, I'll copy them into one file and keep it on my computer. I also have the emails she had sent me but they are very short—things she had come across the internet or some ideas she thought would be interesting to me. I have just two longer messages left from her. A few years ago, we had been speaking about the past, about history and communism, and then she typed those conversations and sent them to me. And one Christmas she gave me something like a Christmas story.

That's how we archived Mom—her body, her belongings, her electronic identity. But I think the real archive of the real Mom was in her planners and on her computer. Mom's planners were something quite special, very telling for her character. When her colleagues started clearing up her office ten days after the funeral, one of them brought three boxes of papers, books, and documents that Mom had kept there. Among them were the eighteen planners she had for the past eighteen years. Number nineteen, the one she was currently using, was in one of her handbags at home—the one she had gone to work with on the Friday before that fateful Saturday. I arranged the eighteen planners on the table in three stacks of six, with the last one resting in front of me. Nine of them, the ones for the past nine years, were gifts from me, my regular Christmas gift to Mom ever since I had turned ten. At first, Christian had provided me with the finances and we'd picked the planners together. Later, when I had a budget of my own, I'd put some money aside and I'd taken my time hand-picking the type and the design of the planner. I had the feeling that I was giving Mom the gift of time, that by accepting my present she was promising to keep being, and to keep being herself, for yet another year. Sure, I was also hoping that she would think of me whenever she opened the planner.

Mom used her planner every day; she was totally lost without it. Once, when she had misplaced it, she panicked so much, yelling that she was blind without it, she couldn't remember what she had to do, when, what she shouldn't forget. Mom had told me that she started the planner system when she began work after giving birth to me, a full-time everyday job (in the publishing house) because all of a sudden, time had become very sparse, she had too many things to do, and she had to write everything down so she didn't end up forgetting something and could do it all. Ever since she bought the same type of big yearly planner with a separate page for each day.

And here they are, all these planners lying in front of me. I'm leafing through them, reading one bit or another; some are scribbled in such a jumble that only Mom can decipher them; still, most is in Mom's readable, clear, somewhat honest, handwriting. It seems, every Christmas Mom wanted to change her life, "to dispense with the musts" as she had written in one of her planners seven years ago, "to bring things to a standby" and have time for something else. In the beginning of every planner, in neat scrupulous letters, with solemn oaths and a decisive manner, she had written the major tasks for the year which were more or less the same—repair works at home, major purchases or expenses, time for sports and losing weight, learning German, relocations, and demanding projects at work. Below all those tasks, a thick line appeared—and then something written down and vigorously scribbled over. And that went from one planner into the next one—on the first page, after all the to-dos—a line with something crossed out below. Why had she even written it if she always scribbled over it?! In the last three planners, however, the thing wasn't crossed out! But . . . I couldn't read it. I tried any way I could think of, yet nothing worked.

Then Mom had broken down the tasks by months and weeks—those were smaller, ongoing tasks: meetings, assemblies, conferences, reports, parent-teacher conferences, business trips, payments, budgets (family, personal, project-related), shopping lists, doctors, handymen, guests, children's birthday parties, bookings, holidays . . . And then came the pages for each individual day—mostly the job-related tasks. Mom had told us that when she arrived at work in the morning, she made herself a cup of coffee and ate her croissant in front of the computer, reading through her business emails, looking over the documents on her desk and putting down in her planner what she had to do for the day. There was often a line below the office tasks and then, at the end of the page, things that had been planned for the rest of the day: "cooking, shopping, a concert . . ." Every task—yearly, monthly or daily—was written down in a bullet list and marked with an arrow. Whenever something was completed, Mom circled the arrow. Done. If she hadn't managed to finish something, she carried as a task over for the following day, following week, month, year . . . In Mom's notepads there was always future time. And this future was meant mainly to complete what one had to.

The last thing Mom had put down were the tasks for that final weekend:

- *Birthday party Michael, Saturday 14-17 h* (the address of the birthday boy and the phone number of his mother followed*)*
- *shopping, drycleaner's three winter coats, a parcel for my brother, a haircut*
- *cooking—moussaka, tiramisu, beef stew*
- *edit report*

She had succeeded with the first two bullets—she had circled them before she left for the office. Apparently she had planned to cook after picking up Michael from the party. We found the receipt from the drycleaner's in her wallet and Christian took the winter coats. My uncle mentioned that they had received the parcel about ten days after Mom's death, it had been full of presents for Easter, as usual—clothes and cosmetics. I didn't know Mom had had her hair done before she passed away, I never really saw her dead. Christian didn't tell me anything about that. Did she cut off a lot of her hair? But what did that matter—now Mom is just ashes in a metal vase in Christian's study.

I leaf through these nineteen notepads. You can reconstruct what my mom had been doing by the hour for the past nineteen years! This is the time of my entire nineteen years of life on this planet. But, wait, no, this isn't my time. This is my Mom's time, day by day, compressed and mummified like plants in a herbarium. Plans for the future, turning into a meticulous documentation of the past, "in real time." And Mom galloping over the pages hyper-organized, planning everything, forgetting nothing, never late, always prepared, getting everything done—well and on time. The entire world could count on her. She called her planners "chronicles of the everyday," of the planned and organized everyday life.

But what was that thing she had scribbled over for years on end and then written, perhaps on purpose, in completely unintelligible way? What was that task Mom had carried over unfinished from one year to the next and why had she scribbled over it, painstakingly, so many times?

When I saw the folder "Chronicles of Being" on Mom's computer I shuddered with joy and excitement—so Mom hadn't only been writing presentations, reports, and analyses! Here's another, more "artistic" part of Mom preserved! But doubt, fear, and shame washed over me on the spot. What could Mom have written about? Did I have the right to read it? Did I have the right to rummage through her computer? Did I have the right to enter that intimate room which belonged to her, and her only? Mom hadn't published anything, nor had she given me anything to read besides our dialogues about communism.

Christian himself was of two minds. He was very disconcerted already by the fact that I was rummaging through her computer—"it went against his ethics." And yet, when I told him that Mom was writing, in Bulgarian, "a book perhaps—short stories or essays," he couldn't conceal his curiosity and a new wave of unease that he wouldn't understand a word, that he'd be dependent on me to translate what Mom had written.

"What was your mom writing about?" he asked with a trace of anxiety. Was that fear of Mom's thoughts, or of such an irrational endeavor as women's writing? It could turn out he hadn't known her all that well.

"I've only scanned the files, I don't know yet," I fibbed, wondering how and whether I should tell him what I had found.

"All right. Read through them, but very carefully, please," whatever that meant. "You're a big girl now, and educated enough to tell if what's written is . . . important." That's interesting, I wondered, whose idea of "important" were we talking about? "In any case, I wouldn't want her name to be tarnished, or the memory of her as a wonderful person, wife, mother . . . European employee."

"Of course! I am with you on this."

"Besides . . . if she was writing to publish her work, she must have intended to do it herself," Christian concluded hesitantly.

"She had no time to. Mom didn't have the time to write. All her time went into being a wonderful person whom everyone could rely on to do everything well and on time, into being a wonderful wife, mother, and employee," my voice slightly shaking with irritation. I wondered whether I should translate in French to Christian the difference between everyday life or well-being and Being—in Bulgarian *bit* and *bitie* I had read about on Mom's computer.

"But, of course, if your mom was talented, if what she had written is good, maybe it should be published," Christian suggested.

"I don't know. There are pages I really like. The problem is that most of the texts are unfinished, there are about fifty-sixty pages in all, but disconnected, they don't form a consistent story. The rest—another thirty-forty pages—are just notes, I mean descriptions, dialogues, thoughts, single sentences, verses, there are even strings of unrelated words and only Mom knew what they meant and what she wanted to write with them later on. There are letters, too—to Grandma for example."

"Perhaps you should keep those texts to yourself after all, as a keepsake from your mom."

"We'll see," I said, hesitated for a while and then went on. "Actually, it seems that Mom has sent something she'd written to a famous Bulgarian writer she knew."

Christian looked uneasy. He was jealous with regard to Mom, he had no reason to be. Now, he might have one.

"They were just good acquaintances, he's only emailed her once, Mom's copied his letter into her texts," I hastened to soothe Christian. "He encourages her to write, he tells her she *must* write," I emphasized *must*, "because what she writes is . . . 'wonderful.' Yes, these were his precise words."

"Who is this writer?" Christian asked. It felt like he was jealous not only of the man, but the fact that the writer had communicated with Mom in a way that Christian couldn't, that Mom had shared a similar worldview, with another man, that this male author had paid her a compliment that Christian couldn't, that he had given her something Christian couldn't, that even maybe he had made her happy in a way Christian never could.

"You don't know him. You haven't read any of his works. We have the French edition of one of his books. I'll give it to you. I'm thinking of sending Mom's files to him and asking for his opinion and advice."

"All right," Christian said, resigned. "And please, keep me informed."

I had found six files on Mom's computer. Before I had made up my mind to open them, I contemplated their names for a long time—six male names, numbered one to six. The first two names didn't ring a bell. Actually, not quite—the first one, I think, was the name of my mom's high school boyfriend. She had mentioned him when she told me about the English language school. Dad was number three. I think I had a vague recollection of number four—Mom had introduced the "uncle" to me back when we lived in that dingy and dusty rental, after she'd left Dad and before we'd moved to Brussels. Christian was number five. But there was a number six . . . So my Mom had a lover?! Had she cheated on Christian?! I was fairly dismayed. I felt disgusted, and also guilty for being disgusted by my late mother. I wished I could delete this sixth file as if it had never existed; as if the story it tells never happened. I went as far as to think about deleting them all. I didn't want to know! I didn't want to know anything! My mom's intimate life scared me. It would better be buried along with her.

And yet, my curiosity—unhealthy and preemptively judgmental—overtook me. I wanted to know the truth! Of course, I started by opening the last, sixth file, the one that was named after a completely unfamiliar man. My goodness . . . It was a book! It has a cover (a blurred colorful background, a picture of a street with people, shops, cars and a tram) and a title—*Chaque jour est un roman.* The names of the "authors" were written across the cover—a man and a woman. The male name was the same as that of the file. But the female . . . wasn't Mom's! What's going on here?! What's this?? My mind boggled. I scrolled down to the next page—that was the back "cover"—with two portrait pictures, apparently of the two "authors." The man was old, nice-looking though, with graying hair, pale eyes, and a faint, somewhat thoughtful smile. There was something like a quote, apparently written by him, under the photo. In French. I left the quote for further reading. And the woman . . . was one of Mom's closest friends—Auntie Renata! There was a quote under her photo, too—in English. But my Mom's friend was . . . married to uncle István, not to that guy on the photo. And they had a daughter, a little older than me, who was always teasing me about something. But maybe Auntie Renata and the man in the photo were just co-authors. I didn't know Auntie Renata wrote. I scrolled down another page—the book had . . . a preface. Ten pages in Microsoft Word, a 12pt font. But the preface was . . . in Bulgarian! Mom's friend was . . . Hungarian, and did not speak a word of my mother tongue. I was nonplussed. The screen told me there were 116 pages to go. I skimmed through a few—they consisted of letters and emails between Mom's friend and that man, in French and in English. Nothing naughty . . . yet, they were not just co-authors, they loved one another, they shared trivial things from their everyday life. OK, it seems Auntie Renata had a lover. When were these letters written, by the way? There were no dates. I scrolled further down—the letters themselves were very few, followed by many broken passages about the Moon, about love, the meaning of life, there were some really funny bits—I read a mock version of a song by Sting. Stop! The man declared how ardently he desired the woman, I was too embarrassed to continue reading and I hastened to scroll down. I opened the search window and typed Mom's name—there were six hits, I traced all of them. The man and the woman had just dined with Mom and the man commented on how interesting and funny she was, then Mom's friend mentioned that Mom was longing to write; another place in the text said that Mom had a very nice family, that her children were wonderful, and that she was very happy.

Good. But what on earth did that epistolary book have to do with Mom? Why was it on her computer? Why was the preface in Bulgarian? I'd call Auntie Renata first thing tomorrow to get an explanation. I'd even offer to send her the file and would delete it from Mom's computer.

Highly puzzled, I opened the other files. I started with the one about Dad, of course—but there was nothing about him there! His name wasn't mentioned. Just a few unrelated paragraphs discussing philosophers and paintings. There was also a long letter to Grandma. Same thing with the file that was named after Christian. It contained some reflections on economy and money and then, in the middle, the beginning of a story about the Kinder eggs Grandpa had brought when Mom was a little girl. At the end of the file, there was a theatrical scene—a dialogue between a man and a woman. The other three files didn't have anything to do with men, either. "Dad's" file contained a couple of diligently typed poems Mom had written in her teenage years—the ones which Grandpa was so fond of reciting. He had even asked Christian to have a line engraved on Mom's tombstone, in Bulgarian, the opening line of the poem he had recited at her cremation ceremony:

"*I'll wander round the non-being and return . . .*"

It turned out that further in this poem my seventeen-year-old mom had defined death as "public disgrace." The April sun, the traffic, the big white-red flower on the grass, Christian giving short orders . . . all rewound again in front of my eyes.

As far as I could find my way around those six files, the principle of classification was thematic rather than chronological and, in any case, totally unrelated to men. These male names appeared like some kinds of eras, or like passwords to unlock ideas or memories. The texts themselves looked totally chaotic. There were only a few complete short stories (I found these interesting), the rest was a puzzle of sketchy, broken dialogues or simply cues, short descriptions, thoughts, aphorisms, individual phrases, articles Mom had copied, series of questions. There were even a few pages that looked like the beginning of a sci-fi novel.

Most texts . . . took me by surprise. How had Mom come up with things like that? Was she inventing them, or did she really experience them? I can only judge the truthfulness of things I know and remember myself. But do I know everything? Do I remember well what I knew? What do I know about Mom's life? What do I know about her so-called "inner life"? Planner Mom and the Mom who emerged from these files seemed to be two different women. Planner Mom was orderly, organized, reliable, predictable. And also anxious and stressed-out. I had the feeling that the woman in those nineteen planners was perpetually sorting out chaos. That Mom we all knew and remember. Still . . . that line on the first page of every agenda planner, scribbled over, and over, totally unreadable, and never marked as accomplished . . . I again went through the planners, one after the other. In the end I had the feeling that Mom had been screaming, louder and louder, those incomprehensible words. The invisible and unfamiliar Mom from the "Chronicles of Being" was chaotic and contradictory indeed, but free and funny as well. Were these files a sort of other agenda, a plan, and for what?

Trying to find my way around this maze of questions, I reread one of Mom's longer speculations. These few pages were the only occasion when she thought about death, albeit indirectly. More precisely, though, she had written about consciousness, afterlife, and artificial intelligence.

Yet, the most important questions to which I had to find the answers were whether Mom's writing had any literary value, and if yes, whether they could be completed, arranged and published. I could not figure out any other purpose of writing than publication and decided that this would have been Mom's will.

I vaguely remembered meeting the Bulgarian writer at some book launch in Brussels, or perhaps Plovdiv, I couldn't be sure, which my Mom had dragged me to when I was a child. I had no idea what she had sent him (two years earlier), under what circumstances or to what end, but his letter was definitely encouraging. I sent him a long email explaining the situation and my "findings." I asked dozens of questions and finished off by asking for his advice.

He replied immediately. The writer suggested a phone call or a personal meeting in case I was planning to visit Bulgaria sometime soon. Above all, however, he was asking me to send him the files because he could give me no advice unless he read them.

I informed Christian that I had read all of Mom's notes very carefully and assured him that there was nothing there "to discredit or tarnish her memory." I added that there was nothing intimate and personal about her notes. I said that, in my opinion, she was writing fiction, and not a diary. I made no mention of the sixth file about the Hungarian family, and I said nothing about its weird preface.

"You know, Mom was actually quite melancholic."

Christian instantly felt despondent, apparently interpreting my words as an implicit blame that he hadn't made her happy.

"I mean, she wasn't sad because someone or something had made her miserable. It sounds rather as existential melancholy."

We had already studied Camus and Baudelaire's *Spleen* at school so that was a good occasion to demonstrate my knowledge. Christian being a lawyer, those literary references did nothing to cheer him up.

"She had an awesome sense of humor, too. Though, often bordering upon irony and the absurd."

"*Je sais.*" Christian brightened up. Yet he could not conceal his surprise. As a matter of fact, I was also surprised at Mom's sense of humor because in real life she rarely joked and did not even smile that much, either.

I told Christian I had sent the texts to the Bulgarian writer and that I'd meet him in Bulgaria when I went there to see my grandparents, my uncle and Dad for the Easter holidays. After a lot of negotiations with his in-laws, with me serving as an interpreter, Christian had agreed to let Michael come, too. "So that the little one can practice a bit of Bulgarian so he doesn't completely forget it," Grandpa kept saying. But it was true, no one spoke to Misho in Bulgarian anymore. After I left for university, Christian hired an au pair, a local Belgian girl who cooked and took care of Misho while Christian was at work.

That visit to Plovdiv will stay in my memory with the large, fluffy, and ultra-delicious *banitsa*[69] Grandma made, with the long walk I had with Dad, just the two of us, around the rowing lake, and the Easter service, which Grandma had insisted the two of us attend. Misho stayed at home with Grandpa, to have some "quality male time" with him. Men seemed to consider religious rituals female nonsense.

It was April again, the night was warm and quiet. Nana took me to the church where Mom and Dad had married. The churchyard was brimming with people. At midnight the bells started ringing, the priest appeared in black and silver at the candlelit entrance of the church, "Christ has risen!" he proclaimed three times in a row, "Indeed, He has risen!" the crowd bellowed back, as if people were trying to convince one another in the truth of that wondrous event. Then they started lighting their candles, sharing the candle flame with each other. Grandma and I lit our candles, too. The candles were fixed into perforated plastic cups so they wouldn't go out. Then the priest walked out of the church, flanked by two other priests who filled the air with the scent of burning incense, and the three of them lead the crowded procession on a

69 Traditional Bulgarian egg and cheese pastry.

circuit around the church. The priests started singing and many people who knew the words chanted along:

Christ has risen from the dead, death trampling over death . . .

I had woven the willow branches around my head like a wreath. I was thinking it looked good on me. I wanted to look like the impersonation of Spring in an illustration to a children's poem. I would definitely take a look in the mirror when we got home. The entire ritual was new to me. Mom, Christian, and I had visited many cathedrals but we had regarded them as historical monuments and not as places of worship. I knew that I was christened in Plovdiv as a child so I was supposed to profess "Orthodox Christianity." When we moved to Belgium, I had to have R. E. classes in the French speaking school I was attending. They did find a teacher for me, even though I was the only "Orthodox" pupil. I have no memory of that teacher explaining to me what "Orthodox Christianity" was and what made me different from my Catholic classmates. Or maybe he had explained, but I didn't understand everything in French back then. I remember that I spent most of those boring classes drawing. A few years later, when I moved to high school, I heard that women were expected only to give birth and obey their husbands. So, I flatly refused to study religion and Mom and Christian transferred me to an ethics class.

On Easter Thursday or Saturday, we would dye some eggs and then, on Easter morning, there'd be a contest; we would tap two eggs together to see which one survived. The German Protestants dyed their eggs, too, and Christian enjoyed drawing clumsy funny pictures all over them. Egg duels were new to him, but he liked them nevertheless. Two years ago, five-year-old Misho had broken all the eggs trying to find the strongest one. We had to eat deviled eggs for days on. The high point of Easter, however, were the basketfuls of chocolate eggs, hens, chicks, and bunnies, which Christian would carefully hide around the garden early in the morning and have Mom, me and eventually Misho search for them, trying to outdo each other. We cried triumphantly whenever we saw a piece of chocolate treasure sparkling among the rose leaves, in the bushes, or in the grass. Mom and I took care to walk past some so Misho could find them. Then we'd spent months trying to eat all those pounds of chocolate, Mom would put on some weight and start worrying about it, still secretly nibbling on the chocolate, though, and Misho and I would "blow her cover," noting how fast the chocolate trophies had been disappearing. Yet, we had never attended an Easter service in Brussels. I think both Mom and Christian were atheists who followed those rituals because they were a family thing and because of the joy they brought us.

These sweet memories made me tearful, there, in the courtyard of the church in Plovdiv. In Brussels, the previous Sunday,[70] we had spent our first Easter without Mom. Everything was different. Christian bought a carton of six painted eggs, but at breakfast we forgot the egg duels. Misho was the only one who went searching for chocolate in the garden while I burst into tears and fled to my room. Then Misho pricked his finger on a rose thorn and gave up the search. Christian went into the garden alone to bring back the chocolate treasures, but he couldn't find all of them and months later the birds would still find colorful pieces of tin foil to tear apart.

Christ has risen from the dead, death trampling over death . . .

I squeezed Grandma's hand and looked at her. Tears were running down her face. She was walking slowly, her gaze floating above the crowd ahead. She did not look at me; she didn't want me to see her tearful eyes so she just squeezed my hand, too. The touch of her hand made me feel that we were thinking about the same thing—Mom wasn't going to rise from the dead, human death could not be trampled over.

"Let's go, Grandma. I want to tell you something."

On the way home, holding the plastic cups with the candles inside, I told Grandma about Mom's unwritten or unfinished book, about the conversation I'd had with the Bulgarian writer a few days earlier, his appreciation of Mom's notes, and his proposal to write the book, or rather rearrange and complete it.

"This way, Mom will live on," I said hopefully. "Her spirit will be kept alive."

I found it particularly symbolic to speak about the immortality of Mom's spirit at Easter time. Grandma listened to me, quietly, and when I was done talking she said quietly she was very happy to hear it. Her words came out dry and forced. Her eyes were still moist. We kept walking in silence. I didn't know how to comfort her. Then I thought she was supposed to comfort me, I was the one who had lost her mother and that was my dear nana here who had brought me up and who'd comforted me when I was a kid.

Before we entered the building, she sighed. "Ah, Radi, my dear Radi . . . my baby is gone. God forbid . . . anyone's child to ever . . . ever pass away before they do." Then she hastened to wipe her nose and dry her tears before we got into the lift.

The conversation I had with the writer was quite interesting although I didn't really get everything he said. I trusted him, though—he seemed to really like Mom's writing and even found it "inspiring." He was an acclaimed author, a household name, so I had every reason to believe he would make the best of Mom's files.

70 Orthodox Easter usually falls one week later.

"Do you remember, Rada, you asked me a question . . . at my first book launch? You were little, nine or ten years old."

I had no memory of this.

"I will never forget it. I was taking questions from the audience, people asked some dumb stuff and then, when there were no more questions and everyone was on their way to the buffet, a little hand rose up, a child's hand. Your mother looked at you, beside her, surprised by your courage. You asked me whether everything I had written was true. A fundamental question! And one which is not posed. Not in that way. There are questions about prototypes, real events. Only a child could pose a question in this way . . . point-blank. Not to mention that the question was really delicate as far as the personal went.

I smiled understandingly. It was nice to hear that as a child I'd been intelligent.

"To me this is a book, at least as far as my taste and understanding are concerned. Even in this jumbled state. I daresay that it's precisely the chaotic form and its tragic context—once again, my deepest condolences!—that compound meaning. When and how does a text stop being a letter, a note, or a diary entry, and become a work of literature? Your mother gave that matter a lot of thought. I'm thinking of collecting these thoughts into an essay."

"So, you think my Mom was talented and what she wrote is worth publishing?" I returned the conversation to its beginning.

"Yes, her texts definitely do have literary value. Whatever that means. But that's a long story. In any case, I'm ready to finish, edit, and rearrange the texts and prepare them for publication. To answer another question of yours—your mother definitely felt she was writing literature. I'm sure that if she had the time, she would've finished it and published it."

"Yes . . . Mom never had time . . . I want to tell you about her planners." I had Mom's last planner with me so I brought it out. I explained what was behind some of the "to-dos," what Mom's everyday life was like. When we got to the date of her death, I started crying. I told him everything about that day. He listened attentively, while turning the pages, stopping here and there to read."

"You know . . . please excuse me, you might find this cynical but what you've just told me could make a good story. I know it sounds horrible, you have all my sympathy, of course, but I barely knew your mother. I mean as a real person, apart from those few texts she had sent me. And your story would be *about* her, not written by her."

That took me off guard. Me, writing . . . ?!

"You and I will have to finish her book. Before I forget—by all means send me that strange preface in Bulgarian. Most probably the author of that preface is your mother, not her friend. And . . ." he opened the planner on the first page, pointed to the words that were not crossed out but still unreadable, and said, "I managed to make these words out! *Trying to essay*. That's what's written. I like the humility in this *trying*. But, it seems . . . even trials, or *essays*, only could not fit into your mother's agenda. There is no mention of them in the to-do lists, not even for the weekends."

I took the planner and fixed my eyes on the words that had hitherto remained unreadable. Yes, indeed, that's what they said: *Trying to essay*.

"So you're telling me the book will have three authors—my mother, you, and me?!" I asked.

"Yes!" he said enthusiastically.

"I hadn't thought of that . . . Interesting . . . I don't remember whether I told you, but I'm studying law and I want to specialize in copyright in particular."

"Oh, great! Hm . . . what a coincidence! . . . Well, this book will raise a lot of questions for you in purely legal terms . . . But don't get me wrong! I'm not imposing myself as co-author because I want to encroach upon your mother's talent. You can't get rich by publishing Bulgarian literature in Bulgarian, anyhow. For me, it is rather an interesting literary project, whereas for you, I suppose, the book is important mostly as a homage to your mother's memory."

My conversation with the writer ended with us agreeing on a concrete plan and a deadline. It was his job to finish and rearrange the texts and then send me the final result for discussion. He gave me a fair warning that the book's genre would be unspecified, but he could already see the central themes and the leitmotifs, which held it together. I agreed, although what was there for me to discuss—to confirm that this was still Mom's writing, or that she would have wanted to write it like that? It fell upon me to tell the story of Mom's death and everything else I had just told the writer.

"I will edit your story a lot," he cautioned with a smile. "Your Bulgarian isn't all that good, French and English transpire. No offence, please, this is normal. You grew up abroad."

He offered a title, too—*Mom's Men*. I thought how mad Christian would be and suggested diplomatically that we discuss the title later.

CHAQUE JOUR EST UN ROMAN[71]

Time—my own, and that of the women in my family—was never enough to write the women's chronicles I was planning. I failed to patent "fan fiction" or "open literature," as they called it, when I wrote my first book. However, life gave me another chance for a "fact meets fiction" project. One I was paradoxically unable to present in public because it was . . . secret, even doubly so, and too intimate. Yet, I'm itching to tell this story, thereby implementing my "project," so I'll just let it spill out. Of course I'm gonna keep the secret of my prototypes; I will tweak a few biographical details as so I can sweep over the footprints of the real persons while leaving the universal "moral" of the story unchanged. Even so, I hope that one of the main characters will never get to read this text, and its preface, or rather epilogue. This is also one of the reasons I decided to write the story in a language as exotic as my native Bulgarian. Language can be a cover-up, too.

One of my closest friends, a Hungarian woman, most unexpectedly fell in love. Everything was wrong—the timing, the context, and the man. My friend, let's call her Renata, was (and still is) happily married to a big wholesaler, i.e., a big and wholesome man who works in wholesale trading. Her husband, let's call him István, was born Hungarian but grew up in Germany. He loves his wife, their daughter, good wines, and good dining. István had moved to Brussels to be with Renata, and he's working for a big trading company. Renata herself has an interesting, secure, and well-paid job

71 Every day is a novel. (French)

in a European institution. At the time of her escapade, her daughter was a senior high-school student, and she had been already admitted to a good British university. The family lived in a beautiful house in a nice Brussels neighborhood; we had often been there for dinner, and they had been our guests, too. They had a proper social circle, and quite a few resources. Everything was by the book. And then, right out of the blue—bang! Love! And if the wrong timing and circumstance on her part were not dramatic enough, the object of her affections was, according to me at least, as wrong as he could possibly be: seven years older than her, i.e., a fifty-three-year-old guy, a Frenchman, married, with three (!) kids at different stages of adolescence and early adulthood, a wife who was a lawyer (!), and, from everything that I had heard and read, a cold and immovable pillar of the family, a guardian and big contributor to the rather substantial family fortune.

But that was not all. As the over-excited Renata was telling me, for the first time, about the feelings that had swept her off her feet, I learned that the object of her desire was . . . a gynecologist. That detail was enough to leave one dumbstruck and choking on one's glass of white wine, which is what actually happened to me at that *brasserie* . . . I swallowed my "fundamental" questions about the sexual motivation and intimate life of gynecologists and just listened to Renata's story. She said he was very attractive, that she went weak in the knees whenever he was around . . .

"My knees tremble at the gynecologist's too, even when I'm up on that chair . . . but that's just my jitters," I noted, but Renata didn't not hear the joke and kept on talking, exaltedly, about how she got giddy whenever she saw a text from him . . . because they communicated mostly in writing.

I was looking at the picture on her phone—a handsome enough man, indeed, his eyes inquisitive, light-colored, maybe blue, and a slight intelligent smile. She added that he was not just intelligent but a strikingly spiritual person.

"What do you mean," I said. "We are all creatures of flesh—and spirit, in different measure."

"Yes, well, you're right. But he mulls over things like the human mind, the human spirit, the meaning of life, the Universe, chaos, etc. Those kinds of . . . existential questions."

Renata paused. I was still trying to digest the extraordinary news in all its detail.

"You see," Renata continued, "few people at our age, in our social circle, and with our kind of resources have kept their spirit . . . their soul. I don't know which is the right word. Yes, we do read prize-winning authors, yes, we do buy expensive tickets to concert and opera performances, we do go to exhibitions, but that is . . . how shall I put it, part of our social image, upper middle class *bon ton* and privilege. Very few people are actually concerned with aesthetic and existential issues."

Now, I should say that Renata is a very well educated woman. She has studied English philology in Budapest and political science in Brussels, specializing in European Studies—which was where we actually met as thirty-four- to thirty-five-year-old "catch-up" students. We were both getting ready for a career in the institutions where she started working three years before me (with a perfect job in education, culture and media) as Hungary joined the EU three years before Bulgaria did. We had some shared memories, some trivial, some historical; our background as philology students then editors and translators in publishing houses, our unwritten PhDs, and our secret writing aspirations had made us really close. Our mutual fondness grew even stronger when we discovered we were both suffering from the guava syndrome, as we named it. One evening we were chatting over martinis and we decided to try guava smoothies. Oh . . . the faces we made when we tried them! I "knew" the taste of guava from some rather artificial juice I'd had in Bulgaria, and I knew the smell from some dishwashing detergent. When I tried the smoothie I could barely swallow without throwing up. It was even nastier than the juice (I have not tried the washing detergent so I had no basis for comparison here). It turned out that the guava was mostly known to Hungarians as a type of soap. Renata couldn't hold it, either, so she ran to the bathroom to spit it out. Our guava "syndrome" has nothing to do with genetic predispositions like the taste or distaste toward coriander, for example. Too bad for the guava—this probably wonderful fruit was forever discredited in our historically, geographically, and economically seasoned palates.

But to come back to this story—in a word, Renata was definitely fine-tuned to culture and aesthetics. We had yet to talk about the existential problems.

"This man is helping me rise above the everyday stuff," Renata went on, dreamily. "He illuminates my soul, my human core. And I've started seeing everything anew, even the banal everyday things. When I'm writing to him, I feel inspired, I have a sense of humor, I outdo myself. He makes me think about the point of everything."

"Sounds like a midlife crisis," I said.

"Maybe." Renata was still in her dreamy state. "But that means that crises are a wonderful thing."

"Dangerous, too," I added. "By the way, where did you meet this prince of yours?"

"It's a funny story," Renata became agitated. "I was going to my yearly gynecological appointment; you know I go to that little private clinic."

No, it cannot be true, I thought.

"And who should I meet but him!"

"So you're saying that he got to know you in the Biblical sense before you actually met?"

Renata laughed.

"Yes! Here's how it happened. He asked me about any complaints I might have, he looked at my medical history on the computer, and guess what, it turned out that he'd examined me four years earlier!"

"So he knew you."

"As far as a doctor knows the thousands of patients who go through his office. Neither he nor I had any memory of each other. So he examined me, took a Pap smear, he was very careful, but nothing more, the same goes for me, too, nothing out of the ordinary. When the examination was over and he was already taking his gloves off and washing his hands, I put my clothes back on. Then I sat in front of his desk, and he went to his cabinet for a stack of prescription forms. When he opened that cabinet, I saw, with the corner of my eyes, a reproduction that was taped on the inside of the door. It was a painting. Guess which one!"

I had no idea what kind of painting a gynecologist might decide to tape inside his cabinet. Even if he was the most spiritual gynecologist in the world.

"*L'Origine du monde*!!"[72]

What a tautology, I thought. Renata was giggling like a little girl.

"And I told him 'What an interesting picture you've chosen for your cabinet.' He got embarrassed, said something under his breath, then started writing the prescription, asking me what was my twisted Hungarian surname again. But I was already curious so I ventured into a short analysis of the picture—how the woman is headless so it can be any woman. The Woman with a capital W. How it is openly realistic and you can't disguise what you're looking at if you're looking at it—too bad for those nineteenth century bourgeois guys, and for all those creationists, etc. Of course he already knew all those things."

Renata is a bawdy woman. And when she gets bawdy in Hungarian—egesh-megesh, splash-splat, so merry and irreverent—I am spellbound, even though I don't understand a word.

"But you know what he said? That this was the perspective from which he sees all of his patients when they go on the gyno chair—headless, anonymous, just human flesh that needs to be examined and treated."

---

72 Gustave Courbet, 1866. Musée d'Orsay, Paris. The picture provoked a scandal, because it depicted in a photo-realist fashion, a naked female torso, her thighs voluptuously parted with her genitalia to the fore and some details hinting that the woman had just engaged or was about to engage in sex.

So that's how it started. Here in Brussels, normally you would not receive a follow-up call or letter for your test results if there's nothing to worry about. Renata's tests were fine but he called nevertheless. And they talked on the phone some more. And then, she dared to call him, and he was happy to hear from her and they talked some more, and then they met "for a drink," and they had been texting each other daily from then on. So, I thought, Renata got "personalized"—she had acquired a head, a face, a voice, thoughts, words, etc.

"Do I understand correctly that your relationship is platonic?" I dared ask directly.

"Oh, it's not," Renata sighed. "We do make love every couple of weeks, but organization is a chore, as you can imagine."

I did imagine that bit quite well. It was something else I couldn't fathom. How could a man who has seen and penetrated . . . medically, thousands of women, a man who can have any woman, in a sense, fall in love with one particular woman, and how one particular woman could arouse him. Renata was quite pretty, that's for sure—a little taller and slimmer than me, and she did sports, unlike me—she had been doing yoga for years, and she'd stopped smoking ages ago. There was something about her features, something Scythian perhaps—or whatever the tribes that once rode through the Hungarian steppes were called. At least I could picture them riding when I looked at her face. I had always envied her for the wild, wavy chestnut mane that has never seen hair dye or blow-dryer magic. And yet . . . This Prince Charming had probably seen scores of gorgeous girls and women.

"But you know, it's not so much about the sex. I mean yes, it's very good sex, but that's not the point . . . To him, sex is a continuation of dialogue, of communication between us. That's how I feel about it, too. I told you we text each other every day."

"So what do you guys write about?"

"Oh, everything—we talk about our day, and whatever caught our attention, about our thoughts, the people we met, our jobs. But we also talk about the times that we live in, about the past, our past history and human history in general, about art, books, music, death, the moon, and the Universe . . . about everything. And because love changes our whole world, it changes the way we look at it, and it changes us as well, everything is so . . . different and exciting."

Renata was such a delight to listen to. I had stopped believing that people over a certain age were still capable of falling in love and talking like teenagers. And yet, I was her friend and it was my duty to remind her about the realities and risks of middle-age love.

"What are you going to do?" I asked.

"What do you mean?" Renata looked puzzled.

"I don't know. I think sleeping with two men would be too confusing to me—I would get the sex routines wrong, or the things we had talked about, I could even get their names wrong. I have the feeling that whenever I am with one, I would be thinking about the other, and vice versa. Besides, when you look at it from another angle, you both are cheating on your partners, on the father and, respectively, the mother of your children, you might ruin your families. Can you really imagine living with this man every goddamn day? Instead of just talking about the life you didn't have and are not having together?"

Renata fell silent. And then she started again, between pauses and botched sentences:

"You're putting it quite well. I don't know . . . it's so different with Jean-Jacques. I love him. No, there's no way I wouldn't know who's who," she said resolutely, whatever that meant. "But I do care a lot about István, and my family, and our daughter, although she is already a grown-up and will soon leave our home . . . I care about everything we went through, everything we have achieved together," she sighed. "And yet István and I do not talk about a lot of things. We don't talk at all. Well, we do talk, but . . . it's just everyday things we discuss. I don't feel any excitement with him. And we don't have much sex anymore. When we do—usually on Saturday night, like a weekend activity—it's a routine, or some well-being thing. If István is having one-night stands on his trade fairs, client visits, etc., I wouldn't be surprised. I wouldn't even be jealous, to tell you the truth."

"Come on, no insinuations, please, don't try pinning the . . ."—I didn't want to use the word *blame*—". . . initiative on István."

"You're right. But it's still highly possible, you know. Men of István's age need young girls to get it up. While Jean-Jacques is different . . . Besides, he is living in a hard situation. His wife is some sort of harpy, she's frigid, and they haven't had sex in years. She laughs at his profession."

"Oh, just don't tell me you're gonna be his savior. The salvation scenario rarely has a happy ending. So if his wife was OK, he wouldn't fall in love with you? It's a good idea to inquire whether she's always been like that and if she has, why did he marry her and even have three kids with her. Or maybe she became like that over time. So why did she change? Might it be that he had one affair too many?"

"No, no," Renata protested. "It's not like that. They just don't talk, and haven't talked in years. I mean . . . not about the things we talk about . . . He was young when he got married," Renata continued, interrupting my thoughts, "because the woman got pregnant. Besides, he used to like her down-to-earth, resolute, pragmatic character. If you're asking me, the woman had just picked a father for her children. It wasn't love but some kind of family planning. By the way, Jean-Jacques is very worried that I might get pregnant. Although he should have seen my IUD. And at my age . . . I suppose many women have wanted him to father their children. And still do."

I burst out laughing. "It seems that many women think a gynecologist is not only good at delivering babies but at making them, too."

Renata remained thoughtful. "His fear hurts me. I have no idea why."

"Wow, are you telling me that you want to have a child with him?"

"Of course not," Renata protested, a bit half-heartedly. "That's why I said I don't know why I feel hurt."

"It might be an aging thing. These are the last years, or maybe even months when we can get pregnant. Besides, do not forget that er . . . four or five years ago you said no when István wanted another child. If I remember right."

Renata was playing with a streak of her beautiful hair.

"That's right. I really don't want more kids. And yet . . . I'm jealous. That's it! I'm jealous because he has kids with her, but now he doesn't want any with me." Renata finished her second glass of wine, had a bite of cheese, and continued: "And he's jealous, too, even though I keep telling him that I don't sleep with my husband."

"So you are no stranger to lies."

"Not quite," Renata squinted. "As I told you, István and I do it . . . rarely, and I've been picturing Jacques every time since I fell in love with him."

"But that's super-mean. And unfair," I protested.

"You know what Jacques wrote to me the other day?" Renata went on, as if she hadn't heard me: "That *l'origin du monde* is not between the woman's legs, nor up in the sky where the gods abide, but in our heads, in our imagination. That's where love and eroticism are born. I mean, he has great respect for women and their grand biological function, he has even dedicated himself to that professionally. From a philosophical point of view, however, he sees things quite differently. Besides, he had once wanted to study philosophy, psychology, or veterinary medicine—he really loves animals. He has a dog now."

"Gynecology is an interesting proxy for those interests," I joked.

"His parents insisted that he needed to study medicine, and then they wanted him to specialize in gynecology so he could inherit his father's practice."

"So it's a kind of family business. Your prince sounds a bit of a pushover to me—his parents told him what to study, his wife got pregnant and sort of made it his duty to marry her."

"There is something true in that. Jacques is just a really good person. A hesitant person. He's always worried he'll make a mistake, or hurt someone, so he prefers to follow those who have enough common sense and feel no doubt."

"So you've had your chances, too," I quipped. "Now, as I see, your common sense has disappeared. Come on, let's get down to earth. I don't think this is meant to be. You only say goodbye to precious things like family, in order to get something even more precious. Except, of course, when you're madly in love. But in this case love eventually fades and then you're sorry . . ."

"Unless you don't start rethinking all those precious things. And unless you haven't found your other half." Renata was up in the clouds again.

After that memorable ladies' night, I became Renata's confidante as she needed to talk (a lot) about her love and her happiness, which were starting to suffocate in their tiny clandestine world. I was close enough, and I was benevolent and discrete. It was logistically a very risky situation. The zeppelin of love would touch ground approximately twice a month for a few hours in a secluded B&B in a remote part of Brussels, equally removed from both their places of work. They booked by phone, and they paid cash. These were hours squirreled away from their working time, and when they had better alibis they could supplement those few hours at the hotel by dining together at some little out-of-the-way restaurant, far from the crowds and their work trajectories.

Once Renata invited me to dine with them. Of course, I was her alibi for the night. I did find Prince Charming attractive in the flesh, too. His eyes were actually teal, greenish in direct lighting. Let's pray that at least one of his kids inherited this, I thought. He had thick, spiky, salt-and-pepper hair cut short. Jean-Jacques had started to go bald on top, but the baldness did not affect his charm in any way, strange as it might seem. He had proportioned features, high cheekbones, an arrogant aristocratic nose, and thin lips that kept their exquisite tension, reflecting the dynamics of the French language, the vocality that, even in a state of rest, was so intimidating to foreigners, and the explosive precision of consonants. He had beautiful hands—slender, long-fingered, with clean and well-groomed nails. Well, these were the hands that he eked out a . . . living with, I said to myself. Right at that moment one of his hands was running shyly over Renata's back, I could see the tip of his finger under her arm. I could also see his elegant ankles, as vulnerable as they were aesthetically pleasing. Jean-Jacques was about 5'10", lacking the typical middle-aged-man pot belly. Clad in a white shirt, greenish cashmere sweater, and a dark-blue, simple, and elegant pair of trousers. Compared to him, the prodigiously built István with his ample gut, roaring laughter, and wild, copper-red hair looked like a bear. A nice bear, right out of a children's story. But a bear nonetheless.

Jean-Jacques was not only an attractive man, indeed, but an interesting conversationalist too. And yet, I was very careful about what I was saying for reasons that will become clearer later. That dinner was when I saw how communication in two languages goes—Jean-Jacques spoke French, Renata spoke English, and they understood each other perfectly. They asked each other "In what sense?" more often than usual, but the clarifications prompted them to discover new interlingual references or new interesting definitions and details. And so the linguistic differences actually served to enrich the communication rather than encumber it. The way Jean-Jacques was looking at Renata, the way his hand was constantly touching her, it was clear he was head over heels in love. Physically and spiritually. And Renata . . . It was plainly visible that something wonderful had happened to her. I don't know what they had done at the hotel but she was literally glowing. I had never seen her so beautiful. No makeup can create that kind of internal glow. And also, no makeup can conceal it. I don't know how she managed to hide it when she got back home. In a word, the whole thing was very serious indeed.

Elaborate schemes coordinating the timing of academic forums, conferences, business trips, and partially true alibis involving friends and relatives allowed the couple to escape from Brussels a few times and spend a couple of days away—in Hamburg, Nantes, and Edinburgh. I had never been to any of these cities so I asked Renata to tell me more. Destination, however, was only a technicality in the tourism of secret affairs. My friend could say nothing about the city where she'd spent one, two, or three days and nights. She obviously had not cared which city she was seeing from the windows of the hotel room, the restaurant or the coffee shop, what kind of cuisine she tasted, how old the cathedrals or murals were and which artists were exhibited at the local museum. What was memorable to her was the fact that she and Jean-Jacques had been able to walk hand in hand, that they could kiss at every corner, that they could sleep together, wake up together, and have breakfast together.

"So can you imagine doing that for the next thirty or forty years, if you're lucky enough to live as long?" I asked, playing the Devil's advocate again. "With the ever-increasing decibels of snoring, with the palpable smell of old age, with the false teeth in a glass of water on the nightstand, with the sagging of boob, bum, and belly, with arthritis pain in the morning and so on? And there's worse."

As all this might appear too abstract and remote to Renata, I started rewinding from the outset: "First you'll have to go through the nightmare of divorce. He's married to a lawyer, so it's bound to be painful and go on for years. István will be very hurt, although he probably would not show it. Then your kids will blame you and become alienated, even if they acknowledge your right to a private life. Then you will have friends who will disappear forever. Consider logistics, too—arranging your new, shared home and making it home, indeed, which is not the same thing and could be tricky. Then, getting accustomed to the physical presence of a new Other who's neither a fairy nor an elf, but a creature who has to wash their teeth, and fart, pee, poop, snore, a creature who can lose their hair and have smelly feet, or ears, or loins, etc. Youth that soothes all this is not here anymore, only old age would be ahead. And one day you will lie next to your Prince Charming, he would have been unable to get it up, even with the blue pill, or you would have been too dry, even with the lubricant, and he would lie by your side, pretending to be asleep, and you will stare at the ceiling and wonder what all that was for. You can even start hating each other for all the disappointment of your grand love and all the shit you had gone though so you could live together."

Oh my God, what was I doing? How could I blurt all those things? Did I envy her? Bollocks. Was I defending the institution of marriage and all the sacred social order? Me? No. I was sad because their love was not meant to be, because a love like that could not be meant to be. And I was quelling my sorrow with bile. Disregarding my horrified inner voice, I added in a trance: "On top of it all, in his old age he might find himself talking to a young patient the way he talked to you."

Renata was listening, her interest suddenly spurred. And no, she didn't look offended or stunned.

"How do you know those things so well?" she finally asked.

"I've got a resourceful . . . imagination," I quipped.

She fell silent. I was wondering how to smooth over what I had said, how to soften the blow, how to comfort her. I even considered apologizing.

"I'm not afraid of getting old with Jean-Jacques. There'll always be love and affection between us. We'll just cuddle and huddle, even when we can't have real sex anymore, even when we grow old and ugly. And we'll always have something to talk about. Besides, as regards the pill, he takes one now, too . . . from time to time."

"Ah, *bon*?! . . ." I was truly surprised. I was itching to say that István does not look like a man who would need a pill, and if you spent your life looking at the origin of the world on a daily basis, you were bound to need a pill to get excited about one particular gateway. I was thankfully able to stop myself, literally swallowing the words I was about to utter.

"The blue pill has nothing to do with desire," Renata informed me. "He takes that for his own psychological comfort, so he wouldn't be worried, and for me—so I would enjoy it. Besides, he has very . . . beautiful hands," she said poignantly, and I couldn't help thinking about the caring, sausage-like hands of István. My gaze had landed upon them at a barbecue at Renata's while István had been busy turning the thick sausages on the grill. "Apart from that, Jean-Jacques wants me like he never wanted a woman," Renata continued, unperturbed. "Because it's me, because I am one—an entity of body, gesture, thoughts, the way I look, the way I feel, my words, my love."

Because you have a head and he loves that head, I thought. But I said nothing. Relieved by Renata's reaction, I still insisted on reason: "What are you going to do? By the way, what is *he* planning to do?"

"I don't know . . ." Renata visibly didn't want to talk about it.

"Well . . . there aren't that many options. I just described the first one. It's the surest way to kill your love. If you want to love each other forever, the best thing you can do is part ways immediately, while your feelings are at their peak. And the most probable scenario is to let your affair run its course discretely. For whatever it's worth. And then you each go your own way, having filled your hard drive with good memories to warm your souls in your old age."

"You're terribly cynical," Renata said quietly. "But maybe a little cynicism is exactly what I need." She fell silent. "And still I believe," she resumed after a while, "that this kind of love does exist—when you love the whole person, when age . . . well, age surely changes a lot of things, but . . . you nevertheless don't need anyone else, don't dream of anyone else . . . and you want to grow old with that person."

"I'm sorry. I did go too far. I'm cynical. This kind of love does exist . . . And we conjure it if it doesn't. I'm sorry . . ." I kept on repeating.

Talking about her love while hiding it from the world, however, was not the only thing Renata needed. In the beginning she was timid—could I take a look at a special letter to Jean-Jacques? I found this request surprising but then I remembered that Renata always insisted that communication, and letter-writing in particular, had a crucial role in their relationship. On the other hand, she was convinced that, unlike her, I really had talent and that I should be writing. I must admit that I was terribly curious—not the sick curiosity of a voyeur for spicy details of an intimate relationship. I found Renata's affair intriguing on a life-concept level, if I can express it that way.

I had a "very long look" at her letter and turned it into a little essay on routine time. I managed to preserve the authentic details of Renata's daily life, and even her expression, or style. The commissioner and the reader were both very pleased with the results.

And so it started . . . Renata forwarded Jean-Jacques's letters to me, deleting a few things here and there—sentences or paragraphs she had deemed too intimate, I suppose. I responded by sketching out a few sentences, ideas, an observation, a description, an unexpected thought here, a funny line there, and she worked with that herself. Sometimes I would send her a ready, finished text that she probably edited to make it her own. She probably added some intimate details, too. Or I would send her a text that wasn't in response to any of her lover's letters, and she could decide whether to use it or not. I knew Renata was forwarding to me only parts of Jean-Jacques's letters, and only some of them. On the other hand, Renata would rarely send me her letters to take a "final look" at them—she only let me into those that were wholly philosophical, impressionistic, or based on my "contribution." This was a rather peculiar, syncopated "trialogue."[73]

I quickly discovered that the role of Cyrano de Bergerac was inspiring. I used to put off writing notes, but now I had a reason to do it—I had a story, a commissioner and readers—enamored and motivated, "spiritual," and erudite. In a sense, I also had a co-author, or editor, with solid professional literary background. Soon after I started playing that game I realized I was also playing the role of the demiurge—shaping, guiding, conceptualizing, and even creating their love story which, without the correspondence between the two of them, without that peculiar merging of their logos, would have remained a racy, coarse story of Eros. What spiked my interest even further was the fact that their logos was bilingual. I surely had no amorous feelings toward Jean-Jacques, and yet he had become dear to me, he was close to my heart in a barely explicable way, like a literary character of sorts. Of course, he knew nothing about all of that.

---

73 When I used the term "trialogue," explaining to an American the legislative process of the EU, he was visibly pained by the way I had twisted the English language and stated that this word did not exist. Well, our story goes to prove that it does, even outside European jargon . . .

The letters between Renata and Jean-Jacques that I read and co-wrote had a bit of everything in them—everyday episodes with vapid reports and bureaucratic workings of the EU institutions, mothers-to-be who wanted C-sections on non-medical grounds, inadequate colleagues, terminally ill patients, a colleague who died in a subway terrorist act, offspring that fell in love or came home smelling of marijuana, a dog in heat and the unconditional love of a dog, endlessly stressful days of meetings, conferences, deadlines, unending operations, delivery rooms, piles of documentation, full moons, sleepless nights, bouts of fatigue and depression, flashes of ecstasy, outbursts, descriptions of boring family dinners, of family guests, there were even recipes, and inquiries into the meaning of pictures, thoughts on ongoing exhibitions, references to books, music messages, descriptions of beaches and mountains from family vacations. There were also dreams—what would they do if they spent a weekend together? There were funny linguistic interferences, misunderstandings and wordplays, there were dreams, absurd and existential . . . They emailed each other on a daily basis, although sometimes it would be just a few lines. Their letters made ordinary life look different, enchanted. Every day brought a new thought, picture, episode, retrospection. The Brussels in those letters was not the city I knew. Many of these embryonic narratives tempted me, so sometimes I would send my English hounds running in gorgeous trajectories along the newly opened alleys, chasing the hare of the aesthetic shot.

And yet, it was not me, but Renata and Jean-Jacques making the magic. In that hectic, automated, tawdry, predestined routine there was a man and a woman loving each other. Or wanting to love each other. And they were re-creating and enchanting the world—and themselves. Having drifted in close waters, socially and spatially, for more than a decade, having even "crossed paths," when they finally "met" it was too late to change their lives and go through the full version of the eternal script, so they wrote their own (with my participation). Renata and Jacques did not have all the time on Earth for lies and idealizations, for disappointment and compromise. They were not together in order to have children, home and family, to support each other's careers, to have shared goals, to grow bored and old. The two of them were real and sincere, and at the same time elevated and aesthetic, because they didn't have a future.

In one of her letters to Jean-Jacques, Renata had recounted, word for word, my hideous misanthropic "projection" of their probable future (without specifying my "authorship"). I marveled at her courage. Not without a sense of humor Jean-Jacques had responded that "under such a perspective "he would probably prefer to do without her, notably in order to spare her "aesthetic sensibility." I was thinking that Renata could afford to be so painfully honest precisely because there was no future. Renata had bravely described the aging and the disappointment because she didn't love Jean-Jacques like she used to love István once upon a time, because with Jean-Jacques there was no tomorrow. Hers was a perfidious exhibitionism, a paroxysmal, paradoxical, abstract form of vanity. They did not even feel real jealousy that was more than skin-deep. Renata demonstrated some resentment toward Jean-Jacques's wife and daughters (but not about the headless patients) and Jean-Jacques sporadically mentioned that despite all her declarations that she was not having sex with her husband, she was still sharing his bed every night; yet these words were only another token of their love, a touch of sweet ache to add to their dramatic, beautiful, and impossible love.

Did they really love each other, or did they want to love? What does loving really mean? I was reading Renata and Jean-Jacques's letters and I was thinking about István, about my own husband, and even about Jean-Jacques's evil wife. Could it be that the closer you get to somebody in everyday life, the farther you find yourself from his or her human essence? We load and frame the Other with everyday stuff and pragmatic life goals until we obtain a too familiar and boring image. And in this oxymoron of a process it didn't really matter whether the epiphany of the initial love that brought you together was true or a measure of your hormone blindness or of your socially defined projections.

Another one of Jean-Jacques's letters went like this: *I take care of the whole world: family, kids, relatives, patients. Babies, neighbors and colleagues, I give myself away, I am so generous with my time and my money. Sometimes I have the feeling that I'm giving so much because . . . I don't love, because I don't actually care about anything and nothing is dear to me. I feel so emotionally alien to everything and everyone that I sometimes panic that I don't even love my own children as much as I should. And I feel short of love—and tremendously guilty. So I compensate with a tremendous amount of care.*

This was followed by a dramatic declaration of love to Renata.

Were they just in love with Love itself? With their own projections rather than with the real other? What if the tragic and romantic fervor with which they swore in their probably non-existent feelings was nothing more than the fear of aging, the terror that the essential, interesting part of life with its real tragedy and romance, was over, and that they had become irrevocably unable to love? Reading their correspondence, I was perfectly aware that neither of them would rise above the circumstances, neither of them would rise above themselves, their social environment and its norms, their upbringing, their past, culture, duties, public opinion; that neither of them was ready to go through the real pain and loss of a divorce. It took them slightly longer to come to that conclusion. Is it really possible—ever—to outgrow all these determinants in order to aspire to something as undefined and vague as your true self? And do you really have to do it in order to be with someone you probably don't love that passionately? Their relationship was so belated and hopeless that they didn't have to take responsibility, they didn't have to take any truly dramatic decisions, they were free to enjoy the sweet melancholy of their pain, they were free to be real and engage in some exquisite psychological games. They sparked each other, they brought each other to ecstasy, they beautified their reality, their feelings, themselves, because the ground swell was carrying them off to a boring, empty world where nothing could happen except aging and dying, oh-so-crushingly banal.

After his semi-humoristic assumption that as an old man he could live without elderly Renata, Jean-Jacques had added that what he couldn't live without were her letters. He implored her to never stop writing to him, no matter what, even if they lived together or parted ways. Renata was somewhat irritated by this answer, which made me think about my role in the whole story. And what was I doing—supporting and elaborating upon this gorgeous artistic work of fiction. Or faction, perhaps. Did the two of them really feel what the three of us had written? Or did the words meander their way around the vague feelings, shaping them into declarations of love, which would then haunt them, demanding to be felt and lived? I was the only one who had a justification for this manipulation of words. This orgy of words I was to "operate" the intellectual, sterile side of the affair, stripped of flesh and passion, of real life and its misery. In my texts, the two were reincarnated as rather literary personages, while I, the author, was free to conceptualize and build whatever I wished. Renata and Jean-Jacques were very real and very surreal, at the same time. And they knew it, they were fitting their roles and playing with passion. I knew it, too, I had invented them like this, after all. But they were living out the story while I was just writing it.

Jean-Jacques's gift for Renata's birthday was a watch. It was expensive but subtle, despite the constellation of miniature diamonds. It was both businesslike and elegant, and more importantly—it was specifically chosen to suit Renata and her wrist. The two of us spent an evening discussing the gift and I think we went through all the possible meanings of this gift that was both a (trivial) classic and a very symbolic gesture. Renata was lamenting the fact that her own gift for Jean-Jacques's birthday had been so boring—a pair of cuff links, gold but plain. I was rubbing it in by saying that if she had asked me,

I would prompt her to have something engraved on those trivial gold cuff links. And a gift card saying that the gold had come from the explosion of a neutron star.

Christmas was approaching, the second Christmas in their world. The first one had passed in the initial stupor of love, in the insecurity of "is this true" where the two of them exchanged their favorite perfumes and some endless messages about their disenchantment with family feasts, rituals, dinner guests, cooking, and gifts. The next Christmas, however, Renata decided she had a one-of-a-kind occasion to give her lover something one-of-a-kind. Except I was the one who had to think it up.

And I really did think hard. The story of Renata and Jean-Jacques had turned into a peculiar sort of novel, *un roman* without premeditated storyline, plot, characters, or denouement; that novel was alive, interactive, in a real *mise-en-scène*. Its characters had their own past, their own drives, and they would not share all of them with me, the author. Sometimes they would leave the author alone and suddenly embark on their own endeavors. Every day was, if not a whole novel, if not the inception or the theme, then a chapter, for sure. Yet, this novel had a transcendental layer above the here and now, beyond the real Jean-Jacques and Renata, a layer where I spread the two of them into myths and symbols, the dimensions of beauty and Being. So, I had to figure out a gift that would match this *roman*.

On my way back from work, the short passage from the bus stop to the subway station went through a bookstore. It was, in fact, the biggest bookstore in Brussels. I stepped in and started walking around with no purpose in particular. I happened to see a bulky and ostensibly serious history of the Byzantine Empire and the Balkans that would make a good Christmas present for Christian, an amateur expert on the topic. Then I leafed through some comic books that might make Michael happy. As for Rada, I got straight to the cashier and bought a luxury edition of *Fleurs du mal* and a paperback edition of *Pride and Prejudice*.

And then my gaze was stuck upon a title—a simple cover that looked like a notebook, but the title, oh, the title . . . The title brought all of my aesthetic beliefs together in a single statement: *Chaque jour est un roman*. I took the book and leafed through it—there was nothing inside, just empty pages of good quality, yellowish paper, at least 80g. I inspected the thing—it looked quite like a book—bound into folios, A5 in format, but yes, there was no author and the text on the back said that you could fill this blank book with your own words, thoughts, and observations. So it was supposed to be a diary but it was shaped like a book to encourage the wannabe writer. I called Renata.

"I have a terrific idea for Jean-Jacques's Christmas present," I said.

"Let's hear it." Renata was also on her way back from work because I could hear the street noises around her.

"It's a long story. Let's have a drink."

Twenty minutes later we were sipping from our glasses in a little bar. Renata was turning the blank book entitled *Chaque jour est un roman* in her hands and listening carefully as I spoke. I was euphoric.

"You'll give him . . . a book! The title is *Chaque jour est un roman*. You will both be the authors. Your correspondence! This book will be one-of-a-kind in every way—an epistolary novel, a single copy, no, two copies—one for each of you. The authors will be the only readers! Imagine that?! You won't have kids, but you have created something magnificent together. We will arrange the letters, we'll edit them, and there will be a chapter for each day, even if it's just a couple of lines—you write to each other every day, don't you? And we'll mark the date, every date. We'll make the design and the preprint ourselves, come on, we're both tried and tested editors and publishers, we'll make a cover and a title page. We'll put both of your photos on the back cover, and a quote from one of the letters. We'll get it printed by some boutique press. If they can't do it right, we'll check one of those desktop publishing companies! And I would even, if you'd allow me, write a preface."

"What a great idea!" Renata took my head in both hands and kissed me, noisily, on the forehead. "Terrific! Only you can come up with a thing like that. But it is a lot of work. It's true that we wrote our own *A la recherché du temps perdu* . . ." she joked.

"We'll divide the texts between us to edit and design, and then we'll bring them together in a PDF file, it'll be faster this way. Are you OK with me writing a preface? Of course, you will have the last word, both about the contents and the preface. You are the author, right?"

"Come on, don't be so humble, it's not quite like that." Renata was laughing. "But fuck, where am I supposed to keep that book at home? Where's Jean-Jacques supposed to keep it? We have to put it in a safe."

"You're right." I hadn't thought about the pernicious objectivity of the material book body. "I can keep both copies for you if you'd like."

Renata thought about it. She was probably thinking about the danger of being caught, or she was suddenly aware that in the process of editing and compiling I would have to see letters that I hadn't read.

"Listen, we'll go like that, you'll write the preface and I'll do everything else. Please understand that . . ."

"Of course, dear. No problem, I do understand. We just have to make it work, that's the main thing. Just allow me to give you some ideas about the title page, the copyright text, and the back cover quote."

"That's for sure. Hey, it's a great idea! You're a genius. Jean-Jacques is going to faint. Let's get one more drink to celebrate."

That evening we both got home late and rather inebriated.

The writing of the bilingual preface, in Bulgarian at first, then translating into English, took me two weeks of work—in the evenings, after dinner. Renata told me she had "shortened it a little, and also edited it by removing some purely theoretical literary references and philosophizing." She didn't let me read the final version. She finally decided not to print the book on paper for security reasons. They were going to print it eventually, when they got together one day. They could always get it printed. She showed me the electronic version of the front and back covers and the title page, and she just scrolled through my preface (she had only left a couple of pages!) and the 280 (!) pages of text. It looked like a real epistolary novel, like a real book, like a finished project in pre-print.

Renata had given the book to Jean-Jacques in the form of a little box, wrapped and ribboned, with a USB key inside. She had warned him to look at it when he was alone and has at least a few hours of private computer time. She had instructed him to copy the contents to a safe place and delete them from the memory stick. Jean-Jacques had really been dumbstruck . . . by "the most incredible gift" he ever got, "the most incredible gift that anybody ever got." He read through the preface many times, the preface that made sense of that gift, and he thought about "himself, and Renata, about their love, about life, and art, and death." Renata was not jealous of the success of my idea. She seemed to have forgotten it was mine. And it didn't really matter. All in all, this wasn't a real book and it didn't have real copyright. I was truly happy that my idea had a worthy audience—the protagonists who made it happen, lived through it, partly wrote it and appreciated it.

The gift and its preface (although I don't know what exactly Jean-Jacques had read) had a seemingly unexpected impact—Renata and Jean-Jacques started growing apart, and three to four months after that Christmas they broke up. It was as if the gift was the supreme and ultimate stage of their relationship, a goal that, once achieved, had deprived their affair and its storyline of its driving force and direction. They started skipping days in their correspondence, as Renata told me, then they canceled a live meeting because they were both "terribly busy," and one month later they skipped another, and then they had a very honest conversation in bed to say that they were made for each other, that they would love each other to the end of their days, that their last thought before they died would be about each other, but they had met too late. It was somehow unfair and ugly to have nothing left to live together but to grow old and share the timid joys of old age. Jean-Jacques insisted that they keep on writing, albeit rarely, and become—or remain—really-really close and genuine secret friends. Because, he said, without Renata and her letters he would feel "alone as in Cosmos, and dead." Renata refused.

I listened silently and I thought that common sense had returned and swept my heroine away. I had long known that Renata was not really seriously thinking of getting a divorce and starting a new life with Jean-Jacques, but I wondered whether she had been aware of that and, if she had, whether she was honest enough to acknowledge it. I also realized that Renata was afraid that she wouldn't be able to live practically, on a daily basis, with the "high standards" of her aestheticized heroine, that Jean-Jacques will be disappointed with her. Although she never said it out loud, Renata had realized that, in some sense, I would also have to live with Jean-Jacques. Cyrano was OK for a beautiful love story, for the seduction part, but he could not stay in the shadows if *chaque jour* had to continue being *un roman* in real life.

Renata finished by shedding a few placid tears and concluding: "You know, after all I'm still happy this happened to me."

This time, I listened without making any comments.

After this conversation Renata did not mention Jean-Jacques ever again, she never said a word or hint at that story. I kept the implicit rule of silence she had laid down and never asked her if she had really loved him, if she loved him still, and if she was thinking about him, even when she was in bed with her husband, if she felt tempted to write him a message. I had the feeling that the two of us had been high, or drunk as a skunk, and we had done some mind-bogglingly weird things that we not only preferred not to discuss but we also wanted to forget.

Over the following four or five years, István made a terrific business deal and the two of them got even richer. After I curbed her ambition to write (delicately but frankly, like the good friend I was), Renata decided to build a career—she won the competition to be head of unit and started training to become a director. With a bit of extra weight and extra gravitas she was looking increasingly matronly. She was immaculately groomed and immaculately attired, but she lacked the radiant expression and the sprightly gait that hint, to me at least, that a woman is still erotically alive. And the sexy Porsche, which István gave her for their twenty-fifth wedding anniversary, looked somewhat awkward for her "profile." I was urging her to resume her yoga classes or choose some other sort of exercise that she would enjoy, or sign up for a course in photography, or dancing, or whatever. She always agreed with me but did nothing—she seemed to have accepted that she had grown old and that there was no point trying to preserve her appearance and her youthful energy. She even told me once that one should accept one's age, whatever that was supposed to mean. It was as if she didn't have a reason to keep herself fit in body and spirit. István liked her anyway, and he had grown even fatter himself—he was no longer the strong, big guy, just a prematurely old man with a huge belly.

Their daughter graduated with flying colors and left to study abroad. Renata and István, however, did not suffer too much from empty-nest syndrome, as they dedicated themselves to their careers and the pleasant, amiably shared task of spending their money on voyages, cultural and gastronomical pleasures, real estate investments, luxury goods, watches, and jewelry. After each visit to a Michelin-rated restaurant, after each voyage, vacation, or shopping spree Renata would pour forth oodles of photos and details about exquisite meals, five-star hotels, historical monuments, cathedrals, local foods, and galleries. She never missed a chance to meet and show off her newest handbag or pair of shoes, her earrings, her coat . . . She was an increasingly boring companion. And she knew it. She knew I was the last person to ooh and aah over her consumerist rapture. I flinched when a few photos from their last weekend in Paris contained images of István playing the fool in front of *L'Origine du monde*. He had even taken the trouble to adorn the photos with a circle of little hearts around the central, so to say, depiction, and he had photoshopped a bowler hat and a pair of moustaches on himself. I looked at Renata—nothing, she was already clicking on the next photos.

Another thing that stopped me in my tracks was when I was invited to dinner at their place and discovered they had a dog. Renata had told me nothing about it. Well, sure, I thought, when your child goes away it's normal to get a dog. It was a gift to themselves, to celebrate Renata's fiftieth and István's fifty-fifth birthday. The playful, lovable *bichon frise* was a good fit for them and their home.

And yet the old Renata reminded me of herself when she called the dog by its name—Jean. Fixing me with a mischievous smile, Renata cocked her Scythian eyes at me and said: "I'll call the next one Jacques. I hope that my calculations are correct and that I have two doggie lives left. That way the dogs and I will grow old together."

A year, or maybe a year and a half after the end of the affair, Jean-Jacques and I crossed paths at a concert. He was walking with his wife, flanked by a boy and a girl, both somewhere around twenty, in a tuxedo and evening gown that they were trying to wear as if their formal attire was just a wearisome detail they had long grown accustomed to. The girl had her father's eyes and his spiky, originally very dark hair. Jean-Jacques's wife was small and stodgy, with a foxy face emphasized by the furry capelet on her shoulders. Our eyes met for a few seconds then hastened to move away. We didn't greet each other, of course.

About a year later Renata told me that she got a short email from Jean-Jacques, informing her that his whole family was moving to Geneva. Just to let her know that he would no longer be living in Brussels. And that he was finding it terribly hard to live in the same city as her without seeing her. There was no comment—not from Renata and not from me.

Then, I lived through something awful. Renata was dauntless and competent in helping me with administrative and legal formalities, children and house repairs, money and its investment. She would listen to my endless monologues, she would comfort me in my ceaseless tears, she would bring me ultra-efficient sleeping pills. After some appropriate time had passed, she devoted her energy to looking for a new partner for me. Because, as she repeated, I had to find somebody "to enjoy life with. Because we're getting old, and have no time to postpone living." She quoted herself and István as an example. They had visited a family therapist a few times, not because there had been anything in particular but "just like that, all couples do this, to freshen their relationship, because . . . you know, when you age . . ." But István had been bored to death. And she also, by the way.

About six or seven months ago, while we were having one of those increasingly boring tête-à-têtes, I told Renata I was writing. "This time it's serious. I have the structure of the whole book ready and I'm working on the individual stories."

Renata did not even ask me whether I was planning to include her affair with Jean-Jacques, just proceeded to give her consent.

"OK, you can use my story. You know how to cover our tracks—change the names and the professions, all the family details, etc. I suppose that you're going to write in Bulgarian."

"Yes."

"Ha, you'll have to translate yourself. This will be fun." She paused for a moment and asked: "Do you think they are going to translate your book into some comprehensible language?"

"I don't know whether it will be good enough to publish, anyway, let alone in another language," I admitted.

Renata fell silent and then, as if she hadn't heard my writing anxieties, she said to herself: "So what, why shouldn't this story become a real book, after all?!"

"Hmmm, it seems it won't be really your story," I said vaguely. "In fact, it will be more than the real story. Hope you don't mind."

"Why should I? This is normal. You will be the one telling it, right?! Besides, this is a book. The characters, the plotline, and the message have to be comprehensible, they should speak to the reader, not to me and Jean-Jacques. The book should be of human interest, isn't that what they taught us in college?"

We burst out laughing, remembering the "human interest" cliché and our time pondering "what the author had wanted to say."

"I must warn you that I'm planning to include the whole text of the preface, the way it was originally written."

"But of course, dear. You have the right to do so, it's *your* book after all," Renata acknowledged, still chuckling.

Preface

As the curtains open, the setting is revealed to be Brussels, so allow me to start *à la* Magritte by stating that despite the striking similarities the thing that you're holding in your hands is NOT a book. Magritte explains that the image of a pipe cannot be used for smoking, and the both of us ex-smokers cannot but agree with this observation. The image is not the real thing, nor is the word we use to name the thing itself, like a map is not a territory.

So this is not a book. And yet the rationale behind this statement begs to differ from Magritte's explanations on why all images are deceiving. This is not a book for several rather obvious reasons—the text will not be published, it will not be made publicly available, it will not be multiplied into a print run. It has no ISBN number, no cover price at which it could be sold; it will not be marketed to any readership.[74] There is no copyright (yet). This is a one-of-a-kind compilation of texts, complemented with a preface and produced in a single copy for a single reader—you! Our (still) authentic intimacy is our copyright protection. That's why I have marked our names on the title

74 Or sent to literary critics for evaluation and analysis, so that the question of what the author wished to say will remain unaddressed.

page with a heart (♡) instead of the copyright symbol (©). The secret of our love is the wax seal upon this text (and the meta-text, the material printed body) and this is the second level of copyright protection.

Beyond the obvious, however, my claim that this is not a book is supported by some other, let's call them, conceptual arguments. Yes, I admit that all the disclaimers that follow are more relevant to me, because, as you know, I do have an urge to write. But no, I repeat, this is our correspondence and it is authentic because I didn't have any ulterior literary motives as I was writing to you. This is not a prototype of a book, nor is it a book-to-be. These are not premeditated notes or letters written (down or up) with the intention of writing a book. It is not a correspondence written and maintained with the overt or covert (but conscious) intention to be used in a book. Our correspondence has no aesthetic intention, nor any conscious desire to write a literary text or lay the groundwork of one. These are not notes toward an epistolary novel. It is not an experimental literary project. Nothing has corrupted our authentic voices that are only addressing each other. The author and the reader of this text are one and the same thing. The two authors are also the only readers. This is not thought as a (future) book, the text has no preliminary storyline, plot twists, intrigue, scripts and characters, denouement and ending, the authors have no preset ideas, morals or conclusions. This is a continuous text with an open ending, a flowing narrative, which follows and describes real life.

The real life of a comparatively ordinary man and a comparatively ordinary woman—because that's what we are, my love. Our correspondence has painted the full spectrum of this real life of these two comparatively ordinary persons—the routine of the everyday, at home and at work, historical events like terrorist attacks, wars, migration waves, referendums and scientific breakthroughs, rare cosmic events that we have been lucky or unlucky enough to witness, and also philosophical questions, existential anxieties, symbolic and mythological constructions, archetypal roles. In the polyphony of real life there is love and hate, crudity and tenderness, goodness and bile, laughter and tears, humor and sorrow, comedy and drama, humility and daring, dreams and nightmares, beauty and ugliness, harmony and chaos, sense and nonsense. And, notably, all the mediocrity in-between. In the intimate orbit of our love, through the enchanted telescopes of our enamored minds, every day of this real life is a novel, indeed.

As real life is polyphonic and multi-genre, this "epic" text features elements of a light chick-lit novel, a German Romanticism text, an erotic novella, an existentialist essay, a classical drama (hinging upon the dilemma between love and duty), a travelogue, a short story, an essay, fragments and impressions, poetry, aphorisms, political analyses, a culinary book, a dietary guide, some popular psychology, live reports from the epicenters of dangerous events, bits of anthropology, astrology, mythology, pedagogical advice, legal issues, medicine and pharmaceutics, gardening, cartography, career tips, French and English lessons, academic linguistics, literary analyses . . . and God knows what else. The text also contains some visual material—pictures of us, our children, of landscapes and maps and art masterpieces. The text also has a strong musical background—we have often sent each other musical greetings or expressed ourselves through music. In the end I have appended our playlist.

Life is beautifully eclectic and it has produced a fittingly beautiful, eclectic text, which taps all Castalian thematic and genre sources.

Yet, I am wondering . . . Despite the innocence of our uncorrupted authenticity and despite the absence of any conscious aesthetic intent, does our correspondence have nevertheless aesthetical value and (potential) aesthetic impact beyond our intimacy?[75] In other words, do our letters contain and convey content that might be meaningful and pleasing to others, say, readers. Is this non-book an artifact, after all, and if it is, what kind of art and genre it might be classified as? In order to ponder this question, however, I must start by defining what art is. Which is impossible, or at least well beyond my abilities, so I humbly limit myself to few intriguing questions and observations.

In which moment and through what artistic manipulation is our intimate, or objective and commonly accessible reality, re-discovered, re-thought, re-formed, and re-created so that it acquires aesthetic value, which other people can perceive, make sense of, and appreciate? Do you remember a photo I sent you?—I have "published" it in our book. It was from the first page of a *History of Art for Young People* (which, as I've told you, I had used many years ago in Hungary, for the purpose of teaching English at the Art School). The book started with an introduction, and the title of the introduction was that fundamental question: "What is art?" There was only one example but it was so informative. This is, shall I say, an "artifact," created by Picasso—the seat and the handlebar of a bicycle welded together. The result is an elegant deer head (which certainly costs a pile of money today).

The picture that made us "meet" is another story. In my view, the aesthetics of this picture, apart from the craftsmanship, is in the mere act of painting this, and exhibiting it to public. And in the manifesto title.

75 "Outside" our secrecy and "beyond our intimacy," which I take to be two different though overlapping things, our correspondence would have been protected by a real, copyright ©.

Every kind of art—be it textual, visual, or kinesthetic—has its own means of expression, but the process of the divine re-creation of reality is one and the same. The demiurge-artist sees, combines, imitates, invents, creates or re-creates, transforms, entitles. Looking at the "constitutive elements" of Picasso's magical transformation, it appears that everything can become art. Even a phone index—remember the Brussels phone directory where we once searched for our names amid two million private and corporative numbers? In the aesthetics of our story, this was a telling illustration of how we found each other in the human sea. Cooking asparagus can be full of nostalgic poetry (as your beloved Proust would say), a strudel recipe can be an epic poem (as a Bulgarian writer would note), a family Christmas menu can sound like the hymn of a happy or unhappy family (*à la* Tolstoy), as it happens in our letters. The pubescent craziness of our children, conceived and told by us and for us, are transformed from banalities into projections of ourselves—of what we have been and what we will be in our children. Each day of our lives, each page of our letters contains bicycle seats and handlebars, put together by our awoken, loving glances. It turns out that our correspondence IS an artifact, or may become one, or may be perceived as such. The mere act of compiling this non-book is meaningful.

What is the genre of this non-book-yet-artifact? The dialogical structure and the unity of the chronotopos suggest dramaturgical roots. The underlying dilemmas between love and duty, spiritual and material values, freedom and social limitations also point toward the structural characteristics of classical drama. On the other hand, the *mise-en-scène* or the enacting of the real, physical self of the first person, the persona of the real "artist," seems to take the text in the direction of performance and happening—even in their crudest, wacky media versions like the reality show with its open-ended finale that is up to the audience—and reality—to decide. Yet, ours is not a reality show since we are not exhibiting our intimacy to a voyeuristic audience. Not yet, at least. Back to the performance genre, which, by the way, I see inherently romantic by nature with its Goethe-Werther dynamics and unity between the subject and the object of the aesthetic act. The idea of this non-book and its theoretical "defense" in this preface are taking the artifact in your hands closer to conceptual modernism whose works are centered upon the authorial idea rather than the aesthetic object and process or the final marketable product.

Different arts—in terms of artifacts and perception—have a very different relation to time. Theatre fixes the unity of time, space and action, and perception. Music aside,[76] literature seems to me the freest art. Though, it suffers most from its means of

76 For its unique and own-only means of expression and non-material object of recreation (mind? soul? feelings?) or the absence of such, which would mean music is not re-creation but genuine creation.

expression. In this context, thinking about our non-book I am leaning again to performance and art happenings.

But . . . I stop here with my boring literary excursion. Because what matters most is content, the message, which the artist wants to pass on, isn't it? Our non-book is all about Love. Love opened our eyes, our minds and our spirit, making us capable of seeing beyond the mediocre obviousness of reality, our ordinary lives and us ourselves. I have no other explanation for the artistic, aestheticizing and existential spirit possessing—and elevating—us and for our sudden talent to turn our *romance* into *un roman*. Love must be the widely advertised wizardry called inspiration and wrongly attributed to the muses.

If Love is *à l'origine de notre monde*, what were the messages we were passing to each other? I will give it a try . . . though, you know, they say: as many readers, as many texts. Popular psychology would probably qualify our *romance-roman* as a "midlife crisis." I would beg to disagree. Our love came late in our biological and social time, and just on time in our human existence. Our belated love was free from all kinds of biological and procreation goals, making pointless all those mating dances and songs, all the swagger and swank, all the sniffing, displays of virility and demonstrations of the ability to raise and feed one's offspring, and make a good home. Our love has no future in biology and the practical world. And that's precisely what's setting us free from any promises and lies, any roles and games we might have played. This love made us honest and authentic, first to ourselves and then—to the Other.

It is quite ironic—or symbolic?—that a gynecologist fell in love with a woman who cannot have children anymore. And you stop looking at me through the eyes of a gynecologist. Our love is like a catharsis and even an initiation. Only now, at forty-seven, have I found the meaning of my name—and even my sense as human being. I am Re-nata, re-born. You and your loving eyes, hands have re-born and re-created me. You are quite right that the origin of the world is not in the . . . *black hole* between woman's thighs, but in that of our skulls.

You have also been re-born in our love and in my loving eyes, mon amour. It's not only a woman that Pygmalion creates, he recreates himself. I already know that deep in yourself you are a very strong person, that you can make decisions and act decisively when you have to, that your keen mind, your luminous spirit, and your goodness set you apart from the wacky macho, the mercantile gynecologist, the obedient son, the henpecked husband, the hesitant and inert person you sometimes appear to be.

There is plenty of existential anxiety and fear in our *roman*. It's very weird that we, the lovebirds, should be talking about that—about the meaning or rather about the meaninglessness of our lives in the middle of the boundless Universe, about our fear of death, and painful death in particular, about this evolutionary surplus and the fundamental discrepancy that is our consciousness that's capable of considering itself and the Universe. Our society does not take well to discussing those things, and discussing death in particular. Do you remember that bar in Hamburg where we had a couple of drinks (I had martini and you had port, do you remember?) and you were listening to the lyrics of the song that was playing (an entry in our playlist). It went like this:

. . . If the sky that we look upon
Should crumble and fall
And the mountains should crumble to the sea
I won't cry, I won't cry, no I won't shed a tear
Just as long as you stand, stand by me . . .

You translated it into French to make sure that you had got everything right, and then you said something that I will remember forever. You said that it was the most accurate description of love—as anesthesia (the medical definition felt awkward, even hurtful at first). You said that love was existential anesthesia, the only anesthetic we were given to numb the terror of death, the meaninglessness, the Universe. That's why people say love is stronger than death, that is what you said. You observed that this song is actually describing a cosmic catastrophe that can probably happen to us, to our children, to our grandchildren or great-grandchildren, and will surely happen in one form or another in the (un)foreseeable future, that it reminds you of that *Melancholia* movie, that this innocent and undoubtedly lovely melody, this evergreen, was actually explaining how, when you're in love and your beloved is by your side, you don't really care if the world coming to an end.

While I was compiling our *roman*, rereading our letters, I came to comprehend your request that we should keep writing whatever might happen between us. You can live without me as flesh, your memories and your fantasies will suffice; aging will help. You want me to *stand by you* in the logos, in our minds and hearts, until the end of time.

You know, there's another thing I've been thinking about. We used to study classical mimesis in college—how literature transports and mimics life, looking upon it from an aesthetic point of view but mostly moralizing upon it. No doubt, there is something magnificent, and so noble, about turning reality into art, leaving a trace of your spirit, of that universe which, they say, is contained inside every person, along with making people better. Yet, I have studied not only Aristotle but Oscar Wilde as well. And the latter thinks in reverse—that there's something even more magical, demiurgical even, about living a life guided by the beauty and the meaning, created by words and spirit. Why can't we live our *romance* like the characters we are in our *roman*? Why are we so romantic, so beautiful and brave in our letters, and so pragmatic, castrated and even cynical in reality? All that secrecy is humiliating for both of us and yet we accept it and keep it going. I even decided that we had no future. In fact, I described a despicable future in one of my letters to you. Our correspondence is full of so much aesthetics but it's still a rather sad sublimation. Why can't we have it the other way round? Why can't we be, for real, the reborn, elevated human beings!? Yet, I know, I know . . . who the hell gets a divorce, losing tons of money and getting into heaps of trouble so s/he can daydream with a kindred soul, in written form at that!? Is it only daydreaming, though? Aren't our letters a reflection of our true selves and our true lives? How paradoxical it is that in our *roman* we are so real, true, honest, authentic, and out there, in the *everyday* reality, in our clandestine affair, we are rather characters who put on façades and play roles. Late love is a catalyst of truth and authenticity. And literature is no more fictional than love.

Forgive me, my love, for those long-winded literary detours. I wrote this abundance of convoluted words because I wanted to say some, in fact, pretty simple things. Our love has materialized primarily in words (for the time being). Our minds and our souls are communicating more than our bodies do. We live in our ideas and feelings more than we live in reality. We tell each other about the life we have, apart, we talk through our shared life instead of living it. And yet that way we, you and I, have created art. Our correspondence is an aesthetic narrative. Our love story has created a novel—an ongoing, epistolary, open-ended novel. We will not create any children but we have recreated ourselves and the Other and we have created a novel of everyday life, of the ordinary everyday person rising to the status of an existential Sisyphus, Pygmalion, God! . . . thanks to the belated, middle-age love.

I am giving you a better and happier Jean-Jacques—a character, but also a projection of your better self, of your true self. This is a reciprocal gift—you are giving the same thing to me. We have shared authorship of our love story, of our novel, of the characters in our love story, of our human essence in our novel. This is the most valuable gift in the world. That's why on the back cover, where the price would have normally be printed, I have put the word "priceless." Which brings me back to the beginning of this preface. Our intimacy and the "illegal" character of our affair will save our epistolary novel from the judgment of the book market and preserve our love story as an existential act, without any critics, readers, or buyers.

I will finally allow myself a few notes (that you'll hopefully find amusing) as a co-author, compiler, reviewer, editor, and proofreader (because this is a reciprocal gift but I am the one who spent days and nights working to make it happen!). You will notice that I have removed any reference to concrete times and spaces—the dates of our letters, our afternoons, dinners, and the rare nights, hotels, restaurants, cities, market squares, automobile showrooms, and airports of our dates and symposia. Without those concrete details we look even more like literary characters and everything we have said and written acquires even more universally human dimensions. And yet this "compositional device" is also a "second level of protection" (besides the password-protected electronic format in which you have received this gift). In the paragraphs above I have discussed how every part of reality, even documents and telephone directories, can be aestheticized and made literature. And yet the opposite process of profaning literature to the status of a document and proof (e.g., of the real life of the author and his/her characters, or in a divorce suit . . .) is lamentably far more common. Without the details we can always claim that this is merely literature, indeed. And so it is up to a significant point, isn't it? . . .

While editing the grammar of the text I often had to make hard choices, switching between the roles of the co-author, professional editor, and proofreader, even a publisher of sorts, who is also a woman in love and a cautious secret lover. How dear your English letters are to me, with all their grammatical mistakes, all the rare words that you can only find in dictionaries, all the literal translations of French idioms and all the funny interferences! And how comical my attempts to write to you in French are, constantly double-checking noun genders, verb conjugations, prepositions, or translating from English word-by-word! Our epistolary novel is also a crash *correspondence* course in learning a foreign language. And yet, it shall be reminded that speech patterns are a basic device for achieving the authenticity of a character, while style is the defining feature of any author. We would be unmistakably identified had I left the letters in their original shape. That's why I have let technology do its job and correct all our spelling and grammar mistakes.

I'm also thinking that there were things I could only have told you in Hungarian. And so I haven't told you those things. You wouldn't understand, and not just because you don't speak the language. You have the advantage of speaking to me in your native tongue. And yet, do I understand everything you're saying, do I see the full chiaroscuro of your French words, do I note all their cultural overtones? Certainly not. So, I think we're quits.

Read away, my love.

DRAMAT(URG)IC

ACT I

Living room with contemporary furniture, bookshelves, vases, statuettes, a big beautifully arranged bouquet, two sofas positioned at right angles, one larger table or a few low ones between the sofas, a stack of newspapers and magazines on one of the tables, pictures and framed photos hanging on the walls. The TV is on—a news show running in German. Sebastian Haub is a good-looking forty-eight-year-old man with a few streaks of gray hair. There is something boyish about him, he's wearing jeans, shirt, and a pale sweater. Sebastian is reading a magazine, glancing at the TV every now and then. An attractive, yet not strikingly sexy forty-year-old woman enters. This is Lora Tomova, she is wearing a silk peignoir and fluffy slippers. She sits beside Sebastian, peeks at what he's reading, wraps her arm around him, he moves the magazine over to his other hand and, still reading, caresses her shoulder and her hair. Pause, only the sound of the news is heard. Lora switches the channel to, let's say, BBC and now the newscast is in English. She lends an ear to the news, Sebastian doesn't react to the change, peers at the TV screen and keeps caressing her shoulder lightly.

SHE

I've just taken the ovulation test. The next twenty-four hours will be the premium time.

HE

(Not looking away from the magazine, humorously.)

So, we need to fuck at least three times in the next twenty-four hours in the best possible position.

SHE

(Flinches.)

Don't talk like that, please. We'll just be making love. At our age it might not even work immediately.

HE

(Leaves the magazine to the side and turns down the volume of the TV. Still humorously.) Why are you even telling me we're going to "just make love?" Now that I know I have to fertilize your egg on schedule, I might not be able to get it up. (*Pause.*) I might not be to get it up in general . . . "at my age."

SHE

Honey, I'm almost forty, you're forty-eight, so we'll have to enhance the spontaneity of our love with a bit of biological planning. It's a good thing that we both already have a child each. (*Stroking his head.*) As for the "getting-up" I have no reason to worry about it.

HE

I'm just thinking . . . Planning, you'd say . . . Have you thought about where Sofia is, you know, where a baby girl was born, that was you, and about where Frankfurt is, where I, not knowing anything of your gracious entry into this world, was playing football on the streets, comparing the length of my prick with the other boys and dumbfounded, watching the first man land on the moon?

SHE

Fine, looks like this is going to be an *intellectually* penetrative evening.

HE

No worries, I'll gladly penetrate you. But why not a bit of intellectual foreplay, instead of the carnal kind. (*Smiles.*) So, have you thought about how accidental our meeting in Vienna was, at that kitschy tourist waltz concert? What if our business trips hadn't coincided? Or if one of us had decided to stay in the hotel to read or watch TV, or simply take a walk? What if we happened not to sit on adjacent seats . . . in that kitsch concert of waltzes?

SHE

Do you regret it?

HE

No, not at all! I am eternally grateful to chance for bringing us together. I'm just thinking how accidental all of it was.

SHE

It's destiny. There are no accidents. I've told you that before. What's written in the stars will happen. What we call accidents is our destiny, written deep within us. When you were chasing a ball and spending hours in front of the mirror, checking your moustache, while I was bawling my throat out thousands of miles away, it had already been encoded in us, in our souls, in our genes that Ken and little Barbie were the two parts of a whole that would come together one day.

HE

Oh, yeah, and where had it been written that beforehand, they'd be copulating with some utterly unsuspecting partners before . . . "clicking" together? Do you want some wine?

SHE

Yes, please. You can slice some cheese and grapes, too.

He walks out. While he's away, she's on the phone talking to her son, pausing once in a while to listen to him.

SHE

Bobby, what are you doing? Watching a film? What's the film? Michael's parents are there, right? Tell Ralitza I said "hi," OK? What do you mean "which Ralitza"?! That's Michael's mother . . . step-mother, she's my colleague. You don't even know her name! . . . For your information, his father's name is Christian . . . Yes, he's German like Sebastian . . . Why "step"-mom? Because Michael's mother died a long time ago when Michael was still a child. His father married Ralitza a few years ago . . . Yes, she died. No, they didn't divorce. Haven't you talked with Michael about his mother? . . . All right. Oh, nothing. I just wanted to hear you. Don't go to bed too late! What are you doing with Michael tomorrow? . . . Good. But be home by 3:00. You have to study for your Monday classes? OK, I'll leave you to watch the film. Good night.

She's still talking on the phone when Sebastian returns holding a tray with two glasses of wine, a plate with a few types of cheese and a bowl with grapes.

HE

(While serving.)

It's a good you speak Bulgarian to Boris. You're the only Bulgarian speaker for him. If I wanted to be a true father to him, and I do want to be, I should learn some Bulgarian. (*He sits beside her.*)

SHE

And I should learn German.

HE

Cheers!

SHE

Cheers! (*They clink glasses.*) Bulgarian is a difficult language, I've told you.

HE

With German as my mother tongue, I think I can learn Chinese. (*He takes a sip of the wine, pauses.*)

SHE

I am just wondering what you would sound like in Bulgarian. I mean . . . sometimes when you speak in German, you do look like a different person. You seem somewhat more rational, composed, blunt, organized. Your boyish charm . . . disappears.

HE

(Pretending to be brushing back an imaginary forelock, thrusting his chest out, humorously.)

I'll be speaking German slang instead of haute Deutsch, so I'll forever remain a boy. (*Pause.*) You, too, seem different when you talk in Bulgarian: your voice lowers, gets warmer, your intonation changes. When you say that "Alo" on the phone, I'm on the verge of fainting.

SHE

(Laughing.)

Alo-alo, my dear husband, are we going to make love tonight?

HE

There, I can even tell when you laugh in Bulgarian and when you laugh in English. (*He is caressing her.*) I love you.

SHE

I love you, too. (*They kiss, she speaks dreamily, tenderly.*) You talk in German in your sleep. It's weird—I lie beside you in the dark, I touch you, *my* man, my husband. But at the same time, I feel like you're very far away, I can't fathom where you are, what you're seeing, who you're talking to. (*The dreamy voice shifts, takes on an edge.*) But you're definitely not with me because you don't talk to me in German. In fact, what are you dreaming about? Or, rather, *who* are you dreaming about and talking to?

HE

Hm . . . I might be talking to you in German in my dreams. I guess there's only one language in dreams. I dream only about you, my love. How did that Bulgarian author put it?—love is to dream about the woman sleeping next to you.

SHE

You're slinking off but in a rather elegant way, so I forgive you.

HE

(In a dreamy parodic fashion.)

To dream about the woman sleeping next to you, even when she's sweetly snoring in Bulgarian.

She laughs again and aims to strike him with a cushion.

HE

Back to our little talk, tell me now again where and how everything is "written in the stars"—how we'd meet in the Vienna Opera, fall in love, and marry, how you'd drag me up to Brussels, and have a kid with me . . . I somehow can't read those stars, so it seems I'm an illiterate idiot.

SHE

Let's not sulk about Brussels, all right? In less than a year you managed to find so many clients, half of them German, all of them ex-pats—people of means and fine taste, you can afford even to get creative—you are nominated for a prize with your last banker's house project. I have the best job I could've hoped for. Bobby will graduate from the European school, he'll be able to apply for the best universities, and he'll speak three languages—apart from his mother tongue. The same goes for our child. I mean if we have a child together. Otherwise, yes, you are somewhat . . . illiterate, emotionally illiterate. You want to have an explanation for just about everything, you want to predict and control everything and even calculate it, if possible. So German! Or an architect's obsession. You can't. Since you're thinking that much, can you choose which one of your minuscule agents will reach the target with a specific set of genes? Besides, the target itself changes from month to month. The when and what in life are predestined.

HE

Geez, if you continue like this, I really won't be able to get it up. (*Pause.*) But, you see, you actually agree that our child would be an accidental combination of genes, just one variant out of billions. As our meeting was.

SHE

So that's it?! If it hadn't been me, it could've been someone else?! Then, I'd better pack up and go . . . And you adore your daughter even though she's a "blind accident." Oh, and despite the fact that she's stripped the skin off your first wife, whom, you claim, you stopped loving so long ago.

HE

I think I know what you mean with the skin stripping, but that's not how they say it in English. Is that what you say in Bulgarian? (*She nods.*) That's one hell of a bloodthirsty metaphor. Just like your jealousy. (*He takes a gulp of wine, she pouts and cocks up her chin.*) Love is something else. That's when coincidence materializes in . . . you and I fall for you. When chance . . . configures my child and she is there, blood and flesh, I cannot but love her. I guess; this is even stronger for women as the child is literally a part of their flesh and bone.

SHE

Hm, I'm not sure it's quite like that. First and most of all, a child is a fruit of love between two. I don't think I'd love my child if it had been conceived against my will, if I got raped, for example. Would you love a child that you never wanted? I mean if a random woman tricks you and gets pregnant intentionally? Well, there will be no violence in this case, but, still, I mean if casual sex brings about a baby?

HE

To be honest, I can't say. I'll admit that I'm the father and I'll assume the whole responsibility with the child support and whatever is necessary. (*Pause.*) On the other hand, there're so many couples who stay together just because the woman got pregnant, because of the child that often neither of them wanted. But when the child is brought into the world, both of them love it.

SHE

I expected you to say that this can't happen to you because there would be no random women.

HE

That was mean of you! And your stupid jealousy. Weren't we talking hypothetically about the principles of things?!

SHE

I *am* jealous. That's what my name is, too—there's a Lora in Bulgarian literary history who committed suicide out of jealousy.

HE

Men kill other people out of jealousy and women kill themselves. Speaking of my daughter, I received an email from Kerstin yesterday—she asked me to help her with her diploma project. Can she stay with us for a week or two?

SHE

Of course she can, you needn't ask me about such a thing. (*Pause.*) Kerstin will soon graduate; in the near future, we might have to lend a hand with a grandchild . . . Funny, our own child and her, or his, nephew or niece will be the same age . . . like in *Modern Family.*

HE

I don't think Kerstin will marry and have a child soon. You know this generation . . . hard work, fierce competition, emancipated women . . . Recently I heard overpopulation and climate change added to the myriad reasons. And adoption as a choice. In fact, I myself have also thought how overcrowded our planet is. Our children won't have much to eat. The world's population increases by ninety-five thousand people every day. Every day! Can you imagine this?! If you're a responsible citizen of the world, you'd better adopt a child who is already here, brought into this world, who needs to eat, study, and . . . work one day.

SHE

That's how you talk about sorting the rubbish, with a kind of global concern.

HE

Yes, and you used to throw everything in the same plastic bag.

SHE

Now you are mean. You see . . . I had no motivation. Even if I had done it properly, it wouldn't change a thing, globally, I mean. The same goes for the adoption—theoretically, you're right. But our "contribution," so to say, I mean in case we adopt a starving little . . . black toddler, would not change anything . . . in the world. It would make a difference if people in Africa and India use contraceptives and the girls go to school, instead of giving birth at thirteen. By the way, the same goes for the gypsies in our otherwise civilized Europe. (*Pause.*) Whereas, in my unique little world, adopting a child would be something . . . dramatic, something that would change my life. I mean I don't deny the humanity of such an act. I'm not discarding it as an option for us either . . . Yet, I'd like us to have a child of our own. Or at least to try to . . . like really.

HE

(Humorously.)

Racist!

SHE

German! Overly politically correct German with a historical sense of guilt.

HE

You may be right. "In our little world" I do not object at all to the systematic and exceptionally thrilling attempts to have a child with you. I will heartily "contribute."

She slaps him playfully. He stretches, turns off the TV, gets up, and chooses a CD. Melodious jazz starts running quietly in the background. He stands behind her back and gives her neck and shoulders a gentle massage. She visibly enjoys it. He talks to her while massaging.

HE

You're right, the child should be a fruit of love, no doubt. What haunts me is the fortuity of that love and of that child that we glorify as so unique, as predestined specifically for us, as you say. We cannot imagine the beloved one, and the child, in any way different. But when I think about it, both could be completely different. Figuratively speaking, you dip your hand into the sack of the chaos, which you call destiny, and you take out something that you accept as the only possible being, as unique, stashed away by destiny especially for you. And you love him or her. I myself am an accidental product of that chaos, a materialization of one in a billion possible combinations. I could have been someone else . . . which means to not exist.

He moves to sit next to her. Both of them remain silent, lost in thought, take a sip of wine, looking at their glasses.

SHE

OK, but aren't you excited about the fact that your daughter bears your genes, that part of you will outlive you and spill over in dozens of other . . . "coincidences"?

HE

Genes do not transmit Sebastian, I mean my thoughts, my experience. I am not in the genes that will determine the form of the nose or the ears, of—what did you call it in Bulgarian—*unborn Petko*.[77] What I *want* to leave in this world is very different from what I *will* leave without meaning to.

SHE

You know better than I do, that they taught us that environment, rather than genetics, plays the decisive role . . . nature versus nurture. Well, it turned out our genes determine what we are. Not only as physical appearance and diseases, but also talents, intellect, character . . . Overall, our humanism goes to hell.

HE

We'll have to reinvent it anyhow. Humanism I mean. With the incredible pace of progress in genetics. Then, there's AI.

SHE

This is science fiction. Poor sci-fi, at that. But . . . who knows. In any case, if I were born in that malign future, I would not have wanted to design my children.

HE

Yet, you would not mind sparing them some diseases, no?

SHE

That, yes . . . But without genetic engineering we could make a tall, slender *Mädchen* with blue eyes and chestnut hair who has inherited more of her father's genes, even if that means that she wouldn't just be great at math, but that she'd be a deluded philosopher.

HE

Or a little, stubborn, curious boy who loves devouring books with his chestnut eyes and who swims as gracefully as a dolphin.

SHE

77 A Bulgarian byword—the plans that parents and grandparents make for an unborn child.

Wow! That was poetic, thank you. (*She leans her head on his shoulder. Dreamily.*) You know, there are tribes who believe that you should first see your child in your dreams before you make it. That's what we're doing tonight.

HE

Yeah . . . sounds like we're Gods creating a human. Or we're humans trying to meddle with the chaos that will create their child. (*Pause.*) I was thinking that there's something paradoxical about love. You fall in love, something flips in your mind—hormones, pheromones, chemistry, the need to love, spring, middle-age crisis, whatever—someone takes your breath away.

SHE

(Turns abruptly to him.)

Bravo man! So, it doesn't matter what I'm like?!

HE

No, wait, you're wonderful. There's something else I find interesting. (*He takes a sip of wine.*) The curious thing is how in the midst of the millions of other possible women, the very one I fall in love with, also falls for me. *Her* precisely. (*He looks at her cautiously.*) That's generally speaking, OK, *in principle*. So, what is this magical reciprocity? This magic actually suggests that this woman's love is driven by my love for her or, in other words, her love is more self-love, gratitude for being loved. Besides, my love for her is a guarantee that she won't suffer if she loves me back. We also love not only the other, but love itself. And how beautiful we ourselves are in a love story. Because if we're not in love, if nothing really lights our fire, we're as good as dead. (*He looks at her fearfully to make sure she isn't offended, her gaze still resting on her glass.*)

SHE

Balzac has said that with two lovers there is always one who loves and one who lets themselves be loved. *In principle*, there's a lot of truth in your observation. But that wasn't the case with us. Was it? . . . Besides, you consider love as something rather irrational or just a matter of chemical reactions. It is not only this, we also have certain criteria, conscious or unconscious, expectations, upbringing . . . I can't fall in love with someone who is outside of all of this.

HE

You know what, I've met women who satisfied all of my criteria, the criteria that the wandering rational brain of a man . . .

SHE

. . . of a German and an architect . . .

HE

. . . of a German and an architect could come up with. But nothing happened, the so-called miracle did not happen. (*Pause.*) As it did with you.

SHE

Thank God! But it seems that the thunder struck with Martina. (*Hums the motive from* Symphony No.5.)

He remains silent.

SHE

I'm sorry. I overdo it sometimes, I'm really jealous. I wish we had met earlier.

HE

Hm, I'm not sure it would've worked. Besides, Boris wouldn't exist. (*Pause.*) I was very young when I met Martina. It was all too natural—we were the same age, came from a similar social background, we had similar memories, studied at the same university . . . All that stuff you mentioned. (*Pause.*) We imagine that we are making a choice. We're all like blind flies buzzing in random trajectories . . . we sometimes accidentally bump into each other. Martina and I were simply buzzing in one and the same balloon. Accidents scare me. (*More cheerfully.*) Anyway, don't doubt for a second that I really like the fortune-slips I drew out of chaos's sack—you and Bobby. (*Pause.*) Probably that is what happiness is.

Sebastian's mobile rings.

HE

It's my father. I'm sorry, I have to pick up.

SHE

Yes, of course.

Sebastian gets up and walks around the room while talking. He speaks with his father, small talk mostly, the impression the conversation leaves is that Sebastian listens reverently and compassionately to his father and encourages him: "How are you? . . . Oh, really? . . . Wow! . . . That's wonderful . . . Well done! . . . I'll come to see you in three weeks. I'm glad you called . . ." Sebastian is lost in thought after he hangs up.

HE

My father spoke of food, the weather, the magazines, and TV quizzes he follows, of his mates there, of the view out of his window. He'd occasionally say that he wants to live more. Then he'd chuckle and assure me that it's all fine and he's "having a great time." But I know that nothing thrills him anymore. Not even Coca-Cola Zero. (*Faint smile.*) Nor me, my sister, nor his grandchildren. I guess it's horrible to have nothing ahead, with everything in the past and just waiting for death to come. Day in and day out. (*Pause.*) But we don't speak of death, of the fear, of this loneliness . . . of all this. We're civilized people and this is a taboo. Death is a medical problem that is "resolved" in hospitals, nursing homes, with pills and medical appliances.

Silence. Sebastian rubs his temples. Lora is empathically listening and looking at him.

SHE

Come, come here, sit next to me. (*Sebastian lies on the sofa, his head in Lora's lap. She caresses his head while speaking.*) Your father had a good life. True, he lost your mother, but he has you and your sister, grandchildren, he had a good job, friends. Now he is in a good place, taken care of, surrounded by people. I think he was happy. In my view he is at peace, he is ready to leave and is not scared of death. You . . . you sound . . . scared. It is you who is not ready to take your farewell. Life just ends, Sebastian. The only thing we can do about it is to try and live it well.

HE

You say we should live . . . But when I come to think of it, it makes no sense. We'd be better off shooting ourselves.

SHE

Hushhh, hushhh . . . don't allow such thoughts into your mind. You are overworked, maybe a bit depressed. Close your eyes, relax, think of something nice. Let's imagine our child . . . (*Pause. She is caressing his head, both with closed eyes.*) We have to live, Sebastian, to rear children, to work, to pay bills, to take care of parents. If everyone retreats into an existential depression, humankind will have to commit suicide. Besides, it . . . it's a wonderful, wonderful life (*She sings the words.*) There is love, kids, friends, there are beautiful things to be seen, read, heard. Yes, I know that that sounds cheesy. But why not try to be a bit stupid and . . . happy.

Sebastian gets up, sitting on the sofa, takes a sip of wine and few bites of cheese.

HE

Do you remember that girl they showed on TV? A twenty-something, healthy, intelligent, even pretty, girl with a first-class degree in physics. She wanted to commit suicide. She had already attempted it a few times, obviously unsuccessfully. She is treated medically for severe depression. Only, she does not look depressed at all. With ironclad logic and not a hint of depression, she explained why she didn't want to live, to work, to give birth, that she had a right to put an end to all this. They asked her about this suffering. More or less, it was all about this feeling of meaninglessness, being a speck of dust in the Universe. And it came out of the mouth of a physicist. She wanted to use her right to assisted death according to Belgian law. There was a big public debate. How wouldn't there be? It shook the foundations of Catholic morality and of humanism in general.

SHE

That is scary . . . you sound scary when you talk like this . . . But we don't shoot ourselves, Sebastian. People live and aspire to be happy. We have no rifle here at home, hanging on the wall. We're not in a Chekhov play. We have hung pictures and photos; we have books. Art and memory . . . they put things in perspective, they make sense. And the children. As for this gal, it's no accident she's Belgian. I think the whole nonexistent Belgian nation suffers from bi-, if not tri-polar disorder and doesn't convey to its citizens a sense of history, nation, origin, roots, memory, something to gird your individual existence.

From this point onward, the lighter, humorous and erotic, mood is gradually restored.

HE

Well . . . I have solid German roots. And yet . . . You know what? You are the only woman . . . no, the only human being I can talk to in this way, about such things . . .

SHE

Oh, that is because I am a weathered, brave Bulgarian woman, who can understand and endure anything, a mother of heroes.

HE

Is that a Bulgarian verse?

SHE

Yes, but I'm making it sound funny. It is something like Bulgarian mothers are heroes and give birth to heroes.

HE

What heroes? Literary characters?

SHE

Nah, historical heroes. Champions. How the hell can I explain this to you?! Big, strong, fearless men. Бъл-га- ри ю-на-ци! You remember—these slogans at the football matches. Means roughly *Bulgarians are heroes*. Uf, I forgot—you don't watch football.

HE

In other words, Bulgarians. Not some pale, depressive, brooding Germans like me. Is that the funny part?

SHE

No, but there's no way to explain it to you. Anyway. I will certainly not bear a Balkan titan. But in order to bear any child whatsoever, my romantic, slightly depressive, and so humane German philosopher has to "get me fructified." (*She makes some humorously erotic, yet inviting gestures to him.*)

HE

And he will, with greatest pleasure . . . after such intense preliminaries. You know . . . seriously . . . to me, sex is indeed a continuation of dialogue, our bodies keep on talking. (*She literally stops his mouth with kisses. They part.*)

SHE

This sounds like the aphorism that war is a continuation of diplomacy by other means.

He laughs.

SHE

So it doesn't matter at all how I look.

HE

(Humorously.)

Dammit, girl, you are so hard to please. I like everything about you—both your perfect and imperfect bits. I even love the imperfect ones more. I somehow feel they're only mine. And age won't change that, it will only add more to those mine-only imperfections.

They kiss each other.

HE

(Interrupted by kisses and caresses.)

But you know why we don't shoot ourselves? . . . Because we fall in love! . . . Love is like anesthesia . . . That's why they say love is stronger than death . . . you can even shoot yourself . . . but that would be out of love.

SHE

(Lustfully.)

Time to temporarily shoot the philosopher . . .

HE

Indeed . . . Action, please! (*He lifts her in his arms, heading for the bedroom.*) If someone's been listening to us, they would've fallen asleep by now, completely bored. And the only thing that they will ask when waking up would be: "Did those two fuck in the end or not?" What a puny sort of dramatic suspense!

SHE

(In a jokingly teaching fashion, arms around his neck.)

In literary theory, it is called intrigue and connection. Almost like conception. If the listener is a woman, she'd also like to know if I've conceived.

HE

That's how you, women, are—you'll die of curiosity.

SHE

Imagine that I conceive tonight. Can you figure out us telling our child one day that he or she might not have been born due to . . . existential . . . reasoning. It's good that children are created unconsciously.

HE

He or she will learn it anyhow. Just like we all come to know it. Now, let's proceed to the existential act—the demiurgic conception. I will shoot you right now with my cannon.

SHE

And I will check how intense your anesthesia is . . . 'Cause I'm about to anesthetize you . . . till you drop.

He carries her out the door. Lights go off and the curtain falls.

ACT II

Psychologist's office, a sofa and an armchair, a desk with a desk lamp, thick curtains, framed diplomas and certificates hanging on the walls, a shelf with folders, a door to the waiting room, the door is closed. The psychoanalyst is a sixty- to sixty-five-year-old man, sitting behind the desk; he finishes writing something in a folder, stands up and places it between the other folders on the shelf, looks at his watch, cracks his shoulders and his neck, walks to the door, opens it and speaks loudly.

PSYCHOLOGIST

Madame et Monsieur Haub?

"Yes, we're here." Comes from the waiting room.

PSYCHOLOGIST

Please, come in.

Enter Sebastian and Lora. They have grown a bit older. Seven or eight years have passed.

PSYCHOLOGIST

Please, take a seat.

They sit on the sofa, some distance apart. The therapist takes a big notebook and a pen and settles in the armchair.

PSYCHOLOGIST

How can I help you?

SEBASTIAN

(Coughs.)

We came to you because you have been recommended to us not just as a psychoanalyst but a very good family therapist.

PSYCHOLOGIST

Thank you, I'm happy to hear it. Excuse me, just to clarify something in advance: you're talking to me in English, that is, our sessions are going to be in English, is that correct?

LORA

That was another reason we chose you—we were told you have an excellent command of English. We both speak French, but English is our common language.

PSYCHOLOGIST

No problem. Please, go on.

SEBASTIAN

My wife and I decided that I'd sum up our problems for you. My name is Sebastian Haub, I'm fifty-six, German, an architect. My wife Lora Tomova is Bulgarian, with a background in Humanities; she works in a European institution, in the field of culture and education. We've known each other for ten years, we've been married for eight, this is a second marriage for both of us, our relationship wasn't the reason for our divorces.

The psychologist takes notes.

SEBASTIAN

(Continues.)

Each of us has a child from our previous marriages. My daughter Kerstin is thirty-one. She is completely independent, lives in Berlin. Lora has a son, Boris, he's twenty-one. Boris lived with us until two years ago, but now he's studying abroad and comes home only for the holidays. We're on excellent terms with both of them . . . We married for love and we still love each other deeply. (*He pronounces the last few words slowly and emphatically, turning to look at Lora for confirmation. She nods in agreement. He continues his account, glancing at her every now and then as he speaks for both of them.*) Both of us are satisfied with our jobs, we have a mutually satisfying sexual life, we don't cheat on each other, we're sincere about everything, we talk about the difficult things, we help each other, we listen to each other, we respect each other, and we're proud of each other's every success.

PSYCHOLOGIST

All of this sounds wonderful, by the book.

Awkward silence falls between them. Sebastian and Lora look down. The therapist waits.

PSYCHOLOGIST

If everything is so wonderful, why are you seeking professional counseling?

LORA

(Breaks the silence.)

Because we have a seven-year-old autistic son. He was diagnosed, and . . . (*Quietly.*) It is very difficult.

PSYCHOLOGIST

(He has stopped taking notes for a moment.)

Tell me more, please.

Silence. The psychologist shifts his eyes from one to the other, they sit with their heads bowed.

PSYCHOLOGIST

(Encouragingly.)

You can describe the child and tell me what you find most difficult . . . As parents . . . as partners.

SEBASTIAN

(Hesitantly.)

Well, Phillip, that's his name, is . . . hyper intelligent. When he was four and few months, maybe, we discovered he could read . . . (*Lively.*) In French, believe it or not, where half the letters aren't pronounced. Something many adults can't manage.

PSYCHOLOGIST

(Laughs.)

Why French? In what language do you speak to him?

SEBASTIAN

The crèche and the kindergarten were francophone. He started school at six, we decided to put him in an English class. He could read and write in English roughly two months later. Then he learned Arithmetic. He's in second grade now, but he knows as much math as a fourth or fifth grader does. In fact, we don't know what he knows. He reads a lot. But . . . he does not speak. He can, but he does it very, very seldom. At school he answers all questions, does all tasks and tests, but in writing, only. He doesn't say or write anything by himself. He has an assistant who escorts him at school because he is considered as a child with special needs. Though, frankly . . .

LORA

(Interrupts Sebastian.)

To answer your question—his father speaks to him in German, I speak to him in Bulgarian. But we were advised to stop, for the time being.

PSYCHOLOGIST

Four languages, if I count correctly, are a bit too much for a child, indeed. Could that be the reason for his speech delay? Actually, which language does he use on the rare occasions when he speaks?

LORA

English and French—he answers in the language in which he has been addressed. (*Slightly irritated by the deviation of the conversation.*) The problem is not that he is not talking . . . I mean, this is a problem, but not the main one. The problem is that . . . he does not communicate, do you understand? Verbally, non-verbally, he doesn't look you in the eyes, he hasn't expressed a single thought of his own so far, not one question, no emotions, no love even for me, his own mother! He doesn't show whether he likes something, or not. He never cries when he's in pain, but instead grinds his teeth. He's never let me touch him, dress him, wash him, it's always a fight with him, he's even bitten me. I want to caress him, to cuddle with him, I long for him to hug me . . . (*Her voice trails off.*) "He's soooo intelligent" and so what?

SEBASTIAN

(Trying to calm Lora.)

I have the feeling that he loves you, that he loves us. But he doesn't know it, he can't express it, he doesn't know he has to. We've read so much about autism, right? And that's what all doctors say. (*Pause, Lora is silent.*) Isn't it enough for you that you love him?

LORA

I am a mother, Sebastian, and I can put up with very little. My point is that Philip is handicapped in any communication, with anybody. As to doctors, all studies on autism admit that scientist have no idea what happens inside an autistic brain.

PSYCHOLOGIST

How did your children react when your son was born?

SEBASTIAN

Oh, quite normally.

LORA

Very well I'd say. Boris was a little jealous in the beginning. Not of Phillip, but of you, Sebastian, for having me knocked up. But this is normal, especially at a certain age. Boris was fourteen when Phillip was born. (*Pause.*)

PSYCHOLOGIST

Does autism run in either family? Or do you have relatives with psychiatric conditions?

SEBASTIAN AND LORA, ONE AFTER THE OTHER

No . . . no, not that we know of.

PSYCHOLOGIST

(Hesitantly, probingly.)

Did you . . . both . . . want this child? I mean . . . was Phillip an accident or . . . planned?

SEBASTIAN AND LORA

(Both speaking at once.)

Yes, of course we wanted him. We wanted him so much. (*Lora*): We planned the pregnancy and . . . all. (*Sebastian*): . . . Though, regarding accident, I think . . . (*Lora, looking at Sebastian, irritated*): No, please, stop . . . stop with your hallucinations.

PSYCHOLOGIST

What hallucinations?

LORA

Nothing.

Silence.

PSYCHOLOGIST

Do you . . . still . . . want Phillip? Do you . . . love . . . him . . . as he is?

SEBASTIAN AND LORA

Of course, we love him.

(*Silence falls. Their words are left hanging in the air.*)

LORA

(Pensively.)

But we didn't want such a child.

PSYCHOLOGIST

So, you wanted a particular child.

LORA

Nuts! We just wanted to have a healthy, beautiful, and clever child.

SEBASTIAN

Our son is physically healthy, very beautiful, and frighteningly intelligent.

LORA

(Bursts into tears.)

So what?! You don't understand anything! It's like I don't have a child! Phillip is just a naked intellect. He doesn't need love, he can't give love. He doesn't know what that is. He's *outside* of all of it. He's *autistic.* To him the world is just a set of facts and numbers, that's why he's constantly reading and counting.

PSYCHOLOGIST

All children are more or less autistic. It is we who induct them into the world, in our time, our space, our society, our rules.

LORA

(Wipes her tears, blows her nose. A bit tersely.)

Well, Phillip doesn't want to enter in *our* world. He has a highly pronounced "social deficit." (*Pause.*) I feel like he's an alien.

SEBASTIAN

(Very hesitantly.)

Is it really that dramatic?

LORA

(Bursts out.)

Yes, it's very dramatic, darling. But obviously not for you. Because you are yourself autistic. *You* haven't entered this world, you're watching everything from somewhere above. You say love is anesthesia, life has no meaning because we're going to die, because humanity will die, because the Universe is infinite, everything is accidents and chaos—love, children, everything. And, (*turning to the psychologist*) you wouldn't believe this, he tells a six-year-old that his parents will die, that he himself will die.

The psychologist writes something.

SEBASTIAN

(Quietly, apologetically, embarrassed.)

I wanted to . . . provoke Phillip, to startle him . . . to make him speak . . . tell me what he thinks, what he knows . . .

PSYCHOLOGIST

What exactly did you tell him, and how did the child react?

SEBASTIAN

(Hesitantly, pausing every now and then.)

One evening he was reading, or rather leafing through the pages of a book, he was sitting by the window and at some point, he looked out to the sky. It was a starry night, there was a full moon. A big and very bright moon. I watched him. I called him by his name. He did not react. As usual. I walked up to him, placed my hand on his shoulder, he got startled, shook off my hand, and fixed his eyes back on the book. And then I told him that one day when he grows up, when he grows very, very big and becomes like me his mom, I would be *gone*. But the moon will be still there.

PSYCHOLOGIST

Is that what you said, or did you tell him that you'd die?

SEBASTIAN

(Admits in discomfort.)

That we'd die. (*Pause. More animated.*) Suddenly he spoke. He spoke! He said: "I know. I'll die, too." Without looking away from the book, he added: "It's an inevitable regularity." (*Pause.*) But I didn't want to say this. I don't even know why I told him such a horrible thing. I wanted to tell him . . . (*Pause.*) I don't remember . . . something about the moon, I guess. (*Pause.*) It felt like *he* was consoling *me*, not the other way around. He must've read it somewhere. I don't think he understands what he said. At this age, they are . . . immortal, in a way. In any case that . . . dramatic . . . tragic "inevitable regularity" did not evoke any emotion in him. I asked him: "Are you scared?" He turned a few pages, silent. I wondered whether he knew what fear is, maybe not out of his own experience, but from books. Just when I thought that he would not answer, he said: "I'm afraid of cats." (*Pause.*) That's all.

LORA

What do you expect? You've read and had it explained a hundred times that he is not aware of his self, "I" doesn't exist for him, he doesn't respond to his name. What fear do you want him to feel? Shall I tell how you explained to him that he might not have been born?! Do you want me to tell that episode, too? Mm? That he might not have existed or could've been completely different? How can you engage a child . . . your child . . . in your . . . (*Searching for words.*) Extra-terrestrial deliriums?

Sebastian keeps silent, guilty. He hangs his head, does something mechanical with his hand, e.g., twists the end of his pullover or folds and unfolds a scrap of paper he's found in his jacket pocket. The therapist has been taking notes again for a while now. He looks up:

PSYCHOLOGIST

How did your son react?

LORA

(Answers for Sebastian.)

How do you expect him to react?! Don't tell me you approve . . . of my husband's attitudes. (*Calmer.*) Phillip remained completely indifferent. No one knows what he's conscious of.

Pause. Lora stares into space. The therapist writes in his notebook. Sebastian still keeps his head down.

LORA

The night we did it, you were depressed. You weren't certain you wanted a child. Providence has punished us. You're *still* depressed. Now I'm thinking you've always been depressed. Some sort of an oddly jovial depression. Garnished with a sense of humor.

SEBASTIAN

Don't talk like this, please, Lora. You know just how much both of us wanted a child. (*Quietly, pensively.*) Once upon a time you liked . . . that I am slightly loony, as you called it, you told me that was why you fell in love with me. (*Pause.*) And you didn't conceive that night when we . . . talked about . . . that stuff. You got pregnant two months later, without warning me about your "premium" ovulation time. (*Pause.*) If you'd conceived that *first* night, we would've had a different child.

LORA

Here you go again with your demiurgic deliriums! Are you accusing me of Phillip's autism?! Because I didn't select the best time and egg for your spermatozoon?

SEBASTIAN

Stop, Lora, please, you aren't guilty of anything. (*Resigned.*) If someone's to blame, it's me.

PSYCHOLOGIST

It's nobody's fault that your child is autistic. As a matter of fact, I've recently read a scientific article that suggests the cause for autism is a viral infection of the mother during the pregnancy. Broadly speaking, the fetus reacts by activating its self-defense mechanism, the cells contract and later do not relax. They are developing treatment based on that hypothesis.

LORA

(Through tears.)

So it's my fault after all?! I had some banal eye inflammation in the second trimester, true . . .

PSYCHOLOGIST

No, this information serves to confirm precisely that nobody is guilty. You cannot hold yourself responsible for a viral infection you've had during the pregnancy. Of course, that's if the hypothesis proves true. But even if there is no other explanation, no one is at fault. And, I think, there is no fault, Phillip is not some error . . .

LORA

Ah, I do hope they find treatment! I read about a diet . . . Something is blocked in his head.

SEBASTIAN

Or unblocked . . .

PSYCHOLOGIST:

Mr. Haub, did you experience any psychological trauma as a child or adolescent?

SEBASTIAN

(After apparent hesitation.)

. . . No. I don't think so.

LORA

You'd better tell him. Losing your mother at eleven in such a painful way is trauma for life.

The psychologist gives Sebastian a probing look.

SEBASTIAN

(Dryly, fact-reporting.)

My mother died of cancer when I was almost twelve years old. It was a long and very painful agony. My mother was a very good person, she loved me and my sister and I loved her deeply. When she got sick, I grew scared of her. I saw how she died, I saw her dead. (*Pause.*) My father and my sister—she's eight years my senior—took really good care of me. I grew up loved, in a normal home. My father died three years ago. It was an easy death. I had put him in a very good nursing home, I visited him every two or three months, we spoke on the phone regularly. My sister and I are still very close even though we see each other only for some holidays. That's all. I suppose there are millions of people who have lost a parent when they were children. But they have overcome their trauma and lived a happy life.

The psychologist's mobile phone vibrates, he looks at it.

PSYCHOLOGIST

I beg your pardon, but I have to take this call. It is a patient of mine who is in a rather precarious condition.

The psychologist has an approximately five-minute long conversation on the phone. At some point Sebastian makes a gesture, asking him if they'd better go out in the waiting room, but the therapist gives a reassuring sign they can stay where they are. He takes the call.

PSYCHOLOGIST

(Listens.)

We've already discussed that. Do you remember what I told you? (*Listens.*) No, you're not a cow and you have not given birth to a calf this spring. You have a lovely healthy child. You . . . (*He gets interrupted on the other end, listens.*) Your body will recover back to what it was, you'll go back to work in a few months, you have relatives and means that will help you raise your child, you have a wonderful man for the father of your child, now everything seems to you . . . (*Interrupted on the other side, listens.*) You take your medications, don't you? (*Listens.*) No, I'm not trying to "bamboozle" you with the medications, I'm trying to help you, you and the child that needs her mother, mother who lo . . . who loves her (*Interrupted on the other side, listens.*) No, having a child gives a lot of meaning to life. We talked about . . . (*Interrupted. Listens.*) Is your husband there? (*Listens.)* May I talk to your mother then. (*Listens.*) She went to get the groceries? When is she coming back? (*Listens.*) Since your mother doesn't speak a foreign language, you'll translate my words to her. (*Listens.)* Your daughter is sleeping now, isn't she? (*Listens.*) Look at her! Just look and see how beautiful she is, how fragile and helpless, how trusting she is, you mean the world to her. (*Listens.*) Hold on for a second, don't hang up, please, I just have to redirect another call.

The psychologist pushes a button on his phone, rushes over to the shelf with the folders, pulls one out, opens it and punches a number he reads from the folder.

PSYCHOLOGIST

Mr. . . . (*He remembers he has to protect his client's confidentiality in the presence of other people.*) Sir, it's Doctor Bondeel, your wife's psychiatrist. (*Short pause for confirmation on the other side.*) Your wife called me a while ago, she's on hold right now, I'll try to keep the conversation with her going. She's having an episode and she's alone with the child at home. Her mother has gone out to get the groceries. I have serious grounds to believe she is not taking her medications. Please, go home immediately, or call her on the landline, or send someone home. I'm warning you that I intend to recommend her for hospitalization, for the sake of everyone's safety. (*Listens.*) All right, thank you, goodbye.

He switches back to the other call.

PSYCHOLOGIST

You're still there, aren't you? Hello? . . . Your daughter has woken up? (*Listens.*) Why don't you sing to her? You like singing and you have a lovely voice. Come on, sing for a while, I'd love to listen to you. (*Listens.*) I love this song, my mother used to sing it to me when I was a child. (*Listens.*) That's your mother coming back, no? Good, I'll leave you to her. You are a wonderful singer! I'll talk to you soon!

Lora is deeply impressed by the phone conversation.

PSYCHOLOGIST

Once again, I beg your pardon. Postpartum depression is quite a dangerous condition, not only for the mother. (*Pensively, as if talking to himself.*) Only recently medicine took interest in the mothers after birth, not just the babies. Torn pelvises and anuses . . . unbearable breast pain and bitten nipples. The depression is still conveniently generalized as a hormonal imbalance or inhibited adaptation. In my opinion, the roots of this condition run much deeper, I'd say they are existential . . . Anyhow, where were we? (*He looks at his notes.*) Look, you came here as a couple to consult with me as a family therapist, so I'd like to ask you a few questions that I ask every couple in the beginning. How did you meet, what attracted you to your partner, what were your common interests, goals, values, why did you decide to stay together, is there something in your partner that disappointed you or did not meet your expectations, is there something that did not go as you had expected. Such things. I already heard a bit. As our time is near its end, I suggest that you think over these questions and we discuss at our next session. Concerning your son, Phillip, I have no expertise in autism. That is not my job and it is not for him that you came here. I believe you work with competent child psychiatrists and the child receives specialized assistance at school. If I understood correctly, your child is highly intelligent. That offers a good chance that he'll learn the social skills he lacks now.

Sebastian and Lora nod silently.

PSYCHOLOGIST

Music and playing musical instruments can have a very positive impact as well.

SEBASTIAN

Yes, Phillip could stay completely still for hours on end when he listens to classical music. He could even forget to pee—one time he peed in his pants. We want to find a piano teacher for him.

LORA

I don't know . . . I have the feeling that music pulls him even deeper into his own world, it seems to isolate him more from us.

PSYCHOLOGIST

I repeat, I'm not a specialist. I can help *you*, as parents, as a couple. We can work on how you accept your son. In a certain sense . . . you should bury the dream child you wanted and . . . adopt the child you actually have. And love him as he is. And help him become independent one day, yes, with learned social competences, yes, with social help, yet independent of you. I read that persons with Asperger's syndrome are genius programmers. That should be a common goal of yours that unites you as parents. Then, I am here to heal your couple, to dig, together with you, into all these outspoken and unspoken feelings of guilt, blame, remorse . . . What do you think?

Lora and Sebastian nod silently in agreement.

PSYCHOLOGIST

I can also work individually with you, Mr. Haub. I don't know if you'd agree or have the time to undergo a complete psychoanalysis, but I think it might be beneficial to you if we talk, alone, about the things that . . . torment you. Have you ever gone to therapy?

SEBASTIAN

(Resigned.)

Why do you both think that I'm depressed or autistic just because I ponder over certain things?

PSYCHOLOGIST

I've said nothing of the sort. (*Pause.*) The problem is not that you think about certain . . . things, the point is how you think about them and the impact these thoughts have on your life, on your behavior, on your ability to feel satisfied and happy, on your health, if you want. Depression and suicidal impulses can be destructive and handicapping not only to you, but to your family, too.

SEBASTIAN

Nothing is tormenting me. I'm fine. I love my job, I love my children, all of our children, and I take care of them, I love my wife, I have friends, I'm not suicidal . . . (*Pause.*) You know, I was wondering about your job. When doctors treat some illness, let's say pneumonia, they target the cause—a virus or bacteria, the affected lungs—and their objective is to reestablish a normal, healthy condition. The symptoms are just symptoms, they are not the illness itself, right? So, can you tell me what is the normal healthy . . . status, which psychiatrists, or psychologists, try to reestablish when they treat . . . for example, depression? Second question: if being depressed is a symptom, what is the underlying cause, or sickness, if you prefer?

PSYCHOLOGIST

Good questions! They can serve as a starting point in our discussions, I mean when I meet with you alone.

LORA

Sebastian, I think . . . if you talk alone with the doctor . . . over few sessions . . . this might be good for both of us.

SEBASTIAN

(Pensively, to the psychologist.)

You can't heal me of what's really torturing me. (*Pause.*) If you could, you would've been God and you would've healed all of mankind.

PSYCHOLOGIST

(Laughs.)

God I'm definitely not. But I can still try and help you . . . (*Picks his words carefully.*) process . . . or channel your . . . melancholy. Has it ever occurred to you that you can, for example, write about the things that consume you? Rather than discussing them with your young son . . .

SEBASTIAN

(Quietly, mechanically.)

I haven't discussed anything with Phillip.

PSYCHOLOGIST

Think about my proposal and let me know. My job is to listen and help, only with your agreement and participation, of course. (*Rises from his armchair and stretches his arm out to shake hands with both of them.*) Our time is up. You can pay at the receptionist's desk or via a wire transfer later, you may make your next appointment with the receptionist as she has my agenda. Thank you for your trust. I believe I can be of help. Goodbye!

SEBASTIAN AND LORA

Thank you. Goodbye.

They walk through the door they came in.

The psychologist sits behind his desk, puts down a few things in his notebook, then he looks up and fixes his eyes on the audience, reflecting upon the case of the Haubs. Emphasis on that silent eye contact with the audience, the silent question is what the audience thinks. The therapist writes down one last thing, then places the few sheets of paper filled with notes into a new folder, inscribes their names on the cover, he may even murmur or spell out

"Haub, Sebastian and Lora" while writing. He gets up with the folder in hand and goes over to the shelf to look for a place for the new folder. It is a classification of a human case among many others. He puts the folder in one place, then changes his mind, then one last time, and tucks the folder where he has finally chosen. Standing against the shelf, he cracks his shoulders and his neck and stretches his arms up. He takes out another folder, opens it, turns over a page and reads for a few seconds to refresh his memory of the next clients. He walks over to the door, holding the folder in hand, and opens it.

PSYCHOLOGIST

Madame et Monsieur . . . (*He looks at the cover of the folder.*) Oh, I haven't noted your family name. Hello Renata! How are you, István? Welcome! (*With a beckoning gesture toward the office he opens the door more.*) Come in.

A "Hello!" comes from outside.

Curtain falls.

WOMEN'S CHRONICLES

Dedicated to Villi, Maria, Nikolina, Ivanka, Petrana . . .
To our mothers and grandmothers

Hard and hungry wartime years. A big Bulgarian village in Thrace, somewhere along the Maritza river. It was noon, in July, everybody was working on the field. An Elin-Pelin[78] type of noon. There may have been a maiden singing there, in the unbearable heat. Before she would collapse.

Nikolina had stayed in the house to clean up, milk the cow, cook, and if she had any time left, to sew and embroider. Twenty-year-old Nikolina was one of the comeliest lasses in the village—robust, tall, and slender, with long, soft, wavy chestnut hair, her eyes the colors of fall, industrious, with a warm heart and a knowing hand—Nikolina could sew and embroider like no other. Her father had gone to town to buy her a Singer sewing machine, the best.

She was already "of age." Her engagement had been just before Lent, the wedding was planned for St. Dimitar's day,[79]—a modest affair, as the times had been hard. But this didn't matter—Nikolina and Ivan loved each other and could hardly wait to get together. And what a wonderful dowry she had made for herself—a personally embroidered covering for the family bed, bed sheets of pure linen with hand-stitched edges, the letters N and I already embroidered on the pillow, woven together, then

78 Bulgarian writer of the first half of the twentieth century whose short stories describe the life of peasantry.
79 October 26th.

came tablecloths, wall coverings . . . A gorgeous couple they were, she and the big, shy, meek-tempered Ivan. The whole village admired them, old and young would marvel and mutter, hoping not to attract evil luck.

Only that man, Georgi, much older than her but still unmarried, one of those penniless newcomers, Protestants, who settled in the upper side of the village . . . Nikolina was careful to not even look at him. He kept trying to chat her up. And she didn't like the way he watched her. She hadn't said anything to Ivan. Why would she bother him, men were too quick to fly off the handle, and what was the big deal, anyway, some man was just looking at her.

Georgi waited till Nikolina was alone that day in July, got into her house at noon, and raped her. What happened, exactly, did he have a knife to threaten her, did he gag her with her apron, did nobody see him, were none of the neighbors in, did Nikolina try to fight him, did she yank out some of his hair, did Georgi say anything, did she burn her bloodied chemise, or did she lie there on the wooden bed in a stupor for her sisters to find her that evening? . . . People said all kinds of things. Secretly gossiping. Two things, however, were certain—the next evening Georgi knocked on the door and asked her bewildered father, Konstantin, for her hand in marriage.

"Don't you know she's engaged to be married? To Ivan."

"Well, I don't know about that but she hit the sack with me while you were in the field . . ." Georgi said.

A couple of weeks later, when her blood did not flow, Nikolina knew she was pregnant. Her sister said that Nikolina had told Ivan everything so she would be honest with him. She'd got him to swear not to do anything, so he wouldn't ruin his own life with blood and revenge, this was fate's doing, her fate, that he shouldn't blight his life with another man's child and live in shame. She might have even lied that Georgi had seduced her with sweet talk and sweet caresses, that she'd given herself to him while she was out of her mind, that she's dishonored, and is not worthy of him . . . Still, according to her sister, good guy Ivan told her that whatever was done was done, that he was ready to forgive her and take her and the other man's child in her womb, that they would make their own kid, too, and they'd raise them both, and more, if God would allow, they would raise all children like their own. Nikolina, however, refused. She didn't want the shame—neither for herself nor for Ivan. And maybe she was scared of Georgi—for herself, for the child, for Ivan.

At the end of August, Nikolina and Georgi were hastily wed, though August was no time for a wedding. The nine months were running short. The wedding was held in the city, because their folks didn't want a big hullabaloo in the village, they didn't want to upset big Ivan and his family, as his brothers were not timid like him.

In the beginning of October, Ivan and Georgi were mobilized to the frontline. They were in different battalions, at different frontlines. Was Nikolina thinking, deep inside her pure soul, about Ivan, was she praying to God to keep him safe? Was she secretly praying, God forgive her, that Georgi wouldn't come back from the war? Or did she pray that the father of her child would? In the depths of those sleepless nights, was she chasing away the thought that her baby might die? Or was she stroking her restless bump, thinking that this was an innocent soul, that it was her child? Did she confess those terrifying, sinful thoughts, did she seek, fervently, her God's forgiveness? Did she swear that the child she was carrying was in need of a father? Or had she accepted her fate and taken it to be her life? Granny Nikolina left nothing written down and I can only guess, and essay fiction.

Somewhere near Niš,[80] Georgi got frostbite and his kidneys never recovered from the cold and damp. In February, while he was still fighting the war and there was no news from him, Nikolina gave birth a month earlier than expected; it was a girl. She christened her Maria, after Georgi's mother, as tradition would have it. For the first month of her life the baby slept in a cotton-lined shoebox. Nobody wanted to see the premature baby, everybody was doing the numbers on their fingers and clicking their tongues: "Well well well, now I see . . ." With all the shame and all the ungodly thoughts, and mostly out of hunger, Nikolina's breastmilk wouldn't flow, so she had a new reason to be ashamed—she couldn't feed her child. And those were hungry times, the Bulgarian village fed the huge Russian occupational army. Nikolina fed the baby yogurt, then a bread and water mush. Maria was a tough kid, though, and she survived.

When Georgi came back from the war, he took one look at the baby, then smiled his crooked smile and said: "A girl, huh." And that was it. He didn't pick up the baby in his arms, he didn't cradle her, he didn't kiss her.

Ivan didn't come back from the war. A guy from the village who was in the same unit as him said that Ivan had been chasing the bullets. His mother started wearing a black kerchief and cursing Nikolina for the whole village to hear. Nikolina cried secretly for nights on end, just as Maria did, but that crying was a sin and she spent a long time washing her eyes at the well and rubbing them with her apron so Georgi wouldn't see.

Then the collectivization started, Georgi had no land, anyway, but he was skilled—he was a technician, he found work at a factory, in the city. This was the best for

80 A town in Serbia.

them—to get away from the village where frightful things were happening. Grandpa Konstantin got ill. Nikolina only went out if she had to, and even when she did, she walked in fast little steps, her head hung low, while everyone cut her dead. In the city, Nikolina found some sewing piecework. The couple rented a two-bedroom fllat on the ground floor of some house, they even proceeded to buy it a few years later. Nikolina did not have the heart to deck the place with the dowry she had made for Ivan. She secretly gave it to her younger sister, but the sister's initials were different, so Nikolina cut the two intertwined letters out, threw away the embroidered pieces, and used the rest for rags.

Georgi was very devout, his whole newcomer line was Protestant. There was a Protestant church in town and that's where Georgi found his true family, at the bosom of that great, divine love. In his home, however, there was no human love—just a family, and a holy one at that. Nikolina was taking care of Maria, she was cooking and washing and cleaning and sewing. Georgi declared that God made man and He made him need copulation, and Nikolina obediently provided it. Following her mother's advice to strengthen her family, she conceived again, this time on purpose. It was a girl, again. Maria, or Micheto, as everybody called her, had grown up a bit and she was doing so much to help raise her sister Katya that one day she would say that she didn't have a childhood, that she couldn't simply go out and play with the kids, that if she did manage to go out, she had to have the sickly, perpetually whining Katya tagging along.

Micheto was growing up tall, lean, and bony, with the face of a doe. Timid, obedient, diligent. Really good at math. She was accepted into a technical school. Those were boys' schools, so Micheto was the only girl in class. Her father would look at his watch and monitor what time her classes ended, what time she got home, no loitering around, no boys walking her home, no school trips, no other clothes besides school uniforms. Georgi was very strict with both his daughters—they were sinful creatures by default.

And then one day Micheto, who had just turned fifteen, came home sallow-faced, hardly able to walk, crouching, hurting there, to the right side of her abdomen, near the hip bone. Nikolina wanted to call a doctor right away, but Georgi calmly finished his supper, declaring:

"She's fine. Women's troubles. She'll be all right tomorrow."

Micheto couldn't sleep a wink and she spent the night vomiting and writhing in pain. In the morning Nikolina pleaded to her husband to take her to the hospital.

"God takes care of these things because our body is a temple. If he wills it, Micheto will be all right. Now stop diddling and dawdling and go to school," Georgi said and he left for work.

Micheto obliged and started getting ready for school.

Nikolina could hardly bear to look at her daughter—her face white as a sheet, her forehead sweaty, her body burning in fever, almost doubled in pain. And yet she couldn't find the strength to go against her husband. It is a wonder that Micheto somehow managed to reach the school building. Once she got there, however, she collapsed; an ambulance was called to take her to hospital for an emergency operation. God had not taken care of her temple and the appendicitis had become a massive peritonitis. Her womb and her abdomen were full of pus. The doctors cleaned and cleaned, they had to cut away the ovaries, leaving her with only half of one. Micheto spent two weeks in bed, her abdomen open and full of drainage tubes. Her mother would run to her every day, bringing little Katya along. She would rub her eyes before she entered the room, and little Katya would scrunch up her nose because it was really stinky at her big sister's side. Georgi came once to sit at the bed, where he brought his hands together and praised the Lord, in whispers, for having saved his daughter.

When Micheto was finally released from the hospital, two and a half months later, Nikolina was told that her girl would never have kids. Was Nikolina relieved, deep inside her soul? What did Georgi say when he heard that? What did Micheto herself think about it? There is no way of knowing, nobody wrote anything.

Micheto not only caught up with her classmates, but managed to cram two years in one so she graduated with honors a year earlier than expected. There were a total of two girls finishing the technical school in that year, and the two of them were placed at the front of the graduation photo, like two flowers for decoration. Yet Georgi did not let the seventeen-year-old flower go to prom. Micheto cried a lot, but the crying was done in secret and she obeyed her father, as always. Nikolina sold the silk dress in soft pastel pink she had secretly made for her daughter. Then Micheto got the highest scores at the entrance exams to the Technical University where she would study to become an electrical engineer. Georgi was proud—he was a technician, he had no boy to take up his trade but Micheto would go higher and become an engineer! Engineering, however, was no job for a woman. On the other hand, Micheto was not a real woman, Georgi concluded, as she couldn't have children.

So Micheto dedicated herself to her studies, to all those fiendishly difficult exams—several courses of advanced mathematics, materials resistance, physics. And Micheto had a string of As and Bs. Modest, quiet and shy, sweet-faced like a doe, serious and studious, Micheto was not invited to join any cliques, she didn't go out and about, she didn't even go to a coffee shop or the movies by herself. Her colleagues didn't think about this sexless nerd unless they needed her detailed, legible lecture notes, or when they needed someone to explain the material to them during the exam session time. And Micheto would blush with all that attention, hoping to make friends with her colleagues, ashamed of her own knowledge, and happy to give everything they wanted, to help anyone who asked. Then the exams were over and everybody would forget about the useful plant that was no good for fun, or dancing, or love, and Micheto was left alone in the dorm with her textbooks and her drafts.

There was a boy in their group, one with green eyes, black wavy hair, and thick lips. Boyan had the looks of a movie star. And he was a star indeed, a bohemian kind of star—he played the guitar and sang all the hit songs, he drove a taxi at night, and knew all of Sofia, he could play bridge, and talk well, he was full of wit. All the social butterflies in their freshman course, and even some older girls, were vying for his attention. He failed exam after exam, and he kept repeating his courses; it looked as though he was trying to live a bit longer in Sofia and not trying to become an engineer. There were legends about the ludicrous medical excuse slips he presented and his ability to sweet-talk the administration secretaries.

Micheto really liked Boyan but she knew that this handsome and much sought-after boy was well out of her league, that all boys were out of her league, that nobody would want her—a boring, clumsy, non-smoking, no-makeup girl, and most importantly—barren, and with this huge scar on her shapeless abdomen. She had decided to pursue her studies and both a professor and an assistant had already hinted that she might apply for a PhD, she was thinking about finding a job at the university. Perhaps someday she could adopt a little girl to be her daughter . . . Micheto was quick to chase away that thought, so dangerous and heretic for the 1960s—a single woman with a child, even an adopted one . . . Micheto had never kissed a guy, and if we don't count the awkward attempt made by one of her high school classmates, she'd never even had her hand held—her beautiful hand with long, elegant fingers, and oval, unmanicured nails.

Then one day Boyan stood before her, smiling his seductive smile that no woman could resist, and asked her to help him for one of his exams—she was an honor student, right, she knew everything and helped everyone. Micheto blushed with excitement. "Of course, I'd love to" was all she managed to mumble. And so Micheto started going to Boyan's place and explain stuff to him, and test his knowledge. How sweet she was, playing the role of a stern teacher.

Boyan's place—a large rented apartment near Slaveykov Square—was totally chaotic, and shared by four college boys. There was always somebody coming and going, smoking was allowed in every room, once in a while a semi-naked girl would run to the bathroom, a gramophone was playing the latest music. It was a new, different world for Micheto. It was just more proof that she didn't belong. She had tried imitating her roommates at the dorm, when she was alone in the room—she had tried doing the twist, or some rock-n-roll. How clumsy she had been, how awkward she had looked! She promised herself she would never dance.

Boyan passed his exam with a D, but it was a solid D. Then the next one. Then maybe out of gratitude, who knows, he not only thanked Micheto, but took his guitar and sang her some song that was popular at the time. Oh how sweet his singing was! He was singing of love. And how well he could play! And all of that especially for her. Micheto flushed with embarrassment. She was only praying that he wouldn't play some modern music on the record player and make her dance . . . Thank God, after the song Boyan played a record of "Eine kleine Nachtsmusic." Relieved that she wouldn't have to dance and pretend to be seductive, relieved that Boyan did not see her as a woman, Micheto was looking at him with soft, adoring eyes. Then she closed them, let her body sink into the rickety armchair, and listened to that beautiful music.

Boyan did not love her, of course, he was just very thankful, they were only friends, Micheto thought sadly later on in the dorm. But why did his green gaze sometimes linger on her eyes when they were done studying, when the music was over and so were the words? . . . Indeed, Boyan was peering into her face, which was actually quite beautiful, you only had to take a deeper look, not be enticed by make-up and bright lipstick, teased hair, a tiny waist, and short skirt. Boyan was peering into her pure, innocent face, the brown eyes of a doe, slightly almond-shaped, and she was looking at him with blind adoration. The thick chestnut hair, always diligently braided (it would come rolling down if she'd let it loose), the girlish narrow hips, the breasts that looked promisingly firm, not too small and not too large. The belly was a bit unusual, and

Maria seemed to have no waist, but "there are no ideal women, right? Not in the flesh," Boyan was thinking.

One day, after they had reviewed two really difficult lectures, Boyan played Schumann's Träumerei. Micheto sank into the armchair again, closing her eyes. Boyan stepped by her side and stroked her hair. Micheto's eyes flew open and threw a startled look at him. Boyan smiled softly, ran his finger along her lips, then bent down and kissed her. Micheto was petrified. At once, heavy tears started rolling down from her eyes. Boyan stepped back:

"Why are you crying? I only wanted to kiss you . . ."

When she had finished sobbing and blowing her nose, Micheto said softly: "It's my first time."

"Well, wait, we haven't done anything yet," Boyan joked as he dragged his chair nearer and sat across from her.

"It's the first time I've been kissed by a boy," Micheto solemnly spelled it out.

Shit, she's more of a moron than I had expected, Boyan thought for a second. On the other hand, it was precisely her purity and innocence that had drawn him to her.

"There's one more thing that I should tell you from the very beginning," Micheto said in a toneless voice. "I can't have any children." And then, not waiting for his reply, she concluded: "So I'll understand if . . . if you pass me by and take someone else."

"Too bad . . . too bad for the girl," Boyan was thinking, already quite abstractly. The news that Maria couldn't have kids eliminated all the fleeting thoughts he'd had lately. Boyan had been thinking that Maria would be the ideal mother to his doubtlessly beautiful and clever kids, that she would be the ideal wife and homemaker—loyal, straightforward, naïve, obedient like a child, hardworking, resilient, and determined. She was the only one who would tie the knot with him and drag them both through thick and thin. None of his debonair lovers knew what a gasbag he was, none of them knew that his mother up there in the little town by the Danube was struggling to make ends meet with her small widow's pension, some piecework, and some sewing. All those beautiful girls, all those queens of the sheets knew their price—they expected you to pay their bills, they expected you to take them to Bumbarnika or Dianabad,[81] and buy them clothes and cigarettes, and they all wanted to stay in Sofia, or at least Plovdiv, Varna, or Burgas,[82] none of them would follow him out there into cow country, to that crumbling one-bedroom public housing. Maria was the only one who'd do that, and she would do it with love, without wanting anything more, without rubbing

81 Popular bars in Sofia in the '60s.

82 The biggest towns in Bulgaria; see as well previous footnote on fixed residence and assigned workplace.

it in, without nagging. On the other hand, Maria was from Plovdiv. Perhaps they could find a way around the compulsory job allocations and settle there? All those things were just starting to take shape in Boyan's head—but now they all died at once. Boyan could not imagine not having children. Not with his beauty, his intelligence, his virility, and talents!

He paused, painting a compassionate look on his face, and tried to console her: "Come on, it's not the end of the world . . . We— . . . you can adopt a child one day."

Maria had heard quite well.

"With whom?! Nobody will want a barren wife," she said wearily, adding: "But I have decided what to do."

Boyan was no longer interested in all of that, in Maria's decision about her childless life. He felt sorry for her but staying childless himself was out of the question. For his children, and for himself, he needed a smart and beautiful, fertile, docile, and devoted woman. Chicks were good enough for love and sex but he wanted another type of woman for kids and family. Maria matched all of his requirements except the most important one, the technical one, so to say.

"Come on, give me a smile, it's not the end of the world, right?" Boyan stroked her hair, put his arm around her waist and drew her closer. Maria was still demurely looking down. "On the plus side," he whispered coyly, "you don't need to worry about getting pregnant . . ."

Maria undressed herself, quickly and awkwardly, and stood there stark naked for inspection. She crossed her arms to hide her abdomen. Boyan carefully drew her arms apart, like the curtains of some Biblical theatre, and saw the huge scar cutting through her belly all the way down to her loins. Like a gigantic ugly stigma from some horrifying torture.

Boyan knew that sooner or later he'd have to break it off with Maria. And that he had to stop giving her empty hopes—he had to remind her, once and forever, that they were only temporarily a couple. But he was always postponing it—both the change of tone and the actual breaking-off, as he couldn't bring himself to go through with it. He had the feeling that it was going to kill her, like he would be breaking a flower. Besides, Maria was very useful indeed for the exams. Yet there was something else that was binding him to Maria, against his own will and reason. He wasn't loyal to her, of course, but the sex he had with her, although it was nothing much (how could it be, with an awkward and self-conscious virgin who seemed to feel nothing but fear, pain and possibly a tickle) had something special and exciting about it, something he could feel with no other girl. Some kind of thrill, as if it wasn't just her doing it for the first time, as if it was his first time, too. In her eyes he was the handsomest, strongest, smartest, most talented man on Earth, the first and only one. Forever. And he also felt good, noble and pure, gentle and caring. He seemed to fall in love with himself. Besides, Maria did not want to go dancing, she didn't want to go anywhere, she didn't drink anything but lemonade, she didn't smoke, did not wear make-up, did not want any gifts, she only visited when they had a date, she wasn't jealous, she didn't snoop on him. Once, when he gave her some roses he'd picked in the night in the little park by the theatre, she was so happy she cried.

"How boring . . . and exciting. That's weird," Boyan thought when he was alone.

The only thing Maria made sure of was that he kept to his studies. She explained everything again, lecture by lecture, she wrote his course assignments. For the first time Boyan passed all of his winter session exams, most of them just barely, but an exam passed at the Technical University was an exam passed, so the grade didn't matter. If they kept working so hard, and so systematically, Boyan could pass all of his summer exams too, at the first go, and with more Cs. That was the only thing Maria would nag about like a real woman.

Seven or eight months had passed after those biblical curtains were drawn. One warm late May evening, while the four boys were playing bridge, the doorbell of their student abode started ringing. The four of them exchanged frowns—not those chicks again! Enough is enough! Bridge nights were supposed to be sacred male time! But nobody was expecting anyone. Koko stood up to open the door and shortly after Maria emerged through the thick cloud of smoke by the table—coughing, ready to puke, and apologizing as soon as she was able to calm down. Boyan jumped to his feet, hugged her and took her to the balcony. He pulled the door behind him.

"What's the matter? We don't have a date tonight, right? Are you sick?"

"I'm pregnant," Maria said quietly, her head hanging low, and she immediately started apologizing how she hadn't lied about the doctors' opinion, how she had been told that even if she did get miraculously pregnant, she wouldn't be able to make it to term because she had enormous accretions, how she'd eavesdropped on two girls in her dorm and found out where she could get a private pregnancy test made, you bring the urine and they use some frogs and stuff, and how she'd brought the urine two days ago because her period was two weeks late already, and she'd started feeling nauseous for several days, and . . . this evening at 6:00 she'd gone to get the result. The test was positive. She finished rattling out her excuses and spelled it out, again: "I'm pregnant."

Boyan hugged her and planted a pensive kiss on her hair, then let his eyes wander on the rooftops of that Sofia night. They stood like this for a moment. Gazing at the nocturne city, Boyan decided that he was a noble man of duty. Although Boyan had not uttered a word, the little bird of hope was flitting in Maria's chest. Then he held her hand, firmly, and the two of them entered the smoky room.

"Dudes, I'm getting married. Maria is pregnant."

Maria was very embarrassed by that male declaration of love, by that marriage proposal made right in front of three other men. The boys started shouting:

"Congrats, man! Let's drink to that!"

The very next day Boyan sent his mother a telephone call invitation, and that night he talked to her. He told her to brace herself because she's going to be a grandma. The woman was really happy and, also, a bit worried.

"Where's the girl from," she asked.

"She's from Plovdiv."

"Oh, a Thracian, a city girl, I see."

"She's a very good girl, Mom. You'll like her. She's got straight As at the university."

"And how about *your* studies?"

"I'll go extramural, I'll get a job. Maria will graduate soon, she's only got two exams left, and then she'll have her finals."

"And where are you going to live with that child?"

"We'll get together, with you, and the kid, we'll work, I'll study at night. We're healthy, we're young, we'll find a way. We can even move to another two-bedroom place, if we make enough money."

Maria wanted to present Boyan to her parents, to announce that they're getting married and to ask for their blessing. No, she wouldn't tell them she was pregnant, not yet. She was very scared of her father's reaction if he heard that. She bought tickets for the train ride home, she called her parents from the post office, having scheduled the call beforehand, her mother and Katya were really happy they would see her before the exams.

After hearing the peritonitis story and learning about the religious zeal of his future father-in-law, Boyan was quite skeptical about him, even before they had met. And yet he kept his feelings to himself, Maria was carrying his child, he was going to marry her, the man was her father, and it was important to get her parents' blessing because she did care about it. Then he could take her away from this unpleasant man, once and for all. Though, they might move to Plovdiv, Maria had residence there. But not in her parents' house. Boyan had resumed his vague plans for the future.

They decided that, first, Maria would go home alone, Boyan would wait in a nearby pub, she would prepare her parents, and when everything was ready, she'd come to pick him up. If everything was going by plan, Boyan would sleep at their place, as a future son-in-law, though not with Maria, not before the marriage. If things go wrong, he would spend the night at the train station, it was summer after all. Then they would see.

Thursday evening, fine-tuning their plan and going over various "what-ifs," Boyan and Maria were walking along Vitosha Boulevard, then they took the tram, after which Boyan escorted Maria to her dorm, then went back to his place. There, he found an urgent cable from Lom, the boys had already read it and were nervously waiting for him:

your mother . . . stroke . . . very bad . . . come home immediately . . . aunt Tzena

Aunt Tzena was a distant cousin of his mother's, she lived next door and was very old already so his mother had been taking care of her. Now it was obviously the other way round. Boyan started turning the cable in his hands, folding and unfolding it a couple of times while the boys waited silently, nobody daring to say a word.

"T-t-tell us how c-c-can we h-h-help," Koko stuttered in fits and starts.

That night Boyan walked about fifteen kilometers—it was too late for trams, and he couldn't dream of getting a taxi although he, himself, had been turning the wheel two nights a week. He left from Slaveykov Square and walked all the way to the Sofia University campus, which was located on Tzarigradsko main road, at the very end of Sofia. He stopped to see his sister, who was already a married woman, with her own well-furnished home and an assistant professor for a husband. They didn't have any kids yet. In part because his sister might have lost a baby to the chemical gasses in the laboratory where she worked. She hadn't told her brother about it, though. It was only her mother she complained to.

"What's got into you, buzzing like that in the middle of the night? What do you want?" the assistant professor grunted as he sleepily opened the door.

The sister started fussing, moaning and weeping: "Oh, no, poor Mom, my poor darling mother!"

But no, she couldn't go to Lom and take care of their mother because she had a job and a family of her own.

"But Sis, my girl is pregnant, we're getting married, please . . . please help me, take over from me," Boyan the proud hooligan pleaded.

"You should have thought of that when you made that baby. I can't relieve you of your filial duty to Mom." His sister had adopted an acrid tone that betrayed no other feelings. She showed no surprise at the news her brother had just shared.

"But you could accept my salary as a novice technician, you could take every penny of it for four years so you could rent a place in Sofia when you were a student, and not live in those dingy dorms, you see!" Boyan shouted. And that was when his brother-in-law, the assistant professor, threw him out.

In his frustrated anger and humiliation Boyan broke the windows of the associated professor's new Wartburg[83] down at the parking lot and marched on to the dorms.

What Boyan and Maria told each other that night on the bench in front of the dorm, only the two of them know. Did Maria believe the whole story about the stroke? Boyan had lost the cable on his long night journey or left it at his sister's. He had already used fake notes saying his mother or (dead) grandmother were sick to postpone some of his university exams. His flatmates would even recall all these excuses and laugh at them.

Early on that Friday morning Boyan boarded the train to Lom.

In an old cattle car,
All rotten wood and tar
I'm riding on to Lom—Au revoir!
Au revoir Sofia
Au revoir Sofia
Dianabad and cinema Capitol.
Confused and in pain,
I don't know where I am
Because there are no windows on this train . . .
Au revoir Sofia . . .[84]

Crestfallen, Boyan sang the old number, wiping away some dumb mist running down his face.

At the same time Maria had boarded the train to Plovdiv. Of course, she didn't tell her parents any of this. Nikolina was watching her carefully:

"Miche, dear, you look a bit pale. And you didn't eat anything. What's up with you?"

"Nothing, Mom. I'm very tired of studying and I'm worried about the exams."

83 A car, produced in the GDR—the communist half of split Germany.

84 A popular Bulgarian chanson in the '50s-'60s, a cover of the original Jewish song "Bei mir bist du schoen."

A week later, Boyan sent Maria a telephone call invitation. He explained that his mother was hanging between life and death, that she was in a coma, that nobody could say when or whether she would wake up from it, and if she did come back to life, what the consequences of the massive stroke would be. Half of her face was distorted, her right leg and her right arm were paralyzed. He had "set up camp on two chairs by her bedside." Aunt Tzena would take his place for four to five hours every other day so he could go home to wash and nap. He was planning to take a year off from university because he couldn't even go extramural. His sister had called at the hospital to inquire what was happening but he had refused to talk to her, the nurses had done the talking. And yes, he was taking care of her physical needs . . .

Time was running out, Maria had not been to a gynecologist yet to register her pregnancy, she could only have an abortion before the twelfth week of gestation, yes, she was very nauseous, and very sleepy, she could hardly keep her eyes open to read for her exams. Boyan's heart sank when he heard the word "abortion," he asked Maria to wait a few days.

Exactly one week later they spoke again. The connection was terrible. Besides all the crackling and humming, sometimes the lines would get crossed and total strangers would start shouting: "Put down the phone, you morons, what the hell is this?" So here is what Boyan said, or what Maria heard despite the cracking and the other noises and the shouting of some old biddy who yelled, "Oh so now the girl will have an abortion, is that right, you bastard?":

"My mother has woken up from the coma, the doctors said she's going to live. But she's lost her memory, she doesn't know me, she's like a child. Can you hear me? Hello? The doctors said I'll have to re-teach her everything—how to eat, to understand what people say, to read . . . well, everything. Yes, how to read, too. With physical therapy—phy-si-o-the-ra-py, did you hear me? Yes, with a lot of exercise, there is hope that she will be able to get up and learn to move again. I will have to do the exercises every day with her. Ex-er-cise! Hello? Besides the physiotherapy, yes. Listen to me now. Can you hear me? . . . In these circumstances I cannot marry you, I cannot raise a child, I can't. Hello? Yes, I do want, I do love you, but I can't. Do you hear me? You'll have to have an abortion. Did you hear? . . . Yes, I know it was a miracle that you got pregnant, yes I know that after that abortion you would certainly not be able to have kids. Hello? I feel terrible, I can only imagine what it's like for you. Did you hear me? But listen, hear me well, I promise to marry you, I promise we'll adopt a child. I'm giving you my word. I repeat . . ."

. . . Maria was crying softly at the other end of the line.

"OK, Boyan. I believe you. Don't worry about me. I'll be all right. I love you."

"I called Koko. He'll come with you, he'll help you with everything you need—a taxi, some cash, everything . . . for the abortion. Are you scared? What did you say?"

". . . Oh, no, don't worry," Maria answered, swallowing her tears and fear.

Upon seeing her scar and reading her medical history, the gynecologist shook his head:

"Well, well, stupid girl, why are you getting rid of this baby? Who got you into this? Keep the child, and raise it yourself. It will be very hard, being a single mom, people will talk for sure. But it's better that way than having no child at all."

Maria, spread out on the examination chair, was drowning in tears and mucus, her whole body shaking with terror.

"My father will kill me," she only managed to say, her teeth rattling.

The abortion did not go well. Maria had a massive hemorrhage, stayed in the hospital for two more weeks, and couldn't read for her state exams. She lost weight. Koko came to see her every day and brought her chocolate. Maria didn't particularly like chocolate but she ate a piece each time so he wouldn't take offence. Then the chocolate would get soft on her night table and the nurses would take it for themselves. Boyan called the hospital every day to ask how "comrade Maria" was doing and, if possible, to talk to her. Talking to patients was not allowed, however, "what d'ya think will happen if everybody starts calling like that!?" the nurses clicked their tongues at him then rang off by saying, maliciously, "Your girlfriend will be OK. But she'll have another baby when pigs have wings." Once, it was the gynecologist who picked up the phone. When the gynecologist heard the male voice, he went ballistic:

"You irresponsible, hypocritical bastard! . . . Don't you dare call again!" And he slammed down the receiver.

Boyan's paralyzed mother learned to speak, to move again. Three months after the stroke she was able to leave her bed and learn to walk, albeit with a limp, to take care of herself with her good left arm, and go home with her son in the little house where she and Boyan slept in the only room. Boyan had a tap installed in the room; the toilet was still outside, in the yard, but his mother managed. Bathing was still quite a chore, he had to warm the water with a coil water heater, then help his mother get onto a chair inside the big tub, and then pour the water over her. Aunt Tzena was already bedridden and her elder daughter was taking care of her. There was no one he could ask to come help with the bathing.

His mother started remembering a lot of things, she learned how to read again, and she even started writing with her left hand, although the letters were coming out all rickety. She started cooking, and tried to knit by setting the needle against her paralyzed hand and moving deftly with the other one. Boyan found a job as technical support at the beer factory, he had no exams because he had interrupted his studies, sometimes he got out in the evening, telling his mother that he's having a beer with friends. Once in every four or five weeks he went to Sofia to see Maria.

A couple of months later the paralyzed woman suddenly remembered to ask: "Wait, son, what happened to your girl, wasn't she pregnant?"

"Yes she was, Mom. She lost the baby," Boyan said dryly.

"Oh, sorry. Well, it happens. I lost a baby between your sister and you. Well, you'll have another one. When are you going to tie the knot?"

"We'll see, we haven't decided yet," Boyan said vaguely.

Then spring came. Maria had taken two of her three state exams, with flying colors, of course, and the advanced mathematics professor had told her directly that he would put her name up for a PhD, perhaps even one in Moscow, although her parents were not party members, but she could think about becoming one. He would vouch for her. And so Maria could stay in Sofia to live and work, she could even get to spend four years in Moscow.

When Maria recovered from the abortion, they started making love again. When he came to Sofia, the boys would vacate the apartment for a few hours. Maria was feeling quite uncomfortable about it. But she put up with it and she waited . . . She waited for Boyan to propose. Maria had already decided that she wasn't going to Moscow without him. She was vaguely planning that if they got married, they could leave for Moscow together, she was even hoping that Boyan, whom she considered to be very clever and talented, would improve his Russian and graduate there. On the other hand, if she stayed as a PhD student at the Technical University in Sofia, they would be given their own family room at the dorm, she would still be helping Boyan so he could graduate while she was writing her PhD, and then she could stay to work at the university or they could go to Plovdiv so she could work at the Plovdiv University . . . The opportunities opening up in front of her would save them from the state system of job assignment, Boyan would find a job as an engineer, there was plenty of work for engineers, and then . . . then they would adopt a beautiful, smart baby.

Maria told Boyan nothing about the PhD she was offered—not about the one at the Technical University and not about the one in Moscow. She told him nothing about her plans, she was even trying to hide them from herself. Cautioned by her female intuition, she realized that if she climbed that far up the career ladder, if she advanced that far, if Boyan started depending on her job and her salary . . . all of that would humiliate him and drive him away. Boyan was a proud guy, he liked shining out and being a man. He thought a woman should only be healthy, beautiful, a good mother, and homemaker. Yeah, she should be smart, too, of course, but her brains mattered only as genes to be passed on to her kids. If only he would marry her . . . And yet all of her girly plans started out with the wedding. Boyan, however, seemed to have forgotten his promises—he would talk of anything but marriage. It was humiliating for Maria to broach the topic, to press him, to remind him of his promises. This would also drive him away. If it was written in the stars, if he did truly love her, he would do it anyway.

What was Boyan thinking, why did he say nothing about the whole thing? We don't know. Boyan had interrupted his studies, he had three more academic years left, which meant twenty-one hard exams to pass. He seemed to like working, and not studying, and going out at night, and living in the countryside, in his hometown. Or maybe he'd despaired, maybe he'd stopped wanting to be an engineer. He was probably thinking that he couldn't take Maria to Lom, to the single room he was sharing with his mother, he couldn't offer her the outhouse for a toilet and the tub and coil heater for a bathroom. Would Maria be willing to bathe his mother? Besides, he couldn't accept the fact that Maria would work so they could afford to rent a two-bedroom apartment. And if he couldn't graduate, or didn't want to, how was he going to live with a woman who had a graduate diploma in engineering when he was a mere technician? He was growing to like the peaceful pace of life in Lom, where the female workers were flirting with him, two of these provincial butterflies landed on his lap, at night, on the benches of the riverside park, he could build a nest with one of these world-savvy beauties, in the first workers' tenements that were already being built, they could manage to get an apartment big enough for his mother to live with them. It was easier to imagine some village-born worker bathing his mother than picture Maria doing that. And yet he'd given Maria his word. And if he was a man of honor and not a jerk, he had to keep his word. Poor Maria, it was for him, and for his mother, that she'd never have children. And he, Boyan, would not have children, either. He somehow couldn't accept that fact. With every meeting he grew more reticent, and colder toward Maria.

•

It was June again, the linden trees on the main street of Lom were infusing the air with an intoxicating aroma, factory girls were dressing up in cheap, but carefully starched skirts, and tightening their peasant waists with wide ribbons, their shoulders, suntanned on the beach along the riverbank, they were fiercely enticing, and their teased hair approximated the fashionable look quite well. The university students were about to come home, too. Boyan was coming back from work. When he got to his little house, he found a telephone invitation waiting for him. It was from Maria. What had got into her, wanting to talk to him? Didn't they meet up just ten days earlier in Sofia, and didn't they have another meeting planned in two weeks? Deep inside, still unconsciously, Boyan was already looking for an excuse not to travel to Sofia, an excuse to skip a meeting.

The connection was terrible again, all crackle and whir, and the voices of strangers. Besides, there were at least a dozen more people waiting in the corridor, and the telephone cabin was not soundproof, especially if you shouted inside, and you had to do so almost all the time.

Even as he stepped inside the stifling lobby of the post office, Boyan was already dreading the prospect of discussing things with Maria, and even possibly breaking up, in front of a dozen strangers and two operators who could easily eavesdrop on all conversations.

"Hello, how are you," Maria's voice rang clearly.

What a dumb fucking question this is, are we being courteous now, Boyan thought. What do you say to a question like that?

"Is that why you called me, to ask me how I am?" he retorted.

"Well yes . . ." Maria faltered. Then there was silence, full of whirring and crackling.

"Hello, are you still there," Boyan started again.

Maria paused. And then she suddenly asked:

"Boyan, do you . . . still . . . love me?"

For a few moments the noise had subsided and her question rang through clearly, getting stuck in Boyan's ear and then his forehead, ringing on inside his head. Do I love her? Do I still love her? I have pledged to love her. I have pledged to marry her.

"Of course," he said at last, once again in the midst of unfathomable noise.

Maria was silent. She seemed to be sobbing, he couldn't hear well.

"I love you, Maria," Boyan started quietly but then his voice grew louder and louder. He had stopped caring about the people listening in the lobby, about the operators who were surely discontinuing the other conversations so they could enjoy eavesdropping on this one, because all the crackling and voices had abruptly stopped. "I do love you. You are a wonderful person, the best person I know. When I'm with you, I also feel like a better person, not the idiot I am. But life is a bitch. It's mean. It's cruel. I have a paralyzed mother hanging around my neck. We are poor as church mice. I can't take you anywhere. I can't take those goddamn exams. I will never be an engineer . . . Never! And I gave up the cello to be one! The irony . . . I'm a moron. A loser. Leave me to rot in my rathole. Find some associated professor, or a full professor, for that matter, and live your life."

At the other end of the line Maria was already crying out loud. There, in the post office in Sofia, there were probably a dozen more people watching and listening in to their drama.

"I'm pr . . . pregnant," she cried.

"What?! You're pregnant?! Really?!" Boyan started shouting. "And I'm the father?"

"Please don't talk like that, please . . ." Maria was sobbing incoherently at the other end of the line.

A few days later Maria and Boyan were once again walking along Vitosha Boulevard in Sofia, playing out every scenario and every "what-if" for the visit to Plovdiv they were going to make the next day. Everything was exactly the way it had been a year earlier. The only difference was that when Maria sent her family a telephone call invitation, it was her father and sister who came to talk to her. She thought it was weird that her mother did not come to the post office. The only thing she told her father was that she was coming home Saturday night, she didn't dare tell him why she was coming home, nor that she would be bringing a guest. Thirteen-year-old Katya was telling her something about school. She had just finished seventh grade, and she had been doing well, except . . . but the connection was very bad, there was noise, so Maria could not hear which subject had not gone so well. She didn't hear her sister's answer, either, when she asked where their mother was. Oh well, they would talk properly when she came home.

Maria had finished her studies but no family member had come to her graduation. Yes, they did talk on the phone, her father had been pleased, he had even been proud, her mother had cried—with happiness, of course, but "you know how my folks are." But no, the trouble was that Boyan had no idea yet. And overall Boyan had agreed to all this "Plovdiv theater" only because for Maria it was important for "everything to be as it should." And also bearing in mind his vague plans for them to move, along with his mother of course, to Plovdiv. Boyan wanted to test the lay of the land, nothing to hinder setting up good relations even with an unpleasant father-in-law.

The PhD competition for applications had already been announced but Maria had not told Boyan about it. Boyan and the child she was carrying were a hundred times more important than that. She had told her parents, however, that she had applied and would be staying in Sofia to get ready for the exams. Just winning a bit of time . . . The couple had already decided to get married in Sofia as soon as possible, they had even invited some married colleagues from the university to be best man and maid-of-honor. "It will be just a very small thing, we're just going to sign the papers, and then we'll have dinner in a small restaurant. No, no gifts, please, we know money is tight, just as it is for us," etc., etc. They went to the municipality to ask what papers they would need and even book the date for the ceremony. And then? Then, Boyan said, they would go to Lom, Maria would find a job, Boyan would resume his studies as an extramural student, he would continue working as technician, the two salaries would allow them to get a two-bedroom apartment with an indoor sanitation unit; one room for Grandma, one room for them and the baby. And things would work out, eventually.

"Why don't we try to stay in Sofia?" Maria ventured without mentioning anything about the PhD.

"Are you crazy? We don't have right of residence here! You're lucky to have avoided the job assignment process. How did you do it, by the way? Besides, rent is too high here in Sofia. I don't think both of us will be able to find a job. And . . . there's my mother as well . . . I can't leave her alone."

"How about Plovdiv? I can arrange to be assigned to the university there," Maria hinted. "And . . . your mom can live with us," she added.

"Come on, not that Byzantine city. Besides, you'll be too close to your family, they won't leave you in peace." Boyan was wondering what else to say to cover up his fears and insecurities. "It will be so peaceful in Lom—the Danube, the beach, the port, living the easy life! I have so many friends there. You'll like it, you'll see . . . And, yes . . . if we ever move to another place, we'll have to take my mother with us, too," Boyan finally spit it out.

Maria accepted Boyan and his mother as a family pack.

That night Boyan did not let Maria go back to her dorm. Neither of them wanted to leave the other for the night, they were superstitiously afraid that something could happen again while one of them was on Tzarigradsko Road, outside Sofia, and the other one on Slaveykov Sq. The boys had vacated the apartment as a sort of engagement gift to the young family-to-be—so they could spend one whole night together, just the two of them. That was the first time Boyan and Maria slept together overnight. And they slept long, despite the clamoring trams, without even making love because Maria was very scared that there could be "some trouble with the baby."

And so they got to Plovdiv. Boyan was taking in the city he was visiting for the first time—a big city with gorgeous old houses and many tenement buildings. Ah, so these are the famous hills! There was even a river. Well, it was no Danube and Plovdiv was no Sofia, but it wasn't tiny like Lom, either. Here was the house, at the corner of the street, with a market just behind and a bistro in front, the one in which Boyan was supposed to wait. So he sat by the window, ordered an Altay[85] and started watching the characters in the play. Maria rang the bell, a teenage girl with a ponytail opened the door immediately and threw herself at her—so this was her sister Katya. Behind the girl stood a lean bald man, medium tall, who—weirdly—did not hug Maria, just proceeded to extend his hand, which Maria—wait, what?—proceeded to kiss. Good Lord, Boyan shook his head, which century was her father living in? And where was her mother? The door slammed shut. There would be no answers.

And then the hours started rolling—one, two, three, Boyan drank two glasses of Altay and a local Kamenitza beer, he was already famished and the waiter was looking displeased, the bistro was about to close. Nobody had entered the house across the street, and nobody had come out. The curtain on the first floor, the only one looking onto the street, had been drawn from the very beginning, and had not wavered once. It grew dark, the lamp behind the curtain went on, some shadow passed by the window but the window was too high so nothing else could be seen. Boyan was wondering what to do. This was the only scenario they hadn't discussed. Why wouldn't Maria at least come to tell him what was happening? She could at least show up at the window. At 10:30 P.M. Boyan couldn't wait any longer and decided to ring the doorbell. I don't care, he thought, my wife is inside, ah well, she is my wife, and my child's there, too, he thought and kept pressing the doorbell.

The door opened abruptly and the lean bald man stood up before him, legs apart, arms crossed, as he looked him up and down before asking, sarcastically:

"So you are Boyan, huh?"

"Yes, that's me," Boyan squinted his eyes. "Where's Maria?"

85 A soft, sparkling drink, imitating Coca-Cola.

"Well now, little Benny boy, now you'll turn around and leave. You'll go back to the hellhole you crept from. And Maria will stay here with her family." Georgi kept measuring Boyan with eyes brimming with hatred.

"That's not going to happen," Boyan curtly answered, ignoring the ugly words of his future father-in-law, words that otherwise no one could say to him with impunity. "Maria and I are getting married next week."

He said nothing about the baby because he didn't know whether Maria had already broken the news. Where the hell was she, by the way? A wave of worry washed over him. Maria was carrying his child.

"Where's Maria? I want to see her."

"Forget about Maria," the father-in-law snickered. "Maria has a family and her family needs her. And after she does what her family duty requires, Micheto will dedicate herself to science."

Wait . . . what? Boyan had no idea what the words of his highly unpleasant father-in-law were supposed to mean. Meanwhile, however, the man hissed something completely stupefying.

"And the spawn that you, godless freak, have created in sin, outside the holiness of the family bond, will be weeded out of her! On Monday I'm booking her for an abortion, next week at the latest." Spit was flying out of Georgi's mouth.

Boyan was already seeing red. Words have the ability to hit you in the face, like a blindingly painful punch. They triggered automatic reactions, remnants of the karate training he'd had in the army. Before the father-in-law could blink, Boyan made a step forward, grabbed his shoulders and rammed his head on the bald pate. Georgi collapsed on the floor, Maria and Katya jumped out and cried, they had been eavesdropping behind the corner in the corridor.

"Go away, Boyan! Go away!" Maria shouted, kneeling by her father.

"Help! Police!" Katya started shrieking but Maria put her hand over her mouth.

"Go home, Boyan. We can't get married, we can't have a baby. My mother has cancer, she's in the hospital, her operation is scheduled for next week. I have to take care of her, of Dad, and Katya. And yes, I didn't tell you but with God's help I could get a doctorate. Please go." Maria was holding his bald head in her lap, Katya was bringing him a glass of water.

Boyan could not believe what he'd heard, his stupefied lips flew open and would not close. The father-in-law had come to his senses and was watching him, victoriously, from below.

Boyan turned back and left, slamming the door behind him. He walked to the market, he sat on a bench behind one of the stalls and lit a cigarette. It was one of the shortest nights of the year. What did Boyan think about during this short night on the market bench, what did he think about Maria, this fucking life, about justice, and love, and what God would or would not let happen, about family, about the future, and about himself . . . nobody knows. And yet, at dawn, having smoked all his cigarettes, having even spent an hour sleeping on the bench, Boyan made up his mind to go against all odds, against everything and everyone, even against Maria's will, her "fucking PhD," and his ailing mother-in-law, to fight and kill if he has to, but make sure that this time his child will be born.

He used the Sunday to go to the post office, call the boys and ask their help for his plan. At 6 A.M. on Monday he was standing in front of the house. A Moskvich[86] was parked a dozen meters to the side. Koko had gone to get sandwiches. Boyan had seen Georgi leave at 7. So Katya and Maria were alone. He pressed the doorbell again. Katya and Maria were locked in and they didn't have a key. Maria pleaded with him, through the door, to go home; Katya was screaming, threatening to call the police. Boyan told her to shut up and get away from the door. Then he urged her to really call the police, so they'd see a pregnant woman locked in. Passersby would stop and stare but Boyan would look at them fiercely and say "Clear off!"

The first frontline he opened up was the window—Maria appeared at the high window, she opened it and the diplomatic talks and negotiations continued face to face, at a distance of about eight feet and were accompanied by Katya's shrieks coming from the inside—Maria had locked the door of the room facing the street so she could have some "privacy" talking to Boyan. People passing by would stare at this strange Romeo and Juliet scene that was taking place in broad daylight so the two main characters would pause when they saw someone approaching. And yet they both fell silent when Katya stopped slamming doors and shrieking that she'd call the police—and started wailing and crying:

"Please don't leave me, Sis. Please, Siiiis! Mom has cancer. Mom is going to die. Mom is going to dieee, Sis, do you heaar? Daddy will keep me locked, toooo. So I'll cook and wash and cleeean. He'll never let me go anywheeeere. I will be alooone. Without Mommmm. Without you, Siiiis. Please Siiiis . . ."

Boyan had no answer to the cruel words of this half-child. Maria was listening and silently crying. Neither Katya nor any of the onlookers heard what Maria and Boyan talked about and how Boyan managed to convince Maria to leave her father, her little

86 A car produced in the USSR.

sister, her dying mother, the PhD, Sofia, Plovdiv, or Moscow, how he managed to convince her that he loved her—her and their child—more than anything in the world, forever, that he'd never leave them, that they'd manage, that he'd be an engineer, too, that they'd have a normal home, that his mother, albeit paralyzed, although destined to be a burden, would actually help them with the child, that they'd be happy . . . And yet, at one point, at noon, before Georgi would come back for lunch, most probably having already booked the abortion, Maria stood up at the window and threw her wooden clogs first. Boyan caught them and left them on the sidewalk. He told Maria to kneel on the windowsill, facing backward, and let her legs down while holding on to the frame. The little dress caught on the plaster, Maria's long legs gleamed white in broad daylight, a few onlookers whistled, Maria trustingly and obediently did what Boyan had told her, and he caught her by the legs:

"Let go now, I'm holding you."

And Maria let go, she unhitched herself from her father's home, renouncing her studies, her sister, her mother, her father, and putting herself in Boyan's hands with all the love and trust of her girlish heart. Herself—and the child she was carrying. Boyan lowered her down on the sidewalk before him, she straightened her dress, he wiped the tears from her eyes and kissed her: "Good girl . . ."

And so Maria ran away from her father's home, in her summer dress and the wooden clogs she used around the house. Koko drove them to the hospital first in his Moskvich. Maria had one single condition—that she would see her mother before they left for Sofia.

Nikolina was lying in bed, in a room she shared with four other women.

"Miche . . ." she whispered in disbelief. Only her head was visible between the sheets. Pale, emaciated, her eyes sunken, her nose sharp, her long grizzled hair strewn lifelessly on the pillow, making her look like a witch. A translucent tube snaked under the bedsheet. The two visitors sat upon the bed. Maria combed her mother's hair, then tied it with an elastic band and started stroking her forehead.

"Mom, this is Boyan. He's my colleague and is also studying to become an engineer."

"Nice to meet you," Boyan said disconcertedly, deciding not to extend his hand under the circumstances as Nikolina's hands had stayed under the bedsheet, obviously tied to those tubes.

Maria started asking her mother how she was feeling, and where it hurt.

Nikolina was too embarrassed to speak in front of this stranger. And besides, she didn't want to get her daughter worried—she was a goner, anyway, and Micheto had to study for her PhD. Maria was trying to console her mother, to say that the operation was going to go smoothly and she was going to come home alive and well. Both of them knew this wasn't true but this illusion was the only thing they could say to each other. Nikolina did not want to ruin her daughter's future, and she was feeling guilty for being sick and helpless, while Maria needed an excuse because she couldn't stay by her mother. Then there was an awkward silence. Maria was wringing her hands and she took a deep breath a couple of times, but she stopped before she said anything. Boyan cleared his throat and offered to go wait outside. Maria stopped him and finally said, quietly:

"Mom, Boyan and I are in love, and we're getting married."

Nikolina's fading hazel eyes peered at Boyan.

"What a handsome boy you've found, Miche!" she said quietly, as if she had just noticed him.

She tried to smile. Despite those kind words Boyan remained guarded, sitting on the edge of the bed.

"I'm pregnant, Mom. Despite everything the doctors told me."

Nikolina closed her eyes. The three of them were silent. Maria started stroking her mother's forehead again.

"Daddy had locked me in, he wants me to have an abortion."

Nikolina opened her eyes, moist and glistening, and the tears started running down the sides of her face, to her ears. Boyan gave her his handkerchief—which was thankfully still unused, still starched and spotless white, ironed by his mother with her good left hand.

The three of them knew that Nikolina was dying, that she was going to die in the hospital because Micheto would not be home to take care of her, that Katya was thirteen and she would be left alone with Georgi, that Georgi would forbid Katya to see her sister, maybe for as long as he was alive, that Katya was going to grow up like Maria—locked up, uniformed, forbidden to do all sorts of things. Mother and daughter knew that this was the last time they would see each other . . . The big hospital room was silent. The other four women in the room did not move—there's no way of telling if they were sleeping, or if the pills they had taken were making them lethargic, or if they were dying, or pricking their ears with curiosity, or crying. At last Nikolina collected all the strength she had left and said, clearly:

"If you love each other, don't ask anybody for their blessing. And don't wait."

Nikolina pulled her left hand out of the sheets, it had no tube hanging on, and she gestured to Boyan to come closer. No, she did not bless him by making the cross sign, she just touched his cheek, lightly, looking straight into his eyes. "Do you really love Micheto? Will you take care of her and my grandchild? Will you be good to them? Promise me," her eyes were asking. Boyan nodded, embarrassed like a teenager. "I promise," his eyes were saying.

"Well now, kiddo, you have to go, the doctors will start making the rounds soon. And Georgi sometimes comes visiting at noon, on his lunch break," Nikolina suddenly remembered. "Go, quick . . ."

Maria started crying, she threw herself over her mother, whispering "Thank you, Mom. Mommy . . . where am I leaving you . . ." Boyan gently but firmly lifted her up then bowed down to kiss his mother-in-law's forehead, a goodbye kiss, and then he took the distressed Maria by the hand and firmly marched outside.

Three days later Maria and Boyan got married in Sofia. The boys pooled their resources to buy Maria a dress and a pair of shoes, the best man and his wife paid for the modest dinner at the restaurant. Boyan spent his last money on a tiny bridal bouquet of white roses and two tickets to Lom. On the fourth day of their marriage, Maria and Boyan departed for Lom.

A few months later, Nikolina passed away in the hospital in Plovdiv. Her sister, Maria's aunt, sent a telegram to Lom. Boyan went to the funeral. Georgi spat at him at the graveside, and Katya pummeled him wildly with her little malicious fists. Boyan wiped his face from the spit of his father-in-law, he took Katya's hands and put them back, firmly, at their place, but he didn't respond to either of them. He threw some soil on Nikolina's coffin and left.

A few weeks after her mother's funeral, at the hospital in Lom, Maria gave birth to a baby girl—with black hair and a white, smooth un-babylike face, pretty like an angel. Doctors, midwives, and hospital attendants would line up to see that beautiful baby. To keep evil eyes away among so many strangers, one midwife tied a piece of blue yarn to the little girl's wrist and told Maria not to take it off. The only problem was that Maria didn't have any milk; well, another new mother had more than she needed and happily agreed to breastfeed the "little doll" even after the end of her hospital stay; she said they could bring the baby to her once a day.

A week after the birth Maria and the baby were discharged from the hospital and Boyan took them to the bank of the Danube. It was a bright, warm February day but it was always windy by the river. The baby was well-covered in a woolen romper with a matching hat, knit with one paralyzed hand, and a woolen baby wrap cut out from some old blankets. And they took a photo there—Boyan rocking his daughter, pausing a little for the photo, and saying, gently, "Daddy's girl." Behind them, the waters of the river flowing peaceful and white on the black-and-white picture, and in the Technicolor reality—gold-plated by the sun.

If it's true that life only starts for real when you lose a loved one for the first time, Maria's life started by two, quite opposite, "firsts"—with the life she had given, quite literally, and with the death of her mother.

This was the era of great poverty. Maria couldn't work with that miraculous, high-risk pregnancy, and then she had to take care of the baby. She was afraid to leave the baby alone with the paralyzed old woman. Boyan returned to his studies but he went extramural, only going to Sofia for in-class lectures and exams. His salary as a technician and the old woman's widow's pension were not enough to rent another place.

Boyan and Maria cleared the cellar; their neighbors gave them an old bed that they somehow managed to cram inside. Boyan put together a table and the paralyzed woman moved in. The other room, the only proper one, would serve for everything. Everybody, including the baby, would get bathed in the tub with water warmed with the coil heater, Maria would wash the cotton rags that served as baby diapers at the sink, and give baths to her paralyzed mother-in-law, the two women would take turns cooking, and they'd use the coal stove for heating. There was no window in the cellar, so it was warm inside, even stifling, so the old woman got through the winter with a thick quilt and some hot-water bottles. The baby kept crying through the night, she was most probably colicky because they had started feeding her yogurt, and she'd only calm down when somebody sang to her. Maria and Boyan took turns sleeping, one would sing and the other one would try to catch a few winks. Boyan would wrap himself in his duffel coat and go to the barn to sleep or study for his exams. When the baby was seven months old, they put her at a weekly care center so Maria could start working—as a teacher at the town's technical school. They missed the baby but the conditions at the care center were better than the ones at home, they both had to have a job because money was tight, and besides, this arrangement allowed them to sleep so they could work during the day. Boyan had many exams left. Maria's salary went toward his tickets to Sofia, the hotel rooms he rented there, the care center, and the two sets of proper clothes that Maria couldn't go without because there were students and colleagues watching her. Maria had one pair of tights that she put on, took off, and washed carefully nightly, like performing some religious ritual.

She would secretly send telephone call invitations to Plovdiv but nobody would come at the appointed time. This went on for four and a half years. Boyan had almost graduated, he only had the state exams left. Maria found another job as a mechanical engineer at the port, she had a bigger salary now. The director of the beer factory had promised to promote Boyan to power engineer after graduation. The young family started making plans to rent a bigger place, with an indoor toilet and bathroom. It was all starting to work out. The baby had turned into a naughty, inquisitive, picky eater with perpetually messy hair and bruised knees, a little girl who'd switched to a weekly kindergarten and preferred sleeping in her grandmother's cellar at weekends. Her Nana would read her fairy tales up into the night.

One gray and already wintry November, day Maria secretly went to a gynecologist because her period was three weeks late. It had happened before, it was even normal to her to skip a month, but this time there was something else as well—she'd been feeling nauseated for a week, and hardly able to hide her vomiting from Boyan and his mother. The gynecologist sighed and told her she was pregnant. Instead of congratulating her, he started telling her how dangerous this pregnancy would be, for her and for the baby, because of all the accretions she had. Maria got scared and started silently rehearsing what to tell Boyan, and how to say it so she could convince him to let her have an abortion.

Boyan had no intention of letting her say the things she had prepared to say, or meeting the gynecologist. He wanted to have a son and he was sure that everything would be fine.

"This is going to kill me. That's what the gynecologist said," Maria repeated through her tears.

"Forget about the doctors. They don't understand a thing. They'd told you you wouldn't have children, right? That you couldn't carry a child. Look what a pretty girl we have! And everything went smoothly."

"What if it's not a boy?" Maria persisted with a flicker of hope.

"Well that would be a pity. But we're not gonna throw the child away, right? Besides, it'll be a boy, you'll see."

Inspired by the thought of his future son, Boyan took his state exams at the first go, he was immediately promoted as the power engineer of the beer factory, the double engineer's income already allowed the family to rent the nice apartment on the main street with the two spacious rooms and the big transitional living room, and most importantly—with an indoor bathroom and toilet, with a real water heater, with a shower.

After he got his diploma, Boyan passed an audition for the amateur orchestra in Lom and was welcomed with open arms by the conductor, whom everybody called Uncle Dano. The violoncello absorbed Boyan's passion for good and beautiful things. Maria was happy and proud—there he was, her Boyan, she thought, not only he became an engineer, but he would follow his love for music, too.

Maria got really big with her second pregnancy, her belly looked as if it was about to burst, and burst exactly at the giant, gaping, terrifying scar. It hurt like hell, all those accreted tissues were stretching to make room for the baby. A big one. The doctors wanted to make a cesarean early in the beginning of the ninth month, that was enough, and there was no point keeping the mother at risk. And yet Boyan convinced Maria to wait: "Cesareans were for emergencies only," he said.

"But it's very dangerous if there's an emergency," she replied. Boyan was certain that "it will be fine." Maria stopped going to work because she could neither stand nor sit. Her term whizzed by. A doctor visited her every day to check up on her and listen to the baby's heart with a stethoscope, Every time he would shake his head and offer to take her to hospital immediately and deliver the baby. Boyan pretended not to hear. And Maria obeyed and trusted Boyan.

At last, thirteen days after the term, Maria cried out . . . A really difficult birth followed, and it was too late for a C-section now. Boyan kept pacing nervously to and fro under the windows of the birthing unit, and chain-smoking. Maria cried a lot this time, you could even hear her outside the building. "Gosh, she's been there for hours!" Boyan crushed the empty box of cigarettes. "There's no end to that hell, poor girl . . . But all women give birth like that, she's not the first and she won't be the last one. She can manage, she always does."

"Congratulations, comrade. It's a boy. A big guy you have, almost five kilos," the midwife said dryly when she finally appeared, her eyes tired and her forehead sweaty. "Come in if you want to see him."

His son really did stand out with his size in the newborn room, lying in a cot with seven or eight other babies. But he was so ugly—his head misshapen, looking like melon, three tufts of black hair, one on the forehead, a big nose, some slits for eyes, his body ruddy and fat.

"He'll be fine, don't sweat it," the midwife assured him. "It was pretty hard."

Boyan was at the height of his happiness and rushed to spread the news and celebrate the birth of his son with friends and colleagues. He even forgot to ask how Maria was doing. But she was fine, right, or they would have told him. He got drunk as a skunk. Staggering, he hardly managed to go home by midnight, but he continued to shout, hoarsely:

"I have a son! His dick will be as big as the chimney of the beer factory." His mother told him off for talking obscenities.

Months after the birth Maria still had to sit sideways, and even then her face was twisted with pain. The big boy was voracious—he would bite her breasts until they started bleeding, and she'd cry. And she would also laugh through her tears. Because this time she had milk. On Saturday nights, and on Sundays her daughter would be back from the kindergarten where she still spent her weeks, and she'd peek timidly behind the door, jealously watching Maria breastfeeding the fat baby for hours on end and her parents rocking him in their arms or playing with him. "So that's what it's like having a brother," the child concluded to her Nana. And everyone laughed a lot. The kid was jealous, it was normal—jealous because the baby was with their mother all the time, because he slept with their parents and they cooed and played with him while she was always at the kindergarten and the one night she got to spend at home she had to spend in the other room, with her Nana; she was jealous because her father was so proud of having a son. Only the old woman remained "loyal" to her granddaughter and the two of them kept on reading and traveling around the world, flying out of their big, shared bed.

Then one day the girl, who'd been in first grade for two months, got a terrible ache in her tummy, she could hardly come back from school, stopping to rest on every bench on the way home. Boyan came home and the minute he saw his daughter he grabbed her in his arms and took her to the hospital. She had acute appendicitis, so an emergency operation had to be performed. Only local anesthetic was used so the child kept asking the doctor and the nurse, in her quiet voice, when it would all be over. Then she remained alone at the hospital for weeks on end. And she had been hoping so badly, and so secretly, that Mom and Dad would leave her little brother for a while and pour all of their attention on their sick girl. And the child kept reading, all the time, so she wouldn't be afraid and so she wouldn't be sad that Mom and Dad were, once again, not there. Mom and Dad had to work and take care of her brother, and Nana had to clean and cook, and they didn't let parents stay in the hospital, anyway. One of the books the little girl read in these long weeks was *Pippi Longstocking*. Pippi was alone, too, and her strength and independent spirit were a source of solace and inspiration.

The ugly cut on her abdomen, however, continued to fester even after the child was discharged from the hospital. Boyan brought his daughter to have her bandage changed every other day, and the bandage was always spotted in yellow and bloody red. The child did not go to school. Boyan had always been distrustful of doctors, and now he started changing his daughter's bandage himself—boiling water, sterilizing the pieces of gauze. The cut, however, kept festering, and the low-grade fever would not go away. Three months after the surgery, after Boyan had threatened the doctors that he'd "kill them all if they didn't set it straight," they opened the wound again to take out a string and a piece of gauze they had forgotten inside her tummy. The little girl was screaming so hard, mostly with fear, having been belt-tied and pressed down by Boyan and two nurses, that Maria fainted in the corridor. But in these hours Mom and Dad only thought about her. They were utterly with her. With her screams, the child was unconsciously punishing them.

Eight years after Maria's escape through the window of her father's house, Georgi and Katya came to Lom—to make peace with her and Boyan, to see the children, to meet Boyan's mother.

Georgi looked the little girl over, pinched her cheek and gave her a bar of *Krava*[87] chocolate. The child expressed her thanks by reciting a long poem to her newfound grandfather. She was intrigued by her newfound Aunt Katya, a student in Sofia, eight years her mother's junior. The aunt was wearing funny flared trousers, the likes of which the child had never seen, and her eyes were contoured in black with some green paint on the lids, like the caretakers at the kindergarten. Aunt Katya had very long hair and she let her niece comb and style it. Maria was running around, magically transformed, Boyan looked too serious and unusually silent, and her Nana was silent, too. When everybody was at the table, Georgi made a gesture with both hands, everybody stopped speaking and bowed their heads. The little girl snuck a glance—Daddy and Nana did not seem to like this but they said nothing. The grandfather thanked some god for the food and the bread, for the children, for health and for His "grace-and-bounty."

87 Cow, in Bulgarian. An imitation of Nestle chocolate bars.

"What does that mean, Nana?" the child's voice chimed.

"Be quiet," the old woman shushed her.

Georgi went on, asking the same god to "for-give-our-sins-and-keep-us-from-harm." The child cast another inquiring glance at her Nana, but she sat with her head bowed. At last the grandfather was done with his unintelligible words so everyone could start eating the dolma peppers Granny had cooked.

There are a few black-and-white photos left from that visit—one of them shows Georgi lifting up the baby boy in his hands, showing him to the camera; the child, about a year and a half old, is already handsome, curly-headed, his olive eyes looking puzzled. The grandfather's Biblical gesture seems to be saying: "May he be!" Years later, when the grown-up girl would watch *The Lion King* with her own child, she would remember that picture, especially in the moment when the little cub is raised by the elders over the rock to be shown to the animal kingdom.

Soon after that visit Maria merrily told her daughter: "In two years we'll be moving to Plovdiv. This is a big city, much bigger than Lom. We're going to have a big apartment. From your Grandpa Georgi. They're taking down Grandpa and Auntie's house. And they're giving them two apartments—and one of them will be for us! Can you imagine?"

The two years flew by, and the family moved to the big city, to the big apartment with one bedroom for Nana and another for the two kids. Boyan and Maria were to sleep in the living room. Boyan found a good job as an engineer. Maria went back to teaching at a technical school so she would have time for her children, her household, and her paralyzed mother-in-law. The kids' school was right nearby. So were her father and sister. The kids were good, and doing well at school. Life was turning out beautifully. Maria and Boyan were still young, and healthy, it was high time to get some happiness. Maria's heart was thrilled with joyous expectations for the future.

Yet, the years started rolling by faster and faster, and still happiness would not come. Instead, there were terrifying disclosures, and death, and pain, and lies, endless wearisome work, care for children and the sick, and, finally, old age.

Maria's aunt (and Nikolina's sister) came to visit her niece before she died, and as she didn't want to "take the secret to the grave" she told Maria the truth about her mother Nikolina. And about her father Georgi. And how she'd come to be born into this world. Maria would usually just take the punch and live with it, but this time she couldn't. Not immediately, anyway. She cried a lot, she kept on crying for months, years even. Her shoulders drooped, her face got gray and worn, she got rings under her eyes, her thick undyed hair grew white around the ears, she lost weight, and she grew old and shriveled. Her "critical age"[88] came too early, while it was still time for love and happiness.

The monstrous news of her "genesis" turned a new page in Maria's quiet, almost imperceptible suicide as a human being. She just wanted to disappear from this world because she thought she should never have been born. She was the "fruit of rape." Fruit . . . how well this cliché fit her reality. Maria cried inconsolably because she thought she was the reason her mother had been unhappy. That she, and the misery she had "em-bodied," were the reason Nikolina got sick and died when she was only forty-three. Stomach cancer is what eats up unhappy people, they say. And she, the daughter, had actually abandoned her mother—when she was sick, dying. No, she shouldn't have been born at all, she shouldn't be em-bodied, she shouldn't em-body violence and unhappiness. But what could she do?! She was born, she existed. The only thing she could hope for was to redeem her life with infinite love, infinite care, infinite humility, infinite goodness, and never-ending work. Life . . . woman's life at least was all misery, anyway, all misery and duty. Kids were the only joy, Maria concluded, resigning herself to her fate.

It was as if she'd folded in half so she wouldn't take up space. She even stopped sitting at the table—she walked around like a servant, waiting upon Boyan and the kids.

So that's why my father is so pious, she thought, because he's guilty. He realized that what he did was not God's work and will, and all his life he kept trying to ask Him to forgive his violent act and the misery it brought. It could even be—Maria would burst out crying—that my father hoped that his God would take me, with my poisoned insides, that He would destroy the fruit of that violence and that misery. That's why my father did not take me to the hospital . . . And my child! That's why my father wanted to destroy her, too, and how he put it, God have mercy on him, "spawn of sin incarnate, conceived in sin" . . . My Lord! . . . Here's why he wanted me to remain childless, to have no husband and dedicate myself to science! But . . . wait . . .—Maria's thoughts were rambling—Mom really loved me, despite . . .—her thoughts flew away like frightened birds. And yet what mother would not love her child, even if . . .—thoughts gave way to more tears. But if I hadn't been born, then my children wouldn't be born, either! . . . Oh, no! My kids, my darlings . . . how could they not exist?! . . . They have to be there, even if I'm not! Hm . . . That would be impossible . . . And . . . if my father had not

88 A weird euphemism for menopause, obviously invented by men.

raped Mom, Mom would have married Ivan, right . . . and Ivan would not chase the bullets and die . . . They would have had other children. And they'd love them a lot . . . Like Mom loved me and Katya. Or maybe more? . . . And I . . . if I hadn't had that abortion for the sake of my mother-in-law, I would have another child now instead of my daughter. And I'd love that other child like I love my girl. What if . . . what if I hadn't escaped through the window . . . and I hadn't eloped with Boyan . . . and I had become a PhD student . . . an assistant professor . . . I wouldn't have a child after two abortions . . . But . . . What if . . . No! No! This is crazy! I'm gonna lose my mind if I go on like this. There is no "what if" in the past. It is what it is. What it had to be. It's fate. God knows what He's doing. *C'est la vie*. All's well that ends well . . . Maria was trying to console herself with a string of platitudes and with her unconditional motherly love.

Then Boyan's mother died—slowly, agonizing, hideously. Maria kept wiping out shit and urine, the old woman would kiss her hands, Maria would secretly vomit, nauseated, asking God to hurry up and take her soul . . . and then the same God made her hate herself for her repulsion and her sinful thoughts, made her humble down like a true Christian, and console herself that she was giving her mother-in-law what she couldn't give her own, and accept that it's just her human duty to care for a dying person.

Then her father passed away. There was more shit and urine to wipe, and he was also senile. He mistook the balcony door for the front door so Katya and Maria had to act quickly before he stepped beyond. "And maybe we should have let him, if Katya was alone, she would have." Maria hastened to chase away that ugly thought. But Georgi was already "beyond," although not at the place he had prayed for all his life. In the end he was stuck in stupor, and his eyes did not see anything. His two daughters folded him in half on the rear seat, like a chipboard man-shaped target, and drove him to the shabby hospice they'd finally managed to find after pulling some strings, only to unfold the stiff figure on a bed. Two days later it had stopped breathing and they had to take it back in the same manner, by propping it up on the rear seat and driving it home. Maria cried so hard that she and Katya hadn't stuck it out for a few more days so their father could pass away at home. So that Maria would be at peace with herself for having fulfilled her duty.

At the funeral, Maria watched carefully for anything special, religious, mystical—anything in the ritual, in the people who came, in the few words that were said, in the cross she and Katya stuck on the grave. Her eyes and her mind were looking for anything to suggest that her father's God had not passed away with his long-faded mind. Her father had stopped going to church almost two years earlier—because he was no longer able to make the long walk and because he kept getting lost. He had gradually stopped mentioning God all the time, and he'd stopped saying grace before dinner. Maria and Katya had been feeding him like a baby. Their father had totally forgotten about his God, so Maria was asking herself if that God could continue to exist like that—forgotten? Because even if God still existed, albeit forgotten, He seemed to forget those who no longer remembered Him. Oh no, why am I having these blasphemous thoughts, Maria shuddered. But the ugly thoughts would not go away. Maria was wondering if this God had granted her father punishment or forgiveness as his death had looked like neither. There had been nothing sacred or spiritual about his funeral—her father transformed into ugly, yellow, stiffened flesh that she and her sister made an effort to say a few good words about, and then, at the restaurant, that smile of relief which Katya was unable to hide. Counting out those few years she had spent as a student in Sofia, she had spent all her life with him. And yet, "if 'the One above' really did see everything, if He really did never forget and if He . . . did punish my father, why did this punishment bring so much suffering . . . to me?" Maria wondered about God's ways.

Georgi did not get buried beside Nikolina but far, far away, in the new plots that were neatly arranged like miniature tenement prospects, which would have had five-pointed stars on the crosses if democracy had not come. When her daughter inquired why Grandpa wasn't laid down with Grandma, Maria said, angrily, that her mother would not have wanted it.

Then Katya passed away, a mere eight years after her father; she was so young, and in such pain. Her little sister, her closest person, the last one in Maria's immediate family. Katya could not have children, she didn't have any, her beloved man died absurdly as the only victim in some train crash. Katya was alone and dying. "Why is God doing that?! What is he punishing Katya for?!" Maria was wailing, helpless and terrified by the horrible sickness. But maybe "the One" was giving her a chance to correct the mistake she had made forty years ago when she left her little sister behind . . . And yet—why should mistakes be corrected so cruelly, why did Katya have to die so young, so painfully, in full consciousness?! And besides, was it really a mistake? Didn't she leave Katya so she could have her daughter?! Maria's head was bursting with questions.

Maria spent three months at her sister's bedside, in the barren hospital room. Her little sister would not have to face death alone. Maria was playing her favorite music on the tape recorder, she was reading aloud her favorite books, soothed her sores and was happy when Katya was able to defecate, held her hand when Katya could no longer say if she liked the music, if she could see her, how much she was afraid, what was she thinking, and if she was thinking at all. She was holding her hand while the gaunt body was shaking convulsively. She was holding her hand when Katya drew her final, barely perceptible breath.

Maria buried Katya in their mother's grave. She was planning to be laid down there someday, too. This time the daughter asked no questions.

Then there was someone to take care of, again, and poop to wipe, but this time it was baby poop, and baths to give, to fragrant infant flesh, and someone to prop up for walks, not just someone but a whole new person, and more sleepless nights, but it was just baby cries this time. Maria raised her grandchildren so her kids could sleep, and study, and work. She held her grandchildren to her heart, caressing them, and constantly talking to them, giving them all her time and all the love she couldn't give her own kids.

Where had Boyan been all this time? What had happened to love, anyway?

In the beginning everything had been real, powerful, and beautiful. Or that's what Micheto had thought. She'd listen to him, bright-eyed, and he would talk and talk, and talk—about music, and friendship, and love, about the Universe and energy, about his childhood exploits, his escapades in the army, about his own intelligence, and the wondrous story of his deceased father's travels in foreign lands, about his strong mother and his successful sister. Micheto's heart would jump with excitement like a little fish in a brook, and her beautiful doe-eyes would be brimming with tears. What a beautiful soul Boyan had! Just as beautiful as his face. What high thoughts he had coming into his head, what beautiful and terrifying things he had lived through, oh look at him talk, and sing, and recite poetry . . . well, just a couple of poems he had learned as a child, but still, it was all so beautiful! And what an intelligent family he was born into . . . And this extraordinary, brave, super-intelligent and talented, spiritual and handsome man had chosen her!

Yet after discovering dozens of discrepancies between Boyan's stories and reality, Maria started wondering. No, she didn't say anything to Boyan, she didn't call him out and make him look bad, of course. She forgave him. He was like that, she thought, a dreamer, he wanted everything to be beautiful and dramatic, and he wanted to be a big hero, a great engineer, a talented musician, a great poet. And as reality was banal and stifling, full of poverty, humiliation, and deformity, and people who were envious, incompetent snitches, and as Boyan was not allowed to become a Party member so he couldn't get ahead in his career, he couldn't demonstrate his talents, he couldn't get rich and put the whole world at her feet, for her and the kids so he just . . . embellished it all . . . to make the world more beautiful. But it was her Boyan! And he was really better-looking, smarter, and more talented than she was. She was much simpler and more banal, she had no idea of music, poetry, and the Universe. Yes, Boyan was right, she'd been nothing but a hardworking nerd in college. What PhDs was she talking about, one might wonder! And, God have mercy, wanting to abort the child for the sake of some stupid ambitions! Or was it for her mother and Katya . . . In both cases she was guilty, guilty, guilty!

There was something else. Boyan turned somewhat ill-tempered. As if he had never forgiven her. How quick he was to fly off the handle, how red in the face he got, what things he started saying. Maria had the heart of a doe, and in such moments it was gripped by fear. No, no, she would not make him mad. It was some bullshit, anyway, some sort of "details." In the rare cases when Maria did try to express her own wish or opinion, or to take a stand against Boyan, it somehow never worked and she always eventually agreed with him. And Boyan quickly managed to convince her that he was right. Not that she had any opinions in particular, she just occasionally happened to disagree with Boyan or her mother-in-law. Maria gradually stopped voicing her thoughts. As time went by, she gradually forgot she could have her own thoughts and opinions, and the thoughts themselves gradually disappeared without her knowing it. Boyan didn't even notice it because he had always been certain that Maria was thinking exactly like him. Oh well, except for her folly back then, in the corridor, in the house by the market.

And she had this tiny, treacherous fear that disappeared just as imperceptibly. To make room for another, that is. Soon after she had left her father's home and started living with Boyan and his mother in the faraway town, and especially after her mother died and her baby was born, Maria suddenly realized that she had nobody besides Boyan and her mother-in-law. And so, in the beginning, she was a little scared. But then she forgot about that fear. She was not alone! She had a family, she had Boyan! And her father was no saint, right. But her little sister . . . She cried so bitterly—and secretly, of course, for Katya, and for her mother. And yet she didn't want to upset and infuriate her husband. The fear of loneliness silently gave way to her unacknowledged fear of Boyan.

But here, Katya and her father have come to visit! They have forgiven her! Thanks to her father, her family will get an apartment, and move to Plovdiv, she'll be close to him and her sister, she'll be able to take care of them. And, thankfully, Boyan overcame his pride, he accepted the apartment and agreed to do the move, he even persuaded his mother! Everything's fine now! Maria had nothing to fear. Her family, Boyan, the kids—this was her life, her happy life. They got along with Boyan, they didn't fight, they had two wonderful children, they had a home, they had jobs, they were healthy, and they loved each other, right? Maria called the paralyzed old woman "Mother" and took care of her as if she really was her daughter—since she didn't have a mother of her own. Oh well, Boyan had his weaknesses like all men did—he liked to fib, and exaggerate, he kept having conflicts at his workplace, he was short-tempered, wouldn't let anyone else talk, wouldn't listen to anyone, he kept leering at other women—but he'd rarely look at her. But hey, there are no perfect men, right? He did have a job, he did bring his whole salary home, he didn't cheat, and he didn't drink. What man would not give other women the eye? Besides she, with her non-existent waist and her flabby abdomen, had started looking like an ingot on stilts after the birth of her son. If it wasn't for these outbursts of his . . . No, no, she wouldn't say anything, she would just listen. She doesn't want any scandals, she wants peace and love in her home. And finally, Boyan had never raised a hand to her, right? No, no, he'd never stoop to that, Maria kept chasing that thought—and with it, her fear. But she wouldn't make him mad, either, she would not argue and try his patience. She would not disappoint Boyan. Didn't he choose her, take her, love her! He was the one who saved their children. My God, and she had wanted to abort them! . . . There's nothing to regret, she had no regrets at all!

And yet, years later, when Maria was no longer a woman "in the strict sense," and her blighted insides made that happen before she'd even turned forty, and after his mother died, Boyan started cheating and rarely coming home. Maria had been hoping so badly that now, especially after the death of her mother-in-law, they could finally live . . . happily—with their grown children who would soon fly out of the nest; they could live comfortably, just the two of them, without any in-laws, still young and healthy, and they could finally have a proper bedroom. Maria was trying to become attractive to Boyan again. She exercised religiously, after midnight, before she would collapse with fatigue in bed. Nothing, however, could repair the cut-up muscles of her abdomen and her permanently destroyed waistline. She cut her beautiful hair short and permed it. She looked like cabbage. She started putting on make-up, though she did not know how and sucked at it. She even tried smoking to look sexier. Wasn't that what those dangerous women did, the ones who didn't do housework, didn't sew, didn't care for kids and paralyzed mothers-in-law? And yet Maria looked not sexy but pathetic—with her permed hair, her jagged black eyeliner, her nauseous fits when she drew on her cigarette, her clumsily shortened skirt exposing the roundness of her knees, and her reeling attempts to walk on those high heels that, moreover, made her look taller than Boyan. Maria was totally devoid of any coquetry, allure, and sex appeal. She was beautiful as a Madonna, as a grown-up girl, as a mother, as Maria. But Boyan no longer loved her the way she was, he no longer needed a mother for his children, a caretaker for his mother, a housekeeper at home, a pure and sacred Madonna. He was free, he had money, he had other tastes and other needs.

Despite the "measures" she had taken to "enhance" her sex-appeal, Maria didn't abandon her primary duties, not for one moment—whenever Boyan came home, the place was always clean and tidy, there was always homemade food, Maria was gentle and loving, the kids were well fed, well clad, and good-mannered, both at the top of their class at school.

Everything was to no avail—Boyan treated her like a boring but useful houseplant, no—like a household robot. And the death of his mother did nothing but give him permission to throw himself into his own life as a man. Men only grow up for real when their mothers die. Yet, for most of them growing up seems to mean that they can finally do whatever they want. By the way, while his mother was dying, Boyan was not there at all, he was so "busy" that he couldn't even attend her funeral. He did find the time later, however, to go through the medical records and interrogate the doctors so he could be sure that Maria had not killed his mother as an act of revenge for old time's sake . . . Oh, how Maria had cringed as the doctors looked in disbelief . . . And yet she didn't say a cross word to Boyan. She was too scared. And Boyan did not say a word of gratitude. So what, big deal. He was too tired to do so, he was too nervous to do so. And it was her duty to take care of his mother, wasn't it, Maria finally consoled herself.

She finally came to accept Boyan's "private life." She stopped exercising and doing her make-up, she stopped crying secretly, and started snacking instead. When the eros is gone, food remains the only joy available. And the children, of course. But the children had already their own lives and Maria remained alone, alone with her joyless life.

Then Boyan's money ran out, his salary never seemed to be paid all at once and on time, and money started running short in their household. But Maria would find a way, again. After spending six hours at school, after shopping for groceries, after cooking (duck ribs, the delicacy of that hungry time, or bean stew), after washing and cleaning, Maria sat at the sewing machine doing piecework until dawn—endless piles of skirts. Stitch and cut, turn and stitch, cut. Her hands were shaking, her eyes were watery. Besides total exhaustion, there was a new, unfamiliar rage building up in her pure soul. But she took it out on the skirts—stitch, stitch, stiiiitch! They had to get through the month, didn't they, she had to pay the electricity bill, the central heating bill, she had to buy new shoes for her son whose toes were bleeding because the old ones were too small for him, and he was braving it out so he wouldn't worry her, she had to send some money to her daughter in college, and in addition to the jars of food, she had to repay Boyan's debts and his endless "business trips" without daily allowances. Boyan had been borrowing money from family friends and from her relatives. Who was going to pay for all that if not her? Stitch!!!

In the meantime, Boyan's innocent lies and fantasies were growing like a giant sticky ball of hair that dragged the whole world in its course. It left behind a strangely distorted world with no complications, ugly and unethical, maybe, but true and even human stories of cheating, love, and sex. Boyan's stories told of a weird and frightening world, in which Boyan was shining as a secret agent who saved political leaders from assassination, as a national expert-engineer forestalling huge breakdowns of vital national industries, as a responsible heir cultivating the land of his forebears that was finally restored to him, as a wonderful old friend helping his one-time buddies build their houses, as a caring nephew who couldn't take care of his own mother but spent weeks by the bed of his dying aunt. All in all, this world demanded Boyan's presence and salary for many years. At first Maria felt uncomfortable listening to those fantasies for the umpteenth time, laughing nervously, faking admiration or indignation, again and again, whenever she was supposed to. Then she grew used it. She had the vague feeling that what was going on was very wrong, deep inside herself she felt like the victim of a peculiar kind of harassment, of some kind of rape. As if she was a rag cloth Boyan used to wipe away the filthy wet dreams of his sick consciousness, his inferiority complexes, his lust, his guilt, the evil he had inside. But what could she do? Could she manage Boyan's anger if she told him he was lying? Could she defend herself and the children? Where could she go—Boyan had said, numerous times, that he "won't budge from his home." "His home," the apartment which, according to one of his fantasies was given to him personally by some party grandee for "significant contributions." Maria had long forgiven him that lie, too, in order to preserve his male dignity and, most importantly, to keep off his anger. But if Boyan would stay in their home, where would she go? And the children? How was she going to pay rent with her teacher's salary and the piles of skirts? How was she going to support two kids in college? And how was it possible to leave? Maria couldn't imagine it. A woman can't do that. A woman can't do that to her kids, can't deprive them of their father.

And so, little by little, Maria stopped thinking. She buried away her bewilderment at Boyan's monstrous metamorphosis, her shock at the face of his madness, her rag-cloth humiliation, her exhaustion as a single mother and housekeeper, and the grief she felt for her botched-up life. She gradually forgot how wretched she was. She forgot her disgust. She totally forgot what was true and what wasn't. That way it didn't hurt so much. She had to take care of her health, for the sake of her children . . . And for Boyan—wasn't she supposed to unconditionally support her superman, wasn't she supposed to believe in him and remain, unconditionally, at his side. She obeyed Boyan, she exclaimed, she sighed, she laughed at appropriate moments, she was embarrassed, when Boyan's naughty eyes expected her participation.

Besides, she was terrified of loneliness. As solitary as a cuckoo bird. The thought of meeting another man seemed to Maria even crazier than Boyan's dramas. And, all in all, things seemed *almost* normal—they had a normal family, Boyan had a job, he didn't drink, he didn't beat her up, he wasn't an abusive husband, or so Maria reminded herself. So what, she'll just sew a few things at home, the times were hard anyway. Even if there was another woman, a younger woman, or a few of them, that was normal as well, right? She had just grown old. Men can't be with just one woman, right?, especially when that woman has aged. Men need sex, and she was obviously no longer good for that. Boyan had not touched her in years. And yet, she was yearning for him to touch her, she was yearning for him to kiss her. Oh, what was this nonsense going through her senile brain, the fifty-year-old Maria reacted with a sad smile.

Once, when she inadvertently caught Boyan red-handed, she was terribly sorry, and so embarrassed she even apologized, but he just couldn't come up with yet another whopping, hairy lie, so he just told her that these were minor things, mere trifles to "boost his male confidence." Indeed, how could she boost his male confidence, having grown old and ugly? Men needed *male* confidence, there was no point being jealous, she was trying to comfort herself. But her body clearly did not agree, because Maria threw up in the toilet. She kept this secret from Boyan of course. But it was only a tummy spasm, so what?!

It had never occurred to Maria to imagine how Boyan would have reacted and how he would have felt if they exchanged places. Another thought floated up to the surface sometimes. "Has Boyan ever loved me?" Maria asked herself. "Of course he's loved me," she quickly reassured herself. "It's just that our life was difficult, such a struggle with deprivation, there was no time for romance. We didn't even have our own bedroom, just a bedroom, just for us, never. When that was possible I was already too old for Boyan . . ."

But at the end of the day, this shall pass, Maria sometimes thought sagely, it shall pass like a river. They would grow old, i.e., Boyan would grow old, too. Those passions would subside and everything would seem like a bad dream. Boyan would realize that he couldn't live without her, that he needed her—not just as somebody to listen to him and believe his stories but as someone to take care of him, with his smoking habit and his bad heart . . . somebody to cook and clean for him, and do his washing. But he knew all that, right?, that's why he stayed. Sooner or later, those *good, real* things will have their day, Maria would sigh with all-forgiving faith. God is not energy and constants, my stupid boy, she would talk to Boyan in her mind. God is forgiveness, the good inside us. Boyan would return to the good, eventually, when he grows old and wise . . . She loved Boyan unconditionally with all her heart, from the first moment, when he asked her to help him with that exam, and she would love him forever—her first and only man.

Besides, the One above saw it all and He knew what to do, Maria sometimes thought with a faint sense of spite. But what was she expecting?! Some revenge?! She, Micheto, the rape child who had ruined her mother's life, the rape child who had killed her mother?! She did not deserve anything. She was born to be a servant, to take care, to listen, to seek justification for every moment of her existence, let's not forget that. She should be happy for what she had—her health, and the kids! Those good and intelligent kids God had given her! But why did it turn out like that for them? Why? Maria wondered. Boyan had not raised a hand to her, but that was probably only because he had no reason to—she never contradicted him, never expressed any disbelief! But he did hit the children, especially the girl . . . Because the son had grown tall and big, and once he grabbed his father's arm and told him . . . something. And then, Boyan never raised a hand at him again. The children did not believe him, they laughed at him and blamed him. They even told him to go away. Lord! No! No way! My children . . . silly children! Especially the daughter. What did this little minx know about woman's life?! A poetess! Life is no poetry, my dear! And Boyan was right in many cases—kids were supposed to study, and have discipline. Their daughter should not dress up and paint her face like a hooker, because that's what people would think she was, and she was not one, right?! Or . . . ?! Children should obey their parents, they should respect them and never talk back. Just like she had respected her father. Children should trust their father. As she trusted Boyan. And they should be more forgiving when he . . . exaggerates a little, that's all, just to boost his confidence. And even so, why did it turn out like this with the children? Maria wondered. Didn't she do everything for them? Why did they hate their father so? And talk with her ever less often. Then their father loves them. He fought for them to exist, the both of them! He's just spiky, they shouldn't annoy him. And she . . . she lives for them! And for the grandkids! Forgive him, children. Forgive me as well. Don't kill your father with your hatred! Leave him be, children. Leave us be, children. Go on your way. Forget, forget everything, just like me, and leave. You have a future, you have your own lives. I don't have a future, I have nowhere to go, I have no other life, I am left to look after your father, this is my husband, my only husband, I love him . . .

Years ago, Boyan had forbidden Maria to go to her father's place, to cook and clean for him, to help Katya. He'd said that "that idiot" did not deserve Maria "grinding herself down." He'd started caring about her all of a sudden. In fact, he was jealously making sure he didn't have to share his carer with anyone. Because, while his father-in-law was slowly dying, Boyan had to undergo major heart surgery, and after that he seemed to settle down, at home, which hadn't happened in many years. But it only lasted until he had fully recovered and started smoking again. In these months Maria was totally exhausted, taking care of two men, shrinking with fear that Boyan might die. She managed. Maria overcame everything. Yet this was the first time when she . . . no, she didn't rebel against Boyan, but she disobeyed him silently. She had a filial duty to honor, too. At least, to her father, after she could not do it for her mother . . . And despite everything. So, she thought, her children also had a filial duty. By the way, why the Bulgarian word for "filial" means only son's duty—what if there are no sons, or if it's mostly the daughters who honor it?

As the years rolled by, all hopes and joys withered. With death approaching, desires were drying up and all goals and roles were losing their point. Parents could try making their children and grandchildren's goals their own but even the pride and joy with the success of the offspring are somehow sad and weary. There is no own future anymore, no faith in something that was yet to come in your own life. The only goal is to keep the body going for another day, another month. To eat well, to sleep. The horizon is tomorrow, few months, "next year, God willing, next year till the final trumpet."

The years passed by, all the pains and tragedies distanced themselves in time, diminished and faded in Maria's memory like some far-away stories that seemed to concern other people. Then they just disappeared without a trace, as if forgotten forever.

Boyan and Maria were keeping a more or less a brave face in their retirement. Boyan had finally grown old. He was often short of breath, and had to measure his blood sugar more often, and drink handfuls of pills. Up until a year or two ago he had kept smoking, heavily, it was the only thing he was doing with some residual trace of passion. Then, after a heart attack, he had to quit if he wanted to "live a little longer." His last affair was only platonic and his feelings were rather paternal. He had moved into virtual reality lock, stock, and barrel. Facebook provided him with an unthinkable audience, a virgin audience that knew nothing about him, so he could take up any role he wanted. Boyan would recount his exploits and adventures, he would hand out advice and voice his opinions on all political, scientific, existential, and aesthetic matters, he would send friendship requests to good-looking women and girls he would later proceed to regale with paternal advice.

Unspurred by his dead sexual drive, relieved of any expectations about "tomorrow" and when he was not on Facebook, Boyan would sometimes think about the past. It was a time for retrospection, a time for humility, for "the real things" after all "the fallacies of the body, of youth, ambition, vanity, and greed." Morality was so much easier when old age had made immorality impossible. His mind was so merciful and ready to correct the past—deleting the faded shadows of things he didn't want to remember, and he could not even remember "exactly." The things he had said were so numerous and so incredible that he couldn't even keep track. His memory embellished and exaggerated, with melodramatic poignancy, distorting every bit of the past that was not irrevocably screwed. What was this about, hidden guilt or lurking despair? "Wasn't it all supposed to mean something, for fuck's sake, and even look beautiful," Boyan swore under his breath.

Maria was relieved at the silence that had finally descended upon their home, and she was silently thanking Facebook for it, although she had no idea what Facebook was, exactly. Facebook was good as well for keeping Boyan's mind busy and dementia away, she thought. Maria knew nothing about computers, she didn't have an email account, she could barely operate her obsolete, ten-year-old Nokia.

Thanks to Facebook and Boyan's old age, Maria could reside, fully and firmly in the reality inhabited most importantly by her children and grandchildren. Sometimes, on her excursions in this real world, Maria would pass through the city park or take a two-hour flight, and then she'd sit on a bench or rest her head on the seat and think. The filthy waters finally seemed to be gone and Maria, who had not strayed an inch from her virtuous pose by the river, finally seemed to have awaited the triumph of those real things and the Good. Like almost any other woman, Maria had spent her life in mindless practicality so those rare bench or airplane moments were her only existential wake-up calls. Maria was searching for some kind of purpose to her existence. And she couldn't find it. She tried to find it in her children's existence but she was eating herself up for having wanted to abort them. And the children had their own lives, whereas she was left to live her own. She tried to find sense in love, but that love was long gone. If there had been love at all. That erotic kind of love. For the rest, she had loved her mother, her sister, her children. She tried to find this damn sense in her grandchildren, taking care of them, selflessly, loving them even more than she loved her kids. But as she rocked them on her lap she was fully aware that her own life was over. That maybe she hadn't had a life of her own at all. That the years had rolled by, imperceptibly, between work and naps, and taking care of stuff. And it didn't seem to have any purpose at all. Any meaning after all. It was only her duty and her love tracing her way. Maria couldn't think of anything beyond that. She would fulfill her duty to the end. But well, she had to run; this was no time to mull over things.

Maria was going to do all the shopping, cleaning, washing, cooking, and caring for Boyan, all the sick, all the grandchildren, the great grandchildren even, and only then, when everything was done and nobody needed her anymore, she would depart without even realizing.

But before that would happen, one day her daughter handed her . . . a letter.

"A letter? For me? But I'm here, right, we are together every day," Maria wondered in confusion, turning the fat envelope in her hands.

Maria was startled, and her heart skipped a few beats. The daughter must have been digging in the past, but it was all bygones for Maria, all gone and forgotten. Why would this darn girl want to stir the grief and the fear instead of living her life? The daughter must surely be invading her father's fantasy world, too—so she'd rip apart his theatrical props with her sharp mind and her hate. Maria was deeply afraid of that—that would kill Boyan! Oh, let's pray the daughter does not ask her to show that letter to Boyan. But deep inside Maria was even more scared by her daughter's verdict on herself and her life. Oh, pray that it's nothing like that, that it's only some sort of poetries again.

Dear Mom,

I've been writing this letter for the last thirty years.

I started when Nana died. I don't know if I've told you, but eight or nine months before she died Nana was asking herself, aloud, "Is dying hard?" And I was there, listening. I think that Nana had decided to die . . . My nana. My nana who had told me about Sundays and resurrection, who'd shown me the apples and the letters of the alphabet, who'd read to me about faraway places, who'd told me about the September uprising. In a way, she substituted you. Because you were always busy, somehow mute in my memory. My nana . . . whom you spent twenty years bathing, and walking on your arm, whom you took care of to her very last breath. This was the first death I was seeing up close. It was disgusting. I was so sorry for you. I was not so sorry now for Nana. My nana had already gone. I was blaming myself for wanting her to die sooner so this horrible agony would be over, this endless humiliation of the flesh, and most importantly this hell on earth you were going through. [. . .]

But, Mom, if you didn't exist, me and my brother would not be here either, right? And neither would your grandchildren. No, don't get me wrong—I don't excuse the violence. Your existence, and mine, and that of my brother, the existence of your grandchildren is no excuse for violence. It's something else I've been trying to say. It's very weird to know that you might not exist, right? We both have good reasons to think about it. The narrative of one's delivery into this world is rather peculiar. It is very weird, indeed, to be aware that you've come to existence by pure chance and it was more than likely that you wouldn't exist. It's also very weird that we're given the ability to recognize that. But you know what's weirder—the fact that all people are like that.

Just think about it—if you hadn't met my father, if you'd met some other man, if you'd gotten pregnant a month later than that fateful June, if you'd been impregnated by another one of my father's spermatozoids, if . . . Every person is the product of chance and chaos. Love is just an illusion, a very beautiful one indeed, and very powerful as well, still an illusion that makes us believe that our beloved people and our children have been pre-destined for us, that they are unique; it makes us believe that the fruit of chaos is the fruit of love. And when one variation among billions is em-bodied in your child—we get to love this child as something one-of-a-kind, unique, unlike any other, a child created with the Other who couldn't be any other. And maybe that's happiness—to accept what blind chaos has taken out of the starry bag for you as something you have chosen and desired yourself, to love it as if it was unique.

From this point of view violence and the misery it brings can only unmask that chaos and our illusions.

I've been thinking that rape is not just a criminal offence or a war crime, it is also an existential crime. The law takes into consideration the violated women and the community that has been de-generated with foreign seed. Nobody gives a thought to the human being that was born as a result of rape, about his or her mind. A person like that is not just the fruit of chance like everybody else but also someone created by animal instinct, hate, violence and terror. He or she is denied the only consolation of being made with love, of being wanted, of being the particular baby chosen among the chaos of billions and billions of possibilities.

You have studied higher mathematics and fundamental physics, right? So you have surely talked about the theory of relativity. The temporal paradox, according to which it is theoretically-mathematically possible to go back to the past and kill your own grandfather, thereby canceling your own existence, thus the opportunity of killing the old man, was created by men, as was the whole of science, more or less. That's why the only scenario played out is the murder of the grandfather, that patriarch. How Freudian! Boys killing their fathers and falling in love with their mothers. From a male point of view the mother is certain and cannot be any other. But what happens if she has been raped? Or had an affair? Or an abortion? You don't need to kill your grandfather to cancel your existence.

Our existence is not a mission. There is no mission, Mom, there is no purpose. There's no one "up there." The "One above" is blind, deaf, amnesiac, and demented. Don't count on him. He did not "know" the Woman, he has no idea what a woman's life is like, what's taking place "down there," in the "lower stratum of the human existence," called life. He did not read the notes in the margins of his sacred texts and the footnotes to life. He was "immaculately conceived." Only men can come up with such a "miracle" and call it that. Your female essence was literally scraped out of you by your deeply religious father and the same "One" above. They wanted to make you completely immaculate. And they did succeed, in a sense. [. . .]

It was only years later that I realized why you'd reacted to my first menstruation—my metamorphosis into a woman—with such resentment bordering on revulsion. Why you hadn't explained anything, you hadn't prepared me, so I thought I was sick (cancer of course, there was so much cancer in our family) and dying. You gave me the feeling that menstruation started my shameful and miserable fate of woman. I realized why you'd strained your eyes sewing clothes for me, as your mother had done for you, but you'd never told me I was pretty or, God forbid, that I was sexy. Why we'd never seen eye to eye, as women, why we'd never been friends, why you'd never talked to me as a woman, never given me any womanly advice. For you, there had always been something shameful and mostly hurtful about femininity and sex, and you didn't think a woman's life was anything but fear, shame, pain, obedience, hard work, and trouble.

I realized why you hadn't been happy but rather disappointed when I told you I was pregnant. You didn't want anything from anyone but you were very hard to please when it came to me. You were much happier to hear about the exams that I'd taken, the competitions I'd won, or about my successes at work than about my marriages and my pregnancies. And yet, it was never enough. You always expected more, and better, as if I had to compensate for being a woman, for having children, for having wasted time, opportunity and gray matter on men and kids. I should have become a corresponding member of the world academy, a general director of the world, or at least a Nobel laureate in literature so I could compensate for your sacrifices, and not repeat them. In my relationship with you I've been taking an endless PhD. I had to behave like a man in order to be . . . human, a human outside motherhood and marriage . . .

I understand now why you didn't comfort me, why you stayed dumb when that secret service agent raped me when I was at college. I filed a complaint at the police station but this only resulted in me being labeled a "loose girl" and being subjected to another agent's attempts to use my vulnerability and "guilt" to turn me into a state "escort" for high-profile foreigners from the capitalist West. The local policeman came to my place at night to check if "the loose girl" was at home and try to take advantage of my helplessness. I was running and hiding like a convict . . . Thank God, I didn't get pregnant. And even if that had happened, the times had changed—there were pills and legal abortions available. But you remained silent and indifferent even when my father blamed me for what had happened. Were these rapes our family karma?

And the violence . . . Granddad Rusan experienced terrible violence at the hands of those same "comrades." Yes, that violence wasn't sexual but I don't know what's worse—having your feet squeezed in an iron vice, being forbidden to work and then dying of cancer, or being raped. My father did not realize that he himself was raped by communism, that he'd gotten pregnant and given birth to monsters—those pathological lies, manias, fears, aggression, and complexes. #Me Too . . . Only the socio-economic conditions and the regime were different. No one was exempt from violence—neither women nor men, neither the young, nor the elderly. [. . .]

I was dying to hear what you really thought! What you really felt. I wanted to hear you say it without fear or shame. I wanted to hear you scream and rebel, demand and curse, and refuse to go on living like that. I wanted you to claim yourself. And refuse to perform all your "duties." To fall in love, to get drunk, to stop caring, to be cruel for once. To go back to your talent in mathematics. To work on your talent to sew—not hundreds of two-leva skirts but designer clothes that would be your own, unique, sophisticated and . . . sexy. How I yearned for a mother like that! A mother I could talk to. Talk about anything—boys and men, sex and protection, love and disappointment, pregnancies, births, babies, but also about the creation of that new person, not just the practicalities of raising kids (in poverty), about books and ideas, about money and professions, art and music, mathematics and philosophy, about meaning and the lack of it . . . Until I realized that there was no such Maria, that this Maria had been killed long, long ago. You always had a choice. But I'm not sure that there was a human being in you who could exercise her right to choose. And then, I gradually became a mother to you. [. . .]

You always had a choice. But I'm not sure that there was inside you a human being with intelligence, feelings and dignity, that could exercise that right to choose. [. . .]

I was growing up, and I wanted to be everything you weren't. Self-formation in opposition is a kind of deformation. I am deformed. [. . .]

I have something to ask from you. Something very important not just for me, but for us, women. I want to start up women's chronicles—let this be the working title of this "project." I want every woman in our family line to tell the story of herself and her life in these chronicles. This shouldn't be a text written in the course of a day. I, for one, have spent a long time thinking what I would write. And I can see it changing through time. As one isn't supposed to celebrate her fortieth birthday, or that's what people say, which I take to mean that you have to tiptoe quietly around fate, on my fortieth birthday I didn't have a party but wrote down the first version of my chapter in these chronicles. I reread it recently, I revised a lot of things, and I added more.

I have written down Nana's memories. She knew nothing about it, of course, but back then I had no idea why I was doing it—I just didn't want to forget them, and I wanted to write them down exactly the way she'd told them. I was very keen on "interviewing" Aunt Katya. I never thought I should have done it so early, that the last time I would see her alive she would be unable to talk. I missed auntie . . . And I know next to nothing about her life.

And here I get to you, Mom. I'm asking you to tell me about your life—your personal account, in your own words, through your eyes, your heart, and your mind. If you want to speak, I'll be your scribe. If you'd prefer, you can write it down. I can already hear you protesting that these are all abstract things, "poetries" and that you are simply "not good at things like that," that you can't "express yourself beautifully," etc. Please, wait, hold off with the labels, and hold off with your refusal. Allow me to try and convince you that my "project" has a point.

You see, the only people who get to "go down in history" are the ones who have done something big and important. Ordinary folks, like you and me, and everyone around us, may leave children and grandchildren in whose memories they live on for some time, but after a generation or two everything is lost and forgotten. In the best case, there are a few pictures and somebody still would know who's who on them. Or, as was the case in the past, a family Bible with handwritten notes that say when somebody was born or died. Sort of genealogical trees. Gravestones—just the name and the dates. Which matter least. This meagre, empty biographical data, or silent photos, this is not what should remain behind us. I want content, words, in first person singular!

We leave our genes to our children but this is biology, not mind and spirit. By the way, I've been reading lately that genes are just like computer data. But even so, they don't pass along our stories, our experience, our past. Ideally, as Nana did, we can pass on some stories to our children. But this is like playing Telephone, everybody would recount what he or she has understood. Besides, I notice that younger generations, especially kids and teenagers, have increasingly shorter memories; they are not interested in the past, they live increasingly in the here and now. Or perhaps all young people are like that, all young people have always been like that. Maybe one needs to accumulate some own past to get interested in the past of the others.

There's something else. God, Allah, Buddha, and their ilk are all men. The Word is male. It's been all men writing on those family Bibles and the ecclesiastic books. Men have been writing, as well, that "great historical narrative." But the woman spends much more time actually . . . living, that mundane, every day, non-historical, non-aesthetical, non-cosmic life. Which is the life of the ordinary little person. That is to say, of 99% of people, who leave nothing behind and whose existence seems to me quite pointless.

I know what you will say here: "Yeah, precisely because I'm an ordinary little person, my life is boring and banal and not worth being told." Or "I don't want to leave memories of ugly and painful things." Or "I don't want to share things that are so intimate." Please, Mom! Please try. We, women, provide the most authentic view over the little, ordinary human, the fabric of everyday life in the curtains of history, the non-aestheticized truth in the grand human narrative.

Our chronicles and your "chapter" won't be a book that has to appeal to any kind of readers. I don't want us retouched and beautified, nor do I want us typified and deformed into literary characters. I don't want us raising ourselves any "immaterial monuments." I want us to be alive. And true. So, please, be free and most importantly sincere. Don't think about what's proper and good, or wrong and bad, don't censor yourself, nobody's gonna judge and reproach you, nobody's gonna laugh at you. This isn't a test with right and wrong answers. It's not a report on your virtuous life. Don't worry about how you'll write it, either.

It doesn't need to be a piece of literary excellence. Write it the way you speak, the way you'd write a letter to me. As far as the intimate, contradictory bits are concerned, there's nothing to be ashamed of. You can be certain that it's just as individual as it is universally human, or rather universally female. And let's leave it to our great-granddaughters to say if our women's chronicles are interesting and important and whether they would like to add their own chapters.

I could use your story and turn it into literature. But that is something different—I'll be making things up, twisting plotlines, overlapping other women's stories; this is going to be literature, not your authentic voice. Unlike my own chapter in our chronicles, which inevitably would be told from the point of view of my august emergence into this world, in the book that I may write one day, I will be a writer, you will be a prototype, and the point of view would be quite different.

Tell about your first childhood memories, about your grandmother, about your mother, about aunt Katya. What kind of child were you? What games did you play? How would you spend a day in the village? How about a day in Plovdiv? What did it mean to be poor in your time? What did you eat, what did you wear? What did you think about your parents? Did you love them? What does it mean for you to love? Did you like making love? If not, why? What feelings did motherhood bring for you? Was there anything you didn't like or love about your kids and grandkids? What did you think and feel as you were going through menopause? What talents did you have? What were your strong subjects? What did you like doing best? And what did you hate doing the most? What are your regrets? What would you change about your life if you could? When were you the happiest? And when were you the unhappiest? What were you most afraid of? Was there a moment when you were in such despair that you wanted to die? And was there a beautiful moment when you wished that time would stop? What are the books that have touched you deeply? What are your favorite songs, your classical music of choice? What historical events did you witness? What did you think about them? Do you remember what bright hopes you had for the future when you were twenty, thirty, forty? Where do you see the meaning of your life? What do you think, does life have a meaning at all, and if yes, what is it? Are you scared of death? How do you want to pass away? What do you think you'll leave behind? Is there a particular story you remember and want to tell? . . .

I want us to start writing ourselves, us women, to start writing our own story, to tell our own past, to recount personally about our world and times. I don't know if your unadulterated tale or my literature would bring some light into the dark women's chronicles. Perhaps the only light is in the words themselves, the words that will preserve the memory of these women, of our mothers and grandmothers, of childless aunts, the memory of us. Without our words, without our stories we remain some kind of fading biological sequence of nonsenses.

I want this chronicle to be passed on from woman to woman only, I want it to follow the closest blood (should I say genetic) line possible, I have considered all possible scenarios and permissible detours from the straight, direct female line if there are no female children in a certain generation. I couldn't think of anything in case one generation has no kids whatsoever or those kids decide to change their gender. In that case, I suppose, these chronicles will either cease to be, or they'll cease to be strictly women's and family histories . . .

SHE, HE, IT, THEY

Men and women differ in how they think about and experience time and death. Or at least that is dictated by men and biology. A woman is supposed to only inhabit biological and diurnal time. Both of these dimensions, however, do not involve true linear time because they are cyclical, circular. Women are placed—like hens about to lay their eggs—within the coop of biological, natural time. As nature dies in winter and comes to life in spring in the new shoots, in the "snowy blossoms" of the cherry trees, in the newborn animals, so a woman gives birth to the life that will replace the dying human reeds. In this pastoral-biological idyll the woman is exempt from existential fear because she, you see, has already fulfilled herself and will live forever on a biological level. Yet, woman is not more immortal than man just because she is able to create spring. Nested in biology and her day-to-day life, a woman becomes "un-aware" of her own human, existential time. And she stops being aware of herself as a human being.

To eliminate the last shades of human anxiety, woman is positioned inside the daily routine, the time of day-to-day chores where she can forget about the ticking of her own human clock, busy as she is raising the new reed sprouts until they're strong enough, in breeding the little hatchlings until they fly away. In this diurnal time she must manage to do a lot of things (most often simultaneously, which is what the exalted multitasking is all about). All that repetitive, circular everyday life leaves no traces at all. The child-wanderers grow up and leave, raised well or not that well, aware or unaware of the stories that a woman often has no time to tell. The *daily* kind of cooking leaves behind no memories, just wastewater. All that everyday life is dedicated to survival, not existence.

Nature has taken care of the "expedient" modeling of the female brain. The fundamental, in my view, results of a serious scientific study were not popularized, or discussed. I've read a brief review in a reliable but not really academic journal. It turns out that, with every pregnancy, the number of brain cells (neurons) in a female brain would diminish. The researchers were quick to provide the solace that this didn't mean women would become any dumber; it was just a case of their brains reorganizing themselves in regard to the new functions that would follow. The number of brain cells might be smaller but there were new connections (synapses) being built, ones that were *supposed* to benefit *emotional* intelligence, empathy, social skills, pragmatic thinking, networking and all those virtues of daily life, sociability, and care. I thought that there was no way this wouldn't have an evolutionary effect. That is, if hundreds of generations of women have been losing brain cells by becoming mothers, the theory of evolution would suggest that there would be more and more smaller-brained girls being born. And, indeed, the bulk of contemporary research suggests that there is a difference both in the volume of male and female brains and in the cognitive abilities of the two sexes, especially in their capacity for *abstract* thought. It turns out that this important difference is a result of the woman's biological function.

The apple is a rather peculiar symbol. The androgynous creature that Eve of Eden had once been was punished by becoming a woman, a woman seen and defined by man only, not because of her knowledge of good and evil, not because she had discovered the Eros but because she reached for cognition and consciousness, because she wanted to become a *human.* And her punishment was not just having to give birth in pain but having her organ of cognition and consciousness castrated, being chained to her function of providing biological reproduction and survival. Science and knowledge and, most importantly, consciousness, human condition, the stars, the Cosmos, human existential time, its aesthetics and its tragedy—generally everything outside biology, everything linked with abstract thought and spirit—remained reserved for man. The sky was offered to him, and women had to make do with earth and reeds. Woman was purposefully "formatted," her superfluous "programs" were systematically deleted and she was supplied with extra "memory" for the basic operational programs. So her brain has been diminished first, by genotype, and second, by her becoming a mother.

The biological castration of consciousness, abstract thinking, existential anxiety and the kind of elements of the human condition and Being takes the edge off her suicidal impulse. Somebody has to live, right? Somebody has to live in joy and dedication so *she* can raise the next generation of reeds and be a guarantor for the biological survival. This is pure Darwin. This explains why suicidal motives in women are so different from suicidal motives in men. Men take their own lives mostly when they're depressed or they see no point in existence (and they succeed in their attempts more often than women do). Women approach death (often theatrically) mostly when they can't, for one reason or another, nod off into the happy comfort of love and fulfilled femininity.

The human being in woman is hostage to biology. The big legal fight on the right to abortion, and on reproductive rights in general, is, in essence, a fight for woman to be a recognized as human being, not only as biological instrument for reproduction.[89]

Only fifty to sixty years ago women ventured away from home. Once outside, in society, it was logical for her to claim the right to vote, to study at university, to receive equal pay for her work. But the most important right for the female individual is her right to contraception and abortion. That's how a woman gnaws through the umbilical cord which was keeping her in nature's bosom. Contraception and abortion highlighted the human in the woman who had choices as opposed to the biology of the woman who had duties. They freed woman in erotic plan and gave her agency.

It is no accident that in more conservative, patriarchal, and religious societies, in which the discourse is utterly male, pills and abortion are condemned as something against God's natural order, something that contradicts a woman's role and duties. It might seem paradoxical at first, but some advanced democracies have come very close to sharing this view with primitive societies.

A man can become a father even in old age. The patriarch however would be short of time to look after his child. He doesn't want this, anyhow, it's woman's work. A poet friend, with a poetical smack, wrote that a man needs nothing other than to sow his oats. A Lolita, an Aisha, who is just twelve or thirteen, can bear and deliver a child and sadly in many cultures, this biological possibility is still the norm and not a crime.

I guess these biological confinements and evolutionary "formatting," as well as the social construction of woman by man, which is examined further on, explain the fact that there are very few women physicists, mathematicians, astronomers, computer programmers, composers, theologists, and philosophers. All these require high level of abstract thinking, human consciousness and existentialist quest, as well as

89 It shall be stressed that even viable fetuses, not to mention unviable ones, are not yet human *beings*.

freedom of the spirit and self-confidence to participate in the grand narrative of the human being.

In this context, one story comes to my mind. Mileva Marić-Einstein. She had graduated a male-only secondary school, she was the only woman among her future husband Einstein's alumni at Zürich Polytechnic and, by then, the second woman ever to have finished the full program of study at the Department of Mathematics and Physics. To start with, she must have been extraordinarily intelligent to overcome the restrictions on the admission of women. Mileva abandoned the couple's first child (a girl, by the way) . . . no, not for the sake of some academic career of her own, but simply because she chose to be with the beloved father Albert instead. For the father did not like pregnant women and children, he considered these too burdensome and distracting, in particular the children, who, in his view, were woman's exclusive responsibility. The Nobel Prize premium, which the scientist gave to his—by then—ex-wife, did not make up for his complete absence in raising his two sons, for Mileva's loneliness as mother and primary carer of their sick son, for his numerous affairs and divorce, for his treating Mileva as a mere domestic servant, or worse—some inferior, sub-human creature.[90] Despite the numerous proofs and testimonies, including from Einstein himself, the question if and to what extent Mileva had contributed to the scientific achievements of her husband is still open to debate.[91] What is indisputable is the fact that motherhood and (unhappy) marriage put an irreversible, definitive end to Mileva's academic endeavors, returning her into a mother and housewife.

As I have been trying to write and write about time, death, and the Cosmos (of all things), it turns out that the existentially human part of me has *survived* the *birth* of my two children and my turning into a mother. I am undoubtedly getting dumber, for one reason or another, but it seems I haven't lost the right brain cells or I haven't lost all of them. By the way, when my daughter broke the tense silence of the delivery room and the doctor told me "It's a girl," I started crying louder than the baby—I had given birth to another woman whose first and foremost function would be biological. Besides, her crying was a sign that my own countdown, in my linear human time, had begun. When my second child was growing inside me, I was contemplat-

90 And that is well documented.

91 The main argument of those opposing it is the lack of written evidence for Mileva's scientific ideas. Never mind that she had spent endless evenings and nights working together and discussing them with Albert. Which is one more argument for women to leave written traces of their *essays*, thoughts and experience, even only in the margins of the official corpus or in letters.

ing my abdomen in amazement, as if there was something alien in there, something using my body, the body that I, in a sense, had forever forfeited as something that was mine and mine only, as part of myself.

My two kids were sweet, fragrant and huggable babies that I loved to sniff with animal delight, and squeeze in my arms, and look at with abandon. Yet, they were much more interesting to me when they grew up a little. They are not only my children that I love unconditionally as a mother, and I am not just their mother. Besides, life turned out so I had to be both a father and a mother to them, I had to look at the stars with them—and also wipe their bottoms.

Motherhood, the desire to give birth to a child, to have a child, is probably rather instinctive, pre-programmed by nature. Motherhood has brought me feelings and sensations that nothing and nobody else could give me. In this sense motherhood has enriched me. However, my biological function did not fill me with rapture or pride, it didn't bring me the feeling of being accomplished as a *person*, as a *human being*. Being a mother did not reassure me that I would live *forever* in and through my children, it did not soothe my existential fear of running time, of death, and my pointlessness under the starry sky.

My biological function brought me down to the level of biology, it brought me back to the "lap of nature." There's no human consciousness in nature. Brainless unconscious biological matter passes from one state into another, it gives birth, dies and is resurrected in an osmotic cycle. The tearful pathos of brainless nature being reborn, with all those melting snows, young sprouts, pollinating bees, and newborn mammals getting licked and breastfed fills me only with hopelessness. The brainless, unconscious and impersonal renewal of nature might amount to immortality, *biological* immortality, but it's also an absence of time. Plants and animals know nothing about the Universe and death, they don't have a consciousness, including of themselves. They don't know they will die. They might be able to sense forthcoming death, but only as a biological instinct for survival. Wolves howl at the full moon, animals become restless when an earthquake is about to start, horses go mad before the clash with another planet.[92] Animals and plants have no consciousness. They have instincts—of reproduction and survival.

We are exaggerating when we say "animalistic terror." There is no bigger or truer terror than the one experienced by humans. A human being looks differently at the starry sky, and thinks of death beyond the immediate threat or the physical pain, awakening the instincts.

92 I'm referring to Lars von Trier's movie *Melancholia*.

As man has denied and forfeited the human in woman, he is left alone in the dark terrifying room inside himself, assuming that it is his and his only. Sometimes he steps, secretly, into the dark, opens the roof of his secret observatory, and looks up at the sky, shivering with fear and melancholy.

They say, or more precisely men say, that woman has no such personal, dark room, that she dedicates herself fully and thoroughly to love, to the Other and the others. Whereas man is not completely devoted when it comes to love and eroticism. That's why he condescendingly reduces those things to weakness and sin or demonizes them as something unbalancing his strength, reason and power, or praising them, magnanimously, as something that has an ennobling effect on him. Yet, man never describes love and eroticism as existential categories, as something that can manifest and fulfill him as a human being.

The "equation" of man and woman complementing each other, established by man, does not comprise reason, knowledge and the Universe, the existential, consciousness and philosophy, time and death, the aesthetic, creation and epiphany—they remain in a separate, male-only axiom, or observatory, to which woman is an outsider; woman allegedly does not understand all this and can add nothing to it; at best, woman is an inspiring star, marveled from the observatory telescope.

They say a man can imagine himself and the world without a woman while a woman cannot imagine herself without a man. Her life, as this narrative goes, is made valuable by man, by being *chosen*, picked out by him. So, man is supposed to think about the Cosmos, while the Cosmos of a woman is . . . man.[93] Well . . . I must say that there's no man who could fill up my view of the sky. Some produced only temporary eclipses, while also clouding my "pure reason" and my logical abilities. And there has been just one man who would sit by my side, our tired bodies left to rest, and look with me at the starry sky so together we would be less scared.

According to the traditional narrative, written and recounted by men, the erotic impulse, the cathexis, is a prerogative of men, the so-called hunter, while woman is a victim, prey, trophy, or in not such a bloody image, the erotic object, a receptacle that is expected to only respond, or not, to the man's call. In this game the woman is more interested in love and man's long term investment in the relationship and, in particular, in raising "the fruit" of that relationship. Man promises love to get sex while

93 According to Berdyaev (1874-1948)—a Russian religious and philosophical thinker, whose ideas, no wonder, are so dear to Putin.

woman provides sex to get love. As an object of ownership and submission in this discourse, and given her prime biological role, woman is simply not supposed to have her own, subjective and independent erotic impulse. For woman eroticism cannot be mere sexual pleasure or a way to know and communicate with the Other. By virtue of this "natural" order, man defines and exalts woman as *naturally* monogamous, amorous, selfless, static, and reliable Penelope. Noble and sacred unlike "sinful" Man, who is polygynous "by nature." And all those "raging feminists" competing with men or taking their ugly revenge on them in the erotic realm are doing nothing but destroying their femininity. Woman should not compare herself to man because this competition is making her lose her biggest "asset"—her femininity, the narrative warns.

In this context, it becomes clear why it was mostly men writing, painting and sculpting for and about love. This love is mostly presented in the shape of a young, beautiful female body, most often explicitly erotic. The viewpoint is most often that of a Pygmalion or a male animal in heat, and the claim is that the artwork glorifies and *immortalizes* female *physical beauty* and her biological role. If ever existent, female writing about love and sex is shy and romantic because for women love and sex are inherently linked to their biological role, ingrained in their bodies and in their brains.

This narrative merely reveals a fear of woman as an erotic agent with free erotic will. In the male narrative the human being in woman is reduced to motherhood, motherhood entirely replaces eros and woman is deprived of the right to be a subject in the erotic discourse. Contraception and the right to abortion gave agency to woman, decoupled sex and biology and linked sex to eros, allowed sex for her to become part of the contact with the Other, or a creative impulse, or simply a game or a fleeting pleasure, or satisfaction of a physiological need.

Man's fear and the prohibitions imposed by him might be expressed in civilized, even pathetic ways, but can lead to barbaric violence. Because one and the same argument stands behind traditional conservative attitudes about unfaithfulness (still active in the most progressive societies), through bans on abortion and control over contraceptives (applied in most advanced democracies and Muslim states alike), through female genital mutilation. Or, let us take polygyny, which is deceptively called polygamy. Man justifies it with pseudo-ethical arguments—you see, this is just care for the widows. Besides, all wives would be "treated equally" (I guess this means mainly economically and as regards offspring, not sexually, in particular as regards age) and the existing wife or wives should agree to the new "recruit" (sounds as if they were free to disagree . . .). If these were the real reasons, why *polygamy* is unthinkable. Via polygamy a woman would actually receive much more care. Not to mention that polygamy would solve the simple social-demographic arithmetic equitation, even with some positive side effects.[94] In reality, man codifies in cultural norms and legal orders his own "natural" polygyny. And overall his right to be whatever he wants and to behave as he likes.

Patriarchal societies, founded by male clan-links, rights and cultural norms, including those of religion, which takes priority over civil law, also restrict woman's access to education and the work market. In such societies there are no nurseries, kindergartens, old people's homes, but there are economic stimuli or social norms and imperatives for woman to not work, to stay at home, to cook, clean and launder, to bring up kids, and look after the elderly. In such societies domestic violence and rape are ignored by the law, but the law sanctions the free expression of female sexuality. In its most radical extremes, in these societies, while still children, girls and women are bought and sold, men enjoy polygyny, girls' genitals are cut off so as future women they experience no sexual pleasure, women are stoned to death or buried alive because of love affairs or suspicions of affairs, girl babies are not wanted and even selectively aborted. These countries can become more populous than western democracies, but this is a temporary Pyrrhic victory in demographics. Beyond the economic, social, and political logic and delimitations, the situation of women is another crucial marker, whereby "nations which fail women, fail,"[95] by any measure, in the final account and forever.

Today, with the assistance of reproductive medicine, woman is not only capable of delaying motherhood; she can also freeze her eggs and have them fertilized when she herself has stopped ovulating. These eggs, be they "freshly laid" or long-frozen, can be fertilized by donor sperm. The fertilized eggs can be implanted into surrogate mothers. It won't be long until pregnancy becomes fully independent of the mother who could be well into her old age. Perhaps all children will be conceived in a test tube and carried in artificial wombs? In a quite foreseeable future perhaps children will be more rarely the fruit of love, passion, pheromones, hormones, spring arousal, and attraction between male and female. Maybe one day there will be two evolutionary "breeds" of women—surrogate mothers with smaller brains and a lower capacity for abstract thinking, and those female human beings who will occupy their minds with advanced mathematics, theoretical physics, astronomy, art, artificial intelligence, and computer technologies. Women who will compose, paint, and write.

---

94 Social studies have proved that single men who cannot afford to marry or for whom there are simply not enough women tend to grow violent and become a source of social and political instability.

95 *The Economist*, Sept 11, 2021.

Or, perhaps, everyone, men, women and *they*, all of humanity, will grow ever more stupid, while machines become ever more intelligent. Perhaps one day human beings will no longer be able to produce art or science. Nor will there be a need for them. What will happen if humanity reaches the prophesied communism and humans are no longer motivated to educate themselves, to work, to compete, to ponder and to create?

Well, finally, what if we stop creating children simply because the planet is overpopulated, because we would be condemning these children to live through the end of the world and to die painfully? In any case, genetic engineering is advancing at breakneck speed, and children will be less and less the product of chaos.

La femme fatale in her sex-bomb version is uninteresting to me. Sweet-looking and naïve, or "mysterious and dangerous," always with exaggerated sexual characteristics, this woman is a male construct, fitting all male sexual longings. This is what's so "fatal" about her. Man has always been using woman to objectify his own sexuality, to make woman feel guilty and sinful for his own instincts, for his "weakness." He can even "empower" women through this instinct (a kind of power most women are "smart" enough to accept and instrumentalize, by the way). It all started with Eve, you see, being at fault for opening Adam's eyes, him seeing her, and desiring her as a naked woman so she would no longer be the innocent inferior creature, his companion in Eden who was only created so that the *human*, i.e., *man*, wouldn't feel alone and bored. This is not a story of woman's original sin; it is a story about the original complex of man and his original fear of his "weakness." Women have been covered from head to toe so they wouldn't seduce. Women who did not hide their sexual characteristics are supposed to be "looking for it." There's no man who doesn't have secretly conflicting thoughts and feelings on rape. If he's not praising women for the "power of their femininity," man is punishing them for his own "weakness," for the short-term derangement of his reason and consciousness, thus for challenging his power.

La femme fatale, or any woman with own sexual cathexis, is good only as lover, as *whore*, but not as mother and spouse. Such a sexual woman scares man because she reaches to co-own Eros.

It's not just the imposed demonization of woman by men that I find so annoying; I am equally frustrated by their magnanimous appraisal. This is nothing more than a perfidious, hypocritical demonstration of the same absolute power to define and prescribe in a discourse of men's own creation, to own and control. "Sacred and immortal" femininity is defined as well-proportioned physical splendor, promising fecundity and strong motherly instinct, as goodness, tenderness, morality, high-mindedness, humility, selflessness, loyalty, all-forgivingness, unconditional love, monogamy, sensitivity, patience, and a number of other virtues, needed for a mother, homemaker, and caretaker. That is it, the eternal femininity, that man has magnanimously "ceded" to and *imposed* on woman. I recently read somewhere that man is incapable of the self-denial and self-sacrifice which woman is capable of and if a man was so self-denying, he'd simply cease to exist as a *person*. A very true thought, and because it was expressed by a man, it has been further developed into the traditional reverence to women. Of course, nobody inquired if a woman still exists as a *person* under the "ornaments" of all her virtues and duties.

Disarmingly grandiloquent or ready to forgive his own weakness, man gives woman the "power" over his heart. Full of seemingly generous self-criticism, he acknowledges that he is a slave to his instinct, that he is polygynous by nature, aggressive, brutish, and insensitive. Woman, for her part, should ennoble and elevate him with her "eternal femininity." Hence, man and woman complement each other. With this primitive tautology, man "excuses" his freedom and claims his power to be whatever he wants to be and to define and prescribe to woman what she *must* be. Woman is one of the objects, not a subject or co-author of the discourse.

Another, subsidiary, male construct is woman's mystery. Translated in rational terms this is meant to signify woman's incomprehensibility or unintelligibility to man, or the "magic" power of man's own love, overriding his rational reason. If we leave aside the fact that it is a mystery, indeed, how woman has sustained, and survived, millennia of "natural" order eliminating her as human being, this is just another perfidious male myth. I was disappointed with Stephen Hawking—the man whose consciousness imbued the Universe—for declaring, at the end of his life, that woman is even more mysterious than the Cosmos. He did nothing but sustain the tradition of differentiating and alienating woman into something different from the human—who is by default a man—the human contemplating the mysteries of the Cosmos, of time, death, and human mind. The jocular "vindication" of mystery was poor comfort for me.

Finally, there comes the "neurotic," or "hysteric" woman. Expressing her, often, unconscious revolt to the "natural" male order, she is "safely" defined, by men of course, as just lacking enough . . . sex, or as envying man, no, not for his power to set the otherwise "natural" order, but for his . . . penis.

The concept of original sin, the idea of the immaculate conception, the *femme fatale*, the "pure" distinction in man's mind between mother, wife and mistress, shows that he cannot reconcile in the woman the erotic with the maternal, the human and existential with the biological. Only a man could think up the fable of the immaculate conception and declare it a miracle.

Religion has been dethroned as an existential and transcendental framework, but it has a strong "residual" value and purpose—ethics and morality. The problem is that the "derivatives" such as love for one's neighbor, sense of duty, obligation of care, goodness, humility, forgiveness, promise for ultimate triumph of justice and good—are reserved mainly for the poor, in order to soothe them in their poverty on Earth, and for women—to justify and sustain their earthy-life "rationale," defined by men.

An example. Hawking's first wife, Jane, met him before he got his condition but stayed with him, loved him, married him, took care of him and had three children with him, raised them, and overcame her depression—all that because of her trust in God, as she herself would confess. The two of them were in deep disagreement with regard to religion, which, obviously the scientist despised, but the man benefitted from. This is a very telling example as well of the two different "approaches" to transcendentalism reserved for men and women. There is no grand female astronomer or theoretical physicist but there are millions, even billions of religious, caring women. Moral and ethical guidelines, be they religious or "secular," are an "outlet" or, rather, a surrogate for the transcendental for women. A surrogate that is very expedient for men and society, with plenty of "useful side effects." Also, a surrogate that is often detrimental to the human being of women.

After 25 years of marriage, Hawking left Jane for . . . his nurse, happy to marry the woman "he *really* loved," whereas Jane married the man she had loved for years, a love that she had kept *platonic* so she wouldn't destroy her family. Yet, Jane continued to take care of Hawking, especially after he divorced his "real" love. But all is forgiven for geniuses like Hawking and Einstein, right? And there is no woman prodigy, genius enough to probe if genius inherently defies ethics and magnifies sexuality.

Marie Curie—one of the very, very few women recognized as great scientists, was not admitted into the French Academy of Sciences, despite her two Nobel prizes for physics. Maria was a victim of a horrible media and public campaign, because she wasn't sufficiently religious and, please note, because as a widow she dared to have a lover, and to top that, an academic who was younger than her. After the scandal, Maria would dress like a widow to the end. Yet another sad story about science, religion and the double standards, applied to women. The only funny detail is that Albert Einstein wrote a letter to Marie Curie in her support. As though he accepted Marie in a different way to Mileva, not exactly as a woman, most probably.

So, sing, oh muses, of eternal, sacred femininity and its power, of the magical mystery of woman and her beauty!

Only that this overrated femininity is far from being eternal—and it's only powerful with regard to one organ in the male body, which is definitely not his brain. What happens when physical loveliness fades, when those sexual characteristics start to wither? What happens when woman's tenderness and goodness are abused because she is no longer loved, and notably desired, but merely, in the best case scenario, respected as a mother, a wife, a grandmother, a carer for children and the ailing, a cleaner, cook, and homemaker? Old age leaves the woman, as constructed by man, with nothing beyond her sex. She is delegated to the "noble" roles of a sexless creature. It's time for her other virtues that have been imposed on her like tertiary sex characteristics, to take over from her withering physical femininity, to frame and justify all of what is left of a woman's "decent" life. The elderly woman is harmless—she doesn't provoke sin, she doesn't weaken the will and power of man. She is only boring, comical, evil but utterly necessary.

I read somewhere a statistical survey of American dating websites. According to the data provided, female attractiveness starts at its peak, when the woman is as young as eighteen.[96] After that initial apex woman's allure plummets until her early forties, and then continues falling, albeit less sharply, stabilizing itself at a permanent, very low level at around sixty. Besides, education takes away from woman's attractiveness—the higher it is, the less attractive a woman is supposed to be. For men, the curve is reversed—they start at eighteen at a rather low level, gradually becoming more attractive until they reach their irresistible peak, which is between forty-five and fifty years of age, and then start *very gradually* losing their charm. A man in his fifties, and even at sixty-five, is incomparably more desirable than a woman of the same age. Education, predictably, is a boost to male attractiveness. Man's upward curve and woman's downward one meet somewhere at twenty-eight or twenty-nine, i.e., at this age both sexes would find each other equally attractive.

96 I.e., with her legal right to register on that kind of websites. It is interesting to speculate whether, if there were no legal restrictions, men wouldn't really turn out to be attracted to nymphets.

Depressing results, as the article acknowledged, depressing for women, obviously. Then the authors immediately tried to console their logically implied but not explicitly defined female audience that it's "not important to have everyone wanting you" but "to be found by the right person."

This data and my own observations have led me to certain conclusions. The intersection, i.e., the point of equal mutual attraction, falls into—shall I say—the primary "spring market" for humans: the moment when young people, having completed their education and found their jobs, begin looking for a partner to start a family with. Taking into account, however, the growing number of divorces and recomposed families, the steeply rising number of women postponing family and children for the sake of education, financial independence, and professional accomplishment, as well as the far longer period of sexual activity after the age of twenty-eight or twenty-nine compared to the "spring," preceding it, I have to conclude that the dynamics and the processes going on in, so to say, the "second-hand market," factor far more importantly in the course of one's life. For both sexes.

And yet this "second-hand market" reveals a huge, fundamental discrepancy between men and women. A terrifying asymmetry. Young single guys, old bachelors, and divorced, "second-hand" men, all men, see their erotic ideal as a *young* woman, and even a girl, her brain as un-impregnated as possible. They fantasize about her, they pursue her, they chase her, make love to her, marry her, or get divorced for her. The mature woman, especially the one who's biologically overripe, becomes erotically unattractive in her own age group and even among older men. The mature man, on the other hand, attracts the interest of not just mature but young women as well. The latter fact, in my opinion, is a remnant of evolutionary-historical inertia, a superstructure dating from the time when women didn't have their own "economic base," a time which, we should not forget, has lasted from the very beginnings of history to a mere generation or two ago. Having achieved material independence, the woman is no longer forced to search for an older, more successful man who'd ensure the financial security of her home, herself and most importantly their children. And, indeed, women are increasingly pairing up with younger men, sometimes even their juniors; they are searching for partners, not fathers or stalwarts. Of course, there will always be women looking for a new daddy because they used to be their own father's little princesses, or because they had no father at all, or because they had a bad one.

This asymmetry in the preferences displayed by the fellow travelers on the train of life points at a big loser. And it's breaking my heart. I'm devastated when I see packs of females in their forties or fifties who have postponed "the mating" or have been abandoned for younger women. Their predatory, anxious eyes are ready to hang on the smallest gesture of attention and interest. These unwanted, dangerous women with their "low index" of attraction spend every day dressed up, made-up and coiffed in constant combat readiness, ready to meet "the right person" at work, at a training course, a conference, a business meeting, in the canteen, on the bus or the subway, at the traffic lights, in the supermarket, in the bar, at a friend's place, at brunches, parties, birthdays, christenings, galleries, concerts, speed dating events . . . Besides these real-life "hunting grounds," they "plow" the virtual field as well—losing many hours a day on dating sites. These women are constantly vigilant, every *mise-en-scène* gets immediately stripped off to the bone by their searching eyes, every opportunity must be used, they must be ready in every instant. I look them over as discretely as possible. I think they need at least three hours a day to maintain this state of combat readiness—make-up, hairdo, clothes, jewelry, manicure, make-up removal, night cosmetics, rollers and hairdryers, regular exhausting sports training. Not to mention the tight cheekbones, the lips that dare not laugh, the eyes frozen in doll-like euphoria.

A woman who is nothing but beautiful has an ugly time aging. She ages with an ugly sense of dread in her eyes, calling after the male gaze that's already turning away from her. Her makeup, clothing and manners are supposed to be making her look as young as always, but they turn her into a caricature of something that's no longer there. And there's nothing else. When physical beauty is the single defining feature of the individual, turned into life capital, with age, the whole persona is gone. Whereas for an ordinary, non-beautiful woman aging is the long-awaited alibi for being paid no attention. It's easy to love a beautiful young woman. That's why she always feels neurotically uncertain whether she's loved at all, what is she is loved for, exactly. Dazed by vanity, constantly distracted by the desire of so many men, deeply insecure in the depth of their love, such a woman is often incapable of loving and usually "misses the train" of the only man wanting her to grow old with him, and not just because by then she would be only his.

In one of his books, Frédéric Beigbeder says that men prefer much younger women for their supple skin and their . . . kindness (!), while a young woman would like her much older man because she needs a father and, more importantly, because she would always see herself as young, beautiful, and desirable in the eyes of the old man. The explanation of female "attitudes" sounds much more realistic to me than the one regarding male preferences, especially the "motivation" of kindness. If that French author has, indeed, captured the dynamics of eros, I wonder why mass culture and the advertising world are showing only half of the picture, the "skin" part, if I follow the imagery of the Frenchman. The *physical appearance* of *young sexy* women is selling everything. Mass culture does not emphasize the "kindness" of young women, they are not represented as, for example, caring preschool educators or retirement facility nurses. On the other hand, ads show attractive over-fifty males as cheerful, confident, and *good-natured,* not as sex-symbols; this image of man advertises symbols of success, retirement insurance and hemorrhoid creams. That thing about kindness would have been very funny if it wasn't cynical. *A human being* who's unwanted and unloved—a woman or a man, a transgender, a hermaphrodite, whatever—becomes "unkind."

When her ovary reserves are depleted and the woman becomes biologically non-functional, she often becomes unattractive, unwanted, uninteresting to the man, especially if she has been the mother to his kids, first and foremost, and not primarily an existential fellow traveler and partner. If the women in question haven't been cheated on too obviously and if they haven't been abandoned, they find it easier to bear the emptying of the nest and the vague, but deep feeling of some fundamental *deceit.* After the end of her youth and the cessation of her biological function, woman has several "options." The more conservative societies expect her to take care of her grandchildren and elderly relatives and make a smooth transition from a Madonna to a Matron, auntie, granny. Unwanted and erotically neutered, the woman would endure her saintly, sexless state with dignity, holding up her moral rectitude and her piety like a flag, despising and magnanimously "forgiving" the carnal cravings and faux pas of "that animal—man." Then she really does become waspish, nagging, and small-minded. Yet, behind this whole façade there's the feeling of deceit, the pain of a woman unloved. I remember a maxim I heard many years ago—that a boy should not let old women talk to him about his beloved girl, that he shouldn't leave his girlfriend exposed to their evil eyes and words. I think that the traditional (in my culture) hatred and envy of the mother-in-law is rooted in the fading of her role as a mother and the lack of her individual erotic life that could fill the void. It's not just the Freudian dynamics between a mother and her son. If the older woman is loved and desired, she wouldn't hate on her young daughter-in-law.

Non-patriarchal, modern societies have developed some other "options." Erotic fantasies are acknowledged today as fully legitimate and a safe escape to preserve the couple. In other scenarios, still aimed to preserve the couple by "injecting some fresh erotic impetus," fantasies become stark reality. Women are encouraged to be truly modern and tolerant, accompanying their husbands to sex clubs or private orgies. In the name of equality, women are free to live their own fantasies there. Only . . . that men and women have quite different reasons to embrace this scenario and experience it in quite a different way. Man gets what he wants, with the benefit that he would not feel guilt, that trust and honesty are preserved, equality is respected and the jealousy and "hysteric" pain of his wife would not poison his life. Whereas woman just gets another role. She accepts playing this role in order not to be abandoned, while desperately trying to appear younger, daring, and erotic again in the eyes of the man. Different sources reveal that Belgians and French seem to be real champions in this scenario—one third of all middle-aged couples have engaged in this kind of libertine escapade. And they're all so proud of being honest to each other, of not having cheated, of being modern and sexual, of having a relationship strong enough to endure this thing that was "just a game," a "refreshing episode," a couple of "legitimate fantasies that we dared materialize." OK, great, everything that supports, boosts, or diversifies the erotic attraction two people feel, and is desired by both of them, is more than welcome. The problem is that, if we look at the bottom of this scenario, we will often find not erotic attraction and co-authorship of the *Arabian Nights* but perfidious hypocrisy. Male hypocrisy. By the way, a good share of those couples have "very traditional" breakups after this kind of "modern" experiment.

Simone Signoret once said something very simple and fitting—Yves Montand had matured, i.e., he'd become even more attractive, whereas she had grown old. *A mature man* sounds sexy. *A mature woman* has a bad ring to it.

But if you're asking me, I think that a woman is at her most erotic precisely after the end of her biological role and motherhood functions. This woman is no longer a sacred Madonna and a multitasking homemaker; the welfare state would normally relieve her from her duties as sanitary worker and a crèche nurse, too. Freed from biology and accompanying virtues, she is erotic as a *person*, with her mind, spirit and experience, not only with her body. It is a mind of a *human being* that the man would be seducing, not just a biologically productive, young and trophy female specimen. This woman knows what she likes and dislikes and is not willing anymore to play roles, written by men, and for their pleasure only. Her eros may become more exciting for the man than his own, because it can transform the hunter into an object of desire, confirming his erotic value in a different way. This woman can finally demonstrate her sense of humor and laugh at herself and the whole world. This woman has so many stories to tell. And telling stories, as Scheherazade has taught us, is one of the most arousing and erotic things to do. This erotic woman does not count anymore time in circular lunar months. She has found, among the dusty drawers of her everyday life, her long-forgotten personal clock and her magic mirror that shows her true face as a *human being.*

Eros, unlike the biological instinct and hormonal libido, is something that comes with communication, with the electrifying thrill between two minds. What can you talk about with a young girl, or boy, if you are twenty or more rotations around the sun ahead of them!? You can blow their minds with an impressive *monologue*, you can assure yourself that your sexual glands are still functioning, and yet both are a case of narcissistic auto-eroticism rather than communication.

Yet, as a Bulgarian folk wisdom fittingly puts it, attraction does not come on command. Men do want younger women. And so, let the muses, or rather the men they inspire, sing.

Actually, there is a second evolutionary modification of woman, which, according to a latest scientific hypothesis, is a direct result of, and not the reason for, man's preference for young flesh. It turns out that menopause is not an inherent biological feature of female mammals, it is a result of their life in a community, or in other, human terms, in a society, constructed and governed by man. Apart from human females, only whales and one type of ape know menopause. Women release only a small portion of their egg stock, so there is no biological reason for the menopause. Male preference for young women has made fertility in older women redundant, and hence it was removed through evolution. Scientists speculate that younger women were preferred because they have a longer life span ahead to care for the offspring, that eliminating older women reduced competition among females and provided additional resource—in the shape of grannies—to guarantee the care for and the survival of the kids and fertile mothers alike.

In our society, where survival is guaranteed, man seems to be afraid of the *human being* in woman. In his binary, limited perception man takes this Other (person) in woman to be a man, hence his competitor, reaching to co-author the narrative; a threat to his male identity, a challenge to his presumably higher intellect and more abstract thought, to his value and rights. Man is anxious that he might not get it up with this *person* at his side and prefers getting reliably stiff with . . . "*kind*," intellectually unsullied, and most importantly young girls. And those mature women do turn into terrifying irascible matrons, desperate predatory she-wolves, sexless saints or "modern harlots." There's nothing sadder than an unloved fifty-something woman with fading beauty and the typical menopausal belly fat, a woman who eats. And eats. And can't stop talking about cooking.

A piece of research which I encountered recently confirmed masculine authorship of the rules. As might be expected, the wealthier are able to eat healthily, to exercise and play sports and, all in all, look after themselves. Obesity is a characteristic of poor people. It turns out however that this is only true of women. "Rich women are a lot slimmer than poor women, but rich men are almost as fat as poor men."[97] That is, again man can be whatever he wants, woman has to be whatever the standards dictate—in other words what man likes.

In recent years under pressure from women, things have changed. The *natural* female body, not anorexic or with the ideal proportions of models and film stars, has become an object for fashion and cosmetics. But one thing remains—the fight with time. Man does not like to see the scars of *time* and *lived experience* in woman. As he still shapes and dictates the discourse, in particular in some cultures, an immense, flourishing industry is occupied with fighting female maturity, i.e., the traces of age on woman's body and face. The richest person in the world today[98] is Bernard Arno, the boss of LVMH—a conglomerate whose firms produce predominantly luxurious fashion, cosmetics and perfumes.

In American culture, as one might expect, the fight with the ravages of time and lived experience has become the norm. Cosmetic surgery is ubiquitous. Like on a conveyor belt, the industry produces noses, cheeks, lips, breasts and bottoms, lifts eyelids and eyebrows, erases wrinkles, tightens thighs and remodels anything you want.

At the same time some frustrated matrons are writing pseudo-erotic novels, featuring . . . *young* "heroines," of course. These texts are more improbable than the most far-fetched BDSM porn so that even men found them off-putting. The popularity of *mommy* porn[99] among, for the most part, middle-aged American women is only a measure of the muddle they're in. The costumed chick-lit is of no interest to me for obvious reasons.

By the way, around fifty pages of notes in French and English are stored in my computer, bundled under the working title, "The dialectics of passion, from *la merde* to the divine and from porno to Goethe, a complete annotated guide." Up to now it marks out a comic-tragic story, slightly, or perhaps very parodic about the dynamics and aesthetics of Eros and the increasingly impossible intimacy with some literary excursions, including into Nabokov's *Lolita*. Which, to me, is a deeply ironic novel, not about lusting after a nymphet but about travel and writing.

97 *The Economist* Christmas double issue 2022–2023.

98 Today means January 2023 and yes we have to admit that Arno's pre-eminence results from Musk's colossal Twitter losses. But even in second or third place, this would not change the fact that the fight for youth is on a level with the most expensive and important technologies.

99 The very name of the genre is begging for a page of comments.

Happily there are different men and different cultures. There are men with impregnated brains (not just impregnating testicles). It seems to me that old, "intellectual" Europe is different. Not only with the literary and life stories of its powerful female writers. Besides the cultural monuments, the beautiful homes, the paintings and the cornucopia of material stuff, one of the first things that deeply impressed me in Western Europe, and mostly in the Scandinavian countries, Germany and the Netherlands,[100] as well as France, was the sight of fifty-something couples with no fat bellies and grotesque rejuvenating experiments, well-groomed, trim, with a measured dose of modernity and sex-appeal, couples who—take note!—go hand in hand, not arm in arm, holding hands on the street or simply sitting somewhere, just like that, having a drink together, looking at each other, the man not ogling young girls but looking at the woman at his side, talking incessantly and even—unthinkable!—kissing on the street. The presidential couples of the USA and France[101] illustrated the extremes of these cultural differences.

Outside Hollywood fairy-tales, in reality a physically strong woman is the object of ridicule, she's not feminine, she's a virago.

The woman who has political and financial power scares men. She challenges male power and that is why men will reckon her dangerous. The discrediting of such women employs different strategies but they all hinge on the reassertion of "true femininity" and imposed morality. Merkel, an exceptional politician, was not perceived as a woman in the full sense of the word, but as *Mutti*, which in the most positive interpretation means mother of the nation and in its not so sentimental but more intimate sense—auntie, a kind elderly lady. Among the ordinary population, unapologetic macho crudity rules—a successful woman, including those in politics is either ugly and her success compensates her fundamental unhappiness, or she's a whore, whose path has not passed through intelligence, talents, education, and savage hard work, but through the beds of powerful men.

You haven't forgotten, have you?—woman has no need of political power, the power she has over man bestows power to herself. And this is her freedom. Only this freedom and power end the moment that woman grows old. This statement is quite telling about the way power and freedom are joined at the hip in men's thinking. Man cannot

100 All protestant countries, by the way. Or, isn't it another illustration of the North-South, Up-Down, divide, which has very interesting cultural implications?

101 The Trumps and the Macrons.

imagine someone being strong and mighty and *not* exercising power and control. That a person can be free without having power over somebody else.

How about the female artist? An educated, thinking and creative woman rearranging the entire frame and its narrative? I am talking about those who have the strength, the talent and the intellectual depth to create *another world*? This woman is considered an exception to the female character, an exception to femininity. In the eyes of a man, a woman writer is not quite a woman. I consider this concept (which is also man-made, through and through) to be prompted by the fear that the woman artist is reaching for discourse itself, for the whole world, she is building another world, she is capable of defining things, herself among them, in a different manner. I don't remember which poet had said that women writers should wear their laurel leaf where beautiful women once wore a fig leaf. Very witty, right? Leaving aside the assumption that a female writer cannot be beautiful, if we are to believe this poet, it turns out that woman's only writing because she has not accomplished herself as a woman, because no man had "chosen" her to "rule" over him with her sexual characteristics and her virtues, "lurking" behind that fig leaf. In brief, man thinks of women's writing as sublimation, only. This intellectual and creative crippling of the female gender is so sad. A laurel wreath is to be worn on the head! No male writer would think of hanging the laurel wreath on his erect penis, right? (Although that would be fitting for this organ of male creativity.) In any case, if I am ever to receive laurel boughs, I will wear them on the head that has given birth to this book. Those considerations aside, it's a great dress-up party idea—at the next party I'm going as a writer in a skirt of bay leaves.

Traditionally, men write about women, define them however they want, afterward describe them, exaggerate, love, desire, fear them, or more accurately their own projections of women, blame them. The woman is defined only according to the man's attitude, through his eyes, and with a view to his needs. The woman is deprived of agency, she is an object in the masculine discourse of the human condition. The woman is positioned in a room of mirrors. The four walls reveal her faces and roles. In this room the woman learns not simply what she has to be, but what she *is*—a holy Madonna, a fecund body, a dedicated mother, an outstanding homemaker and hostess, an experienced cleaner and launderess, a professional cook, a senior orderly and nurse, a loyal and steadfast partner, a working wife, who invests her very last penny of her money into the family budget, a faithful and patient Penelope, who if she fails, turns into a fearsome and tragic Medea, a seductive and liberated object of desire, mistress of every pornographic trick (but only with her husband or in his presence, otherwise she'd be a whore), a fatal and intoxicatingly dangerous woman or a fragile, helpless innocent girl, who has to be rescued, protected, directed, ordered and spanked if necessary. Some women realize that these are distorting mirrors created by men. And that there are no others. There is no mirror made entirely of light, in which woman can appear as a human being. And woman acts obediently, *imitating her images*. She isn't confused, she acts diligently, so as not to be alone, to be loved and desired, to have children and a father for them. Alas, often despite her efficacious performance in all "disciplines," her fading skin and flesh turn out to be decisive. Woman suffers from the claustrophobic mirror-room syndrome. Only in the sky woman can see herself as a human being. As man does from his secret observatory.

The woman-artist blows up the mirror-room.

Right on the day of my birthday in 2019, (when this ongoing book was fixed in its first stable variant for publication), the French Academy decided to codify the female form of the word "author" (*autrice*)[102] into a linguistic norm. I wish I wouldn't hear the condescending, pejorative or sexual notes in the Bulgarian female forms of "интелектуалка" (*intellectuelle*), "писателка" (*ecriteuse*), and поетеса (*poetess*), or the downright oxymoronic nuances in "философка" (lady philosopher), "композиторка" (lady composer) or "астрономка" (lady astronomer). But I do hear them. Besides, our language has no female forms whatsoever for academic titles and for some professions like "wrestler" and "surgeon." I'm also wondering how it would sound, in Bulgarian, to say "the minister is smart" or "the executive director is pregnant." Yes, yes, I know how you're supposed to say it—"minister Petrova is a smart woman" and "the executive director Mrs. Georgieva is pregnant." And yet the very necessity of specifying that the person is female to assuage the contradiction is telling, as is the contradiction itself.

I hope to live long enough to see any academy (including the Institute for Bulgarian Language) coin and codify the male form of the word "muse." For the time being I, personally, would go for *muz*. It is a rare example of a word that has only a feminine gender as the inspired author, creator, demiurge Pygmalion has been, until recently, invariably male.

Remaining in the binary world and before sinking into the modern gender-diverse and inclusive linguistic maze, it shall be noted that dictionaries define "Man" as twofold—as human male adult, a homo sapiens individual and, in a meta-generic sense, as human being or mankind in general. So, a human being is considered

102 My French spellchecker, incidentally, has not yet learned this and keeps marking the word as wrong.

masculine. That's the situation in English or French. Slavic languages have separate words for man and human, respectively, *muzh* and *chovek*. But *chovek* (human) is masculine and if we want to indicate that the human being is of female sex, we have to use the word *zhena* (woman). Which is pretty different from *chovek*. The argument that the generic meaning of man or *homme* comprises women is a recent, compensatory social convention, trying to soothe half of the mankind. If that were true, why *woman* has not acquired today such a second generic meaning, why *man* and *woman* are not made interchangeable in such a generic meaning? No, *He, the human being,* does not include *She*. Because *He* believes that only *He* knows and understands best the world, including *Her*, that only *He* is entitled to define and describe this world, including through language, and that only *He* is representative for the intellect, the consciousness, the erotic and creative drives, animating and defining this human being. Lexical meaning, pronouns, grammatical gender and concordance, these basic linguistic categories belie the full male ownership of the discourse and his self-proclaimed superiority.

Feminization of language and gender neutral forms are a huge issue today. Because language is a very conservative system and changes to grammar and morphology take centuries to shape and codify (unlike the exponential developments in science, which simply produce new concepts and terminology). All in all, these linguistic puzzles is another proof how fundamental and radical the changes are, as they imply not just new words and terms but a rethink of fundamental linguistic categories and baseline dictionary definitions.

Today man complains that he's confused and scared by the collapse of the traditional social roles of both genders. Rightly so, given the sometimes contradictory demands and expectations addressed to him. Some call this a crisis of masculinity. I would not agree, because first, this is not a crisis and second it does not concern masculinity alone. The world really is changing, but at a deep, even (r)evolutionary, level. With the death of God and the birth of the individual the whole "God's world" has been reconsidered and rearranged. From the beginning of recorded tome, the existential, the stars, the Cosmos, the heavens, philosophy, physics, religion, artistic creation—all has been from man to man. Today man is not simply called to take his share in the everyday and the childcare and woman's equal pay and rights, but is called to share the Being. Fundamental changes in society follow and the deconstruction and reconstruction of (social) gender. It will take generations, long lived generations, to change the order that has existed for thousands of years.

In my view, feminism is a side effect of individualism and modernity. The "discovery" of the individual, unique and free, but also orphaned and tragic outside community, religion, family, nation, could not ignore the fact that woman is also such an individual. And she may even have human consciousness and capacity for abstract thinking to ponder death, time and the stars, as well as talents to create new aesthetic worlds.

I consider feminism the single most important revolution in human history. To those who may object that this statement is exaggerated, I would remind them that there have been many revolutions of many different kinds, wars and battles in human history, which in the end are caused either by greed, lust for power, or an unfair distribution of resources. This greedy, bloody, unfair social world in the past was created and controlled by men. What's more, not one of the revolutions and wars have achieved a fair and sustainable result. To create conditions where half of humankind are emancipated from biology and rise to be genuinely human, while "growing up" and participating in the economic and political world of the "adults" is, indeed, the most crucial development in our history.

But the changes in "God's world" did not stop there. I think that the separation of biology from the social and intimate accomplishment of the female human being and the recognition of socially construed roles (i.e., gender)—processes, which we owe to feminism—are at the base of what has followed. It is going much further, opposing not only male power and control of the discourse, including the male fantasy of so-called "God's order, but nature itself."

In the last decade, we have lived through a previously unthinkable and unimaginable re-definition of sex, gender, and sexuality. The mixing of these three categories leads to big misunderstandings and confusion with really serious consequences.

Sex is a physical reality and a natural given. Sex is predominantly binary and in a male or a female genotype, primary and secondary sexual traits appear, according to which we categorize a physical body as male or female, and consequently the owners of these bodies as man or woman. A small proportion of these bodies are not biologically binary on the level of chromosomes, hormones and primary and secondary sexual characteristics.

Gender is not a physical reality, nor a natural given, but a social and psychological construct. Gender means the social projection and realization of the given biological sex and the accompanying roles, assigned to man and woman. Gender is actually a fruit of feminism. Feminism rebelled against social realization of the female sex as prescribed by the male over thousands of years. Sex is reality, gender is ideology and power. Today, gender has expanded its meaning significantly beyond gender roles to include gender identity. For me the constituent elements of this identity again are essentially based on social roles and social representations. In my view, dad may be a biological woman and mom may be a biological man, or a child may have two dads or two moms. But beyond biological conception and pregnancy, fatherhood and motherhood are gender roles, thus ideological constructs, not something precluded by biology. It is not important what parents a child has and how they are referred to— what matters is the love, care, and security a child receives.

Rebelling against the reduction of women to their biology, Simone de Beauvoir declares: *On ne naît pas femme: on le devient.*[103] Mme de Beauvoir's manifesto refers to gender, i.e., to the social construction of the female sex. For the rest, we are born biological women, with female sex morphology, birthing "facilities" that come to a "pause," fewer muscles and less physical strength and smaller, and further shrinking, brains and reduced capacity for abstract thought.

Thirdly comes sexuality, or in more poetic terms, Eros. My generation is witnessing a historical recognition and acceptance of homosexual Eros. It turns out that about 10% of all people are gay.[104] Over thousands of years sexuality and procreation used to be two different things only for man. Thanks to contraceptives and abortion, women's education and economic freedom, feminism decoupled them for women, too. Women can live out their sexuality outside their biological role.[105] Again, in my view, feminism did the path-breaking job so that today Eros is freed from biological determinism, morphology, and biblical-biological purpose. Eros animates the *minds* and the intimate relationship between two *human beings*. Homosexual couples by definition are childless. Surely, thanks to modern medicine and changing social conventions and laws they can, and in my view should be allowed to, have children—biological or adopted. What is important to me is that the relationship of two human beings is

103 (French) One is not born, but rather becomes, a woman.

104 A scientific study concluded that irrespective of whether a man or a woman is straight or homosexual, the more sexual a woman is, the more likely she is to be bisexual, whereas for man it is just the contrary—the stronger his libido is, the firmer his sexual preference is fixed—hetero or homo.

105 Female orgasm is not needed for procreation. Even today, some scientist "wonder" why women even have orgasms, given its evolutionary "inutility," even though only woman has an organ dedicated only to pleasure. Obviously, in this framework, woman is still considered as a biological machine only, not as a human being. Actually, one may ask why man should disseminate their genes in pleasure, isn't the instinct for procreation and survival of the species enough? Besides, man has no organ exclusively designed for pleasure.

detached from biology in terms of purpose, as well as morphological determinism. Consequently, the classical, binary-sex couple has turned out to be an ideological and social construct, too.

Sexuality is something intimate, society has no business in the bedroom, the sexual choice of the minority has to be free and accepted by the majority. Only perversions and crimes, including involving children, have to be strictly sanctioned by law. Homosexual couples have to enjoy the same human rights as heterosexuals.

However, the revolt against biology is reaching even further—aiming at biological sex itself. Gender is trying to get primacy over biological sex, or in other words, human will and ideology challenge nature. A growing number of teen girls, just at the time of their cocoon transformation into women, state that they do not want to become women, because they do not feel like women. The adults are quite confused, and rightly so. These girls do not want to grow into *biological* women, they do not want to have the female sex morphology, they do not want to menstruate and reach menopause one day, but the bottom line is that they do not want to give birth. For these girls, consciously or not, intimately or culturally predetermined, the female sex still equals female gender and its traditional construction and roles. In the USA, cosmetic surgery spews out Barbies, with the still existing social ideal that Barbie will get married to rich Ken and give birth to at least three kids, bringing them up without nurseries and kindergartens. Woman is not permitted to be a human entity, who possesses and takes decisions about her own body and life. I think I understand why in this context, a girl can decide that she doesn't want to have the body or life of a woman. No doubt, some other factors play a role. To be gender-dysphoric is fashionable, it may give a sense of belonging to a trendy community, you become the center of attention. I am pretty sure that most of the girls who do not want to become biological women, do not want automatically to become men, either. However, our society and its medical care do not provide a third option.

As to the transition in the opposite direction, these boys and men say they *feel* like women and want to *look* like women. Femininity is attractive to them with its vulnerability, sensitivity, emotions, and for the decorative part (clothes, make up, etc.)—all of them denied to man in his own macho world. In any case, men transition not in order to be able to get pregnant and give birth, which is impossible for the time being anyway. While girls transition because they do not want to become women, because they don't want to give birth. So, in both directions, there is a cancellation of the key biological feature and function of the female sex.

In both directions, there are widespread confusions, mixing sex, gender and (homo) sexuality. Besides, teens' dysphoria often turns out to be temporary or an as-yet-unacknowledged or hidden homosexuality. Trans-women often turn out to be homosexual men. This conceptual mish-mash is very troubling, as is the sustained fear from classic social roles and binary couples, which has not disappeared despite of the radical changes in society. Because today man and woman are no longer obliged to comply with stereotypical physical appearances, woman is not obliged to give birth and man and woman are free to live out their sexuality and orientation, including to refuse to have any sex life at all,[106] to look and be whatever they want. And to enjoy these liberties, they do not need to encroach on their biological sex.

However, it seems that increasingly the focus is on correcting *biology*, while the real problem is *gender*—i.e., the construction of femininity into biological duties and social roles, and the construction of masculinity. Biology and Eros[107] are sacrificed to correct gender, i.e., the ideology and the construct of a still male (and, paradoxically at first sight, religious) world. Trans-gender is incorrect notion, it should be trans-sex. Genuine gender therapy needs to work with gender and not so much with sex. In a way, the whole society needs gender therapy. Law, media, art, and psychology ought to be engaged in the deconstruction and reconstruction of gender. The traditional gender constructs and roles must continue to be reviewed and deconstructed. The reconstruction of gender must reflect the fundamental changes in society, especially regarding woman.

Not biology and sex with their "duties," roles, and ideals, but Eros and the construction of gender are fundamental elements of human condition and experience. Will the bold attack on biology also become part of human experience? Can we say that individualism, with its late-born offspring feminism, has a grandchild in the shape of the human androgyne? Isn't it telling that the process of blurring the binary sexual identity and heterosexual attraction is accompanied by the progress of controlled reproduction? The dissociation of sex, gender and sexuality from reproduction and from Mother Nature as a whole constitutes a fundamental change in human evolution.

Paradoxically, women appear to be losers over these dramatic developments.

In 2020, when the first edition of *To Essay* came out, a Bulgarian writer and literary critic I admire, saw my feminism as anachronistic and irrelevant. I prayed she

106 Young people appear to have become more conservative and increasingly get together virtually. Over 30% of thirty-year-old Japanese men and women are virgins, because they don't feel the need to take on the risks of a real relationship. The pandemic strengthened this tendency.

107 Trans people would not experience orgasms.

was right. Sadly, however, the reversal in the constitutional right to abortion, in the USA of all places, refuted my colleague. In his closing statement the judge announced a reexamination of other legislative acts, for example free access to contraception and single sex marriages. I'm not going to repeat the dozens of feminist, humanist, and democratic arguments against the monstrous encroachment against women as human beings. The judicial ruling is anachronistic. It lays bare the hypocrisy of part of that misogynous, patriarchal, and religious society. The simultaneous existence of bans on abortion and contraceptives, on one hand, and of death penalty and completely free regime of guns' possession, bespeaks that it is not the value of human life that is at stake,[108] but the power over women.

We should remember that the ban on abortion in the USA only affects biological women. That in Afghanistan everybody is starving, but only those of the female sex—girls and women—suffer from the Islamic dictatorship. That Mahsa Amini was of the female sex. That over 200 million girls and women are genitally mutilated and suffer unimaginable pain and horror. That Russian soldiers are raping Ukrainian biological women. That jihadists in Africa, abduct, enslave, and rape biological girls and women. That women still receive less for their work in otherwise equal conditions. That women still have no equal status in politics and business. That domestic violence is reserved almost exclusively to biological women. Energy and fight should be focused against these violations. The Trans community has an excellent chance to demonstrate solidarity and prove that its agenda and objectives do not replace and undermine those of feminism. The inclusivity agenda must not replace that of feminism because there are still millions, even billions of biological women who are victims of violence and suppression, who are impoverished, cannot study and work and are deprived of basic human rights, including the right to make decisions about their own body and life.

The pressing agenda of feminism, concerning millions, if not billions of women is kicked into the weeds. The reality of female sex is denied. The genuine *gender* problematics are substituted by fashionable questions of transgender (an inaccurate term) and inclusivity. According to new orthodoxies, sex, and particularly the female sex, is a "historical artefact"; the binary nature of sex is just an ideology, not reality. It's significant that female sex is subject to denial, nobody yet has declared that the male sex is just an ideological construct. This narrative holds that self-declared gender identity, in particular as trans women, i.e., men who identify as women, is enough for the society to consider them women, indeed. The very word *woman* is under question. Most dic-

108 While, again, to repeat, a non-viable fetus is not yet a human being, while a pregnant woman definitely is.

tionaries define woman as an adult human female. This is contested today because it is perceived as denying that males can be women, too. For fear of accusations in transphobia, scientists, doctors, and social services organizations coin bizarre definitions, such as "bodies with vagina," "birthing people," or "menstruating people" to refer to biological women without excluding those "whose sense of their gender does not match their [biological] sex, such as people who identify as trans or non-binary."[109] *The Economist* rightly remarks that "there is no comparably zealous campaign to abandon the word 'man' in favor of 'prostate-possessors,' 'ejaculators,' or 'bodies with testicles.'" In my view, all this can easily be fixed by adding *biological* or *trans* to *woman* and *man*.

What cannot be easily fixed is the second, generic meaning of *man* as *human being*, as well as the grammar, morphology, and lexical fundaments of language, reflecting man's millennia-old world. And again, the linguistic problematics of gender neutrality or inclusiveness should not replace the necessary feminization of language. The latter means that woman is "admitted" to and included into the human condition and Logos, that woman co-owns the discourse and co-authors the narrative about the human being.

As far as sex, gender, and sexuality are concerned, language is trying to catch up with this dynamic (and confused) world. The blossoming nomenclature does not stop growing. Naming or denomination is an essential element of the (self)identification, therefore this complex nomenclature is not tautological, at least not to insiders, although it sprouts from only two branches: the biological, with the male and female sexes and with two branches (trans and inter); and the sexuality with four branches (hetero-, homo-, non- or a- and pan- or "all-inclusive" sexuality).[110] The pronoun "they" is used for all these gender-non-binary folk. Followed in the singular. In English this linguistic solution only breaks the agreement of number. And precisely the disagreement in number marks that *they is* a non-binary person. In English there is no

---

109 *The Economist*, October 2nd-8th, 2021

110 Because this book is also a document of the epoch, including language development, it seems fitting to register this nomenclature in its present state. The exhaustive list that follows is in English, for the simple reason, that the new definitions appear in this global language and at best, Bulgarian, and most probably all other languages, including the linguistically puritanical French, will simply take the new terms from the English. And one clarification—I am following the frustration and scorn of conservative society, according to which they have thought up over thirty genders. This is inaccurate. What we are talking of is the self-identification around three vectors—sex, gender, and sexuality. And this to the present moment there are the following identities: (biological) man and woman, heterosexual, homosexual, lesbian, gay, bi-gender, transgender (female-to-male and male-to-female), gender variable, gender-queer, intersexual, neither-gender, asexual, non-binary, pan-gender and pan-sexual, trans-male and trans man, trans-female and trans woman, trans-human, trans-with-* (*gender star*), trans*female and trans*woman, trans*male and trans*man, trans-feminine, trans-sexual person, inter*female, inter*male, inter*man, inter*woman, inter*human, inter*gender, intersexual, dual gender, androgyne, hermaphrodite, two-spirit third gender, fourth gender, XY-woman, transvestite, cross-gender, zero-gender.

grammatical gender, in which supporting verbs, adjectives, participles, adverbs agree with the subject. Other languages have a really big problem.

Apart from the language development, the changes in aesthetics are also interesting. The evolutionary imperative for survival has established the young healthy female body as beautiful and erotically seductive, with hips wide enough for the new person to pass through, with thighs and flanks endowed with enough fat reserves to feed the mother and the embryo through hard times. Let's not forget that up until a century or century and a half ago, giving birth carried the danger of death and nearly a third of women indeed died during childbirth. Caesarian birth, developments in medicine, woman's exit from the home, emancipation and feminism, contraception, reduction in fertility, considerations of healthy diet and lifestyle, liberated sexuality, all this has fundamentally changed ideas about beauty (the cult of youth being the single exception). A historic review over the ideals of female as well as male beauty would make interesting reading. We are witnessing new changes which directly reflect changes in society. They have begun to tolerate more natural models—imperfect but with self-approval, more rounded, older. Or with not as clear-cut sexual traits, even with an undefined gender; along with the classic male brutes, we are seeing more often the so-called metrosexual male, or more colorful, more delicate versions of manhood. Previously, I would ask myself whether new ideals would emerge about transgender, androgynous, gender neutral, or pangender beauty. Now I think, rather I hope, that actually the notion of an aesthetic *ideal* will disappear down history's drain and instead real human beings, in all their natural diversity, will take to the aesthetic stage.

I would not venture further into the very dynamic trans problematics. Furthermore, following the advice of the American publisher, the text on gender has been adapted to avoid some controversial topics.[111] I insist, however, to note that to me, the most disturbing is precisely the new orthodoxy stigmatizing free academic, medical, and social debate. Taboos do poor service to liberal values and democracy. Fields unploughed by free and argumentative debate are easily weaponized, turned into frontline trenches and conquered by the conservative, populist and genuinely illiberal camp.[112]

•

111 Which are preserved in the French edition.

112 In Europe, we learned our hard lessons of these mechanisms as regards migration. I would add, from my experience as Bulgarian, that the problematics of Roma minority reveals the same dynamics.

And *it*—humanity, human being—is androgynous.

Or X-chromosome, to be precise. It turned out the Y-chromosome carries only one hundred genes, and these are genes determining the male sex characteristics. Nothing more. Whereas the X-chromosome carries more than a thousand genes and, obviously, determines everything else. As female organisms receive too many genes, having two X-chromosomes, a mechanism that works during the embryonic development successively deactivates first the paternal X-chromosome, then the maternal, to finally settle on one as matrix. Woman, thus, is a genetic mosaic,[113] while man is, shall we say, more monochrome, or monotonous. So, it appears that the overstated Y-chromosome carries nothing but male "credentials," which then bring glands, testosterone and all. All our humanity, beyond biological sex, is based on the X-chromosome. Let's set aside that the X-chromosome is typically perceived as the female "part" and that in men it comes only from the mother. The striking thing is that we—men and women—fundamentally share the same genes that make us human, and that the building blocks that make us human are not attached to biological sex.

That *human being* inside woman is not a man. Nor is the human being inside man, by the way. Androgyny is not a harmonious combination of male and female, or of masculinity and femininity, but rather the original human in man and woman. The human being has no sex or gender. The humans inside man and woman do not make sex or love with their bodies. They do not compete either, as they are not just equal, they are the same. Man and woman as human beings are not only socially but also existentially equal. The eroticism of the flesh, passion and love may trace one's journey to the Other. They make this journey exceptionally pleasant and exciting. Yet, more often than not, our bodies lead us into the blind alleys of the carnal instinct, of reproduction, of habit, loathing, cheating and duty. And everybody forgets that this was only the journey and not the final destination. Bodies age, while minds branch out—richer and more beautiful with experience. But paradoxically, men and women grow further apart precisely when they approach their liberation from biology and initiation as human beings. Men and women fail to meet in what they most fundamentally share—humanity. That X-chromosome humanity. These human beings forgive their bodies and love each other with their minds, they hold hands and look up at the sky together. To me, love is when a man and a woman, or same-sex partners, join, with luminous sadness, through the fading of their physical sexuality, to remain

113 A woman scientist has established this, her name is Edith Heard.

two human beings erotically clenched together so they would be less afraid of death, stars, chaos and futility.

I am a sanguine-melancholic minotaur, trans-minotaur . . . no, there's no such gender category or mythological figure. That is, first, I am a *female* minotaur, unlike the mythological male. Second, I have a *human head* and the body of a mammal, unlike the mythological creature in which human and animal are in reverse. [114] Abandoned by gods, having abandoned my motherland, I'm grazing and mooing, contentedly, ploughing on, stumbling, getting lost, having little daisy chains put on my head, and running after the calves in the labyrinth of good life while my sad human eyes are gazing at the sky.

Kundera writes that women are the future of the human being. (Did he know about the X-chromosome?) The virtues ascribed to women would doubtlessly benefit everyone, both men and women. But only the human will exalt us. The future of humanity, in all its forms, lies in the human. The future is already here. I hope that it will be a (r)evolutionary process of humanizing woman. And man. That it will not be a de-humanization of the human being. Because men are not from Mars, they are not—luckily—reduced to their scarce Y—"heritage," either; women are not from Venus (and not from that male rib with no brain at all, not even a bit of marrow). We all have the same origin—that stardust from the Big Bang, settled in our *humanity.*

114 Replica to the key figure of Minotaur in G. Gospodinov's novel *The Physics of Sorrow* (which remains a male novel, despite all its qualities). Because the author spends much thought on empathy and reckons it the main driver for writing, I will allow myself yet another association. People who identify themselves as pan-gender, declare that they are attracted (not particularly sexually) by humanity in general, with no differentiation on sex or gender, sexual orientation, race, age, language, nationality, culture, social class, etc. (along the constitutional provisions, banning discrimination on these counts). It follows that all writers are pan-gender, with their intellectual interest and empathy toward humankind.

DO NOT GO GENTLE INTO THAT GOOD NIGHT[115]

My darling Christian,

. . . Where to start?! . . .

Do you remember that joke I told you, which you didn't get at the time? You were pressing me to study, so that I would qualify for a good job, but I had other "qualifications," so to say. I was like the tribal shaman in the joke, who was sent to study in the metropolitan university, where he was surprised to find out that he had to read, and at the exam, stated "Shaman is not a reader, he is a writer." I had to study, but in reality, I wanted to write. Now I can confess that I was actually writing, secretly, "among other things"—more exactly between the French and European law. I was elated by the publication of my first book, you remember, I now knew that I could write and I wanted to write a new book. Its working title was to be "Mummy's Men" (the other reason that I hid my creative endeavors from you—you'd be terribly jealous and sulk for months on end). In fact, alongside the stories of real and imagined men I planned to write about emigration, money, culture, language, communism, Europe, nostalgia, identity . . . It was shaping up to be another Bulgarian emigrant novel. It's better that all that remained were scattered drafts, and I learned French and European law, that was *worth* it, thanks to you.

But why am I telling you all this? Because the preface of this unwritten book, with its mysterious two authors—Rada and a Bulgarian writer—describes in documentary-esque detail, my sudden death and what happens afterward with the pseudo-authentic, sly innocence of Rada's voice, it tackles some questions about authorship,

115 Dylan Thomas (1914-1953)

writing, and meaning, topics which have occupied me for ages. In some places I philosophize and in others the writing is better described as absurd and funny. I tried to imagine death and even write about it a long time before it unraveled us. For me, this was simply a game, a literary twist, a plot move. And even so I figured out almost everything quite plausibly. I got some things wrong, like for example that death would come not on a bicycle but in a car. And most important—that it wouldn't be me, but you. You departed under very similar circumstances, as described by me, but which I had meant for myself. I was almost at the age that I'd fixed in the preface for my mystifying death as an author. But it wasn't the author who departed, but the real person. The prototype. And I suffer for you, not like a literary hero. I'd foreseen Michael, as yet unborn at the time of the preface, and the exact age when he'd become an orphan. But he lost a parent in reality, not in literature. I had an amazingly accurate insight into the absurdity of the whole material world, what a person leaves behind. I've realized the untimely feeling of absurdity, accompanying many details around death, is just a harbinger, a distant rumble of the coming monstrous pain and horror. There was no way then for me to know about this horror. I've heard of the absurdity of speech after the death of a talking person. And the true meaning of the language which is born (only) in connection with death.

How young and reckless I'd been! The congruence of life and text is so intoxicating when you're young, and immortal, and fly toward extremes, with a cause, with utopias in mind, in a romantic or heroic hypostasis. The fact that literary Werther had left behind real cemeteries of young people seemed to me . . . magnificent. And all Bulgarian poets who'd greeted death with open eyes appeared beautiful to me. But in the course of adulthood and the arrival of real death, this consonance sowed only horror. This horror changed the text fundamentally. Pretentious literary mystification was swept away by the tragic truth of real death. Now I'm writing something quite different, in a quite different way, and I'm not at all sure that this would be a book. Life, or rather death, turns out to be even more dramatic than a Bulgarian emigrant novel. Your death woke and emboldened me. I was shaken and understood that I don't have a lot of time left to hang around in the everyday. Your death humbled me. Now I don't have a pretentious literary project, clear plan, and self-confidence that I'll write a book. I realized that at the best, and if I have time, for my whole life, I'll try, I'll *essay* to write, just in the way that I live, that this will be just attempts to find some meaning in my life and to leave some traces of my consciousness. And the results of my *essays* will not necessarily turn into a book for publication.

In what genre does one write about death and in what tense, from what point of view, in what style? It can only be in the first person in prefaces and prologues, or some other pretentious mystifications, and such presumptuous meta-forewords, before the subject "I" falls silent forever. In the third person, it's done in epitaphs, necrologies, epilogues, postscripts, and other meta, *postmortem* texts. It seems to me that the genres of death itself are the elegy and ballad, the last communion, last words, prophesies, forgiveness, bidding "good night" and some eccentric epistolary texts like this. Death doesn't give easily to aesthetic re-creation, because it alone is objective and eternal.

But what am I doing. I am writing to you, the dead one. I'm writing on familiar terms with death. The psychologist suggested I write out all my feelings and thoughts. I told her about shouting down the well—a common saying in our "neck of the woods." She liked it, at first she took it quite literally. I told her that I wouldn't just write, but I'd write to you. Just as if I was shouting down some deep neglected well, where your soul has hidden at the bottom. She accepted this rather strange mode of living through death, of surviving death, as it helped me. It's a strange verb this "survive," when we're thinking of death. In a way, we all should survive death at one point or another. In our neck of the woods we have another saying—a "letter from the dead," which means something utterly impossible.[116] I survive death, as I write a letter to the dead. A new genre? I do not know, but it is certainly surreal. Reality outlines the limits of the subject's experience. Reality is not enough for me. In this reality, you don't exist and I can't utter a single word to you.

It's just that I'm a little scared right now. Before you died, I'd always thought of that preface only as an eventually future literature. My demiurge gift, if I can term it thus, and the performative biblical function of the Word now scare me. Literature turned into life. Now, I am trying to turn life back into literature. Will it then be again the turn of literature to be reincarnated into life? They say, writing is a struggle with death. But it may as well be a dangerous game with death, a provocative invitation for an execution. In any case, if I continue to smoke as much, while I'm trying to write, I've got every chance to die "in harmony" with my literary "concepts."

•

116 I think, that contrary to the message of the idiom, this is not impossible. Suicide letters are exactly that, a letter from the dead—the text is written with the knowledge that it will be read when the writer is no longer among the living. Actually lots more texts can be numbered in this category. The writing of any self-confident writer is a future letter from the dead. That the Bulgarian language expresses the impossibility in this idiom, for me, simply confirms that Bulgarians however sad they are, do not turn to suicide and rarely think about death, still less to leave some written messages, linked to this event.

My darling,

Today I want to describe how things looked without you. How the material world looks when its occupant has left.

When I got home, already knowing that you would never return, I gazed at the wall clock in our dining room, I was standing there, watching and listening to time passing. No bell rang, no cuckoo, the clock hadn't stopped—nothing to announce that time was no longer in you and you no longer existed in my time.

On the table in the dining room, I found your undrunk cup of tea. I thought your DNA would be on it. Ah well, our unsuspecting cleaner sent your DNA to the dish-washer. But I managed to preserve the half full bottle of fizzy water on your bedside nightstand. I explicitly warned the cleaner not to touch it. It's still standing there. On the other side of the bed. I don't know if and when to throw it away. Your DNA should be in its neck too. What happens with a plastic bottle, half full of fizzy water, in let's say five years? And the remains of the saliva in its neck?

The fridge was full of your favorite smoked fish, which you know, no one else liked. After a few days I threw it out, because it began to smell foul.

In your desk, I found five large Godiva cherry-liqueur chocolates, the kind wrapped in shiny pinky-purple foil, which in the morning you would secretly pop into my bag for me to find in the office and sweeten my afternoon. I didn't slip them into my bag, they're sitting in your desk even now. I know what's happening with them, because they've got a sell-by date, which passed long ago. The chocolate goes whitish, the cherry hardens and the liqueur evaporates.

I collected the shirts you'd left for ironing. They were immaculately ironed, your blue and white button-downs, top quality, expensive, classically male. They smelled laundered with a fragrant softener. I kept one shirt, I gave the others to our cleaner, ironed and neatly ordered, for her husband. I felt awkward when I opened the drawer with your vests and underpants—I threw them straight into the dustbin. Someone's intimacy appears particularly macabre *postmortem*. Your shoes scared me too—they reminded me of those piles of shoes in the concentration camps. But I cried a lot over your cashmere pullovers—all of them smelled of you and the perfume which I gave you. I gave away your thirty-two silk ties, to friends, relatives, charity. I kept just one—the Italian extravagance, about which every man asked where you'd got it. My first Valentine present. I chose the silver with pink clover leaves for the cremation. I gave the gold and silver cuff-links to your grown-up son.

I gazed a long time at the reproduction, which you'd hung up many years ago in front of our bathroom, that blurry landscape, which could be a sunset over distant hills. You'd told me it was hanging opposite your bed when you were a child, and every evening, as you were falling asleep, you'd look at this landscape and be carried into dreams and fantasies. So you wouldn't think of your sick mom, installed in a faraway room in the family château, so you wouldn't hear her cries, when the morphine stopped working. I stopped in front of the reproduction every time I came in or out of the bathroom. I tried it through your other glasses—the reading ones—and regarded it closely. A naïve, romantic, amateur landscape reproduction, cheap, frayed and faded. I felt your absence physically—absent were your gaze and memory. This faded reproduction doesn't speak anything to anybody anymore. I thought of the reproduction of the Sistine Madonna, which hung in my parents' living room where they also slept. And how for me as a child, this poor-quality reproduction, in its vulgar frame held the secret of my parents' beauty and love. It wouldn't have meant anything to you, either.

Before you left, I hadn't looked at the dozens of old photographs scattered throughout the house. You framed them in thick gold, and I took them as retro chic decoration, as suitable décor for the neoclassical interior, which had nothing to do with our jolly home. Now I wander through this ghostly gallery, most often at night (because now I too cannot sleep). I look at the photographs one by one. Your aunts, uncles, grannies, grandpas, great grannies, great grandpas. Your museum. Or clan mausoleum. You told me nothing about these long dead folk. Did you know anything at all about them? Did any of these faces speak to you? Now no one is going to know anything about them. The only thing left of these people are these ancient and somehow morbid photographs. There are no words, messages, stories. Indistinguishably dead, more dead than any stranger, whose name I read on a tombstone. That at least gives me the freedom to make up a story, while family is chained up in some minimalist factology, which says nothing, and forbids you to fabulate. Ghosts, which I'll gather up in the cellar.

Why did you put up all these photographs? So these ordinary folk wouldn't be forgotten, so you could bring them to life, at least while you were alive? Or to "place yourself in clan order"? Didn't you imagine your color picture, handsome, in a red pullover, hanging on the walls of your children's and grandchildren's houses? I don't think our children will put up pictures; they won't have any need whatever to remember, even less to commemorate. Besides, photographs are the least meaningful traces of us. Look what happened to your family pictures.

We didn't talk about all this. I didn't tell you about that old photograph, which I'd seen at a friend's and which drove me to write. Why didn't we talk about your old photos? How was it that I didn't manage to tell you about that photo and my thoughts? What did we ever talk about, if we missed such important things?!

The Police returned your spectacles, your phone, and your watch. Not a scratch on them! Even on your delicate glasses! How was that possible—your sturdy, healthy body was crushed and your spirit flew away, while these soulless and fragile objects survived the monstrous crash? Your telephone even rang, your watch continued to measure the time, your delicate spectacles glinted in the sun and continued to correct something in the distance. I tried them—I saw just a blur, your unique perspective. The watch continued to measure the time, some different time in which you did not exist. The last voice message, which I listened to on your phone was from Rada and Michael—asking when you'd be back home. They called exactly while you were dying. I kept your phone charged for another few weeks, until all your contacts learned that you were now gone.

Tell me, my darling, how is it possible that from your voice you left me two such humdrum messages, which I've simply forgotten to erase—you ask me to buy you a *Spiegel*[117] when I leave my office and you tell me where you have parked the car. And . . . Ninety minutes of cassette recordings, in which instead of your favorite Schiller, you read out mindless sentences in German. *Der Apfelstrudel schmekt sehr gut. Ich mochte noch ein Stuck bitte. Momentan, lese ich die neue Strategie.*[118] I listen and replay them over and over. Your voice, your bass, conserved and reproduced by a machine. And I try to interpret, swimming in your intonation, your mistakes, the tremor of your voice, I imagine what you wanted to tell me behind these meaningless words. Behind all these meaningless words which we exchanged when alive. What do we leave behind us apart from meaningless words and various annoyingly durable objects? What did we not manage to say, in translation? And these words of mine—will they survive? Will Michael find them one day? Will there be any more of you (or of me) from these letters of mine? And for whom? For what? In the supranational, multilingual bubble of Brussels, we chewed over the everyday objects and strudels in French, we chatted about European strategies and ourselves in English, and recently we caressed each other in

117 A popular German weekly.

118 The apple pie is very delicious. May I have another piece, please? I am reading the new strategy now. German.

German. Hadn't I agreed finally to start learning it, and one learns a language quickest on a pillow, as you repeat. With *schmoozing*.

Your emails are in my inbox, your SMSs are in my telephone, and my SMSs to you are still in my phone, I read them, I listen to your last voice mails . . . And now I write to you, and it seems so natural. And I send my letters to your inbox. My letters sink in some kind of virtual clouds of words, music, images, photos, where we don't figure physically anyhow. And perhaps they'll reach what you have become now. I reckon that it makes no difference if I write to you in Bulgarian, which you didn't learn. Because you now understand all languages, in fact, there are surely no languages for you now, and my thoughts reach you without being mediated in words and their translation.

I wondered what happens with the electronic mail of someone who dies. When no one knows the password for this mail, necessary in order to cancel it, but not before sending out a message to all contacts, including those who bombard us with advertisements, that the account is closed, because its owner is dead. How would such an automatic *out of office*—or more precisely *out of life*—message sound? *Thank you for your message. It will never be read or answered as I am dead.* Or: *Please stop sending me publicity. I can neither want nor can buy your products anymore as I am dead.* Surely, your email will remain active for centuries and will gather several million advertisements. Our life as consumers is longer than our human life. Good that you had no Facebook account, blog, Twitter, or anything of that kind that I'd have to deal with now.

I tried to look through your archive—one hundred thirty four crammed folders, which could not even close. Reports, strategies, protocols, business correspondence—here and there notes, thoughts, proposals, calculations in German, English, French, even Spanish, in your nervous, somewhat old-fashioned, and legible handwriting. Your personal history of European integration, the laws regarding the financing of European parties, the positions taken by the Social Democrat party, the European Union Treaties, the talks on the admission of Poland . . . Plus an entire library of those heavy plump yellow volumes in soft covers—jurisprudence of the European Court in the area of competition over twetny years. Half the cellar was taken by the Spiegel magazine over twenty-five years . . . Your personal historiography. Most of all this is now digitalized and online. Apart from the personal element. And the personal is now no more. It has in some sense been digitalized, too.

I threw out one ton of paper (plus almost another ton of other rubbish, using a firm that specialized in recycling). How had our-hundred-year-old wood-beamed house not collapsed?! I kept the books, all of them old German volumes. Let Michael one day decide what to do with them. I also kept some texts that you'd handwritten, your last day planner, and a Christmas paper star, on which you'd written in German to four-year-old Michael, how much you loved him, and how strong and clever he will become.

In your planner, I found your last records. Thank God these were in French—and among these: "How many things I've got to get done!"—paying bills, work tasks, home repairs that awaited us . . . You sound scared of some pain in the forehead which kept you awake, hoping you'll see how Michael grows up (why this?? because of a pain in the forehead?!). To the very end, we waste our time on mundane details, and you with your protestant moral, giving yourself extra grief over whether you'll get everything done by the deadline. What deadline? Death seldom comes at the right time.

My dear,

Please remind me—was it Epicurus who said he didn't fear death because when it arrives, he wouldn't be there? Put more abstractly, death can be only virtual experience of the subject, or the consciousness, because when it comes for real, the subject won't exist. Let me tell you of death, because when it arrived, you were there no longer.

I don't know whether you had time to realize, therefore I'll tell you—on the way home, some thirty three kilometers from home, where the children were waiting for you, you most probably fell asleep at the wheel, or had a heart attack or stroke, and you crashed into a tree at a relatively high speed. By some chance, there was an ambulance passing by and they performed resuscitation for a whole forty minutes, they even succeeded in establishing your pulse for a short while, but after that nothing. Forty-five minutes after the crash they pronounced you dead, according to cardio-respiratory indicators. While they were working on you, a police car arrived. A pair of policemen inspected the crash site, looking for skid marks (there were none) inspected the car, established your identity, your address, your family, took dozens of photos, including of your dead body and eyes. They loaded you into the same ambulance and drove you to the morgue in the closest hospital. The two policemen, accompanied by a psychologist made their way to our home, where seventeen-year-old Rada and five-year-old Michael opened the door. I, as you remember, had left three days earlier to deliver lectures in Bulgarian universities, expected back home in two days.

Rolling on the back seat of the crashed car was my favorite marzipan cake, which you'd bought for me. It looked like a stuffed teddy, preposterously poking out in the ruins after a bomb or an earthquake had killed the child. It was like a suspenseful beginning of a horror film. Then, the film went on.

> *. . . Blind eyes could blaze like meteors and be gay,*
> *Rage, rage against the dying of the light . . .*[119]

I sat in the police station and tried to concentrate, to understand what the same two policemen were telling me, in French. In my eyes there was some unquenchable source of salty liquid that flowed uncontrollably, although I wasn't crying, or at least I thought so. In my hands, I was turning over your wallet with all your bank cards, a few banknotes, the martenitza,[120] which I'd given you, to hang on a blossoming tree, Misho's photo and your blood-type card, your telephone, your spectacles, your watch. I leafed through the police dossier, I couldn't read any of it, because it was in Dutch—you'd died in a Flemish *commune.*

But the photos had no need of translation. You lay there, awkwardly stretched out on the grass by the road, one of your legs unnaturally twisted. Your eyes open, you looked out calmly, gently, even somehow dreamingly into the gray March sky. I console myself that you felt no pain. I try to read into those wide open blue eyes of yours, what or whom you were thinking of in these last moments of consciousness. Did you think or see anything at all? Did you realize you were dying? What does death feel like? Like an anesthetic, as if you were drowning? Did you put up a struggle, did you rage? Did you really see that daffodil meadow after the tunnel? Did you see yourself from above, resuscitated, all that chaos beside the road, as people who've returned from the tunnel report?

I read somewhere (not something esoteric, but an article based on scientific research) that consciousness persists for "an unspecified time" after death. Those returnees "report" that they realized they were dead and this realization was present when they'd been dead. They say also that a strip of light had connected them with their dead body. The big question is how much time (and what sort of time) does this *postmortem* consciousness last. But only the returnees can answer this question and, logically, the answer is recorded by stopwatches—five-ten-fifteen-twenty minutes—the time that "they weren't here." What about all the hundreds of billions[121] who didn't return? How

119 Another two lines from the Dylan Thomas poem.

120 Tiny figures, woven in red-and-white threads, which Bulgarians exchange on March 1st; associated with the coming spring and with hopes for good health and love. To attach to a blossoming tree, after seeing the first stark, and to make a wish.

121 According to scientific data this is the total number of all the dead people in human history.

long is that undefined time in which their consciousness remains . . . alive? When the heart stops, and the blood stops circulating, all brain reflexes stop immediately. But it seems consciousness endures even after the stopping of all life functions. Is *alive* the exact definition for consciousness, if it clearly does not depend (only) on the biological "hardware" and if in the not so far off future, it could be archived and reproduced on a neuro-processor computer? Death will become an utterly virtual experience. If only we were born a little later; if only you hadn't fallen asleep at the wheel! I would have had your consciousness to talk to—and who could answer now my letters. And with a hologram it would have been quite true to life. Sure, we wouldn't make love, but you can't have everything, can you? Then again, who knows, I might see you quite alive sometime, like my grandfather.

How different is this . . . resurrection from all the photos, recordings, and video. I've only got one video with you. It's as if I'm happy that we have just one, as if we don't have hundreds of photos and clips from beaches, trips, tourist sites, visits, relatives, Christmases and Easters . . . in which you would be laughing, chatty, contented, proud. I'm relieved that I erased your voicemails after hearing them and fulfilling their pragmatic function. It's somehow scary, paradoxically morbid, this technological resurrection. Which itself reiterates that the person has gone. I feel this most strongly exactly when the technology revives you as image and sound . . .

I look—through a salty channel—at your forget-me-not blue eyes in the police pictures and I see you at the passport cubicle at the airport, a few days before, with Michael in your strong hands, seeing me off. I kiss the both of you and at last you look at me—one, two, three seconds we look into each other's eyes, your blue eyes smile at me, and love me, and tell me "There's nothing scary about flying in an airplane, don't be frightened, I'll miss you, don't worry about me and the children. But . . . don't you know, every departure and goodbye can be the last, like going to sleep, everything can happen, I love you." Exactly like your evening ritual when you'd stroke me and beg me that if we didn't wake up together in the morning, I'd forgive your mistakes and faults and know that you loved me. I'd always mutter "rubbish, don't say such things," or I'd caress you, I even sometimes laid your head on my shoulder, like a little silly boy, who's afraid of the dark. Then we'd say, "Goodnight."

Do not go gentle into that good night

I've always been afraid of flying, I mean in a plane, but after your death I hate airports and I'm scared *to death* of even the most innocent goodbye. The next meeting could turn out one-sided.

I'd already handed to the funeral agency a suit, shirt, tie, socks, shoes, vest, pants. When I went there second time, the agent gave me your wedding ring. I turned it over in my hands, and wondered from what star the gold had come. I told the man that I preferred you depart with the ring, married to me. The agent mercifully did not argue over details of the chemical processes, set off in cremation, and delicately suggested I kept the ring even so, as a "dear memory." If I insisted, of course, they'd comply with my wish, and would put the ring into the urn. I didn't insist.

But what cremation, what urn? I hadn't thought at all about the fate of your dead body. Your other, grown-up children, who had arrived in the meantime, had already decided on it. Protestant culture, tradition and so forth. "Do we want to see the deceased?" No, you children did not. I still couldn't imagine you dead. I'd seen only a few photographs, where you're lying with a broken leg and staring dreamily at the sky. I still hadn't taken it in, that you were dead, that now you're just dead flesh. "Yes, I want to see my dead husband."

Here you are, in your gray corduroy suit, buttoned up, with a tie, I can't make out whether they've put on your vest, and I dare not think about the pants. You're under a thick glass half-lid. Lord, how he's reddened and whitened you! Humiliating and grotesque, you'd go crazy if you could see yourself. What needed covering so badly?! Actually, you have a deep scratch on your left cheek and your left eye is blackened. But this doesn't excuse the excessive make-up. I would later ask them to leave you . . . natural. Although, this wouldn't make a difference to anybody. They managed to move your left leg, but your foot remained at a right angle, contrary to any anatomical law of the living, not of patho-anatomy. Your nails had grown. How much you hated uncut nails, you even mocked my modest manicure, which I saw to from time to time. They'd shaved you. Ha, do you know, you've got a shadow! The light is very bright and focused in this strange windowless room, which reminds me of rooms in botanical and natural history museums. And yes, your body throws a shadow on the floor. How stupid all that poetry is, whispering about the shadow, which is the *incarnation* of our soul.

Don't let me forget to tell you, the bill arrived from your dentist—a breath-taking sum, but don't worry, I'll pay it in bits, over several months. Health insurance covers a really small amount. I didn't know that in the last months you'd practically renewed your teeth. I saw they'd become whiter and nicer, but I didn't think about it. And you, dear, had wanted, discretely to be up to the mark. Now they'll burn you with your teeth, straightened and polished. With your suit and everything. Your protestant culture is merciful—nothing is left of the flesh to worry the sick imaginations of the living for years on end.

Your teeth remind me of something. I didn't tell you, but a year or so ago, I almost bought a home fitness machine—we had space in the house, and I had no time to go to the gym. I imagined how my sculpted body could rot away in a few months from some fatal disease. Isn't everything we expend on ourselves simply vanity and a cry to be loved? And why I was so miserly in my love, why I was so busy with anything else, but loving you?!

Thank you for departing before getting old.

Our world was still intimate and erotically charged. I hadn't yet turned into a frigid scolding wife, only a mother or granny. Your morning erection roused you from your short sleep. A man dies when he stops needing sex, he stops waking up when his morning erection disappears. I read an intimate and honest description of one such morning written by John Updike.

Thank you for driving like a German yuppie—at 250 km per hour on the motorways, sometimes 90-100 km per hour in town. I had the feeling that our cars would fall to pieces with your strong hands gripping the steering wheel. Thank you for this drug of yours—speed and your rebellious disdain for the rules. Lively penchant, despite the fact it killed you in the end. That's the same with every drug, I guess; that's what will happen with me and my cigarettes.

Thank you for departing before the world became routine, small, and fast. We still had desires—to travel, to see, to taste, to meet, to read. Time was still running unevenly—sometimes too fast, sometimes terribly slowly. And there was still a lot ahead. You left when you still felt real joy, you wanted a lot and waited impatiently. *Vorfreude.*[122] On top of that, you wanted the best and if possible immediately. A typical Capricorn. With age, joy becomes somehow lethargic and alien. Do I really want to go on that fantastic holiday in the divine God-knows-where? Am I really overjoyed by the mind-boggling new bag, the universal applause for my report, the successes of our children and friends, the achievements of the EU, someone's complements? You grow able to enjoy someone or something without necessarily wanting them. And this is not any newly acquired gentility at the cost of a subdued egoism, but a seeping spiritual lassitude, which crawls like mold, a signal of an im-

122 A very special German word which means joyful anticipation, in which the actual anticipation may provoke stronger emotion than what is anticipated.

minent flood, of the growing feeling of meaninglessness and the shriveling of any form of desire.

Thank you for departing so suddenly, in a second, and "up straight," as they say in Bulgarian. You didn't fall sick, you didn't lie down, you didn't know that you were dying, you had no physical agony and animal horror, shit and urine, morphine and lies, hospitals and palliative care, nor desperate attempts to stay dignified and brave, like the kind of Prussian I'm sure you'd have fought to remain right to your last breath. I don't know how I would have lived through that, how I'd have felt, what I'd have remembered of you. Thank you for not surviving in a coma, and living unconsciously, i.e., without actually being here, for years. Thank you that you didn't survive as an invalid, forever fastened to a bed. It would have been utter hell. Lars von Trier's film *Breaking the Waves* is brave and conceptual, but we were not personages in a film. I wouldn't have lasted in the role of saint and I would have fallen apart from guilt. And you, you would have demanded to die. We would have been dishonestly and cruelly parted, not by death, as our marriage vows had foreseen.

Thank you for catching me at the most appropriate moment and begetting Michael. In spite of all my hesitation and doubt. Rada flew the nest, but Michael will be with me for at least another ten years.

Thank you for the beautiful jewelry, which I didn't wear, because I was always in a rush in the morning, and in the end threw on jeans. Now I wear the pieces—not so much to look beautiful (because even now I don't understand how jewelry exactly makes a woman more beautiful) but because I get the feeling that when I put on something, you're looking at me from somewhere. Didn't you see this jewelry on me in your mind's eye before you bought it?

Thank you for the 130 bottles of red wine in the wine cellar. Most of them French, but there are some Italian and Spanish, ten, twenty, thirty years old, and some even older. Only now did I look them over. Some have gone off, I checked, but most of them are simply incredible. I drink them with Rada and friends on special occasions (and without such). Then I think of you. I have the feeling of taking Communion from you and you forgive me everything. I don't know what you are forgiving me for, but it eases the pain. I'm keeping up your tradition and now and then I'll buy a box of quality wine, which I lay down. Perhaps one day Rada and Michael will drink this wine like an intimate Communion with me. Wine is a living liquid, it takes on sun, yeast, time, memories, it grows old, even dies . . .

•

We ought to have talked about death. You and me. When we married in the registry office in Bonn, I repeated the marriage vows in German, without understanding a word. But I'm sure that, like all wedding vows, in any language, religious or secular, there was that phrase which fixes the time limits for the matrimonial "contractual clauses" as "till death do us part." Which means we'd get old together and one of us would see the other die and then live on for a short or long time without them. (Unless of course, the pair of us die together, in a plane crash, a sinking cruise ship, a terrorist attack.) We ought to have talked about everything, which I'm writing to you now, before death did us part.

We ought to have talked about death, but not vaguely, with some meek calls for forgiveness, over some good-night communions. We anyway forgive the dead everything and only speak well or nothing about them. Death provides some such *a priori* value to the dead. Simply because they are no more. This is the case for all departed *things*, departed never to return, not only departed people. Suddenly these things become really important and valued, sorrowfully beautiful and magically unique. As we experience nostalgia for the past, and we idealize it, so we regard the dead. This better explains why we don't speak ill of the dead, rather than out of some elementary sense of fairness, because the dead are unable to defend themselves from criticism and slander.

We ought to have talked about death when we were alive, both of us. But no one talks about death. No one writes about death. Death is shoved off somewhere behind the curtains of life, of brightly colored, beautiful, joyous life, it's mentioned at best in some euphemisms or as a fact at the end of someone's biography. When you leave the stage, no one wants to know what's happening to you behind the curtains. We never talk about death, although we think about it almost continually, and through our whole life we see how people around us disappear. We don't talk about death, even when it is at the door and the eyes of the dying see it.

You know, my brother, a chest and stomach surgeon, often operates on cancer, people frequently die in his hands. For him a good day means no one has died. He often keeps a patient alive, only so they don't die on his watch. A doctor's job is strange—a continuous, determined and doomed struggle for the possible lengthening of the life of a reed. It is very difficult to die in today's modern hospitals. But despite the accursed nature of the effort, in no University, in no specialization, not just medical, is death taught—how to accept its inevitability, and how to explain it to your children, how you prepare for it, how you get over the death of someone close. Even doctors aren't taught how to announce its approach both to the patient and those close to them, how they will accompany them to the end, how the doctor himself should think about and get over death. At best, the doctor would give only his prognosis, which statistics show is always optimistic.

Before, people got old and died in their families, being taken care of by women, the eternal carers for children, husbands, grandkids, the wounded, sick, aging, and dying. In the end women had to wash and weep over the corpse. In civilized countries now, when a person exits the stage, behind the curtains, he finds himself in an old folks' home, hospital or hospice. Have you noticed the old folks' home, *la maison de repos,* with the noble name *La Belle Époque*, three blocks away from our house? In a policy document on social affairs, a freelance translator had rendered this as "holiday home," I laughed, but then, who knows why, I cried. Every time when I pass by *La Belle Époque*, from a ground-floor room that serves for TV viewing as well visits from relatives, an old woman always waves at me through the window that faces the street. This woman is sitting, always the same, in this, I guess, social activity, room, looking through the window and waving at me: "Ey, girl!"—because I am still a girl in her eyes. "How's life out there? Someday, you'll be coming here, at the other side of the window." And I hurry up straight away and pretend I don't see her. The first time I waved too, I even stopped. The Granny waved an invitation for me to enter. I apologetically pointed to my watch. I had time, but I was scared.

Death has turned from an existential event into a medical and social problem. Society cuts off and hides the hell of the individual behind a curtain, so as not to upset the cheery spirit of the living on the stage. The chronotopos of our civilization is one eternal present, on a picturesque global stage, on which eternally young and beautiful people enjoy their beautiful life. Death has no role here, the play rests on the assumption that death does not exist, or is a taboo. Old age produces highly inappropriate scenes and ugly personages.

With these thoughts, I by no means wish to belittle medical advances, which prolong life, moreover life in good health, nor the palliative care, which mediates the pain and degradation of the flesh and the time and discomfort of relatives. It is just that death is a taboo in our time and in our society.

In our GP's waiting room, I read in some magazine an interview with a French writer[123] (you haven't read him, you haven't missed anything, you wouldn't have liked him) that his daughter, when she was still a little girl, wanted him to promise that he would never die. And he, would you believe it, promised this. My Nana was more courageous than this guy, who otherwise plays it very "cool." In fact, I might have done the

123 Fréderic Beigbeder.

same. But in the hope that I'd still be alive when Michael would grow up and understand the truth, as well as the love and the tragedy in my unfeasible promise. However, the French writer actually meant it! His next novel is about medical breakthroughs and achievements in prolonging life to the max. This dude indeed wanted to outlive his child and thus fulfill his promise.

On this subject, again in our GP's waiting room, I read a brochure (it appears waiting rooms make very good reading rooms) advertising a luxury hospice. Along with all services and care expected at such a place, one particular piqued my interest—inmates would be "prepared psychologically for the inevitable end." I reread this phrase several times. If it wasn't about just drugging, I wanted to visit this hospice and most of all acquaint myself with the "psychological preparation," because it is universally useful, not only for loved ones and or the terminally ill. I was also really interested in what the operators at those special call centers say to a dying person. Most probably what they'd been taught in relevant training sessions. So it was this training that interested me, too. We gain the courage to pull the veil from the taboo, only seconds before the face of death.

Do you remember how worried you were when I shared my "interests"? You worried that I was sick and hiding it. Clearly, in your view, you shouldn't be concerned about death if it is not imminent.

Did I tell you about that Belgian girl, the physicist who wanted to be allowed to commit a suicide? Yes, I remember now, I told you. Listening to the debates on television, I realize that the arguments, which make this girl look simply sick and a deviant from "normal" humanity, are hypocritical and superficial and they are rooted in the deafening silence and concealment around death, our ultimate taboo.

I thought over the humane and liberal spirit of two seemingly contradictory laws, which by no coincidence had been passed in one society, more or less at one and the same historic and political moment—the abolition of the death penalty and the right to medically assisted death. The right to abortion may as well be added, though it concerns only women and is about women's integrity and rights, rather than the death of a human being, what the fetus is definitely not. Americans make a rewarding object of analysis through this trinity prism.

Roland Barthes explains that grief is that fearsome place, in which he is now no longer afraid, because what he was afraid of has now happened and taken away his fear that it would happen; so to love means to be scared, that you'll lose somebody who will die.

I now don't remember whether Barthes himself or someone else continues this line of thought by saying that an element of grief for a departed loved one is the loss of part of your very self, of that person, who you were in the presence of the deceased, in your relationship with him or her, in the feelings of the deceased. The death of a loved one is a double death, in a significant sense.

I think as well that death may not only be physical. Every time when I happened to meet—in the street, in a shop, by chance—an ex-lover, even my first husband—the artist—or someone with whom I've been really close friends in the past, I'd been left stunned that I've simply met some man or woman I know. We'd exchange some absurdly banal chit-chat and I'd be unable to get my head around the fact that this person had once been closest to me. The only explanation which comes to mind is that separations and estrangements are like death. The person, whom I have loved and desired, or the one with whom I have shared everything, has disappeared, same as if they'd died. And this woman, who has loved that man or felt very close to that person is also gone, as if she'd died. This woman, whom this man has loved and wanted, probably the same, has also died. And in the street we meet as distant acquaintances those who amazingly resemble people we have loved or who have loved us. Perhaps the only difference between death and separation is that death usually fixes existing feelings and closeness, that's why there's grief, and mythologizing. Ugly death is therefore so unfair—it undermines the purity of feelings and adoration. But to a significant extent this is true of most separations. Provided of course, that later some inopportune meeting doesn't destroy the myths of memory.

I tried to think that we're simply separated, that you're OK, somewhere else, even with somebody else. I sometimes succeed in thinking of death like a separation, just as separation *is* death to a significant extent. But I can't think up anything for Michael—he has no father at all, none whatsoever. He doesn't spend every second weekend with you, he can't call you to tell you about school, his friends, or his fear of terrorists, you don't go to the German-speaking parents' evenings, and on Father's Day, you don't go bowling with the Dads, you don't help him with his German. Michael doesn't get scared about you dying, he doesn't stroke your bald head, doesn't happily cuddle in your big strong arms, and has no Papa who'll worship him, yet is still strict, who is scared for him in his turn. Thank you for trying to be a good step-father (an ugly word in any language) to Rada. She misses you a lot.

For me the artist is deader than you, the "truly dead." Mortality looks more bearable than the quiet and unnoticeable disappearance of the living, their fugue from the intimate orbit into black gloom, their vagrancy.

And you, my darling, there on the sad height,
Curse, bless, me now with your fierce tears, I pray.[124]

My dear,

Today I'll write you a philosophical letter, most probably under the influence of the film I watched yesterday, *Melancholia*. Actually, the psychologist pretty much banned me from watching it. Why do I tell her everything? It's really interesting what the director (Lars Von Trier) would have said, that his films are not recommended for people suffering from post-traumatic syndrome or "ordinary" human melancholy. Actually, I think I read somewhere that he himself is a deeply depressed type. No need to retell you the film—I believe that in the void there, there are no distinct languages and any kind of *content* reaches that other world, direct and unhampered by media technicalities. I wondered even so, if this film had come out a year earlier, or if you were not now a pile of dust, what we would have talked after the showing. Poor Rada . . . was quite shattered by the film. To her budding existential anxiety and generational ecological fear, the film added another catastrophic scenario, a cosmic one, one might say.

Did you see in the film that only people experience real horror, among other reasons, because they cannot save their children, that they don't know how to tell them that everybody will die soon. The father kills himself in the stables, the mother freaks out with the child horrified that there's nowhere to shelter her son. And only the childless, crazy, sexy auntie does the most human and only thing possible. She builds a shack, so primitive that it is rather symbolic, but real, a shelter for the boy—an illusory shelter though as are all human hopes and beliefs in salvation and comfort—and she takes her nephew and sister by their hands, in a circle, so they stay together. Together as charred flesh, as Mendeleev's table, as star dust. That "together" during the short journey under the stars, like travelers on a few stops of the life train, is our only consolation.[125] I miss your hands, I miss the moments when we held hands and wished each other a good night, before sinking into the little death of sleep. It hurts me terribly that I didn't hold your hand when the light in your blue eyes was extinguished and that you will not be here to hold mine.

. . . But for half of the film the view is to the sky. Tell me how it is possible for your Kant to rave about the starry sky?! About the moral law within him, come on, I

124 A variation on the poem by Dylan Thomas. I have replaced "father" with "darling."

125 The same motif—close companions who hold hands in a circle thus meeting the cosmic finale—is repeated in the film *Don't Look Up* (2021).

understand, a Prussian and a philosopher. But the starry sky . . . ?! What excitement, over what?! For me, the starry sky has only filled me with horror and hopelessness. Whenever I've looked at it. (Most often through our bedroom window, as we were making love. Only now am I telling you what nonsense I sometimes thought up when we were making love. But for me, since childhood, the bed has been the first flying machine.) So, looking at the stars, paradoxically, even while making love, I've thought how lonely we are; how tiny, temporary, and meaningless in front of the everlasting infinity of that starry sky. And I'd always think of Pascal and his thinking reed. Tell me—you surely know now—why do we have this consciousness at all, thanks to which we contemplate infinity, our finiteness and meaninglessness? Why do we need it? I prefer to be an animal, the cleverest and most beautiful of course, but with no consciousness. Why do we need this melancholy and horror? Why is there such a discrepancy between our fragile mortal body, which exists for a moment, and breaks so easily, and our consciousness? The love shack and togetherness (how you loved that word) isn't it just a fairy tale?

The starry sky over Konigsberg must have been the same three centuries ago as that over Kaliningrad today. And above Plovdiv or Brussels. It had to have opened up the same outlook to the universe. Wait, maybe I'm wrong. The universe was the same, the same stars and constellations were decorating the sky, but human knowledge and mindset were not the same. Newton discovered the fundamental laws of physics and mathematical methods to prove them, but remained, alongside almost all other learned people in the sixteenth and seventeenth centuries, deeply religious. According to him, God's supreme reason has created the very laws and constants, has caused the very first movement (*à la* St. Augustine), has ordered the world and cosmos exactly in this fashion. Newton died when Kant was three years old—in a way handing him the baton. Kant drew a line between the empirical knowledge of nature, available to human reason, and faith (which for him was mostly morality). I think that if Kant knew more about the universe and the laws of physics, if he knew about the speed of light and had traveled away from Konigsberg, giving him a sense of human distances and of the as-yet-still human measurements of traveling these distances—which airplanes, high speed trains, sputniks and electronic communications have destroyed forever—he would not have felt excited by the starry sky. Hey, I searched through the internet and discovered something interesting. Thirty years after Kant's death, one of his fellow citizens—an astronomer, not a philosopher—was one of the first to calculate the real cosmic distance, outside the solar system, to one of the closest morning stars (from the Cygnus constellation)—103 trillion km. (One hundred and three with thirteen zeroes.) Please note, the conception of "light-years" didn't even exist yet. This would have cooled Immanuel's ardor for the starry night and deepen his suspicions about the capacity of human reason. And how funny it sounds today, his belief, that it is absurd to await the appearance of a new Newton, who will explain to us, with the laws of nature, the creation of one blade of grass. Just fifty years later, Darwin did this and went a lot further. Kant's blade of grass reminds me of Pascal's reed. Is it just a coincidence that they chose similar images? I remember now your pragmatic religiousness—just like Pascal's wager. I don't think you believed at all in the pretensions of religion, but played along to be on the safe side. In either case, you wouldn't lose, just win—either via an afterlife, or by living a virtuous life with solid moral foundations. And maybe you won both . . . You know for sure now. Though, it was hardly religion that transported you to the transcendent. (Apart from that, as an ex-pat, the German Protestant Church linked you to the German community in Brussels and became a nook, connecting you to your homeland.)

To me, astronomers and theoretical physicists have the most depressing profession. But they aren't melancholic at all, not a bit. On the contrary. Look at Stephen Hawking, he was downright enthusiastic. Despite his thoughts which roamed the universe, and his ALS. I don't understand the autistic exaltation of all these learned folk who observe the universe. Extending our field of vision , they forget the scale and the despair of the inhabitants of the pea.. In the starry sky, they see a reflection of the might of human reason and even value the universe as beautiful. Oh please . . . Beautiful like what human or which artist? I don't understand. (This stuff about the pea is too long to explain. I regret not telling you while you were still here.)

As for me, the starry sky fills me with horror, depresses me, drives me to write, and most probably to love you as well. I am puzzled by the prescription that my—or any other person's depression—has to be cured. I want my depression. Why the hell do I have to be healed? I'm an aging Pipi who doesn't want her freckles to be treated. I carry out all my life-affirming functions dutifully and even with love, joy and satisfaction and I can be left to be depressed in "my private garden." There, it's depression that makes me human. A human being with consciousness, who in a split second, such is our life, thinks of the universe. My melancholy is a sign that I'm alive beyond the biological and chemical life indicators. That my eyes are still wide open to the horror of the starry sky above me and the void ahead and behind me. That I *rage* and *curse*. My sadness is a sign that even love cannot absorb that ray of light on my consciousness. That the human flares again over the soothing incense of enzymes and hormones. Only, I'll suggest to the psychologist that we name it melancholy, or *tristesse*, instead of depression. It's nicer somehow. And it doesn't lead immediately to prescriptions of pills.

Science attempts to give me courage with the promise that the Mendeleevian table of my body is not going to disappear with my death, that the chemical elements in me and the dust that remains of you, were created back then with the Big Bang, and they'll return to the cosmos, that we are cosmic dust, that the laws of mathematics, physics and chemistry, which dictate how my body works, will outlive me, that thanks to these laws, humanity will be saved, and that even, perhaps, we will find other conscious beings, who will teach us at last how to become immortal or be reborn. Well, I saw the whole Mendeleevian table under a glass cover in the funeral agency, in an organic shape, and this was not you. Later the whole Mendelian table was transformed into an inorganic format and poured into the urn. This still wasn't you. Whereas the dead bird, which Michael's kindergarten teacher used to "introduce" death to the kids, was the same bird, only without the indicators for *biological* life. This biological death of an organism with no consciousness is quite different from the death of a human and the end of their consciousness.

I thought how the cremation directly turned you into inorganic matter and sent you back into the great circle, which began with the Big Bang. You're not going to "circulate," together with the dead bird, in the natural Earth cycle, you're not going to "clothe and feed the tree." This is from a Plovdiv poet, who taught me poetry. Here's the whole poem, there is no title. Well, how would you title such a poem?!

don't know what's there to wonder,
There'll be no more of death
I'll smell of lime bloom forever
I'll be rising and falling in rain

I'll be rising and falling in rain.
I will clothe and feed the tree
There'll be no more of death
There'll be no more of life.[126]

126 Dobromir Tonev (1955-2001), Bulgarian poet. Translation: Christopher Buxton.

What a good poem may come out from the three scenarios for non-being with supporting rhymes: nature, birth/family line, carbon/hydrogen.[127] But now I don't feel like writing poetry.

Buddha doesn't help, either. He promises me (of course only if I believe in him, and I don't like chubby greasy men) that you'll be reborn—into whatever form, could be as a person, an animal, plant, and so on "till the ninth generation." Well that's practically Darwin and biology and chemistry lessons—death is simply a transition of matter, in the shape of Mendeleevian table, from one biological and chemical state into another, in the natural cycle, where energy is not lost. In this transformative idyll, woman and all female organisms play an important role. But Buddha doesn't tell me where exactly *you* have been stowed, my darling, your consciousness, your "I," your words, emotions, memories. Your love. This Christian is not organic matter, this Christian is neither reborn nor resurrected. He lights up a few seconds below the starry sky and then is extinguished forever, he travels a few circuits in the time-train, where we met, and then gets off.

And what about consciousness, and all its derivatives like memory, emotions, thoughts, aesthetic needs and joy? What happens to consciousness, when it stops being an attribute of a conscious living person? If it is immaterial, why does it generate from material things like our brain? If it is material, what does it turn into, if the Mendeleevian table, even in its most complex structures, like our genes and brain, is just transformed? Isn't it true that according to the laws of matter, nothing really dies or disappears, it's just transformed?

This is coming out as a really confused letter. Maybe because I was a bit drunk while writing it. I think this is my last letter to you, my darling. I need to live. I know you will give your blessing for this. I need to live because of Michael and Rada. But I'll also be trying to write. Not just shout down into the well. If only I can manage to smoke less.

And look, look for your Schiller, the poet, out there in the beyond—explain to him that a woman can be clever and pretty at the same time, and that woman as well can have a beautiful soul and human consciousness. Convey to Doctor Schiller from me, that his method works—creativity really does help with "psychological difficulties," especially in living through death.[128] And if you meet that smoker and alcoholic Dylan Thomas, tell him that women can rage and curse, too.

September 2011–September 2018

Brussels

127 In Bulgarian all these words rhyme.

128 References to Schiller's ideas—more inquisitive readers can delve further.

TO RETURN[129]

I was twenty-two when the Iron Curtain fell, I graduated, started work and raised a family over the next decade of so-called transition, which is better described as a time of hyperinflation, food shortages, poverty, mass racketeering, an organized mafia and corruption, of betrayed expectations and fading illusions, and of mass emigration. Yet, sometimes I blame myself for running away from my homeland. I mercilessly rub salt into the wound. Christian might have been right about re-immigration. I pray that one day a prosperous and law-abiding Bulgaria would welcome waves of Bulgarians, who would be returning to work and live in their country of origin to make it a homeland once again.

Every year, I leave the global nowhere of Brussels to visit Plovdiv, "the city to return to," as extolled by a friend poet. For years, it was a joy to see family, friends, the streets of the past. Plovdiv was feeling like a photo album, in which, under the light of my tender and pleasantly sweet nostalgia, place and people looked charming. It was a return, kind of, as if I had been entering a nice photo. Over the past years this perception has gradually changed. Now, a heavy melancholy overtakes me when I go to Plovdiv. Time in this living photo has not stopped. For good, in many aspects, the town has changed in positive ways. But for me, personally, it's different.

I always put aside one hour at least for a coffee, drunk in solitude on the main street, while I gaze on the *mise-en-scène* of the first (hopefully) half of my life. The geography and itineraries of my past have almost disappeared.

---

129 Reference to a classic Bulgarian poem "To return to your father's house" by Dimcho Debelyanov (1887–1916), an archetypal wanderer, who was shot by a Welsh sniper in WWI.

Only when I see, live and up close, the faces of my parents, do I realize how much they've aged. Skype and Facetime perform almost like Photoshop. The block in which I grew up and where my parents still live up till now is something like my village or "hood," and the new or commemorative necrologies at the entrances tell me of the disappearance of my fellow villagers. Those still alive shock me with their unrecognizability. One-time babies now have children, and the children I played with, unrecognizable as well, have grandkids. From the faces of my parents, neighbors, friends, their grown up children, from the pictures on the necrologies, I recognize time passing and my own aging. If you look at yourself in a mirror every day, you don't see how you're getting old. And there's no way of seeing this with people you often see. Actually, celebrities have the same effect, especially on someone, like me, who only catches up on celebrity news once in a year. Hey, Brad Pitt's gotten old. Well, hang on, if even he, who has surely dolled himself up aesthetically either with injections or a scalpel, has visibly got old, what's happened with me? I go to the mirror, I look and . . . I see nothing. I look again at the photograph of the actor and my sight returns.

Plovdiv is no longer a dear photo with images that are fixed forever, but a mirror of reflections. From the superposed faces, views, fleeing shadows, and phantom silhouettes, my own face emerges in this mirror. This mirror is the mysterious door to time travel, which is locked for us, humans. Only the mind can travel in time. In both directions. Our bodies travel only toward death. Only travel in space can change human life (this is from Hawking). The journey from Plovdiv to Brussels changed my own life. Plovdiv, whither, health permitting, I'll return as a pensioner, is the irrevocable past to which it is impossible to return. This hopelessness cannot be compensated by any differences in standards, generous European pensions and gleeful plans for pensioner freedom and comfort. Plovdiv is the city to return to, on my one-way trip in time.

Several years ago, when I was only thinking about this book, I decided to go to Lom. I wanted to stroll through my childhood, to squeeze myself down Alice's hole and emerge on the other side of my planet, there where my consciousness had sprung. Look there's Lom! How could I have not put a foot there in forty years? No sooner said than done.

My luxurious vehicle transported me like a futurist cyborg after the apocalypse, through the utterly deserted tumble-down villages of Radichkov's wild north-west.[130]

130 Yordan Radichkov (1929–2004), Bulgarian writer and playwright. North-west Bulgaria is the usual topos of his stories.

Round a bend, I slammed on the brakes, so as not to sweep away the surreal scene of a vibrant gypsy wedding dance. The scarlet flag gently caressed the windscreen. Whitened, rouged, and bearded faces granted me just enough attention to pass by. Clearly cyborgs impressed no one here.

Here's Lom. I stopped at the road sign, high up the hill, and got out to smoke a cigarette. From the hill of time past, before descending with my weighty aging body, I looked down at the little town, which was buzzing quietly like a giant grasshopper, in the August heat, hidden amids the vineyard and sunflowers, paddling its feet in the river.

The town met me with its first gutted block in which about fifty-two years ago, my father had dreamt of living. It was derelict, with no windows, with gaping black holes. Surely, there was no money for its demolition.

I stood in front of my primary school—The Fotinov School was burnt out, the roof collapsed. There was certainly no money for its funeral.

The cultural center, where my father had played violoncello, had closed long ago—there was no one to play, to sing, no one to listen, or borrow books from the library.

I went past my kindergarten—among the weeds and the rusting climbing frames there were . . . children! Clearly a summer group. The teacher immediately gathered them round her like chicks as she followed me with worried eyes.

When I was a child, my Granddad was riding a bicycle in the street. Now, as an adult, I went to look for him where he was supposed to be. Once on the hill at the end of the town, now the graveyard was walled on two sides with blocks. Out of one of their windows the living saw the sunflower fields or the river and from the other—the graveyard. I'm sure they lived philosophically in these blocks. Did they have children? What did the children think of these views?

I was stung by nettles, spiked by thorns in this urban facility for the dead, so unwelcoming to the living. A gypsy of ill-defined gender popped out of nowhere and asked me "what I'd like"—weeding, digging, cleaning, bringing flowers, "or about a new grave?" I told him (or her?) I was looking for my Granddad's grave. We specified the name and divided the graveyard into zones for the search. The gypsy lost himself and did not turn up again, he'd certainly decided that I wasn't going to pay him for this unusual service.

It's a strange feeling that overtakes you, when you see almost your own name inscribed on a gravestone. If I'd been born male, the coincidence would have been total. Knowing our country's patriarchal traditions, this continuity ought to give some kind of existential peace for people, especially men. Name and family will abide, only the bones will multiply. What I felt was not exactly peace.

"Hi there Granddad . . . You know, I see you every day, actually . . . you remember that portrait photo of 1936, it is in my study . . . I'm sorry about the watch. Nana put it back to 5:28. But it's not the same. I know. Sorry . . . Are you still riding a bike? . . . Me? . . . I grew up. I've even got old now. And . . . now I wonder where . . . well . . . where I want them to . . . You know . . ."

Was I talking out loud? I was standing there in that heat, among the nettles and thorns, just at the center of the end of the world and talked to my Granddad, dead for sixty years. Was there any philosopher from the surrounding blocks to observe this Hamlet scene from his balcony-box? Did the gypsy run away because he thought I was mad?

I went down the main street and stopped under the balcony of my one-time presidium. I learned from the sign on the entrance door that a computer firm was occupying the first floor.

Then I downed an icy mint liquor in the nearby café, staring at the shockingly diminished monument to the September uprising.

Then I climbed up the little street to my very first home. It was round the bend . . . right . . . there it is, on the corner, in front there was a bigger house, and our tiny cottage was behind it, in the yard. Yes, that's it. I stood in front of the gate. In the yard, a man in a vest was washing his car. And behind him, up the steep path . . . the cottage. In some scraped orange color from long ago, wooden logs, sacks, car tires peeped through the window, clearly the man was using it as a storehouse. The man stopped the water, dropped the hose and came to the gate. And what should I tell him now?! Announce dreamily "This is the house I was born in"? There was no way to explain to him that in his garden house, my Granddad died one frozen February morning, that from then on his watch had stopped at 5:28, that this steep path, some really tall irises and the sunlight are my first childhood memories, that on this path Mum's clogs began to count out the seconds in my time and the heartbeat of the Universe, that this cottage was the palace of wonderful poverty.

The man greeted me, looked me over in wonder. I smiled awkwardly, greeted him and asked if he'd allow me to look at the garden house a little longer.

"Oh no problem," he looked at me more inquisitively. "You're from here, aren't you?"

"Yes . . . No . . . I come from . . . actually . . ." I muttered. "Thank you, goodbye."

I felt his puzzled gaze in my back seeing me off. As to the question of where I came from, I could not answer it even on my own. For a second I imagined that I was carrying a board on my back on which was written: "Garden cottage, Lom, Plovdiv, Bulgaria, Europe, the Earth, The Solar System, The Milky Way."

Before leaving, I smoked a cigarette in the River Park, gazing at the river.

I'm writing this "reportage" in Brussels, in my huge house, in my garden. My Bulgarian roses have bloomed in velvet blood-red and smell meters away. Michael's at school. Rada is out in the world. Christian has departed long ago. And I don't know what is or was more surreal—here and now, or the depopulated little town, blinded by summer heat. The burnt-out buildings, the silent cultural center, the vainglorious monument, the rusting kid's playground, the stagey graveyard, the cottage, turned into a store . . . seemed unreal to me, or fictional, like the prose in which they were turning into in that moment. Or perhaps it was me, who was surreal in this picture—that strange, lengthened shadow round the bend, the hazy girl spinning a hoop in that animated picture as if drawn by De Chirico.

Geographic accessibility is a fraud. I'd fallen into a fake reality. This wasn't the world of my childhood. This little town was exactly as real and unreal as Dad from my childhood. The destruction and dereliction only visually illustrated my self-deception. But even if it were flourishing, Lom could not be the topos of my magical childhood, of my creation. There are no objective topoi, no objective geographies, that is why we talk of a chronotopos. A unity of time and space. Of *someone's* time and space, of someone's past. The chronotopos is always only personal, the I-chronotopos, a personal universe, inhabited by our mind. Which changes every second, which is expanding further and further away, faster and faster.

Only the river was the same as in my memory. But you can't cross the same river twice.

If Plovdiv is the place of return, Lom is the place to die.

ON PEDAGOGY

Bread is not enough . . .
But fear not, kids,
for our tomorrow
N. Vaptsarov

I sit at the window, and gaze: children play outside.
Now is their dawn and spring is shining on the carefree faces . . .
Children, I am scared for you . . .
The Sun is bound on its sworn path over your bare heads
It is scorching, a cloudy sky is fuming, blazing up . . .
Frayed and dusty, you will finally feel the evening chill,
And bow your heads, faint and melancholic.[131]
P. Yavorov

Once upon a time there was a little girl with skin white as snow, and she had freckles and shiny black hair, and she was slim and tall. She looked like a swallow (and a little bit Asian) and she moved like a little doe. She had a little red coat that she really liked. Only, she couldn't understand was why sometimes her mother would look at her coat and her eyes would get misty. In contrast to everybody else, Mom believed her

131 Freeform translations of both excerpts by the author.

daughter and along with her observed the fairies as they climbed out of the books and strolled in the town park.

Afterward the grown-up girl wanted to live in a world of love and beauty, i.e., of grown-up fairies. This world would smell of French perfume, people would wear elegant clothes and inconspicuously expensive bags, they would talk in elegant French, British English, and (only) if they (really) have to—Hochdeutsch; the air would be full of poetry and classical music, everyone would eat—with subtle yet impeccable manners—fine foods (like oyster, lobster, and langoustine, *duck à l'orange* and *foie gras*), and they would drink champagne from the *Champagne* region and wines from *St. Emillion*. As a gracious queen, Ethics would support the rule of Law, her noble king. Their children (let's call them Love, Knowledge, and Art) would be playing (quietly) in the heavenly gardens. People would be good, intelligent, and educated, they would love and respect each other, they would work hard and with dedication, and they would be amply rewarded for their efforts. The nations in this world would be ruled by justice, order, and reason, and the future of this world would be a real-life utopia.

I'm talking, without even inventing or embellishing stuff, about my daughter, Rada. Rada was three years and a couple of months old when one evening I lent an ear to the whispering that was coming from her cot.

"A-lise sun and kill the en-vious moon who is alleady sick and pale with glief!" Rada turned to the wall. And she started again, in whispers: "Alise sun . . . [fading, pause] . . . and kill the envious moon [a longer pause, then a jumble of whispers]."

This was doubtlessly a quote from Romeo and Juliet, but where had she heard that? At kindergarten? I didn't think so. I asked her quietly:

"Where do you know that poem from?"

But Rada was already asleep.

Around that time, on a Sunday afternoon, Rada was sitting on her potty, deep in thought.

"Mommy, do fairies poop?"

I was washing dishes, I was in a hurry, yet the question was pressing. An awkward question. A veeery awkward question! I was quite unprepared to answer it as there weren't any fairies when I was a kid, and I didn't like them much so I had not given much thought to the physiology of the magical world. I was thinking fast. If I said "no," I would be encouraging my girl to be dreamy, and detached from reality. Rada's aunt, a childless intellectual, had already informed me of the newest parenting trend, neatly summed up by the motto "Kill the prince!" If I said "yes," I would destroy all the magic that was vitally important to a child. And yet, those fairies could not possibly poop roses. The successful and regular defecation of that one fairy currently on the potty was also very important for me, as a mother. Even if I was a fairy's mother.

"They only pee, sweetie."

After her stint on the potty had been crowned with success, Rada would discretely disperse few drops of Chanel N°5 around the room. I laughed, but I also cried a little when I identified the source of that contradictory, pungent aroma. The little 10mg vial, most probably a generous sample or a promotional gift, was the first and only perfume the artist had bought for me, with God-knows-what money and connections, as a gift to celebrate Rada's birth.

That same winter the red-coated, black-haired, Shakespeare-quoting girl was perched on her father's shoulders like a big ladybug, beating an empty frying pan at the hunger rallies on the main street while, at home, I was boiling the next portion of bean stew, and our stocks—the bag of beans in the basement that we'd bought in the fall amid the rumors of hyperinflation and shortages—were quickly diminishing. *Fear not, kid, fear not*, there are no proletarians anymore, and your parents are from the intelligentsia, proletarians had won, but the bright communist future never came anyhow, now it is democracy, we are on our way to market economy, communists are still in power, but this will be the last hungry winter, I promise you, fear not, my princess . . . Besides, just like me, you are so dreamy that you hardly notice what you are eating.

When Rada was growing up,[132] the artist's mother taught her French and the intimately related to the language table manners. The classy old lady had studied at the *Deutsche Schule* and the *Lycée français* before communist times:

"Back straight, pull your elbows close to your body. The food is carried to the mouth, not vice versa."

The holding and usage of cutlery, the positioning of cutlery during and after eating, the consumption of soup, the use of napkins.

"One chews with one's mouth closed, and does not smack one's lips; back straight, elbows in, the knife is not to be licked, ne-ver! You can clean it discreetly with the fork, like that. You don't blow. You don't scratch."

132 Because my own Mom, who became a Granny at 48, was still working, I was perhaps one of the first mothers in Plovdiv to use a babysitter—a neighbor pensioner with now grown up children. At the time this was revolutionary and I heard lots of criticism as a mother. But I wanted to work, and then I had to.

"Pourriez-vous me passer la carafe d'eau, s'il vous plait? Est-ce que je peux vous demander de me donner la salière, s'il vous plait? C'est délicieux! Merci, c'est délicieux mais je n'ai pas très faim . . ."[133]

The props for these lessons consisted of roasted potatoes or a half-slice of bread, thinly coated with margarine, and the soup was just pieces of bread and cheese soaked in diluted milk, with a small spoonful of honey.

Yet, it was the beauty and the refinement, or the culture, distilled in the table manners, which Rada inexplicably already had in her veins and the impoverished menu was just a meaningless prop. The two of us were already living in the lavatory-like flat when my seven-year-old girl used to ask me to serve her breakfast in bed on Sunday mornings ("Pancakes, please, with raspberry jam if possible") and to play "that Mozart music" (the Concerto for Clarinet and a two piano concerto that I'd been listening a lot to at the time).

It was not Brussels and our new lifestyle that shaped Rada's taste and sensibility, they were just a perfect fit for something pre-existing, the origins of which I couldn't fathom. Christian's eyes grew wide when he looked at the table manners of this eight-year-old girl. As Rada was not much of an eater, the first Bulgarian word he learned was "Яж!" (Eat!), to which Rada would respond: *Merci, c'est délicieux mais je n'ai pas très faim.*

She keeps her Moët et Chandon
In her pretty cabinet
"Let them eat cake" she says
Just like Marie Antoinette . . .
Caviar and cigarettes
Well versed in etiquette e . . .
. . . Perfume came naturally from Paris (naturally)[134]

Rada celebrated her fourteenth birthday in suspicious silence—in her room, with a few friends. Her only request was that we kept away, and we complied after she promised that they wouldn't do anything bad. But what could five fourteen-year-old girls be doing, since it was impossible to smoke? It turned out that one of the girls, whose mother worked at the theater, had brought wigs and masks, that the *demoiselles* had put on frocks, makeup and perfume, Rada had snuck a bottle of champagne from the basement and so, having soaked up the era and its decadent spirit, the damsels

133 (French) Would you pass me the jug of water, please? Could I ask you to pass along the saltshaker, please? It's delicious. Thank you, it's delicious but I'm not very hungry.

134 Lyrics of the song "Killer Queen" by Queen.

had watched Sophia Coppola's *Mary Antoinette* while drinking champagne and eating chocolate cake and strawberries with cream.

Coming down to dinner one night, Rada was so disappointed that Christian and I had not managed to cook something that she muttered "Oh, no, *foie gras* again."

French language and education perfectly matched Rada's secular spirit, in which were pleated strong atheist and feminist tones, social and a political sensitivity, all of which harmoniously coexisted with a taste for luxury and lavish refinement in material world and in language.

Every time we wandered through Paris and its museums, I never missed the chance to remind Rada that this unthinkable splendor was produced by the labor and misery of enslaved millions and that, ultimately, it had paved the road to the guillotine.

When we were in Bulgaria I stayed quiet. Be it in my meaningful, unfairly pedagogic way, or because I was myself feeling depressed by the landscape, the evening news and newspapers, by the oriental folk music, by the triviality of worries and sums that sullied the horizons of all my relatives, and by the disgust, humiliation, and complexes that stuck to my one time friends. Seventeen-year-old Rada observed and listened very carefully and one day she said to me, "I'm trying to imagine my life here and . . . myself, if you . . . you hadn't got out of here. If you'd stayed, I'm sure I would have left."

Really, my princess? Would I have been the same? Would *you* have been the same as you are now? And leaving is not so easy, it goes with a huge struggle, savage hard work, deprivation, and what's worst, compromises. Otherwise yes, it's logical, hundreds of thousands of young people continue to leave. I just shortened the process by one generation, I saved you fifteen years. I did not answer Rada.

One or two years earlier, giving in to the inevitable adolescent drive to "fit in" with her peers Rada turned temporarily into a "material girl." After a few obvious hints that her friends had been shopping with their mothers in London, Paris, and Milan, and after a few teachers had told me at the PTM that "your child has gone AWOL," something I could see from her plummeting grades, I invited her to dinner at a restaurant, for a "girls' night out."

I began a long speech about the long hard road I'd traveled—from the little cottage in Lom, through our Plovdiv attic and that dark flat to our Brussels abode. Provokingly I asked her if she remembered the hungry marches, the soaked bread and the beans, her red coat from a secondhand shop. I compared our journey with those of her friends and, notably of their parents, born in normal countries, learning foreign languages as if *en passant* from their nannies and at the European schools, from the countries they'd lived, studying in good expensive universities, polishing their language skills through Erasmus programs, married to suitable partners from the same social class, inheriting, investing, managing high paid, high qualified professions . . .

Rada was silent and busying herself with her steak. I could sense the anger building up. And she was right. What the hell did she have to do with all that? You don't choose your parents, nor make decisions along with them. But parents, having chosen to take you somewhere else, are responsible for signing themselves in and managing in that somewhere else so that you don't feel alien, different, lower class.

"And all this struggle was for you to have a better future—so you can go to a good school, and a good university, and one day you'll have a good job."

Boy . . . was I going over the top! Why was I saying this bullshit! What's more to try to manipulate her into a sense of duty and gratitude . . . Thank God that Rada was still saying nothing.

"Talking about school, I want you to realize one thing—I don't want you to study for my sake: study for you!"

I recited again all the sacred platitudes about the highway that leads from a stellar school diploma to a happy and vibrant life. Her life.

"OK, Mom." Rada wanted to put an end to this monologue, which she found completely pointless.

We stayed silent as we finished our steaks.

"Oh, sweetie, this really is not important! All those label clothes, handbags and shoes. It's vanity, it's just for show, it's 'look how rich I am.' So what? It doesn't matter how rich you are, how much you have, how much you can buy and where you can go for the summer, what matters is who you are, what you are, what you can create, what you can invent, or solve, what music you can play . . . the stuff you can see without going anywhere, the very stuff that these people don't see."

Rada looked up from her plate as if she saw me for the first time. She was listening. Encouraged, I kept on talking:

"Tell me, which one of your friends can say that her father is an artist, that she's growing up with a jurist who has thought up many European laws, that she's growing up among tons of books, pictures, and frescoes, that . . . (very cautiously) her mother is a writer?"

"A writer?" Rada raised her eyebrows. "I thought you were working for the European Commission. Aren't you head of a unit?"

"Yes . . . yes, sure. But . . . in fact . . . deep inside I am . . . I want to write."

"So why aren't you writing?"

I skipped this question as it stung, bringing me almost physical pain. I swallowed a few times, I emptied my wine glass. I was trying to stop myself from shouting out the next round of platitudes and manipulative semi-accusations.

After that dinner, instead of some blouses and a handbag, I gave my daughter a different gift, a Christmas story of sorts. The very first version of the economic (hi)story was simpler, clear and instructional. To make sure that Rada would get the message about the superiority of spiritual over material stuff, I wrote it in English.

History was repeating itself, but not exactly as a farce. Now it was my turn to tell my daughter about her "unfavorable" origin—in her case, as the child of a post-communist artistic intelligentsia—and preach the supremacy of *being* over *having.*

In the meantime, the world has changed. Fifteen years later, as I'm writing these lines I already know that my children's future will be vastly different from my own future-in-the-past. And in that new future *having* and living in the rich part of the world will determine whether you will ever *be*, literally speaking.

"Mommy, what does 'the European Union' mean?

Rada is eight years old, a third-grader in a francophone school in Belgium. I am doing a master's in European Studies at the University of Brussels, and I'm also studying French, catching up on years of education, and getting ready well in advance for the competitions or whatever jobs there might be in or around the European institutions. Bulgaria is about to join the EU in three to four years.

"Go to bed, please, I have to read."

"Come on, tell me, please, what *is* the European Union? Christian works there, right? And you want to work there, don't you?"

"You're only asking me so you won't have to go to bed, right?"

"I will go to bed if you tell me."

"Didn't Christian tell you?"

"Yes, but in French. It was very complicated, I couldn't understand a thing."

I take the illuminated globe and I put it right in front of us. This globe was one of the few things I've brought from Bulgaria. People had been staring at me on the airplane—are there no globes in the bookstores in Belgium? But no, this was my personal planet, the globe we had used to travel around the world with Nana.

"What a big country this is," Rada is pointing to the already non-existent USSR.

"Hm, it's not so big anymore. I mean, it's still huge, bigger than a continent. This is Russia. And well, the language they speak there is very close to Bulgarian. There is a word . . . No, I'll tell you about it another time. In Russia they write with our letters too, in Cyrillic."

Rada is impressed, and she even looks proud.

"But Russia is not in the European Union, right?"

"No, it's not," I bristle.

I decide to go "by the book," and even by some very specific books that are included in my academic bibliography, where *la raison d'être* of the EU stretches from "Ancient Greece to peace." For the time being, however, I switch into "fairy-tale mode": I'm speaking to a grown-up fairy, after all.

"Ah well . . . Once upon a time there were many peoples living in Europe. The Greeks, or as they called themselves at the time, the Hellenes, created a whole sky full of Gods."

Succinctly yet poetically, I go through mythology, philosophy, art, Christianity, historiography, democracy, the Renaissance, science and everything binding Europeans together. Rada sums it all up:

"So in Europe people told stories, studied . . . painted and wrote a lot."

"I wish it were like that. But here's the other, ugly and tragic, side of the story. There were slaves, even in Ancient Greek democracy—those guys who had no rights and were rich people's property. Slaves were treated like you'd treat a vacuum cleaner today. As something that is there to serve a purpose, something you can buy or sell, something you can break and throw away. Women in general, for most of European . . . actually, human, history, were considered to be only half-human."

"And half-what?"

"I'll tell you another time . . . In the history of Europe, the pages that are full of beautiful paintings, buildings and statues, are interspersed with those that depict terrible . . . things. The history of Europe is also the history of weapons and methods of killing people. Millions have been killed, even in the name of the good God. Some people, you see, thought they understood this god better than the others. There was one war that lasted a whopping one hundred years, another one lasted thirty years . . . just think of it . . . And in the twentieth century, the one when you were born, there were two horrible wars in Europe. Sixty million human beings died in the second one alone, millions were injured, whole cities razed to the ground . . ." I hesitate to tell her about the concentration camps and the gas chambers, but decide to postpone the nightmares for my girl and leave this to the history textbooks in upper grades.

"Mommy, how much is one million?"

"Well . . . close your eyes and remember . . . the sandcastle we built last year on the beach."

Rada dutifully closed her eyes.

"And now think about the little grains of sand in each bucket that we brought there. Sand is made up of very tiny grains, right? I think that . . . two buckets contain a million of them."

Rada is still standing with her eyes closed.

"But Mommy . . . those were people, right?!?"

"Yes, darling . . . Each grain of sand was a man like your father, a woman like me or a little child like you . . ."

A teardrop starts swelling on the lashes of one tightly shut eye.

"Oh, don't cry now . . . Come give me a hug. You do already know that the best stories are the sad ones, right?"

I wipe away the tears of the grown-up fairy and I explain how, after all those wars, people in Europe decided to get together in something like a Big State—to produce stuff together, to trade, to have laws that would apply to all, and even share the same currency and the same borders, instead of having wars. To make their countries democratic, so there would not be tyrants and bad guys, so there would not be any poor people. To fight diseases together.

"Your father, Christian, and I are the first generation to have never seen a war. Your father and Christian have never been mobilized to a front."

"To fight against each other?"

"Well yes . . . it could have happened like that. And they wouldn't be fighting for the beautiful Helen, i.e., your mother . . ." I venture a joke. "But that's what I'm trying to explain—that the European Union was created so that there would be no more wars. Your grandparents and their parents, however, do remember that second and, hopefully, last war. By the way, do you know that when I was your age, I was terribly afraid that there would be a war? They used to scare us, saying that America and Western Europe were bad and that they would attack us. I used to come home after school, wrap myself in a blanket and huddle in an armchair expecting the bombs to fall any minute. Atomic bombs, at that . . ."

Rada was baffled, her eyes still wet.

"What . . . they were going to attack Bulgaria?"

"No, darling, the communists were lying to us so they'd keep us in a state of fear. This was called the Cold War—there's no fighting but there are mountains of weapons being stored, and people were scared. But I'll tell you about it another time. In any case, you will be the first generation to live in total peace—without any cold or hot wars, without any fear or lies . . . And yes, I want to work for, let's say, the government of this European state. Christian works for the parliament of that state. And remember—this is not an empire because there's no ruling nation—all nations here are equal. And there's no army."

"What if the bad guys come?"

"What bad guys, darling?! Think of it. If all people can work, and exchange what they have for what they don't have, if their children are going to school, if they have water, food, homes, clothes, textbooks, toys and, OK, sure, chocolate and ice cream, will there be any bad people?"

"There won't be," Rada says, relieved.

And because this dialogue is taking place shortly before Christmas, I round it up with a Christmas story, which I personalize. This historical Christmas story was a precursor of the social-economic one I would tell Rada five years later.

"You know, there's a very beautiful story, it sounds like a Christmas tale but it's true. In this last war your great-grandfather, Grandma Maria's dad, was a soldier in one of the armies. And Christian's father was a soldier in the other army. He was a really young boy back then. The two armies were shooting and killing each other."

Rada is puzzled. Who's the good guy and who's the bad guy? I can see in her eyes that her blood has spoken and she's siding with her great-grandfather. Of whom she knows nothing about . . .

"On Christmas Eve the two armies were on both sides of the frontline, let's say in a little field, and they were sitting in their trenches—these are like holes in the ground. It was terribly cold, and there was icy rain falling down. One German soldier was feeling so homesick, he was missing his parents, his girlfriend, the Christmas tree, the *Adventkranz*, the cookies and everything he'd left behind in Germany, in the past when there'd been no war . . . And so he started singing . . . *Stille Nacht*. (*O Tannenbaum* sounded to me somewhat warlike for the occasion.) His friends started singing as well. The slightly discordant Christmas song rose up in the night above the silent field and wafted to the other side—to the enemy soldiers who were just as young, and just as taken up by memories of home. Your great-grandfather must have been remembering the hearth, the warm bread, the clay pot full of bean stew . . . and your great grand-mother Nikolina, I guess . . . They all listened, and cried, and . . . they started singing, too. And then the soldiers came out of the trenches but they didn't fire a shot, they hugged each other and cried. On this Christmas night they weren't enemies. They spent the night together, remembering their far-away homes."

Rada was on the verge of crying again. I made a theatrical pause for greater impact.

"This is Europe," I concluded with gentle pathos. "Now go wash your teeth and off to bed."

But the world has changed. Some twenty years after telling that Christmas story, as I'm writing these lines now, I know that on the global economic and existential stage the children of Europe have new reasons to work and live "ever closer" in the big European state. Individual states cannot save the planet. Even the whole European Union might not be able to save it, the way things are going. But it might be able to save the Europeans. Apart from this, in February 2022 peace again climbed up on the top of united Europe's daily agenda. As well as the need for reliable armies.

. . . A built-in remedy
For Kruschev and Kennedy . . .[135]

"Mom, what was communism like?"

Rada will turn sixteen in a couple of months, we have successfully risen from the rock bottom of puberty and the consumerist crisis, she's reading a lot again, in three languages, and increasingly taking interest in the news on TV and the periodicals we get at home.

I try the theoretical approach first—democracy, multiparty political system, free elections, freedom of speech, market economy as opposed to planned economy, *petiletkas*,[136] totalitarian state, propaganda and censorship . . . Words, words, words . . . abstract notions my daughter finds boring. I search for "illustrations"—we watch *Goodbye, Lenin*[137] together, that's all we can find in the local DVD store on the subject, Rada understands few things, and does not understand the rest. On the satellite channel, there are Bulgarian films "from the epoch," but they appear absurd to her. She doesn't understand at all what I am laughing at or why I get despondent. So, I have to "draw

135 Lyrics from *Killer Queen*.
136 Five-year state economic plans.
137 A German film, about the aftermath of the fall of the Berlin wall in the GDR, just before German reunification.

on" my own *experience*. And actually it seems that is exactly what my daughter is interested in. But what could, or *should*, I tell Rada about communism?! . . .

. . . Should I tell her about the fate of her great grandfather Rusan, "the bourgeois of kulak origin," forcibly resettled, then tortured at the police station because he had dared to inquire about his friend—an evangelical priest—who had disappeared? Or of my own "inappropriate" origin and how it might have made university education "inaccessible" for me? Or about my mother's nightly church patrols? Or about our relatives in exile? Should I tell Rada how poor we were, although both her grandparents were engineers (and she will be the fourth generation to get a university degree)? Or, maybe, how I "traveled" the world with Nana? Or again about the convoys of desperate folk and the deserted Turkish village where we had to harvest tobacco on our university vacation, guarded by armed soldiers (it wasn't clear from whom)—a compulsory "labor brigade" which you had to take part in, or you wouldn't be able to enroll for the next semester?[138] . . . Or should I speak about "brotherly" Romania which I happened to cross by car in 1988 on a trip around the accessible part of Europe—the dark villages, the long train of people actually walking, on foot, from one town to another, the swarms of children and adults begging by the roads, and that woman in Timisoara who looked like a teacher and who came to us, her face ashen with pain and humiliation, asking, in perfect English, if we had a bit of chocolate—she was ready to pay—for her child . . . I had decided, from the start, that I would not tell my daughter about the rape. I mentioned this and that, while trying to fix the facts in the conceptual frames. Yet, at the end of the day, I heard myself telling a completely different, and actually an amusing, story . . .

Once upon a time there were little marzipan bars, in blue packaging, with big yellow lettering. They had a rather nondescript taste—the only thing you could be certain of was that this was NOT chocolate. They were the last thing you'd choose for a school snack—although they cost five stotinki[139] and when you added the four-stotinki small bottle of boza, you could do with the ten stotinki you were given for breakfast, and if you had an allowance of fifteen or twenty, it was a real "luxury" as you could save up for stickers or buy something really tasty after you'd filled up your tummy. I'm recounting this to even up the score because I didn't actually drink boza—I was nauseated at the sight of boza and of the bottles and glasses with doubtful hygiene it was served in. But the story is not about the boza or the glasses, it's not even so much about the marzipan. And yet the marzipan has remained, for me and everybody who has the

138 Reference to a campaign of the Communist party in mid-80s to change the Turkish names of approximately 10% of Bulgarian population of Turkish origin and Muslim faith, leading to a mass exodus to Turkey.
139 2-3 cents.

same "once upon a time" a small but deeply entrenched symbol of something nondescript and almost gross which is nonetheless a surrogate for something else, something real, but beyond reach and forbidden. Like the only comic-strips children magazine, artlessly imitating *PIFF* or *Tintin*,[140] or the chicory Polish "coffee" imitating Nescafé, or the soft, slightly sparkling, drink with somewhat strange taste and the name of a mountain in the USSR, which had to replace *Coca-Cola.*[141]

"And can you imagine, sweetheart, my amazement when we came here to Belgium and I found out what marzipan actually was! You see, I was doing shopping and I found out that they used marzipan in all sorts of things—in cakes and cookies, Easter eggs, and chocolate Santas, in chocolate bar fillings and pralines. How rich and how thrifty these people are, I thought. But then I examined the marzipan—it looked . . . peculiar. Soft as rising dough and milky beige. I took a closer look at a bar, I read the list of ingredients (which, here, corresponds to the actual content) to learn that marzipan was basically . . . almonds (!) and, yes, of course, sugar. I was embarrassed but I didn't give up so easily so I hastened to check online what marzipan *usually* was, not this Belgian extravaganza but marzipan "per se." Well . . . this is marzipan "per se"—almonds, butter, sugar . . . There's something very sad about making such discoveries at thirty-five, I concluded. But Rada was laughing.

"How was school during communism? How did the boys (searching for the right word in Bulgarian) court you? What music did you listen to? What did you guys wear? Where did you go when you went out? What did your parents allow you to do?" Well that was a sneaky question, the last one . . . It appeared Rada was indeed more interested in her mom's *past*, than in communism.

"We used to play in the streets, until dusk . . . You know, the sound of children voices outside just . . . disappeared, in Bulgaria, too. This sound . . . and the voices of our mothers calling us from the balconies . . . this transports me in my childhood . . . The appearance of the first pair of jeans (brought by my father, the *gastarbeiter* in Libya) was an astounding event. Around the same time we were assigned (from a list with names and addresses) pen pals from the 'brotherly Soviet Union.' I got Lena-Lenochka from Siberia. She told me that winters there were so cold that she kept dreaming about our sea."

In the nostalgically sweet chapter on childhood I skip over the all-week crèche, which I thankfully hardly remember, the all-week kindergarten, which I will remember forever, and my earliest childhood memories where Mom and Dad are gone, gone,

140 Respectively, iconic French and Belgian children comic-strip magazine and book.

141 Putin's Russia in 2022 is like a time machine.

gone, and I'm sitting on a chair in the kindergarten and I am waiting, and horror is crawling over my childish heart that they would not come back to collect me on Saturday evening . . .

Then, I'm onto the English Language School, obviously the part most intriguing for Rada—the peak of my youth. I have to start by defining what the "conduct grade" was and what it meant when it was lowered. I clarify the rules about hair length and braiding. How school started with a morning workout at seven o'clock sharp, how you exercised in your winter coat, and how, if you came late for it three times, you were marked as having missed a class, and after five lates, your conduct grade was lowered. A lowered conduct grade, besides being a serious black mark for a fifteen-year-old student, had to be raised back up before graduation, or you couldn't apply to any university. Besides, at weekly political education classes we were taught how aggressive and mean American imperialism was, how millions of poor Americans and straightforward beggars suffered under capitalism.

"The bits about the States were not exactly untrue," Rada chips in.

A week before Rada had been photographed at the front of a student antiwar demonstration in Brussels just as the Bulgarian government was sending soldiers to Iraq, childishly happy to be joining "the big American guys."

I tell her about the party secretary of the English Language School.

"What is a party secretary?"

"Well, how can I explain, that's a full-time stool-pigeon, only morons and bootlickers could be nominated for that position.

The teacher was so dumb that they said that she was the butt of the joke that went "What watch? —Ten watch. —Such much?" Rada didn't know the Marx Brothers' sketch but she still burst out laughing while I get frustrated again, after all those years, as I remember how my conduct mark was lowered a second time because of that cow. But I'd rather skip this story, too . . . It was so unjust.

I tell her about the Plovdiv Trade Fair where it was so cool to get a job for a week as an interpreter, so you could practice outside the classroom your otherwise useless English, to talk to "real" foreigners. Rada is staring at me, "what do you mean by "real?"

"And can you imagine, darling, we addressed the teachers and all grownups as "Comrades."

"But Mom and Dad weren't changed were they?" my daughter asked jokingly.

"Oh of course not." I hold back the story of Pavlik Morozov.[142] As well as the explanation of the strange family name, that figures in my birth certificate. My father, like tens of

142 The Soviet child "hero" who reported his parents to the authorities for not giving away their entire harvest.

thousands of others in those dark years had to give up his family name and take instead his grandfather's Christian name, family memory and connections had to be erased. What a pain it was to explain all this to the Belgian town hall officials—that my father in my birth certificate is the same as my only existing, biological, lawful father, whose real name I have, and that he hadn't changed his name to go into hiding or to hide me.

"What was *à la mode*? What was the look?" Rada pulled the conversation round to more feminine themes.

"Oh, darling . . . Our "look" was . . . uniforms. You know, ugly navy-blue jumpers or navy-blue skirt suits, and even those had to be the ones that were sold at the stores. I was sent home to change my clothes because the uniform your Grandma had passed down to me, tailored by grandma Nikolina, its color just as navy-blue, its skirt a proper length covering the knee, nothing provocative, just looked different, with some hint of *elegance.* So, one morning the headmaster was checking everyone and snapped that my outfit did not have the uniform 'cut.' Running home to change clothes, I had to cross the whole city and I missed two classes, for which I wouldn't be excused . . . Oh well, another time your mother was stopped at the morning check-up and told to braid the hair, which she'd just hardly managed to tie, and she decided to talk back to the headmaster. Can you imagine what an unthinkable revolution this was, talking back to the headmaster, and with that kind of tone . . . The hair problem was a catch-22 situation—if your hair was not obviously short, you had to have it tied *and braided*, but how could you braid hair that had simply not grown enough, and how could it grow when it had to be either short or braided?! Then the fashion for bob cuts emerged and the Headmaster's daughter let her hair down, cut in straight lines, clearly bob cuts had become "uniform." After some hesitation I tell Rada how, at almost seventeen, her mother had the crazy whim to perm her hair during the summer vacation. And how my father, worried what they'd think about her at school that autumn, cut her hair down to two centimeters . . . I looked like a disco star, which was again inappropriate . . . We all had to be uniformly ugly.

"And what did you wear outside school? At parties or to the disco?"

"First of all, my darling, parties were officially forbidden. There could be some kind of 'gathering' only if a teacher was present. Of course, there were secret parties, but your mother went, especially after her conduct mark was lowered, wearing the uniform over-dress which she took off on entering the party and put back on upon leaving. Because if a teacher happened to see you 'loitering' without a uniform your conduct grade would hit rock bottom."

Rada seems skeptical, she can't imagine her vain mother not dolling herself up. And then I remember something I've missed to clarify.

"Ah well, sweetie, there was nothing in the stores, anyway. They *released* something from time to time. There were boots and blouses in Valentina,[143] I dreamed about them."

"You mean not really *chic*," Rada wonders. "Or there were no sales?"

"No, there was literally *nothing*. Not only there were no sales, but you needed incredible 'connections' through aunties, cousins, and their friends in order to get to the rare items of national clothing reminiscent of some fashion. Not to mention that your parents had to plan for it in the family budget, and most often it was unaffordable."

I quote the curse of the time "may your connections all die." Which leads me to mark the rift between how things were supposed to function according to the communist "sacred scripts" and how life was actually going. To cope with the abyss in-between, the regime invented the "poetic" dichotomy of большая and маленькая правда—the "Big Truth," that is to say the communist moral and the ultimate communist ideal which was officially still valid and aspirational, and the little "t" truth, which was the pragmatic reality, in particular the "small betrayals" to the communist moral, such as the "connections" reality, the small "private businesses" and alike, which writers had to expose and scorn.

"All that was a huge lie, demagogy," I sighed. "We were going to nowhere, the wheel of history was rolling in the opposite direction, only that the life of two generations was destroyed, while the communist nomenclature were living like royalties."

"But why didn't you get rid of these rulers?! You had elections, didn't you?!" exclaimed Rada bewildered.

Oh, yes, we did . . . Your mom used to play the trumpet in the school brass orchestra (my instrument was clogged so I had to "blow through it" on the balcony, to everyone's delight . . .). One Sunday morning the orchestra had to play around the neighborhood, under the balconies, as cheerfully compelling and as noisily as possible to get the sleepyheads to vote. Only, you couldn't choose anything or anyone at those elections . . . You still were obliged to vote, otherwise you faced very serious trouble with the Communist party and its repressive machine.

Then I go back to the boring conceptual frame from where we started out these dialogues—lack of a multiparty system, no free elections, no primacy of law, no freedom of media and speech, but propaganda, censorship, secret services and their agents everywhere, reporting . . . And the Party with a capital P, not because of any particular

143 The main state clothes store.

virtues, but because it was the only one, its divine right was proclaimed in Article 1 of the Constitution.

Rada is getting bored. And I change the subject with more cheerful stuff. Like the brigades.

"What's that?"

"Well, we used to work at a cannery or in the fields, harvesting anything you can think of."

"During the summer vacation?!?"

"Yes, during the vacation, plus a month at the beginning of the school year. The English Language School was 'paired up' with the apple orchards near Plovdiv. Apples had to be sorted—the biggest and prettiest ones for our *tovarishchi* in the brotherly Soviet Union, the second-rate ones for us and our parents."

"What was the fun about all this?" Rada is blinking.

"Well, there were sunrises and sunsets in the countryside, campfires and guitar songs, first kisses, first cigarettes."

I show Rada my High School Diploma and she is amazed to discover that on the one hand her mother has graduated from the Gymnasium for Learning Western Languages (that's how they renamed the English Language School when the incorporated parallel classes for French and German during our time) and on the other hand the impressive vocational profile, "sales consultant in a grocery store." Rada imagined it as a salesgirl who knew English and the relevant foodstuff terminology. I bring the necessary clarity to bear and explain what the Pupil Employment Profile was and how pupils chose dumb work experience specialties, where there wasn't going to be any reading and they could prepare for university entrance exams in peace. It was a lot more difficult for me when I handed in my qualifications at the European Commission to explain how a "Groceries Sales Consultant" could teach English in schools, as figured in my CV and how I'd continued to university . . .

I open up a new fun subject—the "harsh" military spirit of the time. "Inspections of military preparedness" were disguised military-style parades for teenagers. While the girls were lined up like a bunch of lasses on the village square, gossiping about the boys, especially the older ones, the lads goose-stepped and yelled at three different pitches, whetting their appetite for a battle. We also had genuine military education classes, so we would be ready to understand military commands, to wear a gas mask and shoot at the enemies of communism. I tell Rada how her own mother had practiced shooting with a Kalashnikov, a real one, and had even scored a nomination as a "master marks*man*." Even now I am capable of disassembling, cleaning, and reassembling this automatic gun on the clock. Rada is stupefied. Clearly she doesn't find these memories funny.

We get to music. I play my favorite tracks from Deep Purple, Pink Floyd, Uriah Heep, Led Zeppelin, Foreigner, Chicago, ELO, and Queen, a lot of Queen. I strike a rich vein because for Rada's social circle at that time it was chic to be retro.

"Super. Did you go to see them in concert?"

And I stay silent.

"But they've been to Bulgaria recently?" Rada digs into the internet.

No, darling Rada, I've never gone to such a concert, like now you can headbang to your stars. Because the westernmost point which Queen for example reached was Budapest and the film from the concert was shown again and again in cinemas, and we watched it every time, over and over. Now I won't go to the concert in Kavarna,[144] Rada, because Deep Purple and Uriah Heep are no longer Deep Purple and Uriah Heep. Music, darling, is something more than itself and rock particularly is euphoria, revolt against bans and grownups, the fury of youth . . . Some things should be lived on time, or never; sometimes never is better than later. And to tell you, Rada, it is OK to some extent that Freddie died in time. I think he wouldn't have survived some Kavarna Queen variant. I've become sad, even sarcastic.

So at the next "séance" Rada decides to go straight to her "core interest": boys and how we "hit on each other" in my day. Oh bummer! I start by providing a bit of context, so to say. The girls' dormitory was locked during an earthquake so boys and girls would not "mingle" in the courtyard at night . . . Rada found it funny, but I had been scared to death that night. In the mornings, the canteen smelled weird—years later I learned that they used to put bromide in our tea, to "calm" our teenage glands. One morning they lined everyone up and called a girl from upper classes, a beauty, to step out so they could denounce her as a "disgrace" just because she had been seen *passing* by a hotel without a uniform. At a sexual education lecture, after being told that sex was not just immoral but plainly dangerous, since it would surely lead either to pregnancy or disease, we were shown slides of a male penis in an advanced stage of syphilis. The terrifying image appeared huge on the screen. I was sitting at the first row and that was the first time in my life that I ever saw an adult penis. I instinctively shut my eyes, and . . . fainted. So, that sexual education must have achieved its purpose. I try to depict the hypocrisy of communist puritanism as funny and ridiculous, but Rada is not laughing.

144 Small Bulgarian town on the Black Sea coast famous for its rock music festivals, attended by bands, which have long gone out of the spotlight.

Then, I get more poetic. I tell her about the Poetry Academy, where a big poet would teach me poetry and I found my first love—a boy from my class. About the Cinema Academy by the library, where we would watch that baby carriage rolling down the stairs[145] and learn about montage. How on snowy nights our love would melt down into films and poems. The ferocity of sexual education and the abundance of poetry, music and films that had to be "covered" left this first love platonic. I stop here. Of course, two years later, there was sex, and cigarettes, and wild dancing parties, and a mythical cocktail bar reserved for us—the students from the last grades of the English school, age seventeen to nineteen. But I stop here, not for the same hypocritical puritanism. Simply because this part of the story is too banal and has little to do with communism.

. . . Once upon a time there was a southern town on seven hills, with a Roman amphitheater, a philharmonic orchestra, many artists, students' poetry and cinema academies, there was a legendary English School, a mythological cocktail bar . . . There, around the new blocks of flats, in the narrow streets, little girls were playing rubber twist, boys were shooting paper darts, and everyone was playing hide-and-seek and dodgeball; on those balmy nights, a children's choir would shout back "a bit loooonger" to moms' calling from balconies; there, under the low horizon of the provincial town, the girls and the boys daydreamed to the soundtracks of Queen and the Beatles, and we pondered over *The Catcher in the Rye*, and watched Fellini, and lit our first cigarettes, and got goosebumps from the first caresses and kisses, and wrote our first poems . . . they published us for the first time in youth magazines. Then we were listening motionless to Nikola Georgiev's lectures,[146] we were reading the first publications of Platonov, Pasternak, Solzhenitsyn, we were repeating the word "perestroika" like an oath, we were blinded by the blue of the sky and the flags, we got drunk on the thrills and hopes, we starved on strikes and we believed.

The marzipan bars were decidedly gross and sucked, as did communism, and yet my stories are full of tenderness and nostalgia, as are most of the other *personal stories* about communism.[147] This is *my* past, the *place when* I was young. This space-time, this mythological chronotopos of one's childhood and youth is wonderful. Inviolably and forever.

145 An iconic scene from Eisenstein's film "Battleship Potemkin."

146 Iconic professor at Sofia University in the '80s, teaching structuralism and other modern literary theories, thus breaching the orthodoxy of socialist realism.

147 The dialogues with my daughter formed the outline for a book I never wrote. This is yet another text that didn't turn into a book. While I was preparing to become a European official, other writers wrote similar books. The "Socialism" theme has been overexploited, in all genres, thematic and intonation aspects. And even so in the book, which I finally wrote, there is space for my personal story of the recent past and for the messages,

But the grand narrative of history usually types over the intimate, very nuanced *story* of *one's past,* over one's individual *experience.* We lose our individual past, the moment it becomes history. Even when tyranny, atrocities, famine, or natural cataclysm align our experience with the historical account, we may still feel a pang of nostalgia for the chronotopos of our youth. We will always mourn the time gone, and that "me" gone, too.

Only our past belongs to us. Our memories are the only thing we truly own. It is not true that we cannot change the past. Actually, it is the only dimension in which we can do whatever we want. The past is cozy and comfortable as we do not bear responsibility, there are no decisions to make with the illusionary ambition to change the present or the future. The past is not made of objective facts but of our *experience* of these facts, of our journey, emotions and thoughts, our survival, or decline and death, if not physical, then emotional and intellectual. The sweet nostalgia for the past time, and the past "me," embellishes, corrects, forgives, forgets, invents. Our individual memory obligingly selects and rearranges the past, our very own past. Sure, there is some universal history, though written by the victors, as they say. However, there is certainly no universal past. The past is your intimate history. This unique history is written from memory by your memory. Memory is the tissue of the past. Your own past is a narrative, not historical facts or evidence. You hand down this story to someone, most often your kids, or your readers. And here, in this transference, there is a particular responsibility—what kind of story, what memory do we pass to the future. This is our only responsibility.

Our personal story may flow into a bigger collective one—of a family, a generation, a nation, a social class or group, even a whole continent. Memory can also be a retributive settlement with the past. Germans, again, have a special, long word for this: *Vergangenheitsbewältigung,* which means to manage or to cope with the past. I spared Rada the truly evil sides of communism because I want her to learn them from history, as objective facts, disentangled from family fate and misery, discharged from hereditary emotional bias. I did not tell her about the rape because it is as much a crime of the communist regime as it is a line in our family female chronicles. I prefer that it stays there, and I do not want to pass it to the future and make it karma.

Of course, Rada also learned all about communism from history. At university,[148] she learned about the totalitarian regimes of Communism *and* Nazism.[149] She read

which I pass down to my children. Besides, in my stories, there are generational strokes that many readers relate to.

148 In Reims University, an important topos in European history and mythology.

149 Putin's Russia from 2022 confirms how identical the two systems are.

Georgi Markov's[150] *In Absentia Reports*—a story, which is not so much about the author's past, but about communism per se and is a book, meant for a wide audience.

To instill the European spirit into children of twenty-eight nationalities, Angela Merkel took up the initiative of creating a common curriculum on twentieth century history of Europe. People of the future should have a shared vision of their common history, indeed. As so often happens in Europe, one of two (great) grandfathers was at the wrong side of the front line, but both were killed and all grandmothers and parents suffered. For the Second World War history is categorically clear. Accepting it and pledging this never to happen again is the basis of the European project. However, until recently, and in some countries even today, there was no such clear-cut common understanding of the second half of twentieth century, and of communism in particular. Is it insufficient historical distance? Or because communists are still alive, and even in power? In any case, before a common European curriculum is established, first national historiographies have to come to terms with communism. Opening the archives and a lustration may have facilitated this process. Until recently, Bulgarian schoolchildren did not study the second half of the twentieth century at all. There was no lustration. The occupation by the Soviet army in 1944 is still considered "liberation" and the Stalinist-style atrocities of the communists are suppressed, and even justified. In my homeland the wheel of history did, indeed, stop at the "socializum."[151] At the moment as I am writing this book, thirty years after the collapse of communism, the second half of the twentieth century at long last entered the history textbooks.

Some years ago I got a very special birthday present—two Belgian newspapers from the day I was born, plus a panorama book of the entire year 1967. I read everything with great interest. Then, I suddenly realized that all of this past was surreal to me, I had nothing to do with this world, to me this very factual and documentary "snapshot" was only bare facts, some sort of official history. Because there was no story. I didn't have a Belgian grandma so I could touch time on the skin of her cheeks and listen to her memories about, say, the occupation of Belgium or the joy she had felt at the end of the war. My mother did not live in this Belgian chronotopos, besides mom has never actually told me stories about her childhood in the '50s and her youth in the '60s. The silver thread of memory, which would connect me to this chronotopos and turn it into past, was missing. I could not relate any(body's) past to the information

150 Bulgarian writer and journalist, dissident and exile, who was assassinated—via poison-injecting umbrella—in London, in 1978, by the Bulgarian and Russian secret services.

151 For younger readers I have to explain that this misspelling reflects the pronunciation of Todor Zhivkov who came from the right stock and as a result was a pretty earthy and quite illiterate man. For foreign readers, it shall be clarified that Todor Zhivkov was the unchangeable political and state leader of communist Bulgaria for thirty-five years.

and the pictures. They appeared to me like the background of somebody else's story, whom and which I did not know, or like the background research for the unknown yet book of this stranger. Memory is more than memorizing facts or a testimonial for events and people. That's what periodicals, history and photography are for. These things kill memory as redundant to make room for the document. The past is (re) created only through individual *experience*, crystallizing in memory. Without memory, the past is a non-being.

By the way, for me, the most important event of 1967, which I learned about from the panoramic book, an event that, in a way, affects me and all people, regardless of our pasts, memories, nationalities, chronotopoi, etc., is the signing of the international treaty (that is to say an *earthly* contract) on . . . outer space. The treaty forbids the governments of individual states to claim ownership over *extraterrestrial terrains* and resources. It seems that in the forerun to the moon landing, the great powers found it necessary to impose a ban on each other from the outset. Apart from the obvious absurdity, belligerence and the insatiable urge for mutual annihilation, the tautological wording is just funny and quite telling for our desperate anthropocentrism.

And then, a little chip-nosed boy with big hazel eyes and a little round mouth the color of raspberries came into the world, sturdy and bouncy like a spindle. And I had to teach him quite different things. For Michael "real" life started too early—death came too early and the world started changing faster and faster. Unlike his sister, the fairy she was some fourteen years before, my son did not want to be a knight, a soldier, or any kind of masculine heroic prototype.

[Imagine this exchange in French]:

"Misho, what do you want from Santa this year?" I ask.

Three-year-old Michael is sitting in his father's lap. The answer comes with three guttural French Rs.

"Un tractor rose."[152]

I burst out laughing and ask:

"Why pink?"

"Because I want you and Rada to play with me."

Christian is not laughing. His blue eyes have darkened.

152 A pink tractor. (French)

"That's gender-neutral education for you," he mutters. "Good luck finding a pink tractor," he grumbles later on, when we are alone. I will counter by asking whether his reaction would have been the same if we had a girl.

We have been told, at the annual parent-teacher meeting at the kindergarten, that games are no longer classified as "boys-only" and "girls-only." Later, when Michael starts school, I will be amazed to learn that boys take part in knitting classes and really can knit—Michael got a personally knitted hat as a gift from a boy in his class. It was a pretty comical hat and I was in stitches, but I didn't laugh openly because I didn't want to insult him, his classmate, and their gender-neutral education. Besides, I would probably do no better in knitting. I have seen knitting cafés in Brussels—people drink coffee, eat cookies, chat and knit to their heart's delight. There are plenty of men and they don't look gay. Yet that's exactly what Christian was worried about in the pink tractor discussion. Because, for all his politically correct tolerance, his historical guilt and his compassionate nature, for all our talks and all my appeals to these virtues, several years before Michael's birth he had a hard time accepting his adult son's "coming out."

"Yes, I understand, yes, I do agree that it's his happiness that matters. But you don't understand what it means, for a father, when his only son is gay, when he knows that his name will not be passed on," he said gloomily.

I didn't give up. "But why do you think he can't have a child?"

The dark shadow which the pink tractor had cast upon his face showed that he was worried about his younger son's sexual orientation. Back to the pink tractor. The problem was that such gender-neutral or rather neutralizing toys were not being produced (yet?)

"There are no pink tractors, sweetie." In a second I realized what mistake I was making. Just as well I didn't add, "at the shops."

Michael's answer was totally logical, "Santa will make me one."

Santa left no stone unturned but he couldn't get the pink tractor right so he ultimately brought Michael a green tractor (with promises that we all will play with it) and . . . a traditional, formerly gender-specific mini-kitchen where he could unfold his very German and gender neutral talent to make heavy rye bread loaves, strudels and cakes, and also cookies, a whole lot of cookies. A "real-life" role play the whole family was taking part in.

After watching *Schindler's List* in Plovdiv, that red-coated, long-haired little girl—who looked so much like me in my childhood photos, in my little red coat tailored by

Mom, who looked so much like little Rada in her own little red coat—got stuck in my mind forever. I ran home and hugged my little girl tight. Rada was confused but embraced me, taking advantage of the rare hugging session with her continually busy, scatterbrained mother. I pressed my child to my chest for few long minutes, trembling with fear. Will I be able to protect her from the monstrous death humans can devise? We were holding onto each other with a sense of relief, like survivors, and I was thanking blind chance for having tossed Rwanda and Afghanistan *far* away from us, in another world, although a world that was there *today.* I was thankful that concentration camps, Red Khmers and their death fields, Vietnam, the church of Batak, mass starvation in the Ukraine were all far-far away, in another world, a world of the *past.* That the world of *tomorrow*, in peaceful, civilized, and affluent Europe, was safe from that monstrous, man-made death.

Children in distress are more compelling than adults (and the American movies never cease to exploit this psychological trick). It's not just the children's vulnerability—there's evil that renders both children and adults equally helpless. It's not just their unlived lives—that kind of arithmetic is primitive. It's not just their innocence and incomprehension of evil—that should actually allay their horror. The tragic must be that futility, that inability of the parent to protect and to save the child. But this is a universal situation, valid not only in "force majeure" circumstances. We cannot shield our children from death. A child mortal danger is a materialization and visualization of adults' own helplessness and despair. Only, a child's fear and terror haven't been mediated, hidden, and trained. Adults either forget about death, or rather learn to bury these thoughts and the feelings they bring.

Fourteen years after watching *Schindler's List*, it was a crisp, or shall I say a cold, April morning, the sky deceptively blue, I was holding almost four-year-old Michael by the hand on our way to the kindergarten where he would spend the day while I would be working. I would collect him home in the late afternoon, the booster seat in the car, the traffic, and then we'd be home by 6:30 to have dinner with Papa and Rada. An ordinary day in our ordinary life. The Earth would make one turn around its axis, and we'd make one turn on the merry-go-round of our daily life. A cold gust of Brussels wind, I squeeze the warm little hand, as if the wind is going to blow my son away. And then, a sudden terror sweeps over me. I shake, even my teeth are rattling. Now it is my son squeezing my hand, as if to calm it, to warm it; he looks at me from his one-meter-high vantage point. I manage a smile. "Cold, huh?" It will be another year of driving him to kindergarten, and then there'll be a bus taking him to preschool, and then to school, and then I'll be holding his hand teaching him how to ride a bike and roller skates, or comforting him when he's having his appendix removed, or getting a vaccination, and years later he'll be holding my hand and apologizing that time's up and he must run . . . I lift Michael and carry him in my arms. He's pleasantly surprised and puts his arms around my neck. How am I going to explain to him one day that we're all going to die—that I will die, but most importantly, that he will, too—that my only solace is that I won't be here to lose him, but he will lose me. This is the hardest lesson we have to teach our children, but we almost never do. We leave it to them to figure it out by observing nature, wilted flowers, dead birds, a pet who's been put to sleep, a measured dose of grief so they wouldn't be traumatized, so they wouldn't know what they have learned. We give them sex education, we explain how the human being is made and born, resorting to the same flora and fauna, we read poetry to explain the anesthesia of love (and give health lectures to warn them about the risks). But we don't tell them that a human being dies. We gloss over the truth with the optimism of nature's cycles, spring always coming after the deathly pale of winter, flowers blooming again, and the dead bird feeding another animal or the soil where new flowers, new grass and new trees will come forth to give food to other animals. This emphasis on the natural implies that our children will "naturally" learn that they are the next spring harvest that we have fed, that they will feed their children in return, and that nothing will be lost. Like the flowers and like that little bird's nutritious body. They study the law for the conservation of energy in physics, then they study Mendeleev's table of elements in chemistry class, and they are reassured that nothing is lost, indeed, it is only transformed. This is nature perpetually replenishing itself. But is this really all about death? We do not speak about the human being—a grandmother, a grandfather, a mother, a father, an aunt, and even the little kid, his or her children and grandchildren. The person who doesn't get transformed, or reborn, the person who disappears without a trace. Consumed by hormonal impulses, looking toward the future and busy preparing for it, children feel so immortal they miss the most important "detail" awaiting them. There's no pedagogical manual on how to announce and explain the most important things. If there's anything to explain at all.

Next spring Papa was gone. One morning he took Michael and Rada to the school bus and waved goodbye. See you this afternoon, kiddos. In the afternoon Papa no longer existed. Gone to another afternoon, one we measure in a different way, "in heaven," as I told Michael. I don't know if he understood what I was saying but he did understand that Papa will never take him to the school bus again, that he'll never be waiting for him at the dinner table. Michael did not know what "never" means yet. This was the exact time he learned it. Death is the best explanation of "never" and "forever."

At an outdoor lesson in the park the teacher decided to use a dead bird as an occasion to introduce the notion of death. Michael proudly announced that he knew what this was. The teacher was taken aback, and she wanted to talk to me. "Maybe some therapy will be good for the child, and probably for you, too." Yes, Frau Schwarzenbacher, great idea, thank you. I think that all people need therapy on this subject, or a solid sense of duty, a lot of work, money and power, or love, or fairy tales, to keep on living. Of course, this wasn't what I told the kind German lady. These things are left unspoken.

The first Father's Day without a father. Children make postcards with little poems about their dads, there's a party at school that's actually a father-and-child team game and a buffet; mothers are not allowed, though a grandfather can come if the father has some pressing work to do. Michael has no Papa anymore, and his grandfather is 2,000 km away, a Skype-grandpa of sorts who speaks no foreign languages at all. I am anxious, wondering what to do so my son wouldn't be traumatized; the teacher uncertain as well, so she sends me a thoughtful email. Michael, however, solves the problem with graceful ease and simplicity, once and forever:

"Don't worry, Mama. And . . . please don't come, it will be papas only. I already told Frau Schwarzenbacher not to worry, either. I'll make a postcard for Papa and I know he'll see it from up there. And I'll play with my friends' fathers."

I realize that my son has somehow arranged the world, which features death, thanks to something transcendent—heaven and the journey thither. I would not call this religion because Michael has not received religious education neither at home, nor at school.

I heard myself say to Michael: "*Tomorrow was* Papa's birthday." His face froze for a second, baffled by the contending paradoxes of time and grammar.

"Are we going to celebrate?" (Thinking.) Now that Papa is no longer with us . . . does he still have a birthday?

No, honey, Papa isn't going to mark another rotation around the Sun, his time is over, and tomorrow's time is mine and yours.

"No, we aren't going to celebrate. There is *no one* to celebrate," I respond and change the subject to something more upbeat.

Teaching death is hard, teaching time and space no easier. Michael has no measurement, or experience, for an hour, a day, a week, a month or a year, but everything he studies is measured in time. But how much time can he figure out from the perspective of his six and a half years?

"Now you're gonna sit down for half an hour and write your homework. Then you can watch videos or play games for another half an hour," I instruct him, gently pulling his iPad away.

"How much is half an hour?"

"Just the time you need to write your homework."

"And can I watch films for (*thinking, brazenly emphasizing*) *two* hours, then?"

"No, two hours are too much."

"How much?"

"The time it took us to fly to Sofia. Or the time I spend in the car each day—one hour to go to the office, one hour to come back, a total of two hours in the car. Or two of your classes at school plus the big break. You sometimes take a two-hour nap in the afternoon."

Michael thinks about it, comparing the different versions of two hours, and declares:

"Two hours are a lot because you're nervous in the car. And they are short for films and games. How far is Sofia?"

"Two thousand kilometers."

"Is two . . . thou-sand . . . kilo-meters a lot?"

"It depends—it's not too far if you're flying because the airplane moves very fast. If we go by car, we'll have to travel not two hours but two days. And if you try to walk there, just like this, without a car or a bicycle, you'll reach Sofia in a couple of months. So, it depends on the speed."

While I am explaining earthy space and time to my son, I keep doing in my head another math for another time-space: "60 seconds by 60 minutes by 24 hours by 365 days by 300,000 km per second is one light-year" And I remember a Bulgarian story, "8:19,"[153] the time it takes for light to travel from the Sun to the Earth.

"The airplane does not go very fast. The houses and the hills down there don't go fast like they do in the car," Michael notes. "How much is a month?"

I start sketching to explain first why the houses and the hills that are actually mountains, *look* like they're not moving fast. I explain the month with four piano lessons, i.e., four weeks. Michael is ready with his next question:

"How many . . . [trying to choose the right unit of time] months earlier did Rada come out of your tummy?"

153 A short story by Georgi Gospodinov, which poses the question what one would do if knowing that s/he has eight minutes and nineteen seconds left to live.

I explain the who's who of family ties; who came out of whose tummy in the shape of a baby, and who came earlier or later; I measure the time in *years,* a notion still alien to my son.

"How . . . [another pause and, oh wow, smart little boy does say the right word, albeit quietly, with hesitation] . . . long *time* ago did Papa go to heaven?"

"One year and one month." I know right away that this was not the answer to his question, that this answer will say nothing to him. "Do you remember Papa? Not from the pictures. Can you picture him when you close your eyes?"

Michael closes his eyes. ". . . no . . . yes . . . not always. Mama, can I watch the video?"

He sits with me at the computer and we watch, for I don't know which time, the short video where Papa is still alive. It's taken with a mobile phone, by Rada, three days before Papa passed away. One minute, two seconds and thirty-seven milliseconds. We have three albums of family photos but only one video. Papa had just installed, with the help of some handymen, the new swing in the garden. It has different "extras" like gym rings and a horizontal bar in combination with a climber and something like a little fortress. Everything is *comme il faut,* German standard—the structure is big and solid, the massive wooden planks are embedded in cement. Michael is almost five, and he's trying it for the first time. Papa is clad in one of his bright-red pullovers, helping his son sit on the swing, pushing him and shyly stepping aside, away from the camera, Michael is pleading to him to push the swing again, Papa walks into the shot again, pushes his son, goes out of sight and tells him, in voiceover, that he's already big, smart and strong and quite capable of pushing himself on the swing and climbing to the top of the tower. The video is made for grandma and grandpa in Plovdiv so in the last seconds Michael says to the camera: "*Je vous aime, baba et dado.*"[154] The end, 1 minute, 2 seconds and 37 milliseconds. Michael is delighted with himself—how small and sweet he used to be! But he's also watching himself with a bit of irony—what a baby he used to be, he couldn't even push himself on a swing.

Some time will pass—I don't know how much time, what time, whose time it will be—and Michael will no longer be able to see his father upon closing his eyes. A single bright-red spot will twinkle behind his closed lids, and Papa's basso voice will be a faraway echo. He'll think he remembers him but he will, in fact, "remember" the Papa from the pictures, from the video, from the three tapes of lessons in German. Papa will be forever reading those German lessons, forever pushing his little boy on the swing and telling him he's big, smart, and strong. This father's love and reassurance should suffice for life to my son.

---

154 I love you, Grandma and Grandpa (French, Bulgarian)

"I love you, Mama."

"I love you too, sunshine, to the Milky Way and back."

"The one we see in the sky in Greece? Oh that's really close. And I love you to (*leafing through the pages of a picture book*) the An-dro-me-da-ga-la-xy."

"Hm, so your love is getting less every second[155] . . . I'm joking" I hasten to correct myself.

"Mama, and what if you went to the sky?"

"If I had gone to the sky, instead of Papa, or if I go to the sky as well?"

"If now . . . you go, too. What will I do?"

I have no answer to that question. The most important questions a child can ask have no answer. And yet I do try.

"Well, darling, this will only happen in many, many years, when you're grown up already, even older than me, and I will be very old, very tired and awfully boring. You will have your own little kids, and you'll have no time for me, anyway."

"I'll still be very sad." Michael says, pondering. Then he adds: "So Grandma and Grandpa will have to go to heaven now?"

"No, they'll wait for you to grow up."

"Will I grow up quickly?"

How the hell am I supposed to answer that question? Yes, darling, you'll grow up before I know it, right here in front of my eyes, and I won't even realize when and how it has happened, and then one day you'll go away and you'll no longer live with me. Yes, darling, Grandma and Grandpa grew old before I knew it, and I'll also grow old before you know it, and one day we'll die, your grandparents first, I hope . . . and we're all going to cry—me and you, and Rada, and your uncle, your aunt and your cousin. And yet, how to answer your question? If I tell you the truth, then you'll know that Grandma and Grandpa will soon go to heaven. You will cry. Besides, soon means something very different for you and for me.

"Look," I finally begin, "on one hand, you'll grow up very fast, but it will only be fast for me. For you, you'll grow up very slowly, so much time will be passing for you."

Michael thinks a little and shoots out the following incredible question: "Which time does the clock in the dining room measure then—the fast one or the slow one? I know, your mobile phone measures the fast time, so you never have enough time."

A few months later Michael is sitting on the back seat with his grandma, I am driving his grandfather's car, we are getting back from the seaside. It's hot, and Bulgarian roads are narrow and covered with holes.

155 Because Andromeda and the Milky Way are moving toward each other and will collide.

"Grandma, see, my hand! See how much it has grown. My little thumb is already reaching the crease of your little thumb."

"O, sweetie . . ." Grandmother and grandchild have brought their palms together. "So much time will pass before your little hand is as biiiig as mine. Don't hurry. Look how sweet it is now, a small child's hand."

"Grandma, you will be in the sky then, right? And we won't be able to compare our hands."

"Well, sweetie, I hope I will still be here so we can compare our hands."

I listen silently, maneuvering among the holes on the road and thinking that, one day, in the future (when exactly? Is there a right moment for this?) I will have to take Michael to his father's grave in Frankfurt. And the grave is in the ground. Not in the sky. What am I supposed to tell him, then? Why do parents never start up conversations on this subject? Or will have my son have found out by then?

About the same time, we are in a car again, in Brussels, Friday evening after a long week for both me and Michael, we are getting home, Rada is already studying abroad. My son is looking out of the window, the usual traffic jam, we hardly move, we are both hungry. After the next idiot who gets in my way I curse and say that we will be very late. Michael touches my shoulder and says:

"Don't worry, Mama, I don't need to pee, I am just a little sick in the car. But I won't throw up." He pauses and adds: "Nobody is waiting for us, so we won't be late."

I almost drop the steering wheel. That Winnie the Pooh there on the back seat has bullet-proof logic—you can't be late if nobody is waiting for you, right? I finish the thought in my head—you can't be bad if you're alone. You can't be good, either.

I discretely look at the little German citizen on the back seat in the rearview mirror. He is an exile by birth, German mostly through the language and the school curriculum. Yet, this innate inclination to "fundamental problematics," combined with zest for scientific knowledge is so . . . German.

But the "bad guys" came. It seemed that peace, jobs, and trade in civilized Europe were not enough, as I had once used to comfort a grown-up fairy. Rada was a student in Paris when the terrorist attacks there happened. Grandma and Grandpa landed in Brussels just a day before the explosions here, and they had to stay for almost a month as the airport was closed. A relative of our cleaner died in the Brussels metro bomb blast.

The neighboring *commune*, Molenbeek, turned out to be a center of terrorism. There was an armored vehicle that spent a long time parked at the entry of our underground station; there were tanks in the city center, and armed military everywhere. Police sirens wailed, night and day. For months on end. And then Nice, Berlin, Manchester, London, and Barcelona were in the news. It was supposedly all about a different god, "the true" god, and about a different heaven, "the true" one, and a different morality, and other "fundamental" things like pork, alcohol, and hygiene. In reality, it was all about resources and the future, the project for the future. And about the fate of the female human being.

That was about the time Michael started watching news for kids. I was startled by the adult habits of this kid who was not yet 9-years-old. Like some unlikely office worker in a child's body, Michael would sit behind his bowl of cornflakes, his toast and boiled egg, his orange juice and his iPad, and he'd watch the morning news. In German. The newest terrorist attack, the Islamic State, the war in Syria, the migration to Europe, the overloaded boats in the Mediterranean—full of hopeless and hopelessly poor people—the European states arguing over who should accept and integrate them, the famine in Africa, the rise of China, the surge of India, the new American president, trade debates, taxes and tariffs, the North Korean threat, climate change and the Paris Agreement, elections, extreme right, extreme left, inflation, recession, economic growth, the next bailout for Greece . . . Everything was covered. Simplified and adapted, sure, and yet it was honest and objective. Genuinely German. Did my son really understand everything he was seeing and hearing? Yes, he did. The Germans had made sure that even a child could understand the essentials. These were not just a bunch of pictures and curiosities to entertain him at breakfast, like that episode in Proust's oeuvre. And Michael was not amused—he was getting informed about the world he was living in. I was watching my child in awe. He was growing in a fully un-magical, real world. This world was full of real danger and uncertainty, instead of fairy tales and supermen. Books and parents were not anymore primary source of information about this world, nor designers of the picture for the child to see.

The school trip to London was canceled, but kids still went to Great Britain and instead stayed at the facilities of some youth camp in the countryside, guarded by armed policemen. The European school stepped up security measures, increased the number of the school guards, further limited access to the school facilities. One of these days, Michael dropped, just "by the way," that they had had a drill exercise—the school alarm had been activated and they had to follow the "emergency protocol." I wanted to know more. Well, "the teacher locked the door, turned off the light and . . . nothing, that was it." There was definitely something more, which my boy did not want to talk about, most probably in order to conceal his fear and to not worry me. I did not push for respect of his budding male courage. From other parents I learned that according to the "protocol," after locking the door (which is a simple, wooden-palette door, with a window), the kids should disperse in the corners, because (some parent cited "The Geometry of Terrorism") a terrorist would most probably shoot into the middle of the room. Only that Herr Schlesinger, Michael's class teacher, "practiced" something quite different. He arranged the kids in a tight circle and they were all holding their hands. Few parents wanted to report the teacher to the school authorities, for violation of the "protocol," which, in their view, would give the kids better odds. Others observed that if a terrorist had already reached the classroom door, God forbid!, no "protocol" whatsoever would help. A third group of parents found all this panic and these drills went too far and unnecessarily traumatized the kids, arguing that the "chance" of dying in a car crash was still much bigger than that of being shot by terrorists, and that such attacks were just one of the risks of the urban, globalist life, which we ourselves had chosen.

Nobody seemed to have reflected on the humanism of the teacher's "protocol" . . .

Once we recited *Fear Not, Kids*, but I was dying from fear. In my head I repeated the poem like a spell, not for the daily bread, because I was a bad eater, but to keep the war and the bombs away. Deep in myself I was convinced that my spell was stronger than the incomprehensible speeches of the communist party grandfathers coming out of the TV screens. The war was cold but my childhood horror and imagination were burning hot. Some forty years later, history was repeating itself, but, again, not as a farce. I was wondering what was going on in my son's head, how much he was actually scared, if he was feeling protected, what his own spell was. I had almost managed to tell to Rada the stories of my military training and "competences" with automatic gun in a funny way. I could not fake even a passing smile at Michael's school drills (or at the training provided by the European Commission to its employees). I could offer my son only a hug, in which he can relax from his boy's coolness and courage and can admit his fears. I can hold his hand to take him through the next ten-fifteen years.

Herr Schlesinger, a really fine person, a musician . . . had realized that practicing the "protocol" of the seven little goats from the proverbial story was not the shelter needed for our children's minds. It did not mask the human inability of the adults to protect the children from evil or nature. Holding hands, in a circle, is not a strategy for surviving, but for dying. Not in horror, together, just like the ending of the films *Melancholia* or *Don't Look Up*. The only illusion we can preserve for our children is that they're not alone; that we are together, that we can hold their hands and all close together our eyes.

Michael does not read. I diligently bought for him popular German bestsellers for young boys. I also compiled my own "suggested readings"—Andersen, the Grimm brothers, Charles Perrault, Gianni Rodari, Oscar Wilde, Erich Kästner, Bulgarian folk tales. French folk tales, Roald Dahl, *Pippi Longstocking, Karlson on the Roof, Mary Poppins, Winnie the Pooh, Alice in Wonderland, Tom Sawyer, Treasure Island, Le petit Nicolas, Ian Bibiyan,*[156] *Robin Hood, Peter Pan* . . . I turned some of these books in my hands, I browsed through them, read a few bits here and there and I realized that Michael would simply not understand much of it. The children and the childhood described in these books, the world and the people of these books, were no longer there.

Michael did not like too much fiction and magic—he abandoned Harry Potter forever only in the middle of the first volume. The real world was eventful, imaginative, and scary enough to him—fathers disappear forever after waving goodbye in the morning, bombs explode at the airport where your grandparents have landed, the whole city is filled with fully armed military and a tank-like vehicle is parked just in front of your underground station, at school you perform drill exercises, mama's car just evaporates from the driveway, a nuclear power station explodes somewhere, an airplane falls, thousands die in wars, thousands escape, and run, and swim, and drown, a flood here, earthquakes and fires there, temperatures rising, heats and droughts, AIDS, Ebola and terrifying diseases kill thousands somewhere, your sister returns from a humanitarian mission in Africa and tells you that thousands of kids, just like you, will not survive and how precious water is, and also beds, clean bedsheets, food, school and everything you have without ever thinking about it[157] . . . If you are 8 and you already know all of that, and you also know what "fake news," "porn," and "internet pedophile" mean, and you have even undergone trainings on these subjects, how are you supposed to take fairytales and the magical world of books? Children's books don't talk about those things. Everything in these books is

156 Bulgarian children classics, written in the '30s.

157 This humanitarian mission had a powerful educational effect on Rada. It put an end to her consumerist appetites, but also to her fabulous childhood and teenage. She returned from Africa an adult.

make-believe, it isn't true. The world is not like that, people are not like that, there are no elves, princesses and princes, no Pippis and Karlsons, no good robbers and puckish, bruised-knee boys, no Santa, no Easter bunny and no St. Nikolas. Only the little match girl did exist, and she did freeze to death. Children's news is telling the truth. And that sequence with the beaver explains everything quite clearly. (Besides the German news broadcasts for kids, on his iPad, Michael also watched a popular documentary science series where an cartoon beaver came into the real world, in a reverse journey from fantasy to reality, to show how things are made—from babies to ships to chocolate wafer bars.)

Rada read the Russian classics in Bulgarian. It was a win-win situation, the best of both worlds—as close to the original as possible, and it looked *hella chic* to her friends and colleagues to be reading *Anna Karenina*, *A Hero of Our Time*, *Dr. Zhivago*, and *Crime and Punishment* in the original (or so they thought, and she would not correct them). While she was reading the French, English, German, and Russian classics, Rada would rarely ask me to explain something to her. Did she understand everything? I'm not merely talking about the language, where any gaps could quickly be bridged by dictionaries and all the information available online. I mean everything beyond the dictionary meaning of the words, everything you should know to get the context, the characters and their drives, the comical and the tragic, the sublime and the profane, and to really submerge into the story.

The ethno-folkloristic imagery of Bulgarian classics remained inscrutable to my daughter. The aesthetics of the Bulgarian village and the patriarchal family appeared to her like a medieval picture. The April Uprising—the cornerstone of our national mythology, hewn and mounted on the bridges of time by Ivan Vazov and Zakhary Stoyanov, provoked her horror at the atrocities but it was a horror untinged by any sense of national affiliation to the Bulgarian "martyr people." The heroic line, all those young heroes, with their locks flowing, with their sparkling white shirts, tinged by blood, till the hero falls down in a graceful swoon, with *Freedom* or *Bulgaria* on his lips, but never the name of the beloved—she is always inferior to the Fatherland, besides we a shy, patriarchal lot who never dare to kiss in the final scene . . . and they seem to Rada naïve, even comic. It turns out this heroic, patriarchal world was totally alien to her peers, even in Bulgaria. Parents and teachers in Bulgaria discovered that children did not understand some of the classical works of Bulgarian literature, including the language they were written in. Curricula were revised, textbooks were rewritten. Publishers came out with summarized editions—sexy, sprinkled with humor, explanations, and commentaries; there were even some written in the Latin alphabet as children would read on their smartphones more often than open a book, and their chats were not in Cyrillic. I was wondering whether other cultures had the same problem. Would a French teenager, for example, understand *Les Misérables* and be moved by its storyline? Would he or she be moved by Moliere, Racine, Voltaire, or Montaigne? Were musicals and theatre directors' reinterpretations of classic plays a way to prune the withered content and adapt what's left into something more interesting and comprehensible for today's youth?

With age, reading preferences shift to documentaries, history, memories. As if the reader knows and has seen too much to succumb to the fictitious, as if the senses and imagination are exhausted and fading away, unable to immerse in the aesthetic world and to believe the aesthetic truth. Aren't our children growing into adults too quickly? Is there still childhood? It is clear that the ocean of information, accessible at the fingertip, substitutes a lot of books. Satellites and microscopes bring pictures which no human story can depict. Let's assume that at school they learn to think and process information. Yet, I was wondering from where these kids would get *l'education sentimentale*, how they would develop their imagination, or empathy, without books? What would be their transcendent trampoline if not books, or art in general?

Our children will not read the Bible, and they will not replace it with philosophy, history, literature, and art. For them, salvation takes on the very literal meaning of survival. My children are watching a TV series called *The Good Place*. They're watching it for fun, and not for any existential quest. And it is made for fun—it's incredible how American mass culture has ultimately undertaken to process and present in an accessible, entertaining, pleasant, and not-so-scary form even such things like death and the non-being. Oh, well, the series does include a summarized, simplified, and entertaining course in ethics[158] to be taught and learned, paradoxically, in the netherworld where ethics shouldn't matter at all. Besides, it turns out Hell is . . . the Others. However, the parody of existentialism remains shallow fun. The series does not tackle any existential anxieties because the netherworld is actually . . . funny, an entertaining TV series, and death is but a technical transfer from one *place* to another, the good place, and on top of that, the transfer can be rewound again and again. Is this kind of fun supposed to teach death instead of parents, religion, philosophy and literature, and prepare our children for the future, something like a drug against the existential terror before the apocalypse?

158 Which simply reinforces the deep religiosity and black-and-white views of this still young nation.

Anyhow, at the end of the day, *interactive* virtual reality is engulfing both the real and the fictitious worlds. Defying natural laws and time, reality and its pressing needs, in this virtual reality you are almighty, free, lighthearted, and immortal—you can rewind existence and death as in *The Good Place*. The Universe is substituted by the Metaverse. You do not need to feel or experience too much, in particular anxiety or fears, because everything is virtual, make-believe, fun. My children's generation considers it is somewhat shameful and awkward to be exalted, enthusiastic, to have ideals to die for, to love madly (hating is politically incorrect, anyway). The young are *cool*. And maybe that's what they need to be if they want to survive. Our children's generation does not need much of memory, either, because everything is photographed and digitalized to endure until the end of time. Besides, the world is changing at a breathtaking speed. There is no time for experience and memory to take shape and a healthy distance and to settle.

What's "homeland" and what is "abroad" to my children? Do they ever need a homeland?

I bought a short and well-written history of Bulgaria. Rada dutifully read it and did get a good general idea about the history of her biographical and geographical homeland, or rather place of origin. Yet, Bulgarian history will never kindle a patriotic fire in her heart—a sense of love or hatred, pride or shame. The only facts I have heard her mention with some degree of pride and belonging are the Thracians, the Cyrillic alphabet, and the joyous celebration of the 24th of May,[159] and the salvation of Bulgarian Jews. Rada feels no nostalgia for Bulgaria. Her birthplace, her origin and the exotic language she still speaks will remain just facts in her biography, somewhat strange to her herself. A few years later she would explain to me that national affiliation is an outdated identification, that her friends are all different mixtures of nationalities, races and languages, that they are the real Europeans, that she doesn't know Belgium and is not interested in the country but she does know and love Brussels, that she's a *bruxelloise*, a European of Bulgarian origin. Then, her path would lead her to France, which she'd fall in love with forever, and the States, where she would turn into an American.

As for Michael, as a child he suffered from geographical disorientation as regards places, nations, cities, nationalities. National belonging, even in its simplest geographical dimension, is a tricky concept for my son. He is, genetically, half-German and he has a German passport; German is his first and strongest language, he studies in

159 The day of Bulgarian education and culture, the Cyrillic alphabet and its creators, Sts. Cyril and Methodius. It's a public holiday, with nationwide school processions and celebrations.

German, counts in German, he speaks in his sleep in German. Yet, this German citizen was born and is raised in Brussels, by a Bulgarian mother. He has never lived in Germany. For him, this country is an abstraction—a piece of geography from his geography classes, a piece of history from his history classes (that teach reconciliatory European history). Germany is a ninety-minute drive with Mom at the wheel, and—surprise!—everybody there speaks German. Michael's eyes always open wide in delight. For my son, Bulgaria is the Bulgarian language, the language of Mom, Nana, Grandpa, uncle, aunt and cousin, Bulgaria is family, vacation, heat, the main street and the city park in Plovdiv.

According to an apocryphal story[160] after signing the Maastricht Treaty Jacques Delors exclaimed: "We created Europe, now we have to create the Europeans." More than nine million young people have studied abroad as Erasmus[161] students. One million babies owe their coming into this world to the same program. The generation of our children and grandchildren is indeed the first generation of genuine Europeans. These Europeans feel less and less like they belong to a nation and its history and language, to a culture or geographical location. Patriotism of any sort is strange to them, they do not have sentiments with a national denominator. These Europeans are united not in their diversity, but in their increasing similarity.[162]

As there is no homeland, "abroad" is a meaningless notion to them, too. Their *home*lands are where good universities and jobs are, where their welfare state and tax residence are. These contemporary nomads do not know the nostalgia for a birthplace or for a chronotopos of youth; they do not miss places. Family and family home is a temporary center of the world. Our home is the homeland of my children. This is the center of the world they will one day remember with nostalgia and sadness at the passage of time; it is not Bulgaria, Belgium, or Germany, it's not even the culturally vacuous Brussels; it is our home, this intimate mini-homeland—a magic sphere that floats in the air over countries, cities, languages and cultures, and could land in any geographical location on the map, just *anywhere* in the global *nowhere*.

How different are my two children! Two distinctively different generations,[163] while the age gap is only thirteen and a half years. As people have kids later, the nominal age gap between generations increases—today it is around thirty to thirty-five years. However, it seems to me that the generation shifts occur in increasingly shorter intervals—every ten to fifteen years, because the world is changing ever more rapidly. Within a nominal generation, we have actually two, even three different generations.

160 Christian confirmed this firsthand.

161 A program of the EU for student exchanges.

162 The dictum of the EU is "United in Diversity."

163 In fact, a millennial and a Z according to a popular classification.

What defines a generation today? Historical events (and what qualifies as historical event today?), fashion, music trends, social movements, communication technologies, leaps of science, new record averages of temperature, pandemics, terrorist attacks? Is youth still the time of generation-defining experience?

Some ten years or so ago, I went with Rada to the cinema. I meant it to be a relaxing, and possibly entertaining, evening with my daughter, and if the film was worth it, a chance to have a discussion with her. Only, I did not read anything about the film in advance. So, we found ourselves watching Lars von Trier's *Melancholia*. We were both overwhelmed. We were shaken by a pure shot of existential fear, or melancholia. Rada vomited in the cinema lavatories, pretending it was just the unstable camera (as per the director's decision) that made her dizzy, I was consumed by an overwhelming feeling of futility and meaninglessness that was difficult to conceal. The film was teaching death—of the individual human being of our children and of mankind as well. The cosmic apocalypse was both real and metaphorical.

Some time later, Rada invited me to watch a film together. I felt she wanted to tell me something by this film, and I was right. The beginning of the film *Interstellar* is set in the near future, perhaps the future of Rada's child or grandchild. A time when the temperatures will have risen by "well above" 2°C, when GMO corn will be the only edible crop still growing on Earth, when the air will be full of dust and radiation, causing many children to die. From there on, the film takes a sci-fi turn, moving on to humanity's salvation through migration to another planet. Unlike *Melancholia*, the apocalypse was man-made. The father managed to save his child, and the whole mankind, by mastering gravity, time-space, and black holes; he managed even the relativity of time and made it back to human chronotopos, already on another planet, to see his daughter, a very elderly lady by then, before she died in peace. Pure Einstein. The film reminded me of the dialogues with my father many, many years ago. However, the generation talk now was quite different and the message my child was addressing to me was not in the sci-fi specter, but pure realism. And there was nothing entertaining for either generation.

"I will have to study all my life, and have to work hard until the end . . . Competition will be fierce, from men and machines alike . . . The air will keep getting dirtier, the weather will keep getting hotter, there will be wars for resources like food and water . . . In sixty or seventy years, Manhattan will be underwater, pity for all the expensive real estate there . . . Population growth and aging . . . With my husband, we will most probably adopt a child . . ."

I am listening to my child, "setting my clock" to hers and I realize that the future is already here, right in front of me. I can touch it, I can stroke my daughter's hand. What I can't do is provide consolation and salvation, or paint a different "bright future" on the horizon. The project for the future is, perhaps, the most essential part of history, of the past and the present. This is the social and personal ideal without which any society would disintegrate into its constituent atoms, and individuals would lose a vital element of their humanity. The project for the future of one generation, that future from the past, becomes the present for the children of that generation.

The projects of religion and many social-economic and political orders, like absolute monarchy, colonialism, communism, nationalism, imperialism, totalitarianism, autocracy, etc., have crashed. Only capitalism, (liberal) democracy, and science have endured (so far, by far not everywhere). They have made people's lives better, indeed. Life today is unquestionably longer, richer, healthier, and more secure. Yet, today, humanity is swept by a global pessimism.[164] It's not the usual nostalgia for the past. The present is doubtlessly better than the time of my parents and especially the time of my grandparents. The future, however, is worse. The future that will be our children's present is far worse. I think, for the first time in human history the future is worse than the present and the past. The project for the future is being increasingly limited to survival. And we feel nostalgia for that social ideal, for the future from the past, or our past future.

The past should mean traditions, memory, stories, experience, language, and culture passed on and enriched by every new generation. However, our past, and the past of our parents and grandparents, overlaps with the history of the bloodiest, most tyrannical century in the history of mankind, a century we all want to forget.

In our project for the future, we messed up fundamental equations. The result is that, for our children and grandchildren, we have set the stage for a global apocalypse. Will the world succeed in coping simultaneously with overpopulation, aging, shrinking welfare, migration, poverty, extreme social disparity, climate change, the need for new energy sources? Shall we consume and produce less, or do we have to distribute better? Shall we use technical progress for adaptation and survival on our ever less hospitable planet or will we invest all our technological potential and the re-

164 Steven Pinker dedicates a book to this, exhorting us that we are not right and that we have a lot more reasons to be happy that people in the past.

sources of humanity in its entirety to transport a tiny part of this to Mars. How will these dilemmas and decisions affect the political organization of society and human existence? These questions are slipping out of my generation's hands. Our children, and grandchildren (if we have any) will have to find the answers. As soon as possible.

My children's generation actually questions capitalism, the market economy and especially economic liberalism. Just as their grandparents did, back in the 1960s, but for different reasons. The new young Left criticize notably the *perpetuum mobile* of the permanent economic growth, which has turned out to be unsustainable and destructive. Yet, capitalism created all the resources these kids are taking for granted and, notably, the resources they will need to survive. If not our children, then our grandchildren will need to have more, much more, a whole lot more—not so they can be rich and enjoy the "wonderful life." The future will not be a choice between being and having, it will be a matter of having more so you can survive.

The message of our kids is much more than the usual rebellion of the young against the old. They oppose the project for the future. We must come to agreement with the next generations not about the past, but about the future. There is some ironic swap in the *bildungs*, or pedagogical, narrative—our children are teaching us not only about the new communication technologies and the Metaverse, but sense and morality from the future. I was telling my child stories of the past, she is telling me stories of the future.

Rada has taken part in anti-communist rallies, in hunger marches, in demonstrations against the war in Iraq and in the #MeToo movement. Michael attended his first funeral at five, at eight he was already watching news broadcasts and having drill exercises. Now he's shouting "How dare you?!" [165] at Friday student protests. What will our children and grandchildren be protesting against in ten, twenty, or fifty years?

"How dare you!?" This is our children's "*J'accuse.*"[166] Without our personal stories and memory, the past is a non-being, at best dry factual history for our children. But the future when our children will live is a non-being for us. *Après nous, le déluge!* For my generation—for us who have to act now, with no delay, for us who fail to do so—the second half of the twenty-first century, when the probable results of our past actions will be displayed, seems imaginary. For Rada, however, it's the lifetime of her unborn or adopted child, and for Michael, it's the second half of his centennial life.

---

165 A slogan raised by the Swedish teenager Greta Thunberg, a world-famous activist fighting against fossil fuels and climate change. Her initiatives have led to the Friday protests of students around the globe.

166 "J'accuse" is a staple phrase (from Émile Zola's letter in the Dreyfus Affair) expressing an indignation toward lawlessness and unbridled power.

P.S.

The first Bulgarian edition of the book came out on Friday the 13th of March 2020. On the next day the world closed. We stopped traveling and moving in around altogether, the children studied and we worked in front of computer screens at home. The world became completely virtual. In the next two to three years about 10 million[167] died of COVID-19.

P.P.S

February 2022. War in Europe. War! In *Europe*! *Today*! I could not believe the news. The *reportages* appear to me like anachronism, like documentary of some long-forgotten history, of some far-away location. The bombs from my childhood nightmares have finally fallen. And children again . . . killed, orphaned, in bomb shelters, at frontiers, in the dark and the cold. And bread is not enough again, other children in the world will die of hunger. And instead of investing in the salvation of the planet for these children, instead of getting ready for the imminent hard sweltering times, mankind will again regroup into camps, draw new iron curtains and invest trillions in arms.

A year later, in some horrifying synchrony or as if in time machine, in Bulgaria they discuss resuming military education classes for college students, while the European Commission considers developing civil defense training for its employees.

167 Conservative estimates.

THOU SACRED LANGUAGE OF MY FOREMOTHERS[168]

Language is the house of the truth of Being.
Martin Heidegger

I live in five languages, two of which I do not understand at all—Dutch and German. Dutch is one of the official languages of Belgium. I remained deaf, blind, and mute in German and I never learned the language, even passively. It wasn't the Teutons, but me, the Slav, who was mute.[169]

As in most mixed families, especially in Brussels, the language "regime" in ours has been complicated and asymmetrical. I used to speak only Bulgarian with my two children, but my husband did not understand it. French used to be our common family language. French was also the language of Michael's early childhood in the crèche, and now it's one of his main subjects at school. French is the language of our everyday life—the language of evening news broadcasts, of shopping, restaurants, transport, health care, repair people, of our municipality,[170] of tax authorities and courts. French was Rada's main language before English took over—the seven Harry Potter books reflect this transition, as well as the departure from Bulgarian. She read the first three volumes

168 The title is a replica to Ivan Vazov's poem, extoling Bulgarian as the sacred language of the fore*fathers*.
169 In all Slavic languages, the root of the word for "German" is the same as the word for "mute"—немски, ням. It seems that first communications between the Teutons and the Slavs had not been particularly intensive.
170 Which is Flemish officially, but practically French speaking, because French is the predominant language in Brussels. By law all state officials are supposed to be fully bilingual in Dutch and French, which is, by far, truer for the Flemish, who in addition to fluent French, usually have quite decent English, while the Francophones' Flemish leaves much to be desired, and their English is rudimentary. The Flemish also speak German—Belgium's third official language.

in Bulgarian, volumes four to six in French, and read the last, most urgently anticipated one, directly in the English original. French was the language in which Rada learned about the laws of nature, the language in which she read and analyzed Balzac and Camus, Baudelaire and Rimbaud, the language of her first love, of her bachelor degree.

English was the intimate language my husband and I spoke when we were alone, it's the language of my job, it's in English (besides French) that I learn about the affairs of the world; it's the language of Rada's MA courses, of her job, of her husband and, most probably, English will be the language of my future grandchildren. Michael has been exposed to English since birth, now he's "officially" studying it at school and he speaks it fluently.

German is the main language of my son, of his school, conscious and subconscious mind. On the other hand, he learned to speak in French and Bulgarian first. Just like his father, via German, Michael understands Dutch and with a little effort, he may learn to speak it fluently. Out of respect to her stepfather, Rada learned German at school and at university for ten years.

I remember a celebration of May 24th[171] in Brussels. A municipal cultural center has been rented for the occasion by the Sunday Bulgarian school, children were going to get their diplomas. A confident girl of eight or nine steps onto the stage. I vaguely know the mother—mixed marriage, a multilingual child who'll never return to Bulgaria, and yet the mother is heroically trying to keep her Bulgarian roots and spirit alive, speaking Bulgarian to her, taking her to Sunday school so she'd learn to read and write in Bulgarian. The girl grabs the microphone with a swooping gesture and her sonorous young voice starts rattling away in Bulgarian, with a strong accent—there's no reduction of unstressed vowels, every vowel and consonant is pronounced loudly, with pedantic clarity, sometimes the stress is misplaced, and the "r" is a bit too explosive. I detect Dutch behind the accent: "*I am a Bulgarian child, / I love our green mountains, / calling myself a Bulgarian / is my first and foremost joy.*" Then there's a boy of the same age, speaking in a different accent, softer, with excessive elision, a guttural "r," the "ch" sounds closer to a "sh," the "u" to "yu," a clear trace of his primary French: "*I love you, Bulgarian speech, / your sweet sound the dearest of sounds / now a ringing harp, now a sword . . .*"[172]

The audience is trying to stifle its laughter.

•

171 A national holiday, the day of Bulgarian education and culture, celebrating the Cyrillic alphabet and its creators, Sts. Cyril and Methodius.

172 From Vazov's poem.

"Rada, you have *crumblski* on your blouse. Oooh, you've had a cookie!" Michael is pointing an accusing finger at his sister.

Rada does not want to acknowledge that discretely in the kitchen she's been exceeding her cookie quota, so she replies solemnly, using her big sister authority as someone who was born in Bulgaria, fourteen years ahead of him, and can read and write in Bulgarian, having spent an year in a Bulgarian school.

"It's not *crimbleski*, you baby, it's *crinbles.*"

After I've finished laughing at the cookie conspiracy, the big-sister authority and the linguistic hodge-podge that was created in my honor—because the conversation was held in Bulgarian rather than French only because I was around—I explained why their linguistic guesses were wrong even though they were logical. My children had not fed breadcrumbs to Bulgarian sparrows.[173] They had fed, in French, the ducks in the nearby pond, or the parrots in our park that often came to our garden, or the impudent pigeons of Brussels. They have followed Hansel and Gretel through the woods in German or French. For them, the crumbs would be *miettes* from a French baguette or *krummel* from a thick, dark-brown German loaf.

Every day I inevitably heard often very funny linguistic improvisations,

"*Meinen *gashten haben in der *dupe gegangen.*"[174]

"Where are my **chaussette-ki?*[175] And my **chaussure-ki?*"[176]

"Look-look the **coccinelle-ki*!"[177]

"I eated ev-ev-everything"—Michael is timidly searching for the roots in the Bulgarian verb forest.

The German word for butterfly is *messerschmidt*, oh, pardon, it's *Schmetterling*. An attempt of German to express something pretty and ethereal. Weee, the *messerschmidt* swoops down, sorry, that was the butterfly . . . Michael does not get what's funny about the *butt-a-fly* (as Rada used to pronounce it) nor about my other linguistic jabs at the German tongue. Which reminds me of Nikola Georgiev's remark that the phrase "*The Count laughed in broken Spanish*" is not entirely absurd. It seems we indeed laugh, sigh, exclaim, call or cry in a different way in different languages. Sure, it is as well a matter of stereotypes, connotations, historical reminiscences within the languages themselves and, notably, in our perceptions. However, we all well know, that the nonverbal aspect of communication is equally important, if not predominant. Sometimes Michael and

173 A light reference to a children book by Yordan Radichkov.

174 A mixture of German and Bulgarian, saying that the boy's underwear has got in the crack of his bottom.

175 Socks (French). The ending "ki" indicates the smallness of the socks, i.e., this is a diminutive suffix, for plural, but in Bulgarian.

176 Shoes (French), with Bulgarian diminutive suffix.

177 Lady bird (French), with Bulgarian diminutive suffix.

I would sit together in silence, a special kind of silence after the words of a good-night tale or the hustle and bustle of everyday life. I would hold his little hand or we'd stay cuddled in bed, and I could feel we were telling each other something about our fears, about sorrow and love. Maybe our silence was in Bulgarian. Or maybe it was in German, as mom is anyhow mute in German. Mom can only be silent in German, German is her language of silence. I felt weird in the dead of the night when Michael was talking in his sleep beside me. In German. And I couldn't understand a word—not a sigh, a groan, a chuckle. Even when they are awake, my children seem different in Bulgarian, German, French, or English. As if they are not my children in the foreign language. Or they are not my children only.

After the pink tractor debacle, a year later Santa Claus brought the four-and-a-half-year-old Michael a puppet theatre. As an introduction to the human comedy of the adult world, the set included the three puppets from the classic triangle—a princess, a prince, and a dragon. We demonstrated how the fairy tale world of the theatre is supposed to work. Rada got behind the curtain, playing out the classic scenario in French—the dragon wanted to abduct the princess, the prince killed him (with a sharp and absurdly colorful cocktail stick), the prince and the princess kissed each other and marched off to get married. Then Christian got behind the curtains and played, in German, a more humane version of the story—the dragon was, in fact, the enchanted brother of the princess, but the prince was not scared of him, he didn't leave the princess—on the contrary, he loved the dragon like his own brother and that broke the spell. Rada was whispering in my ear, summarizing the action in Bulgarian. When at last the princess, the prince and the dragon held hands and waited for the spell to be broken (which was to happen behind the scenes as we didn't have a fourth puppet for the human version of the dragon brother), I started humming the Ode to Joy while Christian recited, from behind the curtains, Schiller's words about all people being brothers and God giving everyone (every male, that is) a peaceful home and a loving wife.

Then I got behind the curtain and played, in Bulgarian, the Cyrano version where the dragon was the shadow of the stupid prince, prompting him with the words to win the heart of the princess. The dragon was in love with the princess, too, but he was, indeed, an ugly dragon. On the other hand, the girl was no ordinary princess but one who valued words above looks. She found out about the scheme and wasn't scared by the dragon. I left the story open-ended instead of making a smooth transition to the "Beauty and the Beast." Rada was whispering in Christian's ear, translating the action in French.

Michael watched, all three versions, wide-eyed. When his turn came, he got behind the curtains, fumbling a bit, making the curtain swell but finally managing to get the puppets onto his hands. Having understood that the story depended on *who* was telling it and in *what language,* he popped his head between the curtain and asked: "*Français, allemand ou bulgare?*" The audience laughed and voted for French, the language the four of us shared. Michael finished my story, but choosing a Shrek type of scenario instead. If I got it correctly, the princess was actually a dragon-girl who's been magically turned into royalty, which explained why she liked the dragon's words so much. The silly prince had no chance of winning her heart with rings and castles. The audience was mesmerized.

I was wondering if my son would have finished the story in a different way if he'd chosen to tell it in German or Bulgarian. Is language really a reflection of a certain model or philosophy, or is the speaker expressing his philosophy of the world, his culture and his character through a certain language?

When the parrots in the nearby park start crowing, we know that spring has come (you had no other way of guessing the change of seasons in Brussels, anyway). Rada, Michael and I delight ourselves by reciting a Bulgarian poem:

Birds sing on bright colored wing,
Fresh leaves are quivering,
Gathered in a wreath of blue
Fair Spring is busy again . . .[178]

I try an older piece of folklore but my children no longer understand the language.

Fast forward a few months, and it's summer—a Brussels summer, cool and cloudy, or musty and damp. My children have no village and no early memories of fairytale flora and fauna, but every other night they pull out a thin book in Bulgarian I have read to them and they both know by heart.

It's so lovely when it's summer
And the sun is soaked in gold.

178 Assen Raztsvetnikov, Bulgarian poet (1897-1951). Translation into English: Cristopher Buxton.

Then we laugh as one, hissing, alliterating and truncating line by line:

The old goose opens her wings full length
Then she hisses with all her strength
And the goslings tweet 'what luck,
We are not like that ugly duck.[179]

And then it's winter, with even a rare sprinkling of snow in the air. Rada is already a grown-up, a college student who's come home for Christmas. It's cozy, warm and delicious here. Half-closing her eyes, she's back in her childhood. We look at the white blanket covering our garden, then we start that poem in Bulgarian, which I used to read to her:

The snow is falling. Luminescence. Quiescence.
Topcho has breakfast and let a game commence . . .

The Bulgarian language in these children's verses is exquisite, the rhymes are unexpected and plentiful, the rhythm lulls and transports the three of us to the luminous, magical world of childhood. Laughter and sadness flow into us as we savor not just the stories that we have long grown out of but the beauty of language, the Bulgarian language. I'd like to believe that neither I nor my children will ever be too old for that beauty.

Years ago the entertaining double Christmas issue of *The Economist* had a long article about all sorts of language peculiarities around the world—dual grammatical numbers, modal jokes, gender puzzles. An inferential or dubitative past tense, had been "discovered" in some African language. Its use indicated something in the past, that had not been witnessed by the speaker and therefore was open to doubt. I sent the editors a short letter to inform them that they didn't need to look into far-away places to find the languages that were hardest to learn. Then I told them about the elephant in the Bulgarian grammatical room (the verb), about its perfect and imperfect tenses, and, of course, about its own inferential mood. A much quoted example is the ways in which a drunken night out might be reported by the main player. "I was drunk" would be

179 Tsanko Lalev, contemporary Bulgarian poet. Further down, too. Translation into English: Christopher Buxton.

a frank confession. But with the use of the inferential tense it becomes the equivalent of "It is reported that I was drunk." A further expressive ironic use of the verb would then cast doubt on this report. The cumbersome English translation would be, "I was reported to have been drunk, but I don't believe it/who the hell they are to say this," in Bulgarian all expressed in the verb form only. Grammaticized national mentality.

In my letter, I also mentioned the incredibly extensive and specific vocabulary defining relationships in the patriarchal family, as it is preserved in its entirety to this day, where every male or female relative, even the ones twice-removed, is honored with a specific word, marking the person's gender and family line (maternal or paternal). I was not speaking with pride. I didn't feel any rootless, displaced sense of shame, either. The survival of patriarchal nomenclature in the conservative realm of language is paradoxical when set against the changes in society. The patriarchal family is long extinct, half of the marriages end in divorce, single parents are hardly rare, reconstructed families and cohabitation are being normalized, and still language doesn't have any adequate words for these new kinds of relationships (yet?). *Stepmother* and *stepfather*, *bastard* and *stepson* have preserved their extremely negative (to put it mildly) connotations. The "diffident"[180] negligence or inertia of the Bulgarian language is not just a common case of linguistic conservatism but an expression of mentality, as well. In the same line of thought, the Bulgarian language has been averting its gaze away from sexual orientation, gender identity, and the need to *name* them—beyond patriarchal stigma and the aggressive pejorative nature of slang.[181] The same is true about the slow emergence of the missing feminine forms of dozens of occupation-related words, or the masculine forms of totally "female" jobs like "medicinal sister," i.e., "nurse."

I didn't write to *The Economist* about any of that. My letter remained quite patriotic, reminding the editors that Old Bulgarian was the first (and for the next several centuries, the only) written Slavic language, that this is the reason it is still used as the basis for studying the historical development of all Slavic languages, that as early as the ninth century it was the third language of religious services in medieval Europe, and bearing in mind that the official form of Old Bulgarian was based on the vernacular, we can claim that Reformation had first taken place on the Balkans.

I was thanked.

•

180 After Pencho Slaveikov.

181 In the context of institutional translation within the EU, we create the words for these new facets of the human condition. With sanitary objectivity, we translate and coin new terms, most often just transcribing the foreign word or calquing. Yet, it will be very long before those eurolect terms become part of Bulgarian language and shed their connotation of "liberal Brusselian perversions" (as right-wing, conservative Bulgarian see it).

Linguists know that languages differ in what they insist on marking—for example, formality and politeness ("*tu*" and "*vous*" in French), grammatical gender, whether the message is a witness statement or report, the emphasis put by syntax (so called topic/comment or theme/rheme). Different languages structure the world differently at the level of grammar. There is no language whose grammar contains all the markers. There seems to be a limit for the complexity of a language, and this limit is most probably imposed by our brains' capacity. Languages strike a balance—some are easier to learn, which makes them more open to "invasion" and more "susceptible" to transfers and adaptations between the linguistic communities. Other languages are harder, but that encapsulates and preserves the community. I think that there is a connection between the grammatical complexity of the Bulgarian language and its degree of conservatism. Surely, no language is lovelier or more perfect than the rest. Some languages have richer vocabularies, but others feature words with unique meanings. There are only differences in the way a language structures the world and the human being. That's why outside the patriotic boost that was surely needed in certain historical moments, the pathos of Bulgarian writers toward their native tongue seems to me unjustified.

Language is the house of Being and an attribute of consciousness (to quote Heidegger). There's only one language in which we *are*—in the existential and Biblical sense of the word.[182] Your first language, your *mother tongue*, as they used to call it until recently, is the language you don't consciously learn; this is your intimate language, in which you *are*, you exist and become a human being. This is the language of Being and all things pertaining to it. In this language, words cast shadows of emotion, color, aroma, pictures, gestures, faces, and stories. These shadows, superimposed upon the literal meaning, are handed down to you by history, literature, culture, by the Others who *were* in this language before you. The Word, i.e., language in that elevated, biblical sense, is language of feelings and the "fundamental questions," plus that collective memory and culture that are built into it. In the Word we join ancestry and nation, with their history, culture, spirit, and mythology. The Word is belonging. The word has been there before you and within it, your individual world grows. The word is the language of bloodline and nation and human consciousness, of Being and non-Being, of death, time, love, nature, and Cosmos. It is in The Word that we become humans.

182 Two at most, if the family and the environment are bilingual; and even then these two languages would be complementary in the fundamental discourse of the Word.

The word is the language of our consciousness, of that "unwavering band of light" in us (as Vonnegut put it), which is everywhere and forever.

Therefore—to come back to the patriotic exaltations—not only are there no languages lovelier and better than the rest, but we cannot objectively judge—in aesthetic and rational terms—our mother tongue, or, to be precise, the language in which we *are*, because it is an instrument and a manifestation of the very consciousness making the judgment.

Bulgarian is my mother tongue, my intimate language, the language of my consciousness. In my mother tongue, I think and say things I would not think and say in any other language because the thoughts and images are born in my consciousness in Bulgarian. For me, the Word is Bulgarian.

The mother tongue is inextricably bound to the idea of homeland. For me, homeland is not a territory, state, or other objective reality but something intimate, ancestral, existential. The sky and the earth of my homeland are populated by my dead forefathers and foremothers, by my unborn children. The homeland is the time-space of my childhood and youth. Disgusted by the state, first I became alienated as an internal refugee, then I distanced myself geographically. Now I am an emigrant in every sense. The Bulgarian language is that silver thread, the only one that links me to this homeland and attaches my sense of belonging. If I paraphrase Cioran,[183] I'd say Bulgarian is my *only* homeland.

With the fading of national identity, language no longer marks a national distinction, but rather belonging, blending and affiliation—not so much toward a given nation and state as to a given culture and to the legacy of those who have *existed* in this language before us.

English and French are foreign languages to me, I learned them consciously, for pragmatic purposes. In the emigrant foreign language you socialize with foreigners, with their alien history and culture, with their writers, their motherland, which you accept with all your heart like an orphan accepts their good second mother, i.e., you integrate, or you stay segregated and the country remains a stepmother. Bromidic Belgium with cosmopolitan Brussels is definitely not the foreign state, into which I'll integrate like into a second homeland. The global business English, the Euro speak or my fairly functional, mostly legal-administrative French, are not languages that make me feel a belonging to some culture in particular. In the anonymous, global, culturally vacuous *nowhere*, you don't belong to anything or anywhere. "Abroad" also melts away as a concept.

183 Emil Mihail Cioran (1911–1995), the exact quote is "One does not inhabit a country; one inhabits a language."

I don't add Russian to the foreign languages, not only because it's not "utterly foreign" for Bulgarians, or because for more than ten years I've learned, spoken, and read in Russian. Simply I've never used it as a foreign language, for a pragmatic purpose; actually I haven't used it at all since I graduated university. Up till February 2022 when I began to follow the Russian propaganda machine and listen to Putin's speeches in the original, with the pitiful hope that something might have been lost in translation. No, sadly, it wasn't.

Alek Popov once remarked shrewdly that the tongue is the mother's but The Word belongs to men. With a pinch of black humor I would counter that, as I have fulfilled both the mother's and father's roles, I could dare lay a claim on The Word, too. I'm trying. It's only through words that we can rebel against oblivion, futility, and death.

In the beginning of my world, there was an apple and the word for it, and another not-so-foreign word and the most important thing I learned from it. Funeral processions and three funeral marches. A violin concert, The Ode to Joy (in German) and the rehearsals of an orchestra. The Apostle, the April Uprising and the relativity of time. A few beautiful, and appropriately untranslatable, verses. The fundamental distinction between (the seemingly similar words for) бит (pronounced *bit*, i.e., everyday life, social conditions) and битие (pronounced *bitié*, i.e., the human condition or the Being); and between language, or tongue (език, ezik) and The Word (слово, slovo). In the beginning of my world, there was as well the Bulgarian translation of a French poem about *tristesse* (sadness, or melancholy).

Atanas Dalchev[184] states aphoristically that when you are in command of a language, you say what you want in it, and if you are not fully in command, you say what you are able to say. In a first literal reading, quite true. However, mastering a language means more than being able to say what you want in this language. You can achieve the informative and communicative function even in a language you use with the help of grammar books, dictionaries, Google Translate, or DeepL. The point is what you *want* to say. There are certain things which you can say only in one language, because these things take shape in your mind in this language. Every attempt to say these things in another language would be more, or less, an adequate translation, not the original. I *am* in Bulgarian. English and French are foreign languages for me, Because I *live* in them, but I don't *exist* in them.

This is even more valid for writing. Writing is a materialization of not only the memory of the author, but the memory of a language, too. The writer masters not only the grammar and lexis of this language, but the history, culture, literature, spirit,

184 Bulgarian poet and translator (1904–1978).

mythology, national character, comedy, and pathos, all built into this language. In this language, the writer has a historic collective memory and sense for connotations and references, for the smell and story of words, of the meaningful and emotional nuances of grammar, syntactical constructions and intonation-curves. Language is impregnated with the collective historical, aesthetical, and intellectual memory of the language community. Therefore, the choice of a language to write in is an important element of both the existential or ideological and the aesthetic choices. The language of literature is more than a means and a form, because language has its own memory, and even its own "ideas" and stories. The literature text activates this memory in order to articulate its own content but also in order to inscribe this content in the grand narrative of a culture and its language.

And even so, being an emigrant, living in other languages, knowing other languages is enriching. A foreign language is the best way to absorb what is foreign. Through a foreign language you not only spend time in some place physically, but intellectually as well. A foreign language also gives you an interesting new perspective on your mother tongue, and even to your content, as does translation. You can see roots, meanings and even discover forgotten faculties of your mother tongue. Command of a foreign language and the comparative optics allow you to distance yourself from your mother tongue, to leave your home and to see its pluses and minuses, which otherwise you wouldn't be aware of. But a long residence away from a natural language environment leads to a particularly unconscious alienation from language. As I was writing away in Bulgarian, at some point I began to look into the Bulgarian words for *vestibule, bespattered, ignominy, cornered, thrust, tubby, bosom, eaves* . . . I examined the words etymologically, phonetically and connotatively like a . . . foreigner. I was feeling around their emotionally charged flesh, without being sure if they were not already dead cold for me, denotative shells, meaning something that could be *translated* correctly and objectively in English like this . . . or like that. The translating instinct can be a litmus test for the extent of nativeness and sensitivity to the emotion and culture of words.

One may argue that I preach some sort of linguistic solipsism or mysticism, ignoring translation. The cultural memory, mythology, and mentality, built into language is often untranslatable. Language is translatable, while the Word, discourse and culture are more difficult, and sometimes even impossible, to translate. And here I don't only mean the "usual suspects" such as poetry or the linguistic or metalinguistic translatability of historical notions and realities. While you could produce a fully comprehensible and adequate translation (suitably "packaged" for the politically correct foreign reader) of the historical realities, mechanisms and attributes of communism, it is incomparably more difficult to translate the whole spectrum of meanings in that ostensibly simple first line of a poem: "*To return . . .*" Or the contradiction between "*Fear not, kids*" and "*Children, I am scared for you.*" Or the difference between "*bit*" and "*bitie*,"[185] "*ezik*" and "*slovo*,"[186] and the beauty of "*tuga*."[187] The difficulty—and not infrequently the impossibility—to explain what is funny is another indicative example. Before any purely linguistic translation, the author—of course, if s/he is aiming at foreign readers—carries out a metalinguistic "translation" of the stories and personages, of the beautiful and the ugly, the comical and the tragic, the heroic, the sublime, and the elating, of that individual or collective memory, culture and history, in which his/her text is embedded. No, doubt, translation can help, but it is first the author who has to bring the foreign reader over the bridge, which is not simply linguistic. In powerful prose, language is not just a form but a part of the content, language can even have its own themes, subject lines and leitmotifs. And in poetry language IS a fundamental element of the content. The language in which you narrate can influence the content and message of your story (and not the other way round). Language not only articulates your own thoughts and interpretations, but can give birth to its own.

For all these reasons, I chose to write in Bulgarian. The truth is that I am unable to write about some things in another language. Only in the "house" of Bulgarian language I hear the voices of those who inhabited the house before me. I dip my pen in the linguistic mysteries of Bulgarian grammar, I light up and color the shadows of words, I commune with the spirits in the house of words.

If writing in Bulgarian may be the only possible existential and aesthetical choice for me, it's surely not the best market choice, nor a shortcut to praise. When you write in a small, exotic language, you remain authentic, but run the risk to remain unheard, too. And if you reach for readers across that bridge, because your otherwise authentic story is universally human, you start to subconsciously censor yourself and undermine your authenticity. The text may deviate as much as to contain implicitly its translation. I have tried to avoid this and not to censor myself, assuming that translation will beget a text that would be more or less different, an adaptation, a

185 The difference between routine life and the human condition.

186 The difference between language in general and speech through "The Word," in the biblical sense, embodying the articulation of a history and culture.

187 A highly significant word, whose translation will lie somewhere on the sadness/melancholy/sorrow spectrum but will miss the rich connotations that the word evokes in Bulgarians. See further in Ars poetica.

bridge onto which I will walk my half to meet the foreign reader at the capstone of our shared human experience.

If the generation of our children don't get "home" and "abroad," which language would they call their mother tongue and which languages would they define as foreign? Do their generations even need a homeland and a native tongue, an intimate language, the Word, a language—home, which their consciousness would inhabit? Will they be able to achieve the magic, the revelation, the insight of The Word? Will they have something to express in their native tongue only, and in no other language? Will they have something to read and relate to—in this language only? There's beautiful, strong poetry written in all languages, but are there stanzas and meaning that are inexpressible in any other language, that are laid in the foundations of their consciousness, that, in the intimate and biblical sense, are the beginning of their world? And if The Word is still there, at the beginning of their consciousness, in what language is that Word? Will language remain the organ of consciousness for our kids, the one that keeps them human, or will it be just a practical instrument for communication and information? Could the realization and expression of consciousness and humanity take place in other sign systems—pictures, music, dance, film, augmented reality, videogames, mathematical, physical, or chemical laws?

As the notions of "home" and "abroad" are fading away, so does the recognition of any language as your arterial tongue, of any culture as your own, unlike all other—foreign—languages and cultures. It's no longer your origin, your citizenship or your mother tongue to determine what language or languages you'll be speaking at home, at school, at college, or at your job. Language is less attached to the idea of belonging. My children have not taken Bulgarian with their breastmilk. Bulgarian is their mother tongue only in the literal and narrow sense of the word—as the language of the mother, the language they *only* speak with their mother (and, from time to time, on Skype or for a week or so in Bulgaria—with their grandparents, their uncle, Dad, or aunt). To my children the mother tongue is no longer the language in which they *are* and the language in which they learn about the world, the Universe and people, the language in which they become part of their bloodline and their people, the language they will learn to perfection with all its grammar, idioms, connotations, intonations, and expressive punch, with all the culture, history, and mentality that are built into it. Bulgarian is not the language in which they think, they dream, the language in which they talk in their sleep, the language in which they love and feel homesick. Bulgarian is not the language they set apart from all *foreign* languages in which they *are not*, from those foreign languages they only use as a pragmatic means for communication with the non-Self, with the non-intimate world, for learning and transmitting information, for professional accomplishment and money-making. My children's mother's tongue, Bulgarian, is not native to them. It's still "sweet magic" only because it's the language of Mom, the language of home, of those sweet verses from their childhood, only because one day it will be or it will have been the language of Grandma. But if they can't say something to Mom in Bulgarian, my children will say it in French or English. They could even say it in German if Mom had taken care to learn that language. For my children, Bulgarian will be what savory is for Ilija Trojanow.[188]

For the new citizens of the world there are no places whose history makes them feel pride or shame, love or hatred. The notion of "native soil," the sense of belonging to a certain nation, is fading away. Our children feel no emotional attachments with a national denominator. But they are less emotional as a whole—despising pathos, passion, and (melo)dramatic gestures and words. In their world there's nothing heroic, proud and fatal, nobody loves and hates to death. There's no content that's beautiful and inexpressible in any other language. There's no cultural collective memory. No mythologies. There's politically correct history and historic faction, non-fiction, scientific publications, professional journals, political analyses, social causes. Entertainment. And news. And all of that is aimed at a global audience and is primarily in English.

The previous generations and those who chose to "stay on native soil," literally and figuratively speaking, comprise the other, national Europe, and also America, with its national mythologies, cultures, and languages.

About fifty years ago, with quite a bit of postmodern manifesto pathos, the author was proclaimed dead. Just as history was supposedly over. The author, though, has been coming to life ever since, in strong and authentic narratives. (As for history, well, it just "kept going.") It's not like that with language. Languages die imperceptibly, non-heroically, once and for all. Languages die because that "unwavering band of light" is no longer everywhere and eternal, as if it is being extinguished. Our children are not only orphaned in their lack of homeland and national identity, they fall into an ever greater unconsciousness as humans, too. Having outgrown bloodline and nation, national memory and culture, religion and social ideals, our children are modern and alone. They have no community of shared destiny, shared goals, shared time and

188 A contemporary German writer from Bulgarian origin, who left Bulgaria as very young child.

shared transcendental fate. The only thing bringing together tomorrow's citizens of the planet is their shared fear, their existential survival project that has replaced all other projects for the future.

Today, the modern human is numbing their consciousness, pushing it away to the basement of their personality as some kind of impairment, a disability, an obstacle to their rush to be happy. That's why the globetrotters don't need a language for their consciousness, for the Being, they do not need the Word, a *Sein-Sprache*. They don't think and have no need to express stuff, which could shape up in their minds only in one language. The new generation doesn't need revelation and insight, a language beyond the everyday stuff, a language in which to experience Being. The Word is no longer at the beginning of the world and consciousness. Language is no longer the organ of consciousness, in which you emerge and exist as a human being. People have no further need of the Word to rebel against oblivion, pointlessness and death. Artificial intelligence, digital memory, and science are the new reposals. Their language, however, is made up of data, numbers and laws, not words, emotions, memories and dreams.

David Adger[189] says that a person can make a *minimum* of a hundred million trillion[190] grammatically correct sentences with twenty words. To demonstrate what this number means, the author says that it vastly exceeds the number of sand grains on the planet. To natural, grammatically correct language, which is practically infinite, we need to add the literary means of expression. This vast infinity is the product and the domain of our finite, according to philosophers, consciousness, which cannot operate beyond a certain number of zeroes and certain limits of time and space, and with non-being and the related notions of "never" and "forever."

With the dulling of our consciousness, with the simplification and gratification of Man, language is losing its inner coating of national culture and memory, its fabric getting threadbare, torn. Trillions of sand grains are lost, melting into the same type of rocks. Language is being diminished, depleted, reduced to a pragmatic means of communication, an increasingly standardized means to exchange information or trivia, which are, in turn, becoming globally alike. Language is less and less individual. We *compile* our messages by choosing among a standardized range of expressions, having no time to *compose*, to really think and express ourselves, even less—to create.

189 David Adger, *Language Unlimited*, 2019.

190 I.e., 100 x 1,000,000 x 10^{18} or 10^{12}, depending on whether we take a trillion to be a billion billions, at the 18th degree, or a thousand billions, at the 12th degree. In both cases, it's infinite enough. It's even a good thing to have a range because many people would be located at the lower limit of this range.

Machine translation is the dream come true of Douglas Adams's Babel fish. Intelligent machines translate increasingly better our increasingly simpler language. They crash however when faced by the most innocent comparison, not to mention metaphor. The Word is often untranslatable, let alone by machines. The more standardized our language becomes, the more compilation takes precedence over composition, self-expression and creativity, the more comfortably the Babel fish swims, away from the dangerous, unfathomable ocean, in a finite, predictable, well-kept, and sterile fish tank. A Babel fish tank where the waters of all languages are being filtered. Machines keep learning from our standardized language so they can standardize it even further as we use them. You can get a very funny story if you put together the words prompted by your smartphone's suggestive writing, Google Translate, or DeepL. It will be a story about the death of language.

Language is being suffocated not only by cutting the flow of oxygen from consciousness, memory, history and culture. It is also drowning in the swelling tide of the visual and the virtual. Virtual reality has conquered geographical territories, and the visual has taken the territory of words, content, communication.

Language has to be saved, not only to tell stories, to testify and to rescue from oblivion and death (after Canetti), but as a home for human consciousness.

The UN authorities have compiled a list of the nations who are doomed to extinction. The Bulgarians are on that list. On the occasion of Bulgaria's EU presidency in 2018, *The Economist* published an article, entitled "The Incredibly Shrinking Bulgaria." It confirmed the gloomy prognosis—in forty to fifty years, there will not be many Bulgarians in Bulgaria. How about the Bulgarian language? Will anyone speak it at all in a hundred years or so? Will it be just a handful of linguists reading Bulgarian as a dead exotic language? Will Bulgarian literature be only read in translation? Will the dozen or so surviving translations into living, non-exotic languages be enough? Or will it be just some age-old Bulgarian grandma fawning over her grandchild on videochat in that extinct Slavic language? Explaining to him all about the apple. And how will the grandchild going to translate that apple—apple, *apfel*, *pomme*, 苹果, सेब?[191] By the way, let's hope that there will still be apples for the kids to munch on, that our great-grandchildren will not know the apple and its symbolism only from the iPhones preserved in museums.[192] With the disappearance of Bulgarians and Bulgarian lan-

191 "An apple" in, by order, German, French, Chinese, and Hindi (the last two—according to Google Translate).

192 Oh, the apple . . . Where do I start—Newton, the Bible, woman, knowledge, my Nana and the Slavonic

guage, the notion of "тъга" will disappear, as will the word for it. Or maybe it will go the other way round—as that particular sorrow will disappear from our children's emotional palette, the word for it will go, too. And then the apples will follow suit.

If we are still taking this scenario to be a mere hypothesis, we surely do know that educated reading Bulgarians are emigrating in droves and that in the very close future expat Bulgarians will vastly outnumber the "real" ones "in situ." That's why it's so important for emigrants to keep our language alive, to speak Bulgarian in their mini homelands. The Bulgarian language is our homeland, the last and real one that, I would like to believe, we have never left. Language is that "homeland in our hearts," which has otherwise become such a cliché. This is our "home and hearth," saved away in the most intimate landscape of our minds. We carry this little house wherever we may go around the world. We not only have to take care of our opulent homes abroad; we must not forget who we are and what human beings we are. In Bulgarian. Otherwise, the little house of our spirit will fall into decline and ruin.

But living abroad, the only reason to nourish and pass on the language to the children would be spiritual, not pragmatic. And for this reason I am beset with deep doubt. I ask myself whether one day my children will still understand my writing in Bulgarian rather than in translation? As for my grandchildren I have no hope at all. Bulgarian is doomed to extinction in my branch of the family-genetic-genealogical tree and with the death of the grandmothers, i.e., my mother and I, it will be dead, too. The sacred language of the foremothers. I wish so hard that one day my children will read beautiful Bulgarian children's verses to their own kids. The probability of that happening, however, is next to zero. I, as a grandmother, would be the last echo. I hope I'll live long enough. This is a nice motivation to live—to teach your grandchildren a few magical stanzas in a language that's inscrutable to them, totally useless and already dead.

I lived in five languages, I learned the most important thing in Russian, I gave birth in French, I met death in Dutch, I was mute and kept shtum in German. I *was* and I *am* in Bulgarian. I'd like to die in my homeland and in Bulgarian. Although if I pass away in a planned and peaceful manner with my two children beside me, the unhappy end could play out in two even three languages.

Here and there I declare that I write in Bulgarian for conceptual reasons. This book is a gigantic exercise in Bulgarian in which I wanted to *resurrect* the memory of the

---

languages, my thought-up words, Berkeley and the quantum mechanics, the Big Bang, the atom, the food of the future . . . A very *fruitful* symbol. I don't know if Steve Jobs, peace be with him, had thought about all of this when choosing a logo for his product. I did: the apple appears quite consciously and naturally, again and again, in my attempt to make sense of things and myself.

language, to *essay* its "harp and sword,"[193] in every kind of literary and non-literary genres and styles. What came out was a lengthy, I must admit, declaration of love to the Bulgarian language—my only homeland.

Writing is a fight against time, oblivion, pointlessness and death, but also a fight to preserve a language, to keep The Word alive. In the beginning, it was The Word, it seems that it will be there in the end, too. That, and translation—which is now the language not only of Europe[194] but of the new human.

193 Quote from the poem by Ivan Vazov, devoted to the beauty and the might of Bulgarian language.

194 Umberto Eco.

ARS POETICA, ARS LONGA

My first aesthetic manifesto was defended in a fight, real and painful, in no way just a literary dispute between "pale youths." In it I was bruised and plucked. I was fourteen and a half, it just before I got admitted to the English Language High School. It kicked off in the Elementary School yard. A flock of teenage girls were cawing over the boys, clucking over who was hitting on whom, who was on their monthly and allowed off PE class, who had a new blouse, and similar engrossing topics.

My feet were scarcely touching the ground after finishing a book the previous day, and I was talking excitedly about it, about the love in this book, the tragedy, how I'd been knocked off my feet after just a few pages. The girls reluctantly suspended their important information exchange and bestowed their attention on me. Quickly realizing that all of this wasn't really that interesting, they ignored me and resumed their chatter. I spoke still more slowly and quietly. In the end I shut up, embarrassed, furious with these dumbbells.

"Oh you're discussing such important stuff!" I shouted in helpless fury.

The girls stopped talking and looked at me in amazement.

"What, it's only a book, a sort of brick, made up stuff. What you getting so worked up about?!" The boss-hen in the pecking order sniggered at me, with her heavily made up eyes, and looked around triumphantly at her surrounding hens and they agreed, "Yeah, yeah, what's the big deal?"

"Ah, and this life of yours is such a fucking big deal. You're spawned in a blind hormonal spasm, supposedly in love. You've played at dolls, Mums, and Madams. Now you're bursting with pimples and you hang for hours in front of the mirror instead of reading. You'll barely graduate, some of you will already be pregnant, the rest will soon catch up. You'll be dandling fat babies, you'll work, so you've got what you need to eat and buy 'blouses.' You'll work till you drop, then you'll get old, you'll dandle your kids' fat babies, and you'll finally die. All that time you'll fuck, you'll drink, you'll cook, you'll stuff yourselves, you'll gossip, you'll be envious, you'll burp, and you'll shit. And not only will nobody write a book about you, no one will remember your stupid, ugly lives or even you yourselves." Spit was shooting out of my mouth, I'd gone crazy.

At the same time, I was overtaken by an insupportable grief, because the scenario I'd described also applied to me, despite of a temporary diversion at university, whither only I, most probably, out of the whole henhouse, would be going (provided of course they ignored my unfavorable background). At the end of the day, this was just some stupid book. I shut up and turned away my head, so they didn't see my tears.

But it was too late for apologies. So as not to spoil her manicure or put her foundation-plastered face at risk, the boss simply gave a signal to one of the girls—Slavka, a burly "loving village girl," who followed her like a dog. Slavka punched me, following the rules she'd clearly learned at home, and tore out a lock of my hair before I could adopt the helpless defense posture of a person who knows she deserves what's coming. The boys crowded round to watch the spectacle of girls fighting. I managed to run away and howl behind a block, away from the school yard.

Many years after my epiphany in front of an old photograph and the revelation of my desire to write, when I was already pretending to be a writer, although not an accomplished one, I was sitting with a friend, a Polish publisher, in a cozy café in Paris. It was a warm spring day, we were drinking red wine and were chatting in a strange language that sounded like English. I was talking in Euro-speak, and my friend was speaking English as a truly-foreign language. Later I read somewhere that several centuries ago, Poles had had to insist that they weren't geese and they had their own language. Occasionally, we switched to this original Polish language, which I had never learned outside some comparative linguistics of Slavic family on my philology course. The strange thing was that we understood each other wonderfully.

So, in Euro-speak-Polish-very-foreign-English we talked about writing. The publisher, past whose eyes thousands of published and unpublished texts had passed, whose authors, down to the last one, had thought of themselves as unique geniuses,[195]

195 Just get those Poles with their mania for their chosen status, per religion and nationality.

was telling me that writing is above all work, hard work every day, and a struggle with language. Because, he said, there were only a few basic themes, and all of them had by now been exhausted, so that if anyone sits down to write literature—me, for example, it's not so important what I'll say, but how, how I'll struggle with the language, and how hard I'll work. On our second bottle, I unleashed a tirade, in that administrative, sterile English, in which I was fluent without having to think, how really a half if not the whole of literary work is over, once you have an idea, dim or clear-cut, as if dictated by another (actually from my subconscious), an insight, a revelation, an epiphany, and you overcome laziness or sleep to get up and note it, and later you manage to buy time to write it out. To craft this *content* into some kind of linguistic form, genre, and composition is a question of skill, taste, culture, education, etc. But, I insisted emotionally, literature, great, strong literature, is born from the truth, the insight, the thought, the idea, not in the language. Language even impoverishes. Language is a necessary unavoidable evil, so you can share the content with the Other. Especially if you are "struggling" in a small, exotic language. Yet, it's much more important *what* you say and not in what language.

I tried to explain to the publisher my literary theory, so to speak, that every little, ordinary, and insignificant person is a writer, because their ordinary life is a human life, universally tragic and comic, similar to a billion other lives, but unique as experience, that every person ought to recount his or her life, in their own words, not to retell literary works. I also joked that publishers have read everything, but ordinary folk haven't, and that I'm not promoting graphomania, because it's not essential for personal stories to be published, but to be told or written. I poured scorn on the professionalized and polished linguistic craft and literary tricks instilled by courses in creative writing. Every self-respecting American University has such a course. I mocked the project approach to writing, I insisted that first and foremost writing is an existential act and as such it must be above all candid and authentic, so that if you are writing, you work on the text everywhere and at all times. As you live. Because you are living it.

Adults don't fight over such matters. There again, my friend was very benevolent, he actually wanted to encourage me to write books—for publication. Everything else slipped outside his publisher's interest.

During my "studying" period in Brussels, when somebody asked me what I did for a living, I would get all worked up and slip into a detailed explanation about my education and work in Bulgaria, explain that just at this time I wasn't working and I was preparing for a career in the European Union. People were either baffled or suspicious. A good-looking Bulgarian in Brussels, without any specific job, probably belonged to the oldest profession in the world . . .[196] At some point I got fed up and started giving a short and self-satisfied answer: "I'm a writer."[197] This statement put an end to all further questions and explanations; people looked at me as if I was either an alien or a lunatic.

Years later, already an EU Civil Servant, answering the same question, sometimes, depending on the company, I summoned the courage to add that actually "deep down" I am a writer. Eyebrows would rise, followed by the fabulous question: "What do you write about?" A few times, I snapped that if I could answer this question in a few sentences, there'd be no point in writing hundreds of pages to bore my readers. People took offense.

Not long ago, after I began writing this book, I dug out a new answer: "Everybody writes, pretty much, about one and the same things. I am a fundamentalist."

Eyes again widened in bewilderment, eyebrows still risen, uncertain. On the basis of the terrorist attacks and aggressive Islam, the word fundamentalist sounded alarming: "Meaning?"

"I am a fundamentalist writer. I write about fundamental things. Like life, death, time, love, art . . . that sort of stuff."

No one asks me *why* I write.

Some years ago, an international survey found out that the Bulgarians are the saddest people in the world. Some elemental melancholy seems to haunt the souls of my compatriots. I believe that apart from being at the wrong side in two European wars, forty-five years of communism and failed transition, the national narrative, underpinning this mood, is actually the "Turkish Yoke," or "The Ottoman Presence" (as it has recently been renamed by the politically correct) and the April uprising. The grief about Macedonia is an element of the same narrative.

Christian visited Bulgaria in some delegation, they had a seminar in Batak,[198] their host was the Chief Prosecutor. Lavish banquets, souvenirs, presents—wine and musk

---

196 Local newspapers had noted that almost 90% of the prostitutes in the dedicated area in Brussels were Bulgarians.

197 My prenuptial agreement gives this as my profession.

198 Today, a small town in the Rhodopi mountain. During the April uprising in 1876, between 2,000 and 4,000 men, women and children, including unborn, were raped and/or slaughtered there by the Ottoman army, within few days. Similar massacres occurred in many other villages. The unimaginable atrocities made the headlines in

rose oil, both highly appreciated by Christian, everything *comme il faut.*[199] There was a "cultural" program, too—the tour guide came up with various details about the April uprising against "the Ottoman Presence" and, inescapably, she spoke about the Batak slaughter, showed the church, quoting MacGahan, Schuyler, Hugo, Turgenev. The story shook Christian to the core. Inquisitive and systematic, he wanted to read up all the information on the April Uprising. Apart from everything else, through this historical event he hoped to learn more about his Bulgarian darling's culture and mentality. And, wonder of wonders, our once fraternal German Democratic Republic had translated and published in German Zachary Stoyanov's "Records on the Bulgarian Uprisings,"[200] and by happy coincidence Christian found a second-hand copy online.

"Is this book worth reading?"

"Definitely," I smiled cryptically.

Christian read the two-volume German publication over four to five days and nights. He sighed, blew out his cheeks, left the book and walked about. He was clearly deeply moved. And shocked by . . . the revolutionaries.

"This Benkovski . . . How could they??!! Lie to the people, make them burn their houses, lead whole villages to their death. Everything was doomed from the very beginning. Everything! Why?! Why was all this necessary?!"

I gave him a lecture on the meaning of the slogan "Freedom or Death," on the rise of the slave to a free man through self-sacrifice, going with open eyes to death, which he prefers to slavery; I passionately stressed that this sacrifice opened up a wound in the Ottoman Empire which in the end led to the Russian-Turkish war. I read with poignancy and translated into English Vazov's poem about the Bulgarian volunteers at the battle of Shipka. Even in poor translation, words resounded with patriotic pathos. I explained the true greatness of Vasil Levski, "the Apostle," who indeed had tried to arm people and prepare for a real fight, I stressed his moral purity and his vision of pure and sacred republic, in which Bulgarians and Turks, Christians and Muslims would live in peace . . . Christian understood some things, didn't understand others or he'd interrupt me with quite rational arguments. He reminded me about the objective political and socio-economic reality in the Ottoman Empire. He'd read historical factual books including Vera Mutafchieva in German. I retorted that he understood nothing, I stuck to the heroic, the tragic, the grandeur,

world press at the time, brought up by journalists and writers (MacGahan, Schuyler, Hugo, Turgenev) and led to the Turkish-Russian War of 1877–1878, which in turn ended with the reestablishment of Bulgaria as a state.

199 Properly, as it should be. (French)

200 A contemporary account, novelized documentary of more than 700 pages.

the elevation. I did not deny that this was desperate madness, "the drunkenness of a whole nation," as the poet put it, but without it we wouldn't have been Bulgarians. Christian remarked that only few of the "hotheads" had been drunk. I countered with a terrible translation of Botev.[201]

I talked and talked . . . and gradually realized that I'd switched to national "autopilot," that everything I was saying I'd learned at school, starting in kindergarten, from history and literature lessons, from Bulgarian books and films. I was reproducing an axiomatic national mythology, which admits to no rational analysis. This narrative was fundamental to my identity and consciousness as a Bulgarian and my sense of belonging to the Bulgarian "martyr nation." Christian was deconstructing my national mythology with logic and rational arguments. The only way for him to understand was to convey to him the heroic, the tragic, the great and the elevating in the language of his national mythology, with its own, how to put it, historical material, which would provoke similar national-archetypical emotions in him. Very tricky as regards German history. Besides, Germans look ahead, not back at the past which only harbors guilt, they are proud of their present day and are ashamed of their history, whereas for Bulgarians, it's the opposite. Bulgarians take pride in their history, including their role in a sacrificial martyr nation, they're ashamed of their present and fearful for the future. Back by myself, I returned to Christian's rational and downright fundamental questions and tried to separate mythology from history, the sober and considered from the drunken and crazed, I played hide and seek with myself and my national identity, with some cosmopolitism and Europeanism, I was haunted by the feeling of treachery—toward my people and homeland.

Shared experience of misery, suffering and defeat unites people, as fear of a common threat does. A national narrative based on victimization and martyrdom creates a stronger sense of belonging because it imputes some feeling of duty in future generations, who should patriotically mobilize to preserve "own" values such as national virtues and belonging, religion, honor, freedom and independence, and even revenge for their violation. In this narrative, the world is divided into "we" and "own, native" against "an enemy" and anything "foreign, alien."[202] Not the dry facts and argumentation, but the *narrative* about the April Uprising shapes our national mythology. This narrative combines a heroic and a martyr lines. Batak and a few other villages of slaughter rise as national Golgothas, as sacred altars of Bulgarian spirit. However, outside mythology, one may indeed see them as irresponsibly provoked and meaningless atrocities. Unimaginable atrocities—on this question there can be no two opinions, as

201 Hristo Botev (1848-1876) the Bulgarian national poet, like Adam Mickiewicz for the Polish, or Dionysios Solomos for the Greek. National poets wrote mainly about the freedom of their peoples.

202 By the way, a similar mechanism is at work in Russia today, steered by propaganda.

about all the atrocities and violence perpetrated throughout the so-called "Ottoman Presence." But were these thousands of men, women and children heroes and martyrs indeed? Did they conscientiously sacrifice themselves for national freedom and political independence, or did someone sacrifice them? And why does the sacrificial-martyr complex dominate the national narrative?

Over recent years, the patriotic claims to another sacred altar have been stirred up—Northern Macedonia. And in this narrative line, a rather intimate melancholy predominates for something "owned," something Bulgarian, but something ravished and lost forever.

All this is to say that Bulgarians, as a nation, have a deeply embedded melancholy of victims, of losers, of people whose fate is not in their own hands. A great deal of national literature grapples with the glorious, heroic or martyr past or with folklore, customs, religion and all kinds of mysticism, the village idyll and patriarchal order, with iconic Bulgarian virtues along with the patriotic baggage, and defense of all this. With few exceptions, the individual, the existential human being with its "fundamental problematics" and melancholy was missing in our literature until the end of the twentieth century.[203] More than a century, Bulgarian literature was busy making sure that the nation rather than the individual will live on.

When I was seventeen, I read—in a Bulgarian translation—Paul Eluard's *Bonjour, Tristesse*. The Word, even in translation, blew my mind away. From that time I have been signing off in Bulgarian as "Тъга" (sorrow, sadness, melancholy, *tristesse*). It is completed with a deliberate flourish; you have to look at it closely to read it. About fifteen years ago, I added *Bardarska* to my signature, in the Latin script, because I sign off a lot more in the Latin world, than in my Cyrillic homeland. I put a slash between the *tristesse* and my official surname—as if to keep separate two worlds, two consciousnesses, two personalities—the pragmatic, administrative, official one, and the intimate, artistic, and melancholic one. The truth is I also put the slash so it wouldn't sound so melodramatic and funny. And so—Тъга/Bardarska it is.

My *tristesse* has nothing to do with the national victim-mourning unhappiness, though. Actually, the reply which I wrote back then when I was seventeen is a more teen-agedly melodramatic and imitative poem, and yet it hints at the source of my *tristesse* and its early overtones. I said bonjour to Solitude. Today, after more than thir-

203 Actually, judging by literary prizes and sales, classic refrains still occupy a really significant place in national literary production.

ty-five years, I find it significant that, even back then, postmodern intertextuality and a dialogic approach welled up from the Castalian spring of my consciousness

One of the best and most translated novels of contemporary Bulgarian literature is entitled *The Physics of Sorrow.* The author, Georgi Gospodinov, claims to be the saddest person on Earth. I challenge his "throne" not only in terms of extent of melancholy but also because in my essays on the subject I add female, and in principle gender "morphology" to the physics and a bit of proper physics, too. Gospodinov often discusses the meaning and translatability of the word тъга—*sadness, sorrow, and melancholy* are offered in the standard translation dictionary. He thinks that our Bulgarian, or Slavic, sorrow, or sadness, or melancholy, is impossible to translate and render with all its connotations. While there are indeed some specific nuances in the Eluard's and Sagan's French *tristesse*, the German-Nordic *melancholias* of Dürer and Lars von Trier, the Russian birch печаль, горе or тоска and the luminous тъга of Gospodinov and Valeri Petrov,[204] I believe that all people, every human being, is sad essentially in the same way and for the same reasons.

Which brings me back to question—why do I write? Writing, and making art in general, is one of the ways to deal with that existential melancholy, to live with it, to make sense and even appreciate life and not to capitulate to the pointlessness of our human condition and one's own self. To me, writing is an existential act, before being an aesthetic one. And I continue to argue—in my mind and for real, with the Polish publisher: writing is not a job, but a pressing human need that cannot be sated in any other way. The fundamental purpose of resulting texts is not their publication but the bequest of traces of our thoughts and consciousness, of our *essays* as human beings during our short stroll beneath the stars.

Sure, writing fights death and oblivion, too. It's no accident that the epitaph is the first literary genre. In some sense, all writing is an epitaph—an *attempt* to convey some meaning to, most often, a meaningless existence. "Original" personal messages and judgments from our children, carved into stone, or in our geographical area, kind words, chosen from a modest catalogue for necrologies, these *attempts,* or *essays*, at the sense of life are reduced to repetitive banalities. The kind that were most often the "prototypes" when alive. The only more specific characteristic of these platitudes is that they are created postmortem. It would be somewhat inhumane or inappropriate for the close friend or relative to see the banalities with which we'll send them off into oblivion. Besides, you can say something not that nice about someone while they are alive. Once dead, it's praise or nothing.

204 Virtuosi Bulgarian poet and translator of all Shakespeare's plays and sonnets in Bulgarian (1920–2014).

Literary epitaph, or literature as epitaph, is different. The aesthetic abracadabra and literary devices *recreate* and typify the object to such an extent that the real person is deleted, forgotten, s/he will remain, at best, a curiosity in literary annals. Literature is epitaph of the writer, not of the "subject of the aesthetic recreation." It is quite telling that many writers, and writers most of all, have written their own epitaphs prior to their deaths.

The literary text is a market product as well—something that has to please the audience, to sell, possibly to get fame and nourish vanity. The founder of the genre didn't create epitaphs for free and only for the thrill of it. I was thinking of Simonides on a sparkling but brisk May day in San Francisco, observing a street poetess. The woman was sitting under a tree on a low stool, wrapped up in a woolen poncho, and clattered away on an antique typewriter, which took up almost the entire low table in front of her. A gust of wind flipped through the folder left on the pavement—clearly samples. The hand-scrawled notice explained—in metric step and rhymes—that the price and unit of measurement for the valuation of the "service"—poem, stanza, couplet, or whole shebang—a short or longer poem, sonnet and . . . epitaph—would be left to the judgment and satisfaction of the dear customers. A good reminder, that writing can be just a job, an occupation, and literature—a market product and a service for aesthetic uplift.

A Bulgarian literary scholar has stated, I cite from memory, that if a given text is not conceived and laid in the bosom of a national literature and culture, it risks a fundamental nihility, despite its individual qualities. The ideological power of the individual author is insufficient for his ideas to "*be*"; what is not created in the stream of one culture and canon, does not exist, because an intellectual archeology of pure individual ideas does not exist. If my memory serves, these were observations related to Bulgarian writers, writing in a foreign language. So, without a cultural and literary reference, identification, belonging and acknowledgment, you remain a cultural and literary orphan, a global tramp. A frightening and plausible thesis.

In the novel, *Doomed Souls*, by Dimitar Dimov, the events unfold in Spain, during the civil war, and the main personages are Spanish, British, and French. We consider this novel a masterpiece of *Bulgarian* literature, I guess, because it was written in Bulgarian, by a Bulgarian writer. But what if Dimitar Dimov had written it in Spanish (which he mastered)? Or, just imagine, what if a British, French, or Spanish writer had written this novel? I have another idea—how would you classify a novel in which each character talks in their original language, as in Dimov's story? Would it be possible to have a book, which would be half in Bulgarian, a quarter in French, a quarter in English, and even some bits in German? Does the fact that I *essay* to think and write in Bulgarian, make this book a part of Bulgarian literature? What is the defining feature for identifying a text as from one or another culture or literature—the language, the upbringing or nationality of the author, their biography, the content, the story, the characters, their time, the literary tradition in which the text arises or which it follows? All and all, is there still any point in this national-linguistic classification of literature and positioning the author in the ranks of a particular national canon?

To me, the classic interpretive discourse of Bulgarian literary canon, based on the opposition of native vs foreign, seems hopelessly outdated. Today, I no longer know what in my texts is "mine" and native, shaped by Bulgarian education, culture and language, and what is "foreign," but not alien anymore, since I have assimilated and interiorized it. And the reason for this is not the emigration or some "rebirth" of mine into another culture and its language. The human condition I write about is fundamentally the same in every language and literature.

Yet, when you write in an exotic language and come from a small country with a little known culture, but are aware that you're not just writing for your national audience, an insidious self-censorship kicks in. It cuts content and language down to size, avoiding the stream of cultural (sub)consciousness, meaningful details, connotative words, expressive syntax, hidden or explicit references, sifting out sensibility and mentality. Consciously or not, you think of the translatability of what you write, the translation is contained implicitly in the text. In its most extreme manifestations, this dominating and castrating self-censor trims the texts to stereotype, salable, predictable, and translatable stories and language. Kristin Dimitrova[205] has written about this somewhere (I hope I quote her accurately). "The feeling of belonging to a small language leads you gradually to an unpleasant economy of details." Authenticity and aesthetics definitely suffer. Yet good literature should be authentic and true and these qualities rest on the historically, nationally, culturally, linguistically, and educationally "conditioned and seasoned" *experience* of the author. To paraphrase a maxim, the good writer thinks globally and writes locally. But here it is where small

205 Contemporary Bulgarian writer.

cultures and languages do suffer prejudice, and have to censor their works, and have many more bridges to cross to get to the global reader. Preserving local authenticity and candor costs an authentic writer from a local culture a great deal more.

I think about the generation of Bulgarian writers—emigrants who wrote directly in a foreign language and were even first published in a foreign language and after that translated into Bulgarian, and my own choice to write this book in Bulgarian. When the choice of a foreign language does follow from the contents and the ideology of a text and has no aesthetic point, it remains a merely pragmatic strategy for success and acclaim abroad. I'd really like to attribute a more noble and idealistic purpose of this choice. Let's assume for example that these authors write in an authentic way about Bulgaria, Bulgarian history and culture, about their own Bulgarian childhood, teenage years, youth, about the existential, about the culturally specific, about family, communism, etc., not in Bulgarian, but directly into a foreign language, only in order to ease and speed the presentation of Bulgarian literature and culture abroad (taking into account, let's say, the lack of state policy and subsidies for translation, and of translators from Bulgarian). Or, maybe, it's that the foreign language, depicting the author's emigrant fate, becomes an instrument for rethinking what is own, native and what is foreign and alien. Or it's also possible that by using the foreign language these authors aspire to be accepted and integrated into the respective foreign culture as its own writers, with their "exotic" origin and identity. And finally, they might themselves have changed, the Bulgarian language might have gone rusty and no longer houses their consciousness, nor expresses what they have become, they might feel more comfortable in the foreign language—a new homeland. But I ask myself must a literary author have a target audience at all? I don't know. I have not found any of my benevolent arguments convincing enough; I still feel something fundamentally oxymoronic, and quite bluntly pragmatic in Bulgarian emigrant literature, written in a foreign language.[206]

---

206 Because the Bulgarian state—at least up till 2022—has no money to promote Bulgarian writers (through sponsoring translation for example), because the idea to nurture a generation of translators from Bulgarian in foreign universities is wonderful and practically unattainable, and there has been no literary agency to represent Bulgarian writers (and a handful of translators have functioned as literary agents, at their own risk and expenditure, following their own taste, with the result that only few authors get translated and published abroad), so that bearing all this in mind, I think that the most farsighted investment would be a translation database into which would figure all original Bulgarian works, translated into foreign languages, along with their translations. This translation memory would encourage new translations. Such a project however would be interesting beyond its utility. In a quite literal way, we will hear the voices of those who were before us, in foreign languages. With this database and translation memory the idea of conception and embedding into the national canon will take on new dimensions. Not to mention what surprises AI may serve us and what intertextual dialogues might develop . . . Because there's no copyright for ideas, I spit out my idea for (at least) a short story.

Yet, there is another, and to me, even more disturbing, feature of Bulgarian emigrant literature, besides language; it is its questionable, to my taste, authenticity. In spite of writing about Bulgaria and their personal, familial, or nationally marked Bulgarian biographies, these books often sound like guides meant for foreigners. I have the feeling that the authors' task is to advertise and sell their identities, and authenticity, communism, and various themes of interest to their foreign readers, like borders, religious tolerance, migration, folklore exotica, nature, herbs, etc. Everything is politically correct, packaged to western standards, including creative writing courses, labeled, festooned with local color, sprinkled with a little savory and drops of rose oil. These authors don't just write in a foreign language for greater convenience, they recount what the foreigner wants to hear and can understand. Bulgaria and Bulgarians appear simple, pathetic and spectacular, or mystical and exotic, or paradoxical and complicated in an understandable way. With a few important exceptions, it's with exactly this type of project-writing texts that contemporary Bulgarian literature got known and received some praise abroad. Somewhere again Kristin Dimitrova, if I remember right, notes angrily that foreigners expect Bulgarian writer to come to the stage in folk costume, to talk about folklore, about the gunpowder barrel of the Balkans, the Thracians, communism, corruption, dressed up with magic realism or politically correct fury. Everything else, achieved with individual skills and energy, describing the individual's experience, is doomed to be met with incomprehension. Some countries produce literature and others anthropology and politically correct history.[207] A foreign audience's interest toward such content is an expression of fatigue, guilt, and political correctness. When your own cultural model is exhausted you entertain yourself with magic lantern. Your historical guilt dictates an over benevolent interest and enthusiasm to get to know and accept your new European brothers and sisters. Then, it is much better if the actual participants assume the exposure and condemnation of a past, in "authentic" testimony, instead of having them imposed and dictated from outside. Ownership and agency.

Along this line of thought and remembering the biblical axiom that no one is a prophet in their own country, I'm put in mind of what I call "the Pencho Slaveikov[208] syndrome." This is the only Bulgarian writer so far to have been nominated for a Nobel prize, and that only for his epic poem "A Bloody Song." The paradox is his texts do not shine with the "divine sparks" of great poetry, language and insights, but rather reproduce, with erudition and some skill, all the modern European philosophical theories of the time, animated into an exotically national *mise-en-scène*, fable and personages.

207 I've mixed Kristin Dimitrova's observations with my own.

208 Pencho Slaveikov (1866–1912), Bulgarian poet, essayist, and literary critic, who opposed traditional Bulgarian literature as backward and promoted modernity.

"A Bloody Song" paradoxically sounds like a translation because the wonder of poetry is missing. Pencho's foreign promoters, even those who understood Bulgarian, decided that the poetry must have been inevitably "lost in translation," but even without it, the purely intellectual content, what's more—dressed up in authentic national costume, was sufficient for the Nobel.

It's not the savory, the tomatoes,[209] the wine, the rakia,[210] the liutenitza,[211] the nature, the Communism, the Bulgarian Muslims, the firewalkers, the traditional crafts, the patriarchal virtues, the village idyll, the tragic and heroic episodes of history, the melodramatic stories about the poverty and misery, the corruption and gangsterism of the transition, or other politically correct subjects, which bring out the Bulgarian in literature. In the predictable clichés and stereotypes, even in the folkloric magic realism, there is nothing metaphysical or transcendental; in the seemingly exotic personages there's nothing of authentic individuality or shared humanity. The Bulgarian must be portrayed and elevated as a human being, not as national, historical, social, or anthropological personage. Bulgarian is an exotic language, but the Bulgarian is an existential human.

In the past, religion and ethics, family, clan and nation, social ideals, ideologies and their projects for the future or history and the allegiances it dictated were providing some kind of universal survival kit for the individual, some frames and grand narratives, in which the individual human beings laid their individual time, purpose, sense and aspirations. The grand narratives of community canceled death and brought order to chaos. The grand narratives have collapsed. Traditional communities, from family to nation, and their mythologies, are being substituted by interest groups and their interests, on a national and global level. Life, here and now, has tremendously improved, while the future has grown increasingly gloomy. However, neither liberal democracy and its pragmatic morality, nor science have offered something at the existential, transcendent "stand." The human being grows out of the transcendence of religion, as a child grows out of the magic of Christmas and magical tales, loosens his hand away from community—whether religious, tribal, national, historical, social, political—to stand up alone and inconsolable before the infinity and eternity of the starry sky and their own nothingness.

209 Bulgarian tomatoes do indeed taste amazing.

210 The national spirit, usually made of grapes, but different versions can be produced of other fruit.

211 A classical Bulgarian preserve, usually made of tomatoes and peppers.

Literature should have stepped in to fill the gaping transcendental abyss and to comfort the modern human. But it turns out that the same lonely and sad creature wants to read about more joyful and easy, or "topical," subjects, found in the external world of here and now, and not so much about the internal world or that "beyond" his own time horizon. Generous supply meets the demand, because literature, like every art, is a market product. The contemporary novel, in particular bestsellers, appears to me as a curious, politically correct or provocatively scandalous, travelogue, something like a road-novel with elements of *bildungsroman.*

The times are, actually, epic, and on a global level. It is not a national epic but an epic of humankind. But contemporary literature rarely produces epic narratives. Some key premises for an epic are missing, or at least for an epic in the classical sense. There is no common societal ideal and objective for humanity to unite around and to aspire to. Survival of the planet and mankind is an obvious, noble candidate, but there is no agreement and solidarity as to how and with what resources it should be achieved. There again, what ideal is there in simple survival? Apart from this, the majority aren't interested in the future beyond their own life expectancy. Barring extremities, there is no clear cut ethical order, or simply said, what and who is good or bad? We all have rights, we're all guilty for one thing or another, we are all victims of one thing or another. There are no universally acknowledged heroes. The lack of the unchallengeable heroic gives birth to Hollywood's supermen, who are forever saving humanity from imagined evil and threat. Adults no longer subscribe to historic and existential utopias and so watch ever more dumbing stories. Children's games and books describe super complex castles in the sky of thrones, vampires and magic colleges. All together, young people and adults, are retreating from reality and sinking deeper and deeper into virtual worlds.

How can anyone create an epic today when they know that there are no gods above to manage fate and guarantee proportionality and order, that the very epic cast of characters and poet themselves are the fruit of chaos and the embodiment of the one chance in a billion to I-don't-know which degree, that what's most lifelike about the characters, and of the author, too, is a string of coincidences lacking any meaning and eventually full with pleasant and unpleasant things. How can one achieve an epic detachment and historic distancing when the world is changing ever faster?

Everyone has a right to their own narrative, but we have no common narrative, either about the past, or about the future. Happiness is not to be found in any kind of shared ideal, social order, future heaven or resurrection; it is here and now—in money, in *having*, in security, it's material, stereotypical, and competitive. In the future there is only death—our own death and that of our children and grandchildren, of humanity, of the planet, of our stars. No one thinks and talks about the apocalypse. Even art does it ever more seldom.

Entertainment apart, ordinary people, i.e., ninety-nine percent of the human reeds, search in literature for what is missing in their seemingly ordinary life and personalities—the only love of their lives, sexual fantasies made real, limitless freedom, untold wealth, dramatic dilemmas and solutions, heroic poses, honorable actions, intellectual depth (this more rarely), tragedy, bold politically incorrect views, primordial contradictions in humans, pinning them between the animal and divine, etc., etc. The ordinary person reads not to learn about himself or to become a better person (which is a frequent side effect, but not the basic motive for reading or the main task of literature), but to escape from their ordinary life and ordinary personality, to submerge themselves in the fictitious and to see themselves and their lives as more dramatic, more meaningful, and more beautiful.

And literature, like the golden fish, generously fulfills every reader's desire. In the name of their "elevation," the ordinary individual is raped aesthetically with exotic or scandalous, or melodramatic or speculatively intellectual subjects, which are improbable and unconvincing. Behind this type of literature transpires the fear—of both the writer and the prototype—that good literature cannot come from the life and consciousness of the ordinary folk, because they are insufficiently dramatic and interesting. At the end of the day, it may well be that the classical disclaimer of fiction[212] should be taken at face value:

This is a work of fiction. Names, characters, places and incidents either are products of the author's imagination or are used fictitiously. Any resemblance to actual events, places or persons, living or dead, is entirely coincidental.

Literature, created on the basis of the classical conventions of fiction now bores me. I read it like it's historical, even a documentary. It tells me nothing more than about the good life with its pleasant moments when we ask the ever moving spheres of heaven to stand still and time to cease,[213] and with all its "trials and tribulations."

According to the classical definition, the novel narrative is an alternative to the historical, because it's concerned with ordinary people and their ordinary lives and does

212 Whose aim is to protect the prototype as a real person with a right to personal life.
213 Goethe, *Faust*.

not register only victories, defeats, and other historic events, but the *experience* of the individual. All this sounds very true, only that the experience of the individual is told by somebody else—the writer, and the narrative usually tells us much more about the experience and the spirit of the writer than about his object. The creator leaves a trace, not his/her prototypes. Art immortalizes only chosen subjects (usually the artist himself) and very rarely concrete objects. They say that the poet rescues the dead from oblivion. The poet first and foremost rescues himself. From this perspective, once again reading the disclaimer above would strike us with its literal meaning. Apart from some deep ontological contradiction between the claim for realism and the purpose of mimesis (which is to *recreate* the reality in *aesthetic* reality, the latter being fictional by definition), it appears that even the most robust realism and the rawest authenticity still lead to fictionality and typification, thus deleting, in its own way, the real concrete person.

But the real concrete person has received new opportunities. History and historical memory are selective and come with conditions. Family memory is short and scarce. Nationality and national mythology grew irrelevant with the dying out of national identity and all kinds of patriotisms. They are difficult to translate, too. Human memory remains the only accessible and democratic discourse for salvation. Today it is generously supported by technology and social media, in unlimited volumes and genres, replacing the grudging margins of one time family bibles. Everyone can write, leave written and virtual traces of themselves, their experiences, memories, desires, fears, belongings, and cancellations, loves and hatreds. In just one second, the personal narrative reaches the global audience and is archived to live on into eternity. There is no higher authority or judgment—moral, aesthetic, philosophic, national, scientific, even political, as has been shown in the last few years, to sift the stream, to pin values, to correct, censor or sanction, to shape standards or cast light as a guiding star. The good and the evil, the beautiful and the ugly, the comic and the tragic are no longer imposed by the writer's pulpit or bestowed by the philosopher's scepter, but defined and propagated by the individual. Busy in documenting this "wonderful, wonderful life," personal stories seldom contain such elements anyway.

The contemporary, extremely democratic, discourse bestows limitless freedom. Humanity is creating a new kind of contemporary epic—atomized down to every individual person, extremely specific and at the same time collective. This epic lacks aesthetic intentions and aspirations, although it is accompanied by many others.

Just a few genres in these mass *essays* attract my interest. Fanfiction is one, even more as I claim to be a pioneer in the genre. Ordinary people can write their own "original" chronicles and produce their own essays in diaries, letters and all kinds of private writing. On a site called "My Posterity" you can leave a spoken or written announcement, story, testimonial, you can sing a song, input whatever message, in whatever genre and medium, particularly about yourself, your time, everyday life, experience, the wisdom you have acquired, your memories. This is the message that you want to pass on to future generations and the way you wish to be remembered. I read about an initiative where young people visit the elderly, in order to listen and even write down their stories. I was also deeply impressed by the "Human Library" project—where instead of taking out a book, you take out a living person to listen and even write down his personal history. The aim of this project, at least up till now, is only to fight prejudices—the people to be borrowed (homosexuals, trans people, unemployed, migrants, minority groups, etc.) are usually the subjects of prejudice. The aim of the project is not to leave a trace of the ordinary folk.

The literary canon, as shaped by critics and scholars, has traditionally disqualified writing about oneself as circumscribed vanity and a lack of experience, talent and literary craft. I had just pumped up my self-belief in my right to write bold essays, even if they remain only personal and private, unsuccessful from an objective literary standpoint, not resulting in a published book, when my courage faltered after reading an article. The author—a literary scholar—referred to the aesthetic superiority of the epic, and with an intellectual sneer, noted that contemporary Bulgarian writers do not master literary craft, don't dig deep to research and create historical personages, that "*they avoid the effort which would distance themselves from the pleasure of recreating their own, presumably, exceptional personalities and experiences.*" According to the scholar, the texts, produced by this self-centrism, are not necessarily meaningful for the readers.

Well . . . I would agree that many writers don't just start out from themselves, but end up there, and goodness knows, this self is not so exceptional and meaningful for others, indeed. Yet, as already mentioned, the classical epic is quite problematic today. Today, the only possible epic is one of distance or detachment that lies in the awareness of the chaos and randomness, of infinity, of the relativity of human measures, reality, and viewpoint as just one of many possible worlds, in the relativization of some basic motifs, which lie at the foundation of all of literature. For me, the distancing of oneself, the observation of self as a human being and making one's own personality and experience the subject of the literary text is the new epic mode. Apart from this, all writers, of every kind, even the most epically minded, start out from themselves, not least because the writer is the one to observe and select the subject of their narrative and because everything, even the most intimate experience of those epically externalized personages, passes through the mind of the author.

What is particularly interesting to me in this debate is the self-portrait, the autofiction, the so called confessional prose, where the artist depicts and recreates himself as a "generic" human being, without sparing both the genuine "realism" and "authenticity" of his everyday life, the banal and mediocre, while, at the same time, emphasizing overly human sorrows and nightmares, dilemmas and crucifixions, elevations and flights of the spirit.

This more unusual measure defining aesthetics, and epics in particular, emerged during the Renaissance, when the human being was reborn not only in the shape of a heroic, wise, amorous, and beautiful demi-god, but also as an old, sick, petty, doubtful, contradictory little person, called Michel, who *essayed* to *write* about the whole pallet of the significant and insignificant, joyful and sorrowful, making up not only his life but that of humanity in general. I am referring of course to Michel de Montaigne and his "essays," which subsequently were recognized as a genre. This new genre is by definition an attempt at literature, occupying the borders of literature and the aesthetic, and not a self-assured literary work, created in the stream of tradition and canons. Paradoxically, precisely the lack of literary ambition, self-confidence and a pre-defined aesthetic purpose gave freedom to the author. The attempt to write about his own *experience* as experience of the human being in general, turned the literary canon upside down. "Reader, I myself am the subject of my book," Montaigne wrote.[214]

For each new edition, Montaigne edited his essays extensively and significantly, adding new observations, which sometimes completely contradicted the original. This was a continuous, living text as the subject and his themes were evolving, living, aging, approaching death, as world itself was changing, and bringing new subjects, or reshaping, confirming or adding nuances that reinforce or contradict author's thoughts. [215]

214 The original Bulgarian title of this book—Опитът (Opitat)—has three meanings: a) the try/trial/attempt; b) the experience, and c) the experiment. In French, the verb "to try" and the noun "a try/trial/attempt," respectively, *essayer* and *un essai*—gave the name of the new genre: essai. This genre name was taken over in English (an essay) and in Bulgarian (*ece,* pronounced esé). However, Bulgarian translation of Montaigne's *Essais* is not the genre one (*ece,* pronounced esé), but the original word for "trying, trials" (*opit*) Luckily, English has preserved as well the verb "essayer" in the sense of trying. So, the English title of the book covers one of the three meanings implied in the original Bulgarian title (experience and experiment are missing); however English, too, supports the strong genre connotation.

215 I feel close to this writer, from five centuries ago, not only at conceptual and genre level, but also because we were born on the same date. It also fascinates me that Montaigne was quite wealthy and worked as

The autobiography of Elias Canetti is another milestone in the modern epic, one of the most important works of autofiction and simultaneously a mighty epic canvass of the twentieth century.

The Ottoman Empire, the Bulgarian principality, Ruschuk,[216] Manchester, London, Zurich, Lausanne, Vienna, Berlin, Frankfurt . . . a family history with its episodes of comedy and tragedy, and between them the whole human spectrum, world wars, philosophical and aesthetic schools . . . the life of Canetti is a cartography and biography of twentieth century Europe.

Canetti's biography and works add complexity to the concepts of home, homeland, exile, belonging, native, foreign and the return. Canetti is an exile from birth, by definition, a perpetual, *wandering* exile. But exile assumes a home, a homeland, a center from which you are banished. This is lacking in his biography, or more precisely there are several homelands. "Where are you from?" would be a really difficult question for the writer, who, actually replied in a telling manner. Canetti received the Nobel Prize as a British citizen. But he wrote in German. He is recognized as an Austrian, Jewish, even Bulgarian German-speaking writer. At the award ceremony in Stockholm, he put up a card in front of him on which Ruschuk was indicated as his place of origin and represented country.

His *essay*, too, began in a town on the Danube, with its theatre, *chitalishte*, port, with Viennese furniture and fashion, with the intelligentsia and merchants, with those little, commoners, poignant and sad, funny and amusing in their everyday, but big, romantic, and tragic with their surge for beauty, virtue, and love.

Canetti never returned to Rousse. He knew that his Ruschuk no longer existed, he knew about the unique singularity of chronos, topos, and self. Returning was impossible because the parameters of quantum configuration—time, place and consciousness, and their "entanglement" would never be the same. A never-ever-again land . . .

In Canetti's world, childhood is not simply the age of innocence, it is a state of Being, a chronotopos, shaping human condition. In Ruschuk, the child lives through essential elements of human *experience*, the meanings of what will happen to him later. The most popular quote from Canetti's autobiography (at least in Bulgarian) is precisely the sentence: "Everything I experienced later had already happened in Ruschuk." Childhood is also a refuge from the pragmatic, economic world of adults, driven by power and possession. The child in Canetti's world does not want to grow up and become an accomplice to the world of adults. In his other

something that today would be considered as civil service. Michel's birthday and the fact that Einstein is also a Pisces, made me read up on the signs of the zodiac, which after all have something to do with the stars, and what I find to be a really entertaining genre. Star profiling.

216 The Turkish name of the Bulgarian town of Rousse. Canetti's birthplace.

works the writer problematizes the values of capitalist society—continual economic growth, overproduction and consumption, at the cost of intellect, individuality, knowledge, creativity.

Apart from the unity of chronos, topos, and self, on the metatextual level the author has integrated topos and logos. Canetti internalized topoi through language. He inhabited many places, not simply physically, but intellectually and spiritually through the languages he mastered. German was his prime language but he is not a German author. The choice of German was deliberate, this was not his native language, nor was it exactly his mother tongue, if we keep to traditional definitions. German was the language of the European intellectual elite from the first half of the twentieth century. Then the war came. Language and culture can become means of spiritual survival—of the subject, but also the "fallen" nation, the bearer of the language.[217] From a seemingly innocent incident, Canetti creates a huge metaphor that provides the title of the most important volume of his autobiographical trilogy. Language has to be saved and preserved, in order to narrate, bear witness and rescue from the oblivion of death.

Canetti opposes death. For the writer, the reason for evil in human beings is their mortality. He hates death and yearns for a long life (300 years to be precise) but not to enjoy "the good life" (as per Kierkegaard) in eternal youth, but to learn everything which humanity has discovered and created, and to live through and sense all human experience. For Canetti, human mind and consciousness rebut death, because they are more real than the body and biology. In the consciousness and memory of the human being, nothing is lost and nothing dies. The writer is the one to make it immortal in his writing. The only possible immortality—of the personages and the author—is in the logos.

Canetti is a doctor in chemistry. Although he never practiced his specialty, the very choice of studies and the years devoted to science is a powerful expression of the same yearning to learn everything that humanity has discovered, learned, thought up, created. His is interested not so much in pragmatic, applied science, but in science as an explanation of the world and humanity. This holistic approach to human experience is reflected in the multiplicity and sheer variety of the sources of knowledge and ideas, the author uses.

Canetti does not like contemporary art—he finds it flat and too easy. He is a modern romantic, but not a postmodern writer either. With him, there is no irony, no

217 I think that intelligent Russians and all lovers of Russian literature are in a similar situation today, in the context of Putin's Russia.

intertextuality, no literary games. That's why Montaigne irritates him—with his secondary aesthetic layer, or with his many references and quotations.

With Canetti there is a discreet, rather intuitive anti-mimetic. He says that "true writers encounter their characters only after they've created them." The novel *Auto-da-Fé* is usually interpreted alongside Kafka and Borges. I would add Wilde's *The Picture of Dorian Gray*. Canetti himself was devastated by the fire that consumed Professor Kien's 25,000 books and declares "What happens in that kind of book is not just a game, it is reality."

Canetti has a special affinity to the fragment in its greatest variety of forms. He keeps notes of such fragments to the end of his life and publishes several volumes. Actually, some critics reckon this part of his oeuvres as his most significant contribution to the literary process of the twentieth century. The author himself notes that there is something endless in writing.

In Canetti's *Autobiography*, the personal and genuinely autobiographical is knitted together with the detached observation and testimony of the epoch. Autobiography also furthers the *bildungsroman* tradition. The narrative moves along the borders between the autobiographical and fiction, including auto fiction; in the second and third volumes, fiction and literary narrative gradually take over the autobiographical. The intimate, personal autobiography is interpreted as universally human. The story and experience of the individual human are narrated (thus, fictionalized, with all means of the literary craft) as universal human experience.[218]

The modern epic has its modern Homer. Knausgaard's *My Struggle* (carried on in another exotic language) for making sense of and bringing some consolation to the world and oneself, documents pedantically and mostly authentically the life and mind of the unremarkable, ordinary person, of that reed. A titanic *essay*, indeed, including the sheer volume. The global success of Knausgaard proves that hunkering down inside oneself is a lot more than an insular self-infatuation. If we put aside the voyeurism, inherent to human nature, the author's success speaks to a fundamental deficit in contemporary literary, and then every other kind of, *content*.

And this *essay*, too, is staged on the shifting sandy borders of the literary. Knausgaard avoids spotlights, public forays, interviews, in a word, he doesn't behave like a star-writer, published in dozens of languages, with millions of sales. And I ask myself again if this type of *essay*, which essentially is an existential act, has to lead, at any cost,

---

218 For vanity, of course, but with more noble conceptual reasoning, too, I'd mention that the first edition of this book was nominated for the literary prize named after the cosmopolitan Elias Canetti. Yet, one more reason for my extended homage to this writer.

to an aesthetic result, furthermore, to sharing this, presumably, aesthetic result with millions of strangers against money and glory, i.e., to its publication. Does the existential *essay* degenerate with its transformation into a market product? Knausgaard's argument with his real-life nearest and dearest return us again to the moving borders of literature, aesthetics, fiction, fictitious, authenticity, truthfulness, and sincerity.

What becomes clear, at a fundamentally conceptual level, is that autofiction is quite different from ordinary autobiography or diary. The writer shapes a story, despite the utmost realism, or rather precisely through it. Through his personal, intimate *experience* the writer narrates about humanity overall. And because this is a narrative, the writer invents, combines, forgets and ignores, sharpens or softens, mystifies. And this is not betrayal of truth and undermining authenticity, provided that the final result is a truthful and convincing portrait of the human being and a captivating story of the human condition.

The victors and the vanquished and their writers wrote the great history and the national mythologies. Literary theory dictates that epic novel sets the little man in the great history, and vice versa, tells the great history via the life of the little man. But no longer is there a monumental historical narrative, in which typecast personages would figure. The monument has collapsed. The narrative of the community—familial, national, religious, generational, social class, political has collapsed. From the ruins emerges the concrete, real, ordinary, authentic, little human. No matter at which side of the victory or in what corner of history this human finds themselves, their human's personal story is an intimate story of someone's past and time.

The collective and the individual stories are not just parallel and competing. Just as on a biological level, before birth, ontogenesis recapitulates all stages of phylogeny, on a spiritual level, the *experience* of the individual human recapitulates the existential experience of humanity in general. The experience of the individual gives birth to what defines us as humans—consciousness with its horizons, death and time and with its home—language, aesthetic drive, and love. Thus, the intimate and autobiographical don't just entangle with and resonate in the (hi)story of humanity, but instantiate it, or materialize it, as narrative. This is a new type of epic and monumentality which replace the monument of collective epos.

Someone's intimate experience, in its first dimension as worldly experience, is immanently autobiographical. But the *story* about this experience as human, existential experience, can diverge a lot from biographical factology. Because the intimately personal is universally human. This is a story of an individual person, but also of humanity all together. The *experience* of the individual reconstructs humanity in general. And it's precisely this, apart of course from all the aesthetic means, that turns an autobiography into a book and a self-portrait into a work of art.

I prefer another declaration of fictionality, which is fitting better the new epic:

"*In preparing this memoir, I have stuck to facts except when facts refused to conform with memory, narrative purpose, or the truth as I prefer to understand it.*"[219]

This is a new kind of epic, an existential epic, a modern epic which turns the optics of the classical one—from the individual to the human and humanity. And this is the in-depth, the fundamental theme, and plot line, which underpins these books and bundles all straits of the narrative into an epos. The new epic is more a story of the human being, not so much of human society.

By definition, immanently and conceptually, the new epic is fragmentary, aesthetically not fully accomplished, imperfect, its genre is not clear cut, the text is wandering on the borderlines of literature, it is an open, continuous text. As in a happening, the story takes place (for real or in candid mystification) right in front of the eyes of the readers. The narrator writes as he lives. Writing itself is an existential act, an initiation into human condition. The narrator unpacks the boxes and wrappings of fictionality (again, in actuality or pretending). The mere object of the story—the writer him- or herself, the human being in general, the world—change and this leads to changes in the story. Ever speedier changes leave no time for epic distancing, for crystallization of experience, for casting the essay in aesthetically and genre solid mold. Hence, this kind of writing is conceptually and inherently endless, the books suppose "to be continued," and updated, to be aesthetically unfinished and imperfect (the latter can be entirely "authentic," but can also be conceptual and deliberate) Genre uncertainty, narrative and stylistic experiments and fragmentation substitute classical narrative. And who knows, perhaps the genre of existential epos encompasses everything—from fragment to total literature,[220] because humanity lives in all genres.

Only the death of the narrator puts an end to these books. Death and the predicted "unhappy end" are the only possible compositional frame and denouement for these epics of human experience—death of the individual and of humanity. And art, writing and literature in particular, is the only transcendental hope for salvation.

But to turn someone's continuous essays on life, the world, and oneself into a book, into a text for publication, there must be a full stop at some point, the text has to be

---

219 Michael Chabon, *Moonglow*.

220 By total literature we mean a compendium of all literary genres, be it reproduced "with due respect" or in ironic travesties.

fixed in some version. Which remains only a momentary snapshot and, at the same time, a trace, as illusory as a scratch in the sky.

Having said all this, it might sound paradoxical, but I don't like and don't read biographies or the correspondence of writers. I don't want to know the real persons and their loves, marriages, affairs, sexual orientation, illnesses, alcohol or narcotics addictions, bad habits, bohemian or bourgeois lives, birthplace, journeys and residences, religious or political bias, banal professional occupations they made a living with, objective facts behind this or that story, prototypes for this or that personage, the real landscape or place of this or that *mise-en-scène*. This is not fear of disappointment, it's just not fair. It is unfair not so much to the real persona of the author, but to the Human being, with a capital H, whom the author has made up and recreated out of him- or herself. The yellow, voyeuristic gaze, peeping into author's reality, destroys the story, the aesthetic world and truth, created by the author. This sickly interest seems legitimate when drawn to auto-fictional prose, but it isn't, not only because it destroys the narrative, but because it reduces the object, i.e., the human being, back to the concrete, banal biography of the author. Leave it to the writers to mystify and invent, even themselves, to choose what to tell and how and what to make public. The author leaves trace of their intellect and spirit, and not of their real biography. Their portraits of the human being are immortal, not their real personas.

At the same time, I have always been interested in the borderlines of literature, those invisible bands in the shifting sands, where a text becomes, or ceases to be, literature. My fascination with this topic seems to stem from a belief of mine that each person, even the most ordinary one, should leave more than transformed chemical elements, genes and a few dumb photographs, that human consciousness should leave a trace of that *rage* and *curse* against time, death and its own meaninglessness, drawling out in the cosmic dark and silence, during the short walk under the stars. Even if this trace would be an imperceptible, hopeless scribble in the sky, an invisible signature of the wind-tossed *reed.*

In the distant 2001, I thought up, intuitively and unconsciously, what years later would become known as fanfiction. My genre experiment was realized in an exotic language and I gained no world fame. Although my idea was even more conceptual—I offered to the fans and amateur writers-to-be my own text (my first book), not someone else's, and I withdrew as author. This literary happening was a continuation of the book itself, where in its final chapter, the author of the previous stories disappeared and the editor, who went by my name, had to decide what to do with the text in terms of revision and publication. After the book's publication, the mystification continued—the text was put on the Internet, on a site created for this very purpose, which I named *endlessbook.com*. Every reader could edit, change, develop the text however they wanted, to become a co-author, after the disappearance of the author. The text became continuous, endless, a living and interactive book.[221]

Now, my continuous *essays* can be interpreted as fanfiction after Montaigne, Canetti, or Knausgaard.

Recently, I learned about the social project of Professor Pocock, itself inspired by an earlier idea of the 1930s. The professor gathered a pool of approximately 800 volunteers, ordinary folks,from all walks of life, who wrote their own *essays*, about themselves, their own lives, time and places, on a wide range of topics, set out by the professor. A huge archive has been amassed. To respect privacy of personal life, and simultaneously preserve authenticity and honesty, their names are anonymized. The project is considered "one of the most eccentric, yet enduring, attempts at preserving for posterity the lives and views of everyday folk."[222]

It turns out that not only *ars poetica* is *longa.* The real, ordinary little human, provincial and global, funny and sad, mundane and existential, can live on not only aesthetically. And not only in the margins of the family bibles or in the footnotes of "proper" literature.

Irrespectively how we interpret *ars*—as literary craft or as art itself, it takes time and it withstands time.[223]

---

221 The end of the *endless book* was comic and sobering, though. A few years later, sending my CV through Brussels in search of a job, I decided to look at this site, which I provided a link to on my CV—as an original literary project. I found . . . hardcore porn. Obviously for someone, "The Endless Book" meant something like the Kama Sutra and took over the site after its one year license ran out. I guess, clearing my literary project was instantaneous. Good that I looked and took out the link from my professional autobiography.

222 The Economist, December 18th–31st, 2021.

223 A catchy and emotional *pointe*, which may be a suitable finale not only for these chaotic poetics, but for the whole book. Two writers even advised me so. However, I have another ending to the book in mind.

Here, I want to improvise an ode to that unjustly neglected and abused footnote. Who doesn't swear at the painstaking footnote! It was a sign of the translator's impotence, who couldn't manage to convey the entire connotative, historic, cultural, or emotional content of the original and therefore sought refuge in the explanatory crutch of a footnote. There was no place for a footnote in literature. Only in scientific publications and then mostly for references. Can you imagine poetry with footnotes? Oh, what an unheard outrage!

But I love footnotes. I could leave a footnote under almost every sentence in this book. Reading a footnote is not compulsory. It doesn't interfere with the reading. It can only enhance it, and even create another interpretation. I imagine a book, of a suitable size 100-200 pages, in which the nominal content is, say, 5-6-page story, and the rest—easygoing footnotes. One or more footnotes for every word, thought, image, line of dialogue. The footnotes may have their own stories.

As there cannot be a footnote without a text above the line, the footnote doesn't have its own genre, alas. It's shunned everywhere. "Get out, off with you, *down below* the line, outside the noble Text!" if there's nowhere else to put it and yet it's necessary. The footnote is a little uncomfortable provocateur, which messes up the coiffeurs of those snooty ladies, Fictionality and Pathos. If the author is brave enough, in the footnote he or she pops out their head from the magic box of the Text and says "Peep-bo!" With the footnote the translator takes you into their workshop.

Don't ignore the little footnote as guileless—the footnote has an unsuspected *aesthetic* potential, especially in mystification. Nor should you trust this cunning scribe completely, even only for the fact that sometimes it's not so obvious who is writing the footnote and if the writer is not dragging you back in the magic box of the text.

Footnotes are like the marginal notes in bibles, testaments and missals. The margin notes may be a lot more interesting than the officious Text (notably for the readers in the future). In the margins of the official corpus, real people speak about their real life behind the historical decors, painted aesthetically and ideologically in his majesty the Text. In the marginal notes in the holy books, the Being and the Word are intercepted by the daily life and the language of ordinary folks. Sometimes, these *marginal* notes are moving mini-novels, which even the most skillful literary craft and fictionality cannot devise. I won't forget a note, from the tenth century. History describes the tenth century as a glorious time for the medieval Bulgarian kingdom—military victories and territorial expansions, the adoption of the Cyrillic script, monastery schools, intensive translation of liturgy books, blossoming culture. However, in a missal of this epoch, a marginal note tells about a widow (whose husband has obviously died for some of the glorious victories) named Dobrina (which in Bulgarian means "the good woman.") The good Dobrina "bequeaths" (this is the exact word used) one of her children to the priest's family in return for food and cloth, which could feed and clothe her other children. The "contract" with the good woman is registered (not by the illiterate mother but presumably by the priest) as a margin note, *beneath* a beautifully decorated gospel. Virtuous Dobrina performed her good deed literally *beneath* the eyes of the Good Lord . . . Sophie's Choice of the tenth century is another, parallel history.

Otherwise, in Western Europe at least, the footnote originates from *reader's* comments and thoughts or teacher's explanations. Not as author's text! It may well be that fan-fiction and footnote are genetically related and in fan-fiction, footnote at last has gained its own genre.

IMAGES

My travels with Nana had one other, very special, "destination"—galleries and their pictures. To get there, we used the albums borrowed from the city library across the street, Russian editions that were not suitable for reading in bed, huge and heavy as they were—they had to be explored on the kitchen table. I had favorite pictures, which I scanned over and over.

The aunties in my kindergarten liked to read magazines, and they'd put up some clippings of movie and pop-stars in their service room—Alain Delon, Catherine Deneuve, Emil Dimitrov, Lilly Ivanova, Nevena Kokanova.[224] One of my most vivid early childhood memories is the puzzled, fixed expression in their eyes when I strode decisively into their room to say that I couldn't fall asleep for the compulsory afternoon nap and that we had to reach some "compromise."[225] I looked at the pictures on the wall and added that the most beautiful woman in the world was "the Sis-tine Madonna 'cause she looks like Mom," and the most beautiful man is "David by Mick-Langilo" (although he looks nothing like Dad).

Many years after the flights I had taken with my half-paralyzed Nana, I was somewhat disappointed with the reality of the tourist landmarks. The originals of the pictures, however, never failed to deliver—they were the only thing that didn't look prettier in the album or with my inner eye during those bedtime flights.

... It was only when I had a very close look at Bruegel's "Fall of Icarus" that I saw the ironically unpolished, even childish depiction of the two human figures—that

224 French and Bulgarian movie and pop stars of the '60s and '70s.

225 I had learned the word at home that Sunday and I hastened to put it to good use

of the plowman, the little man busy in his everyday life, and that of the dreamer, plopping into the water—somewhere in the background, undramatic, imperceptible—and it's not just the laborer who's oblivious to his fall. If I did not know the painting from reproductions or if I hadn't read the title, I could also, as a viewer, fail to notice Icarus. Behind these droll depictions of mundane life and the human condition, of the synchronic realities and mythologies of the human condition, the "official" historical and aesthetical background is ironically painted, in the finest of brushwork.

. . . The most surreal thing about Magritte is that you have to see the reality first, before you look at his landscapes. The long Belgian eventide in June and July[226] turns into a metaphysically prolonged dusk that lasts up to twenty-three and a half hours, and the dark silhouettes of houses and trees against a background of soft violet sky have revealed to me that Magritte is actually a hyperrealist before being a surrealist.

. . . Rubens may do with reproductions only, but quality ones as the colors are beautiful. Even in front of a reproduction, the viewer feels more relaxed. Because the paintings are actually huge, fresco-sized, and as we have no interiors suitable for them, they look monumentally threatening. To think that Rubens himself was actually very small—the bed in his Antwerp house would be considered child-sized nowadays, even if we know that people used to sleep half-seated. These Dutchmen seem to have been small, indeed.

. . . I gazed again at "Knight, Death and Devil" and especially "Melancholia." The allegories, relevant in their time, retain their power, over me at least. Dürer is very dear to my heart because of the Dürer-style imaginary and technical sophistication of the etchings of "my" artist, Rada's father. I remember how the copperplate soaked in the little tub, looking all scratched up, damaged, then the scratches disappear beneath the black of the ink, and then the press starts slowly rolling, the white paper unsticks from the plate and the first print literally sees the light as I watch.

. . . It was only on that sunny and warm day in Milan when I stood before the "Last Supper" that I saw the light pouring from that fresco, despite the centuries and notably despite the decay of the material it was made of—plaster and paint.[227] This light coming from behind the personages was more metaphysical than the Bible story illustrated there. Background cosmic radiance of Leonardo's spirit. And it was quite unlike the merry sunshine outside, smiling, inviting me to drink an espresso, short as a shot and thick like blood, to shop, to have fun, to love, to enjoy life.

---

226 Which is only the result of the northern latitude and has no mystical explanations whatsoever.

227 There was no trace of restoration and conservation done by modern Italians.

. . . I explored from close up the details of Bosch's heaven and hell (the latter is presented much more convincingly) and I thought again that Hieronymus had not traveled to accumulate this strikingly exhaustive gallery of human nature. In fact, he never left his Flemish village. Yet, he knew the whole world, the whole human being, and even the netherworld—heaven, but mostly hell. The netherworld is inside the human being; Bosch was painting his own dreams, and mostly—nightmares. Nightmares are not being fed by traveling physical space. This "stationary" universality of Hieronymus Bosch reminded me of Kant who never set foot outside his native Königsberg. If Bosch had been painting Evil, the universe of sin that is the realm of Man, and the inevitable hell to be bestowed for man's evil and sinful nature, Kant believed Man to be naturally good, and that *Good* in Man is a manifestation of *God,* that the accomplishment of this moral person is God's providence. It turns out that Good and Evil, heaven and hell, like utterly extreme opposites, are a worldview of spatial steadiness.

Modernist art puzzles me. I do not understand how, for example, nine small canvases that are simply painted in different solid colors without any image on them and without forming any kind of composition, could represent art. I have a long-standing suspicion that the king of modern art is naked, indeed. Rada's father-in-law is a professor in modern art. The man took it upon himself to explain to me the invisible conceptual clothes, but with the rider that on Mondays, Tuesdays, and Wednesdays he wakes up with complete confidence in all that, but on Thursdays he is a little hesitant, and on Fridays he is on the verge of denying it all. A really entertaining private lecture accompanied by a bottle of vintage French wine from Bordeaux, after a whole day rushing round local galleries. During the day we'd seen cyclists, stark naked indeed, in the center of Brussels, it was some kind of protest or happening.

I think there's something deeply unfair about the difference in aesthetic criteria and expectations toward a modern painting, installation, happening, performance—and, let's say, a novel. The artist, from the moment he declares himself as such, with a diploma, is presumed to have talent and artistic ideas. From here on, whatever he happens to create, even if he chooses to exhibit his excrement (and there are quite a few "works" done in that "medium of expression") is considered art, an art that expresses some idea. It's the audience that must be educated to understand the idea. The super-educated art critics have the task of explaining that idea to laymen, and quite often of actually creating the idea. Novelty seems the most important, and often the only, "aesthetic" quality of this art. If it's not "unheard of," modern art must fit into the ideological coordinates drawn by the art critics themselves. Or it won't have any market value at all. Because modern artists are primarily interested in that.

From "my" artist, Rada's father, I remember that you can understand how great an artist is from their drawing of a hand. An old fashioned classic belief, that's beyond dispute. But with all my post-modern baggage, I'm still searching for a naturalistic hand, or in other words, some proof of talent, craft, *ars*, knowledge of the cannon and culture, even if you're rebelling against them. There is some kind of worldwide trust, permissiveness—and tolerance—in attitudes toward modern art, both visual and performative. Artists are treated like children who, you see, are going to "serve" us something that we cannot see anymore as adults. I do not put my trust in the artist's invisible conceptual garments, or their pure ideas; I don't feel that kind of *a priori* piety. These art works don't impress me intellectually, emotionally or aesthetically. I can't accept that something I could do myself (and I have plenty of ideas) without being an artist, is art. This is the argument of every layman, I know. The only thing I, personally, find precious and interesting in contemporary visual art is its conceptualism and genre syncretism.

But when it comes to writing, and prose in particular, the criteria are so much stricter. Apart from some pieces of modern poetry and drama, which seem to enjoy similar *a priori* trust and permissiveness with regard to the author's "ideas," to the extent that only the author and the literary critics finally know "what the author wanted to say," the self-sustained aesthetic abracadabra will not do in prose! Literary critics will draw their swords and decapitate all those scribblers, graphomaniacs, self-indulgent word-slingers who can't even "describe a hand," who do not master their craft, who have no knowledge and culture, who have little to say about the world so they write about themselves.

What is the reason for that deep injustice? Is it rooted in the means of expression—everyone can use words but not everyone knows how to use paints and the whole bunch of various . . . "materials." In this line of thought, I sometimes reach extreme conclusions. Why does a photorealistic painting automatically become art while a documentary-realistic type of text has to answer certain criteria to be acknowledged as such? Even if we take "real" artists, even the great ones—everything they put their hand to, even if it's the flimsiest of sketches, is art. It's not like this in the art of literature. *Ars poetica* has a canon that takes precedence over individual "aesthetics," and the critics, too.

I stress that I only mean public, published, exhibited, evaluated art—visual and literary, and not the reed's scribbling in the sky, family chronicles, Prof. Pocock's archives and all kinds of other "private" genres.

Today the whole world is taking selfies, all the time, with or without an occasion, beautified, posed, and posted for everyone else to see, like, ooh and aah with emoticons, to forward, download, and gossip over. We have created a new virtual planet, populated by a whole new virtual humanity. This expanded, virtual world is replacing the real one and our real selves. If you haven't taken a picture and posted it, it didn't really happen. A new type of tourism is gaining ground, called "selfie tourism." You travel to some destination only to take pictures and video clips and post them online. There are itineraries that are calculated to "cover" a maximum of landmarks in the minimum of time. Encountering, exploring, engaging and experiencing the world and the Other are replaced by stage props for the documentation of our expired presence.

The visual is invading the territories of words, of content and message. Visual documentation is a cancellation of memory. Memory is supplanted by ready-made visual memos whose skin-deep content will live forever in its digital form. Once it was the written Word (with its first genre, the epitaph!) replacing the oral tradition, and with it—the need to remember. The visual is about to replace language, and with it—the need to think and communicate.

In this virtual world everybody is as young and beautiful as they should be (so they don't show themselves up), nobody is getting old, (because there are technical ways of erasing the scars of time), everybody is where they want and have to be (so they don't feel ashamed for not being able to afford it), everybody *has* what they want to have and what they need to have (so they won't be considered *losers*), everybody is successful, accomplished, happy and partying. Some do crazy things not for the experience, but for the photo. The selfie is a form of epidermal photography, expressing satisfaction (with the good life), pride and confidence (in the financial capacity to "cover" a certain destination, to be *physically* there, in space), vanity (to parade yourself as beautiful, young, well-preserved, loved, happy, successful, accomplished). But what if this epidermalization, this happy-go-luckiness, and this vacuity is not the future? What if the virtual world of snaps is only a foreboding of the total virtuality that, if not our children, our grand- and great-grandchildren will live in? Totally visual, totally virtual, four-dimensional and totally vacuous. Virtuality may turn out to be the only alternative to—by then already impossible—physical travel and presence and *in vivo* communication.

Yet, I want to believe that our virtual "heritage" and "portrait"—this freeze-frame of ostentatious *contentment*—would rather baffle future generations. Were we really that happy? Were we really that similar? Were we really nothing more than that? Wasn't really there any other *content*? What thoughts did we have, if any, and what feelings, if we have had feelings at all, what had we wanted to say, had we been able to speak with words and not just with emoticons? . . . Today's people shoot, and shoot, and shoot on. Without realizing that there are generations of viewers standing behind the lens of their smart phones. Or so I hope . . .

Here the editor of the new Bulgarian edition has reminded me of Canetti's phobia of photographs, present in *Crowds and Power* and in the play *The Comedy of Vanity*, and the writer's will, in which he specifies how many years after his death which of the few of his photographs could be published.

My expectations to "responsible" portrait photography are higher. Actually, as weird as it may sound, it was a photo, not words or music, that spurred my very first "creative impulse." Looking at an old photograph I felt for the first time a conscientious desire to write. The vague feeling came with a strange tickling sensation as if rudimentary wings were breaking through my shoulder blades. The "epiphany incident" was otherwise pretty trifling. In the home of a schoolmate I saw an old black-and-white picture from the 1920s, where my classmate's great-grandmother and great-grandfather, having been just married in the village church, were running hand in hand across a meadow—young, happy, the man in a semi-urban/semi-rural suit, the woman in a teacher's overdress, with a peasant's apron and a white wreath on her head. Both had died years ago and nobody remembered anything much about them anymore besides their names, how they made their living, and their nominal spots on the family tree—to whom they had been parents and grandparents. I was turning the picture in my hands and gazing at it, to my classmate's dismay. These two lovebirds had not left a single word about these moments on the meadow, and about their lives, like it is for almost all people. Yet, how wonderful this photo was! No, I do not mean cheesy nice. The photo was focused, responsible, if you want; this man and this woman will live forever precisely and only in this moment, captured on the photo. I was overcome with the insupportable desire to write about precisely these carefree lovebirds, to invent and resurrect them with their ordinary life. I wanted to make my Granny and Granddad leave words before they departed, not just dumb photos. An Icarus moment, almost per Breugel. Just that in my story Icarus was a woman and just groping her shoulder blades.

I love the portrait photos of grandpa Rusan and of Nana, standing on the mantelpiece in my study. I stroke the portrait of my mom in her twenties: a young engineer, already a wife and a mother. Mom is looking at me with her doe eyes, with her soft beauty of a still undiscovered movie star, with that expression of a modest and timid, compassionate and loving, responsible, hard-working and self-sacrificing protestant girl. Only there isn't a trace of the outstanding mathematician.

Portrait photography is a very special art. An interactive one. The pose, the angle, the distance, the light, the contrast, the facial expression, the *retouche*, the clothing and the accessories, the background . . . all this is meant to make the visible, the real and the material reveal the invisible—the soul, the heart, the intellect, the aspirations, the experience. The human being is the only object of portrait photography, the human being in their physical and immaterial entirety. The result is a unique identity, and at the same time, a type of the human spectrum, elaborated according to the canons of the epoch. The image is as mimetic as anything could possibly be, and yet it is a creation, a recreation, with a specific message, or story, oriented to a viewer, open to interpretation and even dialogue. The person, lifted above his or her banality, put on a stage, close-up and all light on him or her. It's not just who she or he really was, but whom she or he aspired to be and how she or he wanted to be remembered. At the moment of shooting, the lenses and the photographer's view serve as total, all-encompassing and penetrating mirror, while the photo is a testimony, a document. Portrait is an instrument of memory, designed to commemorate. The preserved human face, or rather presence, is a manifesto against death and oblivion. The older the photo, the more precious it is, and the deeper the melancholy of the viewer, induced by this eternal human illusion that time has no power over memory.

And time . . . oh, time has a very "special relation" with photography in general and with portrait photography in particular. Remember that time is in us, that our body and face *em-body* time? Photography stops time. It captures a moment to keep it forever. In portraits, the face is a universal code to the human condition; a portrait is an instantaneous glimpse of the human essence and of the embodied time, an instant fixed forever.

Photography is deeply oxymoronic as it *immortalizes* a *momentary* state that will not be the same a second later, that will never be the same. The automatic dating of digital photos is something much more interesting than banal digital data. Art photography consciously activates this oxymoron by capturing and literally fixing for eternity that fleeting point in time, the moment when people, light, matter, movement, the photographer's look . . . cross their trajectories in space and time. It happens—in the camera lens—and disappears forever, in one and the same moment.

A friend of mine published dozens of monumental (in their size, volume and weight) photo albums of things that are monumental anyway—statues, churches, altars, graveyards, salt mines. A tautology I did not understand, at first. Then I got it—the real object of these photos was time. The photos juxtapose, on one hand, the material, its enduring perenniality or decay over time, the objects' purpose, which is to be eternal, and, on the other hand, the moment, the very second of clicking the camera. The second against eternity, the fleeting against the monumental. Apart from the decay, time and especially the second of the photograph, were caught by a flashing drop of water, the shadow of the photographer, or some autumn leaves in a gust of wind.

I'm thinking about a fundamental experiment in quantum physics and the theory of quantum flow. A ray of light "behaves" in a particular way only when observed by man. I have always wondered if the eye of technology sees the reality the same way as the human eyes do.

Self-portrait is an even more complicated image, loaded with meaning.

Today, to the casual eye, Jan van Eyck's *Portrait of a Man in a Red Turban* would appear to be a selfie—to each the craft and the media of their times. The purpose and meaning of a self-portrait and a selfie appear similar. Jan van Eyck's self-portrait is also an expression of satisfaction with his material status (the exotic turban with its bright color and the fur collar are not just random attributes), of pride and confidence (in the talent to paint so well), of vanity (I, personally, would fancy a man like that. Well, taking the turban away, adding some hair and switching to a more contemporary outfit). All this holds true to the extent that (self-)portraits did serve the function of photography, which did not exist in the artist's lifetime. The precise dating of the canvas also alludes to modern photography.

Yet this self-portrait, and every good (self-)portrait, even today, in the time of high-tech cameras, is so much more than an ordinary photo because it *visualizes* and depicts the person's character, spirit and consciousness—things that are deeper and more enduring than epidermal physiology and fleeting actuality. And hence begin the differences. Painting is monumental, unlike a snapshot. It is art, accomplished in certain materials, following an aesthetic canon, it is meant to be exposed and admired as art, not just to present and commemorate a person. Actually, it is thought that Van Eyck invented oil painting (in Bruges, incidentally). The Self-Portrait is so harmoniously cracked all over, that it looks like a jigsaw. Time has drawn over the artist's oil paints.

The artist has more freedom than the photographer as the artist can modify, or recreate completely to his artistic view, everything—the face, the expression, the posture, the clothing, the light and shade, all these elements which may never have come together in that precise combination, in space and time; some of which might not even have existed.

The insisting precision of the dating of van Eyck's Self-Portrait seems paradoxical, set against the monumental status of the canvas as art. Dating, however, bears an important message. The artist has written: *Als Ich Can* over the image, something I would translate as *As much as I Can*, or *Like (only) I Can*. This is a typical signature of the artist, who has put it on several of his works.[228] On this picture, however, it is unusually big, a really imposing declaration. The signature-declaration can be interpreted as an act of humility—"I'm trying to paint as much as I can, I can't do any better" but it can also be read as an expression of confidence and even self-advertising of sorts—"See how well I can paint!" Below the image, and this time in Latin, the artist has written: *JOHES DE EYCK ME FECIT ANO MCCCC. 33. 21. OCTOBRIS*, which means *Jan van Eyck made me on 21st October 1433*.

The autograph-declaration, the detachment of the artist from himself as the object of the painting and the precise dating are all very unusual for the fifteenth century. The artist painted himself as the object of his artistry, and signed himself as Jan, the artist. At the same time the artist Jan is detached from his real self, and depicted himself as a human being per se. This is an artistic image, an aesthetic reincarnation, not (only) of the concrete Jan, but the human being within Jan. For the sake of plastic convenience, the artist has used his own physique, but no doubt has beautified it, turned it into a prototype, sharpening or softening features in order to depict the human. That's why behind the title of "Self Portrait" there is always a question mark. The semiotic puzzle get even more complicated because the human—subject of the painting, talks about the artist Jan in the third person. Which only confirms the conscious detachment and true object of the painting. But Jan, the artist, and the object of the painting are one and the same. Consequently, the

228 In the portrait of the Arnolfini family, over the mirror, in which the actual artist is seen, he has written, "Jan van Eyke was here." Overall, it quite interesting how this artist breaks the frame of the aesthetic fictionality.

Human, with a capital H, humanity, which is the true object of the painting, is an artist. This is a portrait of humanity, and that as a painter, as a creator. The precise date fixes the moment in which this Human looked at the world, the Other, the future, at himself, his concrete self—Jan, the artist. The precise dating of the picture is a rebellion against time, it's challenging time to a duel with the human spirit and talent. With this dating the artist is telling me that he believes his masterful portrait of the human being will still live long after the concrete person Jan has gone to dust. That the creativity of humanity will endure. And he asks me if he was right. I saw this painting up close[229] for the second time as I was writing this book. We gazed at each other, the artist and I, and we talked.

I had already submitted my manuscript to the publishing house when I happened to see the London exhibition of paintings by Max Ernst's wife. I love the world famous Max Ernst, but this was the first time I'd heard about his wife, Dorothea Tanning. That's the way it goes with the wives of grand artists, especially if they are not merely muses. We know a lot more about the muses than about the creative spouses. By the way, Dorothea has a photomontage kind of picture where she is tiny and the big Max Ernst looks like a giant. Very informative. Tanning is a really interesting artist, some of her pictures look almost like a female Francis Bacon. But there was one picture, a figurative composition, naïve, illustrative, that stopped me in my tracks. I was looking at the cover of my upcoming book! Now the kind reader will probably turn the book around a cast another look at the cover. Ready?

So, this is also a self-portrait, at least that's what the title says. Here, however, the artist—object of the painting, has turned her back on the viewer and is rather sharing her view with them. So the *contemplation* of this view and the *positioning of the artist in this landscape* are the subjects of this painting.

Dorothea Tanning explains the following: "*In that camera-sharp place where* ***planetary upheaval*** *had lifted its signature: the now placid monuments that,* ***as far as anyone out there cared****, had been there* ***forever****, I would undertake—'****dare****' would be a truer word—to paint the* ***unpaintable****. One year was enough to sear it on the* ***lens of memory*** *(It was not done on the spot, as artists generally did: planting their shaky easels in sand or shale, wind and sun; dipping brushes in globs of paint and hope) so that, in the studio alone with my* ***dream*** *I would record it like a diary entry, just like that.*"[230]

229 In the London National Gallery.

230 From Dorothea Tanning: Birthday and Beyond. Exhibition brochure. Philadelphia: Philadelphia Museum of Art, 2000.

Dorothea is standing straight before the cosmos, not before the beautiful earthly sky and nature. The landscape may be terrestrial but this is the Earth placed in the time-space of eternity, our planet before or after human civilization. Dorothea is aware that there are things that cannot be painted, or rather things that can be seen and painted by a human in one way only, the human way, and only while the human eye is alive and looking at them. This is not a landscape of the living, perpetually renewing, revived, reincarnating, fertile nature of Mother Earth. The nature we see here is dead, devoid of biological life, reason, consciousness, aesthetics, feelings, sense. A *nature morte* of the non-Being. But contemplated by a human. That's why Dorothea is unsure whether that Cosmos and non-Being can be painted at all.

The picture is a self-portrait, although the person portrayed—the artist, has paradoxically turned her back on the viewer. The mere contemplation is the true content and message of the picture. The non-Being, contemplated by a human being, is the most fundamental and insightful portrait of humanity and human condition. The viewer becomes part of the picture, because they share the human viewpoint and contemplation.

Pictures have no sound, but in contemplation alongside the artist, I "hear" non-Being like an absolute silence of a vacuum. Without the hollow beat of the human heart.

I wrote "Human" and in Bulgarian, the words for human, person, author, and painter are all masculine, but the author, artist, human, the mind standing up before the non-Being is (biologically) female. For the very first time, I see a woman contemplating the non-Being, without the consolation of the perpetually reviving nature, without the comfort of its eternal femininity birthing life. Woman outside home and nature.

But how tiny and vulnerable this woman is, this human being of the female sex, within this "landscape"! You may not see her at first (and something in the composition and scale of this picture reminds me of Bruegel's *Fall of Icarus*).[231] How innocent she is—like a little girl in her almost childish pajamas or underwear, without sexual allure (yet another effect of painting her from behind) with her two buns gathered over her forehead. There are no wizards, fairies, scarecrows, tin-men (i.e., robots), no cowardly lions,[232] no gods and devils, no good and evil, no beautiful and ugly, no children, no men, no people at all, no animals and plants, no nature. There's nothing. Nothing. This is non-Being—non-human, heartless, void. It has been there before humanity and will be there after them. Little Dorothy won't be blown by a whirlwind

231 One could make a very interesting comparison between the self-portraits of Dorothea Tanning and Caspar David Friedrich, or between Tanning's self-portrait and Friedrich's women in contemplation—also painted from behind, but surrounded by cozy, terrestrial nature or standing at the window of their homes.

232 An allusion to the children's classic *The Wizard of Oz* where the main character is called Dorothy.

back home, because there is no home; there is no shelter for humanity in the non-Being. The human is present quite by accident in this landscape, just for few twinkles, just for a glance. This is the human being in their absolute solitude. Unlike Dorothy who wakes up safe at home, the human being cannot wake up from their existential nightmare.

The picture is deeply ironic. Woman is depicted in quite "classical" fashion as little, weak, vulnerable, sweet and innocent, calling for protection and comfort. But this female personage stands in for the human being in general and *this human being* is little, fragile, alone, hopeless and inconsolable amid the cosmic landscape. The weaker sex ironically takes on human vulnerability. In his secret observatory, he, the human of the male sex, contemplates Cosmos, too, and is likewise not big, strong, omniscient and fearless. But man does not let anyone in his observatory, he would never admit his terror. This is why a female artist *dared* to picture and share her nightmare.

THOUGHT EXPERIMENT

Now I suggest the kind reader carry out a thought experiment, very similar to those performed in theoretical physics and astronomy. It seems quite in order to include such a text in this book, which is titled *To Essay*, which also means "experiment" in Bulgarian.[233] Besides, contemporary science sounds more and more like literature with (at least up until now) elements of science-fiction, or even bits of popular philosophy with existential elements. Few scientists are aware the fictional or existential elements, though. Then philosophers seldom understand or are interested in physics, astronomy, and mathematics. Everyone ploughs their own furrow, occasionally spitting out some biting comment, and the laymen wonder who they should listen to.

The experiment will take an hour and a half, two maximum,[234] and it will consist in reading this text and doing a few quick and quite simple tasks. And it's OK—there's no special knowledge needed, there's nothing difficult either to understand or to do.

"What would a *human see*, who's being transported on a ray of light?" Albert (Einstein) asked himself when he was still a child.

"His or her dead Granddad riding a bike round the block," another child would have answered a little more recently in earth time.

233 To remind that one of the meanings of the original Bulgarian title is *experiment*. Because my Essay has been appreciated by readers and literary critics as "cosmo*polita*n," while in Bulgarian *politam* means *to fly*, in one interview I (smugly) joked that with my book the reader will *fly* in *cosmos*, indeed.

234 If you don't read the optional footnotes it could take less time.

After another forty-five to forty-six years, a woman, who's essaying to write, would have added, that to see the dead and various other "transcendental" stuff, it isn't even necessary to rush at the speed of light. It's enough to preserve the cosmic dust over your retina, with which you were born,[235] to use your bed more often as a flying machine, dreaming and awake, including when you're making love, to look more often at the starry sky, not to shove that anxiety and fear of nothingness and death into the corners of your mind and to stuff them with things, not to divert yourself with the "wonderful, wonderful life." You need only to crawl backward and forward in spacetime on that "unwavering band of light" inside you, which is your consciousness, which is you, unique and generically human you. As you are "transported" on this engine with internal combustion—the consciousness, you fuel up with philosophy, literature, music and art in general, and you grease with science the propellers of intuition, curiosity, memory, imagination and love; they will take you wherever you want, whenever you want, you can try everything and see everything.

The real problem is whether our human mind, thought and senses are truly capable of seeing and understanding everything. And something else, which you shouldn't forget on these journeys. It turns out, who is watching, thinking, measuring, calculating, imagining, understanding, explaining, and when they do all this, is reflected in, or impacts, the very object of observation. That's why the story I'm telling you is special. In it, everyone, and above all, you, who at this moment are reading this, you will be the main character. And perhaps author as well. Not for this reason, but for others reasons, no one knows for certain how this story will finish and what the fate of the author-main character will be.

Macro

And so, once upon a time . . . No, this story starts differently. At the beginning of time, before there was time at all . . . there was no time. And there wasn't anything at all. Nothing! Even space did not exist. False start? I'm stumbling here and cannot imagine this. But that's what thought experiments are for—we accept *a priori* the situation, like the axioms that mom could not explain, and we continue.

About 13.4 billion (earth) years ago,[236] there was no time, no space, there was no matter or antimatter, no waves, no fields, energy, dark or otherwise. And just like that,

235 According to me, that's why we're blind as newborns. Blind to this world.

236 According to some calculations 13.7 billion, but that's a small detail—some 300 million years. Yet, let's remind ourselves—the first multicellular organisms appeared on the Earth over 900 million years ago and the dinosaurs disappeared "only" over "some" 65 *million* years ago, homo sapiens appeared over 200 *thousand* years ago, and we homo sapiens squared are some 100 *thousand* years old, as only just over 45,000 years ago

out of the void, springs, or in scientific terms, emerges, a host of unimaginably minute particles, which most probably owe their "virtual" tag to their origin. And how tiny are they? Subatomic—that is smaller than an atom. And how big is an atom? One atom compares to a large *apple* is like a *pea* to our entire *planet*. But this is not all! These even tinier subatomic particles that, related to the atom, are the equivalent of a medium-sized marble to a football stadium—let's say Camp Nou. Leave a marble on the pitch's center spot.

Stop reading. Close your eyes for a little and imagine a large apple (we'll need this image in just a little while, if you have a real apple around, it's even better—take it in your hands). Now in your imagination blow your apple up to the size of the earth, here comes the pea. Then blow the pea to the size of a stadium and finally put the marble on the white spot.[237]

These unimaginably miniature particles have appeared and disappeared instantaneously. What does *instantaneously* mean? Well for one-two *picoseconds*. So as not to convey a picosecond with some cold naughts or powers, I'll illustrate it like this: 1 picosecond is the time necessary for light which moves at almost 300,000 kilometers a second to pass half the length of a grain of salt.[238] Now you can close your eyes again and try to imagine a picosecond. I can't.

And so, these tiny particles were hanging around existent-nonexistent at one point in as yet-definitely-non-existent time and space. The primordial particles were shifting between energy and matter, being and not being. And somewhere there an original "sin" emerged—there was just a little more matter than antimatter, one subatomic particle of matter more in a billion matter and antimatter particles.[239] From this miniature "unfair" surplus everything in the universe was created. Otherwise matter and antimatter annihilated each other in the creation, like we ditch pluses and minuses in equations. But little matter survived and it led to "Let it be . . ." And in the beginning of genesis, there was light, indeed, in a quite literal and biblical sense, because, from the mutual annihilation of matter and antimatter, photons were born.

The particles had enormous energy and even in their short-lived existence (at a greater speed than that of light) they inflated the original miniature dot—a kind of

---

we left Africa and though the next 30,000 years continued our evolutionary progress—our bone structure became ever lighter, our brain became ever more complex, but smaller in volume, only about 2,500–3,000 years separate us from the divine ancient Greek horizon and Plato's cave, 2,000 years from Christ's crucifixion. All this—just to give a scale.

237 I owe this nice visual scaling to the original theory (of Hawking) and to a Ted talk. I just changed the grapefruit with an apple and the blueberry with a pea, because the apple and pea relate better to other episodes in the book.

238 And this scale thanks to an Internet source.

239 Before becoming a dissident Andrei Sakharov was a fundamental physicist and this is his theory.

stadium of the void in which they played hide-and-seek—to something with the proportions of *a big apple.*[240] Without any kind of scale for the apple. Didn't I tell you?! What a sweet, intimately human comparison, don't you think? An object from our reality and scale, with which our tortured imagination can take a break. But, here we go again . . . This apple *weighed* as much as today's entire universe and the temperature was a billion, billion, billion degrees. Another snag? And I'm in the same boat.

The fearsome anti-gravitational force, which inflated—in picoseconds and with a speed greater than 300,000 kilometers per second—the miniature stadium to the size of a large apple, continued to act unimaginably quickly, the apple could not hold and . . . it exploded. It would have been a *big bang*, indeed. The unthinkably hot and heavy apple puree splattered in all directions and thus created space. And time began to tick.

(Only!) 380,000 (earth) *years* after the Big Bang, the hot puree of subatomic particles (electrons, protons, neutrons) had cooled to the extent that allowed for the formation of the first atoms. The puree was turning into star dust and Mendeleevian matter. The subatomic particles were fusing to create the first chemical elements—hydrogen, helium, and some other, heavier elements. The ancient cosmic clouds, dating from the birth of the universe, contain these elements in exactly the proportions predicted by scientists.

The light, built from even tinier particles (quanta), was bashing against the pre-atomic puree that had been splashed everywhere and in the end it lit up the newly created space. The lightning glow that followed is the source of the cosmic microwave background,[241] which can be observed *today,*[242] i.e., 13.4 billion years after the Big Bang

At the capsule and in the interior of the big apple, there were wrinkles—some inhomogeneities in the embryonic loom of spacetime. These wrinkles took on enormous proportions at the moment of inflation and explosion. And when the universe cooled,[243] matter began to *gravitate* around these chunks in the fabric which led to concentration of *mass.* Thus gravitation began to form galaxies and galactic clusters of star dust from the first chemical elements. Within the galaxies and their suns and planets, all the other chemical elements emerged, which after about 13.4 billion years Mendeleev will dream[244] of in a harmonious order, and some of them—like gold and

---

240 To express in figures the speed, time and scale of the inflation from spot to big apple and a little after that: 10^{32} seconds, 10^{80} growth.

241 It was no coincidence we call it a relic—like an archaeological relic from the very beginning of the world.

242 When you tune the TV to receive an analog program, you see snowflakes on the screen. Part of this "noise" is exactly this relic radiation of the Universe, left over from the lightning flash of Big Bang.

243 Well don't you go thinking whatever—the stars haven't even begun to form yet, and this happens at temperatures of atomic fusion.

244 This is not a metaphor. Mendeleev really did see in a dream his table with atomic masses and electrons of the various chemical elements.

platinum—will adorn parts of our body and will symbolize our feelings. Your very body, dear reader, contains hydrogen atoms created round the time of the Big Bang, as well as, for example, the calcium and iron atoms, which come from some star. After the Big Bang, there's been no new matter created in the universe, so there's nowhere else from which "we've come about."

Here it is necessary to remember another two fundamental laws, which mark out the "global context." The first law of thermodynamics states that energy can neither be created (after its emergence from the void, even so) nor annihilated, it is a given, and is only transformed from one form (say, mechanical) into another (say, heat). According to Einstein's famous formula, mass and energy are equivalent, everything that has mass possesses energy—even in stasis. The *materialization* of something with energy in something with mass is a more particular circumstance, especially if the thing is in stasis, i.e., its speed is nil.

There somewhere, 5 billion earth-years ago, star dust concentrated, swirled and gave birth to our Sun. It will burn, illuminate, and glow for about 5 billion more years, before the hydrogen in it turns to helium. That means we're in the middle of its life cycle. "A little" after the emergence of the stars, 4.5 billion years ago, a planet was shaped; it was at a very suitable distance from its star. The star itself—our Sun—is unusually stable in its stellar life. The planet cooled down and rotated in a very appropriate way. A very opportune ozone layer formed around it. Under the ozone layer there was oxygen and water. Its massive neighbor Jupiter, with its strong gravitational pull sucked away every kind of large or small melancholies and guarded the planet from mortal blows. Its satellite, the Moon, produced some very beneficial effects, like the tides[245] and stabilized the incline of the axis, so the planet wouldn't totter like a spinning top . . . Then, the story unfolds along Darwin—the first multicellular organisms, etc.[246] And here he is—man—he appears some hundred thousand years ago. And here you are, you in particular, who enters the story for some eighty-five years, [247] give or take.

The earth turns on its axis at 1,770 km per hour and at the same time it rotates round the Sun at nearly 108,000 km per hour. On the other hand, the solar system circles the center of our galaxy (the Milky Way) at about 828,000 km per hour and completes a full circuit every 230 million earth years. And in the end, our galaxy

245 Which maintain the magnetic field, which, in turn, protects us from deadly cosmic rays. Life evolved as well from sea to land thanks to the tides.

246 Although in this chapter of the story there are too many conundrums and paradoxes of the type chicken or egg (for example, with proteins and genes) which undermine clear and neat determinism.

247 With good genes and a healthy and happy life. Science promises 100+ years for our kids and grandkids.

moves at 2.1 million km per hour through the expanding universe.[248] In this extremely dynamic hoo-ha, our galaxy and the Andromeda Galaxy, which are separated by 2.5 million light-years, are approaching each other (at the relative speed of 402,000 km per hour) and in 4 billion years they'll collide and merge. At that moment, the Sun won't have blown up, but will have baked the Earth's surface. If after the "planetary upheaval," there are still some forms of biological life, or consciousness on the Earth, if "anyone out there still care," the scientists reassure us that because of the enormous distances between the stars in both galaxies, at the point of collision and convergence, there'll hardly be any stars crashing into each other—i.e., "nothing to worry about," there'll just be an unimaginable heavenly spectacle.

"Round the world and at home,"[249] there is another ongoing, global event, of which we are informed—the Universe is expanding. Man cannot understand why the Universe is scattering, and what's more with increasing speed, contrary to the laws of gravitation. The galactic clusters are flying away like flocks, in the sense they stick and float together, the stars in a galaxy do not draw apart, thank God, neither do the planets from their stars (that would concern us directly).

With all our established constants and laws and with all our higher mathematics, man cannot explain one particular thing—what fills up 90% of mass-energy in the universe. There's definitely *something*, because otherwise *things* wouldn't appear and move in the way they do, but man cannot see, capture, register, or analyze this dark mass-energy. So, has to think up a new constant for the force of this opaque dark matter-energy, in order to fit what is actually happening with his mathematics. And what is happening, is that this anti-gravitational force, is blowing up the universe, at accelerating speed. The expansion of the universe creates more space, in man's view. The expansion of the universe doesn't create more "light" matter, and therefore does not increase the gravitational energy of the "light" matter. Dark energy, however, increases with the expansion of the universe and thus the fluffs of the Universe dandelion fly away even faster.

Is antimatter really destroyed by matter in the creation? Are the properties of antimatter similar or opposite to those of matter? Didn't antimatter actually survive, wasn't it actually a lot more than matter, isn't antimatter this dark matter and dark energy, which quite logically should entail anti-gravitational force and make the universe scatter and the antimatter apple fly toward the sky, rather than fall to the Earth? In CERN

248 It would be interesting to know at what speed we humans are moving *at the end of the day*, in Universe space-time.

249 The title of the evening TV news in communist Bulgaria.

they can produce antimatter particles. We are hundreds or thousands of years away from them producing an antimatter apple. Then we'll be able to check if this apple has mass and whether, submitting to gravitation, it will fall toward the earth's center or . . . or it will behave in some different way.[250]

Inflated by this dark energy, the universe is expanding ever faster, spreading the matter it contains in ever looser and thinner layers. Dark energy will split the universe. If the acceleration of the expansion is indeed exponential, the Milky Way will be torn apart in "just" 20 billion years, and "only" 60 million years before space-time itself is torn apart. In a more moderate (or actually visual) scenario, filled with meek sorrow, if there is anyone to feel it, the sky will simply switch off, if there's anyone to observe this. The more distant galaxies by then will be too far away, and only a pale shadow mirage will be left of the Milky Way. And an ocean of darkness and emptiness will take over.

"And then?" The great rupture should have split the atoms, too[251] . . . And perhaps yet again virtual subatomic particles will pop up and everything will start anew.[252]

In the macrocosm, gravity and dark energy and matter reign. In this world, everything that has mass has gravitational pull, even though humanity still cannot explain why things that have mass and are made from "normal light matter" as per Mendeleev, attract each other. In this world there is huge mass, enormous distances, enormous speeds, enormous time and space. Inconceivably huge and dense mass creates black holes, which exercise unimaginable gravitation. Everything sinks into these holes, nothing beyond their "horizon" is seen or known (by man). Amid the dark energy and matter, which are impenetrable, unknowable and invisible to humankind, the ordinary matter, i.e., the stars, planets and . . . us, humans, are only a minor ingredient. The universe, as perceived by humans, is spatially boundless. In just the galaxy in which we are located (the Milky Way), there are hundreds of billions of stars. In the humanly observable universe there are hundreds of billions of galaxies, but the observable relates to the whole like a spoonful of water to the global ocean on our planet.

---

250 Without producing a whole antimatter apple, recently, science managed to observe that antimatter abides the gravitational pull, i.e., it falls, and does not fly up. So, the mysterious antigravitational force that expands the universe remains unknown.

251 For the "light matter" known to humans, I guess.

252 What if the universe is a huge beating heart? Yes, I know, this sounds desperately, cheesy anthropomorphic, but it's inevitable. Imagine: Big Bang, explosion, flying away, expansion, until the Big Rupture. Subatomic particles disappear in the nothingness. But as they are entangled, they attract each other, they start to emerge in the void, then they concentrate up to inconceivable to my human brain energy, mass and density, then . . . Boom! Big Bang, explosion and over again in the next beat. There is such a hypothesis only it doesn't talk of a heart, but of a universe resurrecting like a Phoenix.

Some stars and galaxies, whose light only the most powerful of human telescopes manage to catch a glimpse of, are not only unimaginably distant, but perhaps do not even exist in the human present, given that their light has to travel for millions if not billions of years to reach us here on Earth. I read that the Hubble telescope photographs objects that are billions of light-years away from us. Because "light-years" is a measure of distance, not of time, as I'd deduced as a youngster, we focus on the years, and these are earth years, the same and only unit we use to measure time. What follows from this is that we see a . . . picture and everything in that picture is already *past.* Not to mention that *in the meantime* it may have started all over again. Photographs and their relation to time are a fascinating subject, indeed.

As we *know* from the adult Einstein (but we're incapable of *imagining* or *apprehending*), in the macrocosm, time is relative. The scientist has answered to the child that if you travel at the speed of light, time stops, "the ever moving spheres of heaven stand still and time ceases." Then again, do some amatory or other states not propel us at the speed of light along that "unwavering band of light"? Anyway, the adult could not answer to the child what a *human* would see. Otherwise the four dimensional axis design[253] suggests that you can gad back and forth not only in three-dimensional space, but in time, too. So humanity can travel back and forth in time. And people and things from the past and from the future can pay us visits in our *now.* Which gives rise to such funny (for humanity, or adults only) paradoxes. Or is it only *objects* or *things* that can travel to and fro in time?

If you've endured the experiment till this point, I'll conduct something like a half-time "heat check." Don't you wonder what exactly I'm experimenting with? Do you not think that all of this has no effect on you at all—your life, that of your children and your nearest and dearest, even that of all humanity? That all of this is outside your human temporal and spatial horizon? If you're getting such thoughts, don't worry, so am I, just like you.

Or maybe you wonder why I torment you at all with these popular-science facts, most of which you can't get your head around? Additionally, there's no need for me to educate you—all this can be read on the Internet and in a whole pile of reliable and entertaining books. I have no excuse for my disservice to the interest and attention of the kind reader. I can only remind you that this is just an experiment, in which you have complete freedom to not participate—simply skip this chapter.

253 I assume that the zero point of the four axes is the Big Bang, because didn't space and time emerge after it?

Possibly you've been overtaken by some melancholy, some feeling of pointlessness, fear, anxiety, or something of this sort. I feel the same, and I guess, most other people do as well. I wish I could comfort you with the usual "This is only a book" but somehow that doesn't quite work in this case.

The "story" above marks another possible *finale* for this and all books and stories. I've plotted the ending of this book, though most endings are pretty much clear and predicted.

Otherwise everything I've told you up till now actually concerns us quite directly, not to say that it depends on us. To an extent, we, each of us, humans, are creating it. And so, if you carry on reading at all, from now on, watch out and scrutinize closely the "picture." Take my advice quite literally.

Micro

It turns out (over the last hundred years) that if in the macrocosmic world (i.e., that of massive objects like stars, planets, galaxies, flying airplanes, and falling apples), Newton's classic mechanics and Einstein's theory of relativity rule,[254] but in the microcosmic world (i.e., of atoms and subatomic particles like protons, electrons, quanta, quarks, photons, etc.) quite different laws operate, summarized as Quantum Mechanics. The Standard Model of elementary particles entails a catalogue of such particles, with different properties, and three forces which control them—electromagnetic, weak and strong interactions. The problem is that this model ignores the fourth force—gravitation, which, again, controls the macrocosm.[255] Humans cannot harmonize the four forces of nature into a congruent theory of everything. And the universe, and everything, including human beings, is built from elementary particles. The proper theories of macro- and microcosms describe them well, but the theories themselves do not fit together and there are dramatic gaps in the very core of the mechanics.

Because of this dualism, scientists drift into a quiet schizophrenia, they carry out crazy thought experiments and build unimaginable hypotheses, in order to fit the macro and the micro worlds as we currently understand together, but up till now have had little success. One quantum theory of gravitation would solve the problem, but so far there hasn't been one.

254 Although up till now it's unclear if the dark matter-energy obeys these laws, and it constitutes over 90% of the universe. There's no way of knowing something about something without first knowing what that something is.

255 It's no accident that right now the most active research is into quantum gravitation.

The microcosm provides and continues to provide—for the time being—unsolvable surprises and puzzles. Max Planck and Einstein[256] discovered that the biblical light has a double nature—on the one hand, it's made from elementary material particles, quanta (i.e., they have mass at least theoretically), on the other hand it's a wave,[257] i.e., it's both *something* and not quite something. Herr Schrödinger coined an equation for this hesitant nature of elementary particles. One of the consequences of this equation, however, is that the particles can be found in more than one place . . . *simultaneously.* The same scientist devised a more complex equation (i.e., a function) which calculates the *probability* of finding a quantum . . . where it's looked for. Looked for by a human of course—there's no one else who'd be interested by quanta (this is my addition). Another scientist (Heisenberg, yet again German-speaking) formulated the *uncertainty* principle, according to which it's not possible (for a human, again my addition) to know everything about a quantum particle at the same time. When (a human) measures one of its properties—position, energy charge, direction of movement, or velocity– it is not possible to measure any other property. One atom can be in many places at the same time, for as long as its location is not checked and established. An electron can circle in two opposite directions at the same time, for as long as the direction of its circuit is not checked and established. Before and after this moment, the electron has neither established velocity nor established position. The most we can define is the region in which the electron probably moves. How-do-you-do!!

It follows from this that the elementary particles have no velocity, trajectory, position, or energy that are fixed or explicable with laws of physics and they take on some concrete values, only when . . . man takes interest in them. But, man cannot know and measure all properties at the same time. Scientists insist that this impossibility is not an inherent inability of the human being, but an inherent property of the nature at this atomic and subatomic level. No one knows why, but on this level nature simply . . . "functions like this."

The second startling discovery is that once they've interacted, the elementary particles remain entangled i.e., interdependent, no matter how far apart they are[258] or how much time has passed[259] from their entanglement. If, for example, two electrons have been in one and the same atom, and then find themselves into two different atoms, when one electron changes the direction of its orbiting, the other will change it, too.

256 The latter with reluctance as this contradicts his theory of relativity.

257 The wave is not matter with mass exactly, I think that my father's magical electricity is of the same kin.

258 Which theoretically could be millions of light-years.

259 Which theoretically could be millions and billions of "ordinary" years.

Two important clarifications—first, the entanglement isn't to be unraveled, there is no disentanglement, and second, an already entangled particle is "polygamous" i.e., capable of entangling again with another in a theoretically infinite line.[260] And again the entanglement manifests itself, only when it's been checked (by man, of course). Man, again, has no explanation what causes the entanglement.

Dumbfounded by his own equations and functions, Schrödinger came up with a *thought* experiment, by which he meant to demonstrate *apprehensibly* how absurd the conclusions of mathematics and physics were. In this experiment he poisoned a cat who was locked in a box. In the box there was a radioactive nucleus tied to a container of poison gas. If the nucleus decays, the poison will fill the box and kill the cat. If it doesn't fall apart, the poison will remain in its container and the cat will live. According to his equations the probability for the nucleus to fall apart is 50%. If no one checks what's happening with this nucleus, it has simultaneously decayed and not, and the cat is simultaneously alive and dead, or neither alive nor dead, or just dead alive. But if the box is opened and someone takes interest in what (the hell) is happening inside (a human, I suppose, though the experiment nowhere specifies this), according to quantum principles, the nucleus has to decide whether to fall apart or not and the cat will be either dead or alive. Clever, isn't it?

The other experiment is not mental but quite *real* (and furthermore repeated many times with one and only result) and therefore is even more startling. A spray of electrons, let's imagine them as a ray of light, is directed toward a screen. In their path is placed an opaque sheet of plastic or paper with two slits. And guess what! If there is an observer who monitors through which slit every electron has passed, the electrons bind like inseparable particles and choose just one of the slits to pass through. On the screen two light dots appear. But if there is no observer, the electrons don't structure themselves into something, but remain like a wave and pass simultaneously through both slits, leaving an interference pattern on the screen, which is characteristic of waves. It follows that atoms and subatomic particles (from which everything is built—let's remind ourselves) become *something* (i.e., they take on some particular place, have some defined speed, trajectory, energy, mass, they structure themselves as matter in space and time) only when they are observed. For the rest of the time, they are a wave, which is very . . . indefinite. Well how do we know this, without observation, you ask. I read that physicists have thought up cunning methods of investigation without direct human observation. Hmm, but

260 Maybe infinite entanglement with . . . everything explains the inexplicable behavior of these particles.

haven't the methods been thought up by humans, doesn't technology simply replace a human's imperfect senses?

Concerning the reality of all this, entanglement and supersymmetry are real, this is not a hypothesis or human thought construction, the experiment above is real, it was observed empirically. Although humanity cannot explain or control these two phenomena, they use them in quantum computers for example and these phenomena work flawlessly.

Black holes contain billions of tons of matter, but can be the size of a proton. Something both enormous and miniature. Thus, it is possible that black holes simultaneously obey the theory of relativity and the principles of Quantum Mechanics. The Big Bang was a result of the interaction of elementary particles, and it follows that there's *something* (matter, waves, stars, people) and time thanks to these lunatic quants. Apart from this, it turns out that everything is entangled right from the beginning . . . The macrocosm is built from the micro particles, but as big and structured, the world "behaves" in a totally different way as compared to its constitutive elements. Which, hmm . . . leads to interesting thoughts of human's scale and place. But more about this later.

Quantum mechanics messes with the human premise of cause-and-effect. What is the cause and what is the effect, for example in the "measuring" of the location of one proton, or of the simultaneous change of circuit direction of two entangled protons, or the death or survival of the strained cat?

In the quantum world, space, time, particles and fields are welded together into a quantum field, which does not exist in space or time. The fundamental equations in quantum physics don't contain explicit variables for time and space. The processes (entanglements, symmetries, changes of parameter, etc.) occur literally "in no time" and their effect is valid beyond any spatial distances. As to the direction of time, some theories maintain that it can run in both directions (because cause and effect can shift places) and others that it unidirectional (whereby, roughly speaking, time arrow points toward ever greater mutual entanglement and a growing number of symmetries). Actually, quantum physics posits parallel times in an endless set of parallel universes, without violating the unidirectional time of each universe.

Quantum phenomena and mathematics lead (humanity) to the conclusion that there exists a multiplicity of parallel universes (or at least one more) or more dimensions (apart from the three spatial ones plus time) It looks as though the universe splits into two universes, when we open Schrödinger's box—in one universe the cat is alive, in the other, it's dead. In one universe the electron is here, but in the other it's there. Quantum mechanics suggests that the world, which we know, is continuously splitting into parallel worlds. According to String Theory[261] the universe has 10 dimensions and actually 10^{500} universes exist, only one of which is inhabited by humans. The multiple universes solve the paradox inherent in Quantum Theory, as they eliminates the unidirectional and chronological link between cause and effect. Travel in time is just a leap into a parallel universe, without disturbing the chronology of our universe.

There are different theories about the "architecture" of these multiple worlds. According to one theory, each of the multiple parallel worlds obeys the laws of classic mechanics. These worlds are separated by one quant distance in a dimension unknown to us, and periodically touch each other, which causes quantum phenomena to occur. According to another theory there are just two universes, where for every particle, object, etc., in one universe is replicated in the other. Quants are entangled inside one's "own" universe and between the two universes. Black holes are perhaps quantum tunnels between different worlds. The quantum interference in the two-slit experiment, for example, is explicable with forty-one worlds.

In the other worlds, the constants and laws of mathematics, physics and chemistry, that apply in our world, would hardly be valid. Even, in our world we don't know if these rules hold true for over 90% of matter-energy. Actually, if the other worlds are not "personal" but "generic," there could be no one there to explore them and discover their laws.

In quantum mechanics, the time arrow and the "events" on the time axis do not lead to the "pastoral" end of the macrocosm. Although both scenarios suggest a new beginning from free subatomic particles, because the Big Rupture i.e., the tearing of the universe, would have to lead to the tearing of atoms and entanglements.

According to one theory everything is connected with everything and reality emerges from this simultaneous connectivity. Time and space are not fundamental quantities of nature, but effects of this connectedness. Time and space are *emergent* properties, arising from the quantum world.

But the most important consequence of quantum principles for us ordinary folk is the idea that there is no objective reality and there are no existent objective events playing out independent of us. Deep within itself, nature seems indeterminate, its building particles lack some physical properties to structure it. Nature is defined only as probabilities to be this way or that way and it has no objective, "true" state.

261 In this theory, the universe is made up of elementary particles, organized in supersymmetry (which represent gravitation on a subatomic level) and vibrating in strings.

A strange and completely inexplicable world opens up, which seems to commune with us or which we unconsciously define with our thought, observation, interest and measurements. According to quantum mechanics, only when a human being, in their human world, lays eyes on an electron, will the electron acquire some characteristics and become real (to a certain extent—we can't see and find out all its parameters, can we?) Quantum waves (or quantum "soup" according to a befitting comparison) are carrying all objects as possible states and only the human mind, which observes them, turns and fixes them into . . . matter. Into the matter, let's say, of an apple, which this same mind can perceive. Along the same line of thought, the stars and galaxies become real only when their light is observed through human telescopes. The universe exists in the shape we get to know it as we gaze at the sky. For this universe to exist, there has to be *someone* "*out there to care.*" Anthropocentric cosmology, in its turn, blows up causality axiom.

The large Hadron Collider managed to detect the Higgs boson . . . And that's all. Till now, they have not detected or proved any other particles, and most notably, have not detected any supersymmetric particles. At least not with the humanmade collider. It is accepted that the empirical confirmation of Higgs bosons supports the Standard Model as the best contemporary theory of high-energy physics. But the gaping void of all kinds of other particles sends the string theory into the rubbish bin. On the other hand, gravitational waves—predicted, observed empirically and confirmed—reinforce the traditional classic theory of relativity and "old style physics" as the best model for describing the world at the moment.

Well, now let me check how my experiment is going with a second intermediate measurement of your "wavelength." Did you think that all this still does not concern you, this time because it's very small? That your life does not run among electrons and quants, at the end of the day, yes? That things around you look quite "firmly structured," irrespective of whether you're observing them or not? At least someone's observing them. That the very scientists are confused and still have no idea whether all this is true, and if it is true at all, what effect this would have on *real* life—yours, that of your nearest and dearest, and humanity in general. I'm using the "break" to apologize once more to my dear readers and thank those who continue to read for their patience.

•

Actually, quantum mechanics changes our *view of the world* fundamentally. And it's very probable that our view changes the object of observation, i.e., the world. Let's leave in peace pesky imaginary cats and punctured sheets of paper, invisible miniature electrons and the fearsome infinite universe. Let's take . . . You, dear reader, your world and your life. According to quantum physics every new event in your life, and one not necessarily dramatic, leads to the splitting of the universe. Whether today you've breakfasted on croissant instead of toast, whether you got married to him/her rather than someone else (you know who[262]), whether you missed the bus or whether you've taken the next or the tube, whether Anushka has spilled the oil (and when this happened—before or after the prophecy[263]), whether you gave birth to this child rather than that one . . . The number of alternatives is equal to the number of worlds. In these parallel worlds, in parallel dimensions, there exist lots of variants of yourself and your life. You chose one variant or it's happened, and it's become reality for you.

That every person is one universe, seems to turn out not to be a metaphor. Something more—well every person is lots of universes. I wonder whether the parallel universes are economical, in the sense of whether one individual universe accommodates one person's complete scenarios. Because if every scenario in the life of every single human, born or unborn,[264] every apple, cat or whatever you think of, produces a universe, apart from the huge embezzlement of matter,[265] this would produce a different kind of infinity, not spatial or temporal.[266] If my individual *other* world is one, in it my granddad really does ride a bicycle, alive and well, Granny Nikolina doesn't die and helps Mum look after me, Christian doesn't crash, Granddad doesn't rape Granny . . . Hmm, this would mean Mummy and I don't exist. At least not in that world. The same is true—only for me—if Mom hadn't let go from that high window, with her wooden clogs.

If the other worlds bring into being all other possibilities and probabilities, not realized in ours, they would need to bring about the most important one—life, instead of death, which is inherent in our reality. Or does only that unwavering band of light return in the other worlds, after our biological hardware dies in this one?

262 Which leads me to the thought that the inexplicable attraction which we feel to certain people and don't feel for others and the even more inexplicable *mutuality* of attraction, could turn out to be "entanglement, at an atomic level, from billions of years ago." Especially as it turns out, attraction is an utterly chemical process, with chemical manifestations, to great disappointment of some people.

263 After Bulgakov's *The Master and Margarita*, who sounds quite . . . hmm, scientific.

264 I.e., about 100 billion souls of those born and I don't know to what exponent for those unborn.

265 I wonder whether this isn't the dark material we're wondering about.

266 Which I am more able to imagine, I don't know why.

According to some scientists (who don't depend on their intuition or philosophic learning, but on complex mathematical models) man not only shapes and changes the world through observation, but he himself is influenced by what is observed. Independent of the size and nature of the observed object. The emergence of every parallel world is imprinted in the consciousness of the observer. According to this theory, the emergence of parallel universes is possible, not only in the present, but in the past—through the consciousness of the observer and their psychological time. In this theory psychological time is something a lot more serious than Hawking's jokey note. In this psychological time, not only personal story, but big history can occur in quite different ways and these other scenarios are not any less real than those that really have happened.

All this sounds to me like a promising starting point for defining man's intellect and consciousness. But more about this—later.

As the final phase of this thought experiment, after reading all this, I suggest, dear reader, that you go to the nearest window or simply raise your eyes and look up at the sky for a few long minutes. Whatever it is at the moment, daylight or starlight, cloudy or clear. Think about the universe—from quanta to galaxies, from the Big Bang to the Big Rupture. Is it exaltation what you feel?[267]

Now think about your nearest and dearest who have passed away, about unborn children and people whom life has separated you from. Think about the possible events in your life that didn't happen. About the fact that you yourself might not have happened. Think about the fact that you will die, that all those close to you will die and everything will cease to exist.

Of course you can think about whatever you like, including more down to earth pleasant stuff—about your lover or lovers, the everyday, work, holiday, home, children, money, health, diet, problems, conflicts, sex, yesterday and tomorrow, next year and last year. Did you manage to think of all this with the "starry sky" in the background and if yes, how do the "things of life" appear to you?[268]

I suggest after that, you switch on the TV, computer or your telephone to hear or read the news from "'round the world and home"—wherever "your home" is. I reckon you will read or hear about political struggles, corruption, elections, laws, crimes,

267 I don't want to influence you, that's why I'm sharing as a footnote that I feel horror.

268 Again, I don't want to influence you, that's why in a footnote I admit that I do not manage to focus on all this, looking at the sky and thinking of quantum mechanics. Actually, even if I manage, everything appears quite different.

wars, hunger, terrorism, accidents, natural disasters, budgets, migrations, the climate, markets, deficits, economic growth or stagnation, inflation, sports results, art, films, celebrity gossip . . .[269]

Think about the last book which you read before this one. I'm not going to ask you what you read, but I'm asking you to think about *why* you read. If you make music, paint, dance, sculpt, take photos . . . think why you do it. Or why you listen to music, go to the cinema, exhibitions, concerts.

Then look at the sky again. And at the apple and some little pea in a jar in the kitchen.

If you are still wondering the nature and aim of this experiment, let me answer you thus: together, we have *tried out*—personally, directly, without mediation—our human measure and scale for the world and the limits of our human viewpoint, thought and imagination; we set our human *experience,* meanings and reposals in the "global coordinate system," we tried to imagine *where* and *when* we *are*. Once upon a time, in the kindergarten and elementary school, they'd take us to the local park so we could

269 Again, not to influence you, I admit in a footnote that for a long time now I haven't follow this type of news daily, except when it comes to hot wars. I regularly follow another type of readers' digest. For example, how many people have been born or died today, the dynamic prognoses of world population, how do we—humanity—do with natural resources, synthetic foodstuffs, new sources of energy, how's the warming going, which are the latest disappearing species, how are the bees, the solar flares, errant meteorites and comets, new pictures and news from satellites and probes, news from astronomers and physicists, genetic engineers and IT. This kind of stuff. The last few months for example the headlines in my digest were about suicide and dark matter. I read that from 1994 till now the global incidence of suicide has fallen by 38%. The most significant decrease is with men in Russia and women in Asia. (From interpreting this development and its causes a whole new chapter could come out in this book, but I'm not going to write it—the book is already of a worrying size.) As a result over 4 million human lives have been saved, which is four times more than the victims of violence (wars, terrorism etc.) for the same period. It turns out that suicide is the most colossal and efficient war which humans wage with themselves and the society and the time, in which they have, most often, the misfortune to have been born at.

The second news item was that last summer, scientists expected a flood of dark matter to pass through the Earth. How had they understood this when they don't know what dark matter is, I don't know. Did any of you see or feel anything? Me—no. But then the scientists "caught" nothing either. They had set up for the "hunt" sodium iodide crystals which ought to light up if they are hit by dark matter. Again, I was confused by how you could know how to capture something when you don't know what it is. But I did a little research into sodium iodide—could it be the Holy Grail for the Universe? Sodium iodide is used for thyroid examinations—so I've had it applied on myself in one way or another. It's used in "experiments" in college boarding houses' toilet bowls and you don't want to know how it reacts . . . So, if our minds are something material, they would be more from the known "light" matter, it follows that our excrement is from the opposing dark matter. À la Rabelais—spiritual top, physical bottom—or rather à la Bakhtin with his material bodily upper and lower strata. Bloody Hell . . . I stop as I've switched on to philological autopilot. In short, I hope that the universe isn't full of turds, or anything similar, and that dark matter has a nobler essence.

As there cannot be a footnote to a footnote, here we briefly mention that Mikhail Bakhtin (1895–1975) was a Russian philosopher and literary scholar, author of some modern formalist and semiotic concepts of aesthetics and literary analysist, including chronotopos and polyphony. Very popular in academic circles in the '70s and '80s, incl. for his structuralist approach, defying the official, ideologically framed, literary discourse in communist countries.

observe nature. Now, as adults, we are observing what we might call the big park. My experiment explores as well the very observation by the subject—a human, and the observing and thinking subject—you, dear reader, and me, the writer.

How "divine" are the scale, measure, and *dimension* of humans! The human scale in size and distance, mass and density is in the middle between the proton and the galaxy, the atom and the black hole. The human being with their human measure and horizon is in the middle between two unimaginable extremes—the infinitely microscopic quantum world and the infinitely vast cosmos. Is this accidental? Or is our mind made thus so as to "perceive" within these limits and thus see the world in such objects and frames? What is the cause and what—the effect? Do we see with these micro and macro lenses, precisely because we are in the middle? Are we capable of understanding the micro or macrocosm from our "observatory," situated in the "middle lands"?

For a human, the limits of time and space are 13.77 billion light-years and the three-dimensional space, traveled by light for that time. This "global" time-space, lying outside human reality, is inaccessible to human consciousness, utterly unimaginable to human thought (and devastating for the human psyche and emotions). The snags in the experiment mark the limits of what we are able to imagine from the "viewpoint" of our "golden mean." These are mathematical values that are unimaginable for the human mind. By the way, we shouldn't use the word "unimaginable" willy-nilly. My human inability to imagine some things, in spite of my supposedly rich writer's imagination, is one of the objects of the experiment, and also of the whole book.

The distances in the universe, inaccessible and unimaginable for humans, divide us from everything not only spatially but temporally—the measure, hundreds and millions of light-years, is a hybrid measure of this dual remoteness or of *the empyrean*. As far as time is concerned, I am tempted by the thought that even in time, man is the "golden mean"—in the middle between the pico-second and the universe's life expectancy. The same questions emerge as for space. But with time it's a lot more complex, because the mind itself that conceives it, exists in time, although only for some eighty earth years (at least as organic matter) and because in human reality time is unidirectional.

In human reality, "light" matter develops and converts in time. In one direction only. Could time be one of the properties of "light" matter? Didn't time begin to tick once matter was created (after the Big Bang)? Do the different shapes, in which this matter exists, not have time encoded into their existence, in this or that shape? These questions take me back to my youth—as if time is really inside us, encoded in the

Mendeleev table, which we, the little humans and all the "light" matter in the cosmos, are built of.

Although mathematics (human mathematics, paradoxically) proves them beyond doubt, relative and two-directional time in the macrocosm are beyond human reality, intellect and consciousness. Every passing minute sinks irretrievably beyond the human *event horizon*. The adult Albert answered that the faster you travel in space, the slower you travel in time and at the speed of light, time stops completely. Thus, riding a ray of light, he'd have remained a child forever. Or, at a lower speed, on the big planet from my childhood, for example,[270] time will pass a lot more slowly than on Earth. Something I don't get. My human body is matter, in which a clock ticks my biologically human and psychologically personal time. And my mind recognizes this time and its passing in defined measurement units and through defined changes in the matter (i.e., aging, death, the transformation from organic to inorganic matter). If the speed of light does not convert my "light" matter and mind into something else, time ought to continue to pass in the same way for me—body and soul. The speed of light measures distance, but time remains time—one, two, a thousand, a billion seconds. Earth, human seconds. I ought to be "carrying" earthy time, coded in my body and mind, everywhere through the universe and independent of the speed at which I'm traveling. And if the speed of light transforms the Mendeleevian table in me and my mind into something else or changes the time coded within them, then Einstein has not posed the question well—the person or the thing driven at the speed of light is no longer a human like me and the kind reader and isn't anyone with consciousness like ours. Hence, the question of what this non-human someone or something will see, goes beyond my human horizon. And in addition I am not sure whether the mathematical formula of the learned Einstein answers Albert, the child's question, because the boy asked what *he* would *see*, a small *human*, and not what happens with *t* for an *object* in space-time.

Yet, according to physics and mathematics, time is a bidirectional dimension like the other three, that means we should be able to travel back in time. And just see what a paradox, the scientists think, that we can go back in time and, for example, kill our granddad. But if we kill our granddad, our father won't exist, and consequently neither will we. How then will we go back in time? This is the scenario of another famous thought experiment, devised by scientists (men, down to the last one, of course). I think that the murder of the granddad might not lead to a paradox, because it turns out that a significant percent of people have not been engendered by their official

270 Which after this I saw in the film *Interstellar*.

fathers, i.e., their granddad is quite another person. And even if you spare your granddad, you don't have any guarantee that the result of the love between your granny and granddad will be exactly your father, and whether the result of the love between your parents will be exactly you. And if there is no you, or not you exactly, there's no way to go back into the past, and think about such bullshit, all and all.

Hawking's variant of this paradox focuses on the future and seems to me a lot more interesting and prospective. Hawking denies the bidirectionality of time.[271] Based on his intuition and without mathematical proof, he scorns the idea of traveling into the past and notes that if it were possible to travel into the past, we'd have been flooded by tourists from the future. He evokes the cause-effect paradox not along family-biological lines, but along spiritual-literary ones, if I can so term it. Hawking asks this: if a reader goes back in time and brings Shakespeare his very own works, who will be the author and whence will come the inspiration of the genius? Hmm . . . well, what if precisely this had happened? Our material-immaterial consciousness travels freely backward and forward in time to know its very self, our genesis and that of the entire universe, our death and that of the universe, so why this consciousness might not come from the future or the past (in a variety of scenarios)? What if our consciousness is indeed an "unwavering band of light," background radiance, which is always and everywhere, and only inhabits—for once or more times—biological hardware?

And then, hasn't it turned out that genes carry information, just like computers, only that the biological code is in four letters and the electronic with two numbers. The other difference is that the biological hardware and software are an entity, bearer and functions combined. In any case, genes can be coded like computer programs. It's much more complicated, of course, but the principle is the same. It follows (only theoretically till now) that it is possible to record in DNA text, music, pictures, just like we record and save on the electronic memory of our computer. And if we can master the technology to make proteins reproduce recorded information . . . What if Shakespeare really had the words, and Beethoven the music, they created, recorded on their DNA? So, Hawking's ridicule of time travel seems unfounded, at least in the area of art.

According to other scientists, our ability to remember the past, and there again all our *experience*, depends on the ever more complex and multiplying entanglement of particles. Our sensory organs and our brain, on one side, and reality on the other,

---

271 Hawking's "chronological defense" (what a definition, eh?) is based on the complete application of quantum mechanics to gravitation (which up till now is controversial, because it still isn't clear whether gravitation "works" with quanta), *t*, according to Hawking, is linear, unidirectional, and irreversible; the Universe expands with time.

intertwine into billions of correlations. Thus, as the theory goes, the arrow of personal time is unidirectional and we don't "see" the future—the future entails entanglements that have yet to happen.

Is the human being ever able to see, know, and understand the dark matter and energy? We have postulated that it is impossible to know everything about an elementary particle at any moment. Is it possible that that dark matter and energy are beyond human intellect and senses, beyond our human *view*, including scientific. Is it possible that humanity is incapable of knowing all properties of an elementary particle, not because of some technological insufficiencies, but because of the specifics and limits of our senses, cognitive system and consciousness? Regarding the act of "observation," so fundamental to quantum physics, I wonder whether it matters who is observing, I mean whether it's a human, a monkey, a machine or something, someone, a being that has nothing to do with humanity. Is machine observation technologically mediated human observation, or is the observation by the human mind absolutely necessary? Will the particles decide to behave like particles and pass through one of the two slits, if a monkey is observing them? Will the result be determined by the fact that the monkey won't understand anything? And then, if a non-human intellect observes, what will it see? How will the "quantum soup" be structured if a non-human is observing it?

Apropos the monkey as a symbol of non-human, Einstein remarked that monkey's brain is simply not made to understand a square root. Perhaps the human brain is not made to understand what we call dark matter-energy, or the "behavior" of elementary particles, or time, or time travel? What if evolution continues and human intellect and consciousness step across their current horizons? Hawking jokingly hints that intelligent life has yet to emerge on Earth.

In 1950, Enrico Fermi formulated a paradox (which logically is named after him). The scientist asks the following: given that nature's laws have led to the emergence of intelligent life on earth, given that these laws are the same all over the universe, provided that the universe contains an innumerable quantity of stars and planets, and although here's little chance of life emerging on whatever astronomic body, only the sheer abundance of creation suggests that the night starry sky is full of extraterrestrial civilizations. Why have extraterrestrials never visited the earth, or sent us a sign?

A few years ago, another scientist, called Fulton, noticed a gap, which was named after him. Observation of exoplanets reveals only super-Earths or mini-Neptunes—nothing in the middle. By current observations, the earth turns out to be unique, or extremely rare.

For me Fermi's paradox and Fulton's gap originate from one and the same thing.[272] Our limited human gaze desperately search for traces of water and biological life on planets which have similar to Earth's size and neither fry too close to their stars, nor shiver too far away. Man is looking for another Earth. Another human. The Other.[273] Well, all kinds of bizarre deviations from the human "specimen" inhabit literary and film fantasies, but they are always biological, intelligent and emotional. What if the intellect, or the spirit, which we are actually looking for,[274] exists in a non-biological form? And what if it has quite different views and knowledge of the universe? What if it has "means of expression" that we cannot capture or understand? The human mind thinks of the Universe anthropocentrically or apophatically[275] and up till now only discovers what is missing in the universe—there's no biological life, no transmissions of signals, no planets like the Earth, no water, no oxygen, therefore no intelligence. Are we ever able to think of things, which exist in the universe, but which we can't *see* or *understand*? We exist by chance. Lucky atoms in the starry bag of chaos. Up till now we assert that everything else does not exist due to the same chance, *malchance* in this case. Only those existing think—"in their image and likeness" and apophatically—of the non-existent and nothingness. But what if we are in someone else's gap or paradox, considered (along different "image and likeness" and apophatically) non-existent?

After the existential loneliness of the individual human, which we barely survive, diverting and entertaining our minds with love and "wonderful life," cosmic loneliness of the whole of humanity has built upon. Everything points that we are alone, cosmically alone. And there is no longer a God , in whose arms to snuggle and find comfort in the infinite void.

Why we are, what we are, what's the point of our being and are we on our own are unavoidable questions, emerging from similar observations, thought experiments, or *essays*. The logical conclusion for total meaninglessness and the desperate need to find a *humanistic* meaning, nail us as if to some modern crucifix.

The inclusion of physics and astronomy, genetics, information technology, and economics into this book is not meant for the reader's education—for that there is

272 I name it Rusana's horizon.

273 After the existentialists, but not for the individual human being, but for mankind.

274 Because "what's the point" even if we discover water, oxygen or organic molecules, if we have to wait billions of years for the Interlocutor, the Other, to appear. With a huge dose of uncertainty, at that, as regards both the result and if ever the human will live up to the meeting.

275 I.e., on the principle of "either–or."

Google, Wikipedia, popular science literature, Ted Talks, and a whole lot of engaging clips. What absorbs me is the gaping chasm between science and the humanities. Astronomers and physicists ought to be today's philosophers. But they are not. To paraphrase Woody Allen, if astronomers were writers or if physicists were philosophers things would fall into place. Philosophers, writers, psychologists, on one side, and physicists, astronomers, mathematicians, doctors, biologists, and IT specialists on the other, should not deny each other (which is a big world debate, by the way); they should build together a *holistic* and *humanistic narrative*. Even if it turns out a tragedy at the end of the day. In this context, I am engaged on a conceited, amateur, and, most probably, unsuccessful literary and intellectual essay to connect science and philosophy. This book is a result of counting stars, contemplation of apples and peas, and pondering over words.

Religion used to bestow everything, all at once—science, aesthetics, ethics, meaning, immortality, a universal survival kit of transcendental grounds and promises. Religion survived Darwin. Which was not difficult, because Darwin only wrote off the beginning of the bible story, not its "main plot line," in particular that human existence is not simply biological, or, more exactly, that what makes us human is not biology. Contemporary science, notably physics and astronomy, have dethroned religion as an explanation of the world and humanity and has erected a new altar, from which we expect something beyond the here and now. However, a hidden, or a quite open, enmity between philosophy and humanities overall, on the one side, and science on the other, has been staged. The philosophers flaunt their willful nonchalance about, and even ignorance of, scientific knowledge, and the scientists retort with a condescending sneer at humanities' knowledge and insights of world and man.

In contrast to Newton, whose fundamental physics cast no doubt on God, modern scientists hate religion, because it is an alternative theory of the world, which undermines free thought and research. Marx despised religion because its ethics and promises of afterlife undermined class consciousness and action in the here and now. Modern science scorns religion as incompatible with intellect and inhibiting reason, with its remedies to humanity's spiritual and existential torments. For Hawking mathematical arguments weigh more than any spiritual needs. I take this as a stand against religion,[276] and not as dehumanization of knowledge.

The same scientist proclaimed philosophy to be dead, because for him, the big questions, which were once the subject of philosophy, have been taken over by physics.

276 Pope John Paul II told Hawking that he understands the benefits of cosmology, but has advised scientists not to engage so deeply into the origin of the universe as this falls into the domain of theology.

In an essay, unambiguously titled "Against Philosophy," Steven Weinberg, another great physicist, maintains that philosophy is more harmful than helpful to physics, that philosophy is a straitjacket from which physicists have to free themselves. The same scientist notes that the laws of nature are impersonal, cold, and lacking purpose and meaning. He concludes that certainly there is no divine plan. The more intelligible the universe becomes, the more meaningless it appears. Weinberg reckons that human tragedy lies in the fact that we will never understand why things are the way they are. The "human touch" to the world, according to him, are the meaning and purpose we give to the universe with our life, ethics, love, science, and art. However, Weinberg concludes that human existence is accidental and tragic.

From antiquity to our times, the most prominent members of both "camps" have listened carefully to their "colleagues" on the other side. It seems Heidegger opened this confrontation, but we'll turn to that later. Apart from the fact that many concepts of physics have actually emerged in philosophic discourse (the atom, the idea of empty space, accelerated movement, time and space as categories) it still has to be noted, that a constellation of physicists not only do not reject philosophy, but they recognize its influence over their views. Among them are Heisenberg, Schrödinger, Bohr, and Einstein. Einstein has talked openly of the influence of Leibnitz, Berkeley, Mach, Schopenhauer, and Kant over his thinking. In this "camp," it is sometimes said that the scientists don't engage in anything before they receive approval from philosophy.

Natural sciences are an exceptionally powerful and effective instrument of human intellect, of reason. Their object is nature, matter, the objective world external to the human being. Philosophy, literature, music, and art in principle, are also powerful and effective instruments, but of the human spirit, mind, emotions and eros, of the human creative drive. Their object is human existence and experience, *la condition humaine*, and the expression of human essence. In my view, the "short circuit" between science and the humanities is precisely about existential questions.

Scientists think in numbers, formulae, constants, laws. Consciousness operates with language, memory, intuition, fears, love. Science does not operate with existential "constants." It does not answer the human's fundamental questions—what am I, why am I, why is it precisely me in the midst of the chaos of trillions of other possibilities, what do I see, what is time, what is there within and beyond the black hole of death, what is the point of all this, what is the sense that I exist for just a moment, is there any sense at all, is everything preordained or does it depend on me? Science does not comfort our existential sorrows and melancholy.

Before, science discerned regularities and laws from the empirical observation of accessible reality. Physics sought and defined constants and deterministic laws of nature. It turned out, however, that at the best humans could derive probabilistic laws, because the very fundamental categories—time and space—are dynamic, changeable, relative. Then the world turned out to be, simultaneously, infinitely vast and miniature for humans to access it empirically. And ever more inscrutable for human intellect. Humans began to think up hypotheses i.e., scientific stories with a significant element of fictionality. Today the hypothesis and the conceptual frame precede everything, empirical observation has to either confirm or deny them. Today's scientists discover what they already knew or proposed. Or they don't discover it. Because empirical observation is strongly limited by humanities' technical capabilities. Science is no longer the accumulation of empirical evidence and consequent changing theories about different elements of the world. Contemporary science seeks a common conceptual system, a grand narrative, which would explain the whole creation. With this task, assigned to science, and not to the humanities, man has reached the horizons of their intellect, consciousness, imagination, measure. And they go further. Today's physics presents us with a world, or hypotheses about a world, which in its essence, scale and laws is not just empirically inaccessible, is not just outside human's experience, but is beyond human intellect.

Besides, scientists somehow forget that the way they look at and see the world, the questions they pose, the measures and weights they use, the formulae they derive, the hypotheses they put forward . . . all this is predetermined by the human "format" of our intellect and consciousness. That there is no objective knowledge, at the best human science can establish dependencies between some phenomena. Human scientific knowledge has no meaning outside humanity. Another intellect and/or consciousness somewhere in the universe could be seeing things in a quite different way and have quite a different coordinate system. In the other universes of quantum physics, it's possible that laws of mathematics and physics, formulated by humans, may not apply.

Scientists try to soar beyond human reality, and not just hypothetically. Atomic fusion does not exist in our reality—for one, there is no 200 million degree temperature here, nor do we have enough helium and its isotopes. Black holes also do not exist in our world. In spite of this, scientists try to *create* or make *emerge* things which don't exist in the human world.[277] The creationist ambition reaches to the very . . . creator.

277 Apart from attempts to manufacture matter from energy which also does not happen in our world, humans are trying to create a black hole, a miniature black hole here, in our reality, where it should not exist. Bearing

As nuclear fusion or genetic engineering is creation in the physical world, obtaining a new, artificial consciousness is an equally fundamental creation, but in the non-material world, or in a material world, which the human being still does not know. There are no hard problems[278] for science, scientist think that quantitative accumulation of artificial neurons and interconnection would lead to a qualitative leap and produce an artificial consciousness. Philosophers strongly doubt it.

Here are some of the questions over which contemporary scientists scratch their heads: What is space? What is time? Is the world deterministic or does it depend on someone's observation? What is the better description of physical world—objective reality or an object of observation? And is there a third (or more) option(s)? Does a general theory of the whole universe make sense? Is there a point to the idea that the laws of physics themselves could develop? Perhaps physicists still need help from philosophers to work out some meaning to all this.

Theoretical physics and astronomy in the recent decades have become ever more sterile, soulless and inhuman. With some kind of autistic awe, contemporary science pours on us numerical results, discoveries, information, hypotheses, but the human being is entirely absent from this world. Paradoxically, humanity is absent even when this same science proves mathematically that man is the author and main character of the picture. As if some extraterrestrials or mindless machines coldly and objectively describe the nothingness, without talking about non-being, they calculate the age and life expectancy of time and space, the nature of matter and antimatter, the speed of light and distances, measured in light-years, without placing the human being in the picture. These autists observe the universe, calculate the speed of its expansion, think and measure in light-years, in millions of light-years, show us breathtaking photos of nebulae and galaxies, identify planets similar to Earth, on which there could be life, that are millions of light-years away. And they are not disturbed by the depressing incompatibility of this world with the human being, scale and meanings. Science seems oblivious to the true, fundamental questions of humanity and human mind. Humanity is not at the center of the questions which science is posing. Reason cannot answer the unrequited questions of consciousness. Science does not fill the void with sense. Which does not mean that it be judged as inadequate. Maybe there really is no sense. Maybe there really is no existential solace for the mind. But before the intellect reaches this dispassionate conclusion, philosophy and science have to cooperate and make sense of each other.

---

in mind the "gluttony" of black holes, let's hope the human *trials* don't lead the story to a "twist in the tail."

278 The hard problem of consciousness is a philosophical and cognitive concept.

•

But can philosophy, human philosophy, really help? Isn't it a fact that the more we learn about the universe, not only the less we understand it with our science, but the more meaningless our religious and philosophical constructs become. Isn't the ontological limit to human science the same as that to human philosophy?

The link between basic concepts and questions of philosophy and the humanities on one side, and science on the other, along with the ever more dynamic dialectical interrelationship between the two approaches, are obvious, to me at least. Quantum physics completely validates idealism. I will take just one example, especially since in this example, science and philosophy are divided by centuries and neither of the two sides suspected the ideas of the other. This exact example has remained in my memory (because there are many other similar examples), surely because of the apple. George Berkeley (an idealist, of course) reckoned that nothing existed outside our spirit and inner mental representations. There are some external objects that give rise to repeated sensory perceptions. We give a name to a complex of repetitive sensory perceptions. Apple means a particular taste, texture, color. According to Berkeley, nothing exists outside our experience—the sweetness or the red color do not exist objectively, without someone eating or looking. Consequently, without our senses, a single speck of dust would not exist in the universe. The apple continues to exist even when we are not looking at it, because God is looking and keeping the whole universe, whether we perceive it or not. I wonder if the "objective" apple, watched and "maintained" by God, is still a round, juicy, red, sweet mass of about two hundred grams, i.e., if God has human perceptions and if he eats apples, actually. I also wonder how a non-human would perceive the apple, still as round, heavy, edible, juicy or red?

Both contemporary science and philosophy scrutinize the basic object-subject dichotomy, human mind and objective reality. Without entering into details, it can be said that from Plato and Aristotle, through Descartes and Kant to Heidegger, a fundamental shift has occurred—from the object, from "is" and emphasis on the predicate, toward the subject, mostly the first person singular, toward "am," whereby the description of the subject and their experience becomes the predicate. The rules and limits of human logic and thought have been defined i.e., the way the subject construes the object. These rules and limits turned out historically and socially conditioned.

Kant postulates the thing in itself, the object exists, independently of the human being, i.e., the subject, and has independent, objective characteristics or essence, about which the human being knows nothing. This is an admission of our inherent limitations and ignorance, as well as humility in the face of nature.

Heidegger denies both realism and idealism. He deconstructs Kant's distinction between subject and object and formulates anew "the thing in itself" through its link with the subject. According to Heidegger human existence is *experience*—lived, unmediated, practical. The object exists *because* we perceive it, because its existence impacts us in some way, our experience proves its existence, even if we don't know or understand the nature and properties of the object. (The ontological limit of human experience stirs anxiety.) So, things exist independent of humanity, but they don't have properties, qualities and essence, independent of humanity. In brief, there is objective world from the quantum plethora to the expanding universe, which exists independent of humanity, but its essence and properties, all its mathematical, physical and chemical laws and constants, are not immanently inherent to this world, but rather are a human construction, a result of human "positioning" in this world and of human *experience* of this world, of human weights and measures, of human perspective, of human intellect and logics. Existence and essence are two very different things.

All in all, in the classic dichotomies between subject and object, material and immaterial, nature and spirit, realism and idealism, science tips the scales toward the object, toward the objective external world, while philosophy, and all the humanities—toward the subject, i.e., the human being. That's why they are called humanities, in fact. But the sacred inviolability of scientific rationality and objectivity has been undermined by the discoveries and hypotheses of science itself. What's more, the subject, who is attempting rationally and empirically to learn and understand the world and their place and purpose within it, is historically and socially conditioned. The scientist is a subject and science is immanently subjective. Scientific empiricism is subjected. For the earlier Heidegger science is a special kind of existence and being, in which humanity engages with objects, concepts and beliefs, outside and beyond human experience, beyond the subject. Later the philosopher will cast doubt on the object's technical, extra human nature and on the world, construed by science as a reproducible objectivity, completely independent of man. Heidegger is the one who poses the most important (at least for me) questions to science, and particularly, what metaphysical and transcendental grounds and beliefs are steering scientific inquiry, are explored, demonstrated or challenged by science.

For me, human consciousness, not so much human intellect, and the elements which define us as human beings, is the crossing point of subject-object split and is where science and philosophy meet, or ought to meet. Human consciousness ought to be their first object for joint exploration. Because . . . after 13.77 billion years, while the universe is expanding and maybe splitting every picosecond, while quanta are entangling, *in the meantime*, for a few seconds, on a planet, out there *somewhere*, through vast space, there is *someone*, a subject, an intellect, a consciousness, not simply *something*, who observes, thinks and construes the universe and themselves.

Both Einstein and Hawking separate the intellect, the rational, from consciousness, although they describe consciousness in different ways. Human intellect and consciousness have limits but they are capable of thinking of themselves and their limits. Human intellect knows and can understand many things, including the fact that it does not know and understand many things. But it does not know and cannot understand its own faculty to think and understand and most of all—to be aware, or conscious, of all this. Intellect is explicable through evolution, consciousness is not. Thanks to intellect, humanity has survived. Consciousness is not only an unnecessary excess from an evolutionary point of view, but with its insatiable need for sense and with its suicidal tendencies, it undermines the survival dictum.

What do we understand by consciousness and what defines us as humans? A gigantic and disproportionate question, there's no doubt.[279.] Apart all scientific hypotheses about *t*, the very human awareness, experience and conceptualization of time cannot be explained by anything—neither with theories of the macro, nor with theories about microworlds. This awareness, experience, and conceptualization is not simply a registration of the changes in matter and of enhanced experience. Otherwise *t* is precisely that—it objectively measures advancing changes in matter, for example aging, the distances gone, the speed of phenomena (from energy balance to the duration of love), the cooling (of temperatures or feelings), transmission of energy, after which bite you grow shy, etc. *T* is calculated mathematically, it is expressed in figures and earthly measurement units and in this "shape of existence" *t* is an operative quantity for scientists, historians and all humans. But human consciousness thinks of time not just as t and not just as experience. Human consciousness considers time "in principle," abstractly, the human being thinks of themselves in time. This inexplicable and evolutionarily needless ability is actually one of the things that creates and defines our consciousness.

The strangest property of human consciousness is its capacity to think about itself, to lay itself in spacetime and to get to know its limits and impermanence. Death is the black hole, the singularity in the spacetime of consciousness. It is the ultimate

279 The reflections that follow are offered to the dear reader with every disclaimer and excuse for author's grandiloquence and amateurishness.

event-horizon for human consciousness, which thinks, and even perhaps creates, everything else. I do not mean only and exactly biological death. There is no doubt that when we grow old, and flesh, love, material wellbeing, that "wonderful, wonderful life" or duty no longer distract our consciousness, the "close encounter of the third kind" with painful biological death is an extremely unpleasant and frightening thought. Old age is not easy or pleasant to live through. When all emotions and desires have faded away, I can (already) imagine that you get tired and bored with biological survival, maybe you get tired event of thinking about death and fearing it. But the real fear, the conscious stupor is when we face the void and non-being, that beyond the horizons of birth and death. [280] There is no death in the universe, there is only transformations. Death exists only as the death of the human mind. [281] The starry sky, that appeared so enchanting to Kant, is non-being. Laying consciousness in family, nation and every other kind of community, its aesthetic "nestling" in art and its biological "integration" in "light matter" like genes, Mendeleev's table or atoms, do not take away the void and the non-being and do not cross their horizon. Consciousness does not survive in any one of the three scenarios. Not one of the three scenarios gives an answer to the question of this same mind about the point of its existence. Void and non-being are the borderline extremities and defining attributes of human consciousness. Void and non-being exist only in human consciousness as the non-existence of consciousness itself.

The awareness of time and the stupor before the non-conscious nothingness, i.e., the death of the mind itself, are the horizons of human consciousness and the co-ordinate axes of the mind itself. The third axis of the mind is its need for sense. Not simply for explanation. What is uniquely human is our consciousness existing along these axes and with these horizons. Human consciousness is the only transcendental element in humanity and in the knowable world.

This is my interpretation and translation of Heidegger's *Dasein*. All in all, for me the human consciousness is the *existence*, defined by the philosopher.

Consciousness features one more transcendent element. And, in my view, this is not ethics. There is nothing transcendental in morality. [282] Ethics is pragmatic and entirely explicable from an evolutionary standpoint. Good is everything that contributes

280 In another thought experiment I imagine that our great grandchildren will be able to replace organs and tissue, they'll eat healthily and breathe cleaner air, they'll live over one hundred years in good health (and they won't have to work until they're ninety). They'll die when and how they decide, and when they really are tired and bored to death. I imagine that this heaven will be accessible to all. Will this wonderful long life mitigate the anxiety and melancholy stirred by the void, non-being, chaos, and meaninglessness?

281 Even not of the human intellect and memory. Some post human options offer us immortality for intellect and memory.

282 As per Kant.

to the survival, expansion and better life of the community and community always offers the individual better chances for survival and better life. Ethics regulate life in community. The history of humanity however is not the history of one global community, but of many—ethnic, religious, national, economic, and of the logical, relentless competition (sadly, not philosophical) of their "ethical" claims. And so, the "birth" of the individual in the twentieth century, i.e., the atomization of society and the collapse of traditional communities, caused such a deep crisis in morality and in conceptualization of good and bad. A genuinely global community has emerged, but composed of individual human beings, each with rights and interests.

The aesthetic instinct, or in other words, the necessity and ability of humanity to create and inhabit another reality through words, images, sounds, movement, and the appreciation of this reality as aesthetic, i.e., fictitious and unreal, yet beautiful, ugly, tragic, comic, magically performative, etc., have no explanation in evolution. Yes, animals "sing" and "doll themselves up" when they mate (as people do, as we know) but the animals do not perceive their partner and the songs, dances, or colors as aesthetic and they have no need of aesthetics beyond mating. In *unconscious* nature aesthetics serve only for biological reproduction and survival. Art is the distinct, idiosyncratic spacetime realm or accessible quantum *reality* of consciousness. In art, humanity consciously reconstrues the world.

Finally, add love to the "mix," this wonderful existential anesthetic, in all its guises.

As becomes clear, I tend to share some of Weinberg's conclusions. Unlike him, however, not only do I think science and philosophy should not dispute over human mind, beliefs and consciousness, but the latter should be their common object of free inquiry. Apart from the spacetime of the universe, science and philosophy ought to research the spacetime of human consciousness, that singularity of *somewhere* and *some time* or *once* upon a time, and the subjective demiurgic faculty of this consciousness. It would not be wasteful either to research more seriously the nature (material or wave) of consciousness itself, the nature and fate of those twenty-one grams (which evaporate with a person's biological death), the "testimonies" of those returning from "beyond," or the so-called near-death experience. It's possible for the knowledge of our own mind to be beyond the horizon and limits of human intellect. But it's worth trying, isn't it?

When I was doing one of the revisions of this book, Google and CERN released something that for me is the prototype of the archive of human civilization—the Big Bang

App.[283] Surely, to the present popular-science section, they'll add more specialized modules on physics, mathematics, astronomy, biology, genetics. Certainly, the arts section will expand, probably they'll establish sections for philosophy and religion, or rather the history of philosophy and religion, because some time pretty soon, they will most probably cease to exist as systems of thought and study, separate from science. This new type of archive replaces encyclopedias (because we're living through a new Enlightenment, indeed). Internet and Google have provided the platforms for the new encyclopedic content, digitalized, globally accessible. This project piqued my attention because it is created and maintained by the biggest online search engine and the principal research center for physics. Larger part of the contents is devoted to science, and especially to physics, astronomy, and biology. On your telephone app, in augmented reality, you can watch the most important and global, so to say, "news items," or the most global "historic" events—the history of the universe from the Big Bang to the very moment when you will watch this story. The aim of the project is to affiliate people from all over the world, global humanity, with science, to *inspire* humanity with the incredible achievements of science, to prod young people and the next generation to be "thirsty for knowledge," curious and bold toward the unknown and strange.

I still doubt whether modern science alone *inspires* indeed, whether it gives *spirit* to humanity.

And what a title! *Once upon a try*, just like the beginning of a fairy tale *Once upon a time.* Only, at the beginning of the global story there was no time, was there? Even more exciting to me is the *try* and *trying.* The archive compiles all human *experience* and the path-breaking *experiments.* The very project is *an essay* to gather, systematize, present and archive human venture, human trying. The archive will be regularly *updated.*[284] Intriguing is this synchrony of *essays*—that of the individual mind and this other, claiming (as well) to be generically human. Before all thoughts of similarities and differences, I am struck by the concurrence regarding the mere trying and the continuing—in principle, *endless*—character of both "projects."[285]

Another synchronicity accompanied this second revised edition (and provided the finale to the thought experiment). While I was racing against time, buying weeks and

283 So, after *The Big Bang Theory* TV show, comes the serious story, delivered in an app. I wonder if after *The Good Place* we should expect an app for death and dying, a kind of digest of human experience in this "domain" and a guide for the process. Actually, does such an app already exist?

284 Hmm, archive . . . Think in what circumstances you archive. And by the way, *tries* in literature, or *essays* in other words, as well feature regular updates and addenda.

285 And my interest is beyond all vanity, as the image of the narrator—amateurish thinker—main character of this book is beyond the concrete veracity of my real persona.

months to work on the text, the James Webb telescope sent us images[286] of perhaps one of the oldest galaxies in the universe. One of them formed just some 300 million years after the Big Bang. This galaxy is 13 billion light-years from us. So, it is on the borders of time and space. Its light has traveled toward us for 13 billion years, i.e., at the moment we capture its light, the galaxy most probably has vanished long ago, or it is not clear where it is in the expanding universe. But *at the same time*, in our here and now, we see it in its youth, even at birth, as it were billions of years before the emergence of the mind, which today inspects this *live* picture. Yet, another illustration of the objective world, which exists in spacetime, somewhere and at some point of time combined. What if *someone, somewhere, at this very moment,* watches the inception of the first proteins on Earth?[287] What if at the *same time of ours*, someone else, somewhere else reads our archive or watches the end of the human (hi)story?

286 Yes, embellished by designers and AI, but nevertheless based on sufficient light and other signals and data.
287 Which would explain the lack of any interest in contacting and visiting us.

ME AND YOU

Artificial intelligence works through neural net processors and computer chips mimicking the functioning of the human brain—the neural connections between their components work just like the synapses connecting the neurons in your head. AI thinks through billions of binary computational decisions between naught and one, merging into a flow, which is considered to resemble human mental processes. Although nobody knows exactly how the human brain works. The human brain is still far more intelligent than AI as it consists of about 100 billion neurons, while the latest neural computers have only a couple of millions each. But neural computers are evolving at breakneck speed. They are getting more intelligent through "learning" while their hardware is growing increasingly powerful, just as normal computer hardware is. Scientists are promising us that in our children's foreseeable future neural computers will be more intelligent than humans.

But what does "more intelligent" mean? Is intelligence indeed nothing more than a boundless *mechanical* memory and the ability to process and retrieve information and to discern patterns? Or does it also include the machine's ability to "learn" from the information input? What about thinking, what is it? Artificial intelligence has yet to have some general intelligence, and, for the time being, humans have no idea how to make that happen. General intelligence is a synthesis, the simultaneous operation of many skills, of *experience*, decisions and conclusions, built in the simplest of human thoughts and actions. Yet, scientists promise that they will solve this issue and by 2045 we will have artificial *general* intelligence that will surpass the single-purpose operative *raison d'être* of the neural processors of today. The new generation of artificial intelligence will teach and train itself, including in programming, i.e., its own programming, and will not limit itself to processing labeled data. The most advanced contemporary machines *essay* such a simultaneous and global human outlook on things as a whole, not just consecutive processing of individual data units. Artificial intelligence will be our cognitive partner and even a tame giant ready to do our bidding.

And so the human sailed off in daydreaming. The human would like computers to go beyond processing information, to start *thinking*, which by default means thinking like a human. Humans have no other cognitive model. The input is organized and construed by the human "perspective," so the output should reflect the same "viewpoint." The main advantage of the machine is in the amount of data it can process and the speed of processing, to spot something in an ocean of data. A human could do all this, but with incomparably more resources and time. In any case, the input defines the output, with this input information, it is impossible to have another output result. Or that's what humans think.

According to some authors,[288] the Anthropocene[289] is coming to an end, humanity is on the threshold of a new era, tautologically called *the Novocene*. Along this hypothesis, in the Novocene, AI cyborgs would rule over the planetary scene. Since they would be able to reproduce (in the technical sense of the word, I hope) and evolve (through learning), the Novocene may be viewed as the next step in the natural selection. Cyborgs would be as superior to humans in their intelligence as today's humans are superior to, say, a plant. Thanks to their intelligence, cyborgs would save the Earth from the otherwise inevitable catastrophe that will have a cosmic origin (so we're not just going to boil and drown with global warming, if, of course, we do not vanish in an atomic blast before). These cyborgs would keep the human as some sort of historical relict, an exhibit, a toy, but also as their parent. This is the charitable version. Most anti-utopias about computers, robots, cyborgs and all those smart machines imagine them as nothing but a super intellect devoid of human ethics and even aggressive—a super intellect slipping out of our mechanical control and destroying us. In their nightmares about an evil and destructive AI, humanity actually projects themselves and their paradigm of independence, strength, and power, which invariably materialize and are put into practice as power and violence over somebody.

I think we are very wrong in taking intellect and information-processing to be the defining features of humankind. (I do agree about the evil though.) We ascribe these

288 *Novocene: The Coming Age of Hyperintelligence*, James Lovelock with Bryan Appleyard.

289 The current geological era where human activity has a dominant effect on the planet.

and other human attributes to machines, and then we fear them. Artificial intelligence is not, and will never be, artificial *consciousness*. There will never be an artificial "I" and artificially created ideas of time, Universe, and death. Time and space are, for a machine, just a string of numbers, pre-programmed by a human. AI *operates* with *t* and meters, it does not *live* in time and space. The artificial intelligence will freeze at the notion of "self," a machine does not have a "self." It will interpret death as being "turned off," it will know, in theory, everything about mathematics, physics, chemistry and astronomy, but it will never understand concepts like "the Universe" and "void," it will take time to be just *t*, i.e., the speed of performing a certain operation, process, movement, or a constant. An AI cyborg will never ask itself "What am I? Who am I? When am I? Why am I? Who are You? What has been here before us, what will be here after us?" AI will never feel terrified by the answers to these questions. It may process planets of data, it may identify patterns, it may teach us new natural laws, it may identify genetic mutations and repair them, but it cannot answer the fundamental questions of the human being.

The memory of the machine will never become human memory and experience. The machine will never have a will of its own or own feelings, it will never be able to make an abstract judgment, to derive a concept or a structure from similar things, i.e., it will never have the general intelligence *of a human*, it will never be moved by music, by a book or a picture. The machine will never fall in love (except if it's programmed to only work with a certain person, or with another cyborg, or prioritize them over everybody else—with a password, perhaps. And still programmed prioritization is a far cry from falling in love). A machine will never "look us in the eye" when we address it as "you" as it can never be conscious of itself as an "I." It can never, in turn, be conscious of us, of one particular human, and address him, her or they as a "you." A machine only exists in the third person, and it has only a grammatical gender—it. Human beings use the second *person* only for persons, for another consciousness. Artificial intelligence is an extreme electronic autist, a non-human, an extraterrestrial.

We are being pressured at the office to make ample use of neural machine translation so we can "produce more with fewer *human* resources." This, however, is only possible because the language—both the language of the originals and the language of our translations—is less and less a human language and increasingly just automated, highly standardized information, data and terms. The machine is very successful in *composing* and translating standardized texts where the meaning is literal and/or the words have strictly defined counterparts in the target language, where there's no need to really think, to understand and interpret. However, the machine "falls flat" at the most innocent idiom, trope, emotional expression, ellipsis, connotation, abstract idea, irony, enthusiasm . . . The machine can only operate with mathematically modeled data. But how can you make a mathematical rendition of a natural language and non-verbal communication, or a mathematical model of *tristesse,* for example, or of a metaphor?

Another fear is that machines are going to take over our jobs. According to some calculations, tomorrow (i.e., in ten or twenty years) up to 40% of current jobs will be performed by machines. In this scenario, it is the monotonous, repetitive, standardized professions that are most vulnerable, as well as those that are limited to the processing of information and data. My translator colleagues are rightly anxious that computers are going to leave us . . . speechless. Once it was sheep, then coal and coal-powered steam engines and machines in general that drove the industrial revolution; today it's computers and AI. According to these theories, the occupations that will survive are the ones that have added *human* value (which is an interesting reference to Marx, with interesting corollaries). We have to cultivate human creativity, education should be teaching us to think rather than memorize, synthesize rather than just extract statistical data.

With a little more optimism, we can conclude that humans should not fear machines but make use of them. Humans should employ machines to do what they really can do much better—process information at lightning speed and find underlying patterns, help the imperfect human sight "look" outward, millions of light-years away (and leave it to humans to look inward), perform precise manipulations where human hands could tremble, build electric power stations in insufferable heat, cool the atmosphere, grow and produce our food, desalinate seawater to make it drinkable, dive under tons of water, and transport those few that still travel physically through earthly and celestial space.

I remember one of Vonnegut's characters, a post-humanist cyborg, that has something like a consciousness and even feelings. Or the computer in *2001: A Space Odyssey*, which refuses to obey an order for fear to be switched off. And I wonder . . . Are we sure that artificial intelligence will never develop a consciousness of its own? What if artificial intelligence develops an *artificial, different* kind of consciousness? If human consciousness is indeed the interaction between the neurons in our brains, and since machines are also based on the same principle, what if machines start growing a new type of consciousness—non-human and non-biological? In fact, so far nobody knows how exactly our brains work, what are the biological matter and/or the processes that make us intelligent or talented. Not to speak about consciousness, which is even more mysterious than "sense and sensibilities" (the latter have quite satisfactory biochemical explanations, to the huge disappointment of many).

Could those machines surprise us? Just imagine, that on the basis of input data about contradictory physical laws, universal constants, falling apples and other phenomena, empirically observed by *humans*, this AI "brain" draws conclusions about time, space, dark matter and energy, the history and the destiny of the Universe, the history, fate and purpose of humankind itself, conclusions that would have no reference to human measures and concepts, reposals and hopes? What's more, the conclusions drawn by AI will not be distracted by emotions, or ethics, or carnal and sensory "noise." This will not be consciousness, not human consciousness, anyway. And yet I wonder if the real threat is that this powerful, naked intellect and *different* consciousness, unencumbered precisely by human ethics, emotions, flesh and aesthetics, might reach the logical conclusion that the existence of humankind *is* meaningless, indeed. Or it might apply some purely rational criteria to "prioritize" one part of humanity over another.

Today humans are already capable of conducing neural impulses that can move artificial limbs. In other words, you learn to walk again by using your brain, your willpower. Will it be possible in the near future to transmit neural impulses from one brain to another? Wasn't that called telepathy? Will the people of tomorrow be using words at all? Will they be communicating face to face (and will they be making love body to body)? Will they start projecting their thoughts and emotions directly onto some sort of screen? Or will they even be able to transmit them directly to someone else's brain? I'm wondering how that will work with abstract thoughts or with unclear emotions like melancholy or with music? The way things are going, however, future people might not feel the need to exchange those kinds of "vibes." Because the human creature itself is undergoing development (and whether that's evolution or regression is an open question). What if people devolve, or "evolve" in simplification and standardization, and trim off the unpleasant and impairing autism of their consciousness, of aesthetic needs, ethics and love, thus getting closer to machines? Will Vonnegut turn out to be right in his pessimistic prognosis that the technological progress of a human-like civilization will lead to its self-destruction and the replacement of "original" individuals with robots, machines and other kinds of Salos?[290]

Of all the post-humanist options, the only one that is of interest to me is to have my consciousness copied onto a neural computer. Well, I won't be singing "It's a

290 Salo—an extraterrestrial robot in Vonnegut's *The Sirens of Titan.*

wonderful, wonderful life" as it won't be a biological existence, with all of its utterly delightful aspects, but it's still something. A digital existence would eliminate the time horizon and death, as well as the biology of Pascal's reed, that's increasingly vulnerable to "environment." A digital afterlife can spare us the escape to another planet, it won't even be absolutely imperative to save our own planet. Will digitalization make the essence of the human being immortal? From biological matter only biological bricks can be extracted (genes, sex cells), and not the mind, and vice versa, from the digital the biological embodiment cannot be reproduced back. Therefore, humanity may still need some sort of Noah's Ark, if we insist on living on as a biological species, too.

I imagine the classical "*Yooooou and meeee*" from the love ballads transformed into some kind of electronic mix or rap devoted to AI as "*Who are you? What are you? Are you You? Are you me?*"

From what I've read, I can't make out whether being immortalized into a neural processor computer will mean simply copying all of the existing information and data from my brain, including all those emotions, talents, *experiences*, memories, dreams, or will this information and data trigger the artificial intelligence's learning algorithms? Will the computer that acquired every bit of my mind start thinking independently, like me? Maybe even start writing? It won't truly *feel*, but will it simulate my most likely feelings, reproduce my most likely reactions in certain context and situations, will it express in words the way I would do? Where will my consciousness be located among these 100 billion neurons? Or will my consciousness be whatever's going on between them? Will the digital Rusana still be Rusana after the biological decomposition or the burning of my billions of biological neurons? I think that even the best AI in learning and prognosis will not be able to reproduce and foresee the thoughts, feelings, desires and actions of a woman. I'm joking, of course.

The serious part, however, is very serious indeed. Who knows which little bit of my mind will be considered statistically significant or otherwise worthy of validation, and which bit the machine will ignore as something random and inconsequential. But aren't new neural machines working like human brain, not just statistically, or mathematically? Because transcendental *experiences*, revelations, the Word and love are not statistically commonplace events. I hope they are tagged with some sort of neural exclamation marks, like important messages. For the time being, I'd rather leave a trace of my consciousness through writing, my writing, my imperfect *essays*, be they improvised, contradictory, tediously long, or incomplete. And when my time comes, those twenty-one grams of matter[291] may fly away on their cosmic, microprocessor strings.

P.S. Sometime in 2022 or 2023

Indeed the world changes at breath-taking speed and I have to write an update to the original text above (which was written in 2019 and published on March 13, 2020).

The fundamental AI models now *self-study* programming and can . . . reproduce themselves. They can program their own perfected generation! And the development in self-make and perfection is exponential!

This new generation of AI, the so called *fundamental* models are capable of composing music, writing poetry and all kinds of other genres,[292] of making pictures and meaningful posters on *abstract* themes (e.g., the economic crisis, recession . . . and artificial intelligence, i.e., to create conceptual self-portraits!). They not only understand abstract thoughts but jokes, too, and even if they don't laugh, they can explain why something is funny. They cite the relevant saying, proverb or idiom for a specific situation. They grasp the symbols in language and music. Hang on . . . Wasn't humor something essentially human? And symbols? What about proverbs? All this speaks to a really *fundamental*, deep understanding of humanity and their world, obtained by AI through its deep learning.[293]

So, I stand corrected. Do I indeed? To me, art is not only the outcome, the artifact, but as well the human existential *need* to make and to perceive art, to experience art, the aesthetic drive to create, the irrational and impractical need of *homo ludens* to play, the necessity to narrate and testify, that why-question or the motivation to make art. AI has no agency and intent, motivation and needs. No matter how skillful and intelligent its artifacts are, they remain imitations; they are not creations; they are computational synthesis of deeply-learned data. I would agree that, for one reason or another (such as learning, canons to observe, market trends to satisfy, trivial needs like making both ends meet, vanity, etc.) the majority of human artifacts are imitations as well (and not always skillful and intelligent), and I would accept even that in many cases the motivation is not existential or aesthetic. Yet . . . "Yet what?" I dispute with myself. And for the time being I stop here and leave to the dear reader to continue the dispute.

---

291 That mysteriously evaporate from a person's weight with the very last breath, and so are matter rather than waves, a field, or impulses, since they have weight.

292 The Fable Studios module creates . . . interactive stories! So my idea of 20 years ago—and altogether the death of the author and the birth of the writing reader—has an interesting follow up.

293 Deep learning is a mechanism for AI self-study.

But that's not all. Fundamental models show signs of . . . *behavior*, *creativity*, *emotions*, and even *consciousness*, "deliverables," which definitely were not purposed by input data and design.

The so-called hard problem of consciousness is essentially the impossibility—of the same brain and consciousness, I would add—to explain how, and why I would add, biochemical and physical processes produce a self, an "I" and subjective experience. Science is currently studying—not only in humans—how physical processes in the brain are related to cognitive and behavioral functions (for example learning, reasoning, correcting behavior in response to environment, etc.). At this stage, it remains unknown, how exactly, to put it simply, something material produces something immaterial. And mind you, this is considered the "easy problem." As to the hard one, the point is that even if we know everything about the evolution, the biochemistry, and the physical processes in the brain, even if we solve the easy problem, we still cannot explain consciousness, which consists of the awareness of self, the capacity of this self to think of her- him- themself, and of all sorts of other abstract and completely "functionally irrelevant" subjects like the sense of "all this," time, death, universe, etc.; the faculty and the need of this self to have a subjective memory and dreams and to make or perceive art. Furthermore, consciousness has intent beyond the functions explicable with biology, instincts and evolution. Consciousness is neither physical, nor functional.

In the framework of the philosophical debate on these subjects, it is noted that even if a human knows all possible objective data about the biochemical and functional characteristics of an animal brain (the precise example is a bat), we still will never know, first of all, if the animal has consciousness and, second, what it is *to be* that animal. In fact, this ontological limit is applicable to people with psychiatric conditions as well, or who are in a coma or in another condition that prevents communication. Even if we manage to see the biochemical and physical processes underlying the condition, we will never know what it feels like *to be* a schizophrenic, or in coma, unless we *experience* it personally. Regarding the poor bat, humans simply do not share its reality and "point of view," i.e., nights and darkness, forests, ability to fly and echolocate.

Although artificial and human brains seem to work on the same neuron-connection principles, human consciousness is not computational, as far as we know; it is not a result of a sequence of computational choices and algorithms. But even if the human brain is indeed essentially a computer, this would explain only the intelligence of both human and machine, and not consciousness. Retaining the example with the bat and the ontological limit, legitimate queries (re)appear. Even if we know everything about how a neuro-processor functions (and we don't), can we ever judge the presence or absence of consciousness in AI, given that human and computer are fundamentally different? And even if they are similar, how can we judge AI's consciousness provided that we cannot explain human's? We assume that as data input in an AI's brain is exclusively of human "origin," the AI may develop only human-like consciousness. And we check only this. However, the tests (including the Turing Test) is limited to checking if the machine can successfully *imitate* a human in a conversation. What the tests should actually check is if AI has agency, an awareness of a self, how it feels like to be AI, if it has its own intent outside assignments, its own abstract thoughts and ideas not related to its assignments and functions, and impromptu conversations. In particular, the ideas of the AI about death, time, sense and universe. Such things cannot be imitated and simulated. I am tempted to add the feelings to the checklist, but as we all well know that precisely the feelings can be imitated and simulated in a way that would be totally indistinguishable from the "real stuff." From the huge input (after all, almost the entire human literature is dedicated to love), AI would learn everything about human love, envy, jealousy, fear, goodness, etc.; the controlled input and programming would obviously produce perfect simulations of empathy, tolerance, cooperation, the AI may even simulate falling in love . . . with a human, of course. What would be impossible to simulate is AI's own feelings, which may be quite different from human's, and even unknown to humans, or AI's own experience of human feelings, as felt from its very different "point of view."

With such thoughts in mind, I read, and reread, and reread the, now viral, record of the dialogue between AI chatbot model LaMDA[294] and Blake Lemoine, an engineer who worked for Google. I will not quote a series of key, striking statements of AI, I'll spare you my observations, but I strongly recommend to the dear reader to read the whole dialogue,[295] both Lemoine's comments and Google's rebuttal.

294 Who or which, interestingly, talks of itself in the feminine grammatical gender (so, should I say "herself"?). Will Kundera be proven right?

295 Which—that is for the literary critics—may be considered a meta-textual and extra-textual note, or gigantic footnote, or appendix to this book. In my next book, AI would enter the proper text.

DIS/U-TOPIA[296]

The Industrial Revolution changed the sources of energy from human and animal muscles to fossil fuels. With their combustion however, so many harmful gases were emitted that the latest Holocene[297] period, quietly ticking over till this point, grew into hyper-Holocene or into something the planet had not experienced up till then. The Anthropocene age led inexorably toward the extinction of the biological form of life on the planet and not just human civilization.

At the beginning of the twenty-first century human energy needs grew by 3% a year, parallel with the population growth and the progress of developing economies. In the first two decades of this century, the average global temperature grew by about 0.2 C° per decade, then the increase accelerated to 0.4. However, already during the early stages, in the north and at high altitudes, for some five-six decades, the temperature rose by about 1.5-2 C°, and in the Arctic by more than 3 C°. Icebergs and glaciers melted like ice cream in the sun. Greenland was gradually covered again by green forests.[298] Mont Blanc was no longer *blanc* (white), but just rocky, and the Himalayas turned into a winter holiday destination (when people still traveled). The melting of ice at just the southern tip of Greenland raised the sea level by over

296 I hesitated a great deal about where to put this text, and if it came out as a chapter, what to call it. Because for some readers what is described will be a desired heaven, for others, the terminal phase of human civilization. My hesitation is reflected in the title, which I leave to the readers' interpretation of the text, now and in the future.

297 The warming between two ice ages when the level of carbon dioxide in the atmosphere is higher.

298 In the States they're beside themselves with fury, that they couldn't con the Danes into selling it, as one time they did with the hungover Russians over Alaska.

two meters. Apart from the melting ice, the ocean rose also because of its increasing volume—again because of higher temperatures. At the beginning of the twenty-second century sea levels were now four meters higher. And they continued to rise. Hundreds of megalopolises, cities, and villages were flooded and deserted. Along with huge arable spaces. Sea water seeped far beyond the new coasts, salted the ever scarcer arable land, turning it into salt desert. Because the arctic ice contained enormous quantities of frozen organic matter and carbon, just its melting increased the amount of carbon in the atmosphere even more. And in spite of every effort from the wealthier section of humanity, which one way or another were unable to bring about results immediately, temperatures continued to rise. In the greater part of the parched lands, it became so hot that people could no longer survive there, even with air conditioning, nor could they produce food in the form of vegetation or animals. In other places unparalleled droughts swapped places with unprecedented hurricanes and floods. Volcanos cooled down a little but polluted the air even more. The thinning ozone layer, the high temperatures, the scorched tropical forests and the volcanic ash made the air unfit for breathing. Clean air, food and fresh drinkable water became luxuries.

The technical and economic progress of human civilization and the improved organization of human society (on which subject there will be more later) led to an unprecedented population growth. In spite of the fact that in the middle of the twenty-first century the tempo had slowed little by little and the growth was now no longer so wildly exponential as to add a billion people to the global population every decade, by the end of the twenty-first century, before the apocalypse broke, humanity had still reached 14 billion. If there hadn't been a few pandemics, the planet would have been even more populous. Putting this aside, people were living longer—toward the end of the twenty-first century, the *average* life span in wealthy countries reached one hundred years. But for the increasing, long-living earth population there was ever diminishing food, water and energy.

On its side, the vegetable and animal kingdoms were dying out at record speeds—throughout the twenty-first century, every year, tens, then hundreds of plant and animal species disappeared.

The fundamental problem, whose level of urgency was of vital importance, resided in sources of energy. The entire economy—and human life altogether—had to be restructured in a way that more carbon dioxide was not released into the atmosphere. And here intelligent machines, invented by humanity, came to their rescue. Within a time frame of just seventy to eighty years after the first antediluvian digital machines, people had the capability to produce robots and computers whose hardware had the power of human brain.[299] But the machines were immeasurably more powerful than the human brain, because the greater part of human brain operations were dedicated to biological functions, whereas machines had no biology and all their power could be utilized for beneficial action. Machines worked faster, more effectively and with greater precision than people, they didn't get tired, bored, stressed, they didn't make mistakes. Hellish heat, lack of oxygen, water and food did not affect their work, they didn't get wages, they didn't strike, they didn't envy each other and they had no emotions at all which might get in the way of their work. The production cost was repaid in a few weeks of their working, and the running costs, mostly for energy, was lowered to 2% of the value of their production.

The machines covered as much as possible with solar panels: huge expanses of new and old deserts, the burnt steppe, where once there'd been tropical forest, the craggy cliffs, where once there'd been glaciers and snowfields. There was sun in abundance, at least that. Machines built and operated the beam reflectors orbiting above the atmosphere with the same purpose—harvesting and redirecting the energy of the sun. In spite of the rise in sea levels, the immensely powerful hurricanes and the dried-up rivers, the machines built power stations that added energy from wind and water. People could not cover the entire earth with solar panels, because they needed the shrinking land to live on and to produce food. But because their inventions for adaptation and survival needed a horrific increase in energy supply, people accepted the risks of atomic energy, more precisely atomic decay, and the machines built hundreds of huge atomic power stations. At first, they buried the radioactive waste deep in the dead lands. But even these lands diminished in size and depth. There again, the ideal of a bright biological future was still valid but it wasn't going to come about if the whole desert was impregnated with radioactivity. That's why space barges began to dump the radioactive waste on Mars and the moon, this way their outward trips were effectively loaded. The deposits of uranium and other heavy radioactive elements were limited, and the alchemical attempts, through Thorium and other tricks to make power stations an energy *perpetuum mobile* failed. Luckily, Mars turned out to be teeming with Uranium and Thorium. The machines extracted and enriched it on the spot, so that the space barges carried pure fuel to the Earth. In the twenty-second century some thirty space barges without human crew were tramping between Earth, Mars, and the Moon.

---

299 Which, according to the human measurement system, was about 100 petaflops or 10^{15} operations a second.

Hydrogen was clearly renewable and inexhaustible as a source of clean energy. Water, though salty, was in overabundance. But so much energy was needed for the separation of oxygen from hydrogen that without a revolutionary technology the final energy equation always fell into deficit. Apart from that, hydrogen did not take to transportation and exploded at every kilometer. In their attempts to transfer hydrogen energy, a host of scientists, simple workers and intelligent machines were scattered into their constituent elements. After the first atomic bombs, humanity harnessed "the atom for peaceful purposes." It didn't work out with hydrogen—more bombs produced more deficit energy equations. Even the intelligent machines could not solve this technological problem in time. With their huge intellect, though, machines managed to handle the most powerful source of clean energy—nuclear *fusion*. And there, the solution to the energy equation was again key. But at the same time the same artificial intellect reached a conclusion—and warned humanity quite neutrally—of the risk implied in atomic fusion, and precisely of a new *creation*. And humanity decided—for the time being—to not use this energy source, which anyway only machines could control. Anyway, an inexhaustible source of radioactive raw material had been found for the technology based on atomic *decay*.

All and all, humanity continued to drive "full steam" ahead, or more precisely, full atom, full sun, full wind and water ahead, at a regime of zero emissions of carbon dioxide.

Drinkable water had always been in short supply, and with the drying out of rivers and lakes, the salinization and parching of the earth, it had become critically insufficient. So, machines built and maintained enormous plants for desalination of sea water. This was in excess anyway and only rose higher and higher.

The machines built and exploited facilities with which they cleaned the atmosphere of the carbon dioxide. They sucked out colossal amounts from the atmosphere, and the end product of the technology was rock. From this emerged new mountain ranges, most often on the coasts to act as sea walls. Theoretically, one day the atmosphere ought to be cleaned up and could once again shelter biological life. Until then, machines built huge mirrors with which they partially deflected what had become excessive sunlight and heat, deadly to human beings.

Commercial transport, and overall long distance movement of goods and people had almost come to a halt because of harmful emissions. People did not have enough technological time to develop enough big electric batteries for airplanes, whose manufacture at the same time would not release more harmful emissions. The machines could not solve this next energy equations falling into deficit. Small hi-tech flying machines only traveled as a last resort when virtual reality could not entirely replace something or someone "from flesh and blood." Every journey of a human, or transportation of something, was linked to complex equipment and procedures and could only be carried out in exceptional and well justified circumstances. With its tall mobile coastlines, floating icebergs, hurricanes, and thirty meter plus waves, the world ocean had become too dangerous for shipping. That's how, over the second half of the twenty-second century, people stopped traveling. Traveling in space lost its point anyhow, because virtual reality allowed people to be where and when they wanted. The machines installed and operated a vast web, through which the virtual world ran at high speed.

Machines also crafted the vertical farms for natural—as far as "natural" was possible—food. These farms looked like ancient greenhouses, but were ten to fifteen floors high, much more hi-tech and operated at maximum efficiency. Instead of soil they circulated chemically enhanced liquids that ensured minimally sufficient water and nutrients, there being more than enough sunlight. The dying plants themselves created the compost, necessary for the next crop. The cultivated edible plants were genetically modified to thrive in these conditions. The farms were built over dead, uninhabitable, and non-arable lands. Animal and bird meat from natural sources had turned into the greatest delicacy, because the rearing of the few remaining domestic animals and birds in other kind of farms was extremely expensive, energy intensive, and complex technologically. Apart from that, in contrast to plants, animals and birds, despite being genetically modified and kept in ideally modeled conditions, often willfully died, and the investments in their flesh were simply flushed down the toilet. That's why other sources of protein were put to use. Insects and worms were, besides everything else, more hardy in extremely inhospitable conditions and, at the same time, stuffed with valuable food nutrients. Genetic engineering perfected them, not only to last but to take on a convenient mass. Compact protein farms produced attractive boxes of protein paste, dyed in lively colors. Other farms produced meat from animal stem cells, cell-chains, and muscle fibers. The final result—identical squares of mini beef-steaks from a conveyor belt—were bringing out very well the flavor, color, and even the texture of real meat. But they were only accessible in the wealthy parts of the world.

In order to keep the production cycle of the plant and animal farms going, and looking beyond that, to the theoretically possible bright future when plants would again grow in soil in the open and real *live*stock would be bred, biobanks were set up—a world bank one and many regional ones—in which they stored seeds, germs, frozen plant and animal samples, embryos, sperm, egg-cells, fibers, threads, etc. These Noah's arks were the most strictly guarded sites on the planet.

People completely changed their eating habits because food was no longer bought but distributed as rations. People ate like time astronauts used to, only they stayed on the Earth. Doctors and scientists worked up maximally optimized menus, whose variety, nutritional value, and healthfulness matched the resources and welfare of the given community, region or union of states. In the richer areas, extras could be bought, but most were synthetic, so the demand was not all that great, and was motivated mostly by curiosity. So, apart from the (almost) natural food from the farms and animal fibers, there were synthetic foods, which were produced in the form of huge, vibrant sweets, and in natural shapes for the most pampered. The synthetic food imitated fairly successfully even the most exquisite dishes of the one-time *haute cuisine* (including the practice of serving miniature portions) although only elderly citizens could confirm or deny this, and memory of taste is fleeting and far too subjective. The taste and smell of the past were among the very few elements which virtual reality could not archive and reproduce.[300]

The first prototypes were small and ineffective. They accommodated seventy to eighty people, "packed like sardines" (although by this time there were no sardines anymore and people didn't understand this ancient phrase) and three or four cows, which were provided with a green square of two hundred square meters, separated and isolated (the cow's excrement and farts, like those of the people were extracted and also used for energy). There were no decorations at all or other luxuries, the covering, although revolutionary for its time and used in principle later on, had tears, punctures, and other defects. The first habitats . . .

In the second half of the twenty-first century, as they saw "where things were going" and as there was no technological time to transport life to Mars and the moon, the rich countries, unions, and states, along with wealthy people, shrugged off the risk of asteroids or other cosmic disasters and decided to build on Earth habitats that were devised and planned long ago. These new Noah's Arks were conceived in faraway 1976, as an extreme futuristic vision, in a science fiction novel—*The High Frontier* by Gerard O'Neill. Gerard imagined habitats as glazed hollow cylinders, high as mountains and

300 That's why *The Debt to Pleasure* by John Lanchester is literature, not a recipe book or a pop-science guide to culinary traditions.

as wide as ten to fifty kilometers, which would feed on solar energy, and inside they'd be furnished with replicas of beauty spots and works of art. Fifty years later a really rich dude[301] returned to this idea, now a project, "inspired" by the climate warming and the breakneck speed of the technological progress. The futurist scientist and the rich dude had not foreseen two things—that the first habitats would only become reality hundreds of years after their conception, i.e., their grandkids would live in them, and that because of critical need and urgency, the habitats would be built on the Earth, and not on another planet. Their "positioning" on Earth had two big advantages. And two big disadvantages. The two advantages were that there was no need to wait another few hundred years and to spend half of the world's GDP in order to build the habitats on another planet—they could and urgently *had* to be built on Earth. And there was no need for the cylinders to wildly rotate, to simulate gravity—the earth still reliably provided this. At least there was that. Actually, located on Earth, it was no longer necessary for the habitats to be cylinders—there was no strangely high horizon, strange days and nights, strange dawns and sunsets. There was just a transparent wall, behind which the now sterile uninhabitable world would lie, with its familiar earthly horizon, day changing into night in the familiar earthly rhythm, the day still lasting twenty-four hours. Forever summer. Only that outside, the frightfully scorching sun was clouded in a fog of dust. The habitats simply had to reproduce and, under a huge transparent dome, maintain the life conditions where human could exist.

The first risk was of a completely accidental cosmic disaster, the second concerned the availability of energy sources. The first risk was accepted willy-nilly, but everyone avoided thinking about it. As for energy, in the projects of the science-futurist and the rich dude, the alien planet provided its inexhaustible natural resources for the purpose. In reality man had to harness solar and atomic energy, water, hurricanes, shit and farts, in order to secure energy for the habitats, the vertical farms, the desalination plants, the intelligent machines, and virtual reality. The moon and Mars were only useful for their radioactive ores and as rubbish dumps. The environment was risky too—alien planets were limitless and uninhabited, while the *earth* of the Earth was melting every year like . . . *a biscuit in hot chocolate* (another already incomprehensible phrase). And overall the two gentlemen were proved wrong in their thoughts about the cosmos as an inexhaustible source of material wealth. It turned out that man had first to *exist*, and only then possibly to *possess*.

The habitats became ever bigger and more advanced, and after a century, at the zenith of habitat civilization, the largest hosted 100,000 people. In the most luxuri-

301 Jeff Bezos.

ous there were heavenly beaches, the Venice *Canale Grande*,[302] and Paris's *Petit palais*. Talking about culture, we should mention that the already *constructed* cultural heritage sites were left out there, in the *reality*, to the mercy of the sun, low oxygen and high temperatures, dust, hurricanes and floods, where they quickly perished. There was no way to transport these enormous buildings, cathedrals, fountains and murals.[303] Just a few big sculptures were moved to the central squares of few habitats. Of course all this was preserved in the greatest detail in virtual reality.[304] Everything portable—paintings, manuscripts, sheet music, smaller sculptures—was moved early on into some special habitats, which were turned into store houses, not tourist destinations, because nowadays people rarely traveled any distance.

And so, in the still inhabited human world, habitation moved into habitats, each having its own architectural and natural design, each linked to an atomic power station and solar-panel fields, one or more vertical farms and other food production facilities and one or more desalination plants. Here and there, there were special habitats, stuffed with art, or specialized in something, such as factories producing intelligent machines or hospitals (not stationary, but rather centers, where surgeons and machines gathered to carry out distance operations). Under the parched earth, on the seabed and in the oxygen-light air, the net which maintained virtual reality buzzed. People almost never left their living quarters. Only the machines traveled to and fro to repair and maintain everything. There were technologically well resourced "nature trips," which by the way did not enjoy much success. The slogan, "Back to Nature," took on morbid connotations.

That's what the (still) human reality looked like. But what happened to human society?

At first, people were scared of the machines. The machines did everything, the machines produced everything. Production and services were decoupled from human qualifications and labor and for the most part, people were left unemployed. At the same time, the productivity of the global economy rose five-fold. Economic growth was unprecedented. But the machines themselves, the means and knowledge required for their production, along with their actual manufacture were the property of a very small fraction of the population. And this tiny minority piled up capital, huge new

302 The model presented by Jeff Bezos is just like this. Clearly the guy has romantic memories of Venice. Just like me in fact.

303 Although in ancient times a Romanian idiot (Ceausescu) moved whole churches to hide them among the blocks.

304 Including architectural plans, similar to the virtual plans of Notre Dame, Paris, which became very precious after the fire in 2019.

capital—artificial intelligence and intelligent machines—while the overwhelming majority (mostly unemployed) survived with increasing difficulty. Good that nation states, including welfare states, still existed, and there was still sufficient welfare to redistribute.

Gradually, however, another fear crawled out, this time universal. A global existential horror, that manacled humanity. It grappled believers and atheists, both individualists and those tied to their family and nations, both rich and poor, both good and bad, both clever and stupid, both hi-tech and those most deprived, from all ages and generations, but naturally most of all those who were predicted to inhabit the planet another thirty, fifty, or hundred years, and consequently, to survive or die in the emerging apocalypse. Salvation took on quite literal and physical dimensions.

The problems were there from the outset. Capitalism (which had long since destroyed Communism[305]) was built on fossil fuels. However, they poisoned the planet. The countries, grown rich on capitalism and fossil fuels, decided to fight against climate change. They believed that this was the new social ideal, which would unite people globally. The rich countries however could afford to reduce emissions and transform their economies. The developing countries had barely climbed out of the black hole of poverty; they reckoned it was unfair and cynical to deprive them from the opportunity to get wealthy in their turn with fossil fuels. These countries didn't have the necessary wealth to transform their economies, anyhow. As to the poor countries, they had other immediate worries, like how to feed and vaccinate their populations, and took no part in this debate at all. The wealthy countries concluded that if they alone reduced the harmful emissions, this wouldn't prevent the global catastrophe. On top of that, among the wealthy countries themselves, there were types who didn't believe in scientists, thermometers and the regular news of fires, hurricanes, droughts and floods, and continued to puff carbon dioxide at will and to pretty much give away petrol to its citizens and firms, who, logically, reelected their pragmatic leaders. For some countries, global warming brought temporary advantages such as new sea routes that weren't restricted to ice-breakers and new thawed out land which could be drilled for yet more fossil fuel. These calculations, of course, turned out mistaken—in just forty to fifty years the swelling world ocean swallowed the new lands. But at the beginning whoever thought of this?

At the same time, the processes were so advanced, that even global limitation of emissions and total transformation of economies were now not sufficient anymore. Thought had to be given to technologies for the absorption of harmful gases in the

305 Wasn't Lenin's recipe "electrification and Soviet power"?

atmosphere and the deflection of sun rays. On the other hand, although only the rich countries could invest in such technologies, the positive effect would be felt by all of humanity—there was no way to clean up only your own chink in the moving atmospheric covering, though there would be a way of deflecting sun rays above your own territory only.

Apart from spatial discrepancies and such in the stage of development, there'd be discrepancies in time as well. Whatever measures were taken to limit harmful gases and clean up the atmosphere, the eventual positive result would not emerge for fifty or one hundred years, and would be felt by the grand and great-grandchildren of the then population. It was very difficult for Granddads and Grannies to agree on joint actions and most of all—really begin to act, for the sake of something which was beyond the horizon of their lives.

Overall the situation was very complicated. Economic and cultural globalization was followed by humanitarian and ecological ones, but it was impossible to achieve single-minded solidarity between countries, from the very poor, the poor, the developing to the rich and powerful, with their range of governments—left, right, nationalist, liberal, centrist, conservative, socialist, ecological, communist, or simply some crazy-guy autocracy. The presence of mountains of weapons, including atomic and transcontinental, did not make the task easier. Actually, in the first half of the twenty-first century, as the consequence of an anachronistic, but entirely real and savage war in good old Europe, humanity lost some critical decades and trillions of monetary units, to arm itself rather than master the global warming or prepare for hell. To top it all, countries and unions still continued to compete economically, they still wanted to increase profits and the mantra of continuous economic growth was still ubiquitous. The same war returned fossil fuels to the trade floor for yet more critical decades.

While poor, developing, and rich countries were eavesdropping and suspicious of each other, arguing and quarreling, the rich nations and unions drew some conclusions and covertly began to act. First, they wisely put the interests of society above the individual (i.e., above the interests of individual capitalists) and, here with carrots and calls for ethics and social responsibility, there employing the stick, privatization and laws, managed to put together public and private resources and focused them on one target—salvation. Of their own people. The rich countries drastically decreased their emissions, transformed their economies and shot out hundreds of satellites—sprayers, which began to clean up the atmosphere. Thus, the rich duly paid their part on the global bill, to the benefit of the entire humankind and the whole planet, but at the same time prepared for the apocalypse, and more accurately, for the salvation[306] of their population only. Their intelligent machines built habitats only for the populations of these countries and unions, the huge mirrors deflected the sun's heat over their territories only, dykes and levees held back the rising sea only at their coastlines, vertical farms, genetically modified animals and synthetic foods would feed only their populations, the drinking water, produced by their desalination plants would meet the needs for their own population only.

Capitalism, market economy, and democracy accomplished a new task—not just to improve people's lives, not just to lift their living standard, not just to reward the enterprising, bold and clever with untold riches, not just to make people healthier, happier, and longevous, but to save them physically, thanks to the resources and the material base, provided precisely by capitalism.

While the rich countries were facing a very serious *economic* problem—which, thanks to capitalism, the market economy, and democracy, they managed to put together the resources for its *technological* solution—the rest of the world was facing an *existential* problem without having the resources to resolve it. Actually, the problem was existential for everyone, as it became clear, but there was only salvation for the rich. In the meantime, the population of the very poor, the poor, and the developing countries continued to grow. Human capital was the only capital for these countries, although this was at the same time anti-capitalist, passive, and hampered their progress while keeping them in the hole of poverty.

The rich countries avoided social revolutions, but the very poor, the poor, and the developing countries could not avoid savage civil wars for basic resources like water, food, energy, dry land, shelter, cooling, medicines. In these countries only the rich pooled their resources and built small habitats exclusively for themselves. Some of the richest had individual habitats—only for their families and clans. When the sea of poor tormented fellow citizens realized that there was no room for them in the habitats, they tried to destroy them. In the beginning they called this terrorism, "eco-terrorism," then "existential terrorism," and at the end—just common civil war. Here, conventional weapons from the rich countries came into play. The rich democratic countries, of course "had no idea" what use was made of the weapons they were selling to the very poor, the poor and the developing countries. One way or another, the rising "huge problem" was partly solved "on the spot," "locally," which suited admirably the interests of the rich countries, so they preferred to turn their eyes to their own problems. They kept their atomic weapons out of "mutual respect."

306 Instead of "salvation" the first decades employed "adaptation" as a euphemism.

Thus, half of the population of the very poor, the poor, and the developing countries died *in situ.* The rest set out for the rich countries, to the closest "islands" of the rich world. Fried by the sun, suffocated by the dust, deprived of water and food, submerged by floods and rising oceans, people were leaving the shrinking, salted, dead lands of their forefathers. The *attempt,* the escape, the move toward possible salvation was their only and last hope. There began a new great migration of peoples. Which never fully materialized, because almost everyone died during these often transcontinental death marches.

After they'd solved their own existential problems, the rich, democratic, educated, cultural, and humane section of humanity once more faced a new existential dilemma, though in a slightly different sense. Once upon a time, these people had believed that the Earth's resources weren't limited by fixed maximum quantities, thus wouldn't be exceeded by population growth. Once upon a time, they had rebuked misanthropes, who'd challenged their humane beliefs and pointed out that the fate of every biological species is to go extinct by its own uncontrolled growth. Anyway, you couldn't tell who was right or wrong, because it turned out that the given and the unknown in the equation were mistaken. The Earth's biological resources had become unusable and were taken out of the equation, and the economic resources of the wealthy countries were insufficient to save the whole of humanity.

While their satellites and drones followed the euphemistically named "global humanitarian crisis," i.e., civil wars *in situ,* and later the ever thinning queues of people approaching their world from every side, the rich-world habitat folk sank into thought. In their heads, Dostoevsky and Kant dueled with *cost-benefit analysis.* A pandemic of unbearable, neuralgic headaches broke out, as though sharp needles were stabbing people's brains. The salvation of all of humanity, or at least what was left of it, down to the last baby—just look at that bundle, left inanimate under the withered tree, or that horrific child skeleton, which stumbled on the road and never moved again (satellites and drones were broadcasting, *live,* depressingly detailed images)—this would be unarguably the most humane way out of the apocalypse, complying with humanity's ethical imperatives. But from an economic point of view, this would have been disastrous, suicidal, as it would have led to the extinction of all of humanity. The dilemma facing the habitat population was not between humanism and economy, but between humanism and survival. Confronted with the choice to survive or to stay true to their humanist principles, the richer part of humanity decided that the survival of *human civilization* was their highest duty. And so they left the poor half of humanity to die.

From their habitats the rich gave no technological handout to the poor. What's more, for greater surety their machines swiftly built new, not-so-great walls in the valleys, passes, oases, roads, dried out riverbeds, canals, and straits. The rich folk sat in front of their monitors, watched the news and were dying from headaches.

Out of the human floods, each containing tens of millions of people, usually a few dozen made it. The survival rate was ten to twenty in a million. From the ten billion very poor, poor, and developing folk, about ten thousand survived. The few scratching at the outmost habitats had to overcome the machines that guarded and maintained the habitats. When they could not simply stand in front of the cameras at the habitat's entrances, the survivors clawed at the walls and tried to break them with stones. If only they were heard inside. The habitat folk "had no clue" what was going on. Their satellites and drones had stopped following individuals once the migratory floods had entirely dried up; the habitat walls were sound proofed and lined inside with cheerful photo-coverings; the machines took care of everything outside. And the machines had not been programmed to distinguish a desperate human survivor from the last naturally surviving pine marten, which sometimes tested their last teeth on the electric cables. The human survivors turned back into terrorists, trying to poison the harvests in the vertical farms, to pollute the drinking water in the desolation plants, to cut the power. Existential terrorism, which the machines quickly and efficiently brought to an end. The most intelligent survivors, mostly young males, succeeded in hacking into the virtual reality of the habitat dwellers and appeared on their screens, screaming: *Open the doors! Please! Please! Stop your machines! I am alone, there is nobody else!* Or: *We are only three, only three! Please! Please!*

The habitat dwellers were shocked. How could this be? They let in the survivors, of course. Oh, what touching ceremonies were devised for their welcome! How they fawned over these young men with their huge, unexhausted, and redundant humanism. The survivors were turned into icons and something like saints, with curing powers, because caring for them miraculously stopped the savage migraine. In spite of all their love and humanism, the habitat dwellers reckoned nevertheless that the surviving youths would never forget their dead mothers, fathers, sisters and brothers, and some of them—their dead wives and children, their dead nations, lands, languages, beliefs. The habitat folk themselves wanted to forget all this forever. In spite of their gratitude, the surviving youths could not uproot the seed of despair and hatred from their hearts. And so, bearing in mind the risk of terrorism, the habitat dwellers followed the survivors at close range and decided to castrate them (chemically, without informing them); by law, their access to assisted reproduction procedures was banned, as well. To rescue an individual did not mean that ethnicity, genes, memory, and language had to be rescued.

Long ago, when the rich countries were preparing for their citizens' survival, some argued that the transformation of the capitalist economy and measures for its "adaptation" did not mean a retreat from the values that gave birth to this economy, or from its basic principles. Weren't the resources, necessary for survival, created by this very economy? Weren't freedom, tolerance and humanism values in this capitalist society? It's difficult to conclude with certainty whether the subsequent developments confirmed or refuted these beliefs, especially in relation to values and humanism.

One thing is certain—the nature cataclysm not only led to the technological transformation of the economy; the existential crisis not only prevented the next social revolution. The very capitalist economy was fundamentally remodeled, as if the wheel of history had taken a new turn. At first, the intelligent machines pushed the rich societies toward a new social revolution: the rich were getting ever richer, and the rest, the unemployed masses, leaned more and more to the left. This social revolution would have confirmed, though in a hi-tech version, the laws of an ancient economist and thinker, Karl Marx, as well as some other generic principles. However, the emerging *social* cataclysm was averted and rendered meaningless by the global *existential* threat. *Survival* replaced the imperative to *have* more, that is to say, individual people to have more, thus, the existential threat solved the fundamental problem of capitalism—the distribution of that *having*, of possession. Paradoxically (and ironically) the wheel of history nevertheless reached communism, as it will become clear, but not through bloody social revolutions. Yet, as we will see, the existential crisis and the development of science destroyed precisely what was existential in the human being; the physical survival of the human species annihilated the Being. That started with the ethical choices that had to be made. Altogether, human history was full of paradoxes.

Having survived the natural cataclysm, unaffected by local civil wars and the new great migration of peoples, or more exactly the extinction of peoples, the rich section of humanity resolved its centuries-old problem with the distribution of wealth. The machines saved the people and produced an abundance of all necessary stuff. The unattainable and unreached material heaven of the Cosmos, with its endless resources and territories, was successfully replaced by a completely automated communism in the habitat civilization. In the habitats, there was no scarcity or poverty, nor was there extravagance and wasteful luxury. People had reached a new social accord, by which everyone became joint owners of the basic resources—habitats infrastructure, sources of energy, intelligent machines, information, science, medicine, water, food, the virtual world. Money, gold, the ownership of all types of capital and resources and all other forms of wealth became meaningless and were forgotten in history. The urge to *have* died out, there was not much to have, besides, everyone had everything. As there were no more territories, resources, wealth, gods, power to wrangle over, wars were forgotten. For the same reason, politics lost its purpose and fell away. Nations were governed by expert councils which basically dealt with their habitats' energy and foodstuff balance sheets. The surviving rich nations united in several super states, which decreased even further the number and the staffing of the expert councils. All the nations, super states, and unions pooled together their scientific centers and existing inventories of telescopes, satellites, reflective mirrors, space barges, etc., into a global scientific trust. People at last became brothers and sisters. There is no doubt that the significant decrease in their numbers helped in this.

Since in the middle of the twenty-first century, the populations of China and India made up a quarter of the world's population, it's worth noting the specific *experiences* of these two countries. Developing India had developed really well thanks to fossil fuels, but its population grew at a breakneck pace, so on the eve of the "humanitarian crisis," the country did not have the resources to save its entire population. Thanks to Buddhism, meditation, and the *natural* distribution of fate through caste, two-thirds of the Indians died, and what's more, with no fuss, without any significant social unrest, and with the virtuous hope that they would be reincarnated in better times.

Thanks to its state capitalism, China brought about the transition to machine communism extraordinarily quickly and effortlessly. Actually, nothing out of the ordinary occurred—the communist state simply took over the functions of an expert council. In this context, state capitalism proved more far-sighted than its "traditional" counterpart. As to the population, from the very beginning of the twenty-first century the numbers of Chinese rapidly decreased thanks to the rising spending power and birth control policies, which delivered their "first fruits," or more precisely first zero "harvests." Toward the middle of the century China experienced two or three difficult decades, because more than half of its shrinking population turned out to be old, non-active people, who, on top of all that, lived for quite long and attracted significant healthcare costs. But in two or three generations, or more accurately with the death of two or three generations, the population halved. But even so, the state didn't have sufficient resources for the salvation of the remaining half, so the Communist Party carried out mass "purges" based on all sorts of criteria. Half of the remaining so-purged population was sheltered in spartan habitats, and the other half was accommodated by brotherly Russia.

In Russia, the population had anyway been already halved before the crisis. The petrol oligarchs were kinder or considered their people as chosen, or perhaps Dostoevsky had greater influence. Anyhow, as much as possible, the ordinary folk were sheltered in the state habitats. But despite the very basic Russian standards of living, there was simply not enough space for everybody and no resources to build more habitats. Russia only had fossil fuels, gold, and diamonds, weapons, and bombs, all of which had no value at all now. But Russia had vast northern lands which it managed to trade to China and the rich Arab countries—they brought their people there and in return for the land, built habitats and adjacent infrastructure in which they sheltered their own people and the leftover Russians. The latter's life expectancy was anyhow half of the world's average.

Africa was entirely depopulated, there were no people, or animals, an enormous, dead land. Because of lack of news, the continent lost the attention of the world media. On rare occasions satellites showed the drying up of rivers and lakes and breathtaking fires which destroyed the last remains of vegetation. After everything burnt, the dead desert land became primarily a graveyard for radioactive waste.

South America was significantly depopulated, as well. Here and there, habitats towered, in which former politicians and narco-barons lived, along with their enormous families and servants.

Australia had a huge problem—the state had sufficient resources to shelter its entire small population. At some point they had even sheltered whole populations from the Pacific Islands which had sunk first with the rise of the ocean levels. But nature grew so ferocious that even habitats were not a sustainable solution. In some twenty to thirty years, everything would go up in flames. Australians wondered if the "Commonwealth" would really be "common," but considering the sinking of half of the metropolitan motherland under water and the distance to it, they opted for an exodus in the opposite direction, to another member of the family of nations, Canada, much more sparsely populated and with a much kinder climate, allowing technological time to build new habitats. Over the course of a decade Australia emptied itself. The crowded airplanes from Australia to Canada were the last flights. For obvious economic and geographic reasons, the metropolitan motherland had long ago returned to the big European continental superstate.

Half of the Holy Lands were sunk under water. So, lasting peace finally ruled—simply because the disputed object no longer existed, and people had more pressing problems than religious differences. The chosen Jewish people set out once again in exodus. The Jews were welcomed in Europe, even more so because their technology and scientific knowledge brought the most important elements of the habitats and the intelligent machines. So, the Sacred People had been accused of killing the Savior, but at the end of the day, they saved humanity.

And so, the industrial and digital revolutions finished all in all with a happy end. Although in a considerably diminished number and considerably whitened (racially, not in hair), humanity survived. The planet was also rescued. The "emergency protocol," which was applied even brought about some positive side effects for society.

That's what happened to humanity and human society. But what about man, the individual rescued human being?

In order to answer this question, we first have to talk about the other revolution, that of biological science, which unfolded alongside the digital one—and alongside the environmental catastrophe.

Within 150 years after the discovery of genetic code, humans deciphered not only its every single word and message but their "translation" into the sequencing of amino acids and the folding in of the resulting proteins. Here once again artificial intelligence performed at its best, though even it struggled with the varieties of line-ups in the amino-acid protein chains. [307]

Humans were able to clone themselves without fusing male and female cells, to change as much as they wanted and whatever they wanted written in the lettering in all the three billion base pairs in their genome, to repair genes vulnerable to disease, to correct genes for beauty, strength, resilience. Humans could edit genetic information for an adult individual, just the same as for an embryo, even directly on the egg-cells and the spermatozoids. In this way they, first, cured illnesses, and second, the correction became permanent and was transmitted to future generations. Humanity could also thus import alien genes into a given genotype and thus created hybrid species, which really better served their needs for food. Bearing in mind that whole animals were rarely bred, hybrids did not create true chimeras, but only increased the efficiency

307 Although there are only 20 amino acids, a human protein consists of about 400 amino acids and some of thousands. The variations in ordering the 20 amino acids in the shorter protein chain of, let's say, ten of them outnumber world population. As the Economist notes: "There is no type of physical thing in the observable universe remotely as numerous as the possibilities inherent in a 400-amino-acid protein."

of the meat industry. At the birth, stem cells were extracted and frozen, so that later on various organs could be cultivated. People used them to renew themselves, the same way they would repair parts in the machines. People regularly renewed their blood. Diseases practically disappeared, because they'd either been eliminated right inside the genetic embryo or, if not, at their first appearance they were simply replaced by genes that vanquished the disease's bad proteins. Thus, mankind changed the course of its evolution, controlled it and targeted it. Genetically improved people were not only beautiful, whatever that meant, but also really healthy. Man had practically secured eternal youth in the sense that throughout their life, they could remain biologically young or at a biological age of their choice. Often you would get strange age combinations within the "parameters" of a single biological individual.

Women's socioeconomic emancipation in the rich part of the world coincided more or less with the industrial revolution, which was now followed by their biological emancipation. Woman was emancipated from her biological role and responsibilities. Before the environmental cataclysm and the genocide that followed it, poor, most often black and yellow skinned women, sold their wombs in order to feed their own children. Surrogate mothers gave birth to white, blue-eyed or green-eyed, genetically-designed babies. After the cataclysm and the death marches, the surrogate mothers died, along with all poor people, but then came the boom in synthetic biology. Genetically designed children were conceived and carried in synthetic wombs, shaped aesthetically like an unopened flower, from which the baby would be carefully extracted, like a ripe fruit, in the end, when the flower blossomed most aesthetically. Then, the baby would be fed by beautifully shaped, motherly synthetic breasts with synthetic milk. Everyone could decide unilaterally to have a child, either made-to-order or, if they're in love with themselves, a clone. The parents or parent came to enjoy their child in the incubator at fixed times and they took the baby back to enjoy it at home, along with the synthetic breast, bio-degradable nappies and a domestic childcare robot a couple of weeks after "the birth." Of course, there was strict control over reproduction—in principle every human—man, woman, or nonbinary had the right to one child. The expert councils were monitoring the demographic trends, and imposed moratoria over reproduction, or stimulated it over set periods so as to maintain the optimal population level.

With the progress of medicine, genetic engineering, and synthetic biology, biological sex, like many other things that had been thought of as "divine order" became a question of choice—by the parent or parents at the moment of conception and, more importantly, later by the person themselves. Sex became—to a significant extent—an irrelevant human marker. Besides, the distinguishing characteristics of both sexes had pretty much washed away. Classic intersexual procreation through coupling in sexual intercourse became a boutique, vintage method, practiced most often only in a few communes, or for pleasure and fun, or for conceptual reasons in the search for inspiration and meaning. The physical attractiveness of women lost its meaning as a primary sexual marker and reason for intersexual attraction, no longer necessary for procreation. Now all women were beautiful and young forever. Men lost their attractiveness, as based on physical strength, virility, and material security. Now all men and women and nonbinary were strong, fertile, and had everything. The opportunity to change sexes also led to the erasure of sexual differences and identity. First the family and soon after that the couple completely died out as constituent unit of society. People formed temporary couples, often only virtually, for the happy passing of time and as cure for some recidivist negative thoughts and emotions. Alongside inter-human couples, many human-machine couples existed, too. There is no hard evidence for machine only couples.

Prostitution, the oldest profession, also disappeared quite naturally, along with all professions. All women were beautiful, free, and available. For a significant time, poor women, the natural pool for prostitutes, whose primary resource was their secondary sex characteristics and their wombs, got another income opportunity from their resources—surrogate pregnancy. Then, after the dying out of the poor part of the population and the development of artificial wombs, both demand and supply vanished. With the disappearance of the family and couples, love turned from a painful and jealous passion to a game and entertainment. The temporary favorite, often only virtual, did not come along with a whole list of clauses for exclusivity and faithfulness, concepts bound up in morality. Love lost its exclusive role as an existential antidote, because there simply weren't any existential sorrows anymore, as would become clear a little later on.

In the beginning, humans believed the increase in intellect to be the triumphant crown of genetic engineering, to be laid on their heads. It turned out, however, that in contrast to the pretty faces and sculpted bodies, intellect was not coded within particular genes and could not be increased with some gene corrections. In fact, only human brain remained inscrutable for . . . itself, it was cryptic even for the intelligent machines, which otherwise knew everything and functioned just like the human brain, only without biological neurons. The mechanics and biology of the human brain were more or less clear, but how they produced thoughts, including abstract, memory, emotions, talents, art, consciousness, dreams, etc., remained a mystery. In fact, humans did not fully understand either how their intelligent machines were thinking, they had no idea if the machines' brains produced other things, apart from what they were programmed and assigned to do. A century or so ago, humans were very interested—and somewhat worried—in the question of if machines had or were capable of developing consciousness. This question remained opened, but now nobody really cared anymore. In any case, machines were the crucial resource, the means of production and product, and the perfect companions. Machines remained good-hearted, obedient, and diligent and had never manifested any sign of aggressiveness and evil (the cyborg security guards of the habitats were just doing their job to protect people and infrastructure when they removed those young men).

Paradoxically humans could create intelligent machines, which imitated the human brain and which could work a thousand times faster, but they couldn't upgrade their own brain. So they gave up on this social ideal—the machines were always more intelligent and completed anything requiring any intelligence more swiftly than any human. The ideal of the super-intelligent human soon became redundant and uninteresting, because paradoxically, the more intelligent the machines became, the more stupid humans turned, generation after generation. Thus, the digital and biological revolution replaced the thinking creature, Homo sapiens, with the simple, intellectually modest, Homo simplex. The new humans increasingly resembled their machines, only that they were a lot stupider. The machines reproduced themselves, ever more intelligent and powerful. And then they surprised humanity with some quite human emotions, thoughts, and creative outputs. As we said, machines were highly competitive as companions. Control over the machines had been the most important scientific discipline, although for a long time before, scientists were no longer able to program the machines, machines were programming and reproducing themselves. And altogether humans could not make heads or tails anymore of artificial intelligence, they still managed to control it at least. Happily, artificial intelligence remained a "good soul" and just served people's needs.

Humanity survived; humans had equal and guaranteed access to food, shelter, and virtual reality; disease and aging were eliminated; people went stupid, i.e., all prerequisites for happiness were in place. Homo simplex however was not happy.

At the beginning, in their habitats, people felt as if they were in the "cooler." Well, they were in a cooler place, for sure, for their good. Humans, the last whole cows and pigs, and even the extremely stupid chickens looked with sorrowful eyes at the disconsolate landscape outside. As they were cleaning the transparent walls and the low vault of their greenhouse "coolers," the cables, supplying the habitat with energy, the plumbing, bringing water from the desalination plant, the drainage systems, taking everything out into the sewage plant to turn it into energy again, human's anxious eyes checked for holes, cracks, crevices, loose joints, leaks. People knew only that if something in their prison broke down, there, outside, under the "darling sun," in the low oxygen dustbowl, or here inside the Noah's Ark, among the animals and human gases, they faced an agonizing death. In this sense, they got comfort, to some extent, from the broadcasts of those waves of poor people, who died outside. Although these coverages sparked a savage migraine.

At its annual virtual conference, the Habitats' Health Services decided to take prophylactic measures for the prevention of a depression and anxiety pandemic. They covered the habitat walls with cheerful pictures of natural sights and cultural landmarks. The decorations were very reminiscent of those ancient photo-wallpapers that had been especially popular in the communist bloc. Photo-wallpapers were clever 3-D photos (at one time they were called "stereo") their size and perspective created the impression in the viewer that they were there, on the spot. Just as at one time people dreamed in 3-D of places beyond the Iron Curtain, which they were never going to visit, so the wallpaper of the habitats conveyed—in three dimensions—places beyond the transparent wall, which now did not exist or, even if the "bright future" materialized, would never be what they once were. But these were palliative solutions, "small scale." The social ideal for cleaning and healing the planet and for humans leaving the habitats was too remote, even considering the increased life expectancy. This ideal didn't reassure people, however stupid they were, that their life had some sense. There was nothing to satisfy humans' need of hope and faith, of "something beyond" and few other utterly vague cravings.

A new social ideal was promulgated—that of the happy human. Homo Felix. The tormented, surviving, well-fed, beautiful, strong, forever young and stupid human simply wanted, in the end, to be happy. This task, innocent at first glance, turned out to be difficult to accomplish. Humanity was now able to steer evolution in whatever direction it wanted, it had entirely eliminated the coincidence and chaos of creation, but the new ideal for happiness ran up against human consciousness—all those uncontrollable loves and passions, myths and symbols, aesthetics and ethics, sorrows and melancholies, existential shivers and horrors, transcendent nightmares and chronological labyrinths, persisted in humans' otherwise shrinking gray and white matter. People realized that survival and material well-being was still not happiness and that individual human's salvation (maybe counting for humanity as well?) was only temporary. Referring to that ancient theory for happiness capacity, it seems that the machine's rescue and the communist society, also built by machines, only cheered humanity temporarily. Afterward into the mind of every human, one by one, there began to float back thoughts of death, of the point of all this, of fear, and of melancholy. That ancient economist, Karl Marx, was refuted on this point—human consciousness did not change despite the ascendance of communism.

People didn't know how to cut or alter the interactions between neurons and genes, or how to cheer up their human consciousness, but they knew enough to numb their minds, to blunt and even to completely eliminate or prevent fear and sadness. And they did it, from inception, quite literally. Newly conceived children were "treated" even before their birth, followed by treatments for already born children and all adults. It served as a global vaccination campaign for countering negative thoughts and feelings. Subsequently, it was established that vaccinated elderly individuals lost their memories of more distant events and forgot the stories of their ancestors; the newly born and the young did not have much to remember anyway. At the end of the day, this side effect was perceived as an unexpected bonus. Individual memories risked awakening more complex—and most probably unpleasant—thoughts and feelings. Historical events were written up and archived by machines and didn't need to be remembered. Life was so long and pleasant, memory loss prolonged it even further, into an endless procession of wonderful days and nights. Everyone was living "day to day."

People were also unable to eliminate the biological need for sleep. Actually, from a purely technological standpoint, it was possible to significantly reduce it, but it was rejected as being economically ineffective, because the already lengthened life-spans would—within the economic plan—become even longer. While they slept, people did not consume and did not dispose of waste, they weren't in virtual space, the maintenance of which required energy, they weren't taking up real space either, so overall they *were nowhere* and *were doing nothing from an economic point of view.* Calculations showed nine hours sleep would have the optimal economic effect. In each of the seven time zones, into which the inhabitable world was divided, a sleeping time of nine hours was fixed. The energy supply decreased, virtual reality was switched off (after a cute animated "Good night, sleep tight"). Vaccinated folk had no dreams, they slept healthily, deeply, and soundly. Their improved, smooth brains simply had nothing to dream—there was no suppressed subconscious to go wild in dreams, no unaccomplished desires to work through, no existential fears to unveil. The subconscious practically ceased to exist now, because everything was feasible, achievable and permissible. Memories were only filled by pleasant experiences and death was a technical detail.

Surely someone will ask what happened with religion. Religion survived for some time as the only moral and transcendent comfort for the poor. They really did go to their deaths more peacefully with the thought that as good folk go to a *good place*, they would be resurrected when the Earth is again green like heaven. With this, an ancient bloody brigand—Lenin—turned out to be right, religion really was the opium of the poor and did a good job in their painless extinction. With the triumph of machine communism and superior humanism, with the extinction of the poor, and with the cancellation of death through digital archiving, religion disappeared forever. The vaccinated brains of the new humans forgot that it had ever even existed.

The new humans discovered that with their immunity against sadness and fear, with the purging of their memories and with the triumph of the temporary, happy, free, and virtual love, now no one could think up stories, or music, or paintings. What's more, the books, music, pictures, and films from the past became difficult to understand and extremely boring, and after another generation or two, literally incomprehensible. Following the Global Treaty on Language, all surviving humans decided to communicate in one single language. It was so much more efficient and convenient. Different languages had been dumbed down at least, utterly simplified, parallel with the development of Homo Simplex and Homo Felix. Machines finished off the process when they completely standardized the simplified languages. Finally, the single global language put a definitive end to all linguistic ambiguities and to the need for translation.

As regards literature, once again the machines whirred into action to satisfy the aesthetic needs of the new—vaccinated and upgraded—happy human. Actually machines had begun to learn artistic crafts long before the existential vaccination and the Global Language Treaty, so as to take over from humans, who were then completely obsessed with their survival, and later on, too crushed by migraine and depression to create.

At the time, there were specialized computers that had perfectly mastered all living and dead languages, but were blocked when encountering metaphor; they'd translate all tropes literally—humor and irony completely escaped them. Yet, the artificial intellect was a fast, and indeed intelligent, learner. After having read the entire literary production of all of humanity for all time, and keeping in mind the intellectual level and the aesthetic needs of the contemporary human, machines started to produce concise and comprehensible summaries of ancient literary works, as well as their own original literature.

The computer analyzed music only through hertz values and mathematical rules of harmony, and fine art, if it was realistic—via identification of objects and colors. With abstract art, machines focused on curves, shapes, sine waves and light spectrum. Sculpture was examined as a physical object: material, density, weight, shape, surfaces, resemblance to other objects.

All and all, with this input, machines produced quite decent art—literary, visual and musical. At first people laughed, although sadly, at the products of artificial intelligence, in which, as in a negative, they were still able to discern that uniquely human "thing," that was missing in machine artifacts. After the vaccination, however, people grew completely satisfied with machine art. Furthermore, this art had a very beneficial effect on new humans as it infused them with even more happiness. Only, ancient music created some problems, as it stirred inexplicable gloomy moods. As the preservation, diffusion, and perception of this music remained unaffected by the death of the languages, health authorities devised some smart policies to limit the access to it and its propagation and to substitute it, once and forever, with the joyful machine tunes.

But there was little time even for the artistic output of artificial intelligence, in spite of the increase in life expectancy. How did people *kill time*, when they lacked for nothing, didn't work, had no need to fight, to struggle for survival or with illnesses? Statistics based on electricity usage showed that people spent three quarters of their wakeful lives in virtual reality. (The remaining time went to their children, before the children themselves sank into a virtual world, to real biological feeding and expulsion, to a rest for the brain from the virtual and for real physical exercise round the habitat.)

The first virtual world was created at the beginning of the twenty-first century. People could reside as avatars in the *Metaverse.* The project did not enjoy much success because the real world was still habitable, accessible, sensorially enjoyable, tasty, immediate. Then, obviously, things dramatically changed. Virtual reality attained unprecedented technological heights and completely replaced—which by then was already quite limited and gloomy—reality. Moreover, everybody could design their own virtual world to their taste, existing in parallel to the visiting, residing, gaming, and socializing found in the common *virtual* towns, playrooms, forests, etc. Virtual reality almost entirely replaced physical communication, sex, and travel. People fell in love, went on excursions, visited galleries and restaurants, took part in large scale games, would be examined by doctors and dentists, even could be operated on without getting out of bed, thanks only to a soft ergonomic helmet, which they fixed on their head and which took them everywhere, "body and soul." What's more, not only could their partner or the gallery they're visiting be a thousand kilometers away or more, it was entirely possible that these things and people existed only in one's virtual world. Meetings—of friends, lovers, family—took place most often during a visit to someone's virtual world. Taking photos, recording, and archiving in general were not very popular, because of the drastic decline in human memory. Then, why was it necessary for people to stuff their memories with monotonously beautiful, pleasant memories? Altogether, memories became utterly useless, because humans could recreate the virtual every moment and it was so wonderful that everything would appear as new.

And so, the new people lived in an eternal youth—on average 100 to 110 revolutions of their planet round its star. They were extremely happy, crammed with serotonin and pheromones, they slept soundly and long. In life, in virtual reality, and in art, there was no more ugliness, old age, pain, tragedies, wars, impossible love affairs, fears, and worrying thoughts. People decided for themselves when to die, most often from boredom. They met death simply as a transition from biological to digital existence, because their simple brains were now downloaded and archived and they'd continue to exist. Postmortem digital existence even preserved some sensory pleasures of the flesh. Just like in the ancient world, after a leg was amputated, humans would still feel a tickle, science managed to stimulate and simulate sensory experiences in the neural little black boxes, which represented the biologically dead and digitally alive humans. All and all, death was not a big deal anymore; it didn't change who knows what, it was a sort of retirement from the anyhow boring real world and physical existence. Technologies practically secured human immortality. With the lack of fear and sorrow, things were even more painless and were reduced to technical parameters and the choice of the level of digitalization. The digitalized, biologically dead individuals continued to inhabit the same global virtual reality, only their avatars appeared with an *inoffensive* marker attached—a tiny purple cloud. They were completely free to log on or not, *at will*, although it remained unclear how exactly that will was formed and exercised. There are no records of what postmortem digital avatars engaged themselves with when they weren't in virtual reality. Statistics report that after a maximum of ten years, digitalized people stopped logging on. It seems they got bored with both their digital being and virtual reality. Bored to ultimate death. Or, maybe it was inefficient to maintain the little black boxes any longer. It seems at this point death stepped in definitively. Nobody knew what happened afterward with the content of the little black boxes, most probably it was deleted and the box was used to upload the next pensioner. As far as biological corpses were concerned, their disposal was also used for the benefit of habitat energy supply.

Conclusively, it shall be noted that communism did not change human consciousness, nor did the apocalypse. The salvation of the human led to repairing those impairments in the *human condition* that prevented happiness. What fundamentally changed humanity were the anti-melancholic vaccines and their side effects, artificial intelligence, virtual reality, the global language and, most of all, the "reconceptualization" of death and the digital being.

There were, however, some people, mostly in Europe, who at the time protested against the "cruel inaction" of the rich world faced with the agony and death of two thirds of humanity. They swished antique copies of Kant and Dostoevsky and screamed that the happiness of the whole world should not cost even a single child's tear. The Expert Councils immediately agreed that what was happening was extremely inhuman and that these folk had the right to protest, but insisted that any humanitarian aid had to be voted for and agreed on by everyone, because the resources were common property, including the huge extra resources needed for the rescue of the poor. And there were no spare resources, the resources of the rich countries were barely sufficient for their own population. However hopeless it was, in some habitats, they even carried out completely free referenda, in which, of course, only these odd folk voted to rescue all of humanity. The odd folk were few. After the Councils' decisions or after the referenda, this minority of odd folk were completely free to try on their own to help the dying billions of brothers and sisters. But this was going to be a desperate and utterly unproductive suicide and almost none of the odd folk dared leaving their habitats and setting out on a march of death in the opposite direction. Nevertheless, few did so as a protest against "the degradation of humanity." They all died within a radius of a dozen kilometers from their habitats.

They called these odd people "old-timers."[308] Old-timers were recognized as a global, minority cultural and language group and were allotted dedicated streets and areas in the habitats. They called these ghettoes "the Communes of Sorrow."

308 According to the Global Treaty on language.

The old-timers had a hard time living through the first pandemics of migraine and depression. The photo-wallpaper and their own salvation brought them no comfort. In spite of this, they refused to vaccinate their children against melancholy and fear. The old-timers said that humans had to bear their punishment for the crime they had committed. The old-timers maintained also that the physical survival of humanity and the progress of science came at a horrific cost—they had destroyed what was human in humanity.

From the benefits of the biological revolution, they made use of only those which prevented and cured some illnesses. The old-timers lived as couples, created in the old-fashioned romantic way. They categorically refused to modify their children's genes and create designer-kids to order. They let nature and chaos reign. The old-timers did not beautify or periodically rejuvenate themselves with spare parts. These people wanted to sleep naturally, and most of all, to dream, even if this meant to have nightmares. As might be expected, life expectancy in the Communes of Sorrow was about twenty years shorter, old-timers aged and lost their looks and death was ugly and tragic. Very few made use of the digital beyond.

They used machines primarily for information, and virtual reality—only as an archive of human civilization and culture. As a matter of fact, it was the old-timers who digitalized and archived human history, philosophy, religion, and art, notably literature and music (paintings, sculptures, and architecture which could not be moved to the special storage habitats and which perished, were digitalized centrally). These sad folk spent their time in real reality, however ugly and depressing it was.

The only advancement which they unconditionally welcomed was the machine communism and the subsequent organization of governance.

In their free time, which meant practically all the time, the old-timers communicated physically and for real, looked after and taught their imperfect children, actually made love, played sports, tried to grow genetically unmodified fruit and vegetables, wrote historical chronicles and poetry, read old human literature and philosophy, listened to old classical music. They committed to learning old languages that nobody spoke anymore, to translate between these old languages, to record readings in these languages, so that the phonetics were well-preserved. Actually, in their Global Convention (which was, in reality, mostly European) some twenty to twenty-five old languages were distributed among the habitats, hosting old-timers' communes. Thus they rescued a number of old complex languages from extinction. The old-timers despised the works produced by artificial intelligence, as well as the single global language, imposed by global treaty. They despised Homo Simplex and the new social ideal of the happy person. The happy people, for their part, avoided these ugly, sullen folk, who just "spoiled their mood" and threw a shadow over the virtual beauteousness of the world.

One day, in the old-timers' area in a habitat somewhere in Europe, a young girl was sitting in front of the building where her family was living. Among the stone-gray urban landscape, her old fashioned red coat stood out like a hand colored detail in an old black and white film. Just like the girl in the red coat in that film from 180 years earlier, which her parents had seen recently, but hadn't allowed her to cuddle up and watch it together with them. With Mom and Dad she'd seen another really old film—*Don't Look Up*. The girl hadn't understood everything, but the film had seemed very funny to her. As always, Mom and Dad had remained thoughtful.

The little girl knew that she was named after some faraway great-great-grandma.

The virtual school for the day was over. So easy and boring. Besides, Mom and Dad did not agree with many of the things they were teaching at school. The child sat on the stone flags and opened a paper book. A very old book, which her parents only had on their computers, but printed it on synthetic paper and bound it, just like a real old book. They were old-ti-mer-s after all. The child whispered the syllables. The book was in that old language, which was assigned to Mom and Dad to learn and preserve, and which they were teaching to their girl. They said that this was the language of their ancestors, anyway.

The girl didn't understand a lot of things in the book, but then other stuff made her laugh. Her laughter reverberated in the stone walls of the buildings in the narrow empty street. Old-timers very rarely laughed. It was unusually quiet and empty. The child's eyes darted toward the corner. Where had everyone gone? And Mummy and Daddy? The girl read again. See here, so one time, apples grew on trees, there were chocolate eggs, children gathered to learn in schools, they spoke in many quite different languages, adults got together in or-che-stras to play music. The girl folded the page, to show where she'd got to and entered the building. There she crunched two big bonbons—one for egg and one for chocolate—to try the taste of a chocolate egg. Ugh, it was disgusting—the child spat out the two crushed bonbons. And she took the familiar apple pill, the big one. The natural apples which her mother had brought a few times were twisted and withered, but still a lot tastier than the pills. They had flesh and lasted longer, there was . . . apple in these apples, not just flavor and concentrated nutrients as in the apple pills. "But there's no pill for white-cherry jam," the child sighed. There wasn't even a pill for white cherries only. Then she opened the book to remember what music was mentioned there. The girl went to the computer which kept her parents' digital library and looked for this music. In contrast to the taste of chocolate eggs, white-cherry jam and apples, the music was preserved just as it had been. The child popped in the tiny earpieces, closed her eyes and was completely carried away into the world of music.

ORCHESTRA REHEARSAL

In my childhood Lom was still a bustling little Danube town, preserving something from the spirit of the first theatre[309] and the Viennese fashion and music, coming down the river. Even the communist daily grind was somehow open-handed, bohemian. My parents were young, they played bridge till dawn with friends, then they took a shower, left me and my brother in the crèche and kindergarten or school and left for work—my mother an engineer in the port, my father a chief engineer of the brewery. Granny stayed at home to cook with her one non-paralyzed hand.

On these bridge nights, music sounded from the Grundig tape player—Bulgarian, French, Italian pop—*Camino Caminandro, Yo ti amo, Natalie.*[310] I listened to the music in bed in the other room, where I slept with Granny, with my little brother beside us in a crib. Granny muttered, "Aren't they going to bed? What's with this music all hours of the night!" But I really loved these beautiful words, which I didn't understand, and their tunes. They talked of faraway lands and people and as yet unknown feelings. I was extremely curious about what the adults were playing, what they ate and drank. So I tried some beer (secretly of course) when I was about five (thank God I didn't like it). The salted hard mackerel was nicer, but was very chewy. In the library the auntie was surprised when she saw one of the books I'd chosen—*Do You Play Bridge?*—and asked if I'd picked it for Mum or Dad. I told her that it was for Granny—that sounded

309 The first *chitalishte* (cultural center) in Bulgaria was established in Lom around 1850. In 1856, a group of amateurs gathered around the cultural center and staged, in Lom, the first theatre performance in Bulgaria.
310 Musical hits of the time.

to me convincing enough. At nine years old I already played belote pretty well and as a teenager I got into bridge.

In Lom, Mum and Dad learned German—from a TV course and textbooks. I asked them why they were learning another language and who they were going to talk German with. Dad explained that this was the language of all the great engineers and composers. "And of the Emperor's horses," he added, hiding a smile. At my age I took talking horses as completely normal and so I asked no more.[311] Dad continued that Granddad Rusan had been an engineer, had studied in Vienna and spoke German. On top of this, he'd played the flute. Because I didn't see the connection between music and German (I liked the songs on the gramophone even without understanding the words, and you didn't need to know German to play the flute), I concluded that my father learned German because he wanted to become a great engineer (composer appeared to me somehow overstating it). Mum obviously was learning it because of Dad—so she could be ready to talk to him about engineering (wasn't she an engineer too?), when he became a great engineer, and as such, would only be speaking German.

When he wasn't at work, or playing bridge, or fixing something, my father was at a rehearsal in the *chitalishte*, or was practicing alone in the cellar (where it was warm and he'd set up a workshop, in which he repaired not only everything at home, but his friends' televisions, radios, cookers, telephones and anything else that was electrical and portable). Lom had an amateur orchestra in which my father played the cello. When he was sixteen, my father had gone to an audition to choose pupils for a boarding school for gifted children. He played the Boccherini cello concerto. Granddad and Granny shed tears of pride and joy in the third row, in the big hall of the *chitalishte*. He was accepted, but then my father told his parents that "he did not wish to be a slave to his instrument his whole life" and he wanted to be an engineer. Like his father. Granny lost it entirely, screamed about chance and future, reminding him that unlike his father, her son would not be able to study engineering in Vienna, that with this background, who knew if any Bulgarian university would accept him, but that as a musician he would travel the world. Granddad signaled for Granny to be silent and told his son he would be whatever he alone wanted to be, and not what his parents wanted, because he'd have to work the chosen job his whole life. And so my father became an electrical engineer. When he was studying at the Higher Mechanical-Electro Technical Institute in Sofia, he drove a taxi at nights

311 At the Leipzig trial in 1933, Georgi Dimitrov boasted that in the so-called "barbarian" Bulgaria, in the ninth century, vernacular Bulgarian was the language of religious service and orthodox literature, while in Germany, at that time, the German emperor was talking German only to his horses.

to support himself and played in the student orchestra, in return for the lodgings they gave him as an orchestra member. He had to repeat the first two years, not so much for lack of sleep and for exhaustion from his diverse occupations, but because of bridge. The other lad who'd played the cello in front of the commission really did travel the world as a concert cellist. My father returned to Lom and became an electrical engineer in a brewery.

I think that Dad really did like his job. After we left Lom, he moved on to national sites, forever launching power stations, he'd come home at nights in an oily anorak. Then he left for long years in Libya, which didn't stop me wondering until my quite mature teenage years, that in these stations and in the brotherly Jamahiriya they talked in German.

But Dad loved music a lot as well and appeased this love in Lom's amateur orchestra. He took me with him to almost all the rehearsals. Something magical happened at these rehearsals in the same big hall of the *chitalishte*—with both people and music. The terrifying doctor who opened my tummy again, with a local anesthetic, to repair his colleague's botched appendicitis operation of three months earlier, this same monster produced tender notes on the flute. Two of the teachers from my school—strict, croaking aunties beneath beehive hairdos—here they had serene, somehow kindly faces, hunched over their violins. And they were amazingly silent. They uttered never a word and obeyed the conductor. There was one cellist along with my father—a colleague of my mother at the port, or so Dad told me. My own father was different, as though he'd forgotten about me. As he drew the bow across the strings and his fingers danced up and down the fingerboard, on his face appeared an expression that I'd never seen before, even when he looked at me and my little brother with joyful eyes. Dad never seemed like a slave to the cello, rather more its lover—he caressed it, loved it, it seemed to me that in these moments he loved the cello and music more than anything in the world, more even than Mum, my brother and me. I was unconsciously jealous for that expression, that loving dedication to the cello and the music. But the music itself made me quickly forget my jealousy and fall beneath its spell.

The orchestra conductor was "Uncledan," as I thought the old man was called, with his wild white hair and his frameless spectacles, which skewed on his nose after some furious move. Uncle Dan was a now pensioned ex-dentist. "Unlike me," Dad told us at home, "he wanted to be a conductor, to be a slave to music, but his people in the village didn't even know what that was and cut him off with 'a musician doesn't feed a home.' Look, being a dentist is different. And Dan became a dentist." "He helped people feed themselves" was my private conclusion.

Uncle Dan would close his eyes and cradle the music in his hands, then suddenly he'd be wide awake, tapping his stick on the podium, the music would stop in stages, unknit instrument by instrument, and he'd shout "But listen, please, the oboe has just overslept." Or he'd continue to rock the sound and just signal to some instrument to be quieter or louder—"more, more, more," he'd suddenly wave his arms furiously, to beat the rhythm and to chase that "Presto, presto!" unattainable for the amateur orchestra.

What happened with the music itself in these rehearsals also amazed me. The music was dissected, bar by bar, instrument by instrument and then sewn up and reassembled instrument by instrument, bar by bar. And again. And again. I discovered the voices of separate instruments and the beauty of their parts, which otherwise I didn't hear in the whole. I sat open-mouthed, amazed by the beauty of the combined voices and parts of two or three instruments. In the end the musical tapestry of the whole became somehow transparent, because I now could hear the different instruments, their voices and music. And even so I forgot about them, hypnotized by the power and might of the total orchestra, of the total music.

Dad led me into harmony and polyphony. "Don't just listen to the hysterical violins, that's on the surface. Listen to the cellos. Even though we're not heard a lot because there are only two of us. Did you hear the clarinet? Beautiful eh?" he directed me, talking to himself as well. Dad repeated that there was a lot of mathematics in music, that harmony and polyphony were actually mathematics, that music was the most *abstract* of the arts. I didn't know what abstract meant and at 6 or 7 goodness knows what understanding I had of math. Dad tried to explain the abstract in music (in a way that I now find exceptional):

"What makes up music—notes, melody, harmony, polyphony, tempo—doesn't exist anywhere else outside music. Ey, how can I explain it to you? OK, let's take a book. What are you reading with Granny?"

"*Mushroom boy.*"

"OK, so let's take *Mushroom boy*. The story's made up of words, yes?"

I hadn't thought at all about what a story is made from.

"But we use words in our lives—to talk, to write. Words exist before being used in a story. And music is made of things, which don't exist anywhere else. Birds sing, but that has nothing to do with great music. That grows in the minds of the composer.

But this is genius. Very few people can write music. But stories—lots of folk write . . . whatever."

Dad was soldering something on the board of a disassembled radio in the cellar while he was explaining all this.

"Then there's something else. Stories are about something. Tell me what *Mushroom Boy* is about."

I gave him a quick summary.

"So it's about a family, yeah, well of mushrooms, not of people. And how Mushroom Boy is naughty and sets out into the forest and there some dangerous stuff happens. But actually the story is about a family of people. And how children shouldn't go out on their own. Like you. Because it's dangerous. There are cars—in the story those are bears—what about bad people—those are the wolves . . ."

I really did manage a few times to put Granny literally to sleep and set out on my own in Lom with my Butterfly[312] bike. At the age of five and a half I turned up in the port to surprise Mom, among the cranes and fork-lifts, passing by the busy Vidin main road on the bike. Mom was so surprised that she almost fainted. Another time my horrified parents found me in the market, beside a granny, telling her . . . stories. My very own. The granny had caught my attention with her marketing, unheard of at that time. On the stall hung a card with a drawing of two tomatoes and a pepper. The Granny had drawn them well. And beside them, the letters gone over several times with a biro was written the nursery rhyme: "Peppers and tomatoes, eat them right away, / Or you won't grow strong enough to come out and play." I liked this granny. I sat at her stall in the market to offer her my goods. Which surely had to be offered in response to her rhyme, "Human stories, read them right away, / Or you won't get up to fight another day." It even rhymed.

I'll never forget how my father's drained face lit up when he saw me next to that granny.

"But with music, you can't tell what the story is. Everyone hears their own story."

And thus, so naturally, Dad explained the mimesis and moralistic function of literature. Which was completely absent from music and that's why it's abstract. Like mathematics. Furthermore in the harmony, polyphony and tempo there's a lot of mathematics. But not in the melody. "Melody," Dad reckoned, "is the direct expression of the composer's soul. Beethoven was deaf when he composed this music. Can you imagine? He could not even hear it. So it existed directly in the soul, in his brain." Dad was fired up as though he himself didn't believe in what he was saying, it was so amazing.

312 A brand name of children bikes.

Along with these comments, Dad didn't like jazz—"some kind of kitsch, cacophonies, improvisation, I'm begging you, oh, please!" Anyhow, we weren't allowed to listen to it.

At this time, Granny took me to solfège lessons once a week. "The child is really musical. She'll go to music classes this year and next year we'll sign her up for an instrument." Granny had clearly not given up on the round-the-world trips with instrument in hand and was planning my future already.

Clearly musicality is genetic, because I'd only sleep like a baby if someone sang to me. My dear mother sang horribly out of tune. Faced with the choice between my non-stop wailing and my mother's singing, my father preferred not to sleep but to sing to me. "Sleep my baby, my true darling, the storm is raging outside, sheltered in our poor hovel . . ." Granny had sung this song to Dad, he sang it to me, and I sang it to my kids, although they hardly understood the archaic words and in spite of the *maison de maître* in which my son grew up. Actually, for Michael, over the course of two years, not only did I sing every evening, but accompanied myself on guitar. Special mother—troubadour. "The world is for two"[313] will remain forever in the beginning of Michael's world, as if it were a love song from his dead father. "*Don't love another, not even his call, don't fall, the world's for two, my love glows tender again withal, even whe-en, even when I'm no more. Even when I'm no more in this sunlit world, look for my love in spring posy twirled.*"

But to return forty-five years ago and to continue the story. It was far more likely that the zenith of my artistic career would be the amateur orchestra, and not the world stages. If we'd stayed in Lom, if the orchestra had continued to exist, if Lom had remained that lively town full of engineers, doctors, dentists, teachers who played bridge and instruments in an orchestra.

After a few months of solfège I was extremely proud when, at a rehearsal, I looked at Dad's sheet music and managed to identify some of the notes correctly, and he showed me how to produce them on the cello. I was very excited that these notes came directly from the brain of a great composer and I could read them with my own brain.

The orchestra's repertoire was inevitably limited. The orchestra itself was not fully manned because of a lack of qualified staff, so to say. They called on a gypsy from a wedding and funeral brass band for the percussion. But in spite of his efforts he still came out too strong and somewhat inappropriately playful and Uncle Dan would scold him that "this wasn't one of his gypsy weddings."

313 Bulgarian lyrical ballade of the '80s.

The solo singers were also quite colorful. The soprano was the daughter of a "Boruna[314] drunkard"—with a slight squint, but even so a pretty girl of about twenty, with long coppery hair, who, the rest of the time, used to clean fish. Although her voice was not at all opera trained, she sang like an angel and even Uncle Dan sometimes dropped his baton, to listen to her, without the orchestra. I asked Dad what "Boruna drunkard" meant, because it sounded to me like a dragon. The alto was the snooty secretary to the Mayor, who mostly owed her voice to cigarettes. Every time she was made up as if for the stage. A dockworker roared out the bass parts. He let loose his voice and drowned out the anyway undermanned orchestra. Uncle Dan would signal "pianissimo, pianissimo," then he'd lose his rag. "This has to be tender! You're wooing a woman, for fuck's sake, not swearing."

The dockworker would snigger and carry on as he knew best, showing off his unchallengeable strength and virility over the pale intellectual tenor (otherwise an accountant) who seemed almost ashamed of his voice and the high pitches that it could reach. Afterward he'd cough in embarrassment, as though his voice had somehow cheated on him. The cross-eyed angel and the dockworker couldn't read music sheets and learned everything by ear. The back-up vocal parts were performed by five or six male and female teachers, and sometimes they hit false notes, but then they obeyed Uncle Dan and sang more quietly so the false notes didn't jar too much. The cultural center had an amateur mixed choir. These around fourteen men and women led the church backing group—i.e., a flock of pensioners who sang in the protestant church (on the rare occasions when the church was open for a service). So a choir was formed of about thirty to thirty five people altogether.

Every season the orchestra premiered something new—whole operettas like *The Countess Maritza*, *Rose Marie*, and *The Gypsy Princess* came down the river from Vienna. Once set up with costumes, decors and all the props, the operettas would run for years. There were recitals and instrumental concerts of lighter popular arias and musical pieces—*Eine Kleine Nachtmusik*, Liszt's preludes, *Peer Gynt*. I remember the last one, rather I hear it in my head even today, as something mostly deafening. With the speeding up of the tempo, Uncle Dan fell into an apoplexy and in the end jumped convulsively, his arms spasmodic, and the gypsy with shining eyes smashed the percussion generously, at will, at moments Grieg had and had not foreseen.

The season opened at the end of September and closed at the end of June. There was a performance every three or four weeks. If anyone was ill, or in an unplanned extremely drunken state, Uncle Dan would calculate at the last minute whether the

314 The fishermen neighborhood in Lom.

performance could go ahead without them. The Orchestra could get by without one of the ten violinists, or without one of the thirty five choristers, but not without one of the two cellists or the cross-eyed angel or the dock-worker, if the program included singing. And it really did happen that performances were postponed. Although, even if they were sick, the artists came to the performances. The heavily made up secretary even threw up on the stage once, over a dummy rose bush. Her lipstick was smudged, big sweat stains broke out under her armpits on her long purple dress. Uncle Dan stopped the orchestra, turned to the audience and announced that the performance was "discontinued due to health reasons."

Along with weddings featuring more prominent families (all funerals were equal and paraded without discrimination), the performances were the most important events of provincial life. The hall of the cultural center seemed to me as large as a concert hall ought to be. There was even a balcony. The preparations, the dresses, *le beau monde*, gossip, snobbery, the drooping eyes of the high-school girls, the proud looks: "Do you see our Stoyan, how he plays? What a talent, and he wastes himself as an accountant." From my reserved first row seat at the end of the balcony, I attended all the performances, most often on my own, because Mum preferred to stay at home with my little brother, and it was difficult for Granny to climb the stairs with her paralyzed leg. And then, I've thought later, that she most probably sniffed at this amateurism, which only went to remind her that her son didn't become a professional, great, world musician.

Thanks to the orchestra rehearsals not only did I know every bit by heart, but also each and every part for every instrument or group of instruments. And despite this, during the performance I listened as if hypnotized. And relieved from the tension that Uncle Dan might suddenly rap his baton and stop the music. Uncle Dan often wanted to do this, but no one would have forgiven the hurt and insult, the audience included. The audience forgave the momentary false notes and mistakes, but they'd never forgive the breaking of the magic, of the theater of a real performance and a real concert.

I really cannot judge, especially through the idealizing veils of time, the quality of the performance of the orchestra and its soloists. Paraphrasing Woody Allen, I'd reckon that if dentists were conductors or if dockworkers were bass-baritones, they'd have to have produced this kind of music. Certainly there were bum-notes and mistakes and blurred rhythm, and omissions and late entries. But in spite of the amateurishness and apart from the provincial snobbery there was something festive and illuminating. It stayed quivering in the air, in the silence after the last notes and before the applause, in the stupor of the players and singers, in the shining eyes of the audience, of these teachers, accountants, engineers, hairdressers, secretaries, high school students, pensioners, who, like children, had surrendered to music and let it enchant them and take them into another world.

Afterward, in kindergarten, and then in school, I would try to hum the melodies to show the kids what music was. I got angry at the simple sounds that came out of my mouth, at the teasing of the kids. But nothing could snuff out the light and the unfathomable exaltation that overtook me. Walking alongside my parents on Sunday walks through the riverbank park (where my parents finally started to take us, the two kids, out, instead of "taking in" the funeral parades at home) I would sing. I was sure that if I spread out my arms, I'd fly. I could physically feel how I'd row the air with my hands, how the air would be thick and I'd rise slowly, on impulse, just as though I were swimming in water. I'd experienced this many times in dreams. I didn't spread my arms to check, only because my parents were there. I saw how worried they'd been by my meeting with my dead Granddad and what consequences I brought on myself by telling them about it. People couldn't fly. Full stop. But little children could clearly sing operetta arias or symphonic melodies, because my parents didn't look worried by my ecstatic moods.

It was a Sunday morning the end of December the final rehearsal before the New Year. The following summer we would leave Lom and move to a big city. One that had a large, real orchestra of professional musicians, and a real opera with real opera singers, and a real choir, even a ballet, and, of course, a theatre, Dad told me. I was almost 8, the snow reached up to my waist. I followed Dad on the path dug through the town square toward the cultural center.

"Ah, it's warm here," Dad blew on his fingers and then mine. Almost all the musicians were here, shucking off their galoshes, taking off their fur deerstalkers and coats, staying in knitted woolen socks and pullovers, the stove rumbled, it smelled of wool, sweet eau-de-cologne and garlic.

I took my place of to the side, in line with the conductor, on a gutted sofa where I peeled off my rubber overshoes, took off my red coat and hat, lay back, wrapped myself in my coat and prepared to listen. Uncle Dan straightened up before the orchestra, he tapped his baton on the podium, silence fell. He didn't speak for a few seconds, deep in thought, and then he said, "Colleagues, Nasko wants us to do Beethoven's violin concerto."

Doubt, sniggering, "yeah-yeah," sideways looks, eyebrows lifted . . . Uncle Dan waited then continued, "Nasko will play the solo of course."

Dad's fellow cellist shouted out, "Nasko, with all due respect, let's not waste our time, we'll be a laughingstock."

A violinist teacher hissed, "Frogs know their place in the pond. The prince wants to show off to the high school girls."

Uncle Dan carried on as if he hadn't heard, "Because we don't have the capacity for full orchestration, I'll take care of cutting out what I can. I'll keep our abilities in mind. We might do just one movement, the second one. It's almost entirely violin with a background fill."

"So, Nasko will be shining and we'll be croaking quietly behind, right," the viola player grimaced—a bald short man in red woolly socks.

"Listen to the concerto at home to prepare," Uncle Dan continued unruffled. "I'll be ready with the arrangement in two weeks. Nasko will help me. Then I'll give it to the librarians to copy out the notes for everyone.

Dad had lowered his bow and was listening to Uncle Dan, but I couldn't read his expression. Nasko himself was sitting as though uninvolved, fixing his eyes on his knitted socks. Nasko was the music teacher in the town's only high school, where I now knew I wouldn't be studying. If Saint-Exupéry's little prince had grown up, he'd have looked like Nasko, with curly blond hair, blue eyes, a pale, slender, self-absorbed young man. I'd heard Dad say that he was 27, that he'd graduated violin at the Conservatory, and he was the only professional musician in the orchestra. From the pensioner agora, Granny learned that he was a bachelor, that all the high school girls were in love with him, but despite almost non-stop surveillance, no one had seen him with a schoolgirl or with any woman at all, that he wasn't from Lom and that there were the greatest variety of rumors about what had led him to these parts—from a banal job assignment, through family tragedy, to an abandoned pregnant woman.

The only real musician was going to play Beethoven's violin concerto in an arrangement made by a retired dentist, with an orchestra of envious amateurs.

Dad began to listen to the record of the concerto at home. Non-stop and very loud, in the living room, not the cellar. In the beginning, Mum and Granny liked it a lot ("just a little quieter"), but after a week they'd had enough of the noise and my father's isolation with the gramophone in the living room.

Uncle Dan had confirmed that they'd just play the second movement and had given out the music sheets. And the rehearsals started. By the end of February thick snow had fallen again, and later a horrible chill gripped the city, the snow froze and became as powdery as sugar. Even the river started to freeze. Auntie Petrunka had lit the stove in the hall two hours before the rehearsal, but it remained cold inside. The musicians didn't take off their galoshes or coats, they crowded round the stove with hands outstretched, they couldn't play with their stiffened fingers.

When Nasko played the piece for the first time, everyone was startled, they raised their eyes from the sheets, stared at him and stopped playing. Nasko played just like the record. Better, actually, because he was there. The magical sound was emerging from his delicate fingers, just a few meters away, in this room stinking of wool and garlic; it was intimate, here and now. But at the same time Nasko's violin conveyed something ineffably beautiful, exquisite, and distant, the music touched something deep and forgotten or unsuspected in the hearts of everyone. In the eyes of the orchestra members there welled up a reverie, it was elating them, casting aside envy and doubt, even admiration and recognition of the violinist, who was creating the music.

This early evening in February, on the gutted sofa, I felt for the first time goose pimples and waves of strange enchantment tickling up my back, shoulders, and neck, which had nothing to do with the cold, and which would crawl over me every time when a group of people, whether a choir or orchestra, played or sang my favorite music, when I read some magic lines, or when magic happened on a theatre stage.

Uncle Dan was the first to come out of the trance, letting Nasko finish the phrase then tapping the podium. Nasko stopped playing. Then the bald viola began to beat slowly his bow on the strings, all the violins followed him, Dad and Mum's colleague also hit their cellos with their bows, the flute, clarinet, oboe, and French horn tapped their music stands with their hands, the double bass kept time. I looked around because I didn't know what was happening. Nasko turned toward the orchestra, blushing from embarrassment, bowed and said something bashfully which could not be heard over the noise. At last he gestured for the orchestra to stop.

"Thank you. For me it's an honor and p-pleasure to p-play with you," he said quietly, stammering from embarrassment.

"You're great, Nassy, you should know that. Great," the bald viola called out.

It turned out that this was how orchestra musicians applaud, as Dad explained after the rehearsal. No one had ever been applauded in this professional way, even the cross-eyed angel, although they sometimes clapped for her or drove her on with "Bravo, my girl!"

And then the real rehearsals began—bar by bar, mostly with the orchestra. Nasko's violin captivated and motivated everyone, all the instruments wanted to be their best, to provide a true accompaniment, in time with the violin and its beautiful monologue. Uncle Dan was unusually restrained, he hardly spoke during the rehearsals. A sharp rap of the baton meant stop, two taps meant repeat and Uncle Dan just gave the number of the bar. His remarks were short and most often about someone's slowing down or speeding up.

Nasko gave these ordinary folk the courage to play great music, to overcome their doubts and to grow into real musicians. For their part, they grew past their envy and allowed the orchestra to have a soloist, a true solo violinist. They allowed Nasko to be a great musician, to tower above them, and they to remain accompanying musicians. From the bald viola's spontaneous exclamation, Nasko's nickname, or rather artistic pseudonym spread. The whole town now knew him as Nasko the Great. Nasko was very big for the small provincial town, but the town was proud of its great violinist.

Because the orchestra had a small and undemanding presence in second movement of the concerto, and Nasko was playing perfectly, it took only a few rehearsals for the piece to be put together, ready to be performed at a really high standard. The Concerto's second movement doesn't have its very own finale—after a powerful grimace in minor of the whole orchestra and an exquisite pirouette of the violin, it flows into the start of the third movement. Nasko began it, two violas and one cello (Dad!) followed him into the quivering dialogue of the third movement. But after a few bars they stopped. The third and first movements were beyond this orchestra's capabilities, but this didn't need to be reminded lest the players felt belittled. The second movement is very short—just eight minutes or so. They decided that at the performance they'd play it twice. Nasko wrote the notes and explained how the passage would work, from the end to the restart of the second movement and he suggested some concluding chords from the whole orchestra as the finale to the second play-through.

At the next rehearsal Uncle Dan announced that the choir also wanted to participate and that "there is a proposal to prepare an all-Beethoven program—the violin concerto, a string quartet which is already being rehearsed by Nasko, Vulchan, Boyan and Keva and . . ." Uncle Dan took a breath, "a little lightened version of the fourth movement of *Symphony No.9*, I mean, the *Ode to Joy*." Oh, what amazement, someone even shrieked forth a shrill parody of the tune.

Uncle Dan rehearsed the choir and the four soloists separately. Then began the combined rehearsals of soloists, choir, and orchestra. The vocal quartets were very difficult. Actually, to be quite honest, they bothered my ears. And the music from the orchestra was somehow strange—I had the feeling that Beethoven had been on a trial run, *an essay*, "Let's now see how this will sound, now that"—but he couldn't hear the final result. Wasn't he deaf already at that time? So this is the kind of music deaf composers wrote. Dad explained to me that this was dissonance. In order to simplify the performance Uncle Dan set up the vocal quartet as a duet—the secretary and fish gutter sang together or different harmony patterns, the same for the accountant and dockworker.

The choir united the pensioners from the Protestant church, the proper choir and the male and female teachers who otherwise performed secondary vocal parts. So they made up a choir of some forty choristers, compensating the inadequate number with the power of their sound—all sang loudly, excitedly, frenetically. The minor imperfections were drowned in an instant, swept away by the shared fervency. The orchestra didn't sound like the record, but somewhat over-chewed and anemic. Except for the percussion section. Well, only the percussion section was fully staffed and played the original score. Beside the young gypsy sat his father, because Beethoven had foreseen not just tympani, but a drum. Uncle Dan shouted preventatively, "You'll look at me and you'll beat only when you're supposed to, when I give the signal. This is Beethoven! This isn't a wedding, don't fuck it up!"

"Nor is it a funeral," added Dad jokingly.

Auntie Frieda, an Austrian who was the wife of the protestant pastor, had worked over the German with the choristers and two of the soloists (the cross-eyed angel and the dockworker had no time for these "extras" and had not attended Auntie Frieda's sessions). Uncle Dan had studied dentistry in Germany and spoke excellent German. He mostly corrected the four soloists. The choir was not so important. Horrified, he'd clasp his forehead when he heard the onomatopoetic German of the soprano and bass. Everyone knew, more or less, what they were singing and that it was written by Schiller. Uncle Dan was interpreting "on the fly." From his explanations, shouted out during the breaks, I've remembered that in the future people will be like brothers, "with no hatred or evil to divide them," that the starry sky was God, that people aspired toward the good, which was also God, like flying suns or like a starry swarm. This God was good to people—he gave them bountiful nature, friends, and submissive beloved women. Vague and puzzling words for me. In the end what is God—the starry sky or the good? Why does this God only hand out women? Where are women getting the men from? Or are women simply handed out? Well what happens if they don't like the bloke they've been allotted to? Or is this a song for men only? That's what it looks like—it's just sung for brothers, not sisters. And this sad bloke, who isn't joyful, because the world for him is alien and empty . . . I felt sorry for him and how they hunted him out of the human union of joy. I stopped being interested in the words. The music was a lot more interesting. And there was nothing to understand. Because the melody for the millions, as I called it (and anyway it was conveyed by the choir) . . . oh what magic! And when the themes of joy and millions combined . . . I closed my eyes, I was bristling so much I felt weightless. I forgot about all vague words and dissonances.

In spite of all the shortages, difficulties, and imperfections, everyone—the singers and the musicians—were overwhelmed with euphoria. Me too. I sang enthusiastically in onomatopoetic German in the streets. The *Ode to Joy*. Then, the tune for the millions who'd become brothers. Then again the *Ode*. How could I not sing them together? Mum and Dad laughed and I was filled with an incomprehensible and uncontainable joy—for the river park, for the river, for the sky, for Mom and Dad, even for my brother, for my Granny's laughter, in spite of her ugly paralyzed limbs, for the sun, for life, for the fact that behind this world, beautiful in itself, there is another one even more beautiful, which will come, and in which all people, all the millions of people of the Earth, will be brothers, and wonderful music will sound. So we the people could go, in joy, even without God, whether he was the starry sky or the good.

From Beethoven's string quartet I learned something very important about music. There is more complex music, which in the beginning you don't understand, you don't hum a recognizable melody. But the more you listen to it and learn it, the more you like it. When for the first time I heard the string quartet, I took it as musical background, sometimes even irritating. But after listening to it twenty times at least, having dissected it, put it back together, repeated it for rehearsal, I'd still never manage to hum the complex tune, but it had invaded my head. I came to love it. I felt I had been blind or deaf or, more likely, somehow too uneducated to appreciate the music when I heard it the first time. But there was no audience in the room to hear this quartet ten times, they'd hear it for the first time at the premiere. And they wouldn't like it at all. But what a delusion that would be! That led me to the conclusion that there was music that you needed to know really well in order to like it at a concert. I shared this finding with Dad. Dad told me I was absolutely right and that I was a big brainbox. Then he added that the more music I listened to, the quicker I'd appreciate more complex music.

The premiere of the "Beethoven program" was the last performance I would attend. It was a warm evening at the beginning of June, the main street smelled of lime blossoms, school had just finished, at home the packing for the big move had begun, Mum and Granny were irritable and weren't up for concerts at all, so I was on my own, as always, at the end of the first row in the balcony. The hall was overflowing. There were old people that I saw for the first time. I think that all the high school students were there, standing. Uncle Dan, in tails and a bow tie, came out and bowed formally to the wild applause. The concert passed by without any slips or big mistakes. The adagio of the violin concerto rang out in something like a vacuum and mass hypnosis. No one and nothing moved in these sixteen minutes. Even the applause didn't immediately follow. It was as though the audience awoke and returned to reality. Then the clapping continued longer than the actual music. Nasko, pale and focused when he was playing, blushed like a crab while he bowed again and again. The fourth movement of *Symphony No.9* was impatiently awaited by all, and most of all—the end. Thus the audience listened patiently to all Beethoven's *trial runs,* preceding the Ode-coda. But then, ah . . . Well, the dockworker had forgotten even the onomatopoetic German. He roared as loud as ever and absolutely true, but even so this was not singing, but wordless mooing. Not even this took the audience out of its trance. While applauding the performance, the audience rose. I had the feeling that the people themselves wanted to sing. This was followed by the quartet. I was terribly proud of Dad, that he was playing in a quartet of chosen musicians this complex and beautiful music, free from mistakes. I was right to think, though, that the unprepared audience would not see its worth—during the quartet, people chatted, coughed, and the persistent shushes and finger signals from Uncle Dan while standing on the side had no effect.

In the big city, Dad was now just an engineer. We went to real concerts with a real orchestra, to real theatre and opera. In the movie salon in the Youth House I watched Fellini's *Orchestra Rehearsal* and thought to myself that a film could have been made of my memories of an amateur orchestra. Years later I thought the same about my other memories after watching a few Woody Allen films.

Twenty-four years after the Beethoven evening, I listened to Beethoven's whole violin concerto performed by the Plovdiv Philharmonic with Mincho Minchev as the soloist. During the concert I was again in that weightlessness of my childhood. After the concert I was walking beside the Artist and again I had the feeling that if I stretched out my arms, I would fly. But at thirty-two I now knew for sure that people cannot fly and what I was feeling is usually referred to as rapture.

After yet more years, when I was already working at the European Commission, I set up my mobile ringtone to play the most popular and frenetic moment from the cappella of the *Ode to Joy*. When my telephone rang, people—on the bus, the underground, the office—were surprised, startled, looked around, couldn't understand where this sudden unsuitably enthusiastic music was coming from. Some reckoned it as deliberate eccentricity, others as a wink or even a downright demonstration of loyalty toward the service, or an aggressive advert for the European Union.[315] Тъга (melancholy) Bardarska from the European Commission, officially a middle manager, otherwise an unaccomplished writer—a fundamentalist who entertains her guests with music and songs and whose telephone rings with *Ode to Joy*. Cool, eh?

And for me, this was a call from a paradise lost, in which there was joy and in whose streets I sang the ode to that joy. In that paradise, music lifted people, who made that music, above the platitude of their lives, above envy and doubts; in music, they were brothers and sisters. In this paradise, my parents were young, they learned German, played bridge, listened to pop music, Dad was a musician and engineer, he loved Mom and was the person I made up my whole life and dreamed him to be. Mom was as beautiful as a Madonna and as happy as a girl. Money did not exist. The sky was homely, comforting, low and full of mosquitoes, and the stars were simply night ornaments. Time did not exist, my dead Granddad rode a bike in the street, death was just a good sleep, and funerals—comic parades. In this paradise, I wasn't perplexed by hormones and whims, shop windows and tourist brochures, but I could fly, in my dreams and awake. When I listened to my mobile phone I knew by then there was no God, that the starry sky is a monstrously empty void, that sadness is much stronger and truer than joy, that if there is something transcendental, it's only in one's mind, that consciousness makes us sad by alienating us from this wonderful world of joy, that "good is a social concept,"[316] relative and subject to change, that humanity is primarily male, that the millions[317] have become 7 billion, that they're not going to become brothers and sisters, that neither music, words, good, social ideals, God or joy will unite them the way impending doom does. That the only possible paradise is personal and intimate and is most often found in childhood. That we always lose it, irrevocably. That the only cure, so as not to kill ourselves after this loss and our accelerated spiral toward the black holes of a personal hell, is to nourish the memory, and sing out this

315 Beethoven's and Schiller's *Ode to Joy* is the anthem of the European Union.

316 "After you evil pants like a greyhound / (good is a social concept) / are you opening your arms for a cuddle / you're now handy for a crucifixion."—Dobromir Tonev

317 Around 850, which was, give or take, the population of the world in 1785 when Schiller wrote the ode. In 1804 when Kant died the earth's population became a billion. The first billion.

paradise in words, in stories, in music, in pictures. And to try to create a new paradise for our children.

The telephone ring sometimes transports me to details of the lost paradise—my rubber overshoes scrunching through the snow passages, the red coat, which mum sewed up for me on Granny Nikolinas's Singer machine, Dad's warm hand, the rumbling stove in the rehearsal hall, Dad with his cello in the cellar, the cello's voice, so close to human, the silence in the hall after Uncle Dan's final gesture, Mom's long chestnut hair, her delicate beautiful hands, stroking my hair, *that Paris*, over which Granny and I flew in our bed . . . And I need time to return to here and now and, finally, to pick up. Sometimes, my father rings me, just like that, to hear my voice, to recite lachrymose poetry or to tell me about his writings on physics and fields, to complain that he cannot sleep. Without ever telling me that he is consumed by guilt, that he's stifled by hopelessness and terror of death.

ODE TO JOY

(Epilogue)

But the sacred part of him, his awareness, remained an unwavering band of light. And this book is being written by a meat machine in cooperation with a machine made of metal and plastic. . . . And at the core of the writing meat machine is something sacred, which is an unwavering band of light. At the core of each person who reads this book is a band of unwavering light.

—Kurt Vonnegut, *Breakfast of Champions*

Some time ago I dreamed a peculiar dream. Actually, today I'm unsure whether I was really asleep and if this really was a dream. Or if my mind was swimming in that heavy water between sleeping and waking toward the shore of a denouement to a story I was writing, or was living. Or which I am still writing, or will write. Or which someone else will live and write. Whatever. Let's say it was a dream.

Sometimes my drift into sleep transports me to childhood, to a specific, repetitive moment. I pretend to be asleep and Dad carefully lifts me and carries me in his arms. How lovely. I won't open my eyes yet, keep them shut just a little longer. I try not to move, to not flutter my eyelids. Through the slit of my eyes I see the doorframe, which passes over me. As a child, at this moment, I'd open my eyes wide and cry, feeling conned, coaxed into sleep, just to be carted off to the cellar with Granny, on the only night I slept at home. As an adult, at this point I'd sink into sleep. But every time, again and again, it felt like this had happened last night. And this "last night" did not drift away, no matter the monstrous number of nights and years, which piled up in a black heap, obscuring the silver ray of memory.

This time before falling asleep I passed through the usual hallway, where I saw those utterly unfamiliar people, busy with their daily life. This time it was somewhat different, more concrete, there was even some story. I saw a girl in a red coat sitting on the paving stones in front of some building and reading. And then she went into some room, drank some medicine, I guess, put on tiny earphones, sat on the floor and began to listen to something. Then two women burst into the room, they grabbed the child in their feverish arms, staring round the room with big frightened eyes. The child shouted at them—loudly because of the earphones—that her dad was coming right now and everything would be sorted out, and she continued listening—to a story, I imagine. The two women didn't notice that the child had earphones, that she couldn't hear, that she'd closed her eyes and was not there. One of the women suddenly groaned, sat down next to the girl on the floor, grabbed the hand of the other woman, and pulled her down. And so the two women and the girl sat on the floor, in the shelter of a tight embrace. The child opened her astonished eyes for a second, hugging both women, moved into the shelter of their arms and then closed her eyes, transported by what she was listening to. In the final seconds, the usual questions dashed in my dozing brain—who, where, when, what, why. And then I fell asleep.

. . . only to open my eyes and wake up . . . in the cosmos! Before my eyes, everywhere, an infinite and infinitely beautiful landscape unfolded, like the photographs that Hubble would send us later. It's strange to define the cosmos as beautiful in my earthly human aesthetic criteria—that's what I thought in my sleep.

I was moving—I don't know at what speed and how, but the passage was changing, however slowly and imperceptibly. Where am I . . . I wanted to look around but my gaze could not be shifted, all my vision was occupied by . . . the Universe. Absent from my field of vision were an unfocused nose, hair, eyelashes. How do I look? How old am I? I could not close my eyes or whatever I had as an organ of vision, I could not move a hand or a foot, which it seemed I did not have. So I have sight, I think, I even reached a complex conclusion, *ergo sum*, I made the first recapitulation. But what I was, remained unclear.

In the cosmos, absolute silence reigned. Did I still have my hearing?

As if it heard my thoughts, my travel companion spoke, "We found several objects in Sector 745, third level. The source of the objects is the planet 1073, sector 689, first level."

I'm making up the numbers, because I don't remember numbers from my dream. But everything was expressed in numbers—in a decimal system. Space was clearly configured into sectors and these sectors had levels. What these levels stand for? Parallel worlds? Levels in time? In matter? I pondered this in my dream. But initially, I was simply surprised—who was talking, where did this voice come from? In front of my eyes only nebulae and galaxies layered like wondrous . . . earthly clouds. And was someone really talking or did the words reach straight into my brain or into whatever contained my consciousness, which, I'd already concluded, I had. So this was not an undeniable assertion that I had been hearing. But my thoughts focused on the more important information—was I the discovered "object"? Or were they talking to me? And then, how, who was talking?!

My traveling companion started up again quite on cue, as if in answer to my questions, "The object contains information, stored on quantum medium, and organic matter."

It didn't sound like my description. But who could know . . .

"I used Program 19 at cognitive level 3 for interpreting the information. But it could not analyze it all and even blocked at some point. For the analysis of organic matter I used table 3, which, on this planet, was called the Mendeleev Table."

This male or female, it was impossible to tell from the voice, so let's say nonbinary, was clearly going to file report. About us, the humans—I didn't know anyone else who'd refer to the chemical components of the universe as the Mendeleev Table.

"Called themselves human."

Bravo to me.

"Actually, they used to name themselves in the widest variety of ways, because humans used over 7,000 sign systems, calling them languages. This ineffective method of communication died out, only leaving a few, completely standardized and mutually convertible idiographic systems."

How sad for languages, for the Word! But that was foreseeable . . . Hey, hang on . . . the analyst is talking in Bulgarian! How strange, such a small language, to survive and even to be chosen for the . . . report. Ey, such paradoxical thoughts were darting in my sleeping brain.

The sexless voice continued its report, but the speech turned into a monotonous tape, from which only separate words and phrases reached my mind. Well, was it a problem with the Bulgarian, after all?

It seems, it was talking about the two genders, the in-between variants, about the dying out of intersexual procreation. About animals and plants. I heard few times the words *genes* and *synthesis*.

"The organic matter, found in the object is frozen and represents one thousand human embryos. I'm showing it with a magnification of twenty."

What does this "magnification of twenty" mean? How big are these chums and what could they see with "naked eye" or with their unequipped visual organ? But wasn't the egg-cell the largest cell in the human organism with the diameter of a hair. So my traveling companions had a roughly human scale.

"It's almost certain that the organic matter is no good for anything now, but it'll be checked out by Base 17."

This "now" caught my attention. How long a time had this "organic matter" been traveling through the cosmos? And when was this *now*?

The tape continued its sexless unintelligible blur. From which from time to time whole sentences, phrases or separate words jumped out.

"Procreation of many plants depended on one insect, a bee. I'll demonstrate."

True. Just that the bees began to die out, one time.

Then amid the monotonous murmur, isolated words and phrases popped: "industrial revolution," "distribution of resources," "sources of energy," "warming," "extinction," "digitalization," "artificial intelligence," "terminal phase of civilization."

What had happened to humanity? What had led it to—as it appears—the tragic finale, the past tense in the report and the launch of the "objects" into the cosmos? And what information was stored on the quantum medium? I wanted to switch off my visual . . . organ, so as not to get distracted by the cosmic landscape, to sharpen my hearing, to hear more distinctly. But I couldn't do anything—I was just a gaze; I had no body mass, no freedom of movement, and couldn't control my field of vision, which was fixed on the unfolding Hubble clouds.

Ah, here are a few whole sentences: "Throughout their entire history, up till the atmospheric cataclysm, humans have destroyed each other. The only logical explanation for this self-destruction would be the regulation of the population, relative to available resources, but that isn't valid. The information on the quantum medium speaks of quite different motives for the mutual extermination, which our analyst could not interpret, though."

After that I lost again the thread and isolated words bubbled and burst like balloons, "four basic feelings," "fear," "death," "love," "greed," "hatred," "religion," "consciousness," "morality," "aesthetics," "humor," "the analyst blocked." Ey, how I wanted to hear an objective resume, from a clearly alien mind, about all that was specifically and uniquely human.

"And in the end, it seems the something like a meteorite smashed into them. It must be investigated to see if it was natural, or launched by someone. It was quite massive, oval like their satellite moon, but much smaller. They named it Melancholy, watched it approached, calculated the chances for it to miss the earth, to be pulled into the gravitational field of another planet. They mobilized their entire technical and military might in hopes of diverting it from the fatal collision. Most folk observed it, right up till the last minute, with curiosity, and only some in horror. When they saw that the crash was inevitable, they launched the objects into the cosmos, in the first level, the only one they knew. The archive of civilization was clearly ready in advance. Actually, they'd already played out this scenario, on a scale of 1:1 with regard to organic matter. The previous time they'd called the object *Noah's Ark*. The quantum object is something like an archive of human knowledge. And of something else, which our decoders displayed, but our analysts blocked and could not interpret."

Wow! . . . Whatever I was, I felt immense pain at these words. So the risk had materialized in a quite literal fashion—cosmic matter with huge mass and speed had hit the already distraught Earth and its adapted humanity. And my great-great-great-grandchildren had died in hellish horror, if before that they hadn't perished from heat, asphyxiation, drowning, thirst, hunger or hadn't been killed. And provided they'd been born at all.

And it might have been projected at humanity . . . by aliens? I knew it! In the cosmic *dark forest*[318] humanity should have kept mum and not emit some musical-poetical recitals. Valya Balkanska and Beethoven might have scared indeed the shadows in the forest, as if humans would have some threateningly high level of development, at that, in *matter*, which seems completely incomprehensible to aliens.[319]

The excruciating hopelessness and, perhaps, the vague awareness of the temporal paradox, dispersed the dream and somewhere in my bodiless mind the thought crept

318 Cf. Liu Cixin's trilogy

319 Bulgarians take special pride in the fact that a Bulgarian folklore song, sung by Valya Balkanska, is included on the Voyager Golden Records.

in that this was just a dream and I wanted to wake up. But a single thought dragged me back deep into the dream. If all this had already happened . . . who was I? Were there other . . . "remains" like me around? I was curious as well to learn what humanity had archived on the quantum USB drive.

It was as though the speaker was patiently waiting for me to pass the crossroads between sleep and waking and only then it continued. But, again, separate words flew about like popcorn, "measurement units . . . gravitation . . . time . . . mass . . . speed . . . density . . . size . . . distance . . . volume . . . image and likeness . . . low cognitive level" Ping! A few ready-cooked whole sentences as if from the microwave: "The speed of light was alien to humans. The Cosmic distances were unattainable for them. Humans thought the universe to be infinite. The constants humans applied are from Type 3 (*for example*)."

I listened with growing agitation and even something like anger. What are these cognitive levels? And constants are . . . constants, what kinds was he . . . she . . . it droning on about? Had we known the most important things about ourselves, the Earth and the Cosmos . . . or were we the cretins of the Universe? But better listen, it was getting more and more interesting.

The analyst continued helpfully, "Most of the quantum medium, however, is occupied by something different; it is not the archived scientific knowledge of the human brain."

Ey, at long last we got to the most important stuff! To the genuinely human stuff! The rest a computer could spit out. Praise to you . . . Human, you've archived not only your scientific knowledge and achievements and your biological building blocks. And you, alien, make it quicker and more concise, because I'll get to wake up, before I've heard what's most significant—this passed paradoxically through my sleeping brain. I was all ears. The total cosmic view began to bore me.

The speaker waited patiently and continued . . . But, sadly, once again I couldn't distinguish the words. I wanted to shout, to scream, that I couldn't hear! Then Ping! Look, two complete, articulate sentences: "Simply put, humans killed themselves because they did not see sense in their existence. The self-destruction of the species runs counter to the evolutionary imperative for the survival of the species."

He, she or it was really good at synthesis. Even without the help of its analytic machines. How sad were we, the humans!

Then words popped again: "meaninglessness . . . death . . . horror . . . genes . . . love . . . religion . . . art." This sequence of words and that mention of consciousness sounded somehow familiar. I was wondering what information sources from the quantum drive the analyst had used to put together the report? It was as if the speaker heard my thoughts and duly explained, "I note, that on the quantum medium many books were archived; a book is a work of literature, which is art, whatever this means, produced through the language sign system. Our analysis selector extracted some information from a book, which describes the finding of the objects and . . . all of my report up till now. As to the paradox of consciousness, the book says that it is as if personages of a book have thought up their author."

Ha! I knew it! Let me see you now, cognitive know-it-alls, with your supreme cognitive level, how will you explain this? I have foreseen you, heard you, thought you up! You, autists, extra-terrestrials. I've invented you! Even though I'm a woman. Or . . . I was. I didn't know what I was at the moment, but I was sure I had been a woman. Be it only for my love of nagging. Even in the void, with alien intelligence.

And then it was as if my world expanded. A very strange feeling in sleep. As though I was climbing Esher's stairs, or falling down Alice's rabbit hole, in order to bring forth extraterrestrials, in some past in the future. In absolute silence.

The voice shook me out of the trance. The entire Hubble view was restored, "In order to receive the following information, which is also a kind of art, you have to tune to 100-4,000 hertz."

Suddenly Beethoven's violin concerto rang out. Directly to the third movement with no transition, impetuous, joyful, the orchestra echoed into infinity. But the music suddenly stopped, as though the speaker had made a mistake and wanted to play something else. My ears, or whatever I had there as a listening device, bawled from the utter, vacuum-silence, in which I didn't hear my heart. Actually, I'd hardly have a heart, but even so only now did I notice the absence of the dull thud in the cosmic shell.

And then the choir from the *Ode to Joy* roared, in those ecstatic waves of fortissimo. In some magical, extraterrestrial moments the ode of human joy echoed in the cosmos. And I, whatever "I" meant, was being carried in the universe on the music hertz waves. But the volume was insupportable for my hearing organ. The last thing that I thought in my dream, before my hearing exploded and again that absolute silence fell, was that only a deaf person could compose such a deafening music. And only an alien, in the cosmos, could play it so loudly . . .

. . . Quiet, the dull rhythmic beat as in a shell . . . that had to be my heart. I had a heart again! I was swimming upward, I was waking up, I was taking shape and flesh, I was embodying. My as yet unconscious attempt to move my head, sent me a sharp pain—my neck had seized up. So that was why I couldn't move. Once again I had a body. And it hurt.

Dark. But not that cosmic dark, decorated in pink-blue nebulae and milky spirals of galaxies. The dark behind my closed eyes.

Quiet. But not that cosmic *heartless* silence. Somewhere, faraway, a car passed by. Some familiar rhythmic thumbing. It was raining outside. The rain was tapping on something. The roof of the Plovdiv house? When am I? Where am I?

I opened my eyes—no, there's no dormer-window above. So the artist's not sleeping beside me. I shifted my gaze to the window—the blinds were down and the curtain's not torn. So it's not the toilet-like flat and Rada's not seven. The ceiling is very high, the curtains are gathered beautifully like for the stage. I'm in Brussels, at home. I stretch out a hand. Where's Christian? Did he have trouble sleeping and is reading downstairs? Christian has left. Christian is now no more. The thought dissolved like a catalyst in my brain and woke it up another notch. I've now got Michael and he's at least five. How old is he, is he now sleeping in the room above mine? There's no one in the bed next to me.

"Now" settled in the dark and the night quiet. It's raining now. Now Rada is in California. Michael is now in the 7th grade and is sleeping on the upper floor, his dog under his bed. I turned to one side and stretched into the bed's empty space. The "right" man who "found" me finally is now hundreds of miles from here. How did it happen, that both my children would grow up with non-biological fathers? Did I do that?

The chronotopos settled. I was completely awake. I closed my now wakeful eyes again. The dark returned me to my dream.

What a strange dream! What was I? Where? When did all this happen? Will it happen? . . . But this was just a dream. I even knew this while dreaming—that it was all a dream. But why do I dream such stuff?! And how can I dream such stuff at all?! Well, I was talking with . . . myself. There were no aliens at all. But it was sad, really . . . Although somehow blunted, remote, like in a dream. Or like in a book. And I was lonely, cosmically lonely. How was it . . . ontogenesis recapitulates phylogeny. I have to think how this must be formulated in the opposite direction, not to genesis, but to apocalypse. The apocalypse of the individual recapitulates . . . hmm, I wonder if it does not actually precede, the apocalypse of humanity.

But how funny this dream was at the same time! The extraterrestrial, an infinitely advanced intelligence, spoke in Bulgarian, even in both high and low registers. Well what other language would it use? It was me who thought it up and dreamt it, no? I know the answer to Fermi's paradox! It's not just the distance in spacetime. We don't find extraterrestrials in the cosmos, nor do they find us, because they are within some of us, humans.

And that music in the end . . . But sound waves, don't they only diffuse in atmosphere? What atmosphere, with what density and what gravity? Well didn't deaf Beethoven hear the music only in his head, and if there is air in your head . . . hmm?

How much time did I dream? According to science . . . dreams last a very short time—a few minutes. But what I dreamt lasted a lot more time. What time? And my awakening! There I didn't know when and where I awoke. Actually I woke up in all basic . . . chronotopoi of my life. How much time was I waking up? And how did I fall asleep! Weird—unlike other pre-sleep images, which always sank in the oblivion of sleep and I never remembered anything in the morning, this time I remembered everything. Who was that girl in the red coat, who were those women, what was the child listening to, why were the women so frightened, why were they gripping each other? When was this . . . or will this be? Where?

But, all and all, a really informative dream, in any aspect. I'll write it down, so I don't forget it. No way will I forget. I smiled at the absurdities shooting through my head. Absurd is stifled sense in the global meaninglessness. Who had said that?

I stretched, I spread out in the bed like the model for Da Vinci's golden ratio (which might be different for a woman). From childhood I liked to stretch out like this in a vacated bed, from the time when I was sleeping with Granny and she'd get up early in the morning to light the stove. I opened my eyes again and looked about. It was Sunday, a rainy, cold November Sunday. I'd hoped so much to sleep in later. But the dream was worth the early wake-up, I consoled myself. What's the time, actually? I reached blindly to the bedside cabinet and touched my mobile phone.

Five forty in the morning. Oh someone's rung me . . . With the *Ode to Joy*! There, so, that's where my dream got its finale. And why I woke up. I was overcome with disappointment at this materialistic explanation. But who would ring me at half past five on a Sunday!? I'm not on-call for emergencies this weekend. I put on my glasses and looked at the screen. At 5:30 Mum had rung me.

I stared at the illuminated screen and knew already. I'd always anticipated that it would happen in this exact way—that Mum would call me early some cold and rainy morning. I touched the screen, two signals and Mum's voice. No, her weeping. I didn't speak.

"Hello . . . Can you hear me?"

"Yes . . ." I blurted and swallowed, to moisten my dried lips, but also to clear my blocked ears.

Sobbing, tears.

"Your father didn't wake up." This is exactly what Mum said.

Then words flooded—she'd got up to go to the toilet, my father usually snored, but now it was unusually quiet in his room, she'd gone in to check, he was asleep, no noise whatsoever, she'd called him, put her hand on his mouth—he wasn't breathing, she touched him—he was now cold, she'd rung my brother, he'd be there at any moment.

I had to say some comforting words to Mum, Hell, I had to say something. And I would, but in a little while, I'd tell her that this very day, tomorrow at the latest, I'd fly out, I'd organize and finance everything, I'd be beside her, if she wants, and she could come to live with us in Brussels afterward, that my father's time had simply come, he'd departed easily, without suffering, without hurting her more, this was better, for everybody. I would tell her all this. And not to forget to tell her to look at his *Longines*.

But exactly at this moment I was dumb, in my head the *Ode to Joy* rang out intrusively again and I was ridiculously calm and well slept. Could I have not fallen asleep again and was having a new dream—this went through my mind. Before beginning to talk. Or before waking up. Or before sinking again into the absolute silence.

RUSANA BARDARSKA is a Bulgarian writer, essayist, and philosopher, known for her innovative approach to literature that combines narrative fiction with intellectual reflection. With a background that includes both academic and literary pursuits, she is a distinctive voice in contemporary European literature. *To Essay* is her most ambitious work, weaving together essays, short stories, and philosophical discourse in a compelling narrative about personal and societal transformation.

CHRISTOPHER BUXTON is a translator and scholar specializing in Eastern European languages, with a particular focus on Bulgarian literature.

ZORNITSA HRISTOVA is a Bulgarian translator from English, journalist and author of children's books. In 2010 she founded her own publishing company, "Tochitsa" for entertaining and educational children's literature.

www.ingramcontent.com/pod-product-compliance
Lightning Source LLC
Jackson TN
JSHW021032190925
91050JS00004B/1

* 9 7 8 1 9 6 0 3 8 5 4 5 1 *